MW01613401

THE PRINCE & THE DANCING GIRL

To Mama on Mother's Day 2007.
You have always been encouraging
and inspirational. I thank you
for your wisdom and care. But
as long as I live there will never
be anything sweeter than my
mother's love.

Your daughter,

Sharron Annette McGregor

THE PRINCE & THE DANCING GIRL

An Inspirational Fiction

(Part I)

Saeed Tiwana and Sharron Annette McGregor

iUniverse, Inc.

New York Lincoln Shanghai

THE PRINCE & THE DANCING GIRL
An Inspirational Fiction

Copyright © 2007 by Prince LLC

All rights reserved. No part of this book may be used or reproduced by any means, graphic, electronic, or mechanical, including photocopying, recording, taping or by any information storage retrieval system without the written permission of the publisher except in the case of brief quotations embodied in critical articles and reviews.

iUniverse books may be ordered through booksellers or by contacting:

iUniverse
2021 Pine Lake Road, Suite 100
Lincoln, NE 68512
www.iuniverse.com
1-800-Authors (1-800-288-4677)

This is a work of fiction. All of the characters, names, incidents, organizations, and dialogue in this novel are either the products of the author's imagination or are used fictitiously.

First Edition

ISBN-13: 978-0-595-42249-4 (pbk)
ISBN-13: 978-0-595-67985-0 (cloth)
ISBN-13: 978-0-595-86586-4 (ebk)
ISBN-10: 0-595-42249-7 (pbk)
ISBN-10: 0-595-67985-4 (cloth)
ISBN-10: 0-595-86586-0 (ebk)

Printed in the United States of America

Author's note

Once, I asked my English professor in college: "Sir, what makes *great dramas* in literature?"

Professor, a tall and burly man, replied, "Aristotle first paid attention to this question. He invented a term: *tragic hero*. What makes him tragic? The *harmatia*, or the flaw. Without the flaw, there would be no downfall. Later, Shakespeare noted that Sophocles and Euripides built their dramas around tragic heroes. There are many tragic heroes in history: Jesus, Othello, King Lear, Oedipus, Willy Loman, Macbeth, Aristotle, Anthony and Cleopatra, Hamlet, Lord Nelson, etc. Writers made their pain known to the world, and it became *literature*."

These characters had a four-dimensional commonality: they had a tragic flaw, gentlemanliness, carelessness, rigidity, ignorance, gullibility, arrogance, ambition, stupidity, excessive pride, or greed. They were, generally, from the noble class. They had very human personalities and they all faced their end with dignity.

The professor explained it thus: " Lord Nelson defeated the French at Trafalgar. He was a hero to his people. His battle and victory are history. He was summoned by the English Parliament to explain his extra-marital affair with Lady Hamilton. That is a story perhaps not recorded by history. The admiral donned his uniform and approached the French. It was either a fact or conjecture that he invited his own assassination. The French shot him. That was a tragedy. In triumph, he became a tragic hero. That was tragedy. Lady Hamilton ended up running a brothel in France: that story is literature, an explication of 'pain.'"

Things repeatedly go wrong in human life. At times we ask, "Is life worthwhile? Is it worthwhile to try when the going gets rough and troubles are incessant?" Those who conclude, "It isn't," give up, either by suicide or by retreating into despair and defeatism. Celia (T.S. Eliot in *The Cocktail Party*) put this aptly when she said, "I must tell you that I should really like to think that there is something wrong with me—because if there isn't, then there's something wrong with the world itself—and that's much more frightening! So I'd rather believe there is something wrong with me that could be put right." Celia is speaking about the most basic and haunting decisions a person has to make.

Does the fault lie in the stars, Brutus? "No, sir," Brutus says. "We did not use our options correctly. The stars are not at fault!" Obligations and the failure to use one's options correctly bring about the tragic hero's fall. We are pained to see it happen; it saddens us. That sadness lives on and lasts in the mind, transformed into literature.

During my military academy days, I read the life story of Prince Maximilian von Hapsburg, emperor of Mexico. I added him to my list of top tragic heroes. Faced with certain death and destruction of his entire power base and value, he did not demur or despair. He died like a man, "with his boots on." History is witness to an endless list of rulers and generals who won great victories, but eventually lost due to neglecting one small military aspect of their situation. In the case of Maximilian, he fought for fifty-seven days. Considering that the French had withdrawn their army two years earlier, it was indomitable. He fought courageously. But he should have known that there would be one moment when he could break out from the encirclement. That moment came early, after about twenty to thirty days. A blacksmith needs to know when the iron is hot. In the case of Prince Maximilian, he did not know the subtle art of breaking through. He was a naval man. Naval admirals have hardly ever won land battles. But he didn't die from shame, like British Admiral Lord Nelson.

History declares it more boldly: the sword comes first, music and revelry later. That is the makeup of Destiny. Our hero, Maximilian, was trained in naval warfare but didn't know land warfare. He could have hired a Confederate general, Early, to beat back his opponent. WE FAIL TO USE OUR OPTIONS AND TOOLS. THEN WE BLEED. We bring on our own tragedy, and then blame others. It is said that "sweat saves blood; brain saves sweat and blood."

This work of drama is the product of a three-person production team: **the author,** Saeed Tiwana, **the co-author**, Sharron McGregor, who tirelessly researched the European portions of the novel, and **the editor**, Catherine Quinn, who extensively researched the Mexican portions. We made use of computers to present a fiction (supported by history) about our tragic hero, Maximilian von Hapsburg. Despite living hundreds of miles away from each other, we assembled this novel in the fashion of an assembly line, with portions coming from one direction to be assembled with beauty and strength from another direction. I thank them both for their committed work on this project.

I would also like to thank my wife of forty-four years, Shagufta Tiwana, who inspired me to write this novel. I used to narrate stories from history. She liked this tale the most. This book has lessons for mankind. Hence it makes this book a perfect gift for the younger generations.

To conclude, I hope future generations can be wiser.

Saeed Tiwana

CO-Author's note

Sometimes I wonder about predestination, the idea that your life is planned out, and you just have to be there to push a few key buttons. I wonder about how much we are involved in preparing ourselves to meet our destiny. After a chance meeting with my architect, co-author, and friend, I have decided definitely that my life has followed more of the latter method.

As long as I can remember, I have loved words and ideas. I love to read, write, talk, debate, and act. I have taught those things in public school and college for thirty years under the titles of English, Speech and Debate, Creative Writing, Acting, Drama, and Literature. I had just retired, so for once I felt I had free time: time to do what I liked. What that was going to be, I didn't know for sure.

But then, in August of 2004, "Senior Citizen" sent me an online chat note that said, "Would you read my manuscript?" My husband Mike typed back, "Sure." After a few minutes, I had an email containing a novel sketch. To this day, I have never told him that it was Mike who replied.

I quickly checked with my father to see if this man was for real. He said they had met, that our respective families had some previous contact, and he seemed like a rational man, so I emailed "Senior Citizen" back with a formal introduction, saying that I might be interested.

My life became a whirlwind after that. There were emails every day. One contained a request for me to create a scene where a Hapsburg prince plays in a polo match and becomes involved with a dancer. I had always been fond of historical fiction, so I whipped something together after reading about how a polo match is played, since I had never seen one. He replied, "Wow!" and I became his co-author. This was mid-August, and in two weeks, he said I "must go" to Europe to research, that he would finance the trip for my husband and I.

Here I must say that the new technology is marvelous. People from a small town can learn about anything sitting in their own homes. But a trip to Europe is mind-expanding and opened this small-town teacher up to many possibilities.

I kept asking my husband and family, "Is this man for real?" But immediately following our agreement, we set a date. By the second week of November, we were in Canada, preparing for a trip to London, Brussels, and Vienna. The next few weeks were fun and exciting. I found myself caught up in the story and in the historical background. Fiction, especially historical fiction, requires background research to the nth degree. I soon learned that the Eastern mind is as different from the Western mind as a man's is from a woman's.

We began our work at the end of August 2004, and he was pushing for us to complete the novel by December 4 of that year. (And for three of those weeks, I was in Europe!) I realized at that time that this was serious and not just for fun. He wanted it done and he wanted it done yesterday. When I began to search for information about how other authors handled deadlines, I found the following quote from Tom Clancy on perseverance: "*Writing a book is an endurance contest, and a war fought against yourself, because writing is beastly hard work which one would just as soon not do. It's also a job, however, and if you want to get paid, you have to work. Life is cruel that way.*"

If Tom Clancy felt that way, I felt entitled to feel that way too.

When I emailed him the quote, he laughed, acknowledged the problem, and kept pushing. We make a good team. I can only say that he was full of "great expectations" for both of us.

I must acknowledge the many family members, pastors, teachers, professors, librarians, co-workers, and friends who provided not only support but sometimes a shoulder to cry on. They all helped to make up the bits and pieces that create who I am, how I think, and how I work. I'm reluctant to give names, but I must thank my husband, Mike McGregor, a local superintendent of schools, who took me to sites in Europe and has always supported me and prayed for me.

I must also acknowledge the knowledge, strength, and ingenuity of Mr. Tiwana, who dreamed the big dream and made me dream it, too.

Sharron A McGregor

Editor's Note

The following is a *partially* real telling of the lives of some *very* real people. It is a story told with a skeleton of actual history to hold it up. Some will pick up this book because of an interest in Benito Juarez, and his staunch ethics and stubborn determination to bring his country out of centuries of chaos and a blatant lack of civil rights. Others, like me, will prefer the idealistically naïve Maximilian, who was probably one of the most progressive thinkers of his time, and immensely talented despite his bad luck.

My greatest hope for this book is that people do not simply look at it as a "history book." There is much more to it than lessons on dates and events. It can fill in information for enthusiasts or be an entirely new story to others not familiar with the history involved. It was a clash of cultures and ideas, a time of waltzes, grand balls, Mexican revolution, rowdy mariachi songs, and sweeping classical works.

While the story has added characters and events, it still allows us a peek into the lives, the minds, and the emotions of people long gone, enabling us to see what things may have been like for them. That alone is fascinating enough to make the reading of this book worthwhile.

Catherine Quinn

A Prologue In Two Parts

Let us go back to the mid-nineteenth century. There we find two characters:

The first is Benito Pablo Juarez (1806–72), twenty-seventh president of Mexico. He was a full-blooded Indian, born in 1806 to a sheep-breeding family. He was a lawyer, a tiny sparrow among the powerful elite. Known as "the Abraham Lincoln of Mexico," his greatest quality was great moral courage and honesty. He championed democracy and worked for the oppressed, and was said to fight for what was right. This controversial Mexican hero was fearless in the face of adversity. He showed abiding honesty and was a relentless champion of democracy. Such is his legacy, now the spiritual possession of all humanity.

The second is Ferdinand Maximilian Joseph von Hapsburg, emperor of Mexico. Born in 1832, he was the second son of Emperor Karl Joseph of Austria. This prince was also an admiral of the Navy, a cousin of Queen Victoria, the son-in-law of King Leopold I of Belgium, and a friend of the French emperor, Napoleon III. With such connections, lofty ideas, and a beautiful personality, he was truly capable and was considered someone who could put down strong roots in Mexico as well. Some say he aimed too high; others say he was tricked into going. Nevertheless, his greatest task was trying to build a monarchy in the foreign land of Mexico. This caused a clash between an emperor and a common man, a Goliath versus an ordinary lawyer, a revolutionary versus a democrat, and an idealistic dreamer versus a pragmatic realist.

This second character was an emperor. He was not directly an oppressor, but he did allow, although reluctantly, state oppression to happen. He was a foreigner imposed on the Mexican people by military force. He tried to make a deal with the revolutionary leadership and suggested compromise.

These two fighters were liberal, democratic, and progressive, with similar ideas but totally different backgrounds. The first was the defender or liberator, while the second was the oppressor, cloaked as a benign emperor, as a European Catholic ruler.

The emperor was denied any compromise. As with David and Goliath, it was to be a fight to the finish. The liberator won because he decided to fight. The Goliath lost because he chose badly. But it is a tragic human story.

Mexico, May 5, 2005
Cinco de Mayo Celebrations
Mexico City

The sun was setting over the city. The descent was almost complete, with only a few deep orange streaks on a darkening sky. A group of children ran down the street in excitement, their dog running alongside them. They giggled as they rounded a corner and came upon the massive Zocalo Square.

An enormous gathering of people had assembled there. Smoke wafted over the children's faces, and their stomachs growled as they took in the smoky aroma of tortillas roasting in hot pans. Girls and their mothers wore brightly embroidered peasant blouses, working over presses to squeeze fresh juice into clay jugs. Their fathers, husbands, and sons carried fresh sacks of cornmeal to the cooking tripods and turned spits, spearing great slabs of roasting meat. It was Cinco de Mayo, one of the grandest days in Mexico. People from all over the city were celebrating the day that their people won a victory over the invading French. It did not matter to them that this victory was later overturned in another battle, because Cinco de Mayo was not about ultimate victory. It was about the bravery of their people in resisting those who presumed to rule them; whether they had won or not, they had dared to stand up to the enemy. The men in that battle would always be remembered, even though many of them died in later battles. They were national heroes, and always would be.

Mariachis stood on a quickly erected stage of wood built just for the occasion. Their horns and guitars were festive, and they wore tight, black pants with silver medallions. People danced all around, laughing and spilling their drinks. Some held their sons and daughters in their arms as they bounced around and danced. Others stood to the side and chatted happily with their neighbors and friends in the festive atmosphere.

Somewhere nearby, a man who had gotten too drunk was picking a fight with a younger man, and everyone around him laughed. Elsewhere, a large group of men gathered in a stable, shouting over a cockfight. A large man with sausage-like fingers held his arm up high, his fist clutching several pesos, as he cheered his bird to victory. He smelled of liquor, but so did many of the men. Their hoarse voices blended with the hoots and songs of the people nearby.

One man placed the last of his pesos on the rail, making his bet on the black rooster. He wavered on his feet, tipsy from the bottle he had continually tipped to his lips throughout the evening.

"Are you going to spend every last coin on those damned birds?" his wife demanded, pushing through the crowd of men.

The man frowned and glanced at his friends, who watched in amusement. "Viva Juarez!" he drunkenly shouted. "I can do whatever I like with my money. Juarez made sure I'm free to do anything I please!"

"Including making an ass of yourself?" his wife snapped.

The man's friends roared with laughter. One of them took the pesos off of the ledge and stuffed them back into the man's pocket. Another friend turned the man's shoulder away from the rail and steered him to his wife. They laughed and shouted, "Viva Juarez! Viva good wives!" as she took the bewildered man firmly by the arm and led him back to the street celebrations.

It was the most wonderful day of the year, a time when people did not have to worry about their usual troubles, their poverty, oppression, or sorrow. Even many of the poorest had managed to save a few pesos and used them now, buying themselves a drink and giving their little ones a bite from their dinner, a tortilla filled with chicken, cheese, salsa, and cilantro. The children squealed in excitement as the delicious food dribbled down their chins.

"Viva Mexico!" was heard now and then, and "Viva Juarez!" was shouted proudly by men from balconies, squares, streets, and windows. They owed their thanks and national pride to Juarez and the other men who had fought for them all, men they would never let slip away into the misty fog of history. Never.

The local casino blazed with flashing lights and the sounds of music, machines, and men's voices. Two late-model limousines pulled up to the casino entrance. Exiting the limos was a mariachi band, costumed in waist-length jackets and tightly fitted pants which opened slightly at the ankle to fit over short riding boots. Pants and jacket were both ornamented with gold embroidery. A larger man with a noticeable paunch and round, almost boyish-looking features struggled and laughed as he asked one of the mariachis to help him climb out of the low-slung car.

The large man, whose name was Arlo, was rotund. Roughly fifty years old, he wore an expensive leather jacket and kept a large Cuban Monte Cristo cigar clamped between his teeth as he entered the casino. His eyes were almost covered by bushy black eyebrows. A black wisp of wavy hair hung in his eyes as he scanned the table games. His face was red with liquor, his eyes sparkling with excitement.

The band members put on large white sombreros trimmed broadly with gold, laughing and making jokes in a carefree manner as they followed behind. Arlo and his entourage sauntered to the VIP roulette table. The crowd seemed impressed by his elaborate show of wealth, and two voluptuous young women quickly appeared from nowhere to grab him by the elbows. Arlo was obviously pleased by their reaction and flirted outrageously. Kissing them both full on the lips, he slipped pesos into the bodices of their dresses.

The ladies energized him even more than he had been, and he boldly handed a banker's check for $100,000 to the manager. The silver-haired man accepted the check gladly and clapped Arlo on the back as stacks of chips were counted out and placed before him. Wobbling on his feet, Arlo moved to the betting area and immediately placed $1,000 on red number five.

"The fifth month, the fifth day, Cinco de Mayo," he laughed. "That's got to be a lucky number."

The women laughed indulgently and nodded, pressing themselves competitively against him.

The wheel was sent spinning by the dealer. The crowd clapped and shouted for their numbers as the wheel clicked loudly and spun around and around. The noise faded as the wheel slowed gradually and the shouts intensified. It slowed more and more before finally stopping on red five.

Cheers and raucous laughter filled the room, some congratulating Arlo and others groaning that they should have picked the same number on that day of all days.

The mariachi band sprang to life in wild celebration. Two violins, two trumpets, a twelve-string guitar, and a deeply resonating round-backed guitar let loose in a skillfully coordinated song of merriment. Mariachi bands traditionally celebrated the great moments in the lives of the Mexican people, and Arlo certainly thought this was one of his moments. He danced around the table with a broad grin, his hands held high above his head and his fingers snapping to the rhythm of the music. The ladies squealed in delight and joined him.

Flushed with victory and full of himself, Arlo finally returned to his place at the table and slapped it with his hand. "Juarez made it possible for me to be a free man and do as I please. This day is for him, and I believe in the luck of the number. Let it ride on five!" He doubled the stack on number 5 and shouted: Go....

That said, he wrapped his arms around the women and squeezed them against him, his hands slipping over the swells of their breasts and caressing their bellies as the dealer smiled and spun the wheel again.

The wheel stopped again on red five!

"Viva Juarez!" Arlo shouted. The singing and dancing began again. He turned to the raven-haired woman on his right and pulled her in for a close and sensual flamenco dance. They stomped the floor in rhythm and the woman twirled her skirts until they rose high on her thighs. Arlo's chubby jowls and round, pudgy cleft chin framed another broad grin. His eyes wrinkled with crow's feet as he pulled the woman up to his chest and ran his hand down her back and over her bottom. The other woman watched anxiously, temporarily forgotten.

Stepping away, Arlo placed his chips among several numbers. "This is Juarez's birthday, 3/21/18." When his numbers did not hit, he celebrated anyway, singing, "No problem. No problem." He smiled and squeezed the lighter-haired woman. "Juarez taught us to remain steadfast when the chips are down. No problem." She smiled up at him, nodding and clutching his chest.

He next put his chips on numbers one, eight, six, and two. "1862," he explained. "The year of our defeat of the French!" One of the numbers hit and everyone again shouted with joy. "Viva Juarez!" Arlo shouted again as the band played "Viva Mexico." He piled large stacks of chips on red five and six other numbers. The crowd clapped and cheered him on as he hit a win again. The pay-off was enormous, and Arlo began passing out chips to all of the ladies nearby, the croupier, and the mariachis that played behind him. "Free drinks for all," he shouted toward the bar.

Soon, everyone held up their free drinks and toasted Arlo, Juarez, Cinco de Mayo, and whatever else someone happened to shout. Arlo downed his drink in one long tip and grabbed handfuls of chips, lifting them over his head and letting them pour down like a mountain cataract. Some of the ladies laughed and pulled their blouses open far enough to catch many of the chips. When Arlo was finished, he turned to the crowd and shouted over their laughter, "Never, never, never give up! I built my life with those words, thanks to El Presidente Benito Juarez!"

Some nodded and lifted their glasses with another. "Viva Juarez!" Others laughed at the man who was drunk both with liquor and with his own sense of victory. Still others crouched on the floor and snatched up some of his chips.

Arlo soon swaggered from the casino to his limo, which had remained waiting outside. He asked the band to play "Viva Mexico," and danced around the limo before getting inside. He threw notes into the air and stuffed several under his chauffeur's hat.

The night hummed around them as the limo pulled away. The city was alive with memories of the past, of the men who had led them to victory and other men who had fallen in defeat. The city had watched quietly, appraising these men as they rose and fell, each one promising so much. Some had delivered over those long years; others had fallen short.

Nations do find, in the end, their heroes and villains. Heroes earn their gratitude, but villains are never, ever celebrated. Thus, on the fifth day of May every year, Cinco de Mayo celebrates the Mexican victory over the French occupational army.

The Hapsburg Curse

"The evil that we do and suffer from is chosen by us and not by God."

"Destroy thou them, O God. Let them fall by their own councils; cast them out in the multitude of their transgressions; for they have rebelled against thee."

—Psalms 5–10

In Hungary, in 1847, a progressive political group was on the rise. The excited people felt directly addressed, as if this group of men truly represented them, and the group won an overwhelming victory in the next election. Austrian Emperor Franz Joseph ignored the vote, one of many actions on his part that eventually led to the Hungarian revolt against his tyranny in Buda-Pest.

On March 15th of the following year, a traveling fair came to town, drawing a steady flow of peasants out into the sleet and cold from the surrounding country-side. A man by the name of Sündor Petofi saw the growing numbers of people in the city and perceived the political power that could be exploited. He did not waste that moment; instead, he lead a handful of conspirators out into the streets and read aloud his "National Song," which he had hastily written the evening before. It was carefully designed to touch the very heart of rebellious sentiment:

> *Rise Hungarians, your country calls!*
> *The time is now, now or never!*
> *Shall we be slaves or free?*
> *This is the question! Choose!*
> *To the God of the Hungarians*
> *We swear,*

We swear we shall
Slaves no longer be!

As Petofi had hoped, the crowd that had quickly gathered began picking up the last line of his song and repeating, "We swear we shall slaves no longer be!" A riot quickly broke out, suppressed with no little effort by soldiers posted there. The square was soon chaotic, filled with fires and thickening smoke. The weeks that followed were filled with many scenes such as that one, an open revolt against Austrian tyranny.

After a long and difficult effort by the Imperial soldiers, the revolt was finally suppressed and several participants surrendered. This was followed by a savage reprisal. Emperor Franz Joseph sent his emissaries quickly to Hungary, where they were to administer vengeance and retribution on behalf of their ruler. Many good and loyal men were executed for their participation in the nationalistic movement, and by 1867 Austria had decreased Hungary's status to that of a mere colony of the Imperial Crown. During the course of the reprisals and executions for revolting against the Austrian government, all of the newspapers in Vienna covered the coming execution of a count of the royal Hapsburg family. There had been many newspaper reports of executions, but this one drew particular attention not just because of the man's status and relation to the emperor, but because he was a handsome and vibrant man of only thirty years of age. He was popular in royal circles, the heir to a vast property.

The young count's mother had run frantically from pillar to post, trying desperately to obtain a pardon for her only son. She had pleaded and wept to anyone with influence, even begging the courts to intervene, but it had all been in vain. Time and time again, people apologized for her plight but turned her away, all the same.

When the woman had exhausted every avenue for justice, she resorted to writing letters to the most influential people she knew of, begging for help. She sent three in all: one to Metternich of Austria, a second to Czar Nicholas of Russia, and a third to her cousin, Empress Sophie of Austria. Her letter was brief, imparting her sense of urgency with its abruptness.

Your Majesty,

I have no one left to whom I can turn. You are my last hope. My son, Count Louis Bathyani, is to be executed in one month. He is accused of rebelling against the Royal Hapsburgs. He carried a packet of strategic documents that were confiscated during the Hungarian revolt, but I swear that he was unaware of its contents. He was simply obeying the orders of his superiors. His loyalty lies with the Austrian government and its right to rule the Hungarians. He would never knowingly carry such incriminating political documents.

My son is himself a man of Hapsburg blood, so you can see why it is necessary to avoid his death at all costs. If he were to die, it would establish a precedent that could allow any royal to be taken and executed. I implore you, contact Emperor Franz Joseph on his behalf. Prevent this injustice.

Only your intervention can save him.

A desperate Mother,
Countess Bathyani

Many of the royals had reacted with displeasure concerning the upcoming executions, and they had indeed tried to dissuade the Austrian emperor from following through. Franz Joseph turned a deaf ear to their advice. The day before the scheduled execution, Countess Bathyani received a letter from the empress, Queen Sophie.

My Dearest Cousin,

My friend, Czar Prince Metternich, and I have explained the matter of your son quite urgently to Joseph. I fear that he is a man of black and white. There are no gray areas for him. He has clearly explained his sentiments in the matter, stating that a pardon for rebels, no matter what their blood, would not be in the best interest of the Austrian Crown. It is with great sorrow and regret that I must tell you that I cannot offer any help in this matter. My heart goes out to you, from one mother to another.

In Sympathy,

Empress Sophie of Austria

Countess Bathyani crumpled the letter in her two hands and pressed it to her breast. She had no words, and could only sink to her knees with great, breathless sobs. She wept uncontrollably for some time before she finally fainted from exhaustion and fell to her side, hitting her head sharply on the floor.

After several hours of unconsciousness, she awoke to the sound of nightingales outside of her window. She stared at nothing at all, even her blue eyes seeming to have lost their color and gone to gray. It took a few minutes before she realized where she was and remembered the fate that had brought her there. Her glazed eyes darted to and fro, as her mind denied the truth.

"It was all a dream," she thought to herself, "a nightmare." But then she felt the crumpled letter in her hands, and the illusion was broken. Slowly she struggled to a sitting position and stared at the crumpled paper, her thoughts mere scattered fragments. "It's too late," she mumbled to herself, tears welling up in her eyes. "Oh, Louis," she sighed. "If only we could have yesterday again." Her mind whirled with her wish, with her need to protect her son, and with the feeling of desperation that seizes a person when all hope is gone. She had no more answers, just lost opportunities. There was no way to go back, and yet she could not bear to go forward.

It was almost dawn on the day of Count Louis Bathyani's execution. The young man gazed blankly through a tiny barred window in his cell. *My poor mother*, he thought. *I must see her one last time.*

"Guard!" he shouted. "Guard!"

A man in a disheveled uniform shouted twice for him to be quiet before sighing and rising with irritation from his chair at the end of the corridor. He smoothed his tousled hair and yawned as he stepped in front of the cell.

"What do you want?"

"Please," the young man replied, "I must send a message to my mother, Countess Bathyani. Time is short."

"What, no priest for your last moments?" the guard mocked. "You want to see your mother?"

"The priest has already been arranged for," the count snapped. "I need you to send a messenger to bring my mother. I must speak to her."

"Who do you think you are? Your royal blood means nothing here."

Louis was desperate. He searched the pocket of his waistcoat, fumbling desperately before his fingers finally touched a smooth, hard object. He pulled it out and tilted it so that it sparkled in the dim light.

"Look," he says frantically, "this is 18-carat gold. It's a very valuable Swiss watch that belonged to my late father. It'll bring a fine price, and it's yours if you send the messenger for my mother."

The scruffy man scratched his head as he watched the gold watch dangle and sparkle, just out of his reach. Greed flashed in his eyes as he grabbed for it.

Louis pulled it back against his body. "You can have it if you send the messenger with my note to Countess Bathyani."

"Alright, alright," the guard hissed between his teeth, stepping back. He waited impatiently for several minutes while Louis sat at a small desk and wrote a hasty letter. "Come on then," the guard moaned impatiently.

Louis finally turned and handed him the note. "You'll get the watch when you bring my mother to me."

"What do you take me for, a fool?" the guard screamed. "I'll have it now! You'll just have to take my word."

"Very well." Louis reluctantly handed his treasure to the jailer. "Please hurry. There isn't much time."

The jailer snatched the watch, clutching it protectively as he walked back down the hall. When he arrived at the entrance of the jail, he glanced around suspiciously to be sure no other guards were about, then opened his hand to examine the watch in the sunlight. An instant later, startled by a sound, he looked up in surprise to see a twelve year-old boy.

"You, boy, come here!" he demanded, trying to hide his reaction.

The boy walked timidly to the jailer.

"What do you think you're doing hanging around here? I should throw you in jail for loitering."

"Please, sir," the boy pleaded, visibly shaken. "Please don't throw me in jail!"

The jailer smirked. "I'm feeling generous today, so perhaps jail is a bit too harsh for my mood."

The boy heaved a sigh of relief.

"But still, loitering is a crime and you have to pay for it somehow."

"Yes, sir," the boy whispered with a faint nod.

The jailer thrust Louis's note into the boy's hand. "Take this message to Countess Bathyani at the old villa north of town. If she's not there, don't stop until you find her." The boy nodded and stared at the folded paper. "Look smart, boy! Hurry up!" the guard snapped, and the boy flinched. He turned and ran from the jail, with the guard's laughter trailing behind him.

The countess, having dressed hurriedly, began anew her search for a pardon. She had already contacted all of her friends and anyone she knew who was in authority, and so she was now prepared to turn to strangers, to anyone, to help her stop this tragedy.

As a result, when the boy arrived at the villa, he found it empty. As he had been ordered, he continued his search, as the countess continued hers.

The time finally arrived for the young man's execution. There had been no word from his mother. He stared wide-eyed at the town square as he was led out with his hands bound behind his back. The square was filled with people and their shouts. They had turned out in high numbers for the entertainment, complete with a priest and a squad of military drums that beat a rhythm that at times was lost in all of the other loud noises of the square.

Louis tried his best to march with dignity to the gallows. An officer stepped forward, his hands held high. The drums stopped and the noise subsided as he announced in a loud voice, "Count Bathyani is to be hung by the neck until he is dead. He has been convicted of the crime of disloyalty and high treason."

As leg restraints were fastened about Louis's ankles, he scanned the crowd for his mother. She was nowhere to be seen. The Officer of the Guard offered the Count a black hood, but he refused it. He wanted to have every possible second to search the throng of faces for his mother.

The hangman kneeled before him, awaiting his pardon. Louis turned his eyes with great effort away from the crowd and looked down at the man. "For what you are about to do," he said slowly and with dignity, "I forgive you."

The priest raised his hand and traced the sign of the cross in the air before turning and walking down the steps of the gallows. A hangman's noose was slipped around Louis's neck.

From a distance, the count finally saw his mother running toward him.

At that moment the general gave a quick nod, and the hangman tripped open the trap door.

Louis's face quickly turned purple as the oxygen was cut off. His mother heaved ragged breaths as she lunged toward the gallows, but several guards held her back. She screamed and fought them, pleading for them to let her go as Louis struggled at the end of the rope. It took over five minutes for him to die, and all the while his mother screamed and wept. The crowd cheered on his death, drowning out her wails.

The hangman finally released the rope, and Louis's body fell to the ground with a thud.

As the guards loaded his lifeless body onto a cart, Countess Bathyani finally reached him, staring down at her son with a hollow and haunted stare. The bells rang loudly and the wind blew harshly, whipping her hair about her pale face. She watched them throw a piece of burlap over his body, covering all but the feet.

She suddenly leaned over the cart and untied the lacings of his shoes. The guards watched in surprise as she pulled the shoes off and kissed the dead man's bare feet.

The cart began to roll slowly away, but she followed alongside it, wailing, "Only your mother has the right to kiss your face now … I'll make do with your feet." Tears poured down her face as she stumbled, trying to keep up with the cart as it picked up speed. She finally stumbled and fell to the road, clutching Louis's shoes as she watched the cart move up the street and around the corner, out of sight.

The countess sobbed and struggled to her feet, running across the street and up the stairs of a church. Inside, she darted into the belfry door, rushing up the spiral steps. Gasping for breath, she stepped out into the bell tower and placed her son's shoes reverently on a stone wall there. After taking a moment to catch her breath, she grasped the huge, woven rope of the church bell and pulled hard. The bell gonged loudly over and over as she wept and screamed to the skies. "Take notice, God! Hear me, God! Remember me, God!"

People on the street below frowned and squinted into the light, trying to make out what was happening as she pulled the rope over and over, screaming, "House of Hapsburg! Remember the evil that we do! The evil that we suffer from! It's chosen by us, not by God!" The wind whipped her hair wildly. "Take my revenge! Take my revenge upon those who kill innocent sons! Let there be a new curse on them! Let their sons be killed likewise innocent! He that kills a mother's son must see his own sons killed!"

With that, she let go of the rope and ran to each of the four corners of the tower in turn. Her face was strained and red as the wind whipped at her mercilessly. "Have you heard me, God? Have you heard this mother's curse? You created mankind! I created my son! You wretched Hapsburgs. How will you like *your* murdered sons?"

CHAPTER 1

▼

RISING FROM THE ASHES

March 21, 1806

It was early morning in the Mexican village of San Pablo Guelatao, the home of the Oaxaca, a Zapotec Indian tribe. A middle-aged Zapotec Indian plowed his field in preparation for planting huaxacac, the type of squash for which the region was named. Birds flew in to pick at the insects. The ground was dry and dusty.

A gentleman-farmer-become-businessman named Don Antonio Maza was visiting his farmhouse in the area, in search of wild boar and partridges to hunt. He held an intricately carved, expertly made gun in his hand.

An elderly Indian woman ran out of her hut and into the plowed fields, crying, "It's a boy! A boy!" Upon hearing this, the farmer left his plowing and running through an acre of plowed fields, rushing to Señor Maza. When he reached him, he panted, "Sir, my wife had a boy. Can you come to my house to give your blessings and suggest his name?"

"Oh, well … yes, of course," said Señor Maza, walking toward the humble house. It was a small duty he was glad to perform.

The perspiring midwife held the newborn baby, small and dark, upside down. His two small feet were clamped firmly in her right hand. She patted the buttocks again and again to no avail. The baby appeared lifeless. She struck the child one last time, holding her breath as if somehow transferring her life breath to him. Finally, the boy began to cry. "That's better," the midwife said, smiling as she gently wiped the baby with a clean cloth.

"Was he stillborn?" asked Señor Maza.

"Well, almost," she admitted, wearily wiping the perspiration from her brow.

The new father beamed. "Sir, you've brought me luck. This is a most fortunate day. A son! How can I thank you?"

"This place is called San Pablo Gueletao," Maza mused. "Call the boy Benito Pablo Juarez. A man called Pablo was a friend of my father, a fine man."

"Decided. My son's name will be Benito Pablo Juarez. What did that Pablo do for a living?" Marcelino Juarez asked, proud that his patron would spare his busy time for a poor man's family.

"He was a clergyman," Maza said, and began to walk away, thinking about the day's obligations.

The farmer ran after him, not wanting to let such a fine moment go. "Then this boy will also be a clergyman. I'll give my daughter Josefa in your service, sir. She's bright and hardworking. She'd be paid for in full, if you educate my son in the service of the Church," he said, hoping he had not pushed the issue too hard.

Señor Maza took a moment to ponder as he studied the girl. *Yes*, he thought, *she is fair and healthy enough to make a good house servant.* "That's an arrangement I'll accept."

The farmer walked his twelve year-old daughter toward the stately coach. Slowly, regretfully, she allowed herself to be led, too shocked to protest. When it was time to climb aboard, the reality of it hit her and she began to weep. Her father tried to comfort his daughter, whispering, "His house will always have food. You'll never be hungry. Weep if you must, but you're going to serve the Maza family for a good cause, the education of your brother."

Josefa sat stoically in the coach as it moved away. Her eyes were large and rimmed with red from her tears. Her black hair whipped wildly in the wind and dust, and she wept quietly as she waved to her father. He walked beside the coach, then ran until the coach picked up too much speed for him to follow. With tears in his eyes, he shouted after her, "Rich men have money! Oh my poor daughter, meek people have no choice but to serve them!"

When the farmer returned to the meager hut that was their home, his wife, Brigida, was dismayed and greatly weakened by the birth. "Why did you send Josefa away with Señor Maza? She's still a child! Besides that, I need her now more than ever around the house," she reminded him, hoping for any reason to be good enough to bring her back.

He sat beside her, picked up his infant son, and gently kissed her and the baby. "I did it for him, for his future." Josefa's mother began to cry. As he stroked his wife's head, he murmured, "Cry, dear, but this son of ours will bring us honor and make us proud."

Oaxaca Town Center

The attractive horse-drawn carriage pulled up to a well-fortified and wealthy house. Señor Maza took Josefa inside his well-kept courtyard and tried to console her. "This, my home, is now also your home. I'm your new uncle. Live here and sometimes you may go back home to play with your little brother. If you love him and do well, you'll get to see him more often, when he comes to be educated by me."

The girl was still visibly upset "What will education get him?" she demanded, tears streaking her angry face.

"He'll be able to select a position in life, any position he likes: baker, blacksmith ..."

"Will he become our President?" she interrupted.

Señor Maza laughed and ruffled the girl's hair. "He'll be a priest," he said with certainty.

"No," she said stubbornly, pulling herself up to her full four and a half feet. "I want my brother to be President."

"That won't be, can't be," Señor Maza said with deep conviction. "Mexico isn't a breeding ground for poor people to become presidents."

"I want to see my brother become a President. I'll work. I'll pray every day."

Señor Maza smiled at the courageous girl. "If wishes were horses, beggars would ride."

Josefa twisted her face and furrowed her brow, trying to understand his words. "What does that mean?"

"Nothing ... nothing. Run along, child," Señor Maza said offhandedly.

"You said something," she said stubbornly, waiting for an explanation.

He laughed as he walked away. "It means don't dream that high, little one."

Turning her back on the man, she clutched her rosary and whispered to herself, "Education will make him our noble President. Beggars would then ride."

Back in the village of San Pablo, the new parents did their best to see their son was cared for, and everything went well enough until the child was a year old. Then, one day while tending the family sheep, the baby's father was bitten on the forearm by a starving and sickly old wolf. He killed it with ease and wrapped the wound with a bandana, going back to work.

Marcelino Juarez became ill a week later. There was nothing anyone could do for him. His fever raged, and spots appeared all over his body. His eyes appeared red and a cough racked his body. He could not keep the smallest sip of water down. Every Indian in the village, including their wise man, prayed and tried every remedy known to them. Herbal healings were tried, using varying doses of plant extracts in mixtures of measured quantity. The disease progressed through various complications: diarrhea, labored breathing and thick congestion. His agony continued for eleven days. Then, on the evening of the eleventh day, his sweat-covered brow relaxed. His body lost its struggle and he died, as his wife cried out in helpless anguish.

Brigida was pregnant again. The next six months were torture for her and her son. She was ill and in a deep depression most of the time. Though the villagers brought food several times a week, Benito's mother was simply too ill to eat. At the end of six months, she died in childbirth. The tiny infant girl was too weak to survive and joined her mother in death. The villagers wrapped the mother and daughter together in a blanket and buried them on the hillside.

The toddler had no understanding. Indians rarely cried, even children. He saw people whom he had never seen cry, yet they were weeping and moaning at this triple tragedy. Young Juarez, now three, was sent to live with his uncle and guard-ian, Bemardino Juarez and his wife, who were poor peasants. They lived in the village of Ixtlan, where the land was still barren and dry. Life was hard and there was not enough food, no matter how hard they worked. Some nights, they all went to bed hungry.

The night Benito arrived at the hut, there was a loud confrontation. Bemar-dino said to his wife, Juanita, "We have no choice but to raise this child. He has no one else. We can't turn him away."

"But we've barely enough food for our own family. He's not old enough to work, or do anything to help pay for the costs. You're taking bread out of our mouths if you accept this child," his bitter wife objected bitterly.

"The decision has been made, woman, and we must make the best of it."

The child Benito heard this, confused and lost in his new world. He missed his family. Nothing here was the same as it was at home. For the most part he was ignored. When his uncle was away, his aunt "forgot" to feed him and, when she did give him food, it was ill-prepared.

The family dog was in the habit of hanging around for any scraps of food left after the meal. Benito's aunt would eat her food and then leave Benito alone to fend for himself. The dog waited until she left, then helped himself to the food.

The boy finally decided that if he must share his food with the animal, he would. The relationship between the two grew, and they became very close.

One day, Bemardino came home from the fields to find little Benito trying to retrieve a bit of his food. His uncle was furious. "Wake up, you lazy woman!" he exclaimed to his wife. "No wonder this child is so thin and weak! Is this how you care for him when I'm away?"

Juanita swung her legs off the cot and said, "Look, the boy is your family, not mine. I've plenty to do around here without being a wet nurse to that brat."

"Haven't you got one bit of human kindness in you? Where's your heart? How can you neglect such a helpless child?"

From that day on, Bemardino saw to it that the boy was fed in the early morning and at night before he put him to bed. They became as close as any two people can be. His uncle talked to him, taught him what he could, made sure he was fed properly, and protected him from his cruel aunt.

A day came when Benito's aunt and uncle took him to the fields. They worked until noon while Benito played with the family dog, stopping to eat the small loaves of bread that his aunt had tied into her apron. From a distance, they saw their neighbor Carlos running through the field, crying in panic, "Help me! Someone help me!"

Bemardino rose from his lunch and trotted to the frightened man. "How can we help you, friend?"

"A wolf pack is circling on the far ridge! They'll attack my sheep and kill all of them if we don't hunt them down. Come quickly!"

Sheep were the most valuable possessions in their part of the world, making all the difference between life and death. Bemardino instructed his wife to finish hoeing the last ten rows and then take Benito back to the hut. Grumbling to herself, Juanita took up the hoe and grudgingly labored until the rows were completed. She was a lazy person and resented all of this work thrust upon her, but she continued to work until the rows were weeded. By that time, it was almost dark and she was hungry. She trudged wearily back to the hut, prepared a small bit of food to eat, then collapsed on her cot and went to sleep.

Late in the evening, Uncle Bemardino returned home, careful not even to light a candle so that he'd not awake his sleeping family. He headed straight for bed and fell wearily to sleep. Soon, however, he began to toss and turn on the bed as a nightmare unfolded in his mind: Little Benito was on the edge of a raging waterfall, the water churning maliciously at his feet. The boy was weeping and calling out for his uncle to save him....

Bemardino awakened from his dream at midnight, every fiber of his being tensed as sweat poured from his brow. He exhaled and rested his face briefly in his hand, relieved that it had only been a dream. Still, the nightmare left him anxious and he knew he wouldn't be able to rest until he checked on the boy. Standing, he made his way to Benito's small cot.

It was empty.

Looking farther, Bernardino saw that the dog was not at the foot of Benito's cot where he usually slept. Growing more upset by the moment, he awakened his sleeping wife.

"Where's Benito?" he demanded.

She rose on one elbow, mumbling in a voice deep with sleep, "How should I know where he is? Perhaps he went outside to pee."

Bernardino rushed outside and searched, calling the boy's name. "Benito! Benito Juarez!" the distraught man called over and over into the black night.

Finally, defeated, he went back into the house, pulled his wife from her bed and shook her by the shoulders. "Think! THINK!! Where he can be?"

"The feeble-brain probably wandered off," the callous woman shouted over him. Breaking free from his hands, she walked away in disgust. "I told you not to bring that brat here!"

It finally dawned on Bemardino what had probably happened. "Did you bring the child back from the fields?" he demanded.

"I don't remember! I told you he was nothing but trouble," she answered, pushing her stringy hair back from her face.

"There are *wolves* in the fields. If anything's happened to him, you'll have *me* to answer to!" Wild with worry, he slapped her across the face.

She staggered back to the fireplace and thumped against it. Stunned and enraged, she reached behind her for the poker and swung it in front of her, keeping him away from her.

"I have no time to waste with you now. I'm going to find Benito." Bemardino ran outside with a lantern and a massive stick for protection. It was three miles to the fields and he ran headlong into the night, stumbling as he called out the boy's name. "Benito, Benito, Benito! Where are you?"

When he reached the fields, he found Benito lying in the dirt, the family dog sitting close by to guard the child. The boy was having a night terror, with tears running down his cheeks. Though his eyes were wide open, he was still asleep, staring out into the darkness and shrieking, " No! Get away! Please don't let it get me! Help! Someone help!"

Bemardino scooped him up and quickly scanned the area for wolves, but there were none. Gently, he carried the boy home, whispering in his ear, "There, there Benito … Everything is safe now. Go back to sleep, little one."

From that night on, Bemardino took over his care completely. He fed him faithfully every morning and night. He was furious with his wife, and they rarely spoke to each other after that. He was cautious and didn't leave Benito alone with his wife for more than a short time after that, rarely letting him out of his sight. A fiercely close relationship built between the man and the boy, who now went with him daily to work on the plowing and planting. The villagers knew that whenever they saw Bemardino Juarez, Benito Juarez would be close by.

His uncle taught him everything a man needed to know about living in the village. Benito was observant and astute, soon learning how to survive. He was also clever, and his mind searched hungrily for more knowledge.

Years passed, and Juarez became a bright, intense boy of twelve, with a shock of black hair. His round, dark-brown eyes took in everything around him, as if he knew he must learn of the world and grow up quickly in order to survive.

Helping his uncle around the household and farm, he worked industriously, eager to please. He contentedly whistled a tune as he worked, whistling more softly as the day went on and he grew more tired.

One day, after his many chores were done, he walked out into the fields at sunset and spread his arms up, wide and high to the heavens, shouting, "Oh, my Creator, give me UNDERSTANDING!"

The boy was a wanderer, an observer, learning about every bush and bird. With his chores done, he walked away from home towards the bushes and water. When he reached the edge of the river, he sat down, whistling, looking intently at the birds as cattle grazed nearby. He watched them for a long time, trying to imagine what they might be thinking. He often wondered about his purpose for being on earth. "Is this all there is to life?" he questioned. "No, there must be more. It's up to me to find out." Like a perching bird, he rode one of the large brown buffalo, whistling and sometimes lying down on the its bare back as his beloved dog trailed behind. Later, he stood up on the buffalo, spreading his arms to the sky, shouting again, "Oh, my Creator, give me UNDERSTANDING!" The buffalo just kept moving and grazing. Even the birds got used to him.

A gruff-looking policeman, passing by, heard the boy's shout. He watched him in secret for a while, hoping the youth would do something with which he could find fault. Always eager to give an Indian trouble, the policeman smiled cruelly and came closer, finally jumping out and seizing Juarez, twisting his ear viciously. "Now, my dirty little Indian, what can you understand from *this* experience?"

The pain was white-hot, unbearable. Juarez, frightened, reacted by giving him a kick to the groin.

The older man reeled back in pain. As he sank to the ground, he gasped, "You … Indian scum … You'll be severely … punished for this!"

The policeman slowly and painfully rose to his feet, then staggered forward in an attempt to catch the boy, but the terrified Juarez slipped out of his reach. He ran as fast as he could, terrified to see that the policeman was in hot pursuit. In desperation, he threw stones at the pursuing man as he fled. One especially large stone hit the policeman's knee and he fell to the ground in pain again. Benito ran without looking back, the wind whipping his hair around his face. His fear pumped energy into his heart and legs. He finally slowed and looked back when he was sure he had escaped.

Back at the hut, Juarez breathlessly told his story to his aunt, hoping that under such extreme circumstances she could perhaps now offer some support and a small bit of understanding. Instead, she raved against him uncontrollably, beating him madly and striking him on the head. Dark blood oozed from his ear, and he began to weep. She shouted, "I have told you a hundred times to be a good boy! You good-for-nothing!"

Juarez cupped his hand to his ear to contain the blood and groaned, finally wailing, "I am a good boy! I'm good …"

His aunt fumed. "Every day, I hear you reporting things against the police and the army men, endangering everyone in this family! You must *want* to go to jail! And maybe that would be a good thing, in some ways—one less mouth to feed! But what of all the money we'd have to pay to the police and court clerks?"

She trailed off and there was a dense silence. Seeing the damage she had caused, and worried about what her husband would do when he saw this, she got up to burn a small piece of silk cloth she had saved for such injuries, getting ready to pack it into his wound. "Your sister will weep, Juarez, and your uncle will worry," she said, trying to give a reason for her bad temper as she softened her position.

"My sister won't have to weep. I'll work hard, and one day I'll become the President, as my sister said. Then *you'll* weep."

Angry once more at his courageous words, the woman sneered, "Hm … Look at your face. You're ugly. You're poor. You're small and stocky. You're an Indian. You have no education. And you think you'll spread your arms, like the prophet Moses, and the sea will part for you? Outrageous. President? Ha!" she scoffed.

Other family members ran in to save Juarez from the ill-tempered woman. Juarez walked out and kept walking. He spread his arms ... but said nothing.

It was dark, far past suppertime, and Juarez had not returned. His uncle was concerned and looked for the boy. He called his name over and over, but there was no answer. After almost an hour, he decided to return home. As he approached the shack, he heard a small sniffling sound coming from the chicken hut. Walking closer, he took a look.

Under the small lean-to, he saw a small form. Benito was hiding there, with a small baby chick in his hands.

"Benito, come out now. It's late and you must return. Your aunt is in a better mood now. She's forgotten all about it."

"But I haven't forgotten it. I'll never forget it. I'll always hear her words in my ears. It's not the beating I'll remember, it's her terrible words. I'm too angry, Uncle. I can't go back in there!"

"You're becoming a man, so come, let's sit on the step. I must instruct you about anger."

Benito, slightly encouraged by his uncle's soft words, slowly followed him to the front porch and sat on the step. When both of them were seated, his uncle took a rag from his pocket and wiped Benito's tears. They sat in silence for a few moments, with the older man's arm around the boy, to take away the chill.

Benito finally asked, "Why is it that I love you and I hate your wife?"

"Because I'm mindful but she's not. I'm careful but she's not," his uncle explained. "I don't mix words and compound them with my anger, but she does. If I'm angry, I may hold my tongue, but she doesn't. She reacts by saying something strange, something inaccurate, adding her rage to it. She's actually hitting you with many things, Benito ... Wrong words, inaccurate statements, anger, arrogance, hate or pity ... You end up getting a mixture. You find it hard to separate her words from her attitudes. At times like these, you're confused."

"It hurts," Benito said softly. "Why does she do that?"

"It's her problem."

Benito looked at his uncle fondly. "You're always kind to me, even when you're angry. Why?"

"Because I've learned to think straight," Uncle Bernardino said. "If I'm angry, I can show my anger, but I don't speak. I don't send mixed signals. If I want to show my affection, I use words accurately and deliberately. A man must weigh everything carefully before he speaks. They say 'A pound a word.' That means you must speak very carefully, very accurately. That will save you so much in life." Bemardino was silent a moment, rubbing his forehead with his hand. Finally, he continued, "Words are like food for birds. A baby chick can't swallow bone with food. Humans can't swallow abuse, anger, frustration, and spitting anger with words. That makes them hate those who hurl it like a pistol shot."

He paused, looking at his hands for a moment before turning to look at his nephew directly. "There's nothing we can't talk about, you know?"

Benito nodded in agreement.

"Benito, let me tell you what my father told me about anger. Anger is an explosive feeling, and if kept inside, it'll eat you alive. The person you're angry with has forgotten, but as long as you hold it in your heart, it hurts you. My papa said, 'the best way to return anger is with humor.' Make them laugh. It offsets the other person. They're not expecting it. There are other tools, like evasion and avoiding the source of your anger. But the most important thing to remember is that, if you choose any of these methods, *you remain in command of the situation.* Being in control is a fine thing, Benito. It lets you decide what'll happen next. Now that you have some tools to use, you can work through any angry time you have."

"Yes, Uncle. Being in control … I like that. Someday, when I'm a leader, I'll *always* be in control." Benito was beginning to form the rigid morality he would one day use to advance to the highest office of his country. His aunt's cruelty was also arousing a passionate, lifelong hatred for anyone who mistreated babies and orphans.

By 1819, Juarez was thirteen and had a daily routine of watching his uncle's flock of sheep. On one such day, he sat watching the flock on the mountain side, sleepy after a long and quiet day. The sheep were grazing peaceably while Benito carved at a piece of wood. He lifted his head from his work … and six armed riders came into view. They rode in close to Juarez and began to take the sheep by force, with drawn pistols. Juarez was angry, but he remembered his uncle's lessons and tried to reason with the men.

"Señors, we're very poor. If you take all our sheep, we'll have nothing to live on for the winter."

They laughed at the boy and began to rough him up, pushing him around in a circle, each one taking their turn to bully him. Some cursed at him, while others hit him. One man, the largest, kicked him several times.

Finally, one of the men took pity on him and told the others, "We're not sheepherders! We'll eat roast lamb for dinner, but then we'll be on our way. Let's have the boy skin this sheep and fix our meal, and then we'll ride on and leave him be."

With tears in his eyes, Juarez did as the man said. Three hours later, the men mounted their horses and rode off. Feeling tremendous guilt over the loss of his uncle's sheep, he despaired. "How can I face my uncle, knowing I'm responsible for this terrible loss?"

He decided he'd take the remaining sheep home and then run away.

Juarez had realized, long before, that he must learn the Spanish language somehow, and that he would never have a chance to learn it in this backwoods town. He knew he could only learn it in the city, not in the hills of his ancestors. He was determined, no matter the cost, to learn the language, learn everything. *Perhaps this incident is a sign*, he thought. *Perhaps it is time for me to go.*

Once he had safely shepherded the remainder of the flock back to his uncle's home, he fled the little town and began the long trek to Oaxaca City, the State's capital. He walked many difficult, mountainous miles on bare feet, managing thirty miles in one day and setting up camp on the windy crags. His drive pushed him not only toward the Spanish language that he so longed to learn but also toward a mingling of races, civilizations, cultures, the future.

When he finally reached the city, he could hardly believe his eyes. It was a large and beautiful Spanish colonial town. Buildings rose higher than any he had ever seen before, with spanning arches of brick and stone. He forgot his aching feet and wandered through the beautifully tiled squares, amid the hum of more people and horses than he had ever seen in one place. Simple Indians sat behind blankets spread out to display their wares, while wealthy people rode and strolled by, in clothes so exquisite that they were finer than any that Benito had imagined. He sat by a fountain and watched it spurt cool, clear water as he rested for a time. Then he drank from it gratefully and moved on.

In Oaxaca, Benito found his sister, Josefa, still serving the family of Antonio Salanueva Maza. She could hardly believe he had come, that her reason for being here all these years had finally fulfilled its purpose. Perhaps his success would make it all worthwhile. She knew their mother had wept bitterly for the remainder of her life after losing her daughter, never truly getting over the loss. Josefa herself had cried for years for her dead mother's sorrow, wishing that she and Benito had been able to know each other. But the distance and their poverty had made that impossible.

She knew that their father had suffered, as well. He had offered Josefa to Señor Maza for the good of the entire family, and as she had matured she came to understand and forgive him. Given how short their parents' lives had turned out to be, matters had ended up being for the best. There was nothing for them back home. Josefa suspected that her brother had had a difficult time without their parents, and she was relieved to see that he had finally come, that he had not forgotten their father's wishes.

Josefa told Benito where to find Señor Maza. He immediately followed his sister's directions and spied Maza supervising a group of laborers in one of his fields. The boy ran to him, catching up with him just beyond the field.

Breathless and perspiring, he said, "Señor, I am Benito Juarez. I'm here for an education. Can you help me?"

Antonio raised his eyebrows in surprise and tilted his hat back on his head. "Well, well, the newborn has turned into a young man. Yes, I promised your father when you were born that I would see to your education. I'll teach you to read and write in Spanish. Because I'm a good Catholic, I'd like you to complete your education and then become a priest."

"Sir," Benito said, "I don't think I like priests much. They're rich, and many take land and money from the poor. I want to be a lawyer."

Señor Maza smiled. "A lawyer, is it? Well, there's hardly any point in debating that now. There's no hurry. Take your time. This is my card. Come when you wish. Your sister Maria Josefa would be glad for you to live with us. Besides, she has *big, big* dreams for you, Juarez."

"*Thank you*, Señor Maza," Benito rejoiced, thrilled to have a chance to gain the knowledge that he knew he'd need to make important choices in his life. He would begin his education as soon as possible.

Antonio Salanueva Maza was the adoptive father of Margarita Maza. Juarez often saw the young girl around the hacienda during his early visits, but to him she was just a gangly adolescent, all knees and elbows, giggling behind bushes and running away.

"A pest, really," he thought.

Seven years passed. It was 1826 and Benito, now a young man of twenty, pushed himself to learn as much and as well as he could, careful not to look back at his previous life. At one point, several years back, he had gotten temporarily distracted from school, instead focusing on running with his friends and enjoying himself. When his grades had begun to slip his sister Josefa put him back in his place. He smiled at the memory.

She had actually attacked him in a rage, tearing at his hair and beating his head and shoulders. "Have you lost your mind?" she screeched as she slapped him. "Why do you think you're here? Where will you be in ten years, at this rate—still playing with your friends? Picking beans to make enough money to pay for your drinking and running around town?"

Juarez had been stunned. He tried to assure her that there was nothing to worry about, but he finally stopped when she reminded him about their parents. "Why did our mother cry at the loss of her daughter? Why was I forced to leave my family, to come here and work all these years? WHY? So that you can let your only reason for being here take a backseat to your own pleasure?"

That had cleared his mind. She was right; his studies had to come first. He owed it to his dead mother and father, whose desires should never be forgotten, even for a moment. Her words made him feel overwhelmed with guilt, and they cried together for a long time after that.

He was touched when she tearfully confessed that every month she went to church and posted letters to God on the walls, praying for her brother's success. She was so sweet and hopeful, so devoted. She told him that, after one such visit to the church, a bird had swooped down over her head as she walked home. She insisted that it meant God had heard her prayer.

"Please, Benito, don't turn your back on what God has planned for you. He heard my prayer, so now you *have* to keep working hard!"

He held her close and comforted her, swearing never again to forget his purpose for being there. They hugged and vowed always to do anything they could for each other.

Juarez studied in the seminary, as was his guardian's wish, but he had no intention of pursuing it. For now, he bided his time and used the seminary's vast resources to get the best education that he could. His face had filled out a little, his mustache thickened to that of a man's, but still he had those round, intense black eyes that appraised everything.

One sunny day, as Juarez entered the seminary, he was invited to a family celebration for the former giggling girl of previous years.

The day was Margarita's *Quinceañera*, a type of coming-out party to celebrate her fifteenth birthday. In their community, the Quinceañera was a significant celebration due to its history of almost instant "conversion" from childhood to womanhood in the eyes of society. Following the ceremony for the Quinceañera, a young woman was eligible for more responsibilities, such as marriage or work in the church.

Juarez entered the gaily decorated old church and was greeted by his mentor, Señor Antonio. "Welcome, Benito. Today, you're to witness one of the greatest events in my daughter's life, and not only witness, but be a part of it. You're like family, so come join in our celebration. I want you to be her chamberlain, her escort."

Juarez was surprised and pleased, quietly relieved that he had worn his best clothes. His patron led Juarez to the back of the church to join in the procession, and there he saw the radiant young girl.

She was nothing like the pest he remembered. Margarita had been preparing for this day for months and was exceptionally lovely. Her long, gleaming, luxurious raven hair was pulled up on the sides, adorned with a small tiara, which symbolized that her mind would never be far from thoughts of God. Her dress was pink and draped over her hips and down to the floor. The matching pink bodice was designed to be worn slightly off the shoulders.

Just look at those eyes. They're soft, light brown, Juarez thought to himself. A second later he thought, *But no, there's a hint of violet near the pupils that makes them sparkle.* He was instantly attracted to this grown-up girl. And all of this was not wasted on Juarez. He knew most of these girls married by the age of fifteen or sixteen. This celebration acknowledged that she had reached sexual maturity and was now of a marriageable age. The most important element of the celebration was invariably a misa de acción de gracias (thanksgiving mass). The birthday girl arrived, decked out in her fancy, full-length dress, flanked by her parents and godparents. She was specially seated at the foot of the altar throughout the service. She was also accompanied by two damas, or maids of honor, and two chamberlains, or escorts: her father Antonio and Benito Juarez, selected from among family and friends.

The culminating moment of the evening came when the festejada (celebrant) and her number-one chambelán (escort) danced to a traditional waltz. As Señor Antonio stepped out onto the floor, Benito knew in his heart that he must have this woman for his wife. She was from a different class than he, and he almost despaired of any chance of marrying her. But after the waltz began, his feet carried him to her side.

"May I have the next dance with your daughter, sir?" Juarez asked Señor Antonio.

"But of course", he said, smiling with pride at Margarita.

During the next few minutes, the two young hearts joined in spirit with few words being said, and they vowed they'd see each other again soon.

"Speech is a mirror of the soul: as a man speaks, so is he."

—*Publilius Syrus*

1826—Franciscan Santa Cruz Seminary, Oaxaca, Mexico

Using the argument that he was not yet old enough to be ordained; Juarez was able to persuade Don Antonio and the Maza family to permit him to take some courses in the liberal arts.

A well-dressed young woman, with long raven hair covered with a black lace mantilla, stepped down from her coach and entered the boarding house of the school. A circular dormitory stood adjacent to a large study. She knocked at a door and it opened. Inside was Juarez the student, writing a long list of names on the blackboard. He greeted her and they tenderly embraced. Looking around but not finding her chaperone, he gave her a quick kiss on the cheek.

"How did you get away without Isabel today?" he asked.

Margarita blushed. "She had one of her blinding headaches. I told her I needed to go to confession, which I have. So she told me to take the carriage and go on without her." She looked around inquisitively. She was clever and didn't miss a thing. "What's this?" she asked, pointing to the blackboard. "Did Uncle Salanueva arrange for you to be admitted here to study Catholic philosophers or these men?"

"I've studied Aquinas and other Catholic philosophers," he explained, pointing to many books with worn spines, "but my heart's just not in official studies on religion. They're not compatible with me. I'd have preferred to learn Rene Descartes's philosophy or the law."

"You're graduating in religion next year. How many more years would it take to graduate in law?" Margarita asked a bit petulantly.

"Seven more years. I can be a lawyer in 1834."

"Seven years ... That long?" she asked. "Why do you want to be a lawyer? Why not a Catholic priest?" suggested Margarita.

Juarez considered his answer carefully. "For various good reasons. Firstly, I want to marry you and also lead a pious married life. Pope Innocent II, in 1139, prohibited clerical marriages. That's unnatural. That's why the sexual scandals of the celibate Catholic priests have continued throughout history. One can remain married to God, but it's the same God who created the basic human passion, call it instinct, to procreate. Either celibacy is a severe test from God or else the Pope has made a serious mistake in this matter. Why should humans be asked to deny part of their nature?"

The girl teasingly asked, "Are you minting this logic only to get married?"

"My knowledge comes from history, Margarita."

"Do I wait seven long years to marry you? I'll be past marrying age by then."

Juarez sighed and walked toward her, looking deeply into her eyes and then kissing her sweetly on the forehead. "Someday," he said, "Señor Maza will come to know about our affair. What then?"

The small, dark-haired girl suppressed a small laugh. "Then … then you would be married to me."

"Just like that?" Juarez grinned.

"Just like that!" she laughed. "My father … and your teacher, Uncle Antonio, he's very fond of you. You know that. He's impressed with your soul but not quite your intellect," she added with a hint of banter.

"What's wrong with my intellect?" Juarez replied, insulted.

Margarita's smile faded and her face took on a more serious look. "My father says that you read the various schools of enlightened thought. That will make you abandon your Catholic faith. You're going to reject religion for secular thoughts. Is this true, Benito?"

Instead of answering, he said, "But they must see my talents."

"What are your talents?" Margarita asked.

"You must see," he said, taking her by the shoulders: "I want to struggle against injustice, arbitrariness. I like freedom of thought. I think like Voltaire. He said, 'Christianity is a good thing for chambermaids and tailors. The elite must look for simple deism.' I want to crush infamous things."

"You think God doesn't exist? " Her eyes widened at the very thought.

"If God didn't exist, we'd have to invent one," he replied, his black eyes flashing.

"If you actually invented God, what would He be doing?"

"Eating corpses or drinking human emotions or, if he's sensible, he'd be making Man realize what He is. Putting sense and sensitivity into mankind!" Juarez walked to the shelf, selecting a book and opening it to a marked page. "This is the Quran of the Muslims. See, it says, 'What has happened to you? How do you judge?' It must be the noblest thing, to judge. Faith is linked to good judgment. Judge well, and judge correctly. That's an awesome responsibility. I want to learn to be skillful in judging. I want to *be* a judge. That's how I can best uplift myself and the society around me. It makes sense. Perhaps He made man because He sought to be judged Himself, to be realized." Juarez walked back to the girl and took her in his arms. "I haven't read anywhere that God loves money and wealth. I want to do something with my life."

"You mastered book-binding, though." Her eyes filled with suggestions. Juarez picked up another book from the table and stared at the book as she spoke. "You were a good book-binder," she said. "With printing presses, the work of book-binding can become enormously well-paying."

"That was years ago. You may be right, Margarita, but I'm not a speculator. A shrewd business sense isn't my forte. I won't be a rich man. Never, ever."

Margarita took the book into her own hands, staring at it as if she could still the confusion of her life through its pages.

"This is about Voltaire," he said, showing her pages in the book, "struggling against judicial arbitrariness. In 1726, he wrote things about a nobleman, Chevalier de Rohan, of the powerful Rohan family of France. That noble had Voltaire beaten black and blue and thrown in jail. The Bastilles and the system didn't give him justice. The law was on the nobleman's side."

"That was unfair and very wrong," she agreed.

"See? Even a typical person would say that's unfair. The ordinary person only considers things on that level. He only thinks that far. A brave person not only thinks but *says* that. The brave *fight* for that. The ordinary person is too worried about his daily bread and butter. He can't say things that might hurt the source of that bread and butter. Those who do speak their convictions are less worried. They're heroes of free speech. Those who fight are truly the brave ones, though the establishment would call them bad names, like rebels or lawless terrorists."

"Outlaws, you mean." Her voice shook unexpectedly, and she fought to control it.

"The very idea that someone is an outlaw is a provocation to bring people *under* the law. Sometimes the law is doing it, sometimes the outlaw."

He could see that Margarita was trying to understand. She paused and then pointed at the blackboard, asking, "This Locke … born in 1632 and died in 1704? What can you learn from such an ancient person?"

"Yes, Locke. An early philosopher, and brilliant. He was the son of a lawyer, a captain in army. He said that it's *understanding* that sets a person above the rest. It gives him advantages and dominion over others. He wanted us to examine our own abilities to *understand* sensibly. Are we fitted to do that? Mostly, we're not." Juarez studied his notes for a moment. On the blackboard was a list of various other authors of the school of enlightened thought. "And Locke didn't like law. He served a Lord and went on to earn his Bachelor in Medicine. I think that law is the best preparation for a political career."

The girl examined another cracked brownish book. "And this Milton? What did he say?"

"A puritan," Juarez explained as they sat at the large, rugged table. "But Blake said he was working for Satan. Milton recognized the absurdity of life and the inherent difficulties of free will. The existentialist praises England, but why praise a king or a parliament that's a general's rubber stamp? It's all about either freedom or faith. He was afraid of the clergy … an artful writer, but he didn't fight the lawless."

Her beautiful eyebrows rose. "Who are the lawless?"

"In monarchies, laws protect the king's will and property. Democracy makes that lawless. The aim of any law is to regulate malfunctions. Civil law should regulate malfunctions in civil conduct, criminal law for criminal conduct, political law for political conduct, merchant law, military law, and so on. In democracy, it's lawful to remove rulers. In a monarchy, that would be high treason and sedition. It's not possible for the king to be asked by his subjects to abdicate. He can't be fired. In democracy, the removal of rulers is a precondition to a better life for the people. So 'lawlessness' depends on the government in place."

"This is all very deep," she replied softly. "Most people don't think on this level. They find it confusing and hard to understand." She leaned across the table and touched his hand, startling him from his own thoughts and making him look directly at her. He was surprised to see that her eyes were filled with tears.

"Benito, politicians here in Mexico have one fate—the firing squad. Generals give them that fate."

"Because the generals regard politicians as their prime competitors for the right to rule," he cut in sharply.

Margarita sat back in her chair and sighed. "Oh, Benito, I worry for you. Law will give you prominence, but I fear that politics will finish you."

"No, sweetheart," he said softly, standing and leaning over the table to put his hands on her shoulders and give her forehead a kiss. "A stout heart plus politics is the key to worldwide fame." He took her into his arms again and they lingered, feeling the shared warmth of their bodies.

After a time, Margarita regained her composure and walked over to read other names, grouped under the heading of philosophers. "Locke, Jefferson, Milton … What's this name? Montesquieu, Voltaire …?"

He moved toward her and the list. "Those are the philosophers of a 'tolerant and just order,' like Hobbes, Milton …"

"And are these your favorite authors of the rationalist school? Rene' Descartes, Benedict de Spinoza, Gottfried William Leebniz …"

"Right. They're called empiricists, like Boyle and Locke …"

"And here," she said, reading from the board, "are the philosophers of the 'natural religion.'"

Juarez was pleased with her persistence in wanting to understand. She adored him, and this love urged her to try and understand what was driving him so. His eyes were shining as he spoke. "These thoughts advance emancipation, freedom. The habitual rulers, kings or generals, don't like these thoughts. They censor it … forbid its literature, banish the philosophers … brutally kill them to clear the path for their own rule."

"So you're planning to compete with the habitual rulers? They're very strong, Benito. They have the armies, the police, and the propagandists."

"They're lacking in any delight or instruction. The old order must change," he said resolutely, "making way for the new. *Democracy* is the new order. *Mexico needs democracy.*"

Margarita moved away, wandering to the far wall and staring at a small, wooden, cross-mounted paperweight lying there. "Benito, kings and generals rule the world. They're becoming very clever. The royal families ask their people to request a prince to accept the throne. The prince provisionally accepts it, then later formally accepts it … then the inauguration in public. And the king holds a general's rank, too. The 'habitual rulers,' as you call them, are getting more skilled at maintaining perpetual rule. Dictators are learning new tricks of the trade. They have tremendous wealth and power." She turned to look at him. "You can't compete against them with your beggars."

"Yes I can and will. It's already happening in Europe," he added. "The people are made to hire a king, then can't fire him. That's still a dictatorship. Those are the dragons the people must fight."

"Do you want marriage, children, and a comfortable family life, or do you want to fight the dragons of the old and new order?" The tears were pouring unbidden from her eyes, and her small hands were now shaking.

"The first is my right. To fight the dragons is my *duty.*"

"You need to be rich to go further," she said, her voice wavering. "You said yourself that you have no ambition for riches."

"I want to make my people and Mexico great and strong. As the saying goes, 'Not gold but only men can make a nation great and strong.'"

"Why can't you be a priest?" she insisted, fighting to keep her voice from breaking.

He thought for a moment and then replied, "My late father and Señor Maza wanted me to be a priest, but my innermost longings are for law and a public service career built around law." He paused, looking into her worried eyes. "And I also want to live my life with you, my dear." He kissed her on the cheek.

Margarita closed her eyes briefly as she was kissed, then opened them slowly. "Your ideas are dangerous," she whispered.

"Dangerous, yes, but they're not sending people to jail for that," he joked, trying to lighten the mood.

Finally realizing that he had firmly set his mind, she visibly gave up, with a slight droop of her shoulders, staring at the floor. She winced at a burning pain in her stomach as fear consumed her. Finally, there was nothing left to do but sadly turn away and leave the room. "Goodnight then, Justice Juarez … or Chief Justice Juarez … " Her voice was heavy with concern as she walked stiffly, like a broken thing, back towards her carriage.

Juarez ran after her and tried to stop her.

She turned and tried one last, vain attempt to reason with him. "Your sister is mad, you know. She dreams that you'll be President of Mexico someday. She's only a house servant, poor Indian women. It's laughable, if your democracy allows beggars to dream that high."

Her words stung but Juarez kept silent. He walked her to her carriage and helped her into it. Then, before it could move, he quickly climbed in, as well, and sat beside her. He put his arms around her and kissed her more intimately than ever before, slowly and deeply. Her lips were firm at first, not wanting to let go of her concern. In a moment, however, they softened as she gave up the struggle and submitted to his kiss. She marveled that such a sweet kiss, such a soft and mesmerizing thing, could come from those lips that so frustrated her. She knew that she had lost the battle, and she also knew that she loved him and would stay with him, no matter what that meant to her own happiness or sanity.

The carriage began to move as they sat wrapped in each other's arms. After a ride of several miles, they stopped at a small café. They could hear music, someone playing a piano. It drew them with its comfort, just as the kiss had drawn them. Margarita hid her face with her mantilla as they entered and seated themselves in the back of the room. They spoke intimately for a few minutes in hushed tones, forgetting their worries.

Eventually, Juarez spotted two of his friends in the café. He got up with a smile to greet them. The three young men looked at each other knowingly and began to whistle as a chorus. The piano man smiled over his shoulder and took his cue from their whistling

Juarez sang:

"Don't leave your memories with me.

What name I should give to your remembrances? I'm your first lover,
mad in love with you.
Don't break my heart, or you'll break yours.
Remember this my beloved..... ."

He approached Margarita and slowly opened her lace mantilla. Leading her to the front of the café, he continued to sing.

"Beloved like this, lover like me."

She blushed and glanced about the room as everyone saw her face. His friends applauded.

Juarez had broken the news of his love openly to all. He knew that the news would reach Señor Maza before the next day. The die was cast. He must ask for her hand soon.

His friends waved farewell as they got up and left. As they stepped outside, Margarita lifted both her hands to the sky and stating boldly, "Oh Creator, give him understanding!"

The next day, Juarez made his way to see Margarita's father. He was resolute as he walked up to Señor Maza, reviewing again and again what he had thought about saying. He stopped in front of Señor Maza and immediately began to speak, pushing the words out so that it could not be undone. "Sir, I know I'm just a poor man's son, born in your presence and educated by you. Nevertheless, I beg of you to make your daughter my wife. Let her follow me lovingly from a thatched hut to a palace."

Señor Maza stared at him sternly, silent and appraising. Then, to Juarez's surprise, he broke into a wide grin. "Well, I would hardly call my estate a thatched hut." He laughed even harder at Juarez's confused expression and clapped him on the shoulder. "This isn't at all new to me. My daughter told me, last year." Juarez blinked in surprised as Maza continued. "You're one year too late in letting me be the first to know that you're taking her to your palace."

Juarez picked up his hand and kissed it gratefully.

Maza smiled indulgently down at the bowing young man. "I couldn't find a better person than you, my son."

"Thank you, sir."

"You can marry my daughter whenever you like. Even today."

"Thank you, sir."

"Don't call me sir."

"Yes, sir."

Señor Maza laughed and embraced Juarez.

CHAPTER 2

▼

THE RIGHT PATH

Mexico, 1831

The chairman of Oaxaca's municipal council rose from behind the long table around which the councilmen were seated. The murmurs of the crowd died down after a moment, and he began his announcement. "Our council member, Señor Benito Pablo Juarez, is a man of law. The town's municipal council is proud of his achievements for advancing the rights of our citizens and the Indian tribes. His industry, forethought, tenacity, dedication and courage are outstanding. On behalf of this council, I say thank you, Señor Juarez."

The room erupted with enthused cheers and applause.

The chairman smiled and waited, finally raising a hand to silence the crowd so that he could continue. "Now I request that our worthy councilman speak his mind."

Every man in the room stood and applauded as Juarez rose from his chair. He walked up to the chairperson and council members, shaking their hands as cheers echoed from the high ceilings and expansive walls. Turning to the assembly, he scanned the men with such an earnest intensity that it captured the room. The applause tapered off and the group fell silent as Juarez looked out at them.

"I was a student of religion, to start with. My father wanted me to be a priest. But I saw democracy next door to us, north in the United States of America. I was curious about it, and since then I've studied it in depth." He paused, leaning forward a bit and resting his hands upon the table. "Democracy is a new word. Not many people understand it.

When military men stage a coup, they claim they're being democratic. 'I'm taking over …' *Yes, sir.* 'I'm promoting myself …' *Yes, sir.* 'Now I'm the President …' *Yes, sir.* 'I won't take off my uniform …' *Yes, sir.*"

Several men smirked in agreement.

"How can a military man be acquainted with democracy when the only training he has is saying *'Yes, Sir,'* even if he's asked to shoot his own people point-blank?"

Murmurs arose from the crowd, as his words were something everyone had heard before, but had never heard stated publicly.

"All of this 'Yes-sir-ing' violates all that we love in this life. It blinds mercy, truth, justice, honesty and fairness. Those who say *'Yes, sir'* without thinking are 'masters of their menials, as well as menials of their masters'. Neither their honor nor their oath is trustworthy."

Men worriedly glanced at each other. "But what of the divine right of kings?" one was heard to mumble to another.

"I'm talking about *democracy*," Juarez continued brusquely, eyes shining. "What is *democracy*? Some define it as 'people power,' but I can give you its definition. The first criterion of democracy is how the minority fares under the majority. That's why I give more attention to the Indian tribes here. I may be an Indian myself, but politics is racially blind."

He walked around to the front of the table, leaning back against it and confidently folding his arms. "The second criterion of democracy is referral to the people periodically for the jobs and their openings. Let the people say who's hired and who's fired. Do they have a say in the hiring and firing of the 'power brokers' of the government, like parliament, prime ministers and presidents? Until the people give him power, *nobody* should hold the top post."

The murmuring began again, though it stayed a low hum as the crowd still felt compelled to listen to the rest of what he had to say.

"The third criterion of democracy is poverty alleviation by sticking to the essence of democracy, *freedom*—freedom to work for an honest wage, or to own your own land or business. Democracy is the best solution for the welfare of any people."

"The fourth criterion of democracy is that it seeks to keep the people united. Democratic principles and institutions do that job. Those who are trained to say simply *'Yes, sir'* must be kept under the feet of the genuinely elected power brokers. It should be asked, 'Why are they saying *"Yes, sir"* so devotedly?' Because they like their position of power, and that position lasts as long as their superior is happy with them. They can quietly reap other benefits—money, women, property …"

"Councilman," one of the councilmen said, interrupting Juarez, "there is no such utopia, not even in the United States."

Juarez raised his voice, his tone suddenly growing more intense. "A society that wishes to travel on the true path of democracy must be aware of the *pitfall* of democracy," he said, stalking toward the councilman who had spoken out. Standing before him, he continued, "And that pitfall is *the minority trying to rule the majority.*"

Despite his prestige and intellect, the councilman found himself suppressing the urge to squirm in his seat like a nervous boy being singled out by his schoolmaster.

Juarez remained where he was a moment longer, extending the moment for its full effect as he finished. "That can take the shape of different governments, with the minority bringing in an emperor, a dictator, an aristocracy … even a general, or conquerors … a system to rule the majority. Mexico is plagued with this."

Many of the men nodded their heads in agreement.

Juarez let the man off the hook and turned to walk slowly along the front line of the seated council. "In the last eight years, we've had six presidents. *Six presidents*, gentlemen. As things are going, we'll have a new president an average of once per year, a new government every year. Imagine ten governments in a decade. Soon, we may well average *two governments* per year … and this won't stop."

He reached the table again and stood behind it. The men seated at the table craned their necks to look at him. Indeed, every eye in the room followed him. "The European Latin race, who, as you know, are comfortably settled in the state capital and many major cities, are actively seeking European Catholic princes to be our ruler—princes like Joseph Bonaparte, Louis Philippe, or his son-in-law from Belgium. These princes have declined, but they continue their negotiations, even as we speak. They'd like to import a nice-looking, acceptable Catholic prince, highly connected with the Europeans. Why do they want someone like that to rule Mexico? Well, they want to get European money into Mexico, but the European powers of England, France and Spain are in no mood to invest in Mexico. We're going to see the moneylender send his armies here to extort the debts we owe them. What they'd really like to do is to attack Mexico, to settle their affairs and to take their moneys back. If we can't negotiate our pacts with them, we're sure targets for their occupation."

An older and well-respected gentleman rose from his seat. His white hair and beard covered a face lined from years of service and honor, and the room grew quiet anew in respect for him. He courteously bowed at the waist to Juarez. "Councilman Juarez, if all you have told us is true, what can we possibly do about it? With all due respect, how can we protect ourselves, our families and land? We need solutions, and I believe there's more that you haven't yet told us."

Juarez bowed his head in acknowledgement. "Sir, I'll explain," he promised. "The minority population of Mexico numbers about one million, while the majority is about *seven* million. The majority, however, is in an extreme state of ignorance and debasement. They want stabilization and foreign aid, but the price that the majority pays for the wishes of the minority is far too high. I'll fight the government of the minority, a government run *by* the minority and serving the interests *of* the minority. I want to see a government of the *people*, *by* the people and *for* the people. This is the way we should go. Mexico needs democracy, and customary rulers must go so that the people can become their own sovereigns and masters of their own destiny. Nevertheless, we must still keep in mind that even this kind of power can be tricked, corrupted, misled and set aside. Kings, emperors, and their generals have learned the art of perpetuity as rulers. The only rule of thumb by which to judge a ruler is *whether or not the people can fire him.* The people must be able to hire and fire their rulers. That's democracy."

Juarez paused to conclude his thoughts, but even then the intensity of his spirit and brilliance of his mind were evident. "This, gentlemen, was but a short summary of my political thoughts. I'm for a democracy, which allows the meek and humble to dream high. Beggars *shall* be choosers. That time has come. Perhaps it can't prevent our nation from engaging in civil wars, but if you have the right ideas for the nation, *rich* ideas, you can prevent it from bloodletting for hundreds of years. Rich ideas can work us toward the utopia mentioned earlier, ideas like constitutionalism," he said, thumping a fist on the table, "civil liberties, peace, internationalism, social and economic justice, due respect to local and national traditions, and the abolition of slavery.

"Let's put an end to extremism and fanaticism. We should put our faith in the balance of powers and the division of authority. My speech will come to a close with two enduring terms: *justice* and *the rule of law!* These are the weapons to use against absolute rulers."

He lowered his voice to a more personal level as his speech concluded. "It's for all to see whether, in the future, I can remain true to my own thoughts. I hope that I will."

With that he took his seat at the table. Great applause thundered throughout the large room, mixed with excited debate among the members of the council.

Vienna, Austria, 1832

The Royal Palace at Wien-Schonbrunn was named after Emperor Mathias, who had discovered the Schoner Brunnen, or fair spring, on a hunting trip on the property. The outside of the palace displayed restrained ornamentation, but the color known as "Schonbrunn Yellow" made it seem to explode, in contrast to the greens, reds and blues of the gardens.

On this occasion, however, the palace was decked in black as a royal coach stopped at the gates, a sign of mourning for the death of the Duke of Reichstadt just a few days before. He had been the unfortunate son of Napoleon the Great by his second wife, the Austrian Archduchess Marie Louise. Arriving as a fragile and sickly boy of four years of age, he had never been allowed to see his father again. Despite that sad beginning, he was generally well-liked, though it was difficult not to pity someone who was so often plagued by illness.

Since the first day Sophie came to the Schonbrunn, they had been close personal friends. She was the Empress of Austria, but her actions were those of nothing more than a kind friend. During the months of her confinement, while she awaited the birth of what would be her second son, she went so far as to care for the sick royal herself, and keep him company as he rested in the gardens. The servants thought her an angel when they watched such an esteemed lady serve as his private nurse. The elite of Austria were not so generous, even daring to suggest in whispered gossip that the child she was carrying could be his own son.

By the hour, Sophie would comfort him by brushing back strands of his golden, curly hair, reading to him and humming softly as the tuberculosis disintegrated his lungs. Sophie had begged Prince Metternich to allow the Duke to go to Italy, where the weather was milder, since the doctors had advised that it could save his life. Despite her repeated pleas, however, the Austrian State Chancellor Metternich refused, afraid of any chance that the presence of young Napoleon might cause an insurrection against Austria in tumultuous Italy. The prince finally relented and said that it would be permitted, but by then it was too late; young Napoleon died less than a week later.

Sophie hated the prince for that. The royal young man, Napoleon Francis Joseph Charles Bonaparte, had been the son of Napoleon I. He was buried in the Hapsburg family vault in his white uniform, with the jacket of a staff officer of the 60th Imperial and Royal Infantry Regiment. At twenty-one years of age, he had died an agonizing death. Sophie had gone into labor that very day, and so was regrettably absent from his funeral.

The gate of the castle-become-palace opened, and a line of several coaches entered. Visiting kings and dukes descended, with their families, from their finely upholstered, gilded coaches. The Austrian emperor Franz Karl and his wife, Sophie Friederike Dorothea Von Hapsburg, Archduchess, stood in the courtyard with their eldest son, Franz Joseph I von Hapsburg. Franz Joseph's hand was clasped firmly in that of his mother, Sophie's, and the dark-haired two year-old yanked impatiently. Sophie's longtime servant, a dancing girl named Adelaide, climbed out of another carriage and joined the imperial family.

Field Marshal Leopold, youngest son of Duke Francis Fredrick of Saxe-Coburg Saalfield (and later Leopold I, King of Belgium), had come from Belgium, accompanied by his aged father-in-law, King Louis Philippe; Louis was the former Emperor of France.

They lingered and talked with their host, the Austrian Emperor.

The children of the kings and dukes of Europe were released and permitted to play together in the courtyard, guided by their governesses and escorts. The royal clown was busy amusing the children with his gestures and frolics.

King Louis Philippe spoke first. "Leopold's refused *two thrones*. He's run through two wives with little thought ... Two years back he refused the Greek crown, and recently he refused the Mexican throne. He's a *stickler*. He even declined to be Napoleon I 's Adjutant. Nobody could refuse Napoleon Bonaparte. Nobody ..."

Franz Karl's eyes clouded over as he walked up the steps leading to the three "Rosa rooms," a flowing unit of rooms made up of one large room and two smaller ones, all of their walls covered with huge landscapes. "I think nobody could refuse me. Come rest and have some refreshment. I'm sure you're tired after your long journey."

Louis Philippe walked to Leopold's side. "My daughter is going to be his *third* wife!" he marveled.

"Indeed your future son-in-law is unique," Franz Karl agreed. Leopold was a colonel in the Russian Izamailovski Imperial regiment when he was a toddler. Seven years later, at ten, he was a general. He actually campaigned against Napoleon. In 1815 he was a British Field Marshal, and had so far refused two kingdoms. He was currently the chief advisor of his niece, Queen Victoria of Great Britain."

"He changes his women like his uniforms," Louis Philippe quipped. Franz Karl sat in a nearby chair. "Excellencies won't have to come to his third wedding because he's neither marrying in the Church nor in a civil office. The Belgium National Congress has recently asked him to accept Belgium's kingship, but he wants to think it over … Probably wants to face elections first."

"Imagine kings getting *elected!*" Franz Karl scoffed. "No heritage, no royal lineage, just elected by the common people. That would be a unique political proposal."

Louis Philippe was uneasy with this conversation. It struck too close to home. He stood and took several steps to the fireplace before pausing. "Monarchs must listen to the new sounds under their thrones," he said thoughtfully. Franz Karl was bewildered. "It's totally beyond my understanding. Who can listen to those sounds? Who can comprehend or understand them?"

"Some people can, and do," Louis Philippe answered.

"Any way to speak with such a miracle worker?" he countered sarcastically.

"I used to consult with one when I was Emperor of France," Louis Philippe remembered. "He must be seventy-five years old by now, lives in Paris …" He paused as he caught Franz Karl's interested glance. "Would you like to see him?"

Franz Karl leaned forward, as if speaking in confidence now. "Did you listen to him? Take his advice?"

Louis Philippe furrowed his brow slightly, then answered with a sigh, "No, I regret to say, and it cost me everything, even my throne. He saw my problem, understood it and suggested a way out. I was hard-headed, unapproachable." His eyes looked far off, as if he could see the younger man that he once had been. "To my sorrow I didn't take that advice," he simply repeated.

"I'll listen to him, Sire," Leopold vowed with a resolute look at the older ex-emperor "Prey send him to me; pick him up lock, stock and barrel, as they say.

I'd need him everyday. I don't need a joker, I need a wise man."

The next morning the royals stood on the balcony watching the parading guard with the royal band. It was a splendid day and the guard was exceptionally turned out. Emperor Franz Karl spoke to Louis Philippe just inside, watching the events through the glass doors. "I'm grateful to you. I read your article on laughter and I agree, your health needs that tonic."

"A doctor told me to laugh during morning walks," Louis Philippe smiled as he spoke. "He thinks that's a good medicine for me. Imagine someone seeing the former emperor of France walking in an English park, laughing alone?" He laughed at his own wit. "The saying goes, 'Laugh and the world laughs with you.

Weep and you weep alone.'" Franz Karl leaned toward him. "Sire, once you were too serious for this life.

"Yes," Louis admits, "There's nothing as sacred as the right to laugh. Many monarchs and administrators can't laugh. Stress weighs heavily on their shoulders. Troubled times are here for all of us. They have to be serious." Louis Philippe explained, his aged face strained with concern. "They've too many matters to deal with in such an impossibly short time."

Franz Karl agreed, "The modern age has only two ailments: stress and seriousness."

Louis Philippe almost visibly shook himself out of his mood, blinking and raising his eyebrows. "But this is a happy, happy, occasion!" he added, his voice rising to a lighter air. "Let's laugh and indulge in some merriment." He smiled and gestured to the clown amusing children on the lawn. "I have a court clown, but not because we all need a daily tonic for health," he explained, "and not to uplift our sunken moods or promote our joys further. I have one to act as a spur to virtue. He's *dead honest*," he chuckled. "Above all I need honesty. Who else can I trust? He's shrewd. His satire allows me to see the common man's mood. He's an older experienced man who has profound observations and isn't deceived by emotions or blinded by fantasy."

"I see," mused Philippe.

"Look at him." Franz Karl walked over to the glass doors and stared out, "He can laugh away his sorrows. His lips are all a smile; his heart is a tearful waste, though."

Emperor Philippe made a calling gesture to the clown. The clown bowed and ran toward the two elder emperors. He bowed low, nearly scraping his large red nose on the marble floor.

"This 'Joking-Majesty' finds two Imperial Majesties asking for company?"

Franz Karl smiled. "See his subtle departure from laughing. Now he's satirical."

Philippe smirked, addressing the clown. "What's the difference between our Majesty and yours?"

The clown hesitated a second and said," Sire, you're thankful when a child is born in your house. I'm not. I say to a child, 'Oh my poor child, my flesh and blood, be not born in my house or you'll regret it.'"

"Again his subtle departure from laughing," Franz Karl noted again, "Now he's critical of the rich and powerful."

Louis Philippe asked the clown, "Do you resent rich people? Do you hate powerful lords?"

"How can I hate something I don't need? As kings and emperors, how can you hate to laugh once in awhile?" he answered. "Well said," Franz Karl laughed, patting the clown on the back.

The clown continued, "By the powers of Your Excellency, my Emperor, I'm to be with kings and emperors at a soldier's salary. I've complete impunity, provided I clothe it in witticisms, to take advantage of the license to foolery which my profession bestows upon me."

"See, Louis? He avoids, hasn't answered your questions."

"Heaven or Hell, which is our destiny?" Philippe interrupted, again addressing the clown.

"If I have self-respect and my opponent has wealth, his destiny would be to earn self-respect … so I'm ahead of him." The clown did a somersault and landed at the feet of his Emperor.

"Would you be happy with a measure of gold?" Franz Karl continued, looking down at him.

Making a broad gesture as if in deep thought, the clown finally replied, "If Your Excellency gives me a mountain of gold and I'm dying … my riches and power would be of no value to me. No resentment or hate … I'd be getting pity instead."

"Right, Mr. Soldier-Shakespeare," Franz Karl said, laughing and gesturing for him to rise.

The emperor waited in the antechamber with the family, repeatedly looking furtively toward the intricately carved door. During all her pregnancy Sophie's well being was Franz Karl's main concern. Thoughts raced through his head. "Will the child be healthy?" Epilepsy did run in the royal line. "Will Sophie be strong enough for the birthing?" Time dragged on and on. The thoughts of thousands of fathers before him tugged at his mind.

The drums began to beat. There was a boisterous commotion of excitement. The Royal Crier paraded to the beat of drums in front of all of the guests to announce the child's name. The drums rolled, then came to a stop. It was completely silent.

The Royal Crier enjoyed his moment under the sun, pulling himself up and announcing, " The name of the child shall be His Imperial Highness, Ferdinand Maximilian Joseph, Archduke of Austria, Prince of Hungary and Bohemia."

Everyone rejoiced and spoke at once.

"Max, baby Max."

"Or Maxi?"

"Maximilian, Maximilian."

"Archduke Maximilian Von Hapsburg," an admiral added A gentleman with gray at his temples reminded someone standing next to him, "He has an elder brother," referring to the Archduke Franz Joseph. "Who'll be the next emperor?"

"Why, the eldest, of course," a lady said nearby.

"Perhaps," another added cynically.

A diplomat commented quietly, "Empires are breaking apart."

Another diplomat in the far corner of the room suggested knowingly, "These boys may be known as just Prince Franz and Maximilian of Hapsburg."

A lady at his right commented, "What a child! A *beautiful* child. He has dreamy eyes!"

Her husband retorted, "That's dangerous. Dreamy generals and kings are dangerous rulers."

"Maximilian is royal. That's his only fault," the clown said with a flourish. "He'd be happier as a commoner."

A courtier heard the clown and asked, "How's that? Nobody can hold him by the collar, drag him by the scruff of his neck. He has noble rights. He has everything at his feet: wealth, position, power, and a future. He's made when he's born. How can he fare badly?"

"A prince today can boast of riches and a stud of excellent horses; however, tomorrow he may be seen getting his shoes repaired by a cobbler," the clown said with a spin.

A diplomat joined in, "What do you mean?"

"Pitiable are less pitiable compared to those who were *not* pitiable. They beat pity itself when they become pitiable," the clown replied mysteriously.

The diplomat was astonished to hear this from the clown.

The royal gathering made a beeline to go inside the palace to see the mother and the newborn. There Sophie lay in the bed with a most beautiful baby, Maximilian.

Franz Karl would remember that scene for many years to come.

He would also never forget another scene three years later. In Vienna at midday Sophie was sitting on thick green grass under a tree. Her younger son Maximilian, by then three years old, hugged her from behind and played with her long, wavy hair. He hid his face in it, pulling at it naughtily and coming forward with a queer, dimpled little smile to see his mother's reaction. She simply put her hair right and kissed him each time.

Franz Karl joined them under the umbrella-shaped tree, more broad than tall, silhouetted by clouds of different shades of white and gray, close to their older son Franz Joseph's school. Sophie was waiting for the school to close so that she could take Franz Joseph home on the carriage. She hardly looked like an empress right then, just an ordinary mother waiting, sitting under the shade of the tree.

Maxi played like a baby lamb frolics around his mother sheep. He was a cute little child with light, thick, slightly curly hair, down to the neckline. Sophie too had long strawberry blond hair, somewhat curly like her Austrian family. She was sitting on her haunches and Maxi was sitting spread across her lap, playing with her necklace and buttons. The wind was shaking the leaves of the autumn tree. Maximilian changed positions in her lap, straddling her with his legs. He clung to her collar and then rolled and squealed, as if in pain. But it was all in fun for him. Sophie looked beautifully young and enchanting. Her patience in waiting with the toddler made her even more beautiful.

Franz Joseph came running out of the school with his black and red bag chopping on his right shoulder. He ran to his mother with his head down and his eyes on his toes. Sophie set down Maximilian, shaking grass from her hair and dress. Franz Joseph reached her and after an impatient kiss, quickly said, "Mama, wait, I'll be right back!"

He dropped his bag at the foot of the tree and raced back to his friends, his eyes still on his toes. Sophie's royal servants came to pick up the bag and bring the coach closer. Maxi stayed with his mother, walking and marching, shaking his head and clinging to her dress. He knew Franz Joseph had gone to play on the slopes and that it must be great fun, but Maxi never left his mother, and today was no exception.

Franz Karl smiled, watching with his wife and little son as the schoolboys played. "Sophie ... Joseph loves you, but Maxi *adores* you. Joseph has a world outside of you, but you're Maxi's entire world."

"Yes, dear," Sophie agreed, "Joseph's closer to you, and Maxi to me."

Franz Karl would also remember one of the times his eldest son, only four years old, was playing with his two year-old brother. Franz Joseph had been rocking Maxi in a cradle but making faces at him. The nannies had been nearby but were too occupied by their knitting to notice. Maxi was making faces in return either because he was frightened or helpless before a bullying older brother. A nanny finally saw Maxi's predicament and scolded his older brother, saying, "Franz, you're a bully."

"No I'm not," Franz Joseph insisted stubbornly, rocking the cradle harder and making threatening gestures.

Franz Joseph used to do that as a small revenge upon his mother. He knew that she loved Maxi most of all, so much that she could not restrain it even in front of her older son. Maximilian was a clever boy, and now he was six years old. He wanted to get even with Franz Joseph for years of that type of persecution. He went to the town and bought a horror mask with a terrible face and stuffed it inside Franz Joseph's peeing commode. Then he went to call his mother to witness the bully's response as soon as he opened the commode's lid. Franz Joseph was asleep during all this, and as usual, he got up to urinate at a certain time. As he opened the lid he saw a horrible face coming out of his commode and threw himself back in terror, crying out.

Maximilian laughed and soon narrated it to all of their nannies. Everyone laughed raucously despite themselves, not wanting to condone it but also knowing that Franz Joseph had it coming to him.

Maxi was not perfect, just a normal child. Sophie wrote in her journal, *"You have no idea how his face changes when he's in one of his tantrums. His under lip and jaw stick out and his eyes narrow in rage, so that he really looks quite terrifying and you wouldn't believe it's the same dear little face we know"* ... *"Max is so good and full of heart, but his carelessness and laziness make me worry for the future and one worries what will become of him."*

Later as they grew up together, Maximilian and his elder brother Franz Joseph become very attached to each other. Both practiced horseback riding, but Maximilian overshadowed his brother. Franz Joseph rode horses without much enthusiasm. On the other hand, the faster and more madly Maximilian rode, the more pleased he became. He once wrote in his memoirs, *"To ride slowly is death; to trot is life; to gallop is happiness; I can't go slowly on a horse."* To gallop on the earth was not enough, and the heights were irresistible for him. *"I still hope extraordinary things from flight, and if the hypothesis of the aerostatic balloons once becomes true, I'll be devoted to fly, and certainly I'll find in it the greatest pleasure."*

Once while in the school library Maximilian, always an avid reader, read Karl Marx's letter to his father. He found it intriguing and jotted down some ideas in his personal journal:

Conclusions:
Karl Marx was once RIGHT.

His theories were incorrect, but one observation (about the main difference between animals and mankind) was right.
*From this we can draw correct conclusions: *Man will never be an angel because choice won't let him.*
**Angel can't be Man because angel has no choice.*
**The great responsibility is educating man.*
**Marx's ideas aim at breaking up empires, nations, sects, affinities, etc.*
But what if communism and capitalism are the same? Where rich become richer and poor become poorer?
That's the point: ideas far ahead … where poor are eliminated, also rich become poor by choice.

Maximilian also had a great interest in science and botany. From early in his life he was curious about plants and gathered all the knowledge he possibly could, even approaching palace gardeners to ask them about planting flowers. He talked about beautifying the flower-decked lawns, making sketches and consulting the head gardener. He wanted the royal palaces and its rooms tastefully decorated with fresh flowers everyday. Maximilian also loved the sea and soon began collecting seashells and studying the oceans. His passion for a subject he had set his mind to was un-bounding.

Texas, 1836

In February 1836 the misty morning was dark with clouds under a huge blue sky. Mexican General Santa Anna pranced on a horse as black as midnight. His uniform was perfection with gold epaulettes and two rows of gold buttons down the front. The red sash across his chest was bedecked with medals and his plumbed black tri-corner hat was set at an angle.

He was taking his forces to the Alamo. No one thought it possible he could reach San Antonio from his position in three days, but these were not green recruits; his army moved with the organization of experienced, time-honored troops.

A sentry from the Alamo had spotted the outriders of the Mexican army before dawn that morning, and by nine o'clock the hills around the Alamo began to be covered by horse soldiers, one by one. The Texans numbered five hundred men, and finally one thousand. The numbers were mind-boggling.

The Americans withdrew inside a fortified mission just east of the town named the Alamo. The mission was pocked with holes from cannon-fire, and one wall was completely breached. The men began a frantic attempt to refortify and build a stockade on the weakest side as soon as they got inside. Trees were felled and a hasty wall erected to provide some cover for the men.

Crockett squinted and spoke to Bowie. "Not much cover around here. This place'll be hell to defend."

"Perhaps we can hold them off until Houston and his army can make it," Bowie suggested hopefully, though his face was etched with grave concern.

"Houston has no idea of our position … and even if he did it would be a difficult march. We must defend as best we can. We have no choice."

William Travis and James Bowie commanded a force of about two hundred Texas colonists and American volunteers, but illness eventually forced Bowie to his sickbed. The men of the Alamo were dressed in everything from buckskin to coonskin hats, most being settlers who had come to Texas years before. The new arrivals, including David Crockett and Jim Bowie, had been assured that the fighting was over and they'd have free land in the new territory that was ready for their leadership. The Alamo had been disputed and fought over many times.

Early in the morning Travis took his sword from its scabbard and drew a line in the sand. Every man who wanted to leave the Alamo was to step across the line, but not one man did. The small band of men was determined to hold the ground until reinforcements could arrive.

The men of the Alamo felt the bleakness of the situation, and it soon became close to desperation as the overwhelming flood of horsed soldiers began their descent to San Antonio. These Mexicans were a sharp military unit outfitted with ammunition and guns. They were an experienced, well-disciplined group who were undeniably a powerful force. Colonel Travis soon began to see the enormity of his task.

Jim Bowie took a long look at the seemingly unending line of horsemen and cannons pouring into the valley. He finally turned to Colonel Travis with an incredulous look. "What's going on? We were told that the Mexicans wouldn't dispute our presence here."

Travis took a deep breath, scanning the hillsides. "It looks like they didn't get the word!"

"We need to make contact to determine their intent," Bowie replied coughing.

"You're ill! You need to take cover!" Travis shouted over the growing din of drums and bugles. "If I'm any kind of soldier I can tell at a glance their intent! I intend to get ready for an all-out defense of the Alamo!"

Once the five thousand Mexican centralist troops were in place Santa Anna sent a messenger with his demand for surrender. Bowie spotted a Mexican officer riding up to the bridge in the distance. "Looks like they want to parley. I'll take two men and meet them."

"You go on if you like, but it's an exercise in futility," Travis said as he readied a rifle, then shouted orders to the men.

Three Americans slowly walked their horses toward the officer at the bridge. Bowie sat slumped a bit in his saddle but obviously took the lead. They spoke only a few minutes before they heard a rebel yell from Travis, soon accompanied by a cannon shot. One of the men's horses reared up at the noise and Bowie gave the order to take cover.

In an instant the three Americans were galloping at top speed toward the Alamo. Bowie shouted as loudly as he could, "Open the gates! Open the gates!!" Quickly the men joined ranks with the other men at their posts.

Santa Anna was furious and screamed his command, "Show them NO quarter! Every man will be put to the sword!"

The officer on his right said with concern, "But general, we have intelligence that the famous Americans Crockett and Bowie are in the Alamo. They're great men, sir. If we don't spare them there'll be a huge protest from the United States."

Santa Anna glared at him with dark eyes glowing with hate. "Death to all insurgents!" he shouted.

After the defiant cannon shot couriers rode out of the Alamo, racing through Mexican lines with messages calling on all Texans to come aid them in this great struggle. The message from William Travis read in part:

I've sustained a continued bombardment and cannonade for twenty-four hours and have not lost a man ... Our flag still proudly waves from the wall. I shall never surrender or retreat ... Victory or Death.

Reinforcements were not as forthcoming as they had thought, and by the eighth day of the siege the number of brave fighters in the Alamo numbered only one hundred eighty seven.

For thirteen days the siege continued. Before dawn on the morning of March 6th the Mexicans, led by Santa Anna, stormed the Alamo with bugles sounding the "deguello" which signaled no quarter to the defenders. They attacked the adobe walls from all four sides. Incredibly the tiny band of men broke up the first and second assaults. On the third try the Mexican soldiers breached the walls and a fierce hand-to-hand battle ensued. The bloodied weary defenders fought fiercely from wall to wall and room to room. When the battle was over the Mexican troops searched every corner and killed the wounded. By midmorning nearly all of the one hundred eighty seven Texas troops were dead. The cost for the Mexicans was high as well, with over fifteen hundred men lost in the battle.

It was springtime as thundering hooves resounded near the Bassos River. A group of Tennessee volunteers were finishing the last leg of their long journey to meet with Sam Houston, the general of the Texas army. As they approached his river camp each man thought in his own way about the treachery of Santa Anna at the Alamo, and later at Goliad. Some outwardly vented their frustrations.

"After a formal surrender, after they promised protection, the American prisoners at the Alamo were just handed over to those animals," one said with disgust, his hatred and contempt of the Mexicans coating every word.

"Show no mercy! Every one of 'em is gonna pay!"

"During the looting I'll show them a sword," one man sneered, making a crude gesture and causing laughter among several men riding near him.

"It was a cold-blooded and atrocious murder," one more thoughtful man said as he rode humorlessly. "Those Americans were the best of the country."

The encampment was set up to gather a strong army to attack Santa Anna. Houston busied himself providing for his army. He was shoeing a horse when one of the men approached and asked, "Aren't there others who can do that, sir?"

Houston shrugged and continued his work. "It needs to be done."

"Will we attack Santa Anna today?" the man asked eagerly.

"No, son," Houston answered, "not today. No one cares as much as I do about this being done right, so we can't rush into it." Some of the men mumbled and complained, but Houston was holding out for more men and further training.

Groups of militiamen and adventurers from Tennessee and other states were being made ready. Houston smoked a cigar as he tried to think of the perfect spot for an attack against Santa Anna. As he passed the time he recited long passages of the Iliad to himself, and more than one of the uneducated adventurers nearby raised their eyebrows.

General Houston was from Tennessee, a tall man with magnificent form and a warm resonant voice. He was a powerful man with immense charisma. His manner was deliberate, self-possessed and restrained.

He also loved books, particularly the ancient classics. His education came mainly from his father's library before he was trained as a lawyer. He had committed much of Homer's Iliad to memory. No matter how dirty the job, he always wore a gold ring inscribed with the word *honor*; his mother had given him the ring back when she had allowed her under-aged son to join the army. She had handed it to him as he left for the army, saying, "Son, take this ring and never disgrace it. Always remember, I'd rather that all of my sons fill one honorable grave than one of them turn his back to save his life. Go and remember too that my door is always open to brave men, but it's shut to cowards."

In April 1836 on a bright spring morning, Santa Anna arrived at the mouth of the San Jacinto River where it empties into Galveston Bay, southeast of modern-day Houston. There he found the local Texans blocking his way. Santa Anna caught up to Houston at San Jacinto on April 19th. He established positions around the San Jacinto river with his back to a wetland, and Houston established his positions across a field from the Mexicans. The following day Houston preempted Santa Anna's attack and led the charge in what was to become one of the most significant battles in American history, the Battle of San Jacinto.

Some nine hundred Texas soldiers mounted an astonishing attack against the Mexican encampment of over twelve hundred men. Although outnumbered and outgunned, the Texans attacked during the afternoon and caught the Mexicans during their siesta. The battle was in an open plain. When the Mexicans attempted to retreat they were forced into the quagmire and defeated. Sam Houston was wounded and the forty year-old Santa Anna escaped. In less than twenty minutes the Texan army had won, taking seven hundred and thirty Mexican prisoners.

Santa Anna was soon captured, and the following day he approached Houston. The general was lying wounded under a large oak tree on the bank of the bayou. The tree was draped as though decorated with great beards of gray moss. Houston examined the man as he came near. Santa Anna was surprisingly small with a sizeable head, the back of which was remarkably large. His face was dark with an olive complexion and a cleft chin. His eyes were described by some as "yellowish black" and were rather deeply set, restlessly glancing about most of the time. Santa Anna gave a warm greeting through his interpreter and sat next to Houston. Houston treated him in a mannerly fashion, but he wasted no time and dictated to him the terms of Texas independence. Hoping to save his life, the suave Santa Anna used the best of his talents of persuasion. He had over five thousand troops, more than enough to defeat the few hundred victors at San Jacinto, but he agreed to order them to return to Mexico. He also agreed when he returned home to work for the recognition of Texas' independence by Mexico's new government, and most importantly, that the Rio Grande would be the boundary between Mexico and Texas.

The next day the Texas army hovered over Santa Anna with promises of revenge and stares of intense hate. The threats were just that, since Houston had magnanimously assured Santa Anna's protection. Happy over his success in getting Santa Anna to order a retreat and eager for more concessions, Houston had caught at a drifting straw of hope. Perhaps Santa Anna was worth more to him alive than dead.

It was Santa Anna's invariable custom to send his compliments to General Houston every morning and inquire as to the state of his wounds. Well he might, for it was Houston who stood as the protector between Santa Anna and the Texan army, who always seemed to be lingering nearby and yelling for vengeance. As Santa Anna put it, "In the critical position in which I'm placed, this proposition is to me what the rays of lightning would be to a poor traveler, who having lost his way in a dark and stormy night, avails himself of the rapid flashes of light in order to trace an unknown path."

About three weeks after his capture by the Texans at the battle of San Jacinto, on the 14th of May, Santa Anna signed the Treaties of Velasco, in which he agreed to withdraw his troops from Texan soil in exchange for safe conduct back to Mexico.

Austria, Vienna.

Since the Revolution, a building had been under construction, southeast of Vienna. Two teams of architects were engaged in its construction. The design was Byzantine mixed with Gothic elements, and it was called "the arsenal." Eventually, it would be known as the Arms Museum (Waffenmuseum), but at that time it housed the Joint Services pre-cadet training school, where the Archduke was a cadet. It was a military complex that included troop housing, arms and offices. Maximilian, encouraged by his family, had joined the navy. With customary enthusiasm, Max threw himself into his new profession and quickly rose to a high command.

A suggestion was made to strengthen Austrian sea power, after it had won Italian coastal areas like Venice. Maximilian was the motivator of that idea. Austria had a navy, but it was collectively called the "River Troops" and served the Danube River areas. The River Troops had achieved a considerable size after the occupation of Venice and, as a result of the peace treaty of "Campo-formido" in 1797, Austria gained an impressive navy. The Hapsburgs wanted their navy to be a major source of power. They were to make new ports like Pola, Trieste and Cattaro, turning them into impressive naval bases.

Belgium, 1840—Royal Residence, Laeken Castle.

One of the most beautiful royal palaces in Europe was the home of the Belgian royal family, the Château de Laeken. It consisted of several handsome buildings just outside of the center of Brussels, in the area known as Laeken. It was built in 1772 on an inlet, with water flowing on three sides. The face of the impressive monument was enhanced by a low relief which represented Belgium. The grounds included formal gardens overflowing with multihued flowers, impeccably cared for and pruned.

The gilded palace gate opened, allowing a stream of ornately carved and decorated royal carriages to enter the palace grounds, one after the other. The horses . were both physically powerful and elegant. The royal family was gathering to welcome a daughter born to His Majesty Leopold I of Saxe-Coburg-Gotha, King of Belgium, and his third wife, Her Royal Highness Queen Louise Marie Therese Isabelle d'Orleans. The royal standard was carried in by a parade of men, and the band stopped playing.

Two boys playing nearby seemed unaware of the ceremonies.

The Royal Crier stamped the ground with his heavy standard. *THAK! THAK! THAK!*

The crowd hushed and listened.

"Here are present the Excellencies, our guests, representatives of the twenty-two royal families of Europe, to witness the naming ceremony!"

The boys went on playing, uninterested, as the crier continued his official speech.

"Here are members of the British, Danish, Swedish, Russian, Hessian, Romanian, Yugoslavian, Italian, Dutch, Spanish, Portuguese, French, Belgian, Norwegian, Greek, Bulgarian, Bavarian, Austrian, Wurttemberg, Mecklenburg and Mecklenburg royal families! Excellencies, you are welcome! *It's a girl!*"

The man stamped the floor again.

"The name of the newborn princess is MARIE AMELIE AUGUSTINE VICTOIRE CLEMENTINE LEOPOLDINE! Her mother is well and happy!"

Everyone applauded. The royal band struck up a marching tune and the royal standard was paraded away. King Leopold I responded to the news with awe." A girl!" He had secretly hoped for another boy, to strengthen the dynasty, and he never seriously expected to get other than what he wanted, but…. "A girl!" he repeated.

The Austrian court minister, attending the ceremony, had brought with him the same Austrian court clown whom Leopold had met years before, at Maximilian's birth. The clown responded to the king's emotional response, "Sire, after hearing your sorrowful words, I'm left no strength even to neigh. I can only fart."

"Hello, Mr. Soldier-Shakespeare," the King greeted the clown.

"A girl after two boys is the best present from heaven, Sire."

The king smiled.

The clown brought out a box meticulously decorated with silk ribbons and flowers, presenting it to the king. "I've brought two Siamese cats from the Austrian Prince, Maximilian. These are for the princess."

"Thank you," the king responded, opening the box and pulling out the kittens.

"Cats serve the purpose of warning their owner regarding the intentions of any visitor, and are quick to indicate or warn off intruders," the clown proclaimed, quite proud of himself.

"How?" the king asked, off-handedly playing with the cats.

"Sire, watch them when a stranger enters your room."

"Hm … Interesting. I didn't know that," the king mused.

"The Prince Maximilian feels that the princess needs the wisdom of cats."

"Really?" The king smiled.

"Your Royal Highness will see marriages of your children into the royal family of Austria."

"Hopefully," the King corrected.

"Hopefully or hopelessly?" the clown pondered.

The king watched the clown, keeping his own counsel as the clown made comical faces.

Mexico, Oaxaca, 1841

The marriage of Juarez and Margarita was to take place in San Felipe Neri in Oaxaca. The interior of the church was magnificent, with frescoed walls and ornately carved wood that covered the altar and nave. After all the rituals of the community and church had been fulfilled, it was finally the wedding day. The bride and groom led everyone involved from Don Maza's hacienda, riding in carretelas (horse-drawn carriages).

Margarita Eustaquia Maza was escorted by her godparents down the aisle of the church, as was the tradition. She wore her godmother's antique white mantilla (veil) over a slim white dress that had large ruffles at the hem, where just a touch of a sheer, light blue petticoat peeked through. Waiting by the altar with the priest, Juarez was dressed in a new black suit with a white shirt and black string tie. That outfit would prove to be his traditional dress for the rest of his life.

During the ceremony, Juarez presented Margarita with thirteen gold coins known as arras, to represent his ability to support his bride. The coins, blessed by the priest and passed through the hands of the newlyweds several times, ending up with the bride. The specially chosen godparents guided the couple through their wedding ceremony. Margarita's madrinas and padrinos served as the wedding sponsors.

After the mass, while the wedding couple kneeled at the altar, a white rope was wound about their shoulders in a figure eight, symbolizing their union. As the priest bound the couple together, he recited, his voice echoing across the vast nave, "Let the union of binding, as well as this rosary of the blessed Virgin Mary, be an inspiration to you both. Remember that the holiness necessary to preserve your new family can only be obtained by mutual sacrifice and love."

Before leaving the church, the newlyweds presented a traditional bouquet of white flowers at the feet of the statue of the Virgin Mary. Don Antonio then invited all of the guests to his home for a fabulous fiesta.

Servants milled around the hall under the watchful gaze of Juarez's sister, Josefa. They served appetizers of Spanish *tapas*, bite-sized morsels of an astounding variety that included pickles, olives, spicy vegetables, cheeses, omelets, garlic shrimp, and chunks of grilled peasant bread. Among the other dishes brought out for the guests were rice and beans, *paella*, *arroz con pollo* (chicken with rice), *ropa vieja* (beef stew), and fried plantains (a type of banana). Dessert was, of course, *flan*, a delicious custard made from milk, eggs, vanilla, and caramelized sugar. It was the perfect way to end the meal, but still more sweets were to be had later when a huge traditional wedding cake was brought out. It was made with nuts and dried fruit, soaked in rum. After everyone had been served their cake, it was time for the bride and groom's first dance. First, the guests gathered around the couple in a heart-shaped ring, and Don Antonio gave his daughter a final goodbye kiss, lightly, on the forehead.

The newlyweds danced, oblivious to everything around them.

Earlier that year, Juarez became a judge, the realization of one of his childhood dreams. His marriage into one of the wealthiest Creole families of Mexico opened further doors to his ambition, and by 1847 he was the governor of Oaxaca. He had left the Church and joined the law, just as he had planned. By 1829, he was engaged in advanced studies of law, and he graduated in 1831. That same year, he ran in the elections for the Oaxaca town Municipal Council and easily won.

That day, a press reporter asked him, "How do you feel?"

Juarez sighed. "Satisfied. I deserved to win. They didn't make me lose."

"Who are *they*?" the reporter inquired.

"*The Establishment*," Juarez replied.

Laeken, Belgium, 1843

King Leopold I entered the luxurious nursery filled with expensive toys, looking here and there. "Charlotte," he called.

No answer.

"Where's Charlotte?" he wondered aloud playfully, searching for his three-year-old daughter. "Charlotte?"

Charlotte waited, camouflaged by nearly three dozen dolls of her age and size. The king looked at the panels of dolls but could not see the child.

"Charlotte? It's Papa."

He heard a tiny giggle to his left and walked toward the sound. He still had not spotted her, but he continued to look intently at the rows and rows of dolls all around him.

At last she winked, surprising him.

The King laughed and walked quickly across the room, swooping her high into the air in his arms. She giggled again. He adored that lovely childish sound. *A girl*, he thought to himself. *I never expected this, but she has strengthened my heart.*

The governess entered, as proud of the child as the King was. Beaming at Charlotte, she said, "Majesty, can you believe it? She can already read!"

"Outstanding!" the king bellowed dramatically as he swung the giggling girl up and over his head. "Never have I seen a child read at the age of three!"

The child laughed with joy as she swooped fearlessly in her father's arms.

CHAPTER 3

▼

THE LOSS OF INNOCENCE

"Every day I count wasted in which there has been no dancing."
—*Frederick Nietzsche*

Archduke Maximilian worked hard to do well in his military career. At the same time, Juarez was on his way to being elected governor of Oaxaca. At the same time, eleven-year-old Princess Charlotte was riding a horse through her father's forests. She was an excellent rider, hunched forward as her long dark hair whipped behind her.

Time was passing by, one year after another, with increasing speed.

Vienna, Austria

Adelaide had been a Bavarian dancer in the court of Franz Karl for a few years, as well as a diva at both ballet and belly dancing. Her unusual talents had delighted the Austrian court for years, and she felt herself lucky to have such a fortunate post. But one would not know that to watch her face on that blustery day in March as she approached the chambers of her mistress, Empress Sophie.

Sophie was embroidering a pastoral scene onto a fine piece of white silk when she saw Adelaide enter from the corner of her eye. The young woman lingered before her, and she finally raised her head, blinking in surprise at the dancer's face. Her cheeks were flushed and her eyes full of tears.

"Adelaide," Sophie said as she lowered her embroidery to her lap. "What's wrong?"

Adelaide lowered herself to her knees before her. "My lady," she gasped in a hushed tone, "Please … I have terrible news and you mustn't tell anyone—"

"Of course not," Sophie whispered, taking her hand. "What's happened?"

"I don't know what I'm going to do!" she whispered harshly, tears spilling down her cheeks. "I'm pregnant."

Sophie paused. "Are you sure?"

Adelaide nodded weakly. "It's been far too long since my last time," she explained, referring subtly to her last menstrual period.

Sophie nodded faintly, absorbing the information.

Adelaide stared at her nervously, trying to gauge her reaction. "Oh, what should I do, my lady? I know full well the punishment for being pregnant."

"Hush. I must not know any more details, and you must keep silent to all the others," Sophie said, her practical side taking over. "You know how fast gossip travels at court."

"Yes, my lady," she replied with a gasp of relief. "Tell me what to do. I can't bear the humiliation of it all." She thought about the punishment she knew was supposed to follow. She would be put into confinement, her head and eyebrows shaved. When the child was born, she would be expected to kill it. The thought of it panicked her, and she wept uncontrollably as she grasped Sophie's hands. "Please, if you know a way of escape, please help me!"

Sophie watched Adelaide grasp her hands, her eyes filled with sympathy. "Hush now. There, there. Put off this crying," she replied gently. "We must have a plan."

Adelaide lifted her head and listened, both relieved and as tense as a coil as she waited for the empress to speak.

Sophie stared into the distance as she thought out loud. "I'll tell my husband and the court that you've pleased me so much that I've decided to give you your freedom. You must go away back to Bavaria. I know a man there who's admired you from afar. He's a man much older than the emperor, but never mind that. You'll be safe and he'll be proud to say he's your baby's father. Make no mistake that the child will belong to him. But at least it will live and you can mother it … watch it grow." She nodded to herself, satisfied that it was a good plan.

Adelaide had agreed, overjoyed that there was a plan at all that would deliver her from the terrible punishment that she should have endured. In two days, she was gone from the Schonbrunn and married to the old man. Six months later, she gave birth to a girl. As Sophie had promised, the man adored the little girl.

"She's a smaller version of you, so we'll call her Adele," the man said at her bedside as they gazed at their new daughter. "She'll have the best of everything, I assure you."

Within five years, the baby had grown into a slender little girl with mischievous eyes, tall for her age and with the long golden curls of her mother. Adelaide began her daughter's dance training, using a small tambourine for rhythm.

One day, her friend Greta was present while the child danced. "Goodness, Adelaide, this child has great potential! Please let me work with her and teach her what I know."

"The violin?" Adelaide asked, picking up Adele and kissing her.

"Yes, I'm sure she'd pick it up quickly. I can also teach her to dance in other ways. I'm no diva, but I'd like to train her in the art of belly dancing."

Adelaide lifted her eyebrows. "Belly dancing?"

"Yes, it's one of the best exercises for young girls, and it helps them to develop better."

"All right, I agree. Do you really think she has the talent for that?"

"Oh, very much so," Greta replied with a smile. "You continue your lessons as before. Just give her to me two days a week so I can teach her what I know."

In the years that followed, Adele's mother taught her ballet and court etiquette while Greta taught her the violin and belly dancing. Once she had learned how to play the violin, she was taught how to play while isolating and shaking just one part of her body. When she had mastered that, Greta suggested to Adelaide that they prepare for the upcoming fall festival of Oktoberfest.

On the day of the local village celebration, both Adelaide and Adele danced with a small group of local women. The townsfolk were amazed and delighted at the show. Twelve-year-old Adele stood out from the rest with her fine footwork and striking style.

One of the town's elders had noticed her talents and approached Adelaide at the end of the performance. "Madam, your daughter is remarkable."

"Thank you," Adelaide said with a small curtsey.

The man nodded. "If it pleases you, I'd like to sit for a moment and speak with you about your daughter."

Adelaide nodded in fascination, following the man to the back garden and having a seat among the festival celebrants. The man accepted a platter of food from a serving girl and made sure that Adelaide was served as well before continuing. "Allow me to introduce myself, Madam. My name is Rolf Bayer, and I'm part-owner of Wagner's Opera House in Bayreuth. You and your daughter must come there for a month so that she can rehearse."

"I'm very flattered, Mr. Bayer. Of course, I first have to discuss this opportunity with her father." She hesitated before continuing. "My daughter is so young, though. Is it possible we could wait awhile? Even two years would give her time to develop."

Rolf shook his head. "I'll need you soon. We're only six months from May. How about if we can plan for then? You'll like Bayreuth. It's a quiet little city in Franconia, Bavaria. And in May the warm weather is very agreeable. Please say you'll come."

Adele again hesitated.

"By the way, what's this little prodigy's name?"

Adelaide smiled. "Her name is Adele."

"Adele—what a fine name for such a great little talent," he said, flattering her. "Please say you'll come," he repeated.

Adelaide paused. "Will you pay for our expenses and find us a decent place to live?"

"Of course, Madam. I'll do that and more. At the end of your month's rehearsal, I'm willing to pay one million florins."

"Done," she agreed, hiding her surprise at his generosity.

By December, Adelaide's elderly husband had grown very ill, and within four weeks he passed away. Adele was quiet through most of the funeral, heartbroken. She had lost the only father she had ever known.

After the funeral, Adelaide took her aside and spoke earnestly to her, almost woman to woman. "Adele, we're alone in the world now. We have to learn to fend for ourselves."

Adele nodded and wept.

In May of that next year, Adele and Adelaide traveled to Bayreuth. The weather was lovely, as Rolf had promised, the edelweiss blooming and the sun shining.

They spent the next month intensely rehearsing for their show at the Wagner Opera House, premiering on the first of June. The show went off without one mistake, and they were both flushed with excitement when they finally left the stage. They cherished those moments on the stage, which allowed them to forget their troubles and immerse themselves in another world for a brief time.

Upon arriving home from their first performance, they found a messenger waiting at their door, dressed in a white turban and fine robes. Adelaide was handed a letter that simply said, "Take all the time you need. When you are ready, I will deliver your answer." She frowned at the note and glanced up at the servant, who nodded. She realized that the message referred to the servant waiting to deliver a reply, and he promptly handed Adelaide an envelope labeled, "To the Most Beautiful Dancing Diva." Adelaide and Adele exchanged curious glances as they hurried inside. Adele sat at an old Viennese writing desk and lit a lamp. She opened the envelope as her mother stood behind her and read the note over her shoulder.

With your permission, I would like to see you tomorrow afternoon at three o'clock.

Signed, Your Most Anxious Admirer

Adele looked at her mother in amazement. She then took out a card and a pen, writing,

Dear Sir,

My mother and I will be glad to entertain you at tea tomorrow at three o'clock.

Signed, Adele

Her mother nodded approval at the reply and Adele placed it in an envelope. Adelaide handed it to the servant. "Good night, sir." The man nodded politely and quickly left.

"What was that all about?" Adele marveled. "I suppose we'll find out tomorrow," her mother mused.

The doorbell rang at precisely three o'clock the next afternoon. Adelaide's servant opened the door and stepped back in surprise as seven tall and dark men entered.

"Welcome, gentlemen," the servant girl managed. "My mistress is expecting you. Follow me to the drawing room."

Malek Basil Bey stepped into the foyer, a full four inches taller than the other men. He wore a dramatic turban of the finest silk, a spicy scent lingering pleasantly about him as his dark eyes scanned the room. He turned and spoke in soft tones to the men about him, leaving all but one to stand guard at the door. He and his adviser then turned and entered the small but graceful drawing room.

Adelaide stood as he entered, offering her hand. He took it and lifted it briefly to his forehead. "Let me introduce myself, Lady," he said in a deep and dusky voice, thick with an accent she could not yet place. "My name is Malek Basil Bey. I am from a prominent land-holding and merchant family in Egypt. We are a wealthy and upstanding family in my country. I have been touring Europe and happened to chance upon your marvelous performance at the Opera House."

Adelaide raised her eyebrows at the odd introduction as he lowered her hand and turned to speak to Adele.

"My dear, I have come to offer you a life of luxury for both you and your mother. I have heard of your father's demise and would like to provide for you and your mother. If you will accept my offer of one hundred pounds of gold, I promise you that half will be paid to you and half to your mother."

Adele gaped for a moment at his sudden offer. "Well ... why would you want to do all of that?" she candidly asked.

The gentleman smiled at her abruptness. "I desire to take you to Egypt to dance. You will dance for my friends. You will be treated as a princess. I promise you that your virginity shall be protected and will be my responsibility."

Adele lowered her head and blushed. Malek again turned to Adelaide. "Madam Adelaide, since your daughter is of such a tender age I realize that the major part of the agreement is up to you. What do you say to my offer?"

Adelaide's thoughts raced at his strange and sudden offer. So much had happened in just a few short months, and there seemed to be no end to the turns in the road for them. Normally she would have balked at such an offer, but now that they were on their own she found herself unable to quickly disregard anything. No matter how strange or unorthodox things seemed nowadays, she had to look at everything as a potential opportunity.

She was silent as she walked slowly to a curio cabinet full of china. "I've wanted to return to Vienna for years," she mused out loud. "If my daughter agrees, you can't buy her but you can give her half of your kingdom by marrying her."

Malek blinked in shock, then turned to his advisors and spoke in hushed tones in their native language. Adele stared at her mother, too surprised to even know how to react, as the man turned back to Adelaide.

"Madam, I must take time to deliberate on the matter. I promise to return this evening to make a final proposition, if that pleases you."

Adelaide nodded and had the servant escort them back out.

As soon as the door closed, Adele turned to Adelaide. "Mother, what are you doing?"

"Securing your future, I hope," she replied, perching nervously on the edge of a chair.

"My future? We don't even know who he is!" she insisted, her face flushing.

Adelaide sighed. "Adele, we knew nothing of Bayer either, and yet we came here and played at the Opera House, didn't we? As I said before, we're on our own now. We have to consider every opportunity that comes along."

"Opportunity? A man wants me to be a dancer for his friends and you suggest marriage?"

"He's thinking about it, isn't he?" she asked, irritated at her daughter's hesitation.

"Should a marriage be formed that way?"

Adelaide sighed again and stared at her young daughter. "Adele, husbands are found in such ways. You know that, as much as we love the stage, too much time up there can affect your chances of finding a good husband. Then where will that leave you? Just be calm and see what he says later."

Adele was tempted to continue but stopped herself, knowing that what her mother said was true. She was still very young, but eventually she would have to find a husband, and if she could not, it would be a burden on her mother. She was torn between her fear and uncertainty of the strange man on one hand, and her sense of duty to her mother and her own role as a young woman on the other hand. She let the matter lie and tried to distract herself with reading until later that evening.

The hours passed slowly as Adele and her mother thought of the possibilities.

Later that evening, the groups met again in the small drawing room. Malek's men and counselors surrounded them. After welcoming him and his entourage, Adelaide stood awkwardly next to her daughter, waiting for her to speak. When she did not, Adelaide finally gave her a little shove.

"What is your decision, sir?" Adele stammered.

"I will employ you," Malek replied in his stiff English and thick accent. He continued, having obviously thought his reply through carefully. "I will give you an extravagant salary. You will remain a virgin and you will entertain for me. You will be my most cherished virgin concubine. You will be allowed to visit your mother once a year under guarded security. I will still pay the gold I have promised. You will live in my harem and I will protect you. If I or anyone else takes you forcibly, I will compensate you with gold as promised."

Adele turned and looked at her mother. Adelaide stared back at her for a moment and then nodded faintly. Adele turned back to the man. She looked very pale and small as she replied, "We accept your offer."

In twenty-four hours, Adele's world changed quickly again. She left her home of Bavaria, the only land she had ever known, and returned with Malek Basil Bey to Egypt. Her mother had tried very hard not to cry, and to encourage her to see it as an adventure, words that Adele now kept repeating silently to herself as they arrived in the strange new land.

The first thing that took her by surprise was the intense heat. Of course, she had heard that it was hot here, being a desert, but it seemed even hotter than the rarest Bavarian summer. There were few trees and no grass, only stone and sand. Their tiny cavalcade passed one after another narrow and dusty lanes filled with people wearing turbans, robes and sandals. On the left was a group of goats being herded through a narrow passage, then on the right was an open market teeming with shoppers. It all went by in a noisy and confusing whirl. She was immediately taken to the sumptuous apartments of the harem. The rooms were large and luxurious, dim and thankfully quiet. They allowed her to rest for a couple of days before sending in several concubines to groom and pamper her. The following day she met Malek's youngest wife, Safiya. The young woman stayed by Adele's side constantly as they selected several beautiful dancing costumes.

The next morning servants brought breakfast, a tray of fruit and cheese along with flat bread and wine. Adele was joined by Safiya, who brought with her another woman whom she introduced as her confidante and friend, Najida—"Clever One"—the expert dancing teacher of the harem.

As Safiya and Adele ate their breakfast, Najida walked in a slow circle around them, nodding appreciatively at Adele. "She does have the body of a dancer," she remarked to Safiya. "Show me your grace, child. Walk to the fountain and do a few whirling steps back."

Adele had never been scrutinized in this way, so she started tentatively, but halfway to the fountain her body relaxed into a natural rhythm. Upon returning, she turned sharply, spinning upon her toes and focusing her eyes past the women. The twirls were perfect.

"Come, sit with me," Najida said as she sat on the floor, patting a cushion beside her. "Let's begin with the reasons for the dance."

Adele sat on the cushion and listened quietly, at times straining to understand through the woman's thick accent.

"In early times, the dance was strictly by women and *for* women. It was used as training for labor and delivery of children. Later, it was used to improve health and endurance. And finally it was found that these dances were exciting to husbands. They were then used in harems or private bedrooms." She set down her bread and turned to Adele. "Remember, you have no need to copy anyone else. The Bey obviously likes and values your dancing style."

"The Bey?" she interrupted.

Safiya nodded. "Your employer, Malek Basil Bey, is known as the Bey. It's a title of respect."

"Oh, I see." Adele knew there was a great deal she had yet to learn.

Najida continued as if nothing had been asked. "I will only try to add grace and interest to your moves, adding in color and spark. You must always dance with a beginning, middle, and ending in mind. If you do this, you'll sense a soothing effect that will help you as well as your audience."

Adele nodded and tried to pay careful attention to everything Najida said. She was determined at least to do the best possible job at her expected task. Perhaps focusing on that would help her to forget how much she missed her home, at least for a while.

The tall and handsome Bey came often to visit his harem, and Adele performed for him almost every time he came. He was pleased with her ongoing progress. She had listened carefully to her teacher, retaining her own style while carefully adding some Egyptian dance techniques and practicing other more complicated moves privately until they were ready to be added to her routines.

Najida seemed a stern teacher at first, but Adele's determination and hard work won her over. Before too long she showed signs of affection. After several weeks they had grown quite close, though they both took their roles as teacher and student very seriously.

After three months Adele had mastered many of the special dancing styles of the region. She was practicing a more complex routine when Malek the Bey entered the harem chambers one late evening.

"Dance for me, Adele," he said wearily as he took a seat. "My mind is heavy tonight. I need to see the lightness of your soul."

Adele nodded and began to dance. He watched her for a few moments before rising from his pillow. "My beautiful Adele, I am pleased with your dancing progress. I have some gifts for you."

From the folds of his robe he produced a collar made of very small gold coins, studded with exquisitely colored fired clay beads strung on fine gold chains. He moved behind her and lifted the delicate chain over her head and about her neck. A tiny bell hung from the center and made a delicate ring as it settled into place in the hollow of her throat.

"Yes, It is worthy of being worn by you, my treasure," he said in his thick accent. "My second gift is this," he said, lifting from his pouch a dancer's belt. It was made of many overlapping gold coins of large denomination. "When you wear this correctly, it will form a lovely V below your hips. Najida will show you how to wear it."

Najida moved promptly to Adele and helped her to put it on. "See now, low on the hips. Yes, that's correct." She stepped back and beamed at the lovely young woman.

"Yes," the Bey said as he left the room. "Now you are ready to dance for my friends."

Adele turned to Najida, her eyes wide. "Do you really think I'm ready?" she asked in a shaking voice.

Najida's eyes were brimming with tears. "Yes, my child, you're truly ready."

Adele saw the tears in her eyes and began to cry, as well. They laughed and hugged each other, feeling silly and endeared at the same time.

Najida pulled back from Adele. "I also have a special gift for you." She took a small box from the table and opened it, revealing a pair of antique Egyptian Sagat finger cymbals. "My grandmother gave these to me when I was fifteen years old, just the age you are now. These are part of Egyptian dance tradition. Use these often but be careful of your music selection. You want the tempo to be enhanced so that your dancing can also be enhanced."

She stopped her instructive speech with a surprised laugh when Adele hugged her tightly. "Oh, thank you, Najida!" she whispered into her ear. "I don't know what I would have done for all of this time without you."

Najida chuckled and returned her hug. "You're a brave girl. You'll be fantastic."

Later that week, the Bey put Adele on his luxury yacht-like flotilla, where he kept only virgin entertainers. He called them his "daughters," preaching skill and piety. He invited his honored guests to visit him there. During their stay they were presented with fabulous food and the finest beer and wine. For their entertainment the beautiful dancing nymph Adele used all of the skills she had worked so hard to attain.

A wooden *kanoun* rested on the knees of another court dancing girl while her fingers, clad in picks, plucked the strings individually to play a lovely tune in the background as Adele struck a pose. Her hands crossed her shoulders as she began with a delicate hip shimmy, rippling in time to the *kanoun*. Her soft green two-piece dancing costume had a richly beaded bra top, and her veils fluttered and flared out as she turned. As her stomach fluttered, she removed the veil from her right hip. Her hips then moved, seemingly in isolation from the rest of her body. She closed her eyes for a moment, using the dance as a tool to express her inner self while her movements interacted with the music.

The eyes of the men gleamed as Adele moved with a deeply spiritual and dramatic style. She finally removed her hairpins, letting her long blonde hair fall around her shoulders. As she used her golden hair as a veil, everyone who watched felt the dance kinetically. She took a few traveling steps using big, deep hip circles, during which she bent over fully at the waist and made a large, sweeping arm movement. She finally lowered to her knees and arched backward gracefully, letting her head rest on the floor in a golden and wavy crescent in front of the Bey.

The men shouted with delight as she rose and knelt at the Bey's feet. He took her hand and drew her upward. When she was back on her feet, he bowed slightly forward, raising the palm of her hand to his lips. He beamed at her, aroused. This virgin woman-child moved Malek. He had not felt such attraction since his first wife.

"I made a vow to you and your mother. Be glad I did, or else you would not be a virgin after this night. Go on to bed now, all of you," he added, turning to all of his virgin dancers. "I have experienced women who can entertain my guests now."

Erzincan, Turkey

Across the blue Mediterranean Sea, a fuming Turkish sultan was sitting on his throne, receiving news of the Egyptian Mohammad Ali Bey's revolt. "Bring in my horse!" he barked. In minutes a gleaming black stallion with a perfect royal head was brought in. The sultan took off his golden coats, swinging up on the ornate saddle. He then drew his sword. "The army is to go under Fawad Pasha and bring Mohammad Ali Bey alive, but in an iron cage."

An emissary from Mohammad Ali Bey, the merchant Saleem Bey, emerged from the back of the room, bowing and prostrating himself before the sultan. He held the sultan's foot in both hands. "Emir Ul Momineen will ask for his capitulation. Send an elephant with your shoe on the howdah," he said, referring to the seat and canopy that is balanced on an elephant's back. "Parade the beast through the city and display the shoe to all its inhabitants."

The sultan failed to suppress a smile as he listened to the man's suggestion.

"When you arrive at Mohammad Ali Bey's estate on the outskirts of town, order the Egyptian fool to save his neck by paying yearly gifts and putting your shoe on his throne. He'll do it," Saleem Bey said. The sultan laughed.

Weeks later the Egyptian rebel king, Mohammad Ali Bey, walked out of his palace and found a huge procession coming toward him. He sighed with dread, knowing what was to come next. The sounds drifting toward him from the procession were mixed: drumbeats, marching, public shouting, pipes, and shrill sounds. The king stood waiting with his entourage as a huge male elephant led the procession.

It was gloriously caparisoned, bedecked with glittering gold *nettipattams*, or frontlets. Its trunk and tusks were colorfully decorated; its body was covered in glittering ornaments and embroidered velvets. Even its huge feet gleamed with gold ankle bracelets as it strode majestically forward, stepping deeply into the soft sand with a noble gentleness. All of the people gathered to watch the elephant sway lightly in his royal grandeur, towering over everyone in his splendid regalia.

When the procession reached the palace gate, the sultan's emissary commanded that the king go ahead of him and lead the elephant himself to the royal court. The king knew he had no choice and agreed. Upon arriving at the throne room, the elephant was made to sit so that the king could reach up into the seat and remove the shoe. Amidst the confusion the elephant defecated on the marble floor. The king covered his nose with his turban as the people nearby groaned in disgust and tried to cover their faces as well. The king finally managed to lift the shoe from the seat. On the shoe was an inscription detailing the fates of those who rebelled against Turkey. It was a very long list. The king frowned and grumbled at that, but he put the shoe on his throne and bowed to it.

The emissary straightened his back and boldly commanded the king to kneel facing the shoe. The king again looked displeased but reluctantly knelt. As the king sat in that position, the emissary read a list of demands from the sultan. The demands were stern, but nothing the king was not expecting, at least until the emissary's conclusion.

"And finally," the emissary stated, "the dancing girl Adele is to be sent to me in Turkey immediately."

The king raised his head in surprise. "Why is the Great Sultan interested in a little girl?" he could not help but ask.

"I am interested, and I am the sultan's son, Khan Kudet," the emissary replied arrogantly.

Malek entered the harem anxiously and asked for Adele. She came quickly and gave a polite curtsey. "Shall I dance for you, sire?"

The Bey shook his head and gestured for her to sit beside him. Adele was startled, never having seen him so distraught.

"You seem so weary, sire. What can I do?"

He placed his hand affectionately on her temple and brushed a strand of hair from her eyes.

His smile was strained. "Simply sit with me and listen. I am a powerful man, but men such as I have few confidantes they can trust. It is lonely on top of this mountain, my dear. There is danger everywhere. But you will not betray my trust, will you, my little friend?"

"Of course not," Adele replied, tears in her eyes. "I've trusted you with my life. The least I can do is listen to you."

"Good, good child … I don't know where to begin so that you can understand."

Adele listened anxiously.

Malek weighed his words carefully. "The Egyptian ruler is a friend of mine, and he had risen in revolt against the Turkish sultan. I tried all the persuasive arguments I could imagine to stop him from doing that, but a man who has set his mind on a course cannot be stopped. The Turkish sultan's army was ordered to march against Egypt. As soon as I found out, I went to the sultan and suggested he not send an army but instead ask for capitulation."

"Capitulation?" Adele asked.

"It means to surrender under agreed conditions. We get to retain our country's form but go under the protection of the Turkish sultan. Our lord would then become a governor for the sultan."

"How wise of you!" Adele exclaimed, hugging him around the neck.

"Wait, Adele. Let me help you understand."

Adele sat back again, her brows knitted with concern. She did not know what this all had to do with her, but she knew it somehow must.

"The sultan's shoe is the symbol of his authority. It was placed on the sultan's royal elephant and sent here, where it was put on the Egyptian throne by our king. The sultan's emissary saw to it himself."

He paused again, touching her face tenderly. "I am afraid that all assurances of your well-being have been taken out of my hands."

Adele pulled back slightly, frowning in confusion.

"I am sorry, my power as your protector is gone. All I can do is give you the promised one hundred pounds of gold, instead of my earlier promise of the protection of your virginity." He handed her a key to his vault, his dark face nearly broken with regret. "My dearest daughter, gold protects. I am giving you gold and advice to protect yourself with it. I shall not be responsible for your pain should you reject my advice."

Adele gasped as the realization of what was happening sunk in.

Back in Malek's silken drawing room, the Turkish emissary paced impatiently. "I want to see the young dancing diva. Tell her to prepare and then come and please us with her dance."

The word was sent to the harem.

Adele stamped her feet. "No! I will *not* dance for detestable men like that!"

Safiya kept her voice low as she reasoned with her. "Consider carefully your next move, Adele. It could cost all of us our lives."

"All of you?" she asked with surprise, looking at the women she had come to love. Her eyes came to rest on Najida's face. "Tell me what I must do."

Najida's expression was hard and afraid. "You'll do what women in conquered nations have done for centuries. You'll survive and help as many others as you can."

Adele's eyes filled with tears as she gasped to catch her breath. Safiya and Najida leaned over her and comforted her until she calmed down. When she finally lifted her head again, her expression was stern and stony. "Yes, I'll dance, but not in the soft green costume of my youth." She turned to Safiya. "Give me your red costume," she said, resigned to her fate.

Safiya shook her head. "My red … No, child. It's much too suggestive for you. It's made for a woman to wear when she dances for her husband's eyes only."

"I know, but the color red matches my anger and passion at this moment. I'll wear it or I will *not dance*. This is *my* capitulation!"

The other women of the harem remained silent, but implored Safiya with their eyes to agree.

"Very well," Safiya sighed. "You'll wear it, but only with some alterations and many veils. I don't wish to be responsible for feeding you to the wolves."

Najida spoke urgently to Adele, knowing they did not have much time left. "Look out for a tall, somewhat fat man with a scar on his lip. He's the royal prince, Khan Kudet. You'll know him by the years of lustful indulgence that show on his face," she added in disgust.

Safiya nodded. "He wears a gold coin with the image of his mother on a big gold chain around his neck. Make no mistake about him, Adele. He may be of royal blood, but he cannot be trusted. He has no manners and he's a dangerous man."

They continued their urgent advice as she was prepared to go. The red dress was quickly altered and covered in veils, as Safiya had asked.

Adele entered the elaborate silk drawing room with her many veils flowing behind her. Her eyes flashed with indignation and resentment as she walked bravely up to the sultan's emissary. The sultan's portly son stood by his side. Adele recognized the prince Khan Kudet by the description Safiya and Najida had given her.

The musicians began to play, softly at first, distracting Adele from her anger and pulling her back into her present task. She stepped back and clutched her veils, crisscrossing them above her head as she slowly crisscrossed her body with the veils down to her navel. She turned and crossed the room, using hip lifts as she shimmied her shoulders.

The men were all smiling by then. Adele moved her hips so that they flowed in a wavelike fashion, displaying moves she had learned with names like 'desert flower' and 'half moon.' The veils over her face pressed against her cheeks as she stepped dramatically forward with classic hip and leg movements, shimmying and smiling as she stepped before the men. All they could see of her face were her piercing blue eyes. They murmured to each other as she boldly executed ribcage undulations with Aladdin arms.

Nothing of the girl remained. All they could see was a fiery red temptress. With every move, Adele used her anger to energize her dance. The tempo of the music quickened as she twirled in front of them, baring her legs for all to see. Then suddenly she fell at Khan Kudet's feet, completely covered in her veils.

Kudet reached for her but was stopped by an elder emissary. "Your father said not to take any of these Egyptian women. We'll travel to Turkey tomorrow and you can consult him on it."

Khan Kudet gave the man a deadly look and left with a sound of disgust.

Adele rose gracefully and exited the room quickly, as well. The eunuch guards escorted her to the harem, where she snuck past the sleeping women to her private suite. She angrily ripped off her veils and threw herself onto the massive bedding, squeezing a pillow to her face so that the others could not hear her cry. After some time, she exhausted herself and fell asleep.

Kudet crept stealthily down the long hallway. He knew that his status meant no one would dare stop him from entering the harem, and this was confirmed as several women watched him silently enter and cross the large room to one of the adjoining chambers; nevertheless, he enjoyed the element of surprise and intended to savor this.

He slipped through a pair of sheer curtains and set his dim lamp high on a shelf to bathe the room in a soft but detectable glow. He squinted until his eyes adjusted and he could see the girl asleep on the bed. Her face was lost in the shadows, but that was not what he was looking at. He watched with greedy intent as her breasts rose and fell in the rhythm of sleep. They looked larger than he recalled her having when she danced for them earlier, but perhaps his desire was making them seem even lovelier. He felt an urge to tear the dress away immediately and bare those beautiful breasts, but he stopped himself. This was going to be slow and delicious.

Kudet lowered himself very slowly onto the bed and briefly tried to make out her face, but all he could make out was the soft line of her jaw before her firm young body distracted him again. He lowered his fingertips to her bosom and traced a line over the swell, brushing the nipple. The young woman shivered in her sleep, arousing him all the more. He opened his hand and gently lowered it just over her breast. With every swell of her breath the breast rose and brushed itself into his palm. He smiled mischievously at her quiet violation.

Suddenly the girl stirred. Kudet shrank to her left as she opened her eyes and turned to her right, confused. She had the vague feeling that she was not alone. The man's chubby face smiled as he savored the tense moment. If she only turned the other way, she would know he was there. She would gasp and he would be forced to attack. It was an incredible moment. He prayed it would last as long as possible.

The girl leaned to her right and lifted her oil lamp to a higher shelf to see by before reaching for her caftan. As she slipped it on her head she turned lazily to her left. She was suddenly startled by a large, rough set of hands around her neck. They squeezed so hard that she could not cry out, yanking her harshly back onto the bed. One of the hands was released from her throat and she tried to cry out, but she was soundly struck across the face, stunning her. The other hand also left her throat and clamped over her mouth.

There was a tearing sound and her dress was pulled open to bare her breasts. She felt a tongue playing over her nipples and tried with all her might to squirm out from under the weight, but the hand over her face pinned her firmly down. A mouth took one of her nipples and suckled as she tried to scream; it was only a muffled protest.

She could feel the lower part of her dress being torn away as her legs were crudely spread. In the confusion, she managed to make out the flash of a gold coin in the dim light, hanging from a chain around the man's neck. She tried desperately to speak to him from beneath the large hand, but he silenced her by clamping both hands around her neck again and choking her. This time, he did not let go, and the room became a hazy silver, and then finally black.

Several weeks later, an armed guard escorted Adele, with her promised gold, back to Vienna amidst rumors of a rape. She promptly moved back in with her mother.

Vienna, 1848

At Austria's royal palace in Vienna, there was a gathering of European kings and courtiers. It was morning, and Prince Maximilian Ferdinand, now a midshipman, was to be decorated by his brother, now the Hapsburg Emperor, for high gallantry in a naval battle.

Maximilian's father, Franz Karl Joseph, had abdicated. Sophie was initially disappointed, but that was soon erased by her overwhelming sense of pride. Their first-born son, Franz Joseph, by then an infantry officer, was crowned as the new Emperor of Austria at the age of eighteen. He was an honorable young man with an extreme sense of duty. Once he accepted the principles of constitutional government, the emperor-king adhered to them loyally.

The palace gate opened for the royal coach, a barouche. It was an elaborate four-wheeled carriage with a fold-up hood at the back, the two inside seats facing each other. It carried Franz Karl, Sophie, and their third son, Ludwig. As the horses were reined in, the attendants hurried to open the pedestals on either side of the ornamental coach. The patriarch, Franz Karl, stepped down with his family. The manicured courtyard garden was full of guests, each having brought their own families and entourages. The ceiling of the great hall, decorated with frescoes by Guglielmi, was hung with magnificent glass lamps. The gold décor and ornate furnishings made this the most elegant area for royal celebrations. The guests were seated comfortably on lushly upholstered couches and chairs.

The trumpets blew. With much pomp and circumstance, the young emperor came out to meet his father. The two men, old and young, moved down the stairs to enter the Investiture Hall. A chief of staff to the emperor read the citation, then called Prince Maximilian Ferdinand forward to be given his award.

"Midshipman Maximilian Ferdinand to receive the Naval Order of Maximilian I." It was the highest for high gallantry at sea.

The prince rose from a wing backed Louis XVI armchair and walked majestically to the dais in full naval uniform. His elder brother straightened with the grandeur of his title, dressed impeccably in his uniform of a white jacket with a double row of gold buttons, as well as red trousers with a gold stripe down each side.

The new emperor of Austria put the medal on his brother's chest. "The fatherland is proud of you," he said slowly, with ceremony, "and so am I, my Maxi." He patted him on the back and gave him a hug. The royal audience applauded, cheering and clapping.

The prince saluted the emperor and Franz Joseph returned the salute. As Maximilian turned and marched back, two beautiful princesses, both from Hungary and visiting Austria as royal guests, rose to greet the uniformed hero.

One princess addressed him eagerly, "You, sir, are the second person in the world I worship most. The first, of course, is my father."

Maximilian laughed, "You, my lady, are the second person I'd most like to see. The first, of course, is my mother." They both laughed.

"I'll come to see you in Hungary when you're ready," he teased.

"Ready?" she asked. "For what?"

"Ready to rub your beautiful mind and body with mine," he replied unabashedly.

The princess blushed but was also flattered. "What if I can do that tonight?" she flirted.

Dancing girls, picked as the supreme beauties of Europe, watched all of this from afar behind veils of curtains. There were women of many types, blondes, redheads and brunettes. Only their eyes showed outside as they peeked through the curtains. Karl Joseph spotted the most beautiful pair of eyes peeking through the curtains. They belonged to his mother's gorgeous head maid, and she was watching him. He took his leave and went to search for his mother in the crowd. While passing behind the dancers, like a policing gesture, he waved his hand and put it on her head. Finding the emperor so close, she jerked her body as if to warn him.

"Just going to bring back my mother," he said. All of the maids scurried along behind the new emperor. As soon as they had left, another palace girl took their place in peeking from behind the curtains, admiring the decorated prince who was right then the object of everyone's attention. Maximilian basked in the spotlight.

His old admirals, generals, officers, ministers, and other kings surrounded the emperor. The former emperor, Franz Karl Joseph, was still among the top nobles of the Austrian empire, and everyone listened as he spoke. "Austria is landlocked, yet it produces brave naval officers. Does someone know why?" he challenged.

"The Hapsburg Empire has seen many land battles in its seven hundred years of rule over Europe," one general replied knowingly. "Now it must fight outside of Europe, in Turkey or in the high seas."

"Well said …" The old emperor Franz Karl pointed to his son Maximilian. "That boy's under great pressure. He's seen how artful or oppressive a state's enforcing elite can be. He wants to pull them off the people. And now he's a hero sailor as well." Many nodded in agreement, aware of Maximilian's outspoken stance for the people and the trouble it could cause. Franz Karl continued, "We have to find him a country to experiment with, something with a limited government … something invisible. Could we afford to put him as emperor here? His elder brother Joseph is from the old school. He's tough, tougher than Maxi."

"We could simply put him on to fighting the Turks," one general suggested. "Fighting the Turks unites us as one fist," he added, clenching his hand into a fist for effect.

Another general agreed. "Otherwise we begin to fight amongst ourselves."

There was a pause as the men thought this over. A field marshal finally added, "But we must only show that we're nearby. Fighting is a waste of resources."

An admiral asserted, "But the Turks always withdraw."

"They're clever," the former emperor acknowledged. "Besides, they don't want to fight Russians and Europeans at the same time, in one decisive battle. The sultans only do that in bed with the dancers brought by their captains!"

An admiral laughingly added, "They have belly dancers to entertain their guests."

"That's why they withdraw in good time. Pleasure is more important than war," the emperor remarked. "Their withdrawal scatters the attackers. They don't know what to do when an opponent refuses battle." Many murmured in agreement. "Somebody ought to write on 'refused battles,' 'refused-flanks,' and all the refused-this, refused-that, in the past battles. That'd make a good textbook for officers of the army," Franz Karl continued, laughing. "They could include stories of belly dancers who refuse sultans!" Everyone laughed. "The first recorded battle is that of a refused-flank between the Thebans and Lucrates. Well, I suppose I now have ample time to do such research," he said, pondering.

A bugle sounded and the talking subsided. The musicians from India began to tune their instruments. There was an announcement from the Master of Ceremony. "Our decorated Maximilian captured a pirate ship. The musicians, its booty, will perform now." The assemblage responded loudly with applause as a piano began to play. "Please be seated," the Master of Ceremony requested, and each guest searched out a seat. An Indian singer joined in with the piano's melody.

This was just one of many celebrations to come for Maximilian, who seemed to excel at everything he set his mind to. Another passion of his had been polo, the sport of kings. The game had fascinated him from the day he was allowed to go to his first polo match with his father at the age of eight. The beautiful horses with their magnificent heads and huge brown flashing eyes seemed like celestial beings with wings. The regal young men riding seemed as if they were part of the horse, swooping, dipping, galloping at full speed only to stop short and pivot, changing their course in the blink of an eye. The manicured hooves seemed to flash in the sun. He vowed silently to work harder for his riding instructor, so that some day he could join the ranks of the sun-bronzed valiant men in their uniforms.

Maximilian had slept restlessly the night before, and the rain was coming down in torrents now. He hoped this deluge, which was highly unusual for this time of year, would not ruin his plans for that day. But finally, after all these years, it was July 6th of 1849, the day that he at last turned seventeen. His mother had to keep her promise and allow him what she had fearfully denied him until this day. In a nearby field he was to play in his first polo match. The French ambassador had vowed to send his country's four best to participate in today's match. Maximilian and teammates Umberto, Paolo, and Philippe had been practicing for months. His ponies Pedro, Nadya, Ludo, Pippin, and Zaiba had been treated as if they were royals themselves, pampered and trained to the peak of perfection.

As Maximilian stood in the pale morning light, he decided to dress quickly before anyone stirred, eager to run to the stables and check the horses. He pulled on his fitted white jodhpurs, then his knee-high brown leather boots, and finally his white shirt with the bright red diagonal stripe emblazed with the royal Austrian standard, his mother's birthday gift.

The rain was letting up as he dashed toward the stable, thinking of the sure triumph of the day. He stamped the mud from his boots as he entered. His groom greeted him with a shy smile and sparkling eyes.

"Sire, you're here early to see your beauties. They're sound and ready for the match," the diminutive man, proud of his skills, said as he pulled himself up to his full five feet.

"Yes, Muti, you've done well," the prince congratulated him. "They're a striking lot. Now I must go to breakfast and prepare myself."

The teammates met in the small dining room close to the kitchen for a brunch at ten o'clock. The young men joked and laughed as they enjoyed their meal. The match was at two o'clock, preparations having been made in a field near the stables. All was ready, although the field was quite saturated from the rain, a dangerous thing for a polo match. The royal family as well as the families of government and military officials gathered around the field, their carriages ranging in appearance from quite plain to gilded and ornate. The French were late arriving and the ambassador was extremely apologetic.

The sun burst through the clouds and began to dry the field. The freshly-mown grass sparkled as the teammates mounted and prepared for the starting shout. A polo match has an atmosphere that is unique, and that atmosphere charged the air with intensity. Maxi's favorite pony, Zaiba, was fourteen hands tall and appeared to have originated from the Asiatic wild horse, with some Arab blood.

Elegantly clad spectators waited for the game to begin. His mother, Archduchess Sophie, and father, Archduke Franz Karl, were in chairs outside their carriage on the edge of the field, servants swarming around them and catering to their every desire. The atmosphere was otherwise relaxed, the green grass soothing their eyes and the sunshine pleasantly warm on their backs.

The umpires trotted out on their mounts. The two teams were lined up facing one another, ready with polo sticks as the chief guest threw the ball between them. The ball was struck and the game began, with everyone away and over the field.

The sounds of the thudding hooves mixed with the cries of players on horses in hot pursuit of the balls. Some bits of grass flew up, clouds of dirt rose. Someone hit the ball out of the scrimmage, smacking it with his cane mallet through the goal post. The red flag went up. A point had been scored. Maximilian had scored the first goal! The spectators clapped and a small regimental band struck up a gay tune in between the quarters. The players rode their ponies off the field to change to fresh mounts for the next quarter. Maximilian chose the sure-footed Ludo and rode on.

Early in the second quarter, a skilled four-goal player for the French named Peter didn't have time to blink. His young chestnut gelding, unnerved by an eight-horse scrum, reared in. The man slid backwards out of the saddle and was deposited bottom-down on the field, right in front of the royal family. Philippe used his misfortune to score before the action was stopped on the field. Maxi grimaced as the man fell and reminded himself again, "The horse and the rider have to be synchronized ... The player should be an expert in maneuvering the horse." Even though Peter was an expert, the ground was soft and treacherous. Since one hand had been busy with the mallet, the reins were controlled with the other, not to mention that every part of him was damp. "He must be careful," he thought.

Before the beginning of the third quarter, Maximilian changed to Nadia, his youngest mare. The main requirement of a polo pony is that it should be swift, steady, intelligent, and above all, have endurance, somewhat like the legendary "Maltese Cat"; however, at this moment, Max wanted utmost speed and maneuverability, and Nadia had those attributes. From the throw-in, Nadia was on fire, five goals being slammed home in the third quarter and taking the visitors by surprise. Their tactics to keep him out of the game backfired as he swept round the arena slipping through the defense, untouchable on his fast ponies. The fast game suited Maximilian perfectly as he challenged every action of the French. Unable to find their own space, the French gave away some unnecessary penalties, which were all successfully converted.

Maximilian was having a superb game. Taking a penalty from the fifty-meter spot, he struck a perfect volley to the center of the goal, and the score was accumulating. In the fourth and final quarter, the interchanging of players in the French lineup did not faze the young team representing Austria. They had the bit truly by the teeth, and despite some brilliant stick work by the French player de Angelis and leadership by Peter, the visitors lost any possible control of the match. The final score was 15 to Austria and 8 to France.

Maximilian joined in a victory shout with his friends and went directly to where his family was, embracing his mother. "See, Mama? I'm well, not one injury. I told you we'd win!" He smiled with youthful bravado and at that moment, he knew what it took to be a man. One must see the prize and work hard, prepare and be patient. That lesson would stay with him for a long time.

His attention was drawn to the rowdy shouts and laughter of his teammates. "Max! See what we've brought you for your birthday bash!" There standing before him were three men and three women, beautiful statuesque blonde Bavarian dancers dressed in traditional costume. The women's bodices were tight black satin, laced in front over five or six pairs of ornamental hooks with a long metal chain, which made the already small waists seem ever tinier. The blouses were fine white linen with short puffy sleeves. The neck draped dangerously low and accentuated the plentiful cleavage festooned with fresh red carnations and greenery. Their long necks were ornamented with black velvet chokers with edelweiss pendants. Their woolen skirts were maroon with two rows of black velvet ribbon around the bottom, while their aprons were a light pink silk with a rose design. Their shawls were trimmed with a seven-inch fringe, gathered by decorative pins on the shoulders and upper back. Their white knitted stockings showed much more of their tempting legs than the fashions of the day normally allowed. This was all topped off with green hats and Trachten-earrings.

At the command of one of Maximilian's friends, the dancers began a lusty version of the Schuhplattler, a centuries-old Bavarian dance in which the men demonstrate their vigor in a raucous but precise shoe-slapping rhythm to folk music, alternating with flirtatious dances with the women. It mimics the behavior of the male bird, which courts the female by flapping his wings and kicking up his feet around in a circle. In the same manner the Schuhplattler keeps his hands raised and, by slapping his feet and lederhosen, imitates the flapping of the wings. The woman spins coquettishly around the man, challenging him enticingly to "catch" her for the waltz.

This hypnotizing scene was enough to make a young man's blood boil.

The strange music had the air of a Salsburg evening just beneath the surface of its notes. It resonated there as a unique key to discovering the soul of its land, its traditions, its moods. The musical and diverse cultural influences had made their mark. Also the alluring women … Maximilian was peculiarly aroused.

At the end of the dance, the young gentry, smartly dressed in regiment garb, presented a challenge to the most beautiful dancer, Adele. She was the ravishing daughter of his mother's servant. There were many ardent rumours about her, including that she had spent some time in the East and learned many exotic things there. Exactly what exotic things she learned was more the subject of tavern talk amongst the young men.

With the empress's permission, Adelaide had brought her daughter back and raised her on the grounds of the palace, where she learned to dance like her mother. She also sharpened her natural talent for sketching by drawing beautiful illustrations of the gardens surrounding her fairytale home.

The young Adele shared the golden-corkscrewed hair of her mother, appraising Maximilian with a glint in her icy blue eyes. She was to participate in a duel, a contest of sorts: a dancing contest against a dancing horse! Adele, heady with the cheers and applause from the dance, had enthusiastically agreed. She thought to herself that the rowdy young gentry would certainly choose her over a horse. She began her dance with slow sensual movements not used previously, which excited the men into clapping and shouting. Her arms stretched slowly over her head, swelling her ample breasts up from the bodice of her dress. The men howled and clapped louder. Her eyebrows arched and her eyes were downcast demurely as she began to bob up and down with her hands on her hips, knowingly bobbing her breasts and straining them against the material of her dress. Many of the women blushed and turned away as the men's cheers and shouts erupted even louder around her.

The magnificent white horse began moving along with every stride of her intricate dance. He flawlessly performed the trot in place, the turn-in-place canter, and graceful lead changes, which created the appearance of skipping. This equine dance executed sidesteps, precise trots, and flying leaps to the rhythm of Bavarian music. It seemed to perform a military maneuver called the levade, used to pull the rider out of reach of an enemy sword, which required the horse to maintain a hunched position at a forty-five degree angle. The men were thrilled. With a series of hops on his hind legs, the horse performed what was perhaps the most extraordinary of all, the capriole. With mane and tail flying like Pegasus in full glory, the white stallion leaped into the air, drew his forelegs under his chest and kicked out with his rear legs in midair.

The crowd cheered and in one motion grabbed the girl with the intent to throw her in a deep clear pool adjacent to the gardens, her apparent penalty for losing the contest. As one man's rough hands and then another pulled at her, the bodice and then the skirt gave way to leave the beautiful dancing costume lying in rags at their feet. More than one slid his hands rudely over her body as she was half-carried to the water. Their hands slipped over her exposed breasts and behind as they tossed her in the water, then turned to the victorious sweating beast and urged him also into the water. Several of the crazed men followed the horse into the pond and forced the weeping naked girl to ride the horse. She grazed her head on a rock in the shallows and was soon thrown into the deepest part of the pond. Momentarily dazed, she began to choke and went under again and again. The men took little notice of her, still too caught up with the splendid horse and the confusion of the moment.

Maximilian stood in shock at the spectacle. Focused on the unfortunate woman, he trotted to the pond and dove in. At first he could not find her, but then he vaguely saw eyes surrounded by swirls of blonde hair, struggling one last time toward the surface. Maxi grabbed her forearm and wrapped his other arm around her waist, kicking to the surface and maneuvering her toward the edge of the pond. He found his footing and with a mighty surge pushed the half dead girl onto a mossy stone. Her body seemed lifeless. His first instinct was to blow onto her mouth as he had seen the groom, Muti, do when delivering stillborn horses. His hands were on her breast pumping water from her chest. At last her eyes sprung open, startled, as she gasped for air. Only then did Maximilian remember he was holding a naked woman in his arms, and his body responded instinctively.

"Come, Maxi, let's celebrate!" The groups of men were then joined by a dozen others shouting and drinking champagne, patting first one and then the other of the polo players on the back.

Adele's breathing slowed a bit as she gazed up at Maximilian. This was her hero as far as she was concerned. Her eyes softened as she stared up at him, then blinked in confusion when the men pulled Maximilian up from the stone and threw a warm blanket over his back, lifting him in a triumphant gesture. They marched him downtown toward the nearby pub that served their beloved beer, eager to drink in celebration and share a snack of cheese and grilled meat. At first he was confused, then surprised, then amused, and finally as riled up as his friends.

Some were appalled at the outward cruelty of the men as they festively made their way to the town, leaving the poor girl wounded at the side of the pond, but theirs was a very different culture. The commoners were simply there to serve and amuse the upper crust, and behavior that would be inexcusable in the lower classes of men was ignored in this spoiled elite of young men. It would seem bizarre to suggest that they had meant no harm, but that was actually true. To them they had done nothing more than played around with elaborate toys, and the thought that they were actually harming someone would have come as a surprise to most of them.

Servants rushed to cover the girl, take her somewhere to rest, and have her injuries checked. The crowd drifted from the scene, most of them more insulted at the nudity of the girl than the actual wrongs that may have been done to her.

The pub was warm, a cozy brown color. This was their favorite place, with the perfect atmosphere for drinking on summer evenings. Here they spent many evenings engaged at their favorite pastime, tonspel. It was a game of throwing coins, and a round of drinks accompanied each score. Maximilian settled into the mellow air, the laughter, the soft glow of the hearth inside, the comfort of his friends, the slight and pleasant dizziness he felt after his second drink …

Soon Adele was rested and fit from her ordeal in the pool. She resumed her duties within a few days, with only a small bump on her head to remember the ordeal by … that and her infatuation with Maximilian. The girl sometimes crept about the palace, gasping when she caught a glance of him and vowing to make him notice her.

Maximilian's mother, Sophie, enjoyed her bath and the ministrations of the older maid Adelaide. The woman had the same light blonde hair and intense blue eyes of her daughter. Though there was the beginning of lines in the corners of her eyes, of smiling lines that never quite faded, she had the body of an athlete and was in her own right a beautiful woman of thirty-five. She had set out to give her queen all of the good and wonderful things she had learned in her country, all of the womanly things pertaining to beauty, health, culture, and wisdom that she could share. These were the things she had been taught first at her mother's knee, then later as she was being trained as a dancer for the royal court. This maid had become much more than a servant to Sophie; she had also grown to be a confidante, a friend, even an adviser.

This was the one time of day Sophie set apart from her royal duties. She knew that taking too many baths was not healthy, as her doctor was constantly reminding her, but it was a warm and beautiful spring day and she could not resist. Sophie had learned of a wonderful treatment for her hair and body called olive oil. It was an extravagance, but after all, she was the empress of Austria. Her maid washed her hair carefully, then applied the olive oil. Sophie relaxed in the luxury of her bath until her maid returned with pitchers of warm water. The maid rinsed the remainder of her body with the warm water. She brought a final pitcher of cool water to make her hair shiny and smooth as silk.

"Stand up, my lady," Adelaide advised. "Lean as far forward as possible, as this will be a bit cold."

Sophie stood and waited as Adelaide rinsed her hair thoroughly. She then quickly wrapped a huge warm Turkish towel around her body to dry.

Sophie's long hair was light with just a hint of golden red. It shone brilliantly in the shaft of sunlight. She was still a lovely woman. As she gazed into her mirror she saw the mole that Maximilian called her beauty mark. He had delighted in playing with it and teasing her about it as a child.

She snapped out of her daydreaming and dressed quickly. The family was to attend a polo match that day.

Later Maximilian and his family were at the tournament, this one an inter-European game. An Austrian player fell from his horse and was injured during the finals, so the judges called for an Austrian reserve player, but nobody came forward. Maximilian had continued his love of polo, practicing every chance he got, so he jumped up from his mother's side, and with a large grin, ran to the polo ground and raised his hand. He loved to ride fast, loved the demanding athletics of the game. This was his chance again, and his mother's gaze followed him tenderly as she watched with a smile.

He was still seventeen and knew that the conventions of the game required one to be at least eighteen to play, but he also knew that when the judges realized this was Emperor Franz Karl's son, they would bend the rules. It was a foregone conclusion, and he was quickly mounted and on the field. The score was England 5 to Austria 2, but not for long. Maximilian scored two goals in three minutes, receiving a standing ovation after the first one. A minute later, he scored again, and the crowd was out of control. People threw their caps into the air. "What a performance!" they cried. His parents, thrilled, beamed with pride.

Surrey, England

Surrey is located in southeast London. Its county town is Guilford. Surrey is primarily considered to be a manufacturing county, famous for its wool and cloth industries. At that time, it was full of large and unused plots of land covered with streams, trees, and small animal life. In days gone by, on a journey through Surrey one would often pass one of several mills. Close by is Ewhurst, a two-tower windmill. It is a quiet and idyllic place.

To everyone's surprise, King Louis Philippe of France, father of Belgium's Queen Louis Marie of Bourbon-Orleans, abdicated as the emperor of France and came to live in Surrey. This is where Charlotte was staying with her mother, who was looking after her aged father. Charlotte remembered the sad day of her grandfather's death.

Charlotte, a lovely child of eleven, played with other children. She had no idea of the coming events. They saw Queen Louise come out of Grandfather's chamber with the loudest possible expression of grief and mourning. The children were frightened and confused by her wails. Charlotte was told bluntly, "Your 'Grand' has died." She saw her mother's mourning and began to cry. She realized that her "Grand" had been everything to her mother.

In the following days, the entirety of European royalty sent notes of sorrow and consolation. Queen Louise was beloved by the poor people of Belgium because of her tireless devotion to extensive charitable work. Queen Louise's sister, the future empress of France, came with her staff to live with Queen Louise for some time.

Philippe was quietly buried with his wife Amelia at the Chapelle Royale, the family necropolis he had built in 1816 in Dreux, France. The doctors who had attended the dying emperor were now worried about his daughter, Louise, who fainted during the ceremony. She soon awakened and again wept inconsolably. Her doctors recommended sedatives and painkillers for her, but that was not enough. She wept day and night until her tears ran dry, and then she continued to bemoan her loss without tears.

Within three months, by October of 1850 in Ostende, Queen Louise of Belgium was also dead.

King Leopold I of Belgium had dearly loved his wife and was overwhelmed by her unexpected loss. He took his two sons and daughter back to Belgium, unsure of what to do with his children. He was a loving father, but he was also a man of many responsibilities, so he hired an especially pious governess to look after Charlotte.

She was devoted to the children, but after observing Princess Charlotte for several weeks, she found her to be lethargic and somewhat depressed. Concerned, she approached the king. "Your Majesty, I'm concerned for Charlotte. She needs liveliness, pep. She needs to go to the beaches in Ostende and to the Ardennes forests, to be more active. She must ride, swim, and learn religious tracts, read Plutarch's life. She must hear Bach's classical music. She needs a strong will, energy, and a positive attitude."

The king agonized, "But I find her grave-minded and critical of everything. Her mother's death has seriously affected her ... changed her."

The governess proposed softly, leaning slightly toward the king, "She needs your company, Majesty. She lights up for you like a flame."

Leopold nodded. "You know, years ago I wished for another son to strengthen my dynasty. I thought I wanted a boy instead of Charlotte, but to my surprise, I was extremely fond of her when I first saw her ..." He leaned back in his chair, remembering. "She was so cute in her mother's arms. But by the time she was two years old, I found her witty and charming. I came to love Charlotte immensely. At only three she could read ..." he reminisced brokenly. "I'd bought her a roomful of dolls, and I could never find her in that room unless she winked." His voice broke and tears welled up in his eyes.

"She's a very intelligent and serious character," the governess remarked softly. "She'll change."

"She'll certainly be intelligent and beautiful," the governess imagined out loud.

"And she's changed since she was a young child," the king added. "She's so wise for her age ... almost like one of my best diplomats."

The governess took a moment and reflected, "All three of your children are going to be the best of the best. Work for them, my lord."

The next day was overcast and rainy at Laeken Palace. Since the death of his wife, Leopold had also seemed gray.

The young, lovely, and sweet Princess Charlotte ran into the room and lit it like a bright flower. She ran up to her father and gave him a hug. Throwing her arms around his neck, she kissed his cheek. "I love you, Papa." She paused, noticing her father's grand attire. "Are you going out?"

The king's eyes had a sudden spark. He smiled and kissed her. "I have to go to church today because it's Father's Day. I'm to hear my father-in-law's ... your grandfather's ... last sermon to emperors and kings. It was *his* mother's dying wish that his sermon be read out to the royalty of Europe on every Father's Day."

The royal carriage rolled toward the cathedral, driven by elaborately festooned white horses. The king's guests were already seated. Leopold twisted his rosary, thinking to himself about his late wife and the father she had so loved. Another Father's Day, and again they were to hear her father speak, but this time from the grave, perhaps with his daughter at his side. Today would be an especially sad occasion.

After the bishop completed the readings from the Bible that concluded the service, he began the sermon.

"We now commence with the last sermon of Louis Philippe, former emperor of France."

The cathedral was full, many of the royalty of Europe listening. The bishop took out his glasses and put them on, adjusting the papers on his podium.

"I, Louis Philippe, former emperor of France, want to leave a message to princes, kings, emperors, majesties, and servants of each and every state. This is that message, call it my last will ...

First there were men, but no leader. All men were free and equal, but then something happened to them and they looked at each other for a leader. The leader was supposed to protect them from known calamity.

Then there were leaders, each vaingloriously content in his own domain. Then someone forced others to give the resources they had in return for protection. That gave rise to chiefs or kings. Then there were kings in different regions, all happy in their rule until the ruled began to revolt. The king was not fulfilling his part of the contract. The strongest king emerged as the emperor.

Alexander the Great left open the question of appointing his heir. Why? Because he knew that the strongest will survive, will become a true conqueror, thus the true emperor. He left it to his generals, like a tournament of power.

Emperors need vast resources for the upkeep of armies. That necessitated expanding the state and breaking up smaller unities to combine humans into a bigger form of unity. Wars cost the emperor vast fortunes, and it made the empire restless. New ideas were needed to break up empires. Some ideas were spiritual, some economic.

The process of civilization started with refusing to be the oppressor inspite of the need and opportunities to do so. To fight back, win, or be butchered. The process of civilization is built like a circle. It starts with revolt and ends in submission.

The kings in earlier centuries had the concept of "the divine rights of kings to rule," which caused much destruction. In the nineteenth century, this gave way to "the divine right of a people to rule." That exported war to other countries and peoples.

The new contemporary theory should be called "colonialism." This means usurping the rights and resources of other people under the disguise of civilization. We are thus about to enter the era of the war of civilizations.

Kingship and emperorship took some time to die. The idea of God's appointed regent died a slow death. The new theory of the day was "God's appointed race." Our friends during the Nineteenth Century had begun to believe that they were the chosen race, chosen to distribute the benefits of western civilization to the backward people of this globe. This theory is more brutal than the earlier "divine right" theory. The former saw internal civil wars, class wars, undisputed kings' wars, and so forth. The latter theory is simple aggression under the veil of progress and development. The aggressors would come upon other people's land to be emancipators and liberators, all in the name of progress.

This much is sure to come to mankind, and it would make an artful history: the oppressor, in search of new resources, will wear the mask of the liberator. The oppressor will have everything, including winning positions by force, cruelty, stolen resources, persuasion, and torture. Anyone with an "empty seat," "conscience," and "stomach" will come running to help the oppressor. If the people show strong political will, they would make them fight each other in a civil war. The oppressors will behave like butchers. They'll seem to say, "Eat your feed or roll in the drum." The oppressed, like poultry, have no hope. How does one defend himself from an oppressor? The will of man, that which refuses to concede defeat, is what makes man struggle against dark and hopeless situations. To simply say that "might is right" is an insult to the very concept of making man the best of God's creation. He has been given other abilities to set things right. Human intellect is therefore the best creation on earth, and it shall make it right again.

Some three hundred years of bloodshed would result from this theory. It would behoove mankind, and especially the rulers of mankind, to avoid this bloodshed."

The sermon was over. The king left the cathedral first, his eyes cast downward.

India, 1852

A beautiful young woman named Reshma Bai approached the small hut where her child and mother lived. She was a young woman, a clever mimic and dancer in the Sikh royal court. She has been trained in the "Kath kali form," a dance drama characterized by mime and facial makeup resembling masks. She was from what was considered by society to be a good family, though they were poor. Her eight-year-old daughter, Zinnia, stayed with Reshma Bai's elderly mother while she made money to support them with her dancing. She was ashamed, trapped in a life of no honor.

She stepped out of the bright sun. The inside of the hut was cooler, and she peered into the darker interior. "Zinnia, my beautiful baby, Mama's home. Come, give your poor mama a hug."

Zinnia got up from sitting beside her grandmother and approached her, her eyes looking down at her feet. Reshma Bai smiled and embraced the child, chiding, "There, there, child. Don't look so sad. Your mother loves you."

She gave the girl a little squeeze and knelt down to look her in the eyes. "It's said that I'm beautiful and that your father is of the royal family. So be proud, Zinnia! Don't look at the ground. Lift your chin and hold your head high," she insisted, tucking two fingers under the girl's chin and raising her head. "Someday you'll be married and have a good life." She looked into the girl's face and smiled, her white teeth flashing against her lovely mocha skin. "Come see what I've brought your grandmother."

Reshma Bai dropped a small sack on the table with a deliberately casual air.

Her mother opened the sack and her eyes widened. "Oh, it's a bag of gold!" A horrified look crossed her face. "Oh, Daughter, what have you done to come into possession of all this gold?" Horrible thoughts of her daughter robbing or even killing ran through the anxious woman's mind.

"No, no, nothing like that, Mother," she laughed, sitting at the table and pulling Zinnia into the chair beside her. "It's my earnings from the royal court. I know it's not the most honorable of earnings, but you take half to take care of yourself and Zinnia. The other half is to be put away for a dowry. I'll add more later ... Zinnia won't go begging for a bridegroom," she insisted to herself.

The young girl glanced at the money, not appearing happy at the thought. "Zinnia," her mother said gently, placing her arm about her, "please give me a smile, sweetheart. I did it all for you. For my love of you."

"But Mama, I don't care about money. I want you to stay with us."

Zinnia's frustrated mother stared down at her, then looked helplessly at the money. Tears filled her eyes and she suddenly began to cry. The older woman reached out to take her hand, but her head lowered into her arm on the table and she wept uncontrollably. Reshma Bai's mother finally rose and walked around the table, standing behind her daughter and caressing her shoulders in an attempt to calm her down.

"Don't cry, Mama," Zinnia pleaded, stroking her hair.

After a few minutes, she lifted her head and roughly wiped the tears from her eyes. She turned to Zinnia, taking the girl's face into her hands and leaning so that their faces were inches from each other's. "Zinnia, I wish for nothing more than to stay here with you. But it's my *destiny*. I can't change it. We're destitute and I'm the only one who can provide. The royals took advantage of me, and now I can never escape this life. *But you can.*" Her eyes pleaded with her daughter's to understand, but of course the child was too young. She finally lowered her hands and sighed, smoothing her dress. "Be a good girl and do what your grandmother tells you," she said in a firm voice. "I'll return soon." She stood quickly and left the hut. Zinnia rose to go after her, but her grandmother held her firmly. "Mama! *Mama!*" Zinnia called out.

"No, Zinnia. You must stay. If you follow, you'll only make it more difficult for your poor mama," her grandmother patiently explained, her heart breaking for the child.

Zinnia broke free and ran out of the hut. She stopped, her grandmother's explanation making her hesitate. As much as she wanted to follow her mother, she did not want to make things difficult for her, whatever that meant. She finally turned and ran to the village mosque. There she found her playmate, Azam Masoud, son of Imam. He was reciting a verse from the Quran. The villagers listened to the boy with complete silence as he translated it for them. The imam, popularly called 'Mianji,' was describing the Muslim faith built around the verse his son was reciting. He explained the concepts of "jihad" and "martyrdom."

"When people work together *towards* what's right and *away from* what's evil, this united effort to root out evil and establish the truth is called 'jihad.' It means to try one's utmost to see truth prevail and falsehood vanish from society. The aim of jihad is to earn the pleasure of Allah."

Zinnia sat on a low wall in the mosque's courtyard as she listened to her guardian Mianji, the village mosque leader referred to as the Imam, recite certain advices from the early Muslim leaders.

"Don't be misled by someone's reputation.

To judge a person, look into his truthfulness and wisdom.

One who keeps his secrets controls his affairs.

Prudent is he who can assess his actions.

Don't defer your work for tomorrow.

Be grateful to him who points out your defects.

Judge a man's intelligence by the questions he asks.

Less concern for material well-being enables one to lead a free life.

Fear the person whom you hate.

It's easier not to indulge in sins than to repent for them."

Zinnia had been listening to such early morning after-prayer sermons for some time now. Young Azam always wrapped up such talk by reciting some verses from the Quran.

"The best jihad is to speak the truth before a tyrant ruler.

The perfect ones are the best of you in character. Out of the best of you, the *very* best are those who are the best to their wives.

He who has no compassion for the little ones or old ones is not from us.

Be fair and just to your children.

He has no faith whose neighbors are not safe from his wickedness.

He's not from us who eats his fill and his neighbor remains hungry by his side.

The best house is where an orphan is well-treated; the worst where he's not.

One who helps a widow is like a warrior in the way of God, Allah.

Actions shall be judged only by intentions. A man shall get what he intends.

God is polite and likes politeness.

Wealth comes not from abundance of goods, but from a contented heart.

The learned are the successors of prophets. They leave behind knowledge as inheritance.

Guarantee me the following and I guarantee you Paradise:

1. When you speak, speak the truth.

2. Keep your promises.

3. Discharge your trust.

4. Withhold your hand from high-handedness."

He closed the book and people began to drift away, nodding their thanks and goodbyes to Azam.

Zinnia approached her guardian, the Imam, and innocently asked, "Mianji, how can there be life after death?"

Mianji turned to the girl and replied, "Because man has a choice to do either good or bad. This freedom of choice, which is not available to the animal world, will be tested by Allah on the Day of Judgment. Hence there has to be a life after death for all villains to be punished and heroes to be rewarded."

"Who lays down the straightest path?" Zinnia asked.

"Quran, the Book of Allah," he explained. "It lays down duties and obligations: be kind to your parents, relatives, and orphans, your neighbors and the needy. It lays down social manners: brotherhood, cooperation, seeking permission before entering someone's house, keeping a promise, honesty and truthfulness, courage, kindness, trustworthiness, justice, chastity, generosity, forgiveness, reliance on God ... everything humans require in their lives."

"What are the bad traits?"

The expert in the Book of Allah continued his recitation from memory. "The Quran forbids backbiting, suspicion, fraud, extravagance, arrogance, hoarding, mischief, corruption, mockery, ridicule, hypocrisy, abortion and birth control, usury and interest, wine and gambling, adultery and theft."

Mianji's son joined them, asking, "Why are usury and interest banned in our religion?"

"Because banks' interests lie in money that flows from the poor to the rich. Zakah is the only tax in Islam on Muslims, money that flows from the rich to the poor."

Zinnia suddenly asked, "Who deserves the best care from me, Mianji?"

"Your grandmother."

"Well, who after that?"

"Your mother."

"But my mother left me for a life in the royal Sikh court. She only comes to give us some money. She hides when she comes. Why doesn't she want me?"

Imam rested his hand affectionately on the child's head and answered softly, "Are you sure that's the truth, little one? Doesn't she provide the food on your table and the clothes on your back? Doesn't she come to see you as often as the palace allows her to? One must always be fair and just, especially to the people we love. Freedom to hurt costs harmony."

"Yes, sir," she whispered. "It's just that I miss her terribly sometimes."

"The Quran teaches us that 'no father can give anything better to his child than good manners.' The same goes for mothers, my child. I'm witness to your good manners, so she must be a good mother," Mianji insisted, smiling tenderly. "She also teaches you to guard your chastity and lower your gaze before men, doesn't she?"

"Oh yes, yes she does," Zinnia answered with a smile, understanding her mother's love more clearly than ever before.

"Then see, my child, you have a careful mother," Mianji said wisely.

Zinnia grew up with insightful talks like that with her guardian, as well as happy times with Mianji's son Azam. They were close playmates and saw each other as brother and sister. The man and his son were splendid to her, sometimes making her forget that she had never known a real father or brother.

Schonbrunn, Vienna, March 5th, 1857

Sophie Frederike Dorthea Josepha was the first child of the twenty-seven-year-old crown prince, Franz Joseph, and his twenty-three-year-old wife, Duchess Elizabeth, nicknamed "Sissi," known to be the most beautiful woman in all of Europe. They were at the palace in Schonbrunn to celebrate Sophie's second birthday, and it promised to be a grand occasion.

Traveling in a royal coach with the family, Archduchess Sophie had never seemed so alive as she did at that moment.

Franz Joseph mulled over who was prettier: his wife or his daughter?

Then he declared, addressing his wife, "All I can be sure of is that you have never been as radiant as our daughter, except for perhaps on our wedding night. Look at her eyes, bright and sparkling, and cheeks the sweetest shade of rose. As a way of thanking you, I'd like to take a moment from your busy day for a few kisses," he said matter-of-factly.

By the time they reached the palace gates, they were giddy with laughter and great expectations for the day. Sissi doted on Sophie, always seeing to the design of some little outfit or other detail with her own dressmaker. She occasionally had special outfits made so that she and Sophie could dress alike, even two magnificent dolls made in France by the foremost toy maker of the realm. She had sent likenesses of Sophie sitting on her knee, both in matching outfits. Sophie had been smiling radiantly, her golden curls falling about her shoulders and tied with a velvet bow to match her dress. The artist had created two dolls, one closer even than godparents. They idolized her, and she always brought a smile to their faces.

Maximilian arrived early in the morning to make preparations for the festivities. Waiting for them in the entry hall outside of the nursery suite of rooms was the darling girl herself.

When Maximilian caught sight of Sophie, she ran with childish faith, diving headlong and at breakneck speed into his waiting arms. She knew full well that her Uncle Maxi would catch her and place her gently on his shoulders. He loved this game, and always carried it out with a happy shout. There wasn't one ounce of guile or pretension in the child, and he delighted in that innocence. Many times he had silently vowed to protect her from all the world's harms for as long as humanly possible.

"Hello, Your Majesty," he addressed Sophie. "And what do you have in mind today for your humble and lowly servant, Maxi?"

This small speech sent the child into a rapture of giggles and childish squeals. "Uncle Maxi!" she laughed. He knew how much she loved his company. No one else was quite the same for her.

In the next moment, she spied her grandmother out of the corner of her eye. "Hi, Grandma!" She wiggled on his shoulders until he allowed her to slide gently down his hip to the floor, where she made another headlong dash and grabbed her grandma tightly around the knees, causing them both to land unceremoniously in a heap on the marble floor.

It was to be an unforgettable birthday. Virtually the entire family was present, including dozens of cousins. The hall was decorated with wonderful dolls, all made to look about two years of age. The dolls rested on marble flooring that was so well-polished that the reflection from the floor made it appear to be covered with twice as many dolls. This made a unique reception area for the birthday celebration.

Maximilian and Empress Elizabeth were the organizers of the party. Maximilian gave orders for the reception ceremonials while Elizabeth happily played with the little birthday girl. The choir of angelic school children sang a birthday song, their music teacher supervising. It was followed by warm applause from the royalty present there. Grandfather, the former emperor, sat and watched as his wife Sophie kissed her granddaughter and namesake with great affection.

Franz later lifted his daughter to cut the huge cake. A parade of little girls followed in ceremonial military uniforms. Sophie was the commander in uniform, ordering the "drill." The guests were charmed by the show and clapped in rhythm to the young marchers.

The party went on for hours, a fantastic affair of games, prizes and elaborate gifts. Dolls were the highlight, earning a special place in the little girl's large collection. Later that afternoon, the children, mothers, and governesses retired for a late afternoon nap. Maximilian and the birthday girl's father, Franz Joseph, sat on a couch together, soaking in the silence now that the party had ended.

"Sophie's two years old today," Franz Joseph mused. "If she becomes an empress like our great-grandmother Marie Theresa, would she be putting medals on the chest of any of her generals?"

"The Marie Theresa Medal?" Maximilian asked his brother with a broad smile.

"Yes," Franz Joseph laughed.

"There're few of those these days. We haven't given any Marie Theresa Medals to generals … that explains why the empire is breaking apart."

"But we have very capable generals," Franz Joseph countered.

"Capable?" Maximilian commented. "None of them has given us any victories."

"We're having some in Italy."

"That's because the Italian people haven't risen in revolt yet. Cross your fingers if they do."

"People can be put down."

"When you put them down by force, you're actually preparing them against you," Maximilian warned, a serious look on his face.

"It's sometimes necessary, Max," Franz Joseph argued. "As distasteful as it may be, coercion is a means to keep an empire together."

"Consider it carefully, Joseph. Did the Roman or Spanish empire succeed in that?"

"No," he answered reluctantly.

"And why not?"

"I can't answer that question."

"I can," Maximilian persisted stubbornly. "Putting down by force means you spend money, and a great deal of it. That money belongs to the people, and you spend it in throttling them. It's counterproductive. The people become angrier, the money goes down the drain or into the mouths of the enforcers, generals and police … and then inflation takes over. Inflation ruins empires, you know."

"Maybe you have a point there," Franz Joseph said, mulling that over.

It was May 1, 1857, two months after the grand little party. A door flung open. A servant woman dressed in a nanny's uniform burst out of Sophie's nursery, trying to shout through her strangled sobs. She staggered against a pillar in the hallway. "Help!" she suddenly screamed. "Come quickly! Call the doctor! Won't someone please *help me*??"

Elizabeth rushed out of her suite and ran to the woman, frantic. "What's wrong, Anna?" she asked urgently, but the woman was leaning hard on the pillar and gulping, unable to speak through her convulsive sobs. Elizabeth took the woman by the shoulders. "Anna, what is it??" she demanded. The nanny tried to speak, but nothing clear came out of her mouth. She shoved the woman aside and ran into her daughter's nursery as guests started filling the hallway from their adjacent rooms, murmuring to each other.

Elizabeth ran to the crib, followed closely by Franz Joseph. They stood together over the crib and looked inside. At that moment, they were neither royal nor majestic, only frightened for the little girl.

Little Sophie was lying quietly on her pink silk sheets in a ruffled nightgown. She was as pale as snow, with red dots covering her face, hands, every bit of skin that could be seen. Elizabeth spoke softly to the girl and touched her face to assess how ill her child was … and found that the little face was as cold as a stone. Sophie was dead.

Elizabeth stared at the girl, mute. She suddenly picked the child up and carried her to the chair where she'd been rocking her only two hours earlier. Franz Joseph was also silent, staring blankly first at the child, then at the mother. His mind was numb, and he could only stand there as the royal physician ran in to evaluate the girl.

"Your Majesty," the physician said as delicately as he could, "I'm afraid she's been overcome by the measles. Please, let me take her for you," he added, gently scooping his arms around the toddler. Elizabeth started to shake her head. "No … nonononoNO!" she screeched, holding fast to the girl. The doctor stood and looked at the emperor helplessly.

Franz Joseph responded automatically, doing what he did best: he ordered everyone out of the room, and they quickly obeyed, with quick bows and murmurs of "Yes, my lord." When the room was empty of all but the little family, Franz Joseph stood before his wife and daughter for some time. He finally sank to the floor and wept at Elizabeth's feet while she sang lullabies into the small rosebud ears that would never hear again.

Seven days later, the funeral procession moved through the gates of the palace, accompanied by palace guard outriders. They turned left onto the road leading to St. Stephen's Cathedral, traversing the long walk to pass the castle for the last time. Many were in attendance and staying at the castle that day, including Sophie's royal cousins and their nannies, and a few other older members of the royal family.

As the hearse approached each junction, police outriders momentarily stopped at the crossing to let the procession through. As they neared central Vienna, increasing numbers of people came from their homes to see the hearse and coffin pass by, draped in the double eagle standard.

In the city center, close to the cathedral and next to the famous Kärntnerstrasse, an absolutely quiet crowd of mourners lined the roads. The imperial burial vault lay below Capuchin Church, a large and solemn building built between 1622 and 1632. The cortege drove along the south side and through the gates, then on to St. Stephen's Cathedral. At this point a large crowd had gathered, some waving small white handkerchiefs and many weeping quietly as the coffin passed by. Sophie's body had been embalmed, with her heart conserved in a silver cup and kept in the crypt of Loretto Chapel. Her intestines had been taken to the duke's crypt in the catacombs of the cathedral. After the funeral mass, the entire royal family was in the graveyard.

The burial of the child princess was a pathetic scene.

After the priest had fulfilled his duties, Sophie's "Uncle Maxi" spoke a few words at the graveside. It took all the bravery of a head-on cavalry charge, but through it all he kept a semblance of composure for both his mother and Elizabeth, as well as for all of the family present. Everyone was still in shock and denial, but the denial was fading as the cruel conclusion was being witnessed.

"Our Sophie, how small and helpless … and yet she brought cheer to all of our lives. She always made us smile even on the dreariest of days, but above all she saw the funny side of life and we laughed until we cried. Oh, how I'll miss those laughs and those wonderful antics … and her innate warmth of life. She was the most angelic and miraculous child you could possibly have, and I was utterly devoted to her, alongside her mother and father. Her departure has left an irreplaceable chasm in countless lives but, thank God, we're all the richer for the sheer joy of her existence."

Nothing could stop the weeping of the child's mother. Arguably the most beautiful woman in Europe at that time, Empress Elizabeth was now beaten and defeated. "What use is kingship if a king isn't safe from disease?" she moaned, both angry and hopeless.

The next morning after the burial, a broken Maximilian received news that his brother was now appointing him as viceroy of the Lombardo-Venetian kingdom. He was to take charge next week. He stared at the correspondence numbly, taking some time to even understand what it meant.

India, 1857

The British-owned East India Company began as an independent trading company. After two centuries the British had become totally dominant over the area. Many of the native resources were removed, including one of the world's largest diamonds, the *Koh-i-Noor*, which would eventually become part of the English crown jewels.

For two hundred years there had been a repressive presence of the East India Company, who had arrived with its own armed British forces. But the local leaders continually put up opposition to total British control. An Indian mutiny finally began.

That year, Zinnia turned sixteen. On her birthday, her mother Reshma visited to celebrate. She gave her a precious veil of the finest materials and workmanship. It was one of the most beautiful things Zinnia had ever seen.

"You're growing up now, Zinnia. This veil is to keep for your wedding day. It's of the highest quality and quite expensive, so take good care of it."

"Yes, Mama," Zinnia promised soberly.

"What have you been doing with yourself these days? Are you taking good care of your grandmother? She's getting quite old now, you know."

"Oh yes, I try very hard to take care of all that she needs. I've been watching the villagers praying in the mosque and listening to religious talks. They have beautiful music that the people call Qawalis. I love the music, Mama. I can't keep my feet still when I hear it," she chattered, always so full of news when she got a rare visit from her mother.

Reshma quickly grabbed the girl roughly by the shoulders and shook her. "Whatever you do, you must *not* dance in public! Someone will see you! Promise me you will not dance outside this hut, ever!"

Zinnia was surprised and frightened by her mother's reaction. She had never heard her mother speak to her that way, and she began to cry. "Mama, don't be angry. I'll do whatever you want! Please stop, you're scaring me!"

Reshma regained her composure, knowing she must seem very frightening to her daughter. She released her grip on the girl's shoulders and apologetically smoothed the sleeves she had wrinkled on her dress. "I'm just so worried about you, child. You're growing up so quickly, and very soon you'll be a grown woman. I have to take precautions against the unholy desires of others."

Zinnia was confused but said nothing.

Her mother left after the noon meal.

"Grandmother," Zinnia said, covering the windows, "you're tired. Lie down and rest. You've worked hard today. I'd like to wear my veil down to the mosque and hear the prayers. As soon as I get back, I'll store it away for safe-keeping."

Her grandmother was weary from the excitement of the day and tiredly agreed, "All right, since it's your birthday you may walk to the corner across from the mosque. But take care to go no further, and come home immediately after prayers."

Zinnia helped her to bed. She then put on the lovely veil, gazing at herself in a rippled bronze platter. She was pleased, turning her head from side to side. "I'll just wear it once, then I'll put it away until my wedding day," she promised herself.

It was a beautiful day. The sun was shining and a gentle breeze played softly with her veil. She did exactly as she had promised her grandmother, stopping at the corner and listening to the prayer of praise. It lifted her spirits, and she felt peaceful. "God is good," she thought. "And grandmother and mother are good. I should try to be good, too."

After a while, the refrain of a sweet Qawalis drifted to her ears and she began to sway with the music. It eased her mind and soul.

"Hello, Zinnia."

Startled, she looked up to find her beloved friend Azam, along with the sisters who lived next door, standing beside her. Azam was a handsome boy of nineteen, with slightly curly raven hair. His dark eyes were fringed with double rows of incredibly long lashes, and when he smiled his face lit up with dimples.

"It's your birthday today, isn't it? Is that lovely veil a gift? You look so cute and grown up," the girls complimented her at once.

"Zinnia is always beautiful," Azam insisted.

Zinnia blushed, flattered by their remarks.

"Come with us, Zinnia," Azam urged her. "We're going to the palace where there's a big parade. The elephants are performing soon. Won't you come with us? We'll come home right after the elephants."

"I don't know." Zinnia glanced back towards the hut where her grandmother was sleeping.

"Don't be silly, your grandma won't care. You're a young woman now," the sisters said as they took her by the hand and gently led her towards what looked to be the end of a brightly colored procession far ahead on the road. The colors mesmerized Zinnia, and she let them pull her along.

As they got closer, they heard the rhythm of drums. The crowd was happy and skipping to the beat. Other youngsters were running and laughing, trying to get closer to the front of the parade where the elephants were. Zinnia and her three friends were no exception, and they squealed as they pressed through the crowds. Soon they were in the luxurious gardens in front of the palace.

"My mother is inside," Zinnia bragged. "She's the most beautiful dancer at the court."

They had jostled their way to the edge of a large circle. Feats of strength were being performed that astounded the children. The magnificent animals were massive and obviously intelligent as they accomplished more and more difficult tricks.

The performance was soon over, but immediately the musicians began to play a soul-lifting and exalting Qawalis. Zinnia made sure that her birthday veil was fastened tightly around her head and then joined hands to dance in a small circle to the rhythms. Azam stood to one side, tapping his foot and clapping with vitality to the rhythm.

It was not long before Zinnia was lost in the captivating music. Her young flexible body moved naturally with the sounds. The dancers were all oblivious to the people around them. The young supple bodies swaying to the music drew men's eyes. Guards standing at the palace gates talked and pointed at the girls.

The girls spun and laughed, dizzy with the sound of the music, the brightness of the sun. Suddenly Zinnia's lovely veil fell to the ground. As she bent down to fetch it she saw a pair of shoes ... her mother's shoes!

"Zinnia, stop that!" her mother screeched. "Come with me this minute!"

She was embarrassed and frightened as her mother grabbed her arm and half-dragged her down the street to her grandmother's hut. Even before they entered, a rain of blows had come down on Zinnia's back.

Reshma Bai beat her with shouts. "Why did you dance after promising never to do so outside this hut?? Don't you see that dancing will give you *my* life? A wretched life without love and devotion?" Zinnia fell to her knees as more slaps stung her face and tore the veil from her head. "Be a good woman! Marry and live without shame!"

Amid the slapping, Zinnia's veil ripped into two pieces.

Both Zinnia and her mother lowered to the floor, weeping.

Zinnia's grandmother picked up the remnants of the ruined veil. She folded it as if it were still precious and placed it in her one possession, a small and intricately carved teak chest that her husband had given her on their wedding day.

That same year, Zinnia saw massacres in Begum Haveli and Punjab, due to the mutiny of the Indians against the British. The commander of that district did not content himself with the practices considered lawful in war by disciplined troops, and the poor girl witnessed cruelty she could never have imagined.

The massacre of Indians by the British commenced with a ruthlessness that made the heart shudder, sadism that made the hair stand on end. Whole towns and villages, once flourishing, were laid to waste. Villagers fled from the assassins, reduced to drifters and beggars in their own country. Even the loveliest districts were converted into a wilderness. In some areas the resistance became violent, and some of the bloodiest fighting occurred in the area of Kumpur.

The British began to encounter even fiercer resistance, and one can only speculate as to what caused these people to suddenly react with such violence after two centuries of oppression. Many men and women were brutally murdered in retaliation, but it did not deter the rebels.

One such retaliation happened in the middle of a village street. After cutting off a man's fingers and mutilating his face with a bayonet, the sadistic henchmen left him to die in the street. No one dared help the poor man, and it took him two days to die.

For survival along the way, the resistance force ate what little food they had brought with them. When that was exhausted, they lived off the land, demanding food from the local inhabitants and collecting forage for the horses. Both sides used several methods of torture besides beating. Two common methods of torture were the "sack" and the "boards." For the first, they filled a sack with hot coals, ashes, and spices, placed it over a person's head or nostrils, and thumped him on the back to make him inhale. The victim either revealed where his wealth was hidden or he died of burns and suffocation. The "boards" derives its name from the two heavy boards between which the soldiers made a person lie on the ground. Two men stood and jumped on them, one on each end, until the tortured person's rib cage collapsed or he told the location of his money and jewels.

British writers also record many other atrocities, such as burning men, dividing children with swords in mid-air, and raping women. On other occasions, they held the headman overnight as ransom. They would progressively send cut-off parts of his body to the village and warn that the next would be his heart if the villagers did not send more money soon. Merchants trembled when they heard it and young women wept. No one felt safe. Other villagers deserted their homes for several weeks and fled to the hills for protection.

The British unanimously agreed with the assertion "that the adoption of vigorous measures for the early suppression of the resistance has become an indispensable obligation of our public duty." Many only wished to plunder, rape, murder, and burn. The unruly hordes commenced a course of destruction that spared no one, not women, old men, or even children. They murdered and tortured the defenseless, hanging the innocent.

In one such scene, a lieutenant inside a tent cried out, "Hang the bastard, hang all of them!" He then went to bed and slept peacefully. The hangings were public. The men were led in a line and made to stand on stools under the gallows. Soldiers kicked the stools out from under the men, some of whom were reciting the Quran as they dropped and dangled on the ropes.

The next night, another set of prisoners arrived. The same lieutenant saw them marching toward the encampment and said, "Hang them. That's the order of Lieutenant Wilson Sahib."

"But they're not for hanging. They only refused to give fodder for the horses," a courier explained.

"Never mind the details. Hang them. The fewer of them, the better," he grumbled. He then again went to sleep in his tent. The courier saw his chance and opened the ropes, letting them all escape into darkness.

With the seemingly unending detention and torture of prisoners, horrible accounts were spread throughout the country.

Zinnia's village was not spared reprisals. Their hut was ransacked and she took refuge in a "Begum Ki Haveli." The English managed to find and attack them with their bayonets but a tommy managed to save Zinnia. She was taken to camp and kept in seclusion while she waited for whatever was to happen next.

One day, word arrived that orders had been given to hang the Imam and Azam, the people who seemed most like her father and brother. She begged to be taken to the gallows and was allowed, and there she pleaded for their lives.

The lieutenant listened to her pleas, his eyes scanning the beautiful girl. He agreed, but with one horrible condition. "I'll let one live out of the goodness of my heart. You, my dear, must choose," he said, smirking. "Your bespoken brother or father? Regardless of which you choose, you must afterwards go with my corporal. He'll sell you and split the money with me."

She agreed, weeping, but was beside herself trying to decide which one she should choose. The father wanted to be hanged, but his son refused. The corporal finally waved his hand. "Hang the son and leave the father." Zinnia screamed her protest but the man only raised his voice and continued. "He's a singer, and he can teach the girl to sing and dance. She'll fetch a higher price that way. Besides, the son might try to follow her."

Zinnia lunged forward toward Azam, but the soldiers held her back. She wailed as she was held fast in the arms of the men. All she could do was watch in horror as they placed a noose about the neck of Azam, the wildly handsome son of Imam. Azam's mother burst from the crowd and rushed to the post, also begging for mercy. Dropping before her son, she removed his shoes and began kissing his feet in anguished desperation. Her words were foreign to the lieutenant, but he did not need any interpreter to understand her words.

Though his eyes seemed very close to softening, he was repulsed at her kissing the man's feet and glanced about awkwardly. She was a sort of animal to him, though a grieving mother just the same. The lieutenant nodded for some men to pick her up and drag her back from her son. Her screams were unbearable to hear as two strong men pulled her back.

The voices of people crying could be heard from the back of the crowd. Zinnia's eyes filled with tears and hardened as she heard abuses in the native language rising from the crowd. The shouts offered pity for the poor mother who sank against the pole and reached out vainly to her son, her wailing making her words nearly unintelligible.

> *"What is a broken heart,*
> *the hollow empty burning sensation in the pit of your stomach,*

The desperation when all hope is gone,
Eyes glazed darting to and fro?
No more answers, lost opportunities,
No way to go forward,
No way to go back;
The mind whirls, wanting … needing … feeling
Extreme anxiety, angst;
What could I have done to make it happen? Where is my guilt in all this?
How did I fail? Aid, assist, help; Prayers?
Only moments left,
Torment, anguish;
Who will help me?
It's too late!
Who has the power?
Men, law, spirit of mercy?
Knowing it's too late,
Oh, to have yesterday again!
Turning to God,
Where can I turn?
Is there an end to this agony, this torture?"

Azam's last words were recitations from the Holy Book. He was at his best:

"Praise be to God, Lord of Universe,
The compassionate, the merciful,
Sovereign of the Day of Judgment!
You alone we worship, and to you alone
We turn for help,
Guide us to the straight path,
The path of those whom You have favored,
Not of those who have incurred Your wrath,
Nor of those who have gone astray."

The man at the gallows pulled sharply on the rope.

Zinnia was never the same.

Because of the Sepoy Mutiny, the East India Company lost its administrative functions to the British government the following year, and India finally became a formal crown colony in 1858. The Crown had an army of its own to take power from the company and its army. During this bloody upheaval, many brutal attacks by the British continued, followed by equally brutal attacks as reprisals by the Indian army.

CHAPTER 4

▼

THE SEEDS OF DISSENT

Mexico, 1853

Mexican General Antonio de Santa Anna had staged a coup and overthrown the government. He was now Mexico's latest dictator. Whether he was enthroned in splendor as president or galloping about in the revolutions, he emerged only as a pamphlet character—a hero to his partisans and a virile monster to his enemies.

Benito Juarez was called for tea. As he entered the stately hall, he was told to wait until summoned because the president, Santa Anna, was busy receiving envoys and dispatching telegrams. From his vantage point he could see an adjacent office complex where clerks and typewriters were placed at intervals, and another office where the principal staff officers were seated and working.

Not having been offered a seat, he paced slowly about, looking at the paintings in the room. One portrait showed the broad-jawed, narcissistic general standing over a pile of bloody bodies at the Alamo, his foot on the dead bodies of Davy Crockett and Bowie. Near that one were huge oil portraits of the general, one after the other, showing the dictator president covered in medals and standing ten feet tall.

Amazed at the vainglory of this man, Juarez thought to himself, "What's being said about him seems to be true. No wonder Santa Anna likes to be called the 'Napoleon of the West.'"

He observed another painting showing Santa Anna's troops executing the Alamo prisoners, all except a few who were supposedly spared to carry home the message that Santa Anna's terrible policy was *no prisoners*. Other paintings of his services to Spain, his visit to Washington, letters to U.S. President Polk, running into Mexico with U.S. help, turning against the emperor in Mexico, fighting the Americans, the French, the monarchists and the liberals …

Juarez suppressed a smirk, thinking to himself, "He'd kill his own parents and then ask mercy as an orphan."

His thoughts were interrupted by a clerk. "The president will see you now, sir."

Juarez entered the room sizing up the man, finding in the arrogant usurper a confident man of advanced age. Santa Anna was by a stand-up working table, his back to Juarez. Half of his left leg was gone, only a wooden peg in its place, but he remained standing. The dictator kept busy working until Juarez finally asked, "May I sit down?"

"Yes," he said without turning, continuing his work a moment longer. The proud general finally sat in a massive leather chair, putting his leg and peg on top of the huge desk that separated them. He did not bother to look up at Juarez, playing with his watch chain instead. Juarez waited quietly in his seat.

"Good morning, sir," the general finally said in greeting.

"Good morning."

The quick-tempered general's teeth clenched and anger surged up his face. "You should call me 'sir.' I'm a politician too, el presidente of this country so many times, the Napoleon of the West!"

"I don't address opportunists as 'sir.'"

"Opportunists?" General Santa Anna fumed. "Hell, do opportunists lose a leg in wars of liberation?" he asked arrogantly, gesturing to the wooden peg.

"You know as well as I that the loss of your leg restored your sunken prestige. I'm well aware of the ceremony in 1842 that began with digging out your lost limb, parading it through Mexico, then placing it on a monument for all to see."

Santa Anna, shocked at the man's insolence, listened with his mouth slightly ajar as Juarez continued.

"You're the artful manufacturer of a personality cult. Not only that, but you're a corrupt ruler. You were defeated at four places in the Mexican War. You're also an inept military commander. Above and beyond all of that, you were a corrupt president for a second four-year term. You want to be known as the hero of Tampico. Anything to help your political career, even these paintings."

"I'll have you know I've struggled, first for Iturbide to win Mexican liberation—"

Juarez interrupted, "Two years later you led a revolution *against* Iturbide, back in '23."

The general glared. "That party was anti-Mexico."

Juarez smirked cynically. "Does that explain your repeated shift of allegiance from party to party?"

"What are you saying, sir?"

"I'm saying exactly what you're hearing," he said, leaning forward in his chair. "You aided Vincente Guerrero to power. After that you revolted *against* him. You helped Bustamante to power, then you turned against *him*. Your brutality at the Alamo and massacres at Goliad make you a bad man, General."

The conceited general's chest swelled beneath rows of medals. "I believe in democracy."

"Democracy under one man's rule?" Juarez scoffed.

"I believe you're beginning to anger me more than either of us should dare!" Santa Anna raged. "The judiciary, executive, and legislature are all intact. We *do* have democracy in Mexico."

"General, you're wrong," Juarez argued. "You're simultaneously head of the state as well as head of the army. Now through your self-serving legal instruments, you hope to justifiably stay that way?"

The general relaxed into his chair and his tone became more condescending. "Sir, we're facing foreign intervention. You're a nationalist, not to mention a legal mind, so you know what that implies. Help me in the larger national interest."

"You talk of democracy and a 'larger national interest.' The reality is that you're un-elected yourself. How can you speak for either?"

"In larger national interests, one accepts a lesser evil."

Juarez was incredulous. "Accept a *lesser evil*? You want to have me on your side to lead others to your absolute authority?"

"You can determine it as a necessity, sir."

"Who gave you the power to determine the state's matters at will?"

"A bit of discretion," the general said, shrugging his shoulders. "My word of honor and good faith are sufficient."

"Your discretion isn't subject to the constitution?"

The general nonchalantly went back to fiddling with his watch chain. "Affairs in Mexico are unique. We're struggling between our past and present. A hundred years to come, my people won't be fit for liberty. They don't know what it is, unenlightened as they are, and under the influence of a Catholic clergy, absolute power is the proper government for them. But there's no reason why they shouldn't have a wise and virtuous leader. They must trust me … as they would a kind papa."

"To top it off, now you're asking this nation for blind obedience. It may not rebel, but attitudes of servility will drain its vigor. If you ask this nation to bend, it'll start crawling." Juarez paused, then said, "Go back to your barracks, General. Already we're split between our opinions of religion and democracy. Your military coup will only install men in uniform in senior positions in the government. Leave us taxpayers alone. We have other worries, too."

"Together we can lead this country of ours out of its worries!" the two-faced general cajoled.

"Our professions differ, General. For me, the greatest pleasure in the life of any politician is in helping others; for you, it's destroying them. Generals look forward best in trenches, not in government palaces."

"All's not well with you politicians either. You're in politics for the people, values and lesser classes. There're many politicians and presidents who work only for the richest, who throw values out the window only to have money to get re-elected inspite of ruling badly."

"Yes, it's true, but the politicians get caught by the complication of the ballot."

"I have the power. I now call the shots," Santa Anna declared with pride. "Look at that painting in my hall. I have my foot resting over the American army's Colonel Bowie and their politician, Davy Crockett. I've also repeatedly humbled Mexican generals and politicians, and now they eat from my hands … you're a poor person of humble origin, an Indian orphaned at an early age and brought up by others. I appreciate your honesty and your principles. You're one of the most capable officers any government could have. Now you're in a privileged position. The military master of the country is soliciting your help. Imagine the new positions you could have … your *family* could have. Also imagine the disgrace, the punishment, and degradation you could have by refusing."

He stared hard at the Indian, letting his suggestion sink in. "What do you say?"

Juarez stood and looked deeply at the resolute general. He answered with conviction, "Your new constitution fuelled the Texas revolt. You used the '*take no prisoners*' policy at Goliad and the Alamo."

He began to pace, weighing his words carefully.

"If a law itself becomes an instrument of the state's fascism, it must not be respected by responsible institutions of the state. I hope you know that jurisprudence. Regarding Colonel Bowie and Davy Crockett, they died fighting a whole army; they did *not* run away. They did *not* surrender. They honored their soil by defending it like true martyrs. It's you who found sadistic satisfaction by getting your foot painted on their dead bodies. Martyrs can't be disgraced. In my eyes it disgraced *you*."

Santa Anna struck his table with an angry fist as he insisted, "My pride is founded on my NEVER having soiled victory with murder. I'm humane and just! During the last campaign, we weren't fighting against a recognized nation. I was forced by law and by the strict orders of the supreme government to apply a penalty to the delinquents … now, that penalty may have been severe, but it was also legal, and I couldn't excuse myself from its application."

"Well, General, tell me why you massacred the Texans of Fanning's command at the Alamo."

Santa Anna's eyes flashed. "Regarding the Alamo, no commander is expected to restrain his troops when a place is being taken by storm. I summoned them to surrender seven times and even offered them mercy, which we'd then have had to take the risk and responsibility of granting, but they refused. They fought to the last, but died."

He continued more confidently, pleased by his first explanation. "The campaign of Texas commenced under a special act of the Mexican Congress, providing that no prisoners should be made. If the law was a bloodthirsty one, hate the legislature which passed it, not the military commander who obeyed and executed it."

Juarez replied, "In that case, you should not have entered a surrender agreement in the first place. But you did offer terms of surrender, and by your own words, you offered them mercy. Once you did that, it was obligatory, and I saw no justification whatever for violating it. As for the execution of Fanning's command, they were prisoners of war under a formal surrender agreement. It was wholly unjustifiable, an act of unmitigated murder—a guilt from which you're not free."

The general stood, towering over the smaller Juarez as he spoke, his voice now an angry hiss. "Mr. Juarez, you were born poor and brought up as an orphan. This is your brightest moment. A master of state is begging your help and cooperation, but the moment may not last long."

Juarez stepped back instinctively, looking fearlessly up into the general's face. "You're right, General. A person orphaned as a child and brought up by the mercy of others must look at his perilous turn in life. This is that turn."

Juarez pulled himself up to his full height. "Here I stand with an almost broken heart and mind. Everything pushes me toward security, safety, tranquility, peace, a 'live and let live' attitude. It doesn't require any intelligence to go that way."

He frowned to himself, overcome with emotion. Only his determination forced him to continue. "But that's the thinking of a *deserter*. He looks at his life, his survival first. He sees the high and mighty master and bends to him. Even the most ordinary intelligence is fitted to go that way. *But it hurts.* The mind and nerve give way to accept the inevitable. I'd hate to be known as a deserter. I can't desert what I understand. I can't desert my education, my morals, my ideals, my senses. If all men bow to you, why not bow to a proper emperor? Why bend to a mere soldier who's forgotten his oath?"

Juarez stepped forward again, closing the distance between them. "Your whole system revolves around one person, which is fundamentally incompatible with democracy. I know that you'll have the money to have a very coercive police and court system. I know that you'll also get a rubber-stamp legislature …" Juarez smirked in contempt. "You say, 'I'm the *master*.' If a master was all that was required, where are all the masters of our history? Why did they go? Why should they go when they have everything? Think about that, General. You have feet of clay. In the pit of my stomach I know that you're fallible. Your mighty position creates people who will humble you in the end. I don't want to be your deputy and have the power to remove you one fine day. That's treachery. You came by treachery. My mind is made up. History is my tutor here, and it taught me to say NO to you, General. Let the matter rest there."

The general raised his upper lip and flared his nostrils, as if he smelled something loathsome, "I had called you to beg your help. Now I'm reconsidering."

"You're about to take revenge on me, so your comments are unnecessary. Have me killed or expatriated."

"You'd rather be arrested than save your own skin?"

"I won't corrupt myself for you and I won't run away," Juarez said. "Where can I run?"

The general answered sarcastically, "You could run to the United States, against whom you took such energetic measures two years ago during the war with Mexico. You raised and sent out three battalions and a gun battery."

"Because our division from Oaxaca was wiped out."

"A nationalist," Santa Anna mused.

"Yes."

"Yet," the general continued, "you prevented me from bringing *my* forces to Oaxaca. Why?"

"Because I feared your schemes."

"You doubted my loyalty?"

"You've proven yourself to be disloyal, General. A man's actions in the past predict his future actions."

"I have the force. I'm now the law."

"Your force wasn't designed to benefit you. You misused it like a lawless criminal. You're as lawless as those who get hanged."

"Politicians and jurists like you talk of democracy, but what good is it if nothing good comes of it? Generations get wiped out."

"Why should generations be wiped out if the same generations elect their rulers?"

Santa Anna sighed and again took on his condescending tone. "The people are pliant. We know how to manipulate people to get the same rulers elected again and again."

"You can't fool all of the people all of the time. Rulers like you aren't wanted in Mexico."

"Rulers have controls and leverages. They can come back again and again. Tell me one who didn't come back inspite of his overwhelming popularity. It's *popularity* that counts for a ruler."

Juarez wasn't buying it. "George Washington was one such leader. He could have been elected again and again, but he refused the third term. Democracy allows for the removal of rulers in a peaceful manner. That's the main reason for its success."

"Sir, don't be naïve," Santa Anna laughed. "Even democratic rulers play tricks on their people. If they're unpopular, they go to war against a scapegoat, a 'sparrow.' They whip up the national spirit and bask in it to get re-elected. They steal money and use tools like the army in their personal deals."

"They can be found out."

"Never."

"They can be impeached."

"They'd have the right kind of money and people around them to stop that."

The general started to stroll around the room. There were files on his table, and he lifted one to present to Juarez. "This is *your* file. Governments keep such files on their principal employees." He flipped it open and turned a few pages. "Hmmm ... it says you made your state, Oaxaca, a model state of the Mexican Federation. You introduced reforms, managed finances so honestly and skillfully that the state's debt of nineteen years was liquidated. Ah, I see you also left $50,000 in the treasury."

"True, and more than that. I was freely elected by the people to rule them. I wasn't a violator or a dictator."

Santa Anna dropped the file and leaned against the table, tilting his head slightly to the side as he crossed his arms. "What would it take to have you on my side?"

"I'm on the side of democracy. You're on the other side."

"A benign ruler is better than a greedy politician."

"A politician is first examined by the people, General. They're carefully inspected. The people won't vote for a paranoid, greedy, corrupt, or ruthless man. Even if they did, they still have the constitutional power to impeach him."

"No, sir. Politicians can hide all of their vices well."

"They can be discovered," Juarez insisted.

"You know, I can appoint you as the prime minister, a very prestigious position."

"To rubber-stamp your orders?"

"I can allow you certain … latitude."

Juarez scoffed. "And then I remain on the other side of our constitution?"

"I see," Santa Anna concluded, knowing now that the Indian would never budge even an inch.

Juarez stared at him, wondering why Santa Anna was allowing him to say all of this, why he hadn't been dragged away to a cell by now. "General, you have me in your custody. Why not kill me?"

The general chuckled, strolling back to his desk. "Oooh, you would just adore that, wouldn't you? Harden attitudes against me … make you a martyr. I'm just starting my new presidency. I have a better idea for a man like you." He smiled humorlessly. "I'll make sure that you're reduced to nothing. I'll keep hoping that you'll join me, but it won't change your demise."

"Your hopes are futile, General. Mine aren't. I have loyalty to my duty, and to the efforts I make on behalf of justice. That can't be futile."

The general's face tensed and his hands gripped the table with an anger he could only barely restrain. His voice was deceptively calm. "So you're all set to see what futility really is?"

"Mark my words, General, loyalty to one's duty and efforts made for justice will *never* be futile. You rule by force … so what? That same force will give birth to rebels who'll get rid of you."

"Benito, Benito," he laughed, shaking his head and looking up at the ceiling with a sigh. "I don't know why I like you … you seem like my teacher, then a moment later you seem like my exterminator. Tell me, why are you so entrenched in your philosophy?"

"You have no time to listen to it."

"Try me. Try my patience."

Juarez paused to think of how to begin while Santa Anna sat at the edge of his desk, facing him. "General, there are two concepts. There's yours, 'might is right,' and there's mine, 'right is might.' I didn't invent it; it's wrapped in the entire history of mankind. Dictators stand for 'might is right.' The small can be eaten by the large. Dictators conquer their surroundings and the humble, pious, and meek are their slaves. Dictators come by force. They promise reforms, but it's just a militarization of the state.

"The state belongs to everyone, but the poorest regions suffer from high levels of poverty and overwhelming destitution. Compare them to the elite, the upper classes. Those people just want to guard their wealth. If the poor threaten them, they employ guards or even the state's police, the army and the judiciary, to violently suppress them. The people don't understand how clever their rulers can be. Before striking the people, they get their intelligence agencies and paid agents to create incidents, accidents, like holding a school full of children hostage. They pin the blame on a chosen opponent and then use the press to make sure that the people believe it. The rulers attract the 'scholars for dollars,' as the Americans say, to help them. The people become angry at the wrongfully-accused opponent, which makes the ruler's punishment more effective. But it doesn't help the poor, and they grow to resent it. Sooner or later they want to fight it. Their fight is then labeled as *terrorism*—"

"The people again, it's always the *people*," Santa Anna spewed with contempt.

"Yes, the *people*! And if the people fight, the government starts 'negotiations.' But meanwhile, they're really preparing to crush the head of the revolt through massacres, jailing, killing, and torture!"

Juarez paused to regain his composure. "When I was an orphan, I needed a mother to love me and a father to protect me. Instead I got an aunt who slapped me at the slightest irritating thing. Then I realized that democracy is the mother who *remains* a loving mother to the small orphans, because politicians need their votes."

He began to pace again, his voice shaking with intensity. "In militarization there aren't any votes, no begging. Just *bullets*. Generals see the job of ruling as easier than caring for the people. Instead of quelling unrest with elections, dictators do it with guns. That's why a nation protects itself from a dictator by agreeing on a constitution … but the first casualty in a dictatorship *is* the constitution. They have tricks of the trade to side-track and amend it. All of the dictator's coins are made so that 'heads' and he win, 'tails' and the other lose."

He could not hide his seething contempt as he paced and scoffed. "And a dictator gets plenty of help from the top intellectuals and religious 'worms.' Martin Luther called the Pope a 'glowing worm in a cowpat.' Those worms are rich, *very, very rich*. They work together in making the people more and more poor. The clergy work for the dictators, and the true leaders of the people are extinguished to make way for the clerics. Then they can attack the rights of the people and call it 'constitutional.' The ruler who stands with the clerics is an enemy of the people—"

"So that's what you choose?" Santa Anna interrupted dryly.

"I choose what's right and I reject what's wrong."

Santa Anna poured a cup of tea for the former governor Juarez, taking his time before handing the cup to him. As soon as Juarez took a drink, Santa Anna clapped his hands. His aide de camp entered the room immediately.

"Put the governor under arrest. Put him in the castle of Ulna. He gets a few days to change his mind. If he's not with us after that time, expatriate him to … the United States. They'll take care of him."

The ADC saluted and came closer. He took Juarez by the arm with apologetic gentleness, finally turning to the president. With his voice shaking in wonder and amazement, he marveled, "But sir," and stopped himself from finishing his sentence. Santa Anna knew that many thought of Juarez as a great man beyond reproach.

"I agree," Santa Anna replied. "This world isn't meant for great people like him."

With that, he turned to leave the room himself, but he stopped when Juarez spoke. "So you choose to leave your affairs to chance?"

Santa Anna turned to face him, surprised. "I've spared your life. If you catch me in the reverse situation someday, just pay me back in that coin. Throw me out of Mexico."

"You have a deal there, General. I'll send you to Texas."

Santa Anna smirked. "That would be as good as shooting me. Not Texas. I've killed Texans by the thousands. Send me to Cuba."

"Cuba then," Juarez agreed.

Juarez was sleeping in his small cell at the castle of Ulna when soldiers suddenly stormed in and took him by the scruff of his neck. A policeman searched him thoroughly and handcuffed him, taking him to the magistrate. Juarez soon stood in a local court, where he addressed the magistrate.

"I'm Benito Juarez."

"That's good," the magistrate stated dryly. "Expelled from Mexico."

"You have no powers to expel me from my own country."

"Who told you that?" the magistrate asked, glancing up from his paperwork with one eyebrow cocked.

"The constitution, sir."

"Can your constitution prevent a military coup?"

"You agree that this is a military coup?" Juarez asked hopefully.

"I don't agree. I simply see it."

"It's your duty to resist it."

The magistrate smiled. "What, and be deported like you?"

"You're adding one wrong to another."

"Be thankful for this mercy. Be deported or be killed."

The judiciary of Mexico knew of Juarez's passionate hatred for injustice. No judge wanted to confront him. Nobody wanted his name added to the list of those who were judged unjustly. Only this magistrate, with ambition beyond his rank, would address Juarez like this. He was double minded, sad but resigned to what he saw as the unchangeable rules of furthering his own career.

The magistrate did not want a confrontation.

"What are you, a judge?" Juarez asked.

The magistrate became breathless. His deep-rooted feeling was, *I'm doing it all wrong!* "Sir, this is no time to argue. Go abroad."

"What if I refuse?" Juarez asked, his jaw set.

"Damn you, they'll put you before the firing squad tomorrow!" he explained, wishing he'd see reason and cooperate.

"Damn *you*. You're a *judge*. Stand up for justice, speak out for the weak and the oppressed!"

The magistrate was becoming agitated. Juarez's upright mind troubled him. "Excuse me," he mumbled and rose from his chair, leaving the room. For several minutes he stood outside, a knot in the pit of his stomach. "This is an injustice," he muttered to himself. His breath quickened and a sense of overwhelming guilt and panic overtook him. *This is wrong! WRONG!*

He exited the room and went to a colonel of the army.

"I can't do it, Colonel. When I hear his voice, I'm filled with terror," the magistrate explained, shakily wiping his brow.

"Just sit down here," the colonel said, offering the magistrate a chair. The shaky man sat down as the colonel stepped a few feet away and spoke quietly to a group of soldiers. The men nodded and left, crossing the court and entering the courthouse. The magistrate listened in horror as the unmistakable sounds of a beating echoed down from the courtroom window.

The soldiers were army boxers, trained in keeping a man conscious so that he could feel all of the pain. Juarez was thrown to the ground, his handcuffs snapping up and hitting his face. His eye blackened as he writhed in pain, one hand clinging to a wall.

The colonel returned to the magistrate. "You can go back in now. We'll have you shot if you waver in your duty again."

The magistrate's eyes widened, but the colonel only stared back callously. The magistrate went back to the courtroom a defeated man and returned to his chair, clutching the back of it as he glanced nervously to Juarez. The Indian was still on the floor, clutching the wall. The magistrate's nervous glance turned to that of pity and he immediately went to help him up into a chair. The kind man took out his handkerchief to wipe the blood from his lips. He glanced about to be sure the colonel was not around, then thought better than to continue this and stuffed the handkerchief back into his pocket. He returned to his own chair and lowered his head to the papers, signing them. Finished with his task, he finally looked back up at Juarez, who was watching him quietly. Their eyes locked as a sort of *thank you* and *you're welcome* passed between them. "Go," the magistrate said. "Go, sir."

Juarez stood, clutching the chair while he regained his balance. "Give it up; it's not for you ... this job."

The judge stared at him, but his own sense of duty and right made him silently agree with Juarez's powerful, precise words.

Juarez turned and walked away.

He was put into a carriage and driven out of the fort. The conducting officer, Captain Juan Alvarez, watched him for a while as they were pushed about on the bumpy road. "You showed great courage, sir."

"It doesn't matter what happens to me," Juarez said softly. "What matters is how I behave while it's happening."

"A good motto for tougher times," Alvarez agreed. The captain looked down at his clasped hands and shook his head. "They've thrown you out of your land. You're an outcast now."

"No," Juarez objected, staring out the barred window. "Birds fly away before a snowfall ... they go thousands of miles away to safety. Man's been given knowledge and guidance to distinguish between right and wrong, and to avoid being misguided. You men in the army only know what you've been taught. But for those of us who know more than that, it's a test. The Creator wants to see if we can use the knowledge given to us to save ourselves from the tricks of dictators and self-styled rulers. I have no cause to be ashamed. Someday in spring, the sparrows will come back to hunt the falcons."

"But it's upsetting ... it hurts."

"Yes, it hurts. It hurts today. It'll hurt more tomorrow. The pain will be even worse the day after that. Every now and then someone will remind us, *taunt* us that we've made a mistake, that we missed a great chance of life. Even my wife will probably be against me in this. I love her and I'll miss her, but I love my principles, too. A clash of two loves is bound to come someday."

Juarez's breath was caught in his throat. He had several broken ribs and was in excruciating pain. He could neither sit nor stand. "Ordinarily, man isn't built to take pain. He's not made to suffer losses. He can't beat fear with fortitude. He's born to be timid, self-preserving, afraid of mishaps ... yet this is precisely the point where he can build himself, grow into something. Adversity has a way of weakening and defeating some, but it only proves to make others stronger. It's a door to prosperity. Not many can see that. The gales, fast winds, hurricanes make a falcon reach greater heights. A man is known by the adversity he can keep."

There was a large bump in the road and the carriage churned to the side. Another sharp pain stabbed at his ribs and he nearly blacked out. It took him several minutes to recover.

"It may well be that I too shed tears on my missing this chance, a chance for wealth and a type of prestige, but mankind has preserved a very important lesson from pain. You have to brave it, stick to your principles. Look beyond the pain ... hope is the word for that. Hoping against hope is the true mettle of any man."

Alvarez patted his arm. "Thank you, sir. I've received an important lesson today. If only I could do more, but I'm too low in the rank and file."

"Low in the rank and file? No, not forever ... you'll get your chance to reach high in the rank and file. Trust my word on that."

"I'll always remember you, sir," Alvarez insisted. "You're a prophet."

"No I'm not, I'm a sparrow."

"A sparrow? What kind of sparrow, sir?"

"I'm just a little sparrow who decided to provide protection to its kind from an eagle. I should learn to hunt eagles," he mused, smiling sadly. "Perhaps then I could bring some comfort, peace and guidance to my people ... to the Mexicans."

The captain frowned. "If prophets do that for all of mankind and rulers do that for their people ... what does the army do?"

"A very perceptive question, young man. The army stays out of non-military affair. When it's time for war, you simply go out and win it."

"But we're always doing non-military duties, like me escorting you out of here." He frowned again at the thought of his duty that day. "This is the most difficult day of my life, you know that? The stone-heartedness of my superiors and my juniors sickens me. I may decide to resign my commission."

"Don't make a hasty decision. Prophets were pelted with stones. Street urchins drove them out of their own cities. Sometimes you have to go through tests and trials in life. I'm also tired and distressed, but I've passed my test. Since the army is your choice, you should go to a library and study the art of war."

The grateful captain saluted him. "I'll be a general, sir. General Juan Alvarez will be in your service someday."

Juarez smiled and put his hand on his shoulder. "These shoulders should be strong to fire a rifle, but they need to be even stronger to save one's nation."

They rode in silence for a while, Alvarez watching the fields pass them by through the barred window and thinking about all that had been said. He finally looked deeply into Juarez's eyes. "One last question for the record. Can you share how you feel at this point? Like a caged mountain lion? Mauled, bludgeoned, degraded but not complaining, handling it like a sparrow?"

"No, not exactly," Juarez replied. "More like the moon when it's getting smaller, but it knows that its fullness is yet to come."

The soldiers pushed a haggard, tired, and badly treated Benito Juarez onto American soil, but once free, he trekked back to Mexico, where he had to do his bit to oust a dictator. He kissed the Mexican soil and said, "I'm back."

He had reached Guadalajara.

General Antonio de Santa Anna barked orders to his staff. "Send troops to arrest all who're able to resist."

"Yes, sir," a staff member answered.

"Yes, sir," another aide echoed. They hurriedly withdrew.

Santa Anna's troops were bound for Juarez's compound near Guadalajara. The stubborn Indian was in Mexico, in defiance of Santa Anna's orders of exile. The troops marched into the building; their intelligence had informed them that Juarez was in. They moved quickly and seized him. He was arrested and thrown into an iron cell.

Upon hearing the news, General Antonio nodded. "He's to die immediately by the firing squad."

As Juarez was taken out to the place of execution, there was a public commotion. The national poet of Mexico, Guillermo Prieto, shouted, *"Brave men, don't allow this man to be assassinated!"* The public stampeded, and there was suddenly a great confusion of horses, military men, and citizens.

Juarez found himself jostled from side to side as the crowd surged with a life of its own. He wanted to escape but did not dare try to maneuver between the trampling horses. He suddenly felt himself pulled up by the scruff as a few horsemen helped him to escape. There was a scuffle before the officers finally captured one of the assisting horsemen, shooting him in the head.

The other horseman leaned sharply over his horse and rode as hard as he could. Frantic orders were shouted from one soldier to another, but it was no use. Juarez had escaped.

New Orleans, Louisiana, 1853

Juarez's companion, Melchor Ocampo, ex-governor and party member, stood outside the cigarette factory where they both now worked, having a smoke break. Juarez walked up to him holding a parcel.

"What's that? You're holding it like a precious gift," Ocampo joked as Juarez opened the package.

"A letter from home," Juarez answered. "It contains soil … looks like coastal soil," he said, letting it run through his fingers. "Someone sent it from the port of Vera Cruz. There's also a very small leaf, as if telling me that spring is here. Mexican soil and a call … " he pondered, lifting the small leaf.

"Soil?" Ocampo cocked an eyebrow and took a deep drag from his cigarette.

Juarez lifted a letter from the soil, gently shaking the dirt from the page and reading it aloud. "Here is the soil of your land which you left … Smell it or come back to it … We eat sorrow, day and night … It's spring now … You said you were a sparrow." He smiled fondly at the letter.

"Who would send such a letter?" Ocampo asked.

"Someone who loves his soil. Someone who met me … someone who knows about sparrows flying away and coming back."

Ocampo's eyes narrowed, beginning to understand. "To hunt falcons?"

"Yes, if it's a sick falcon."

"Alvarez."

"Alvarez," Juarez nodded, turning the letter over and examining the box. "He must have been promoted and posted to Vera Cruz. He's asking me to come back to hunt a sick falcon. Colonel Alvarez or *General* Alvarez?" he wondered.

The two men were organizing a revolution. These unlikely factory workers, sitting on a sunny park bench amid the mossy oak trees and noisy pigeons, were actually the top liberal thinkers of Mexico.

Melchor Ocampo, a man of nearly forty years of age, exuded an air of dignity even in his work clothes. He had a high brow and pointed cleft chin, watching everything around him with deep-set, hooded eyes that sparkled with intelligence. The grandson of an army captain, he had spent two years in Europe before returning to Mexico, where he practiced law as well as pursued his other diverse interests. He was passionate about the concepts of botany and scientific farming, as well as his study of the Indian languages. He had gone on to become the governor of Michoacán, and just a few years before had served as the secretary of the treasury before being exiled by Santa Anna.

The men had met up in New Orleans, waiting out their exile as anonymous factory workers, and they had become quite close. They missed their homeland and used each other to fill that void for creature comfort in a land so far away and different from their own. Only the heat of the Louisiana bay reminded them of the way things used to be, and they spent a great deal of time reminiscing and debating both Mexico's current and historical problems. It helped pass the time, kept the fire in their bellies, and took their minds off of how much they longed to see their loved ones.

"How can we fight our own army?" Ocampo thought that over a moment. "Or more accurately, since the dictator is boss of his army, how can we fight *him*?" He finally shrugged. "Juarez wants to fight, but with what?"

"With his brain," Juarez replied, smiling.

"Well, what does your brain suggest, then?" Ocampo asked, perplexed. "Fighting our own army?"

"Fighting for our own country," Juarez corrected. "Fighting our own people. If the army forgot its duty, we have to put that duty back into its soul."

"What are the chances of not getting caught?" Ocampo wondered out loud.

"Mm … the chances are fifty-fifty."

Juarez's casual nonchalance frustrated Ocampo. "But Santa Anna has the controls. He runs everything … the establishment, the police, the army, spies, money, the press, the editors—"

"We only need one thing: the will to succeed," Juarez interrupted. "And one brave officer," he added, referring to Alvarez.

Ocampo's eyes widened. "How can we go back and fight when we're so handicapped?"

"Go to the right place, get the right supports and ideas, strategies, tactics ... and time."

"Time for what?"

Now Juarez was becoming frustrated. He shifted on his bench to face his friend and began using his hands enthusiastically to help illustrate his words. "Look ... a dictator is always toppled by his closest people. A dictator is a dictator. People close to him get to know that the people are fed up. Topple that dictator with *their* help."

Ocampo frowned and listened.

Juarez continued. "We civilian rulers have secret funds in gold. We let a dictator run afoul, and then we pass that gold to his next man. That's an oligarchy, buying the friend of a dictator to topple him. That's the trick of our trade. When the dictator's been allowed time, that time infuriates the people. Then the oligarchy sends the dictator home. If armies have power, gold has even more power."

Ocampo slowly nodded as he finally began to understand.

Juarez sat back on his bench, his eyes smiling as he stared into the distance and said to himself, "Alvarez should be given the political task of shooing away Santa Anna ..." The smile in his eyes reached his lips as he pondered that thought.

Newly returned from the United States with plans to overthrow Santa Anna, Juarez sat with Porforio Diaz and Alvared in a hideout.

"Diaz, I don't even know your full name."

Diaz smiled and replied proudly, "Jose de la Cruz Porfirio Diaz. It's a pleasure to meet you, sir."

"Finally we can get down to work," Juarez said. "I've heard a great deal about you."

"Such as?"

"I've heard that you believe in positivism and the scientific method."

"Yes, that's true."

Juarez looked curiously into the man's eyes. "I've a friend by the name of Altamirano Ignacio Manuel. He's a novelist, poet, and the editor of 'Correo de Mexico' ... he thinks you're a dangerous man."

"Well," Diaz said in return, "even you're a dangerous man, Señor Juarez."

"But I pose no danger to society, while you have the 'caudillo streak,' as Manuel says."

"He says that, does he? Me become a dictator?" Diaz stiffened. "Never."

"Manuel also says if you teach him the way to uproot dictators, he'll listen very carefully. Then when *he* becomes a dictator, he'll know how to defend himself."

Diaz laughed. "Poets are imaginative people."

"But imagination is the fuel that makes you think far ahead."

"I can see the truth in that," Diaz agreed. "But for now, let's talk about overthrowing our present 'caudillo,' Santa Anna. I don't want other things to distract our attention."

"Yes, we have a job to do. Alvarez thinks that Santa Anna will make a mistake in war, and then we can get him."

"That won't be so easy."

"Even Genghis Khan made a mistake when he planned his battles. He captured over a hundred thousand prisoners from the enemy, then had them all slaughtered. Emotionally beaten enemies usually make mistakes," Juarez explained.

"So what's Santa Anna's Achilles heel?" Diaz asked.

Alvarez, who had been listening intently, answered, "Santa Anna can be overconfident. He could be made to split his forces so that he's weak everywhere and strong nowhere. That's when we can beat him."

Diaz chuckled. "Alvarez thinks a giant can be beaten by a pygmy."

Juarez shook his head. "The study of warfare teaches that that can happen." He paused and watched Diaz for a moment. "You and I are both of Indian origin, though you have Spanish blood. We were both born in Oaxaca."

"Yes, I was born up in the hills, and you down in the valley. My father was a blacksmith and my mother was an innkeeper," Diaz said. "I learned to make shoes."

Juarez smiled as he thought of Oaxaca. "I ploughed the land and had a herd of sheep," Juarez said fondly.

"You had no role in the Mexican-American War. I fought it, I signed up. Such was the common fervor in those days."

"I was a provincial governor at the time," Juarez remembered out loud.

"Sir, many things are common to us," Diaz said, smiling.

"No, you're a soldier. You learned to kill. I'm a lawyer. I learned to serve. In power we'd be totally different in our approach."

"How, exactly?"

"In power you'd divide the rich and the poor, probably ban the poor from coming to the metropolitan cities. You'd match interest groups against each other until elections became a joke," Juarez replied flatly. "I can't do that."

"If one needs material prosperity—" Diaz tried to interject.

"No," Juarez interrupted. "Soldiers aspire to do that. Lawyers aspire to bring moral prosperity."

Diaz got up from his chair without a word, walking to a table spread with food. He picked up a chicken leg and began to eat.

"Alvarez has studied war diligently," Juarez continued. "He considers tactics for taking the advantage when it is offered, or to create advantages when none are apparent. He believes that strategy is all it takes to finally beat Santa Anna."

"Tactics help you to win small. Strategy is what makes you win big," Diaz debated over his meal.

Juarez again shook his head, impatient with the man's limited thinking. "I believe that tactics help you to see what's coming so you can get ready to face it. Strategy is bolder, fancier, and deeper. It seeks to hit the enemy where he's the weakest. Napoleon did that at his victory in Piedmontese, the Italian campaign. He stretched his undisciplined ragtag army in a straight line, parallel to that of the enemy. Then he located the point of his attack, the opponent's commander, and went straight for the enemy's head with everything he could concentrate there in a hurry. Alexander the Great did it differently. He always broke the enemy's flanks and reached his king."

"We have an army," Diaz said, "but we can't bring it out into the open, and our enemies have no flanks. So what can we do?"

"Wait until he divides his army into different routes, then pounce on the king."

"Make the king lay down his army?" Diaz asked.

Juarez stared at him with deep conviction. "Yes, you know what I'm talking about."

"Pardon?" Diaz asked, his eyebrows arching as he finished the chicken leg.

"You understand me well, Diaz … but I imagine you as this nation's leader and I fear you."

"Me?" Diaz was surprised. He set down the bones of his meal and wiped his mouth. "Why fear me?"

"I fear you'll learn all about how to rule indefinitely. You're not democratic, you're an autocrat. Maybe someday you'll realize that democracy is good. Maybe you'll even begin bringing it to Mexico, but by then it'll be too late. Discontent that grows with autocrats ends in rebellion. But I don't think you'll ever be able to understand that."

Juarez got up and left the room, leaving Diaz open-mouthed.

Mexico, 1854

Juarez entered the underground bunker of Juan Alvarez, who was by then a general. The military police guarding the bunker saluted Juarez as he passed by. Alvarez was bending over operational maps, making calculations and taking notes. He stood and put his cap into his hand when he saw Juarez, saluting as well. Then they shook hands.

"What's the situation?" Juarez asked.

"Murky," the general replied. "Here's my rough work, sir." He opened a larger map and put it on the table. "The enemy has surrounded us with a superior force, four times our number. He's dug down and hopes to exhaust our supplies and munitions before launching an all-out offensive. That means we have *time*. Time is of the essence now. If we don't use it well, we'll be defeated, but if we *do* use it well, we can settle old accounts."

"What do you plan to do with this time?" Juarez asked, cocking his head to the side as he examined the map.

"Concentrate forces … attack his encirclement and break out of it, then go to a better region. If we can put our back to the Vera Cruz seaport, that should ensure a better supply and revenue position."

"But the enemy will make a great propaganda of our defeat," Juarez predicted, a shadow passing over his brow.

"Withdrawal isn't defeat, sir. It's redeployment for a better chance in battles ahead."

"Do I travel with you?" Juarez asked.

"We travel close to each other. We have fitted out a coach for you, sir, the black coach."

"Are you drafting orders for withdrawal, General?"

"No, Señor Juarez, *attack* orders. We attack at the obvious targets. We'll then reinforce those sectors, and that should help us to break clean of him. Breaking out from an encirclement is an art, sir. Not many generals know that."

Juarez smiled at the sharpness of the general. "You're clever."

"A general has to be clever," Alvarez replied without a smile, but the twinkle in his eye was unmistakable.

"But generals are usually clever *against* their own people."

Alvarez nodded. "Sad, sad … that's a national tragedy."

"General, I'd like to attend your orders to your subordinate commanders. I need to know something about giving orders."

"You're welcome to, sir," he answered, glancing at his watch. "I have a meeting with the commanders just now. It would be interesting to watch."

"By all means, since I'm here," Juarez agreed.

The general stepped out of the bunker and soon all of the commanders taking part in the operations entered. They saluted Juarez, some also shaking hands. There were field stools sitting in a circle, and all of the commanders were soon seated.

General Alvarez looked at Juarez. "May we begin, sir?"

"Yes, please, General."

Alvarez clasped his hands behind his back and addressed his commanders. "We're here to address our military situation against the ruling conservatives. It's obvious by now that we stand invested by a force four times our superior. We've extended our forces to defend our region. He's bringing forces and supplies and waiting for a better time to attack us. What shall we do?" He searched the room and awaited a response.

A brigade commander was the first to speak. "If we continue to fight this way, being weak everywhere and strong nowhere, we're bound to lose because he's in exterior lines and constantly improving his military strengths."

General Alvarez nodded. "Right. Being in interior lines, we've the flexibility to concentrate forces and be strong somewhere."

A second brigade commander thought out loud, "The question is where …"

General Alvarez suggested, "We have to get to Vera Cruz in order to keep collecting money from customs. He has very little in Vera Cruz, only a brigade."

A third brigade commander added, "But he won't allow us to move in that direction. We have to attack elsewhere, then make a very deep turn towards Vera Cruz."

"We should look like we're going towards his capital, his seat of government," Alvarez stated. He turned to Juarez. "Sir, my brigade commanders know my mind on defensive strategies. We're weak, but we want to win. That doesn't mean we adopt the positional defensive. In fact, it means maneuvering to divide the enemy into a present enemy to be dealt with presently, and a future enemy to be dealt with in the future."

Juarez nodded. "I see."

General Juarez continued. "Generally in military appreciations, senior commanders make a mistake. They tailor their conduct based on limitations. But if limitations dictate surrendering, they're of no use. We're here to appreciate how we can *win inspite of our limitations*. That's the key to successful defense. Defense is really the wrong word; it should be called "winning by decisive engagements.""

"That's a new approach, General … interesting," Juarez commented, thinking it over.

The general nodded. "The first battle must be won. We need to realize that as the very first step in growing stronger over our opponent. We must fix the objective, decide the methods of approach, attack, and encircle the opponent there. The enemy's encircled us, so we move to one place where he's weak and isolated. There we approach him in such a way as to encircle a small part of him, get victory in our first battle. It is a protracted struggle, but we plan it so that we fight battles of quick annihilation. After that we plan all over again for our second victory. That's a long process, sir. It'll take us all night discussing it. I request that you get some sleep. Tomorrow night you can attend orders."

"You want me to go." He glanced around the room and nodded, not in the least offended. "All right, I'll leave." He stood and made his way to the exit. "Good night."

The commanders rose and saluted. "Good night, sir."

Juarez left the bunker.

The following evening, ten commanders sat on chairs in the hall. Juarez entered with Alvarez. The military commanders rose to salute. General Alvarez took his position at a very large field sketch made with colored pencils, stencils, and rubber stamps. It was an enlargement of the battle area, though not to size. Given the time constraints, it was still an impressive sketch.

General Alvarez asked permission to begin, and Juarez nodded. "Gentlemen, please come to me one by one." The ten commanders rose and did as they were asked, and each was handed an envelope. They returned to their seats.

Alvarez pointed to the enlargement. "Phase 1: Everyone takes part. Their roles and assigned forces are given in their respective envelopes … Phase 2: This now splits our entire force into two groups, one in the *holding* role and the other in the *advance to contact* role. We go towards the enemy and hold him, tying him down. Meanwhile the major forces bypass him towards this direction," he explained, drawing a line with his pointer. "Phase 3: Another fixing and bypassing operation. A detour plan. This will put us behind his main forces … Phase 4: Attacking another force, opening the door to our real objective, Vera Cruz … Phase 5: Putting in flank-protecting detachments to prevent the enemy from interfering with our operations … Phase 6: Concentrating all of our forces, then waiting and resting. That should be no more than two nights. Should we fail to concentrate our forces in two nights, we'll be defeated, that's certain … Phase 7: Cutting off the enemy's line of supply by cutting him off from Vera Cruz … Phase 8: Preparation for an offensive on Vera Cruz … Phase 9: Attacking and capturing Vera Cruz."

He lowered his pointer and turned to the men. "Gentlemen, all orders, timings, forces, attachments, detachments … they're in your envelopes. We meet at o-five hundred to sort out any further questions." He paused and held his breath. "Gentlemen, this gives us Mexico and victory over our opponent. Good luck." They all rose and walked out, talking quietly amongst each other.

Early in the morning, all of the commanders were ready. They had all read the orders in their envelopes and discussed them with their sub-unit level commanders. Everyone now knew precisely what he was required to do. They assembled outside of General Alvarez's room for a question-and-answer session regarding their assigned duties. Juarez was already there when the men arrived, and watched with interest. They rose one by one to enter the general's room. Each commander was then given another envelope containing code words for efficient secret signals for each phase.

Juarez asked Alvarez, "General, you've given *two* envelopes to each sub-commander. Is that to keep secrecy?"

"Yes, Señor Juarez. Even someone like you beside me, seeing and hearing everything, would have no idea what the manoeuver was. You also have no way of knowing the commanders' strengths, codes, or signals."

Juarez nodded. "Even I can't divulge your plans, nor any captured subordinate of yours."

Alvarez smiled. "I read somewhere about Mohammad, the conqueror of the Turkish empire. He used to say, 'If my beard comes to know about what's in my mind, by God I'll burn it.'" He laughed a little at that. "In military operations, the most vital thing is secrecy of plans. I got these plans from a very junior officer, someone who's spent his entire lifetime reading operations of war. Nobody knows about him. As the commander of our forces, it's my prime duty to find out such a distinguished military talent first. He and I produced these envelopes." He winked. "Hope it works."

"Ingenious," Juarez marveled, smiling at its clever simplicity. "I'm proud of you, General."

"A general and his army must be like a genie in a bottle. When you open the cork and give him his way, he should bring victory for you and then go back into his bottle."

"Like George Washington."

"Yes, like George Washington," Alvarez agreed, adding, "He lost all of his battles except his last. He was elected president twice. After that he went home voluntarily … yes, like him."

"Are you finished with planning this operation, General?"

"No, sir. The orders were for the general concept. Commanders and troops have been decided. Their objectives have been settled. Now they have to start planning their parts."

"Planning their parts?"

Alvarez stretched in his chair. "See it this way, sir … in phase one operations, I have the entire force under each commander's orders. He'll decide when and how to break out from the enemy's encirclement. After breaking the investment, he hands over his command to the commander of phase two. That commander just has to split his force into two groups. First there are the major forces, which have to go in this direction," he said, pointing to the sketch. "Then the second group gets closer to the enemy here and attacks him, precluding the possibility of his interfering with our marches towards this direction. The commander of phase four has to attack. He has to decide his forming-up places, his route to objectives, what time to attack, and how to do it."

Juarez nodded and smiled wryly. "That's why they say that military commanders should attend to their jobs and not meddle in running a country."

"They can't even do that," the general said critically.

"I agree," Juarez nodded. "War is too serious a business to be entrusted to one ignorant of it."

A soldier brought in a lunch canteen and put it on the table. The commanders had their questions settled, so the general opened a canteen to eat breakfast with Juarez.

Mexico, 1855

One year had passed since that breakfast, and little more could have possibly changed. Alvarez's nine-phase plan of attack had been a resounding success, and Santa Anna had found out all too late that his entire position rested on a foundation of shifting sand. Juarez could not help himself in sometimes smugly remembering the look on Santa Anna's face after he had surrendered to Alvarez's troops following a brief palace shoot-out. The Indian had stood very tall that day, proud of his country. He was soon after made president of Mexico, to the joy of his devoted sister.

Always a man of his word, Juarez had sent Santa Anna into exile instead of executing him, though he could have broken his word after Santa Anna had ordered him shot less than two years ago. He sensed when he looked into the nervous man's eyes that Santa Anna knew Juarez had that right. But still he kept to his original word, and Santa Anna had been sent to Cuba. He went there with his young bride.

Juarez called a conference in Mexico City to discuss the impending French invasion of Mexico. All of the important dignitaries, as well as army and government officials, were invited. Juarez had even taken his sister to the proceedings. The conference was held in the GHQ lecture hall.

The army chief welcomed President Juarez. An ADC whispered to Juarez, "Sir, I fear that the 'brass' may object to the presence of your sister at such proceedings."

"I won't speak today," Juarez replied, "she will. She has a better imagination."

The ADC blinked in surprise and bowed his head, stepping back.

The army spokesman was the first called to speak, and he explained Mexico's debt. Their country owed to several large creditors, notably France, England, and Spain. Charts were draped over easels to illustrate their dilemma. He went on to tell about a secret conference in Miramar, where Napoleon III had been the host.

The naval chief was next. "I appreciate that we can get rid of England and Spain by negotiating a delayed repayment in exchange for additional interest; however, France won't be so easy. Napoleon really wants to send forces. He wants to undo the Louisiana Purchase and deprive the United States of half of its present territories, if Lincoln somehow fails."

Juarez nodded and looked at his army and naval officers. "Anyone who wishes to make any suggestions may now speak."

The generals and admirals looked dumb and the room was awkwardly silent. After a few moments, Juarez nodded to his sister and she rose to address the conference. Eyebrows rose but no one said anything.

"My dear brother, el presidente ..." she added proudly as they exchanged almost undetectable smiles, "... my brothers and sons ... I'm a laywoman. I worked for years as an ordinary servant to help my brother get the education he would need to become el presidente. Did I work so hard and pray so much to see my brother hand over Mexico to some foreign power attacking us? No."

Her voice shook ever so slightly as she spoke, but she paused to take a deep breath and gather her wits. She continued more confidently. "*No.* We won't let that happen. God may be marching with stronger battalions, but stronger battalions must be beaten to convince God that sparrows also can hunt falcons in His domain."

A few men clapped, and it built to applause. Josefa waited until it subsided and continued. "We're sparrows and they're falcons. How do sparrows hunt falcons? First they must keep away from their reach. The falcon must not see us. That's the first strategy."

Juarez stood up. "We're to have no frontlines, no fixed defenses or pitched battles. The question is how to avoid that."

Josefa nodded. "How you do that is to disband the army. Give it one year's pay in advance. Let them take their favorite weapons and ammunition away from the depots. It doesn't matter where they go, so long as they go away."

"Disband the army and arm the ruffian?" a general asked incredulously.

"Exactly," Josefa replied. "The army goes north towards or into America. They hide their weapons inside Mexico or wherever they go in order to disrupt the occupiers. Then the falcon will begin to hunt. It'll fly, go up and down, but it won't find anything. They'll begin to torture civilians. That one thing will turn the ruffian into a patriot. He'll appear, dig out his weapons, hunt, and then run away."

Another general shook his head. "That's a very long and tedious arrangement."

She nodded. "Yes, and that'll only sicken the falcon. He'll change his administrators. The situation around Mexico could change and force their attention elsewhere. We strike where they're weak. They reinforce a sector and we go elsewhere. It's a 'sheep and wolf' game. Play it well and you'll see the falcon fly off. Before flying off, he will try to divide the sparrows, pit us in a civil war. He shall fail because he, having aroused our political understanding, is catching a straw. Then gather your strengths and attack the falcon's lair."

The lecture hall was now humming.

"My brother chased off a wolf, and now he has to do it again. This time a pack of wolves is coming at our sheep. Remember the ancient truth: 'An army isn't responsible for the pots and pans of its populace; it's only responsible to get them to victory.'"

Josefa returned to her seat as the entire hall rang with appreciative clapping. A few generals stood and saluted her. Juarez was pleased to see that one of the men was General Alvarez. Alvarez spoke to the woman. "Many sparrows can keep one falcon away. If they land a smaller force, we must fight and stop them coming at us—though the battleground must offer more advantages to us. But if they come in large numbers, we'll let them 'face the music' that only the sparrows can sing."

Juarez nodded. "Yes, force against force … but strategy against a bigger force. If he's 1:1 in correlation of force, we fight. If 5:1, we withdraw and wait.

The discussion over, he stood. He was proud of his sister, who had given up so much to gamble on him and his abilities. He felt an intense protectiveness toward her and was determined to spend the rest of his life attempting to repay her in some way for all that she had sacrificed. He took her arm with tender affection and escorted her to the waiting room next to the hall. The conference ended a while later and had done much for the morale of Juarez's men.

Abe Lincoln

Juarez sat in his office, talking to an old friend of his. A picture of Abraham Lincoln hung on the wall behind him.

"Good governance means rulers not allowing their governments to inflict pain on the people. So bad governance must mean rulers *allowing* their governments to inflict pain."

"On that we agree," Juan Escudero conceded with a nod.

"On a Friday, in late May of 1787, a group of men met in Philadelphia to design a new government," Juarez continued. "The British government with all its powers fought the government that this group of men produced. Were they rebels or were they freedom fighters?"

"That's clear," Juan replied. "They were rebels against the British and freedom fighters for the American people."

"So they carved out a state from within a state."

"Yes."

"That defines a state, Juan, as having the power to make and enforce laws without the consent of any higher authority."

"What are you aiming at?" his friend asked with a smirk. "Why all this explanation?"

"People can rub off their state and government just as a student rubs chalk off of his blackboard."

Juan scratched his head. "I don't understand that."

"It doesn't take more than a good *idea* to start rubbing off anyone's authority. The foreigners think they can teach us how to run a government. I ask them if they've been successful in running their own government. How can they dictate to us when they have faults in their own governance? Leave us be to design a government of our own choice. There are 2.5 billion people in the world and one hundred and thirty nations. They should come back to us if they find the best system of governing. That brings me to the American rebels, who designed and established a system of self-government. 'We the people' is the most important part of their heroic effort to overthrow foreign occupations. This is extremely rare in history. These rebels, fit to be hanged in the eyes of the British generals, gave the world *democracy*! That changed the course of human history from authoritarian systems like tyrannies and dictatorships, to give a more durable and profitable system."

Juan raised an eyebrow. "You're so much against dictatorships, but that form of government is probably the oldest, and without a doubt the most common form of government known to history. What's so wrong with it?"

Juarez nodded. "That's a very valid question for Mexico. Dictatorships give the power to govern to one person, or to a small, tight-knit group."

"So what's wrong with that?" Juan challenged. "Isn't a benevolent dictator the most efficient form of government?"

"There're many who'd like to use that adjective, but there's no such thing as a *benevolent* dictator. As Lord Acton's epic warning states, 'Power corrupts, and absolute power corrupts absolutely."

"I see."

"It's irresponsible to the people," Juarez continued, "and the ruler can't be limited *by* the people. That's what's wrong with dictatorships," he stated flatly. "Sure, they give the façade of control by the people, with their elections that are actually rigidly controlled with only once choice, or choices controlled by the government. The legislature meets as if they have a say, but they're really just a rubber stamp for the policies and programs of the dictator. Massive propaganda skews public opinion with an artful press and an army of writers. Opposition is put down ruthlessly with the help of a corrupt police force. Only one political party is allowed. Freedom of speech, thought, and association, all so vital for democracy, are not allowed."

Juan nodded. "And they're usually militaristic, gaining power by force. Many important posts are given to uniformed men after crushing all effective opposition at home. But how does a country throw off a dictator?"

"How to bell the cat?" Juarez wondered aloud, laughing. "Yes, there are ways to prevent dictatorship and to topple dictators. That's an important subject for politicians."

"And what exactly are those ways?"

"That's our trade secret. I can't tell even my wife or sons."

"Really?" Juan looked surprised.

"When in power, we set up 'things' that will topple a future dictator. It has to be a fool-proof arrangement, sir."

"Do you have any facts to prove that?" Juan asked, intrigued.

"General Santa Anna took over and had me arrested, then thrown into exile. He thought we'd been reduced to nothing. He later found out that we removed him and forced him to flee." There was a long pause. "If they have force, we have brains."

"What do you mean by *we*? Is that to create a ruling elite?"

"Not at all," Juarez replied, frowning in wonder at his friend's statement. "*'We'* refers to those of us who want to change things in our land from authoritarian to democratic. See, in the authoritarian rule, a man says, 'I own a chair.' Then he maximizes that position for the benefit of his family. In democracy that's called an abuse of power. In authoritarian rule it's called cooperation and facilitation."

"But do you think a country like Mexico is fit for something like democracy? A place where human rights are openly violated, jails are regularly filled with political prisoners, there's no freedom of expression or movement, where there's waste, misappropriations, corruption?" Juan asked, shaking his head in disbelief.

Juarez scoffed. "A country doesn't have to be deemed fit for democracy. It has *become* fit *through* democracy," he insisted, pausing to stare at his friend in frustration. "Juan, if Mexico has all of the problems you say it has, how do we fight all of these menaces? With a *dictator*? Hardly! No, sir, you fight those problems with a democracy. Democracy starts with protecting the fundamental rights of individual citizens. They're protected by the 'collective effort.' Governments are judged best when the general population, not just the ruling elite, is reflected in its actions. Only then can the problems get solved."

"Why is the Church against you, sir?" his friend asked.

Juarez replied, "When in a former government I was appointed minister of justice, I set about making the constitution, including liberal reforms, that sought to take Church properties. Thus began a furious opposition with the Church, who had for a century been the most powerful entity in Mexico.

"The conservatives and the right wing soon joined forces with the Catholic Church to stage a revolt against us. I was forced to flee, but managed to stay in Mexico, setting up a government according to the constitution from exile in Vera Cruz."

"So, even a politician must know how to fight?"

"Yes, fight internal and external enemies of his nation. He must be good at knowing where he stands, where to go, and why," replied Juarez.

Juarez took his hat and stood to leave, pausing at the door and gesturing to the portrait of Lincoln on the wall. "I don't lick Lincoln's feet, as my adversaries say. I admire his ideas and his democracy. We want democracy to set Mexico right." With that, he nodded a goodbye to his friend, put on his hat, and left.

CHAPTER 5

▼

SETTING COURSE FOR A CATHOLIC PRINCE

Brussels, Belgium

The royal palace is situated on the Place des Palais, facing the Palais de la Nation, home of the Belgian Parliament and across the Park of Brussels. An elderly man stepped out of the sun and entered the palace, carrying a letter from the former French emperor, Louis Philippe, to his son in-law, Leopold I, now king of Belgium. He was seated comfortably and given refreshments, soon received personally by Leopold in his courtyard.

"Good morning, sir," Leopold greeted him politely, shaking his hand and taking a seat beside the table holding the refreshments. "It's so good to see you here. The old emperor speaks very well of you. He has a very high opinion of your judgment and erudition."

The elderly gentleman frowned slightly. "Judgment and erudition? Both are worlds apart. It should be judgment *or* erudition."

"Oh yes, of course," Leopold replied, somewhat annoyed. As he took a moment to pour himself a glass of iced tea, his irritation waned to curiosity. "How are they different and worlds apart?"

"Suppose I have children, three boys," the gentleman explained. "They're all adults. Suppose the one who followed my advice became the richest of them all. Would it be good judgment to weld them all together so that they all benefited from his position? Erudition demands that I assess their varied potentials and make each one do what's best for him to do. Judgment follows the *obvious* path, while erudition follows the *real* one. The two are, therefore, worlds apart."

"Hm." The king reflected, not sure he understood what the man was talking about. "Kindly explain it a bit more. I seem to be missing the point ..."

"It's simple," the gentleman continued. "My judgment took the success of one son as a yardstick and others were measured by it accordingly. If I were truly erudite, I'd send each of my children to a profession most suited for that child. I shouldn't put crooked yokes upon their necks, or they may all fall together. Judgment builds or destroys, but erudition can't destroy. Suppose one of the children can become a monarch. Would it be good judgment to put someone like Napoleon under his elder brother who was a tailor?"

This amused the king. He smiled and then laughed. "I see. Yes ... it's normally the case that we want to imitate success. An officer retiring from service usually looks for a successful man, begins to imitate him." He chuckled to himself, imagining the scenario. "I wonder what kind of coats Napoleon would be tailoring with an elder brother?"

"Not the czar's," the sage mused.

"So which is the most important matter in the affairs of ruling?"

"Good judgment."

"Good judgment about what?" the king asked, still amused.

"About men and matters," he replied cryptically.

"Well ... how do you judge a man?" Leopold pressed.

"You have to put him up against another man."

"To see who's better? Or worse?"

"To see them each clearly, you must observe each separately. One may have poor body language, but that doesn't mean the other one is smarter," the man replied, raising a plate from the table and placing a roll on it.

"How's that?"

"The wicked man would have poor body language, but he's profited. His soul's disturbed, but his pocket is full of gold."

The king took a roll for himself as well. "And the other man?"

"The other man has yet to learn wickedness, so he looks clean."

There was a lengthy pause while the king mulled that over. He was beginning to wonder if the man was *so* wise that it took a wise man to understand him. They ate their rolls and drank their iced tea in silence for a few minutes before the king decided to ask more direct questions on his mind.

Leopold took one last sip of the tea and set it on the table. "If you please, I have another question. The czar's army has beaten Napoleon's. What consequences do you see?"

The man hesitated a moment and then replied, "A great defeat coming to the Russian army."

"Defeat?" the king asked incredulously. "The Russians were always trying to look as good as the Europeans. Now they're the *greatest*. They're flushed with an unprecedented victory."

"Exactly, sire, flushed with victory. That'll make them misjudge and want to extend westward. That would create a new European coalition. Europeans are *technically* more advanced than the Russians, and that's how the Russians will suffer a great defeat."

"Defeat … " the king mumbled skeptically to himself.

"That defeat will throw up a new czar in Russia, and he'll launch into the job of progress and enlightenment."

Leopold scoffed. "Russian reactionaries will stop his forward march and probably assassinate him."

The gentleman did not reply to that, and Leopold again sipped his tea, taking time to consider all that has been said. As he reached for the cream, he noticed the shoes that the old man was wearing. They were tough football shoes.

"Why do you wear such shoes?" the king asked, gesturing with a crust of bread to the man's feet.

"Oh, these shoes …" He looked thoughtfully at his feet. "They're the toughest type of shoes. I don't have to buy another so often. Meager stipend, you understand?"

The king nodded politely, never having had to think of such things. "Well, I'm grateful for your advice. Now may I ask what I can do for you, sir?"

The man smiled to himself, the king's words reminding him of something. "You know, Diogenes taught his pupil Alexander of Macedonia how to turn the enemy's flank. Armed with that geometrical knowledge, the boy overturned the flanks of all his enemies and became known as Alexander the Great. When he brought a bunch of vassal kings to his teacher, he asked, 'What can I do for you, Teacher?' Do you know what he said?"

Leopold nodded. "'Move away. Let the sunshine reach me.'"

The man nodded. "Teachers have such peace within. It's called the Peace of Diogenes."

The king walked toward the arch of the courtyard, looking out on the palace grounds. "Truly some people have great peace within." He turned and faced the man, who was still seated. "I'd like to invite you to come and stay in Belgium. Don't look upon it as charity. Honestly, you're like a candle to a man in darkness. You'll have the Peace of Diogenes, I promise you that."

"I thankfully accept," he said, standing and bowing before the king. "France is broiling in turmoil, a political typhoon. I'd be better off here."

"What's your occupation, sir? I mean, whatever you did before, would you like to do it here?" the king inquired.

"My occupation is to think correctly," he simply replied. "That's truly my occupation. I had some property that I gave to my three sons. We lived with them for a while, then they started to quarrel amongst themselves. They quickly forgot that their parents had spent all of their years in bringing them up, in feeding them, caring for them, and protecting them. My wife is an old woman now, but she's my companion and my nurse. We receive a stipend, but that's spent on feeding us or collecting books and newspapers. That helps me a bit to think correctly."

"A bit? To think correctly?"

"Yes, sire."

"I have some land," the king offered. "Take that, sir."

"No, sire. My sons will come running and beg for forgiveness if they hear I have land. Death was created only to give property and assets to the next generation ... but you could increase our stipend. That would be of assistance."

"A stipend, plus land and no visas for your sons," the king replied, chuckling.

Leopold brought the man, whom he now referred to as his sage, to his court. The courtiers bowed to the king and were surprised to see an old bearded French man walk with him, wearing football shoes. The music started and singers began a song. A dozen Turkish dervishes begin to dance. The old man took off his shoes, came to the fore, and started to dance wildly in the manner of the dervishes.

The Mevlevi Dervishes of Konya invented the style of turning dancingly to music. A group of them was amazing to watch, for they all turned harmoniously and in ecstatic unison. They showed marvelously centered discipline, seeming to suggest that their egos were somehow dissolving and merging into some sort of universal soul. "Dervish" literally means "window opening." The Sufi tradition defined the dance as health-giving.

As he danced, the sage came near Leopold and said, "It's good that the brain keeps the heart in check ..." He did an elaborate turn with the dancers. "But even if it's a mistake, let your heart graze over the wild grass sometimes. You've got to let go of royalty. Dance, sire, in your blood!" He smiled, quoting an old persian stanza from Rumi.

"Turn as the earth and moon turn,
Circling what they love.
Dance, break open.
Dance, tear off bondages.
Dance, in the middle of fighting.
Dance, in your blood."

The wise man was a sort of healer whose ideas did magical things. His suggestion took the cold out of the king's heart, blew away his reserve, and chased out his crown.

Leopold got up to dance too.

Falcons or Vultures

After a few days, Leopold visited the new home of the sage. He was curious to see the endless pile of registers, bound and dated. They contained cuttings of different newspapers pasted on thick paper.

Leopold pored over the huge stacks of information. "What's all of this for?"

"This is my intelligence service, my lord," he replied, tapping the volumes. "Every day I pick up tongue-in-cheek types of news from the press. Every day I cut those out and paste them onto a paper. I read them carefully, and often. That gives me the first word of a coming event."

"It's the best one-man intelligence service in the world," the king agreed.

"It is, sire."

Leopold scanned the many articles, curious of the sage's conclusions of them. "What do you see for the future of Belgium?"

"Bring in gold ... not from conquests, but from quests," the sage answered puzzlingly.

"What kinds of quests?"

"Prospecting companies, stocks, growers ... a happy life, museums, flowers ... grow flowers, let the world catch its breath with sweetness and aroma."

"My eldest son is quite fond of flowers."

"Then build him an all-season indoor flower garden. The refinement of glass makes it possible. Catch ideas by the horn."

"Flowers ... what good would flowers do?"

"They're sweet-smelling gold, sire. The world is ready to use flowers as expressions of emotion. There's gold in it."

Leopold turned a page in one of the thicker journals. "What future do you see for my neighbor England?"

"The British army is supporting the second-rate army of its trading company, the East India Company. And why do you think?"

"I have no idea, sir. Tell me why."

"To profit by a rebellion. As soon as the natives rebel, the British can take over the land and rule it."

"But what about the East India Company?"

The sage shrugged. "The company's at fault. They're not passing the riches to the British government. The exchequer is already at the throat of the company's directors to pay more every year."

"Yes, I've heard that," Leopold agreed, "but what right has the British government to ask its traders to give up all they earned abroad? Did they pay for a venture abroad?"

"The same right by which those outlaws Francis Drake and Hawkins stole Spanish gold for Queen Elizabeth."

Leopold chuckled. "Yes."

"Elizabeth saw the possibility of quests. She let others make the money and received her share of it. Wasn't it like taxing the whole world? All of the businessmen of the world? The London Company conquered India. Kings and queens have become very clever, my lord."

The king smirked and nodded.

"Of course, there's one obvious exception. Spain was stupid. Its emperor, Phillip, thought that he didn't need any venture capital except money to raise armies to conquer other people, then take their gold and riches. Phillip I had the mightiest empire in the world. But tell me where it is now. Who ate it away?"

"Who?" Leopold's brow furrowed as he tried to solve the puzzle.

"Inflation."

"Inflation?"

"Yes, sir. Inflation eats away empires. It ate away the great Roman empire, too."

Leopold turned this idea over in his head. Was this starting in his own Belgium? How could he use this information? He sighed and rose. "I see there's some lacking in my education. We'll meet again soon so that I can study this matter further."

Laeken, Belgium, 1856

A deputation from Mexico of prominent citizens, lawyers, and scholars was waiting for King Leopold I. The ADCs showed them the conference hall, where they were served tea by a flurry of uniformed servants. A Yucatan lawyer, José Maria Gutierrez, was leading the delegation.

Leopold entered and they all rose, some raising their hands in salutations. The king acknowledged them with a nod. "Please be seated. What can I do for you gentlemen?"

Gutierrez nodded and spoke. "Sire, we want you … we ask you to accept the emperorship of Mexico. As you know, this is our third visit. Mexico is a budding plant entitled to a place under the sun."

"You don't represent the Mexicans," Leopold retorted.

"We *are* the Mexicans, sire," Gutierrez urged.

"You're the European elite of Mexico, and now you're looking to avenge the defeat you suffered at the hands of the liberals under Juarez. You want to make a hybrid, plant Europe into Mexico. I'd hardly call you genuine Mexicans."

Gutierrez carefully suppressed his indignation as he replied to the king. "Not genuine Mexicans? I'm a respected Mexican lawyer. I was born and raised in Mexico."

Leopold scoffed. "Mexicans wear serapes and sandals. They drink tequila and eat tortillas. They're not interested in *Mozart*," he said with contempt. "They like mariachis and lively folk dances. They sing about cowboys, not German operas." He moved to his desk and began examining some documents.

There was an awkward pause as the men waited, wondering if the king had silently dismissed them or if they should wait further. They decided to wait instead, but the moment was tense.

Leopold looked up at last. "You're the ones who want me, not the Mexican people!"

There was impassioned mumbling in the delegation.

A second member of the delegation countered, "But sire, we're most definitely the Mexican people."

"Wrong. Very wrong!" the king fumed. "You're the minority that wants to rule over the majority. You own silver mines, vested interests, properties. You have influence and you're rich. Your best bet is to get yourself a ruler who's acceptable to the majority." He stared at the men for a moment, irritated. "Gentlemen, Mexicans are a synthesis of their past, and they're very proud of it. They're a fusion of the Aztecs, the Cridlos, and independent Indian tribes.

They're seeking a revolutionary spirit in the nineteenth century and the future. They can be throttled by their own dictators, but not by a foreign monarch with an army of occupation." He stamped a letter a bit harder than was required and sighed, leaning his head into his hand. "Go, I'm staying out of it."

A hush fell upon the delegates. They looked to one another in search of grounds to further their argument. The king had shocked them with his astuteness.

They snapped their heads forward again as he continued his angry lecture. "You asked Napoleon. You asked a British general, too. British Protestants aren't going to suit Catholic Mexicans. The Spanish monarch is ready to sign any paper if your silver and gold are pledged to him. That leaves Austria, the Hapsburgs. They're Catholic, humane rulers, tolerant. They often side with the dissenters. The majority may accept such a ruler. They offer political compromise and don't rule by force. Go to the emperor in Vienna, he's your best bet. But mark this: a Hapsburg never usurps a throne. An Austrian monarch would require a written document reflecting the desire of the true majority of the Mexican nation. They'd require a formal inauguration, just as I required from Belgium."

Leopold paused, then said sternly, "Let me warn you that the people of Mexico are in no mood to accept foreign rulers, hired and fired by the minority. Your people want to protect their silver mines and their gold, but the Mexican people want it for their children. The majority will be easily persuaded by nationalism. They'll fight you. It's basically economics. It's going to be an armed struggle for self-determination against an occupying foreign army. That army will try to make it look like a civil war, but it's really a war of national liberation. They're going to be helped by America and maybe others. The people are up against a racist regime supported by a minority like yours. It's a new idea, this nationalism, but it's built around economics." He nodded to himself. "Go and be established as a *peaceful* minority. Share your wealth with the native Mexicans … yes, that may be the best idea."

The king stood and took his leave. The delegates looked at each other, dumbfounded, amazed, and confused.

The lawyer Gutierrez gained his composure and spoke to the other delegates in hushed tones. "We have an excellent chance now. Let's travel to France, meet the emperor, and persuade him to ask his general for a written document of Mexico's support. Perhaps then we can persuade the Austrians."

One of the men moved to question how they'd get such signatures, but Gutierrez hushed him. The delegates gazed at each other, then rose to withdraw. Gutierrez picked up a drink and made a toast, "To the Mexican counter-revolution." The men smiled uncertainly and raised their glasses. Gutierrez then turned and left with his delegates. He uttered just one word under his breath. *"Redeemer ..."*

The Piccadilly Dancer

Zinnia was living in London with the tommy who had brought her from her homeland of India. There she had started out meagerly, dancing for potato farmers on the city outskirts to eke out a living of sorts. What she made was handed to the tommy, who provided her with food, lodging, and safety. The only mercy she was granted was that the man, for some reason, never laid a hand on her. That was likely due to his controlling wife, since Zinnia was a beauty that most men in his position would have been eager to enjoy.

She began to dance in the city, finding the worldly metropolis a better source of tips. The tommy had objected at first, disliking the possibility of his wife running into her on her trips through the city, but the increased tips were more than he could resist. She dazzled anyone who watched her, entertaining people who had come from nearly every part of the world. She never enjoyed the benefits of the increased tips, still giving every coin to the tommy, but it made things a bit easier at home. The tommy's wife complained a bit less when she found that she could actually afford an occasional shopping foray with her friends.

Zinnia would mold her advantages in any way that she could. Dreams of money and success were the last things she wanted. Right now she only sought a little peace, and she could forget her troubles when she danced.

The High Sea

The Atlantic Ocean churned, its gray water battering the sides of the ship. Prince Maximilian stood on board next to his admiral.

"The wind's good," the admiral commented.

"The enemy knows that," Maximilian countered.

"What do you mean?"

"Because conditions are favorable, the enemy can be assured that we're coming this way," Maximilian asserted.

"So?" the admiral inquired.

"Ambush, of course. If the admiral's ship was captured, it would be a great victory for the opponent," Maximilian concluded, gesturing to the ship they stood upon.

"What should be our next move?"

Maximilian stepped into the main cabin and the admiral followed. He hunched over the marine maps, taking a bearing, plotting it on the map, and calculating it. He finally straightened and pointed at the map as he spoke. "We should leave this wind and take that wind from here. This will bring us to his rear. We'll ambush *him*."

The admiral rechecked his calculations. "Yes, yes I see … good idea, do that."

Maximilian gave the orders for a change of course.

Providentially, Maximilian had come across Karl Marx's newspaper articles in the Italian ship he had captured earlier at sea. Marx's writings in the *Rheinische Zeitung* strongly criticized contemporary political and social conditions. He had also read of Marx in France. Someone had described him as a "baby eater," and Maximilian wanted to see what one looked like.

Marx was a middle-class German. When Maximilian was nine years old, Marx had been studying jurisprudence in Bonn and later Berlin. When Maximilian was ten, Marx had been editing the newspaper *Rheinische Zeitung*. By the time Maxi was thirteen, Marx had become a thorn in the side of German censors. They censored his paper twice, finally giving up and expelling him. Maximilian studied European political economists while in the naval academy, notably Marx. Marx was helping Engels to develop a political theory that would turn the world economy upside down. Even the English expelled him.

Maximilian had seen him in Paris in 1844, back when he was only twelve. He had been fascinated with him ever since. He had noted in his personal diary: "I must read Marx's work, consider it, and try to understand it."

Some of Maximilian's notes on Marx were found later. He wrote:

"Marx says:

Wages are determined by the fierce struggle between capitalist and worker.

The capitalist, invariably, wins.

Combinations between capitalists are habitual and effective. Combinations between workers are forbidden and have painful consequences.

We must find out a new way to assure integration between the worker and the capitalist. The government can replace the capitalist, but not the worker."

Maximilian returned to his room, opening his files. He looked at his collection of essays, notably those of Marx's and Hegelian's views on philosophy and political economy, those of Karl Vogt, the Italian …

team instructors checked the cadets, their weapons, and pouches. The training adjutant took over the parade by 0645 hours.

The commandant of the training academy came with the battalion commander and addressed the cadets. "Gentlemen, the French army has started marching towards Mexico City. They're no longer collecting customs and port duties, but marching to take over Mexico, to topple the government of our beloved Benito Juarez and foist upon the Mexican nation a foreign ruler." He spoke with a loud and commanding voice, adding dramatic language to raise the morale of his cadets. "You're to fight. I want to see your action, not your voices. No talking, no gossiping, no comments. Seal your lips and show me your bravery in the face of the enemy. Make history. You're the first in history to fight during your training. I want only one slogan, 'VIVA MEXICO!' Repeat that with all the heart you have for Mexico. Viva Mexico!" the commandant shouted.

"VIVA MEXICO!" the cadets shouted back.

The commandant ordered the cadet sergeant under officer to take over and march them out to the battle. The under officer ordered, "Right turn … quick march." Horsemen came galloping to lead the marching column, acting as scouts.

The cadets seemed to be marching toward the rising sun.

It was before dawn, still dark in the city square. The "Cathedral Metropolitan" was draped in the silence of very early morning, its rose-colored façade appearing gray in the dim. The cathedral had been carved from red volcanic rock generations before, hovering protectively over a large group of people who stood outside. They were dressed in ragged clothes, many without shoes as they entered the opening doors.

The inner walls were covered with baroque paneling and the church was built in the Doric style. Twenty-One columns supported the vaulted ceiling, 180 feet in height, and the whole interior was richly carved and gilded. The tumbago statues, covered with gold, silver, and copper, held elaborate candelabra. Two flags flew in the vestibule: one was the Catholic flag, the other the flag of Mexico.

Entering from the back was the Catholic bishop Obispo Garcia Juan El Gordo. He passed through the giant arches in the rear, walking through the nave towards his flock. He wore the traditional bishop's liturgical vestment, his purple cassock swaying gently as he moved with a slow dignity. On his head he wore a miter, a somewhat high conical cap. One hand held a ring and the other held the pastoral staff.

He removed his miter as he began the mass, placing it back onto his head when it was completed. He finally turned to address the people. "My children, today has been set aside to demonstrate to President Juarez and our government that the Roman Catholic Church must be supported and allowed to conduct its business as we have for centuries. You are to take up your placards as you leave the sanctuary and follow me singing 'Ave Maria.' Please say a prayer as I speak with el presidente."

He straightened to his full height before the gilded Altar de los Reyes, or Altar of the Kings. It was a very dim section of the cathedral, and the candlelight cast a mellow glow on his face as he began the prayer. "Our Father Who art in heaven, hallowed be Thy name. Thy kingdom come, Thy will be done on earth as it is in heaven." The people joined him in a soft monotone. "Give us this day our daily bread and forgive us our trespasses, as we forgive those who trespass against us. Lead us not into temptation but deliver us from evil ... amen."

The people lit their candles and carried them to the door, stopping on the way to pray at each Station of the Cross. It was a series of fourteen carvings portraying incidents in Christ's journey from his condemnation by Pilate to his being laid in the tomb. The procession through the Station of the Cross ended with the congregation saying the "Prayer to Jesus Christ Crucified."

"We adore Thee, O Christ, and we bless Thee," the bishop chanted.

"Because by Thy Holy Cross, Thou hast redeemed the world," the people responded.

The bishop repeated the Lord's Prayer as they began their procession to Juarez's office building. "Our Father Who art in Heaven ..."

The diffuse morning light sparkled with hundreds of candles, and the lilting sound of "Ava Maria" was heard throughout the area. People looked out of their windows in curiosity, genuflecting respectfully as the group passed. The morning sun strengthened and finally beat down on the earth until the sandy soil was hot under their feet as they finally reached their destination. Bishop El Gordo had led his congregation to a modest hacienda, Juarez's latest headquarters.

The people continued singing outside of El Presidente Juarez's office building as their bishop disappeared inside. His personal men lingered with the singers, squinting in the hot sun.

He was left in an entrance hall while a servant went to the airy library to tell Juarez of the bishop's visit. It did not take long before he was escorted into the library. He strode in confidently and looked Juarez in the eye.

"Good day, sir," Juarez said as cordially as he could muster. The moment was tense, and it was evident from the start that neither man liked the other.

"Good day," El Gordo replied briskly, shaking hands and accepting a seat in a comfortable chair next to the fireplace, with a view out the window.

Juarez sat behind a large desk and managed a pleasant expression. "And to what do I owe this visit?"

The bishop cleared his throat and straightened in his chair. "You're quite aware of the distress of the Church over your commands concerning our lands and properties?"

Juarez nodded. "And you're quite aware of the oppressive behavior of the Church over the Mexican people?"

His blunt response stunned El Gordo. "Everything we do is for the good of the Mexican people!" he replied, raising his voice.

"I see you're well-fed and prosperous, and yet I see my people hungry and threadbare," Juarez continued, keeping his voice steady.

"Church properties and income are for the preaching and expansion of Christianity. Your policies are hurting us."

"Our policies are the same Jesus preached; yours vividly different," Juarez replied.

"Can you explain, sir?"

"Jesus went about doing good; he moved among the dregs of society—prostitutes and tax extortionists. Healing, helping people out of chasms of despair, counseling them in their crises, he went about doing good."

"And what are we doing, sir?"

"Jesus did not empower himself; you do. The people around him saw him and said, 'He must be God.' Nobody says you are godlike. You must have money, power, and better position every day that dawns. Your pope gets it all."

The bishop frowned deeply. "The Church is doing good, sir. The pope dedicates his life to that."

"Jesus said, 'Love your neighbor as yourself, whatsoever ye would that men should do unto you, do ye also unto them. Come unto me, all ye that labor and are heavy laden, and I will give you rest. Ye shall know the truth and the truth shall make you free.' And you, sir, are here to esteem your wealth above all. We were told that the happy people are those who are meek, who weep, and are merciful and pure in heart. But you assume that it is the rich, the powerful, the well-born who are happy. A world of difference between his teachings and conduct of his Church."

"Where would you stand if the Church were to excommunicate you, sir, for blasphemy?" the bishop threatened.

"My answer is the same as what Luther said: 'Under the sky.'"

"The Church stands as the door to Christ between Jesus and people. That is a job we are proud of."

"Yes, just like a doorman. A police commissioner will come or go, but his doorman is at the door forever. The commissioner may be meek and humble, but the doorman is proud of his great job; he inspires fear and awe through his position. People must pay to pass on."

"Are you anti-Church? Do you really want that label?" The bishop collected himself and continued in a tone he usually reserved for the dim-witted. "The Church would have to side with a Roman Catholic emperor, even if he were imported from Europe. Your voters are largely very devout Christians. That's bad politics."

Juarez's eyes narrowed as he shot the man a challenging look. "Your Grace has said many things, blowing hot and cold in one breath. First, regarding Church properties, if you build yourself a castle on a public path, would that please Jesus? If you hurt the people, would that please Jesus? No. I'm not anti-Christ, I'm pro-people—*His* people. The label I want is that I served mankind through the highest ideals and ethics of good public service. If you're bringing an army led by a foreign occupier, what charges should be framed against *you*? As regards Christian votes, you can use them only once and then you have to lose them, because you can't remove poverty and war with prayers and confession."

Juarez looked towards the window, where the crowd's gentle "Ava Maria" drifted softly up to them. He stood and walked to the window to watch them for a moment, then turned to the bookshelf to run his fingers along his favorite novels. His hand lingered at a volume of John Locke's works. "We know good politics," Juarez said, staring at the book. "To unite our people and bring them welfare, to give them good manners and ethics, to make them brave so they can defend themselves. Much of that is beyond your scope, sir. We're far from the twelfth century and you can't pull us back there."

"We're merely defending our rights," El Gordo insisted.

"Do you have any justification to build your properties on public grounds and facilities?"

"Whatever the Church builds, we build on our own land," the bishop replied, his volume again rising. "Señor Presidente, our concepts are merely different. You were born to give testimony about your character, good or bad. We think that a man is born to give testimony about the *truth*."

"Bishop, that's a view aimed at collecting the riches from the world. Everyone born must accept your leadership over all economic and political systems, over all of the vast fields of culture, civilization, and development. Men of God, prophets, they all give away and you collect. This Christ-centric view and everything at your beck and call has emboldened you to interfere in political systems. Stay away from politics. Never, *ever*, threaten politicians at coming elections," he snapped, sitting forward in his chair. "What kind of *truth* are you preaching in a spiritually bankrupt age of material possessions?"

The bishop's voice was calmer but condescending. "Religion isn't your pet subject, sir. May the powers of Christ save you from doing wrong to the Church's property. You're not afraid to shut our doors? We think it's wrong, and the truth is that we own those properties *rightfully*."

Juarez stared at him silently.

"Presidente," the bishop continued, "as I was trying to say, our concepts are different—"

"Have you ever thought about what Jesus would say if he found your palaces on public paths?" Juarez insisted. "Or if you were riding with Jesus on a donkey, what would he say if you saddled Him and let the donkey loose on the pasture?"

"The properties ... they're properties in His name," the bishop sputtered. "Saddling Him would be sacrilege."

"Precisely," Juarez reasoned. "Did Christ want the rich to become richer and the poor to become poorer?"

"Christ gave us moral values to preach, to uphold and live by."

Juarez returned to his desk to pick up a well-worn Bible. He flipped through the pages, challenging, "Yes, and one of those moral values is the equality of all before him."

The bishop's frown deepened until his eyebrows nearly met. "Religion isn't your strong point, sir," he said as he watched him try to find the correct biblical passage. "You left religious education for law, we all know that. And speaking of the law, isn't it lawless to deprive the Church of its properties and means to sustain itself?"

"There's a problem with your 'means to sustain yourself.' You've reserved a monopoly of Christendom. That's your line of business, Bishop. It gives you enormous wealth, power, and prestige. You're here threatening a government with dire consequences if it hurts your vested interests. Well, this much I learned about religion: it's *against* vested interest, the common good. *You* may well be anti-Christ," he said, poking his forefinger toward the bishop.

El Gordo stood quickly with a cold look in his eyes and marched over to Juarez's side of the desk. Juarez stood so that they were eye-to-eye as the bishop spoke in a low and menacing tone. "Should I call you a rebel? The wind won't blow in your favor. We'll see to that."

"Every person who criticizes your ways is called a rebel. Martin Luther was a rebel, too."

"Indeed, he was."

"The wind didn't blow in his favor."

"That's history."

"And history also tells us that when the emperor Nero was burning the Christians, the wind favored the flames."

The bishop stared at him for a moment and then silently returned to his chair. He settled his large body down once again and replied in a befuddled tone but with blind conviction, "We don't know that."

"The Thirty Years' War in Europe involved sorting out such rebels. That's a known historic fact. Do you want that in Mexico, too?"

Now it was El Gordo's turn to fall silent.

Juarez walked around the desk and took the bishop's hand. "Grace, I respect you for your devotion. We're politicians. We're here to worry about providing clean and healthy water, make sure babies are born healthy ... we have to have hospitals for the sick and diseased, and money has to come from somewhere. If a sick mother is about to die in childbirth, would Christ want her to be cured first, or should that money instead be spent to make the Church a bit richer?"

The bishop wrangled his hand free, standing and walking to the door. Anger flashed in his eyes. "You're set in your mind to restrict ecclesiastical powers and property. Very well, we'll see you in the elections."

"'See you in the elections?'" Juarez said boldly, causing the bishop to pause in his exit. "You've gone and betrayed yourself with those words. You're politicians, too. You'll use your power against anyone who seems opposed to your aims and interests. God help whatever politician you end up backing; the poor man would have no idea that he has to make it up to you with enormous paybacks." Juarez shook his head in disgust. "You have a government flag in your chapel, Bishop. If France conquered us tomorrow, you'd be flying *their* flag in there. You're at peace when the people are being crushed and enslaved. That's the difference between our two occupations. We defend and fight."

"In that one thing you're right, Juarez," the bishop agreed, irritated. "We're both politicians, but you're worried about Mexico while we're worried about the entire world. You want unity for the nation of Mexico, but ours is a nation of God's earth. We want to unite all of the nations of the world, not just the different factions of Mexico. We're the seas, Juarez. You're only a river." He again turned to leave.

"Your Christian empire has three parts fighting each other; one part has 154 factions not willing to come together. Where does this diversity take you?"

"Should we abandon Christianity, sir?" the bishop asked.

"Emperors in religious garbs!" Juarez spit out.

The angry bishop turned on the spot and strode forward until he was again facing Juarez, glaring with eyes of steel. "Servants of God," he corrected in a cool, tense voice.

"What do you think all of us politicians should do? Resign, hand over matters to you and let you reign supreme as 'servants of God,' and yet masters of human beings?"

"That indeed would be wise," the bishop said simply.

"If mankind had listened to you, we'd all still be serving under kings and bishops, still under your inquisitions."

"And what are you, Juarez? Just some Indian polishing himself to grab power?"

"What are you, Bishop? Any common man wearing robes to rule the powerful?"

"We are NOT just any men. We are God's servants, ordained through the Church. We've dedicated our lives, our matrimonial happiness, our entire labor to bringing God's word on God's earth. You can't call us trivial names after all that effort. The world is going away from religion. The whoremongers and the perverted have no fear of God," he said.

"Didn't Jesus say, 'Those among you who are without sin cast the first stone'? Who are we to think of making some people good and others bad? What gives us such power? Who are we? God's appointed censors?"

The bishop stared again at Juarez for a beat before asking a pivotal question. "Señor Presidente, would you dare to print that in a newspaper under your name?"

"Taboos, inquisitions ... what did you learn, Bishop? You didn't learn a thing. It's not your fault, sir."

The crowd of voices outside had grown, becoming stronger. The strands of "Ava Maria" seemed to reverberate off the walls. Juarez listened to the singing for a moment before turning again to the bishop. "You men of the Church have your own illegitimate desires. Angels aren't wearing your robes, *you* are. That makes you as susceptible to those desires as the rest of us human beings. God doesn't mind your preaching Him, but He minds if your preaching furthers your own sinful wishes."

"We train ourselves not to have illegitimate desires," the bishop said proudly.

"And *we* train ourselves to take care of those who have such desires. You can go to jail. No ecclesiastical robe can save you, sir." Juarez explained plainly, his spirit taking fire. "We advocate freedom *of* religion, not *from* religion."

"That's a myth," the bishop said with a wave of his hand. "It rests on a misunderstanding, like all myths do."

"Freedom *of* and *from* religion are two sides of the same coin, Bishop. No one has the right *not* to see churches, mosques, synagogues in a nation. All religions have to co-exist peacefully. Freedom means having freedom from rules and dogmas of other people's religious beliefs. A man has to be free to follow the demands of his own conscience, whether they take a religious form or not."

"My, my," the bishop sneered. "You studied law for so long that one would never suspect you were qualified to discuss the role of religion in society."

"One need not be a pope to form an opinion of what function religion serves, sir. The pope is not the only teaching authority. One person cannot be the sole adjudicator of truth and error on life-and-death matters without a sure court of appeal. I feel that religion must satisfy three things," he said, counting off on his fingers. "First, it has to define a system of beliefs that explains the ultimate meaning of life. Then it has to teach religious practices, rituals, ceremonies, and so forth. And finally, it has to somehow unite the believers in a community, to serve as some basis of unity."

"It seems you have no faith whatsoever in God—"

"I believe in God, but my ward is my *people*, His people. They have to be protected and given the best surroundings to grow. It's called *public service*."

The outraged bishop again spun on his heel and left the room with a disgusted "Harrumph." Outside, the large crowd was now holding up placards and marching around the building, singing with more fervor each time they passed below Juarez's windows.

Piccadilly, London, England—April 1856

By 1856, Charlotte, Princess of Belgium, had turned into a beautiful woman. Her world was made up of holidays spent by the sea at Ostende, in the forest of the Ardennes, or visiting family in England. It was on one such visit that she walked around London with an entourage of servants, marveling at the sights. People bustled to and fro everywhere. Some were traveling to work or to the market. Others were just taking a stroll. It was Piccadilly Circus, London.

The name Piccadilly is derived from a tailor who invented a frilled collar called a 'piccadil' for the fashionable elite of London. This was Victorian London, the

London of Dickens and Thackeray, of John Stuart Mill and Thomas Carlyle. During this time, the first London Underground to Paddington was being dug. New coffee shops made the streets a tourist site for people from all over the world. The streets were alive with people from nearly every nation, bustling about with merchandise of every kind to buy and sell. Sellers hawked their merchandise in the open air, making the area electric with excitement. Large sections of the slums nearby were being cleared to straighten and broaden the roads, making transportation even busier.

On a plaque beside a little park, it said that Lord Mosley had made a "trust"— that the property was reserved by him for the pleasure and recreation of the public. The plaque confirmed that all were to enjoy themselves in peace on his property without let or hindrance, and also that police and bureaucrats could not enter that plot of land until they were themselves a part of the public. The Victorian Conservative British Society had morals that did not fit with what was happening inside that piece of property. The newly founded metropolitan police "bobbies" could not enter or interfere with what the general public was doing there. One bobby called it the "Pleasure Garden." Liberals called it "Freedomville."

A handsome, distinguished-looking young man read the plaque aloud:

> "Lord Mosley donated these lands to the city of London to create a 'Pleasure Ground' or 'Recreation Ground' to offer the inhabitants of the town the opportunity of enjoying, with their families, exercise and recreation in the fresh air, in public walks and grounds devoted to that purpose."

The young man promptly remarked, "That has to be the best way to use one's property!"

His young companion asked excitedly, "Royal Highness, can we do this? Would you allow it?"

"This is the future," the young royal replied. "This is what the English citizens want."

They observed the activities happening in the park, and there were many. Some slept, some sat on benches, some sang. There were drums, violins, and acrobats. The square was packed with an avalanche of Irish immigrants who had migrated to London after the potato famine had wiped out the crops in their homeland. In the evening, they gathered at Piccadilly Square for pleasure and relaxation.

The young "man" was actually the royal princess of the House of Holland, Princess Charlotte, dressed up to appear as a young English gentleman. She was visiting her late grandfather's orlean family and Holland. Her friends and body-guards surrounded her as she read the stone, fascinated at its premise. A few hundred years before, a member of the British government had thought about the best use of his property. Now the British government was not interfering with this dead man's wishes, but using it to ascertain what the people wanted.

"What a thoughtful, generous man," Charlotte mused. "Reserving his property for the pleasure of the public only … what a nice way to leave one's property," she sighed softly with a smile on her lips.

A small Indian music band stepped onto the plot of land, taking out their instruments and laying them carefully on the grass. A man with long hair began to tune them. There was also a stunning girl clad in a black and yellow dress, made to look like a Sindhi gypsy. The embroidered silk and cotton dress had *shisha* mirrors and traditional embroidered designs of rich colors covering it, with metallic thread and silk embroidery. The *choli* top peeking from underneath was of traditional east Indian origin, visible as the dress opened down the front and fit the curves of her body. The deep V front left her midriff bare. She had thick raven hair and large, beautiful eyes. Her skin was an exotic golden brown, flawless.

The girl stepped to the front of the band as the older man played a guitar. She began to sing in a sweet pure voice:

"O beautiful face appears in the water.
Hoooo
If you permit me, I love you a little
Oh my love.
Sit with me; I'll fill it with love.
If you get angry, the moon will hide, oooo
My soul."

She began to dance voluptuously as she sang, moving her hips in a forward-and-back motion. The movement was a very tiny and delicate vibration, breathtakingly graceful. Her talent was so great and her appearance so beautiful that she quickly endeared herself to the audience, which clapped and sang along.

Others nearby were soon attracted to the music and the lovely young woman. The crowd built quickly, standing shoulder to shoulder in a large circle. The man kept changing instruments, next playing a harmonium, then a violin.

"A love song it is,

On waves of life.
Life is meaningless
Without our story.
Lalala la.
Meanings of life, find in stories
Of love."

The song and violin were done, and everyone happily tossed coins of every denomination before the little band. The male singer, disregarding the coins, started another song. He sang,

"What's the best story in the world?
What moves the inner feelings?
Is it his birth coming into this world?
Or his death going away from here?
Is it about greatness, is it about divinity,
Ideas, feelings, emotions, cries,
Love, loyalty, sacrifice, honesty,
Bravery, nobility, family,
Success, emperors, angels,
Satan's leaders, feelings,
Remembrances, terror, sadness,
Joy, festivity, frailty, purpose?"

The dancer asked the crowd to clap in a rhythm she had set for them. She smiled and danced around the circle of onlookers, clapping with an exaggerated beat to encourage them to clap along. The smiling crowd enjoyed this song and began to clap enthusiastically as she sang:

"The story of man,
The story of mankind,
His best and worst.
What made him powerful?
What made him weak?
Does he walk, like an animal, day and night?
Busy driving a wheel
In a water-well,
Uttering low and fawning sounds,

To show growling inside,
Or has surrendered will …
Face of sheer helplessness.
Moping around meaningless life,
Showing the lowest character,
or his abject surrender.
Is he the torturer?
Or the tortured one?
Is he the monster?
Makes others do evil.
Is he the monster?
Doing many evil things,
Or docile, life's underdog?
Made to be ethical,
Religious, pious, brave, cunning.
Monster, savage or docile?"

The woman danced wildly as the musicians played their instruments. The crowd cheered in excitement at her energy. She was now singing and dancing erotically, her eyes closed as if dreaming. Someone in the crowd commented, "This sounds familiar. I think these lyrics are the teachings of someone's philosophy. Is it the saint from Sindh?"

The dancer stopped and sang with a smile and a voluptuous turn of her body, striking provocative poses as she continued.

"The best is this, my beloved. Me,
Woman, tempting, alluring, virgin,
Romantic, unattached, available, singing, laughing.
Someone special can bid for me, and all is yours …
I sell not for a night but life … bid for me.
The bidding … let the bidding start … me for life."

The crowd was taken aback, shocked at the very idea.

"Ten quids," a man called out, causing everyone to laugh.

The princess stepped forward boldly, still in her role as a man. "One hundred thousand quid," she bid in as low a voice as she could manage.

"My price for life?" asked the dancer.

"For life," the handsome young 'man' agreed. "One hundred thousand pounds."

"One … two …" the dancer nodded. "Three … anyone? Anyone with a better bid? Me for life?" she asked the crowd in a voice as smooth as milk. "Going … going … *gone.*"

"SOLD for one hundred thousand pounds, the Indian virgin beauty!" an Englishman chimed in.

A middle-aged man appeared and bowed to the highest bidder. "Sir, I get half of the pounds. I own her."

The handsome young bidder looked at the dancing girl, who nodded in agreement. "Yes, he bought me from my parents. He gets half of all that I earn."

"Manager or pimp?" someone shouted rudely from the audience. The crowd laughed and jeered.

"Think what you wish," the girl responded.

"All right, you also come with me," the young 'man' said to the girl's owner. "You'll get your money from Belgium. That's where my treasury is located."

The former soldier responded quickly. "I'll follow you anywhere for fifty thousand pounds, sire."

"And another one thousand quid as a tip for the musicians," Charlotte added, still careful to keep her voice lowered.

The Indian man with the long hair pleaded, "We're part of her, sire. She dances and sings, we play the instruments. Please keep us together."

"No," Charlotte replied. "I have little use for you."

The dancing girl lowered herself to her knees. "You've got them all, sire, for the price. I'll pay for their substance and quarters."

"All right," Charlotte agreed with a shrug. "Get into the coaches, all of you."

The musicians did as the young stranger told them. Charlotte took the girl into her coach and they were soon moving. The horses were whipped and they began to trot, then gallop.

Charlotte relaxed in her seat. "So explain your music to me."

The Indian woman nodded. "My songs have a different view. It's not the story of a man, a woman, or their relationship that makes the best story in the world. It's the clash of ideas that defines human intellect and directions. Those simple ideas can change mankind's condition for centuries."

"How's that?" the princess asked, keeping her feminine face lowered a bit.

"The present century was forged by the ideas of earlier centuries. That's the political story of man, and it makes the best story. The depths of intellect are the true story of life itself."

"You seem knowledgeable. Are you educated?"

"No, sire. I have no formal schooling."

"My, how did you learn to speak English so well?"

Zinnia smiled, pleased. "To communicate better, I arranged for a tutor to teach me everything she could about the language, manners, everything about the local culture. I made sure to learn how to communicate in several languages since I came to Europe," she replied proudly.

"Well, what do you think the best story for a song is?"

The woman was glad that her new owner was interested in her ideas, and she answered gratefully. "To me, the best story is when there's a person of great noble birth, great fortune, and enviable reputation. That person is gentle and genuine. He has great ideas about developing life and human happiness. What if he's set against the ideas of another person of low birth, someone of misfortunes, poverty, and a disputable character, but that person has ideas on how to develop greater human freedom instead of just a luxurious life? It's a unique clash."

Then she sang softly: "Oooooo … mine is a secret love, secretly and helplessly I have fallen in love. I have not cared for the honor of my parents."

Little did the princess, who had purchased this dancer for a hundred thousand pounds, know that her own life would be playing this drama. She could not have known then that her life would qualify the words of the Bible, "The meek shall inherit the earth." This clash would someday take place, and not too far in the future. The lowly, the meek, and humble one would triumph. It was to be an Indian boy, poor and illiterate, an ugly "half breed," simple and powerless. Benito Juarez would triumph over the scion of the Hapsburg emperors. He would be a David overcoming a Goliath.

After days of travel over land and water, the coaches halted at a sentry post outside Laeken Castle, which was near Brussels. An old servant of the former emperor Philippe looked inside the first coach. "Is that you, young lady?" the head watchman asked as he gazed dimly into the coach.

The dancer gasped, "Are you a girl?"

The princess took off her hat, relieved to be able to relax and let her long hair fall onto her shoulders. She smiled at the old man. "I've been away visiting London. I bought this lady. Her musicians are in the other coaches."

The head watchman was not sure what to do. He finally managed to say, "Highness, she and her goods must first pass through security. I'll take care of that. You may walk into the palace alone."

The princess descended from the coach. She took a checkbook from her coat, writing two checks for 50,000 pounds each. She handed one to the dancer's manager as he stepped out of the spare coach. The other she gave to the dancer. "Here you are, paid in full."

The dancer was bewildered. "But you said we needed to visit your treasury."

"A princess needs no treasury. Their face is the treasury," Princess Charlotte explained.

"Then why didn't you pay me in Piccadilly?" the man asked, barely hiding his anger.

"We royals are trained only to pay huge sums if there aren't any witnesses."

The dancer examined her check. "Is it cashable in London?"

"Take it to the Bank of England or anywhere you like. They'll make the payment in three days, after confirmation."

"50,000 pounds," the girl marveled with a smile. "I only earn twenty pounds a day."

The princess smiled and walked to the palace, tired but happy to be home.

The following day the princess was relaxing in a quiet garden. Her father, King Leopold I, sat beside his daughter.

"Is what I hear true, Charlotte? You paid 100,000 British pounds for a whore? I can't believe my ears."

"She's a beautiful singer and dancer, not a whore. She's my jewelry, Papa. Prince Maximilian is visiting us next month. I've planned festivities for his arrival."

"Thoughtful or vain festivities?" he asked knowingly.

"Thoughtful," she answered coyly.

Leopold smirked. "What's the plan? Dazzle the prince with the full lush of your adolescence, or present him with corrupted girls?"

Charlotte smiled. "I'm simply following your teachings. You always said, 'Prepare for the villain.'"

The king chuckled. "Yes, I remember."

"We need attractions to draw things to us."

"But Charlotte, why the whore's whole entourage? Why did you buy all of them?"

"The old man is a singer as well as a musician. He's very good on the piano, I hear. In fact, I've called him and here he comes. Please, Father, be quiet and listen to him carefully."

The king nodded, watching the singer as he came forward and saluted.

Charlotte was intrigued with his manners and style. "Singer, where did you learn to salute so perfectly?"

"I was an Indian unit's religious teacher, an imam of a mosque in the unit barracks, my lady."

"Oh, I see … well then, how is it that you sing so well? You have talent."

"Thank you, Your Highness."

"What was that chorus you all sang and clapped in rhythm?"

"It's our 'Qawali.'"

"Qawali," the princess repeated, liking the sound of the word. "Why is this Qawali so admired by all of you?"

"It touches deep religious emotions, Your Majesty."

"Qawali," she repeated. "It sounds like a psalm."

The old man continued his explanation. "What I've learned, I sing. I teach, share … the dancer attracts the crowd."

"Where did you get your knowledge?" she asked.

"The Quran, the holy book of Islam," he explained patiently, pleased at her curiosity. "I was a teacher of the Quran in an Indian unit of the Punjab regiment."

"Do you find it a sufficient education?"

"More than sufficient if one undertakes that education seriously."

"What is it?" the king chimed in. "Some book on philosophy?"

"It's much more than that, sire. It's the word of Allah, God."

"Oh, my, my," the king muttered to himself, not really understanding.

Princess Charlotte quickly changed the subject. "What makes your songs so full of rhythm?"

"I see mathematics even in music. I was singing the number eight: *da da da da, da da da da.* There are songs of slow rhythm, number three. A child hears that: *da da da, da da da.* Some songs get closest to human nature. It's like when a mother sings a lullaby to her baby, trying to put him to sleep. That's the first rhythm a baby learns. Then there're shouting songs, numbers eleven or twelve. Songs based on number eight attract a crowd more because they have rhythmic clapping," he explained, clapping *1,2,3,4,5,6,7,8.*

The king was entranced, himself an artistic man. "Wonderful. I'd like to hear it."

The man made a gracious bow. "I'm at Your Highness's service."

Princess Charlotte had also been listening intently. "Wait, your first song wasn't based on the number eight. It was mixed with other numbers, wasn't it?"

The singer smiled at her cleverness. "Correct, Your Highness. You're very observant. The mixture makes 'ragas,' which touch emotions. Some emotions come during rain, some at night, some in spring, others in winter. In India, the 'ragas' are the center of all music."

"So you know how to perform such ragas?" Charlotte asked.

"I know some."

"Good!" she exclaimed, now even more satisfied with her purchase. "We're having a guest from Austria, a very special guest. Maximilian Von Hapsburg is coming here next month. Prepare a few songs to honor him."

"The Hapsburgs are some of the few rulers interested so deeply in music. They're rulers as well as singers, guitar players, piano players. Music is in their genes," the king added.

The princess laughed. "You may go now, Teacher," she smiled at the old man. He saluted them both and left.

"Well, daughter, your plan is …?" the king asked, summoning a servant for lunch.

"The archduke will visit and we'll entertain him with our newly bought asset. I think you should send my eldest brother to the coast to receive the prince," she suggested, referring to the Duke of Brabant.

"Yes, I've asked him to do that," he replied off-handedly. "But my naive child, what if Maximilian falls for the *dancer*?"

"It'll quicken his proposal for my hand in marriage."

"Thoughtful … artful," the king laughed.

"Practical," she whispered with wisdom beyond her years.

Later upstairs in the princess' chambers, the dancer rubbed soap onto Charlotte's back. It was nighttime and the two young women were alone in the ornate shower room.

"You're my personal body servant now," she instructed the dancer.

"In my country we don't say 'body servant,'" Zinnia commented, "just 'servant.' They're considered to be friends, soul mates of their mistresses. We call them *saheli*, each a part for the other."

"Hmm …" The princess pondered the idea. Zinnia rubbed the rich soapy foam onto her neck and back, pouring some water from time to time.

"Kings used to have body servants," Charlotte commented thoughtfully.

"Were they good-looking boys?"

Charlotte laughed softly. "Maybe!" She paused, becoming more serious. "Are you truly a virgin? You said so."

"Yes," Zinnia answered confidently.

"I can't believe that. A woman bought by a tommy, kept as a street dancer?"

"It's not such a mystery. It's quite easy to find out if I'm not."

The princess was incredulous. "How?"

"The lady's finger will not penetrate my body."

Charlotte blushed. "I was never taught about such things," she mumbled, examining herself beneath the bath water. "My finger goes in!" she exclaimed, giving away what she was doing. "I'm a virgin, though!"

Zinnia smiled behind her, continuing to wash her back. "But Princess, you ride cycles and horses. Your lifestyle is probably rather manly."

"Oh my ..." Charlotte could only reply, blushing harder and hiding her red nose in her hand.

"Blushing?" Zinnia teased, trying to be friendly.

"My lifestyle may be manly, but I'm a girl, too ... how do you know these things?"

"Knowing such things could be a matter of life and death in India. We have a custom called 'karo-kari,' which means 'honor killings.' After marriage, every daughter has to prove that she was a virgin on her marriage night. The family gathers after the wedding night to see the blood on her bed sheets. After the blood is shown, everyone gets up to congratulate the parents of the girl for bringing up a true virgin. If the blood isn't there, the father has a right to kill his daughter there and then. They *call* it honor killing, but it's just plain murder. There's no honor in murdering anyone, but our laws allow it."

"That's unbelievable, just awful!"

"Yes, I can see how you would think that. But it's a custom that keeps India's daughters virgins whether they live in deserts or large cities. They'll fight, scratch, *claw* to preserve their virginity."

"Get naked and get into the tub," the princess suddenly commanded.

Zinnia was reluctant. "But I'm only your servant."

"Obey me," Charlotte said with mock seriousness.

The dancer took off her clothes and entered the foamy tub.

The princess carefully examined Zinnia for herself.

"It's true ... even my little finger can't go in."

"That's virginity, Princess."

They giggled and splashed water on each other when the awkward moment ended.

"Do you mean to tell me that every girl is a virgin in your land?"

"No. Each girl decides who is to take her, whether it's her husband or her lover. But they eventually face the consequences, which are well-known."

"So that's what's meant by 'giving him all you have'?"

Zinnia nodded. "A common girl has only the honor of her virginity to give up."

"Honor has a different meaning in the west."

The dancer got out of the tub and dried herself, quickly dressing and bringing warmed towels for Charlotte.

"I'll take some wine. You can sing me a song."

Zinnia stepped out of the room and returned with her violin, starting a slow melody. Then the violin changed to a fast track, stopping suddenly. She began to sing.

"Aaaah … Ooooh …
Some evening come into my heart.
Some moonlit night, think of me.
When you are gone, come back.
If I go away, call me.
Aaaah … Ooooh …"

The violin began again.

"Day, night, life is passing.
Another sweet refrain from the violin."

She leaned her head over the violin, playing wildly. Charlotte had dried herself and slipped on a robe as she listened, and both were soon up and dancing in ecstasy. They finally fell onto her bed, laughing and out of breath.

Zinnia rested on the soft mattress. "Am I your servant?"

"Not anymore. You're my *saheli*."

They embraced.

The next day Zinnia was perched on a footstool in front of Charlotte, cleaning her toenails.

"You have beautiful feet, my lady."

"At least I'm not flat-footed," Charlotte responded practically, turning her feet to look at them.

"I'm flat-footed," Zinnia confessed. "I can't run fast." She lowered her head as if to appear that she was working more carefully, sadly remembering the many times in India when she had to run for her life.

"You don't have to run, Zinnia," Charlotte said, as if reading her thoughts. "You're in a civilized country now."

Zinnia's face betrayed how naive she thought her mistress to be. "What if I'm made to run?"

"Who would dare do that?"

"Well, there are people above you."

"Only God is above us," the princess stated flatly, using the royal "us."

Zinnia was quiet for a while, deep in thought. She looked as if she was deciding whether or not to speak. Charlotte said nothing, waiting until the girl finally did.

"We believe in an afterlife, heaven and hell. Do you?"

"Yes, of course, the priests teach us that. What does your religion say about who goes to heaven or hell?"

"One of our sayings goes, 'Sell yourself for others, but don't sell others for you.'" She paused, thinking over how best to reply. "Heroes will go to heaven and villains to hell. Hate, secret, silent murders, ruthlessness, lack of pity, blood letting—those with negative attitudes will go to hell. Those who think positively and act correctly, people who aren't only made for themselves—those people may go to heaven."

"Where did you learn all that?"

"From the village," she replied. She did not discuss the Imam, though he was always on her mind.

CHAPTER 6

▼

COMING TOGETHER

Schonbrunn Royal Palace at Vienna, Austria—1857

The young Adele continued her persistent infatuation with Maximilian. It was not easy, finding an opportune time to make him notice her, what with the prince's frequent trips out of the palace and the legions of both servants and eager young women around him so often. She did not dare compete with her betters, the royal women who came with regularity to visit him, and she also had to be careful not to interrupt family time, when the prince was finally lacking his entourage.

One evening, the prince happened to be walking through a courtyard, taking a shortcut from the dining room to his private chambers. Most evenings, Adele kept track of his movements and tried to be prepared for such brief chances to "run into him." The sun was low and orange, casting a mellow golden glow on the small garden. Bees buzzed lazily among the flowers as the birds chirped and the soft breeze rustled through the trees.

As the prince rounded a winding path, the place that Adele knew was the least visible from inside the palace, she stepped out to face him.

He paused and appraised her with open curiosity.

The sun shone on the back of her head, catching her yellow hair and giving it a dazzling halo of bright gold. She held a white shawl around her shoulders, open just enough in the front to offer a glimpse of the swell of her breasts, artfully lifted in a tight bodice. The white dress hugged her body, curving in at the waist and billowing out into beautiful skirts. She looked like an angel.

"My lord," she said softly, looking up through her thick lashes, "perhaps you don't remember me, but I wanted to thank you for helping me, the day I was thrown into the water at the polo match."

"That was you?" Maximilian asked in wonder, leaning forward a bit for a closer look. "Ah yes, you have those striking blue eyes, just like your mother."

"You know who I am?" she asked, pleased.

"Of course." He moved in closer than he would have dared to with a princess, but Adele was only a servant. The girl's breath caught in her throat and her heart beat faster as she carefully tried to maintain her composure. "How could I forget a beauty such as you?" the prince added, coming even closer, so that their bodies almost touched.

Adele's face flushed slightly as her breasts rose and fell with each deepening breath. She had spent quite some time idolizing him. His interest in her now was the answer to her prayers.

Maximilian reached out boldly and lifted her necklace from her throat, his fingers brushing her skin as he held it up to examine the pearls set in gold. "I hope you're not too uncomfortable speaking with me after … all of that," he said, referring to her nakedness on the day they had met.

"Not at all, sire," she answered so boldly that he lifted his eyes from the necklace to look into her eyes. Her breath caught in her throat again, but she ignored it and continued in the same confident tone. "I'm not uncomfortable at all."

Maximilian found her false bravado alluring, and his own heart beat a little faster. "Really?" His hand lowered to place the necklace back against her throat, his fingers almost stroking her skin this time. "Are you sure?"

Adele's eyelashes fluttered briefly as she was overcome with desire, a thick and palpable sensation that she had never felt before. "Yes, sire," she whispered.

His fingertip touched the edge of her bodice slowly, tracing a line over the swell of her large breasts. "Does this bother you?"

"No, sire," she whispered.

His fingers lingered, taking the tip of one of the laces in the bow at the top. "Does this bother you?" he repeated softly.

"No, sire," she replied breathlessly, her eyes half-closed.

He slowly pulled down on the lacing, opening the bow. "This?" he whispered. His fingers gently pulled the lacings from their eyelets. "This?"

Adele did not reply. The bodice loosened and finally fell away, revealing the under slip. Her breasts pressed against the white gauze-like dress as she felt the breeze play over them through the light material. Maximilian's hands glided softly over the white dress, stroking her breasts as he paid careful attention to her response. She inhaled deeply and did not shrink away from his touch. One of his hands cupped beneath her right breast as he leaned down and gently kissed the nipple through the material. She gasped, her blood hot, as an electric thrill raced through her body. His tongue played over the nipple until it was fully erect, as if it were trying to push out of the dress.

Adele took the neck lacing and pulled the bow free with a sigh. Maximilian teased the dress open and lowered it to reveal her perfectly shaped breasts. She moaned softly as he opened his lips and took her nipple into his mouth, his tongue stroking it boldly. She was soon lowered to the grass as he tasted one breast, then another. "This?" he whispered, the question more for his own arousal than her reply.

Her fingers wove into his hair as he excited her. She writhed in ecstasy. She felt one of his hands sliding up her skirts, caressing her knee, then her thigh as he moved his way up between her legs.

Adele gasped as his fingers stroked her expertly; his head lifted so that he could watch her face. Her eyes widened in surprise at the first jolts of energy she felt in her loins. He was very accurate, knowing just where and with how much pressure to press and stroke her there. He watched in aroused anticipation as her eyes slowly closed, her breath deepening to gasps when she inhaled and moans when she exhaled. She finally whimpered loudly, her hips tilting instinctively upward as she was swept through the full wave of her pleasure. Afterwards, she struggled to catch her breath as the wave subsided, opening her eyes in surprise. She had heard about this feeling but had had no idea it would be so powerful.

Her surprised pleasure was more than he could bear, and he finally opened his trousers and lowered himself onto her, pulling her skirts up. She wrapped her legs around his hips and her arms around his neck. As he pushed, she gasped at the pain but reveled in the knowledge that her hero was the first man ever to have her. "The only one," she thought, holding him tightly against her.

They spent much more time together, after that. Adele waited eagerly every day in hopes of seeing him, of stealing away somewhere to have him take her again. Sometimes, when he was tired, she would let him lie on the grass and rest his head in her lap, stroking his hair and pretending to herself that they were lovers soon to be engaged. Other times, she would make detailed sketches of the palace and the gardens, or of him on his horse in a polo match, and she would surprise him with the drawings when she saw him next. He seemed enamored as well, and she secretly hoped that his feelings for her were as profound as the love she felt for him.

Prince Maximilian was in his mother's bedroom after dinner. Sophie had a large bed covered with fine damask and Belgium lace. Her pillows were of the softest down, covered with silk pillowcases embroidered with tiny silk eagles. She reclined on her pillows with her three tiny dogs, as Adele stood to one side.

The prince kissed his mother playfully once, twice, then three times.

"Mother, my very dearest mother," the prince laughed. "See what we have as a court dancer?" He gestured at Adele. "She's fantastic, dances like an angel. And she's more than just an exotic court dancer; she's also a brilliant pencil painter. I find her so accomplished."

Sophie smirked. "Brilliant pencil and chalk painter. Yes. But you cannot be serious about her."

Maximilian laughed and winked at her cleverness. "Touché." He sat at the edge of her bed. "Surely you'll allow me an occasional lapse of reason?"

"Yes, well, perhaps some of her gifts were unknown to you until just this week," Sophie teased.

"Oh, Mother, may I send for more maids from Bavaria?" he asked, his tone joking but his expression more sober as he gazed out the window.

The queen's smile faded. "Royal servants can't be obtained so easily. They can't come near us until we're assured of their personal loyalty," she warned, not sure whether he was serious.

Smiling mischievously, Maximilian perched on the edge of her bed and put his arm around shoulders. He whispered into her ear, "Ask your papa, he'd tell you. She's of royal blood, but born to a royal maid. She doesn't know that."

The queen bristled. "Promiscuous court dancers are not allowed to give birth to royal blood. That's the law."

"What if she gets pregnant from some man of royal blood?" Maximilian asked, still smiling.

"Then the royal *law* takes over," she replied shortly, and dismissed Adele. When the door was closed, Sophie turned back to her son. "You know she has to murder her child, then be married off to an old servant. All future offspring belong to that old man."

"So that all future births are of common blood?" Maximilian asked flatly.

"She dare not name a child of hers as royalty."

"Because of the sword of royal law, murder hangs over her head?" Maximilian scoffed.

The queen nodded matter-of-factly. "It's to prevent the spread of bastards in royalty."

"Royal men can't be bastards?" he bantered.

The queen laughed and tapped him gently on the cheek. "Oh, stop it, Maxi. Don't tease me!" She feigned another soft slap to his cheek, then relaxed into her pillows. "Tell me, are you interested in Adele?"

"My only interest in life is the woman whose eyes I first saw, whose lullaby song I first heard, who kissed me a hundred times a day. No matter where I go, she's always with me."

Sophie laughed and kissed her son. "That's me!" she beamed. "I'm extremely proud to say that I was born from an emperor and empress. I've been an arch-duchess, the wife of an emperor, and now the mother of an emperor. If you go to Spain or Italy, I'll be the mother of *two* emperors." She paused, looking carefully at her son. "They're thinking of finding a new country for you to rule. Revolutionary leaders and politicians in exile from Mexico are asking for you to be the emperor there. That would be a superb situation for you, son. Napoleon wants it as well. He's your window of opportunity."

"No, I don't count kings, emperors, or armies as windows of opportunity. The true window of opportunity is a wise friend, someone loyal and farseeing. I'm simply a sailor." He looked out through the window again. "Going nowhere. Just your son, Mama." He came and laid his head on the pillow beside her, his gaze straying to the bedside table. He lifted a portrait of two brothers, in army and naval uniforms, and looked at it thoughtfully before holding it up to his mother with a soft smile.

She sighed heavily, "Ah, yes, when Franz was in battle in Italy and you were on the high seas, I thought about both of you constantly. My heart was broken. I missed both of you so much. You're my beloved, sweet sons … a soldier son and a sailor son!"

"Yes, but I missed you more at sea," he teased. She made a face at him and he laughed, kissing her cheek before settling back down into the pillows. "I saw uniforms, marching, medals, parades … but my greatest desire was just to see you, Mama. You always pushed me towards things I didn't like because Father wanted it that way. You know, even when I was running a mile in the naval academy, I used to fantasize that I was looking at you, remembering how you energized me. I'm thankful I wasn't the oldest son, the emperor. Thank God for no such weight upon my shoulders."

"No, you can't mean that," she said, frowning.

"I've always said that I'd abdicate the throne of the world for just one hug from my mother. Give me a hug and take my kingdom." He kissed her hand.

"Yes," she assured him, "I'm always with you in my heart. But now you have to decide about your date of marriage."

"So I have to marry where it already stands decided?" Maximilian asked, knowing the answer but looking concerned over the subject.

"Yes, son. Hapsburgs can't marry out of emotion, or love, or fancy. Indeed, few Hapsburgs are ever asked when they will marry. That stands decided before they're even born. They're the breed of kings, and their fate is settled before their parents even see the baby's face. It's our way of building a larger empire, through marriage."

"Yes, I know, there has been a plan for all our lives. The Hapsburgs have had immense success in ruling ... but I don't understand the reason for that. How have they done it?"

Sophie considered, then shrugged. "First, you must have huge amounts of land. Seven hundred years ago, the Hapsburgs started with land in Switzerland, France, Austria, Italy, Germany, and Hungary. Those holdings gave them riches and allowed them to wield huge resources and power."

Maximilian picked up the thought. "And the Hapsburg kings were cleverer still. They didn't pretend to be the regents of God, as the English or Russian kings did. We're not anointed as the viceroys of God on earth, right?"

"You are correct, son. What a man needs is youth and health. If he has it, he's a king. When that is gone, he is a beggar. As for kings, they can stand on the steeple and piss on the people. The clergy helps them do it. Strange, but in the year 1300, a bishop started a doctrine and called it the 'reformed Christianity.' He said, as I remember,

Worship the king.
Serve the Lord.
Learn the word.
Enrich people's lives.
Build lasting friendships."

"Yes," Maximilian said. "I remember now. Bishop Neumeister was his name. Kings used his doctrine to perpetuate their rule. The Church saw him as a heretic and burned him at the stake."

The queen's lady came to tidy up her bed. The two continued their conversation, ignoring her.

"*We* put up kings who are hired by the nations to live happily ever after," the queen responded.

"Not entirely true, Mama. We used to say, 'The king is God's shadow on earth.' We've abandoned that theory, but now we have a more brutal theory. We say, 'We're a chosen race, chosen by God to distribute the benefits of western civilization to the backward areas of the globe.' The people in those areas often don't want those benefits, and they certainly don't want the control of their lives that accompanies it. We don't care, because we have a sense of mission. Britain is doing exactly the same thing, nowadays. And France wants to do it far away, in Mexico. I believe we started to feel that way after superior weapons came into our hands. But we need policies to rule, not weapons."

His mother nodded. "In the olden days, kings did exactly that. Your generation of kings lives with the people and thinks of their welfare, their happiness …"

He paused in thought for a moment. "But they snuff out brave people who have brave ideas. The people have to be brought up to be brave if you want to build their national spirit. That alone protects a king's sovereignty. That's the reason we princes or emperors go into battles so often." Maximilian walked to a large, ornate armoire on the other side of the room. "Mother, Franz Joseph just returned from the Piedmontes battles. He must be asking himself why people rise in revolt."

"Why, indeed," Sophie huffed, her forehead furrowing.

"It happened because our regiments were deployed to stifle the revolution in Saint Lucy," he insisted, referring to Italy. "Once the people tasted their first baptism of fire, no occupying armies could stop the spread of revolt. And now the same thing has happened in India."

"Dissent, defiance, and mutiny are what commoners give rulers as thanks for their work," Sophie interjected.

"Mother, we just changed emperors. The regions of Lombardy, Veneto, and Friuli have also risen in popular revolt. They made Father relinquish his throne in favor of Franz Joseph. The Houses of Savoy and Piedmont are still helping the rebels. After each revolt, we see fewer nationalities in our empire. Revolt is like a wolf that takes away one sheep at a time. Our flock is threatened. Why is revolt spreading as it has? I am convinced that the answer is simple, Mama—the myth of emperors is gone. We must come to terms with that, before it is too late."

"We've been subduing them all to the emperor's authority for hundreds of years. We can do it again," Sophie insisted.

"Suppress them with brute power?" Maximilian retorted.

"If necessary."

Maximilian kissed her again. "That isn't you speaking, Mama. Not my sweet, gentle mother! That is the archduchess, married to an emperor. That is the mother of one or two emperors, a *queen*."

"Maxi, it is what our family believes. It is our policy for ruling. It is part of the Hapsburg secret," Sophie insisted, looking perplexed and tired as she responded to him.

Restlessly, Maximilian returned to the window, and saw Adele and Prince Ludwig getting down from a palace coach, followed by two girls.

Where did they go together? he conjectured.

"Mama, I see two girls. Who are they? And why is Ludwig flirting with Adele?"

"Ludwig treats Adele like a sister," his mother said with a dismissive sniff. "He took the other two Hungarian princesses, Luloo and Venice, out for nail care, a haircut, and some shopping."

"Luloo and Venice? Have they grown up so tall and womanly?" asked Maximilian.

"Yes, indeed," replied Sophie.

"But they were little girls only yesterday!"

She laughed. "Little girls grow like vegetables, overnight, not only in their bodily forms but in their minds."

Maximilian left his station at the window curtains. "Oh, Mother," he said gently, coming close and looking directly into her eyes, "I was never impressed with all of that. People can no longer be subdued by force. They must be subdued with the myth of 'people power.' Today, we need to sell the idea of kingship like a product. A better product will sell. What makes a king an emperor? His customers grow. What causes that growth? Product loyalty. We Hapsburgs have followed that basic rule for selling a product, but today we're outdated and we need new customers."

Sophie gazed into her son's eyes, trying to understand, wearily brushing a strand of hair back from her brow. "Maxi, sometimes I wonder where all of these strange ideas of yours come from."

Maximilian quickly changed the subject when he noted his mother's weariness. "Franz Joseph has returned from the battlefield. His palace is now full of the prettiest girls in Europe. Should he forget his battle lessons and turn to pleasure? Look after those girls?"

"Flirt … " his mother smiled. "Monarchy is too dry. To him, pleasure is nothing more than a duty. You know your brother won't sit with them. He has his eyes on marriage, as is his duty. Indeed, he has fixed on the most beautiful woman in Europe, Princess Elizabeth. And he'll marry her. Beautiful girls who come here and hope for that honor are mistaken in their hopes. Maxi, go and present them with roses. Send them away. Your elder brother is too busy to pacify his opponents. He'll soon be married at Wien-Augustinerkirche. His only preoccupation is to learn how to run the empire, and he has strong friends to help him."

"But in the days to come," Maximilian interjected, "I'm afraid that he'll start to see his friends disappearing, little by little, as well as his ideas about the supremacy of the emperor. The political and social progress of modern times is unstoppable. Soon, his empire will lose vast holdings and regions. He may rule the longest, but I fear he's going to be a very lonely and sad ruler, Mama." He leaned over the bed and gave her a hug. "I want him to flirt with girls, even my girlfriends."

"Why *your* girls, Maxi?" His mother was amused, a small light returning to her eyes.

"They're all incredibly beautiful, that's why! He has to show that he has life. Men respect that."

With a kiss, he bade her farewell and left his mother's chambers. He walked down the marble staircase and crossed a set of rooms, stopping to look at a half-closed door. Quietly, he opened it wider and saw the royal guests, the two princesses from Hungary, sleeping on a giant bed. On tiptoe, he came closer and looked at both sisters.

He remembered how these little girls, little princesses, used to come to their palace. They had been so perfect that no one could distinguish them from made-up dolls. Now they had grown up. And he was to marry a princess. Perhaps one of them?

Which one? he asked himself. Both girls were stunningly beautiful. They were called the most gorgeous pair of girls in Europe.

"What are you doing here?" The maid lying close by opened her eyes.

The prince placed his hand gently on her mouth. "Just a sailor," he joked. "Permission requested to come aboard."

The princesses were now awake as well. One rubbed her sleepy eyes. "Don't be afraid," she assured her maid. "He's a Hapsburg. You know how they are. Hapsburgs get arranged marriages before they are born. Lover boys they can be."

"I came to bid you goodnight," Maximilian said.

"He actually wants us to accommodate him until morning, sister," said the first princess.

"Two virgins," the second princess mused, without even a blush. "Have you dreamed of having two virgins in the same bed on the same night, Prince?"

"No." Disengaging, he left the room, grinning. "What dream?" he muttered wryly to himself as he left. "Having *more* than two, *that's* a dream!"

The next day, the two younger Hapsburg brothers were visiting in Franz Joseph's study. It was a modest room with typical furnishings. Maximilian said to his younger brother Ludwig, "You saw one of the princesses naked today?"

Ludwig nodded with a grin.

"Do you recall that poem our old tutor taught us about the virgins making much of time?"

"You mean the girls?" Ludwig replied.

Max laughed. "Let me see if I still remember it," he said, looking every bit the naughty schoolboy.

"And while ye may, go marry;
for having lost but once your prime,
you may forever tarry!"

Ludwig said, "The best time to court girls is when in they are teens. After that, they become old and demanding."

"That's what I was telling Mother. In youth, all investments in sex look easy and remunerative. In old age, it's begging with a bowl."

Both men were laughing loudly by the time Maximilian was finished. After they stopped laughing, however, Ludwig looked guilty. "I didn't mean to spy on her. I thought *you* were having a bath."

"But you saw the silhouette of a girl through the drapes!" Maximilian insisted.

"After that it was pure curiosity, eh, brother?"

"It was a silhouette behind the glass of a naked girl. How was I to know she was a princess?"

Maximilian winked. "Now I have a reason to reject that girl. Yes, it's unfair, but people do get punished through no fault of their own. They're all yours!"

"I can marry one if you like," Ludwig quipped.

Maximilian laughed, walking down the hall to his own room. "Ludwig, you're going to set a record for marriages to any girl who appears to suit your appetite. And you're not even going to ask the important questions. Is she intelligent? Has she studied words? Has she beautiful eyes? Does she love you?"

Ludwig joined in the laughter. "I hate cats," he called down the hall after Maxi. "They came with four Siamese cats!"

"Carpe diem!" Maximilian called back over his shoulder as he entered his bedroom. He took off his clothes and fell on his bed, still chuckling as he drifted into sleep.

As he slept, a lovely girl crept in and kissed him on the top of his head.

Maximilian peeked from under the quilt and saw Adele standing close by, taking off her clothes. When she was naked, he reached out sleepily to catch her and put his quilt completely over her.

"You asked for it," he said happily.

They kissed with passion, but she soon drew back. "You're leaving tomorrow?" she asked petulantly.

The prince covered her mouth with kisses. "Tomorrow is too far," he moaned.

In the morning, Maximilian opened his eyes and found Adele still in his bed. He slapped her naked bottom. "Go, go," he said, half-teasing.

She hurriedly rose from the bed, a pillow clutched in front to hide her body.

As he began to dress, Adele asked, "Are you reporting back to your admiral post?"

"Yes, I'm now to serve as ADC to the naval supreme commander."

"Will you wash his socks?" she asked with a sweet smile.

He paused, smirking at her. "If need be. But an admiral's store has more than a hundred socks. I can help him plan a naval battle, too," he added proudly.

"I want to be in that battle."

"Why?" He raised an eyebrow.

"To soothe your nerves." She walked to him and began rubbing the back of his neck.

"You're doing well here," he said, reaching behind him and pulling her into his arms. Her skin was smooth and silky, her breasts sliding against him and arousing his desire again. He lowered her back to the bed to continue the previous night's games. The woman's virginity was a distant memory; she now had many tricks of the bed yet to share with him. He moaned in delight and wished he could stay with her all day.

On a warm day in April, Sophie and Adelaide discussed their children as Adelaide worked on the empress's coiffure of the day. They continually danced between their roles as servant and royalty to that of best friends, doing so with an ease that many years of togetherness had fostered. Sophia had just had her bath, where Adelaide had washed her long reddish-blond tresses, now streaked with silver.

"And what's happening with your daughter these days?" Sophie asked as she sat before her oval mirror, watching Adelaide brush her hair into soft, gentle waves.

"Oh, Adele is the picture of health, thank goodness," Adelaide murmured with a smile as she continued rhythmically brushing. "Her beauty is undeniable, if you'll pardon a mother's pride. And her dancing is better than ever. I would love for her to dance for your family soon."

"That would be delightful," Sophie agreed. "On the thirteenth of May, we're going to hold a celebration for the late Empress Maria Theresa's birthday, and also in honor of my son Maximilian's trip to Brussels to seek a bride. Adele should entertain then."

"My daughter would be most honored, my lady," Adelaide agreed with another smile. "I'll have her make preparations, starting today." She drew Sophie's hair up and pinned it into an elaborate twist, studded with diamonds.

Both women were quiet for a few minutes, then Adelaide laughed.

Sophie eyed her speculatively. "What?"

"Oh, I was just thinking about how the men will perform at the celebration. They're bound to have some duels. I thought it might be amusing if there were a sort of 'dancing duel.' You know, between two dancers."

A smile spread across Sophie's face. She began to giggle at the thought, and then finally laughed out loud. Both ladies laughed as if at some conspiratorial private joke. Sophie spoke between bursts of laughter. "Yes indeed! Let's mask the entertainment, to mock the men! It'll be something just for the ladies of the court!"

"It's a wonderful plan, my lady. How will it be arranged?"

"Franz Joseph will leave all of the details up to me, as past mistress of the palace. Empress Elizabeth isn't too fond of entertaining, so I'll take care of everything. And I'll ask a second dancer to join in the fun." Sophie stopped in mid-thought and walked over to her velvet chaise lounge, reclining lazily. Her expression was thoughtful as she worked out the details in her mind. "I know how we can structure the 'dancing duel'! First, we'll have a dance from each of them, to introduce them to the audience. Something short, perhaps only a minute long. Then we'll have an 'all waltz' so everyone can dance. Finally, we'll let the dancers choose their music and dance in any way they wish. Maximilian can choose the winner."

"Will it actually be called a dancing duel?" Adelaide asked.

"Of course," Sophie said firmly. "How will the men know we're mocking them if we don't point it out plainly?"

They both laughed.

Later that day, when Adelaide went to her home just outside the Schonbrunn gates, she wasted no time in finding her daughter. "Adele, you've been exceedingly blessed," she beamed. "You've been asked to dance for the Imperial family."

Adele's eyebrows arched as she lowered her sewing to her lap. "They asked for me? Really, Mother? How exciting!" She popped out of her chair. "This is my chance to perform for all the important people!" She paced. "Oh, Mother, do you know how important this could be for my career? I must get some new costumes! I saw the most darling little shop in town today. They were selling items from Turkey and the Mediterranean. They carried *tikas* and *Parandas-Satrangi*," she babbled, naming some of the costumes she had learned about during her time away.

Adelaide laughed at her excitement. "Stop! First things first, darling," she said, taking Adele by the shoulders. "We must wait to buy pretty baubles. We have a lot of work to do with the dancing. Everyone will easily notice how lovely you are. It's more important to work on your technique, so you can astound them. I'll contact Greta. I'm sure she'll want to assist and accompany us to the performance."

Adele looked excited enough to jump out of her very skin. "Can we practice some techniques now?"

Adelaide nodded and cleared the floor of chairs to give them room. "Let's begin with arm movements. As you know, arm movements are crucial to all effective dancing, because they help you communicate the story you want to tell. I'll demonstrate, and you can copy for me. First is the move called 'above the head.' It's used to show tall objects such as a building … or your lover."

Adele mimicked the movement perfectly.

Her mother nodded and then demonstrated the "opening" maneuver. Her arm pressed against her chest and then swept outward in a circular movement, finally stretching out straight ahead.

Adele copied, pausing as her mother repositioned her fingers and showed her the proper way to hold her hands.

"Good. Now let's work on the 'circular movement.'" She showed her daughter the technique, which gave the impression of brandishing a sword. They moved on to the "crossing arms" movement, and finally the "reaching arm."

They repeated the movements over and over until Adele had mastered them. It was tedious work, but Adele applied herself and learned quickly. After two hours, Adele was instructed to add the movements to her dance. She incorporated them aptly, and they then moved on to wrist and finger work.

But all their efforts went for naught. Maximilian insisted that the function—and dancing duel—be postponed until his return from Belgium. And he left.

The dashing, elegant Austrian Prince Maximilian was twenty-four years old when he traveled over seven hundred miles, by river and through mountainous terrain, to Antwerp. From there he went on to Brussels and Laeken Palace, a few miles beyond. As Maximilian's coach drove up the long entrance road of the Chateau de Laeken, he allowed himself to speculate about what—and who—he would find waiting at journey's end.

He remembered that introspective moment with startling clarity when finally he beheld Charlotte, beautifully adorned in a gown designed to show her figure to its best advantage. She looked ravishing, though a dark woman in the background distracted him.

When she met the handsome prince from Vienna, she found him to be charming, handsome, witty, and lively. He spoke perfect court French when they were introduced, charming her even more. Despite the no-nonsense attitude she had been known for since the death of her mother, Charlotte fell for him instantly. Not long after that, she was said to have remarked to her brother, "He's so sweet and handsome. It's difficult not to fall in love with him."

King Leopold I visited his guest in the royal guest apartments. It was a sumptuous suite, rich forest green in color, with five-hundred-year-old tapestries of pastoral and hunting scenes. Each tapestry was a perfect composition, providing the room with an airy, outdoor feel.

The prince sat listening to the first of what he would later call "Leopold's sermons."

"The Austrian Hapsburg royalty has successfully ruled the best portions of Europe for over seven hundred and fifty years. Its present emperor, your brother Franz Joseph, is watching as his empire loses its holdings in Italy and Germany. He must be very sensitive to any losses, and determined not to allow further decay. He must hold on to the Balkans and Serbia. He has to exert authority and control, if the Hapsburgs are to rule on."

"Yes, sire. That's the traditional view," Maximilian replied. "It calls for greater government, larger armies, police, controls … which I regard to be anti-people. We shouldn't be masters, but rather friends to the people."

"That would be unbecoming of any ruler, including the Hapsburgs," King Leopold retorted.

"We've gone past that policy," Maximilian objected. "So much has been desired by the establishment, and it's already caused further losses. There's a war with France now, and possibly another coming with Prussia. The establishment's policy has gone bankrupt. Times have changed, sire."

The king was surprised. "You call a policy that's been tried and tested by emperors 'bankrupt'? It's not bankrupt."

Maximilian held up a hand, not wanting to offend the man. "What I'm saying, sire, is that force by the establishment on its own people destroys that establishment, because the people won't defend it in war." He paused, finding the right words before continuing. "Policies like that weaken their sense of unity, goodness, and bravery. The people's determination to protect their system is weakened. That's the starting point of all revolts. We mustn't raise armies. We should provide food, clothing, and shelter. Give them surroundings not built on force, and that'll become the strongest basic necessities in their lives."

"Basic factor …?" Leopold repeated, confused.

Maximilian nodded. "You see, I believe that man has only six basic factors that determine his direction: food, clothing, shelter, the absence of force in his surroundings, sex, and leisure," he explained, counting them off on his fingers.

Castle maids arrived to serve tea, interrupted the discussion. By the time the tea was served, the king had calmed himself and was able to proceed in a jovial manner. "We'll have a gala night in your honor this evening, with music, young and beautiful girls … the flowers of Europe."

"I'd be delighted to attend, sire," Maximilian replied with a broad smile.

The king wiped his mouth with a napkin and stood. Maximilian stood as well and followed him out of the suite and into the courtyard. The prince felt good about this visit, and he smiled to himself as he watched the king ride away to the main castle.

"I would believe only in a God who can dance."

—*Nietzsche*

Since well before dawn, the servants had been bustling with activity. A thousand details had to be seen to. There was to be a gala night in honor of the visiting Prince Maximilian, and their superiors wanted everything to be perfect.

Midmorning in Charlotte's chambers, Zinnia was freshening the room with a vase of flowers. The sun from the window behind gave her an angel's halo and made her skin appear to glow.

"Oh Zinnia, you're so beautiful," Charlotte mused from her seat at her dressing table. "Please teach me your secrets. I want Maximilian to find me desirable."

Zinnia walked to the dressing table, topped with an elaborate oval mirror trimmed in alabaster. She picked up the silver-backed brush that belonged to Charlotte's toilette and began brushing gently through the princess's raven tresses. "My lady, your youth is sufficient beauty for anyone, but I will advise you, if you wish. We'll begin with a luxurious milk bath, and after that we'll wash your hair, condition it with olive oil, and rinse it thoroughly. Clean, smooth skin and silky hair is enough for most days."

"But tonight Maximilian will see so many attractive royal prospects for his bride. How will I compete?"

"You need only perfect your best attributes: your lovely body, your beautiful hair, and your attractive eyes. Have you selected a gown for this evening?"

"Well, yes and no ... let me show you." Charlotte rose and opened her wardrobe. Pulling out a dress, she held it in front of her. "You see, this one is silver-gray with black ruffles. They say it's the latest style. And see how low the neckline is? Surely he would notice me in this!"

"Yes, he'll notice the dress ... but will he remember you? I think that dress is a bit too stark and mature for you."

"You don't like it." Charlotte was on the verge of tears. "But what *should* I wear?"

Zinnia smiled kindly, knowing how nervous young mistress must be. "Show me the other two dresses that were delivered today."

Charlotte's chin was quivering as she opened the armoire and brought out the other two evening gowns. Zinnia brought both over to the window, spreading them out in the light there. One was a lavender gown with a corseted bodice and mutton sleeves. "This one is beautiful. It would work wonderfully for a night at the opera. But the second one, let's see ... what a flattering skirt! Layer after layer of white lace ruffles ... these ruffles around the scoop neckline would be striking against your raven hair. And the pale pink bodice makes your skin shine. Let's slip this one on," she suggested, lifting it up. "The fringe around the bertha collar and the short sleeves are both enchanting. The bodice dips down in the front with a V at the waist. That should make your little waist look even tinier."

"Are you sure he'll notice? These colors seem pale in comparison," Charlotte observed.

"Have faith, Princess. Let me help you," she offered as Charlotte slipped out of her nightgown and stepped into the dress. "I'll just do up the back … yes … yes! Look in the mirror," she insisted, triumphant.

She stood behind her mistress, pulling her tresses up on the sides as Charlotte looked at herself in the mirror. "First we'll prepare your hair in soft curls. Then we'll use four of the lovely diamond pins from the jewelry closet to draw it up on both sides, to show off your pretty neck. For drama, we can add baby's breath and four of the coral rosebuds I saw in the garden today."

"I think I see what you mean," Charlotte conceded, examining the dress and turning her head from side to side to look at her hair. "Will you continue to help me, Zinnia? I don't want to be alone. The time passes so slowly that way."

"Yes, Princess, I'd love to help. I'll need a few minutes to prepare myself, though you're welcome to come to my room with me while I dress. But you must sit quietly and have a light lunch with your feet up. There will be much dancing this evening."

CHAPTER 7

▼

THE PRINCE AND THE DANCING GIRL

The grand ballroom was decorated to the hilt for the occasion. More than 30,000 carnations decorated the marble staircase and ballrooms of the palace. The walls were also adorned with magnificent decorations and set ablaze with glittering lights, evoking an atmosphere of elegance and tradition. As the guests arrived, they enjoyed a champagne reception, then the opportunity to pass through a formal receiving line to meet the king. The ballroom where the main festivities were to take place was the largest room in the palace, 125 feet long and about 40 feet both high and wide.

Fifty large chandeliers of Austrian crystal were surrounded by gilded and delicately ornate scrollwork in the baroque style, illuminating the room with a warm golden vivacity. Each was a unique piece of art. Venetians had probably acquired their crystal-making techniques during the Crusades, through their contacts with the Near East. The Venetians provided the link between the ancient and modern crystal-making arts, combining the best of both worlds. Their crystal was noted for its brilliance and for its light, imaginative form. The tradition of this noble art, handed down from father to son for centuries, was revived in the hands of the crystal master with grace and musicality.

At the top of the staircase of honor, the prince entered in his admiral's uniform of navy blue, with many metals pinned on with gold braid on the shoulders and cuffs. He was particularly debonair that night, causing whispering among many princesses in attendance. He was announced, "His Royal Highness Prince Ferdinand Maximilian of Hapsburg, archduke of Austria, brother of the reigning Emperor Francis Joseph of Austria. admiral of the fleet.

Following the guest of honor was Charlotte's brother, heir to the throne, Leopold of Brabant and his wife, Princess Marie-Henriette. Prince Philippe, the younger brother was announced. then other princesses and princes were announced.

Next, the royal prince from England was announced, "The Royal Consort Albert Francis Charles Augustus Emmanuel of Saxe-Coburg-Gotha, Prince Consort to Queen Victoria of England." The most noticeable aspect of Albert's face, stature, and deportment was his stiffness and formality, as if he worked at being unapproachable. King Leopold and his sister, who was Albert's mother, had been instrumental in arranging the union of Victoria and Albert. He was born on August 26, 1819 at Schloss Rosenau near Coburg. This made him an alien prince who was initially unpopular, but in time, the English came to admire him for his irreproachable character, his devotion to the queen and to their children, and his deep concern with public affairs and diplomacy. His mother and uncle Leopold adored his stiffness as well, having known all along that it covered a very caring man inside. Following Prince Albert was a myriad of visiting princes and princesses, dukes, and duchesses. Other notable guests included Prime Minister Charles Rogier and other top bureaucrats of Europe and Russia.

Charlotte was finally introduced as "the Princess of France and Belgium, Her Royal Highness Princess Marie Charlotte Amélie Augustine Victoire Clémentine Léopoldine." She was a vision of spun sugar. The fabric of the dress was a very fine silk taffeta woven with pink satin ribbons, with the slightly trained skirt cartridge-pleated entirely around the waistband. Leather slippers of a soft pinkish-cream color, decorated with a subtly embossed pattern, encased her graceful feet. They were designed especially for dancing, edged in narrow pink silk ribbons that matched her dress perfectly.

Charlotte moved with graceful elegance down the staircase towards her father, who was outwardly glowing with pride. He stepped forward and took her arm. "My child, you're the prettiest woman in Europe tonight. Let's show these royals how we entertain imperially."

She giggled. "You see me through a father's eyes, but I do feel pretty. Is Prince Maximilian here? Has he been introduced yet?"

"Yes, he's standing over there by the fireplace."

Her eyes moved slowly across the room, so as not to be too obvious. "Oh, Papa, isn't he wonderful?"

Leopold laughed and handed his daughter off to a young admiring duke so that he could greet his other guests.

Duke Henri was delighted. "May I sign your dance card, Your Majesty?"

Maximilian watched King Leopold closely as Charlotte entered. He leaned towards a Belgian admiral to his left. "Remind me just who that beautiful young lady is?"

"King Leopold's only daughter, Your Majesty." Maximilian smiled and nodded his approval.

A hush fell over the crowd. The dancer emerged adorned in her elaborately beaded costume, veiled and mysterious as she swayed to the music. She was smooth and seductive, as if somehow she and the drumbeat were one. The moment was hers. She was resplendent in an embroidered dress of orange and black, in the highest traditions of royal India. Her beauty and Indian music took the royal audience to heights they had not known before. She was magnificent. No one had ever seen this style of dance, music, or costuming before this.

She was tall and her skin matched the orange of her garment. She had rubbed turmeric powder on her body before her bath that evening, bathing in the turmeric water to cast a golden glow on her complexion. Her skin was silky and her hair gleamed, framing her dark almond-shaped eyes. Everything she did was with a dynamic, whirlwind presence.

The music began.

The woman danced on the notes of the song, lifting them to new heights. She was pure movement and joy, projecting a beauty that came from the inside. The bottoms of her feet pushed against the floor, feeling the connection with the earth and the debt she owed it for her constant support. As in many Eastern traditions and arts, there was a strong sense of grounding and connection to the earth. Her bare feet staked a claim on the space. Her shoulders soon caught the energies and her arms rose up to take charge of the space over her head.

Within this scope, there was the beauty of creating a blend of stories, tableaus, and personal reflection. There were no restraints in her art, only her imagination and spirit of creativity to take the royal audience to the edge of a limitless scope of possibilities. The artist initiated her moves from the center of gravity, the belly and hip areas. The moves were delicate and elegant.

As the energy built, Zinnia danced faster, until the power burst forth in leg lifts and leaps. It was finally too much for mere forward and backward motion, and she broke into circling and turning. A moving spin was actually an incredibly complex set of events. Her body turned, her foot went out, her chest and shoulders followed, and her arms followed or led her chest to maintain her balance. Her head snapped around to the new direction. All of this happened beautifully, with perfect balance maintained throughout. It happened without thinking because all of it happened, must happen, too fast for stringing out words. Zinnia disappeared in the flow of energies that passed through and around her. Her veil fluttered gracefully behind her as she flowed to the music. She was pure delight and grace, every movement filled with a natural and elegant beauty. She was actually unaware of her sensuous, graceful, and powerful womanly presence as the others witnessed her ecstasy.

She showed such charisma and strength that the audience was compelled to silence. When she spread her arms, it was a choreographic delight. Her own band was in attendance and clad in black, matching her orange dress with orange *pagris*, a type of headdress. Zinnia introduced her little band, which added one serene tune to another.

She then asked the audience if they knew Allah. "Allah, Allah!" she called.

As with anything extremely different or new, a hush fell over the hall, and then the whispering began. "This couldn't possibly be a dance to take seriously," someone murmured, appearing ill at ease at this strange spectacle unfolding in front of their eyes. Zinnia was both beautiful and powerful, and this dance was designed for a woman's body, appreciating and using the natural curves and roundness. And, ah—the veil! Therein lay the greatest magic. She appeared like a princess, an angel, and a mythical beauty while floating across the floor with that shimmering chiffon catching the breeze!

Confident of her abilities, Zinnia attuned herself to the drummers' rhythms and matched their intensity. Her dance techniques were so completely natural that she applied them at a moment's notice to the always-changing music, swirling her five-layered skirts. The Arabic music was not only marked by artistically rich and ingenious musical compositions and lyrics, but also by impressive vocal talent from both Zinnia and the Imam.

"Allah hu, Allah hu."

She asked the audience to sing with her, "Allah hu, Allah hu."

Zinnia began clapping, asking them all to clap. The singers added shades of different notes to the chorus of "Allah hu."

Eventually the entire audience, royalty and servants alike, was singing and clapping "Allah hu." Then she stopped and proclaimed, "You see, Majesties, we all sang and became one before Him."

They applauded. Two types of musicians, European and Indian, were seated opposite each other. "Can you sway all the people? Make them clap together? Or swing together? Or sing together?"

The emperor commented, "See how she's rubbed sovereigns in dust?"

Zinnia sang, "We come from dust, we go to dust ... Allah-hu ... He will not return to dust."

The emperor smiled. "We're here for now. We rule."

She responded in song, "He was here before all emperors. Only He will live forever. Allah hu."

The emperor opened his mouth to speak again. "We—"

"Only He ... " she sang.

"Allah hu," the assemblage chanted, caught up in the emotions of the moment. There was resounding applause when she completed her performance and breathlessly curtsied before the noble assembly. Leopold faced the crowd and announced, "Come, everyone, we'll have a splendid dinner in the rotunda dining room. Then we'll return for dancing and our final toasts." A trumpet announced the dinner hour.

The oval table was around twenty-two feet long, draped in a pristine antique Brussels lace tablecloth. It glowed and glistened with exquisite candelabra adorned with sparkling Austrian crystals every five feet. The food was presented on large glossy golden platters, and the wine was in huge urns with elaborately worked handles. The table was set with royal china and the silver gleamed with just-polished brilliance. The guests' dishes were made from pure gold, each one containing the crest of that particular guest's house.

The table decorations, centerpieces, trays, serving bowls, serving pieces, place settings, silverware, and other utensils on display were proof of the great wealth of the country. It was an occasion of splendor and pomp. There was porcelain from East Asia, Sèvres, and Vienna. There were "panorama plates," Faïence china, gold work, Vienna court silver, and the "Grand Vermeil Service." It was an elegant table service for 140 people.

Throughout the gourmet dinner, violinists played softly in the background. The best servants dressed in sharp white uniforms with red trim served the guests expertly. There were mussels in aspic, salmon tartar, and rabbit pâté served with fresh grapefruit and champagne cocktails. Next they were offered a codfish carpaccio that was rimmed with fried leek shavings. A supreme pheasant was accompanied by endive, wild mushrooms, and a mashed potato encased in a sliver of celery root.

Maximilian and Charlotte found their nameplates directly across from each other, and he wondered quietly to himself if the princess had something to do with the arrangement. During the dinner, they were conversational and gracious to the diners sitting on their left and right, but their eyes met several times during the course of the meal. They both reached for the tray of seasonings and their fingers touched lightly under the golden dish. Sparks flew. The princess felt an unfamiliar sensation deep in the pit of her stomach. Maximilian smiled knowingly and winked while Charlotte only blushed and glanced around to see if anyone had noticed.

Dessert featured poached pears and prunes in a red wine sauce, paired with ice cream made with Armagnac brandy. A tray of petits fours encompassed miniature babas, cherries in fondant, chocolate-covered orange peel, and scallop-shaped cinnamon cakes.

After the sumptuous meal, the doors leading out to the gardens were opened. To the guests' surprise, there was a volley of fireworks, and the sky was ablaze with bursts of brilliant color. As they poured out into the courtyard, they saw an entire Roman world set in flats and scrims throughout the grounds of Schonbrunn Palace. The Gloriette was even seen in the background, the ancient Roman ruins that the Hapsburgs respectfully left alone in their gardens.

The ADC announced, "For the guests of King Leopold, in honor of Archduke Maximilian, there will be a military tattoo, a tent-pegging competition, fireworks, and hot air balloons for your pleasure." There were gasps and squeals of delight from the ladies as the men immediately began discussing the engineering of such a huge display while somehow keeping it secret from all of the guests.

The other doors were opened to view military bands, and horse guard formations performed in time with the band music. These formations looked rigorous and impressive up close, but from a distance they were almost hypnotic. The area teemed with color, spectacle, and excitement.

Next a dazzling show was spread out on the Laeken Castle grounds, a whirling and colorful kaleidoscope of music, dance, and display. It was exciting and breathtaking, with reenactments of battles and exotic Turkish music and dancing.

Then the audience gathered themselves together for the finale, the Viennese military tattoo. About one thousand or so performers were on the castle grounds. Column after column of marchers, dancers, and bandsmen ended in a grandly choreographed flourish. The tattoo audience joined in a great chorus of singing, cheering, and applause. Cries of "Bravo!" were heard before a hush fell for the singing of the evening hymn, the sounding of the last post, and the lowering of the flags on the castle. The hussars doing their musical ride dazzled the audience with their precision and varied line formations and movements.

The royal bodyguard was doing a drill. The captain's commands could be heard. "Shoulder-ARMS! Close order ... forward ... MARCH!"

On the west side of the garden, there was a splendid display of tent-pegging by the Laeken imperial cavalry. In this competition, the rider, using either a sword or a lance, was to charge across the riding arena and attempt to pick up a wooden block of four inches in size. If he successfully carried the block to the opposite corner, he was given a full point. If the peg was picked up from the middle of the arena but not brought to the opposite corner, then half a point was given.

Another show featured thirty-two cavalry men in their trademark red uniforms executing a series of intricately choreographed riding maneuvers set to music. The performance had its roots in cavalry training. Riders bearing lances moved in sections, half sections, and singly, their horses trotting or cantering. The horses and their riders created beautiful figures like wheels, domes, and carousels, often surprising the audience with smooth, coordinated, yet complex transitions from one figure to the next. The finale of the half-hour show was the charge, an exciting surge of rider and beast with lances leveled at the imaginary enemy. The exquisite horses, carefully bred at the royal stables, were sturdy black mounts. The royal family operated its own stables and had been breeding them for decades. The second section of the tattoo began with a mounted arms competition in which members used sabers, guns, and lances to perform feats of skill while racing on horseback over a certain course.

The band used special instruments that most German bands employed at that time, including flugel horns and flat snare drums. There was also the palace horse guard, dressed in full uniform. The parade maneuvers and the quality of the horses and regalia were impeccable. They marched and pranced in impossibly intricate formations.

While the guests were astonished at the fantastic sights, the dishes and tables inside were whisked away until only the chairs were left. Leopold, with generous pomp, presented the head of each royal family with a thoroughbred prancing horse. He gave away about four hundred that night, a gift made even more elaborate by the fact that the horses had been transported by ship from Spain.

As the last strains of the nation's hymn died out, the orchestra, hidden in the alcoves and upper balconies, began to play. Fifty couples joined hands for the grand promenade. A specially prepared cotillion of young ladies and gentlemen performed a formal opening dance. The elegant attire of the participants, scenery, costumes, floral displays, and brilliant shimmering decorations against the backdrop of splendid architecture made for a dazzling display.

About one hundred members of Belgian, Austrian, and other European royalty prepared for the dance, which was to be a polonaise, a kind of ceremonial dance. Ladies wore glamorous white dresses and the young men black tails. Afterwards, the master of ceremony proclaimed, "Alles walzer," which meant that everyone could then join in to dance.

They began waltzing, and number after number was played for the enjoyment of all. The murmur of dinner conversation and the music ended suddenly when the trumpets sounded again, signaling that the time had arrived for the Grand March. Gowns rustled as participants hurried to find their places, then the music began and the march was presented for the royalty and dignitaries. Couples filled the dance floor, whirling lightly in three-quarter time around the room.

Tradition demanded the dance card, which ladies used to list all of their dances for the evening. Young men would reserve dances by writing their names next to certain dances. Maximilian was first on many of the princesses' dance cards, and he loved that fact. It was not as enjoyable as he had hoped after dancing with two other less attractive princesses, finding himself glancing over his shoulder to keep track of Charlotte. He spied her whirling and dancing with handsome young men who were obviously caught by her charms, and Maximilian finally stayed out of the next dance to go speak to his mother's friend.

"Mother, I've never been so put off by this silly tradition of the dance card. Why is it I must wait on the lady of my choice when I feel she'd really rather dance with me?"

Charlotte's godmother, Countess of Hultse suppressed a smile. "Maxi, my dear, don't be so impetuous. This is a way for many in society to mix and be introduced."

"That's all right for them, but I'm a Hapsburg! I have to pick a lady of royalty for my bride. This is just a waste of time, an impediment to the entire reason I'm here." He tapped his foot in restless irritation as he waited for the song to end. Timing his move carefully, he stepped between a young man and Princess Charlotte at the end of the waltz.

"Hello again, Princess. I don't believe you'll be needing this any more tonight," he said, taking her dance card and ribbon from her wrist and slipping it between his vest and shirt with a small bow to her.

She was shocked, giving him a questioning look. She then looked around at her family, afraid that there might be some political consequences if she broke the unspoken contract of the promised dances. "Prince Maximilian, this is just not done! It's not according to etiquette."

Maximilian took her firmly in his arms, smiling that wicked little smile of his, and waltzed them into the center of the other dancers. "Princess, I'm impressed with your father's style and splendid treasures. Tonight I intend to steal the greatest of those."

"Steal? You must be joking, Your Highness."

"I'll steal it only with your sweet permission."

Charlotte blushed, finally understanding his meaning. After a few moments of dancing she relaxed. She looked up into his happy face and said with a small smile, "You know, you just might cause a small war."

Of course the various gentlemen on the princess's dance card were upset. Duke Henri was particularly enraged. "That swine! What does he think he's doing? How can someone of his royal breeding be so brash?"

Other young dukes agreed, some of them feeling that the Hapsburg prince had taken advantage of his station and position as the honored guest. Just the same, not one of them dared to step up to him, a Hapsburg, and demand their right to dance. Maximilian's bold move did not go unnoticed by the king, who at that moment realized that this man was destined for his daughter.

"Well, well," the king commented to his sage. "Our prince is quite sure of himself."

"Desire's made more than one army go to war, sire. Remember Helen of Troy."

For the next hour, the young princess and prince danced every dance together like a betrothed couple. They gazed into each other's eyes as if looking for the answer to some puzzle. Young and old took part in the dancing, but when it was close to eleven o'clock, the more mature couples followed tradition and sat comfortably in chairs lining the rotunda, drinking champagne or their favorite local beer while watching the younger couples dance. It was getting later and one by one, the couples took their leave of the king, hurrying off to their wonderful guest suites for the night.

It was just after midnight when Maximilian and Charlotte walked out into the garden. After that, no one saw them for the rest of the evening. Early risers on their way to work were reported to encounter the couple, still in their evening clothes, with cashmere shawls draped over their elegant coats as they strolled through the royal park.

The next morning King Leopold visited Maximilian in the family breakfast room, anxious to continue their previous discussion. The two were like debaters in a class.

The king began. "How do you measure human destiny?"

"First things first," Maximilian stated. "Humans need food, clothing, shelter, sex, the absence of force in their surroundings ... once he has all of that, he wants leisure."

"Your six basic factors, as you call them," the king recalled. "So man's rise has to do with such requirements?"

"Yes, sire."

The king continued, "But the decadence of the English started only because the people had plenty of leisure. Leisure starts a race where nobody wants to be left out. They strive and struggle to push and shove each other in order to reach the prize. Leisure destroys the integrity and priorities of man. Only the yardstick of leisure measures civilizations. The merciless attitude of soldiers against conquered people and their leaders and resources only shows that the conqueror has plenty of leisure, which makes him heartless and inhuman. He treats the enemy as an animal. Isn't that true?"

"That's a unique thought, sire, but I think it's farther from the truth than my theory."

The king gestured to the prince and they walked out to the magnificent gardens. Wide curved paths were lined with manicured box hedges that stood two feet tall, surrounded with well-kept roses. "You know, Max," he said familiarly, "flowers contribute charm and tranquility to ease the hectic rhythm of life." Leopold's love of flowers was evident in every room, each adorned with lush bouquets of flowers from the royal gardens. His pride for his gardens was obvious. He stopped to smell a rose. "Yes, yes," he continued after a moment, "Man wasn't made to be an animal, to suffer like the water-wheel bull. With due respect to the evolution pundits, man isn't from the animal world, because the animals can't ever shed their animal lives. Their education is limited to their living modes. A horse will remain a horse."

He smiled to himself, plucking a petal from a rose and stroking it as he spoke. "The wisdom of ancestry isn't available to animals. The pen was given only to mankind. The animal is endowed with a given set of instincts, while humans are endowed with faculties that can be cultivated and developed. That's what education is. A hen's chick has no instinct to wade into water, but a duck's chick needs no educating to wade therein."

As Maximilian listened, the king led him back to the special part of the landing where many servants dressed in crisp uniforms were serving his private breakfast. The two men were seated and the servants quickly brought the king his eggs, prepared just as he liked them. "Try putting duck eggs under a hen," he challenged, spearing some eggs with his fork. "Then put the hen on the eggs near the water. The chicks that come out are a mixture. The hens haven't learned to swim in water, but the duck's chicks would go right in. This means each non-human living thing has a fixed, unalterable, living mode and set instincts. But try putting two babies alongside the water or near a snake. They need education to avoid danger."

The men paused to eat some of their food before Leopold spoke again. "Inspite of education, man takes to vice."

"Is that the reason why the education of man takes the longest?" Maximilian inquired before sipping his coffee.

"Yes," the king replied. "The four-year-old horse can run in a derby, but a man doesn't have the capacity to compete at the age of four."

Behind the glass doors, Maximilian spied the delightful young princess. He smiled and said, "Sire, your dear daughter Charlotte is waving at me from inside the house."

The king was delighted to see his daughter take so enthusiastically to his plan and said laughingly, "Oh, please go. The young should spend time together. We can talk tomorrow." He was pleased with himself as he watched Maximilian stand and eagerly trot into the house.

Maximilian ran through the French garden doors of the palace and up to Charlotte. She was dressed attractively, with much attention to detail. He leaned against her with a sigh. "Your father talks about things I've yearned for so long to hear, but he can be so *boring* about it! Thank you for rescuing me."

Charlotte smiled flirtatiously and backed into a corner out of general sight. "Daytime belongs to Father and his kingdom talk, but the nighttime is *mine*. No talking now, just kisses." She placed her hands on either side of his head and stood on her toes, kissing him passionately. The gamble paid off and he embraced her, returning the kiss. He then lowered his head so that his forehead rested on hers, smiling and whispering, "I'll have to marry you, I think."

"We don't need a license. I love you."

"It's hard not to love you back," the prince confessed, kissing her on the forehead.

The next day, the king came into the elegant dining room called the Hall of Mirrors at breakfast time. It was early morning and Maximilian was waiting to eat.

"Good morning, Prince," Leopold greeted him.

Maximilian was hardly awake and suppressed a yawn. "Good morning, sir."

The king sat before his breakfast and continued their previous discussion while eating, taking up where they left off. "Maximilian, what's civilization?" The prince opened his mouth to reply but stopped himself when the king began to answer his own question. "Civilization is man's refusal to use power, or his contests against power. It's an historic record of his education, his will, backed by his intelligence in different times and settings."

Maximilian had another cup of strong coffee, attempting to attune himself to the king's chosen topic of the morning.

"The pen records his experiences to benefit his farthest progeny. Apes or monkeys don't enjoy that! Man's evolution is a cyclical record of his civilizing, or the renunciation of force, and his decivilizing, or resorting to the use of force. Civilization starts from refusing to use force, and it ends by refusing to resist it. That starts man's animal life. It's not the animal who moves from animal to man, but rather the man who moves from man to animal. That cycle is called *life*."

Maximilian listened half-asleep, though his years of practice at boring official ceremonies and speeches had taught him how to make others think that he was extremely interested. He caught the cue and nodded in agreement. Leopold had meant to make it look like a spontaneous discussion, but Maximilian suspected that it was really a carefully practiced speech.

The king lectured on. "Nature's made millions of experiments to collect the essential lessons for how mankind can shed his animal life. One eternal truth is that man was never an animal, but he's sometimes forced to live like one. That's man's social and economic burden. Hindsight helps mankind to shed that animal life. The history of man is full of examples where man becomes man. But when does that happen? When does man become man?"

Maximilian sensed he was supposed to say something, but since he really hadn't followed along, he had no idea what to say. "That makes some story," he finally managed.

The king was suddenly distracted by a beautiful woman who had strolled in to have her breakfast. "Which story?" he asked off-handedly, watching the woman take a seat.

Later that day, Maximilian was dining alone with the princess. They were in a small private room with high ceilings. The richly ornamented furniture was white with expertly painted gold filigree. They sat at a round table inlaid with rare woods, set with delicate china and crystal. The meal was nearly finished. The butler waved for the other servants to leave.

Charlotte took the last bite of a chocolate croissant. "Mm, that was sweet."

Maximilian nodded to the butler. Well aware of the prince's intent, the butler backed gracefully from the room, closing the wide heavy doors as he left. Maximilian winked at the princess and kissed her.

"That was sweeter," he said.

"Are my kisses all that sweet?" she asked coyly.

"Yes."

"Well, how many do you need?" she asked with a smirk.

The prince was taken aback. "As many as I can get," he laughed. "A million kisses! After that I'd still like another slice."

"So don't eat more," she suggested, laughing. "You'll ruin your appetite."

Maximilian rose and walked around the table. He lifted her into his arms even though she was still eating and headed towards his bedroom.

"If it's a million kisses, you can present that check!" she laughed. "It would be cashed."

"A million?" the prince joked. "Plus another slice," she answered. "She calls it a 'lop-off.'"

"Who is *she*?" he asked, looking around as he placed her gently on a chaise in his antechamber.

"Patience, please," she said, taking a small ribbon and hanging it outside on the doorknob as a token to indicate that they were not to be disturbed. She closed the door and turned the key, a mischievous look on her face.

Charlotte walked Maximilian to his bed. He lifted the guffy quilt and blinked in surprise at the naked Indian dancer lying there.

"Welcome on board, sailor," Zinnia greeted him with a smile.

"You?" Maximilian said in surprise. He remembered her vividly from even before his arrival, back at the duel. Whatever she had on her skin earlier to make it look more orange was gone, and her bared skin was a rich golden brown. He was finally permitted to gaze at the breasts he had daydreamed about, and they were as plump and lovely as he imagined. Still he carefully controlled his reaction, flustered and confused by Charlotte's presence.

Charlotte giggled. "This is the 'lop-off,' my betrothal gift to you. Enjoy," she said, stepping behind a drape to exit the room via a private entrance. What Maximilian did not know, however, that she never really left, instead hiding behind the curtain and armoire where she could watch them clearly. She was curious about what happens between a man and woman, wondering to herself how Zinnia could take the first violation to her virginity so amusedly.

"Another slice? This is the whole pie," Maximilian said, his eyes wide with wonder.

"It's more than the pie," Zinnia added mysteriously. "My duty is to fulfill your dreams, if I can."

Maximilian saw the edge of a china plate on the mattress, mostly covered by the quilt. "What are you eating?" he asked, barely hiding his laughter.

"My dinner," she replied, laughing.

"You were having dinner under the quilt?"

"I can't eat under the quilt?" she teased.

"Well, you can … you can eat whatever; ask for it." he declared.

"No, you ask for it, sire," she giggled. "This is a once-in-a-lifetime treat. I'm a virgin."

The prince threw the dishes out of the bed. Two delicate Bavarian rose porcelain plates crashed to the floor, the rattling echoing off the walls as they took some time to settle. The dancer used her most bewitching smile and asked, "Some face death amusedly, don't they?"

The prince paused. "But you're about to be deflowered. How do you feel?"

"Like every girl in my village on her wedding night."

"But … there's no wedding."

"This is my wedding," she explained. "The princess wanted this for you and she's the one I obey, but I wouldn't give myself unless I wanted to. I like you, sir. I want to give you the most precious of gifts. I'm the princess's body servant, her *saheli*, and it's my duty to take the burden off her body. Never mind my karo-kari."

"Karo-… what's that?" he asked.

"For this lop-off, I'm willing to die later on, if need be," she replied seriously. Then she jumped up on the bed, taunting, "Let the adventure begin! Bring on the wolf! Little Red Riding Hood is waiting in the bed!"

Maximilian left a candle burning so that he could watch the beautiful girl dance her sex in bed.

Later, after both were satisfied, the dancer got up, wrapped herself in a thin sheet, and walked gracefully to the window. The moon was so beautiful. She took a furtive glace towards the princess, who was still hidden, then picked up the violin. She started sweetly, picking up speed and finally playing with such abandon that it could make the heart break. She sang,

"A love song it is.
On waves of Life.
Life is meaningless
Without our story.
Lalala la.
Meanings of Life.
Find in stories of Love."

The violin kept playing. The prince got up naked and walked to the dancer. She threw her thin body wrap off and danced wildly, ending the dance in a gracefully seductive Turkish fold.

"Lalala la."

He captured her with delight and tossed her lightly on the bed, covering her body with his.

After Maximilian fell asleep, Zinnia tiptoed from the bed to her mistress. They both snuck through the private door and entered the adjoining chamber, where they conversed in whispers.

"My mother would *kill* me if she was alive, but it's been decreed that I must marry a Hapsburg. Many princesses dream of the opportunity I had tonight. My father needs me to do the proper thing, and this Maximilian is a handsome prince. I'll have little trouble getting him to marry me now, I think … and he seems so sweet," she said rapidly, as if to convince herself.

"Yes, my lady, I've made my choice and now you must make yours. Believe me, you'll have few regrets about this night. Go now; meet your destiny."

She took the princess by the hand and escorted her gently back into the chamber, walking her to the bed where he slept. She kissed her sweetly on the cheek and whispered, "Now the mystery will be gone. Lie beside him on the bed near enough to feel his breath on your face. Soon you'll know ecstasy."

Princess Charlotte lay beside him wide-awake for some time. She thought back on the scene she had just witnessed between Maximilian and Zinnia. She could not get those images out of her head. Of course she had heard rumors and stories among her friends about what men did to women in bed, but to actually see it had been more erotic than she had expected. It had been very difficult for her to remain still and silent as she had watched Maximilian taste the dancer's body, run his strong hands over her breasts and hips … by the time the dusty light of dawn began to fill the room, she was overtaken by her desire for him. She began softly kissing his hands, his chest, and his cheek.

The prince awoke to find a second virgin in bed. He was both surprised and delighted. This one's beauty was as great as the first one's had been. "Charlotte," he whispered. "Now you're here with me? Has there ever been a night as magical and exquisite as this?" he asked hoarsely as he kissed her neck, her breasts, as his need for the virgin beauty finally overtook him.

Zinnia struck a pose. She wore the heavy makeup, abundant jewelry, and bangles of her native land. It was the following evening, and she stood in the princess's antechamber. The room was lined with gold draperies and filled with furniture upholstered in rose-colored silk. Zinnia's hands were full with *hina* tapestry, and a thin veil covered her eyes. She was the picture of loveliness and desirability. Her musicians struck a tune and she sang, "Chori-chori, I have allowed myself to love you."

"What's chori-chori?" Maximilian asked Charlotte quietly.

"It's Indian for a thief. 'Chori-chori' means that, like a thief, I've given up my prized possessions."

Zinnia sang to the couple, blushing at the lyrics that now had such personal meaning for her. After the concert, she personally served them dinner, all of the dishes having been made by Indian cooks.

"What's all of this, anyway?" Maximilian asked as he licked his fingers.

"Zinnia's *walima*," Charlotte replied. "It's a dinner hosted by the bride's people for guests and the groom."

"The dishes are tasty, but you were both tastier," Maximilian joked.

Charlotte blushed prettily.

Zinnia reached beneath a sofa, retrieving a white Egyptian towel and approaching the royal pair. She knelt and showed it to the prince. It had blood on it.

"What's this?" he asked, bewildered.

"Blood," she answered simply.

Her statement surprised him. "Whose?"

"Ours," she said, gesturing for the princess to kneel beside her.

The prince looked at the large red stain absorbed by the towel. "Two kinds of blood, is it?" he asked.

"One kind. The blood of two virgins," Zinnia said.

"Well, mixed blood," he corrected.

"No, there aren't different kinds of blood. Blood is blood, whether it's that of a rich man or a poor man, a poor girl or a princess," she sighed.

Maximilian frowned a bit as he thought that over.

"When the lights are off, all virgins are equal," she explained. "All their blood is the same color. No royal blood or commoner's blood. You've taken two virgins, my lord. She's yours from her heart and soul. I'm only the lop-off, but we'll pay the same price for loving you."

"Well-said," Charlotte agreed, taking the towel from Maximilian and putting it on the floor by his clothes.

The prince kissed the hands of both girls.

"She doesn't have to die loving you, but my death is certain," Zinnia explained.

Maximilian looked shocked. "But … I can buy you from your parents. No one will dare harm you."

"But they'll ask you to marry me."

"But you said so yourself, I already did marry you, in a way," he replied helplessly.

Zinnia was delighted with his response. "That calls for a song and dance tonight in my friend's bedroom. Thank you!"

"You're welcome. The pleasure's mine," the prince smiled.

"Ours," Charlotte corrected him.

"Yes, ours. She's now a postscript," he whispered breathlessly as he took Charlotte and drew her to his chest.

When the prince came to Charlotte's bedroom that evening, Zinnia was standing with a silver tray of drinks. Instead of wine, the prince picked up a cup of orange juice and took a sip.

"Good evening, sir." Zinnia said.

Maximilian asked, "Are you a Muslim girl?"

Zinnia replied, "Yes, I am."

"Do Muslim girls sing and dance?"

"Faith has nothing to do with profession."

"But it has been claimed on good grounds that a Muslim is a man marching with sword aloft and followed by a long train of wives," Maximilian offered.

"The sword first. The Quran does not counsel turning the other cheek. It teaches forgiveness and the return of good for evil when the circumstances warrant. But these are very different from not resisting evil. We are not doormats for the ruthless. Our Holy Book allows punishment of wanton wrongdoers to the full extent of the injury they do. Otherwise, morality evaporates into impractical idealism and sheer sentimentality. Jihad is extending it to a man's social life. About wives, would you like to see widows earning for their children from prostitution? If not, a man has to bring in widows and their children to give them sanctity of a home."

"Where did you learn all that?" asked Maximilian, surprised.

"From the life of our Holy Prophet, when we read the Quran with translation and explanations at age 10."

"The Quran allows polygamy?"

"No. The Quran has verses that forbid polygamy under normal circumstances. Marriage is sanctified; the sole locus of the sexual act."

"What was that?"

"Last night? I obeyed my mistress. I can be killed for that."

Zinnia walked away. Charlotte was nowhere to be seen, so he has time to scan the room with interest, trying to see if he could discern more about Charlotte by studying the décor.. The raised ceiling was covered in gilded woodcarvings as well as massive moldings. The armchairs were adapted to the taste of the nineteenth century, in the style of Louis V. They were covered with expensive robin's egg blue damask. There were three chandeliers, one large and two small, all painted in gold leaf and dripping with Austrian crystal. On the far wall, there was a large fireplace framed on either side by two Corinthian columns, and at the base of each was a small stool covered in the same blue fabric. A delicate oval mirror adorned the wall above. His observations were interrupted by the sound of women's laughter coming from the dressing room.

After twenty minutes, Charlotte and Zinnia entered the room, still laughing. Charlotte's cheeks blushed with pink when she noticed Maximilian standing before the fireplace. He turned to greet them.

Zinnia made a graceful curtsey, wearing her best makeup and dance costume. She remained in the curtsey until he recognized her. "Rise, Zinnia," he said, taking a long and appreciative breath as he smiled at them both.

Charlotte fought the sudden acceleration of her heartbeat and said calmly, "Good evening, Prince." Her beautifully arched eyebrows rose as she gestured to Zinnia. Zinnia lifted her head, her lush lips turning into a smile. She took off her shoes, took a violin, and turned slowly as she sang, "Oh, my lover has come to make me his beloved. To honor me, ohhh."

Her bare feet touched the floor lightly. It appeared almost as if she were floating as her veil and skirts rose with the draft. Her shoulders soon caught the energies and shook rhythmically, her arms rising over her head in a majestic motion. She created a story with her movement as she continued her song.

> "Our beloved has come
> To get a bride.
> I fall on your feet in gratitude.
> What's your regal status? What dust am I?
> Our beloved has come.
> What have you made of me?
> Something from nothing.
> You are majestic. I'm only dirt.
> Stars and moon have touched me.
> Where has love brought me?
> How far I have come.
> You have made me beautiful, graceful, and peaceful."

She danced, touching the prince. The three wrapped themselves up in each other until the following early morning. Maximilian and Charlotte were fast asleep. Zinnia quietly rose to set the room in order. She went to cook their breakfast and eventually returned with a huge tray. The couple did not stir, so she opened the curtains to let the daylight in.

"Breakfast in bed," she called.

They did not hear her, still sound asleep.

She took a silk handkerchief and moved it softly against the princess's face, then the prince's. They slowly opened their eyes, yawning.

"Good morning," she said softly as she moved the handkerchief. "Breakfast, Your Excellencies."

They sat up, Charlotte pulling up the sheet to cover her. Wordlessly they watched Zinnia rush from one place to another, getting their meal ready.

"Is she going on our honeymoon, too?" Maximilian teased.

"She'll go ahead of the bride," Charlotte chuckled.

"Ahead of the bride?" he asked.

"You saw her musing and singing while having sex in the bed," she replied. "She was singing when she was taken? I can't do that."

"What was she singing?"

"Oh, you know, a rapturous sort of slow song ... it started something like 'tut tut ... tastes so sweet, you ...'" She tried to copy the tune but soon gave up.

Maximilian laughed softly and hugged her affectionately. "My mother is arranging a gala night of dancing; there's a competition. I think Zinnia should take part in that. Belgium versus Austria."

Maximilian entered the king's office the following morning. It was an ornately paneled chamber, inlaid with burled wood with colorful tapestries on the walls. The king was busy with a stack of papers on his desk.

He had come to say goodbye.

The king greeted him fondly. "What are your plans now?"

"I'm going back to supervise the construction of a new fortress in Trieste."

"Ah, by the sea … lovely. Before you go, I want to give you one last lesson, the most important lesson for a future king and emperor."

"And what's that, sire?" Maximilian asked, joking to himself that these speeches might just force him to break off his betrothal pledge to Charlotte.

"You'll find revolutionaries, heroes, figures important for your people … artists and nationalists. They might be caught overthrowing your kingdom, but when they fall, forgive them. 'If they fall to you, give them pardon,' as the saying goes."

Maximilian considered that. "I think I understand your thinking."

Unknowingly echoing the words of an Indian somewhere in Mexico, Leopold continued. "But there's also something that we call chutzpah. For example, if a man kills his mother and father, then asks for mercy because he's an orphan, that's chutzpah. Don't forgive him."

"Enlightening," the prince mused. "I'll remember that, sir. Reluctantly I must now go now. My mission awaits me."

The king stepped out to watch Maximilian ride away in the royal coach. He was strangely sad. Zinnia watched Maximilian leave from a window, also sad.

Austrian hussars, or royal bodyguards, accompanied the coaches as they traveled through the beautiful countryside. And in the meantime, at the palace, the king asked his chosen lord to go after the prince and negotiate his marriage to Charlotte.

Mexico

It was early morning. The rising sun was breathtaking, its rays of heat cutting the skyline in hues of orange and red. In this agricultural area, a gram crop was grown over a vast area. In the green fields were a father, his two sons, and three horses.

The father was riding a black horse at top gallop, pressing to go faster. His eldest son was sitting on a tree branch trying to measure the speed. The horse pushed through the knee-high crop, some three feet in height. This required more strength than running at a gallop. The crops were dipped in morning dew, and the horse trampled a thin line. The younger son watched, wondering if the owners would yell or object.

The trampled line faded as the crops restored themselves, but the horse seemed to be indulging in a futile trampling exercise. The crop was wet and thick, and the horse made a great effort to speed through it. His coat was lathered with white foam after the rapid run through the standing crop. The elder son wrote the timings in a log. His father, a police official, was Señor Carillo. He rode to the solitary tree where the two boys sat, climbing down from his horse. He then took a second horse, a chestnut, and walked him to the starting point. He mounted, positioned himself, and then waved his hand. The young timekeeper took note, and Carillo was off. The chestnut ran laboriously at first, soon racing at top speeds through the crop.

The younger son watched intently, his eyes bright and wide with excitement. When his father arrived again at the tree, he examined the various speeds scribbled on the scrap of paper.

Carillo turned to his sons and said, "The chestnut is the fastest. We'll buy it."

The younger son asked, "Father, why do you come to Grandpa every year to buy a horse?"

"Because the swiftest horses are found here."

"Why do you select only the swiftest?" the little boy asked.

"Because I'm a police officer, son. I need a swift horse to chase the bandit."

"I don't need a horse to chase a bandit." The boy smiled as he proudly raised himself to his full height.

Carillo suppressed a smile of his own. "And just how would you capture him?"

The youngster scratched his head for a moment, then straightened up again and replied with bravado, "I'd ambush him on a bridge or something."

Father laughed and hooked his arm around the boy's neck, pulling him against him. "You're clever."

The three went to the horse trader, Morrito, where Carillo asked the price and paid cash.

Inspector Carillo was taking a siesta with his wife. The covers on the bed had been thrown aside; the woman made a mental note to make the bed again when her husband arose. She got up to check on her sons in the next room, moving quietly so she would not disturb her husband.

A healthy woman who looked too young to be the mother of two large boys, she paused in the doorway of her children's room. Wiping her brow with the back of her hand, she asked, "Isn't it too hot here?"

Vickers, the younger son, replied, "Yes, I'm going to sleep outside, Mother."

"Me too," Carillo agreed, having suddenly appeared from behind her and slipping an arm about her waist. She gasped lightly in surprise and then smiled, leaning against him. He looked to his son. "We must sleep as much as we can, since tomorrow is Uncle Antonio's most important day."

Vickers's eyebrows rose. "His daughter is getting married, so shouldn't it be *her* special day?"

Carillo nodded. "It's a very important day for her, perhaps the most important day of her life. But it's also a special day indeed when a father gives away his daughter's hand in marriage."

Vickers nodded, having to agree with that despite his lack of full understanding. They walked outside and lay down on wooden cots stuffed with straw beneath a one-hundred-year-old shade tree. The light breeze soon lulled them to sleep, and they rested quietly until later that afternoon.

A pounding on the Carillo family farm gate resounded through the yard, reaching the distant cots as a faint thumping. Three people with four horses were attempting to enter the gates, but they were closed. A man's voice outside the gate shouted, "Is there anyone here??" This woke Vickers up, and he reached to stir his father awake.

Carillo lifted his head as a faster and harder banging started on the gate. He quickly retrieved his gun from beneath his pillow and trotted to the gate, opening it cautiously. A policeman stood outside.

The man was out of breath and his hair disheveled. He wasted no time and said to Carillo, "Sir, Inspector, robbers have sent a message from the house of the goldsmith James. They say, 'We're here. We've robbed your goldsmith. We're raping his women. Tell Inspector Carillo to come and get us.'"

Inspector Carillo frowned and thought for a brief moment, then turned to his son. "You go to the police station with him," he said, nodding to the policeman. "Tell Ramos to get to the goldsmith's, and then you come back to the house and sleep inside this time."

The boy nodded and left with the policeman as Carillo saddled his horse quickly. He slid his revolvers and rifles into place and raced off at a full gallop. Soon after that, his deputy, Ramos, received word from Vickers and began giving orders to his subordinates. A guard of mounted police was soon stampeding towards the crime site.

In the morning, Vickers woke up in his mother's room. She had insisted he stay with her that night, ignoring his protests to stay in his own room. He heard a commotion outside and went to a window. There were at least four hundred people outside, all standing or sitting near a cart that held the corpse of what had to be the robbers' ringleader. The dead man appeared very tall and broad with an exposed hairy chest. Even dead, he frightened the boy. He had just one wound, a pistol shot to the head. Vickers rushed to the door, but his mother stopped him and handed him a glass of cool water. "Take this to your father."

He rushed outside and moved as fast as he dared without spilling the water, weaving through the crowd to try to find his father without getting too close to the cart with the scary dead man in it. He finally found him sitting on a table with other officials. He was recommending Deputy Ramos for the "kill." Even the young boy understood that the one recommended for the kill would get a cash reward, as well as a medal for gallantry and promotion. He was surprised to see his father do all of this for his junior deputy. He handed the glass to his father, who thanked him and pulled him up to sit beside him. The other officials had concluded their business with his father and were beginning to disperse. The boy could not help himself, and he stared at the nearby corpse, at that single shot to the head. His father noticed his expression. Theirs was a world where people often saw death, but not always so close. He examined the boy's face and saw fear, but something else as well. He finally leaned down to the boy, softly asking into his ear, "Vickers, are you all right?"

The boy spoke, but his eyes never left the body. "Father, every day you wake us up with one more bullet in the tree stump. It's such a good shot, it always looks like the bullet went into the same hole." He finally turned and looked up at his father. "Only one man can strike in the forehead like that with a single shot. That's you, Father. Why are you giving your deputy the kill?"

"Because my deputy has a low education and can't be otherwise promoted to higher rank. Here was an opportunity to give him a promotion."

"That's a good thing to do, Father, but I think it's wrong."

"Why?" Carillo asked, surprised.

"I have a strange feeling, Father," Vickers answered. "I think your deputy Ramos is trying to get you out of his way."

"That's negative thinking, Vickers. See the bright side, not the dark one." He pulled the boy against him. "Besides, what would make you think such a thing?"

"I think that," Vickers continued, "because I know something of his past."

"You should think positively, act correctly, and know that you're made for others, not for yourself. I'm giving him this honor because I don't need it for myself," his father lectured.

"My point is that he found out about the crime and sent you his policeman. Why couldn't he first go himself and then inform you in the meantime?"

"Son, that kind of thing happens. Subordinates don't have initiative. They want orders."

The intelligent boy frowned at that. "So he can't make the decision on his own. He has no initiative. Why promote a man like that?"

"Vickers, you read too much. You argue too much. Just don't argue with me," he snapped. "Just like my father, unaware of things happening under his very nose. Brave, courageous, ethical but ... ignorant," he finished, almost talking to himself at that point.

Vickers shifted in his seat as his father grew more aggravated, then decided to ease the tension with a smile and a hug, his silent apology. His father's mouth curved up slightly at the edges despite himself and his muscles relaxed. The boy saw it was working and smiled broadly. "So how did you kill the robber?"

"I sent the police from the usual direction. I waited for him on a bridge and he came. He shot my hat, I shot his head. Just one shot each. He missed and I didn't."

Vickers grinned at his father's explanation. His father grinned back, shaking the fluff of his hair. But he still felt an urge to help his son to understand the point of helping Ramos, to use this moment to teach his son a valuable lesson in life. "Can you see now why I'm giving Ramos the kill? All of my men there saw what happened, and they'll be pleased to see one of their own being helped by an official. You have to earn the loyalty of your subordinates if you want to rule them."

"So, your subordinate gets rewards for *your* bravery?"

"He lacks education, son. This was one chance I could give him."

"Tomorrow he'll be showing his bravery medals proudly, even though he didn't earn them."

Carillo shrugged. "Just a part of human nature."

The boy forgot himself again, unable to understand or see his father's side. "But is that the right thing to do? I mean, fooling the department? Promoting someone who now has a uniform he doesn't deserve?"

"It's not that simple. He's good for the department, so a promotion will extend his services to that department." Vickers thought about an earlier lecture from his father, and began to quote him almost verbatim. "If all professors of 'evil emeritus,' like the sea pirates, crime lords, tyrants like Genghis Khan … if they all stood dressed as Santa Claus in the Town Hall, handing out candies and gifts, would you like to be a child believing them?"

His father chuckled. "Deceptive, but that's their art."

Vickers was confused. "You told me that was evil camouflaged as good. I think you should take off the mask. Ramos is a bad police officer, Father. He looks frail and innocent, but he's the cruelest police officer in the province. You should know that before acting for him. He's the Devil."

"How do you know he's a devil? How can you, a child, know the Devil?"

"He knows he's your favorite deputy. Before that, I already knew he was evil. I heard he has important higher connections, and he uses his title and uniform for them. The baker says he works under the red … floor." He paused and frowned, knowing he did not repeat the term correctly.

Carillo smiled. "You mean the red carpet."

Vickers nodded. "What is that?"

Amused, he explained, "Grandfather was a very good judge, and he once told a lawyer that there's something called a red carpet. This means it hides the places it's laid upon. Normally we say 'red carpet' to show elegance, but it actually hides and helps the swindlers, the false men, and the tyrants." The boy was still unsure, so Carillo paused in thought for a moment and continued. "Grandfather said that if you want the police to harass someone by entering their home without a search warrant in the middle of the night, train the police to say nice things while doing it. Use a 'red carpet.' Or if you want the citizen of a rebellious town to be punished, you put a red carpet on them. Pretend that you're hunting terrorists. Send the army to attack it, but let women, old men, and children get out of the town. Keep the males of combat age inside the town, and then attack them. The bloody streets are 'red carpeted,' and the army is free to kill. Half of the rebellious town's punishment is that the people who are safely out of town are later easy targets for looting after their younger men have been punished. The government can use the red carpet to punish as well. Your grandfather was telling how a wicked government can violate peoples' rights using policemen and army officials trained in the art of the red carpet jobs. 'Roll the red carpet, and don't let them see the surface below.'"

Carillo paused and then hugged him, whispering, "Be kind to him, boy."

"But that helps him, not us."

"You see everyone as a devil."

"Yes, unless he proves himself not to be."

"All right," Carillo sighed. "But how should you treat a devil?"

"We do the opposite of what we should do with devils. In church they say that the Devil is stronger when he sins ... so we should make people who can stop the Devil from sinning stronger. Whenever the Devil comes with an innocent face, we should call him the Devil. But we don't do that, we ... 'red-carpet' the ones who look good, but they're not."

"You're a difficult one." Both Vickers and his father stopped talking for a moment, turning to look at the body again. The last of the lower-ranking men were leaving, and the cart was being led away. The man's body shifted with each bump in the road, his head rolling from side to side. Vickers's mother stepped out of the house, glancing nervously at the cart and gesturing that it was almost time to leave for Carillo's brother Antonio's. Carillo nodded at his wife and she went back inside.

The boy's eyes narrowed in thought. "How did you get him, Father? Was it when he was galloping towards you?"

"Simple ballistics," he answered with another faint shrug. "First I had to ensure that I had him dead center. I had to come to the bridge and face him squarely. I corrected my centerline. Because he was racing towards me, I had to hit him a little lower, aiming at his chin. A steady nerve and allowing him to get nearer ... that did the trick."

"But he shot at you first, and you still didn't move?"

"He wasn't in control of his accuracy."

"Odds were against him, huh?"

"Yes."

"Ramos didn't even see him running? He couldn't try to shoot him first?"

"Ramos delivered. He led the man to me."

Vickers scoffed, "Tomorrow's paper will add a medal and citation to Inspector Carillo's deputy Ramos."

"A fortunate thing, son. My promotion and publicity would have prepared him against me."

"What? I don't understand that."

"Weaker people may not have the means to beat the stronger people, but if the stronger go on treating them wrongly, it finally prepares them *against* the strong."

"But Father, what if we treat them right, but they're evil? Is it just too bad for us?"

"Your judgment here is wrong. Good judgment is a skill men need in order to live, Vickers. You must think it through more."

"Well, how did you judge this?"

"Last night I was told about the robber. He'd been in jail and had just completed his sentence. On his release, I sent him a message saying never to come into my area, but he dared to anyway. I judged that this meant he planned to kill me." He raised his hands and used them to illustrate as he continued his explanation. "See, the goldsmith's home that the robber had raided had two approaches. I sent the police detachment to block off one route, and then I used my fast horse to cut him off at the second one. That was common sense, because I judged that he'd run away from the police by using the exit farthest away from them. When I reached the bridge, I got down and paced the same distance that I had measured from my tree to our house." Vickers smiled, knowing that 'my tree' meant the tree by their house, the one he shot a new bullet into every morning. "I decided to hit him from that distance, since I was best at that. It worked."

"So being daring didn't help the robber ..." Vickers concluded.

"Nope."

"He died because ...?"

"He died because he wasn't intelligent or wise. Have you ever seen a squirrel lying crushed in the road?"

"Yes ... that means that death is accidental? I thought it was pre-ordained!"

"Would you occupy a position that your enemy has vacated?"

The youngster nodded.

"No. *Never*," he replied louder to make it clear, "because the enemy knows that area. His artillery fire will be the most accurate. Like my using the distance to my tree to set up the shot. So surviving ... *living* requires intelligence."

"How do you know you have intelligence?" the boy asked.

"If you can give the correct reaction in the shortest possible time."

"How's that?" Vickers asked.

"Well, suppose a tree is falling and you're riding a horse at full gallop. Someone sees you and frantically warns you about the falling tree that's about to land on your head. There are two things you can do: either rein in the horse or speed it up. You have a split second to decide. The correct decision saves your life, and the incorrect one kills you."

"So the robber just wasn't intelligent?"

"I don't think he was," Carillo laughed. "Committing a crime and then calling the police to catch him is just stupid. Then trying to escape in a direction well-known by the police is a second stupidity. Then going towards the only place nearby that was narrow and would restrict his movement, the bridge ... that was a third stupidity. Firing at me from a galloping horse was really just a half-hearted attempt, not bravery."

"Was it a punishment from God?"

"Nope. God gives His blessings. He gives life. It's up to us to make it or destroy it. He allows us to unfold our myth, set our course right, to set right our choices, even our mental and physical health. This desperado should never have turned to bad things. He could have gone on to have a life. He'd served his time in prison, so the police had nothing against him."

"The police had nothing against him? But he was a bad guy. Wasn't that enough?"

"No. The police are not the judge. Police can't interfere in civil matters, only criminal matters."

"Then why do we have the police, Father?"

"To protect people from those who try to take the law into their own hands."

Vickers remembered his lessons about the police, quoting, "To protect, to serve, to uphold ethics. To prosecute the guilty and the unethical. There's a law. It's not in everybody's hands. Everybody has surrendered his right to take the law into his own hands. The police prosecute those who do it, the lawless people."

Carillo nodded, not surprised. The boy was brilliant beyond his years, and seemed able to quote so much of what he read.

"But, Father, what if the police make a mistake?"

"There's someone like a judiciary to correct that. Suppose, as a policeman, I found your mother guilty of murder. Suppose I arrested her, put her in hand-cuffs." Vickers giggled at the very idea. "Suppose your grandfather, a retired judge, took up her case as her attorney. Nobody believed your mother except an old man, her father-in-law. Before the judgment, suppose he brings a witness to the court who demolishes the entire case against your mother. The man who's been seeing criminals before I was born is proved right. What role have I played as a police officer of integrity?"

"A negative one," the youngster answered.

"Exactly. It's beyond the police to judge things, son. We have a judge trained to do that. In Mexico, the courts must stand as a major guardian of individual liberties. When a policeman is scheming against you, they're there to help prevent that. If the whole world is blaming you for defrauding them, a judge must listen to your side of the story. He has to weigh the testimony. Are you guilty or innocent? And if he's a corrupt judge, on the payroll of the government that wants to punish you, we also have the jury system to stop him. The entire judiciary system is built around *giving justice*. Anything preventing it is a judicial malfunction."

"How do you judge a man?"

"Who is a gentleman? Does he tip his hat, pushes in ladies' chairs, and the like? In French, the word 'etiquette' originally meant 'what's on the outside of a package indicates what's on the inside.' Fully adequate and poised, a gentleman has the approach of the idealist host who is so at home in his surroundings that he is completely relaxed, and being so, can turn his full attention to putting others at their ease. And he needs nothing himself; he is wholly at the disposal of others. His approach to others is not what he can get, but what he can do to accommodate. He holds always to his own standards; however, others may forget theirs. He is friendly, but not familiar; the inferior man is familiar, but not friendly. He is well-bred and dignified, but not pompous. The ill-bred are pompous, but not dignified. As Confucius said, a gentleman is the brick of great foundations."

"Yes."

"It's simple for me. A rogue is *not* a gentleman. Either he's a rogue or he's a gentleman. Either he's sane or he's mad."

"What's the difference? Rich gentlemen can be bad men, right?"

"A bad man who's rich can never be a gentleman, Vickers. A rogue is more articulate, in command of himself. He speaks well, and he's often rich. A gentleman is a simpler being. Would you trust a rogue or a gentleman? Because I'd much sooner trust a gentleman. A rogue is a schemer, but a gentleman isn't."

Vickers laughed. "Yes, Father, you always say, 'Smell a person. If he's a rogue, he'll be stinking. Put two people in a debate, but don't listen. Just smell them.'" They both laughed at that.

Vickers pushed himself back onto the table and folded his legs beneath him. "I've seen politicians debating before elections. Is there any way to choose the right one?"

"Yes, I think so. Look carefully at those men, Son. Listen to them, but also study their demeanor and ask yourself three questions. First, who's richer? That'll give you his educational background, lifestyle, morals, inclinations. Second, who's simpler? A gentleman has to be simpler than a conniving crook. Third, who has sincerity? He'll be the one who's more competitive in life, because he wants to win for the right reasons. Sincerity always wins in the end. And all along, keep asking yourself if you can trust a rich man, a crook, and an insincere person. You'd get the answer."

"But what if he keeps his true nature hidden?"

"I think you learn one's hidden nature by sitting with them in silence. Be patient, then hit their mind with great joy and then great sadness. Watch their reactions; a window will open for you to see their soul."

"Did you learn all of this about human nature from being a policeman?"

"A lot of it, yes. Animals don't need policing because there's no disorder in their set course. Only man needs policing. Why? Because he's different from the animals. He's been given the ability to choose between right and wrong. He may go his set course, or he may disobey. The *choice* to obey or disobey needs guidance, which is education." He smiled and quoted a verse.

"Knock at the door of reality;
Shake your thoughts,
Draw the right conclusions.
Now you are alive;
Your mind is now *open*."

Vickers shook his head. "I think the ideal person is a *lucky* one. He's born poor, but becomes the richest. He leaves his secure job and becomes a president. He's like Midas, and whatever he touches turns to gold," he explained, smiling faintly at the idea.

Carillo gently interjected, "The path to ruin starts from success ... and the path to success can start from ruin. Do you know this aspect of life?"

"No, but ..."

"The education of man must teach him to be steadfast, show kindness, be truthful, stay healthy, respect his parents and teachers, and be honest, mannerly. He should learn to keep silent but help others, be generous and remain safe. He should learn to behave these ways no matter where these behaviors take him in life, son. On the other hand, he should learn that he must never lie, backbite, and be of a suspicious nature ... never be disorderly, jealous, angry, proud, abusive, or hypocritical. These are negative traits."

"Education is in school, but they don't teach us all of that in our exams," Vickers replied in a mischievous manner.

"Real education must instill willingness to work for what's good, what's right and to keep away from what's evil. Evil brings evil, but good begets good."

"Where did you learn all of this?"

"From life."

Vickers smiled. "You're more a teacher than a policeman."

"And you're my most intelligent student."

"How do you judge my intelligence?"

"I judge a person's intelligence by the questions he asks and by the suggestions he gives." He winked at the boy. "Of course, as many questions as you ask, I believe you may be the smartest boy alive."

The boy beamed, taking it as a compliment. "So you think I'm the right kind of person."

"You're a good boy, Son. We all have our defects, but you work to correct them so you can be wiser as you grow older."

"What are my defects?"

Carillo thought and then quickly asked, "Would you spare me if we were at battle and I came under your sword?"

Vickers hesitated to answer. "Would you spare me, Father?"

"No."

Vickers stroked his chin in thought, remembering. "You didn't spare Vail," he commented, referring to his older brother. "You arrested him even though the department asked you not to. You said, 'A policemen takes pride in arresting other people, but even more pride when he arrests his own people.' You led him out in handcuffs even though Mother was crying."

"Yes," Carillo agreed, a shadow of sadness moving over his face.

"Why? He's your oldest son."

"Why? Because I should be sincere with whom I deal. I can't have different yardsticks for dealing with people. Honesty is truth, and dishonesty is untruth. One should be truthful or untruthful. The choice is ours."

"How about destroying one's life by choice?"

"Yes, and how about having anarchy, chaos, unrest and civil war in one's life, and that, too, by choice?" his father challenged, quoting another verse.

"In the slaughterhouse of duty, only the best
Get killed, because they can't run away
From what it's right to do.
Others are only dead meat."

"Amusing … very amusing," his son replied bitterly to his poem. "But what if *both* sides are in the right? The mighty and the weak? Pharaoh and Moses? The Greeks and the Trojans? What if a terrorist was only doing what his patriotic duty asked him to do?"

Carillo pounded his fist into his open hand. "Every evil starts from the word *right*! The path to hell is paved with good intentions, can't you see that? Judgment, *good* judgment, is *good religion*. A police officer who arrests his own wife for someone's murder is a sad, sad person. He matches the handwriting, fingerprints, evidence that his wife was in that room. He could take the extreme step to burn down his own house to hide the evidence, but what he doesn't know is that his wife was admitting guilt only to save her husband's sister. Whether he did his duty as a police officer or violated his oath by hiding the evidence, he was *wrong*. Even a sense of duty can be wrong, Vickers."

"I'm not going to be a police officer," Vickers suddenly announced.

"You'd better not. You're good for the army."

"I like the army, but is one career better than the other?"

"A policeman can be an angel if he wants to. That's difficult to do for a man in the army."

"But the army is always stronger than police."

"Only if they violate, Son."

"I can only apply for the army after finishing school."

"No need to plan it just yet. That isn't until next year."

"What future do you see for Vail, Father?"

"His choices will decide the outcome."

"Vail wanted to marry Uncle Antonio's daughter," Vickers recalled sadly. "Too late now."

"Vail's too young. We knew that."

"Do you both mind??" They both looked up in surprise at the voice. Vickers's mother stood outside the house, smiling with her hands on her hips. She leaned forward playfully towards her husband. "I told you we have to get ready to leave, and you engage our son in one of your never-ending debates?"

"She makes a good point, Son. Enough talking for now. Go and get ready for Uncle Antonio's."

The Wedding at the Inn of the Sun

The Carillo family arrived at the hacienda of Antonio the banker, Carillo's cousin. They were amazed at the wealth and beauty surrounding them. The hacienda, known as the Inn of the Sun, was set on twenty peaceful and secluded acres of natural desert landscape. Historic adobe buildings sat filled with the finest examples of old Spanish colonial architecture.

Carillo smiled at his wife. "I knew Antonio was doing very well for himself, and that his wife is quite wealthy … but I never imagined anything *this* grand."

As the family entered the grounds, they walked through an inviting covered entryway and into a breathtaking courtyard. In the center of the yard stood a double fountain ten feet tall, decked in red and yellow flowers. The pathway led them to a rich garden carved with aqueducts and streams, designed to support many tropical species of plants. The water made the area cool in the shade of the Mexican fan palms.

Mariachi musicians wore black suits, their pants laced with silver, as they serenaded the guests in the courtyard with delicate music. In preparation for refreshments, rustic tables were laden with traditional foods, including spicy rice, beans, tortilla dishes using chicken and beef, salsa, and meringue. Sangria, a cold drink made from wine mixed with brandy, sugar, and fruit juice, was served.

Antonio greeted them and introduced the bride and groom. The bride wore a mantilla veil and a slim dress with fine embroidery, as well as a matching bolero jacket. In lieu of carrying flowers, she held a fan. The groom wore a matador's outfit of a bolero jacket with tight-fitting pants.

Before the marriage ceremony could begin, a limping ragged beggar approached the master of the house, Antonio. The guests fell silent as the beggar picked that moment of all times to ask for alms. Antonio searched his pocket and took out a wad of notes to give to the beggar. The beggar began to bow and kiss his hands, but Antonio grunted and shook his head, helping him to stand. The beggar then lowered his hood and removed his robes, revealing that he was actually clad in the best of clothes. He took from his pocket a gold watch and cuff links made of diamonds, smiling at the collective gasps around him. Antonio smirked and joined the others as they surrounded the man.

"Why did you do that?" one of the guests asked.

"Do what?" he asked playfully.

"Come to Antonio dressed as a beggar?"

Antonio clapped his hand on the man's shoulder and turned to his guests. "Once long ago, God sent his angel to three men—one a leper, another one bald, and a third one blind. He wanted to test their worth, so the angel first asked the leper what he wished for. The leper wanted his healthy complexion back, so the angel waved his arm and the leper was cured."

"'Anything more?' the angel asked," the strange man piped in, helping to tell the story as he winked at Antonio.

"'One camel, for traveling,' asked the leper," Antonio continued with a grin. "The angel waved his arm once again and a pregnant camel was found sitting close by. Then the angel went to the bald man, who wanted his hair back. His request was granted, and when the angel asked if he wanted anything more, he said, 'A cow to give milk.' A pregnant cow appeared, and then the angel went to the blind man, who got his vision back and asked for a goat. A pregnant goat appeared."

The strange man interrupted again. "The camels, cows, and goats multiplied!"

A few children giggled at his flourish as Antonio suppressed a chuckle himself and continued. "Many, many years later, God sent the same angel to the three men. The angel went dressed as a beggar and asked the leper he'd cured for a camel. The man who used to be a leper said, 'I have a lot of duties and responsibilities. I have no camel to spare. Go away.' The angel said, 'But you were given one camel, a pregnant one, by an angel, right?'"

"'No, no, my father and grandfather had many camels,'" the strange man said, pretending to be the leper in the story.

"The angel's deep blue eyes pierced through the man as he asked, 'If God gave you so many, why can't you give one away?' The leper was outraged. 'I have other worries!' he said. 'Don't stand there, begging. Get out!'" Antonio exclaimed.

The man again picked up the narrative, still leaning familiarly against Antonio. "Then the angel went to the man who used to be bald. He had no cow to spare. Riches had only made him stonehearted. Mercy and compassion were gone from his heart. Then the angel went to the man who used to be blind, asking for a goat."

It was Antonio's turn to interrupt, holding out his hands and pretending to be the formerly blind man. "'I was blind and God cured me. He gave me one goat and it multiplied. He's been very good to me. I can't give God a goat, but I can give you many. Take what you like, but don't thank me. Thank God.'"

The stranger nodded. "Thanksgiving is to be thankful. Being thankful is to be merciful, full of compassion and magnanimous. God loves the thankful folks. God left the goats to the man who'd been blind. The other two men, the ones who used to be bald and a leper, lost their entire herds to a deadly disease that swept through as their punishment." Antonio grinned. "My friend and I used to listen to that folktale from my grandmother every Thanksgiving. She would cook the nicest meal and we'd listen to her favorite stories. He came here to test me," he explained to his guests. "He came to test his own friend."

The man laughed at Antonio's faked indignation. "I'm actually a fortunate man myself. I'm a gold miner and came today, traveling all the way from Europe, to attend this marriage and test this blind man. Now I know he's in God's stead, even now. He's still very rich of heart and not ready to be poor."

"What made you so rich?" someone asked them both.

Antonio looked at his friend. "Our beloved grandmother told us the formula."

"What formula?"

Antonio's friend explained, "We always split our income into three parts: one part for us and our families, a second part for the needy, an interest-free loan, and a third part we plough back into our business to make it grow."

"What about the income tax?" someone rudely called out in the crowd. "Don't you pay the income tax?"

"We pay all the taxes. But we don't take or pay interest."

"Why not?" someone else asked from the crowd.

"Because our grandmother taught us that interest is taxing the poor for the profit of the rich. Giving alms or interest-free loans to the needy empowers the poor and is a tax on the rich."

Another guest shook his head skeptically. "You pay your taxes, then you divide whatever's left into your three parts. How can that formula make anyone rich?"

Antonio smiled. "My grandmother used to say, 'When you get God's helping hand, you'll get help out of nowhere.' We see it happening in our lives. She repeated that lesson every Thanksgiving Day to all her family at the table."

Everyone murmured as the man took a special place in the wedding party and the ceremony officially started. The bride was brought out to the assemblage, led to stand before her father.

Antonio stood up and opened his portfolio bag, removing rich gold jewelry. "My daughter," he said, "I'm giving you gold, but do not love it. All the gold in the world is not worth a day, an hour, even a *minute* of life." He then reached into the bag and lifted out a large heart-shaped piece of gold jewelry, placing it on her head. "It's best if you use your head instead of this." Then he put two beautiful earrings in her ears. "It's best to listen to good advice instead of these." He put a necklace on her. "It's best to wear around your neck good deeds instead of this." Then he put a beautiful golden band on her upper arm. "It's best to trust your strong arm rather than this." He finally placed gold cuffs around her ankles, which spread out over the tops of her feet. "It's best to remain steadfast rather than to wear these."

Everyone began to clap. He looked around fondly at his friends and family and added, "It's best to sing now."

CHAPTER 8

▼

AN EMPEROR WITHOUT AN EMPIRE

By 1856, the construction of the fortress of Trieste was well underway. It was designed for the safety of the Austrian emperor, and Maximilian was supervising its construction. The castle was located on a rock that had been levelled and refilled with dirt. It looked out on the sea, surrounded by an Italian garden. From its wide terraces one could view the Istrian coast, and sixty feet below there crashed twenty fathoms of water. The view went on for miles. The grounds sported conifers from all over Europe, including fir trees from the Himalayas and cypresses from California. There were walks above the bay and formal gardens, pavilions, a greenhouse, and numerous ponds, all well cared for by a staff of gardeners.

Maximilian had decided to focus his skills, energy, and resources to design the castle so that it might reflect his adventurous personality. He knew that although this was technically being built for his brother the emperor, he was really the one who was likely to enjoy it. He therefore designed and decorated his study in an exact replica of his cabin quarters on the frigate *Novaro*, on which he had traveled the world's oceans. Having explicit duties and being highly intellectual, he had become one of the best-traveled royals of his day and dubbed himself the "sailor prince."

Out on the balcony there was a huge umbrella positioned over four chairs. Prince Maximilian, dressed simply in a white shirt opened at the neck and well-tailored trousers, talked with the French diplomat, Count Rene.

Count Rene began, "Our revolutionaries, Danton and Robespierre, toppled a ruling royal dynasty. Then Robespierre cut off Danton's head, only to lose his own head to others. It proved the saying that a revolution devours its children. It's an ancient principle of politics, but we saw a dictator end in a monarchy. Why?"

"That's called chutzpah, revolutionaries killing their comrades, anti-kings becoming kings, anti-dictators becoming dictators …"

"Yes," the count answered, "but I wonder which part is chutzpah and which part is history."

"That remains to be seen."

"We *hope* we see it," the count continued. "History is really just humans changing. History doesn't change a thing, it's *character*."

"Character?" Maximilian repeated.

"Yes, it's a trait born from temperament and environment. There're basically four types. There's the idealist …"

"That's me," Maximilian interrupted with a smile.

"There's also the rationalist, the guardian, and the artisan. The idealist should marry the rationalist type."

"That means I should marry Charlotte," he said rather gleefully.

The count continued, "The guardian should marry the artisan."

"Where did you learn all of this?"

"From sages, wise men," the older man replied.

"This is all very thought-provoking. Your advice somehow makes me comfortable. I can be my own self now. I feel … human again."

"What have I said to deserve this?" the count asked, feeling both honored and slightly amused at the young man's dramatic words.

"I was going through a devastating time," Maximilian explained. "I was suffering from within ever since I came back from Belgium. I didn't know where I stood, where to go, why, who I was. Where was my world? I struggled to find the meaning of life and what my purpose was. Now I know. I *must* marry Charlotte."

"The matchmakers are talking to your parents," the count divulged.

"How do you know?"

The older man smiled. "Sire, it's a diplomat's job to know the mathematical struggles between his state and others. Ever since you went to Belgium, the French Foreign Service knew that Belgium would be seeking a marital alliance with Austria. Your marriage to Charlotte, 'by hook or by crook' as they say. King Leopold deputized his confidant to go after you and negotiate the terms of marriage. We knew that, and now our foreign service can do one of two things: prevent the marriage or, as I think and deem it necessary, allow it. Positive thinking brings positive results."

"How very candid of you," Maximilian marveled. "But how would it bring a positive response from France?"

"The establishment wouldn't like it, of course. Their kind of thinking is too narrow. The marriage would stabilize Austria and Belgium, and that would leave France with no other alternative but to go along and befriend the Austrian empire. Besides, your marriage in Belgium to a cousin of the French king is a good thing."

"Wouldn't it mean war?"

"Heavens, no! Napoleon's gone. Marshal MacMahon is ruling now, advising the young king. France wants to pay debts. Our main worry right now is to pay the debt Mexico owes to the Europeans. The emperor was thinking of sending you with an army as the emperor of Mexico to get Mexico to remit its debts."

"So ... France is facing two revolts, one in Mexico and the other in Paris. A dangerous situation for any ruler." Maximilian thought about it and then concluded confidently, "The Paris revolt has succeeded. The Mexicans will also succeed."

"Those are military matters, Sire."

"You're French. Your king is removed. Why not remove the policies as well?"

"Yes, why not?" the count replied.

"Generals in charge of troops can change their minds, can't they?"

"The Parisian garrison's general was the apple of Napoleon's eye," the count laughed.

"General MacMahon? He proved to be an opportunist, a dealmaker. That goes beyond simply changing your mind."

"I can't comment on that."

Maximilian insisted, "He made a deal with the revolutionaries to get promotions from a new monarch."

"Hunt with the hunters, run with the hunted?"

"Exactly," Maximilian said, pleased with himself. "And now you tell me that Napoleon wanted to use me as a tool to tear at Mexico?"

"No, Sire, but I did advise Napoleon that 'our man' Maximilian would be more likely to dig in his heels in Mexico as a good Hapsburg emperor. Your set of ideas would have helped you to overcome a difficult situation over there. Of course, the presence of a French army there is a precondition to your success."

"I wouldn't have accepted the emperorship until the people really wanted it. They would have had to show me their approval and support."

"I know that," the count said wisely.

Tea was served and both men stared out at the sea.

After the refreshments, Maximilian amused himself by watching the Adriatic Sea through a telescope on the balcony.

"Well, what do you see?" the count asked.

"I see a European war at hand. There'll be tough times ahead for both Austria and France."

The diplomat Count Rene again met with Prince Maximilian outside the construction at Trieste. Maximilian was pacing as the diplomat entered the terrace gardens.

"How can I be nominated as a French emperor in Mexico when *your* emperor has met with the prime minister of Piedmont-Sardinia? Now he's busy discussing *Italy's* future!" he ranted without the benefit of a greeting.

Count Rene smiled. "I have great respect for your foreign service and spies," he complimented, since everything the prince was saying had indeed happened. "It's true, they met at Plombieres and discussed Italy's future."

"Cavour and his ideas on the unification of Italy are well-known. He wrote it all in his newspaper," Maximilian said, staring out at the ocean.

"He's the man uniting Italy, we know that," the count agreed.

"Which means that Cavour could start provoking us into a war because the French emperor has told him to proceed?" the prince insisted.

"A sound conclusion."

"Then it's war," Maximilian stated flatly.

The count walked to a large flat stone. He nodded permission to be seated and the prince granted it absentmindedly. The count took his time to begin, measuring his words carefully.

"We can persuade Napoleon to renounce Cavour. We have the cards."

"Have you?"

The count nodded. "Napoleon is your personal friend, Sire. He's in need of a Catholic prince for the job of an emperor in Mexico. The British are Protestants, so they won't install their generals in Mexico. Spain can be taken out after a deal. That leaves the French. The American president is busy sorting out his Confederates. He has a long, drawn-out civil war on his hands. It brings one single conclusion: Napoleon needs Austrian help to dominate Mexico. He's even thinking of taking back Louisiana. That makes you the most important part of this affair, Sire."

"You've put your cards before me honestly but cleverly."

"Sire, a diplomat plays his cards by being straightforward, by honestly putting his cards down and showing them on the table. I regard the marriage between you and Princess Charlotte to be the catalyst that'll bring peace between Belgium and France. Belgium would be strengthened by the marriage."

"I see," Maximilian said thoughtfully.

"I have to remain loyal to my country, but I also have to win your heart. I can accomplish both by always thinking of your welfare," the diplomat explained.

The half-built castle stood in the background, silhouetted by the setting sun. Maximilian began to walk towards the castle, kicking a stone on the beach. He turned to the count with an ironic smile. "You should be a spy instead of a diplomat."

"Master spies become master diplomats, Sire."

"I disagree there. Master pimps become master diplomats. Master spies are great soldiers."

They entered the new construction laughing.

Soon thereafter, Maximilian informed the diplomat about the dancing duel in Vienna, inviting him to see the Indian and European 'divas.' Then he himself left Trieste and traveled to Vienna.

March 30, 1857

A revolution had broken out in France against Napoleon III. He ordered 24,000 troops to suppress it, but General MacMahon staged a coup and joined the rebels. They installed nineteen-year-old Prince Louis Philippe as the king of France, and Napoleon was exiled to England. Once there, he received news that the traitor MacMahon had become marshal of France and been declared a war minister in the new royal cabinet. Ideas of ruling Mexico through a European prince were shattered along with all of his other plans. His very thoughts could have gotten him arrested for high treason when he heard that Louis Philippe had been formally crowned at Rheims on April 28th, 1857.

Maximilian had his own bad news as well. In the Treaty of Pressburg in 1858, Austria recognized Hungary's independence and ceded Slovenia to Magars, granting sovereignty to the Czechs and creating Galicia, just when Maximilian was to be its grand duke. Now Austria was reduced just to its German and Italian regions. Revolts were beginning in Bohemia, Moravia, Slovakia, and Slovenia. Austria offered France an alliance and King Louis Philippe agreed. Under the Nuremberg Pact, Bavaria was to remain an Austrian holding.

The Treaty of Prague established a Russo-Prussian group of nations and Maximilian stood disinherited from all of his previous titles, including the ones from Romania and Sardinia. The Austrian currency declined in value with the loss of Lombardy, and Maximilian was now left only with a single Venetian dukedom. So much had changed in only one year ...

At the end of July 1858, the diplomat Count Rene met with Prince Maximilian at Trieste. He greeted Maximilian with the quiet respectfulness one uses with someone in a state of mourning. "I'm sorry for your losses, Sire. All of your empire lost in just two short years ..."

Maximilian simply smiled. "And now MacMahon is your minister of war."

"Yes, and what a fine general he is. Napoleon's removal has emboldened other patriots."

Maximilian was irritated with the count. "Hungary instigated a revolt against Austria. My brother sent 24,000 troops to pull it down. Czar Alexander found an opportunity to help us but refused, and the revolt spread like wildfire. We had to fight a volunteer army that was helped by Prussia. We had to come to France for an alliance. France is threatened on three sides now, so how are we supposed to fight our revolts when France has so many of its own troubles?"

"You can't fight everyone, sire. War isn't the solution when dissolution is the order of the day. A treaty and an alliance are what's called for now."

"You mean granting sovereignties to rebels? A bonanza for the rebels!" he countered. "That's a unique thought!"

Versailles

Count Rene had traveled to France to meet Empress Eugenie in her garden at Versailles. She walked across the garden to meet him, lovely in the morning light. They stood near the chateau by the intricately designed flowerbeds that stood in symmetrical patterns, dotted with ornate fountains and sculptures.

"I told the emperor that we should give Mexico to Maximilian. But ..."

Empress Eugenie's eyebrows arched. "But?"

Count Rene tried to read the empress's face. "The emperor says the vote has to be rigged. French soldiers holding the referendum won't satisfy Maximilian."

"Maximilian is wise. I'm afraid he'll see a lack of enthusiasm in the Mexican people and end the monarchy before it has a chance to begin," Eugenie predicted with a frown, trying to figure out a way to convince both Maximilian and her husband Napoleon that a Hapsburg emperor was the best idea for Mexico.

"There's a pestilence right now in Mexico, Your Highness. We can blame the plague for low attendance," the diplomat suggested.

"Yes, we can do that, but Juarez is popular. Many people support him, and he has armies getting Lincoln's military support."

"We can attack Juarez and put him to flight."

"My advisors told me you were a wise man. I agree," she said with a smile. "There is a way out. We can ask our general there to make attack plans now."

Royal Palace, Vienna, Austria

A Belgian coach driven by both a sharply uniformed coachman and footman drove up to the front entrance of the Schonbrunn. The butler hurried down the stairs to greet the driver. They spoke briefly before the butler hurried back inside to find Maximilian.

Within minutes, the prince was opening the coach door for Zinnia. He helped her down from the coach, sending her old singer, the Imam, to the kitchen to send word for food. He gave her a warm hug before holding her by the shoulders at an arm's length, slowly taking in her beauty. She was lovely, draped in blue silk and chiffon trimmed in tiny gold specks. Her dress fit snugly at the waist and flared into a skirt that fit nicely over her feminine hips. The sight of her touched him profoundly, and his eyes shined with approval. A smile was set on his face.

"Welcome, Zinnia."

Zinnia had come to Vienna with a letter from Charlotte to the groom. "From Belgium with love," Charlotte had written on the front.

The prince laughed when he read that, and led her to the lantern room, which opened onto a large gallery that served as a waiting room for servants and guests of the emperor. It was adorned with gold stucco, and there were paintings on the walls of Joseph II, Leopold II, and Franz Joseph I.

Sophie was reclining on a chaise, reading. She set the book down with a small smile as Maximilian presented the beautiful dancer to her.

"Here she is!" Maximilian announced.

"Who is she?" Sophie asked, looking Zinnia over from head to toe.

"God sent a fairy from heaven for you, Mother."

His mother examined her further, joking, "Am I dead? Am I in heaven?"

"No, Mama," her son laughed. "She's in your service from today onward, a gift from Charlotte."

"Oh Maxi, she looks like a princess. She's almost more beautiful than Sissi."

The old emperor entered the room in search of his wife, stopping when he saw the trio. He looked closely at the charming girl, taken aback. "Is she European?" was all he could think to say.

"She's Indian, Father, of the desert people. She's a singer and a dancer, a gift from Charlotte," Maximilian explained.

"Charlotte has an eye for beauty," the old king said approvingly.

"Come here, child. If Maxi likes you, then I like you," Sophie said gently. "Come sit by me." The two talked softly for a while, eventually giggling and then laughing. In very little time, they had made a deep connection.

The king walked out to the anteroom with his son, seeking privacy. "Look here, Maxi, she's no longer a guest. She's part of the royal household now. For safety reasons, you must have the dancer inspected by a doctor first. We can't take any chances."

"But surely since she's a gift from Charlotte—"

"Gift or no gift, it's the family's safety at stake," he interrupted. "She must be checked out."

Later that day, Prince Maximilian returned to his mother's stateroom.. She was still reading on her chaise lounge. He greeted her with a kiss and hug.

Sophie looked at her tall and handsome son. "Maxi, have you decided to marry Charlotte?" she asked outright.

He smiled. "She's intelligent, artful, small, and dark. I'm tall and light. That's how it should be. She's fluent in several languages … she has beautiful silky skin … yes, Mama, I think I'm in love with her."

"We've settled your marriage then. If you're pleased with the princess, then I agree. You can ask the terms from your father." She was trying to sound reasonable and methodical, but Maximilian could tell that his mother was delighted.

"But Mama, she's rejected two rich and powerful suitors. One of them was even the Spanish ruler's son."

Sophie smiled. "Did she tell you that she loved you?"

"Yes, she said it was love at first sight. I know she loves me, but they say she's usually very pragmatic, practical. What if she changes her mind?"

"Maxi, if she said that she loves you, it's a good as done," she said firmly.

He smiled like a boy. "I'd enjoy life more with her by my side."

Adelaide, the Bavarian dancer who was the queen's confidante and personal maid, entered the room. Her steps were quick and graceful as she brought medicines for the empress. Sophie looked at them all with a sigh as the maid hastily left.

Maximilian glanced at the medicines. "I must beg leave for now. I'm tired, and you also need your rest," he said conscientiously.

After a week of arduous travel, Zinnia had arrived with her entourage at the Schonbrunn. She had been sent by her mistress to compete in some sort of contest, and she did not want to disappoint her. Still, she was flattered by the special attention she was being given, having expected to be treated only as a servant. She was delighted to find one of the rooms totally emptied.

Zinnia visited the prince's bedroom to tidy up after delivering medicines to Sophie. Completing what she came to do, she quickly started for the door.

"You've been avoiding me. Why?" Maximilian asked from his seat by the fireplace.

Zinnia hesitated at the door. He sprung up from his chair and blocked her exit. "You'll force me to come as the blood-hungry wolf and frighten you to death at night," he warned with a smile.

She lowered her eyes and looked to the floor through a thick fringe of lashes. "I sleep naked, Sire. It may give the wolf's teeth some trouble."

"I know that body of yours. It doesn't frighten me," he whispered intimately.

Zinnia laughed.

He took her in his arms and kissed her deeply. They went up the back staircase to his suite of rooms. As they entered the prince's rooms, Zinnia changed her demeanor. She became flirtatious, provocative, and highly sexual. Maximilian was also different there, succumbing more to the impetuousness of his youth. He reacted to every move, every sigh.

She was in control as they entered the antechamber. At that moment, she was royalty and he was her servant. She removed one piece of clothing after another, slowly, sensuously. This was different than any other tryst he had ever encountered. He was mesmerized by the change in her as she became the initiator, and he submitted to her control.

"Zinnia," was all he could manage to say, his voice soft and vulnerable as he watched her. Soon she stood naked like a goddess before him. It was a fitting analogy, because he worshipped her body. "Zinnia," he whispered again, his voice deep with emotion.

They came together like a fragile mirror, breaking and flying into a million pieces, cast off and reflecting light in every direction. It was another amazing afternoon of lovemaking. Their bodies always responded to each other like it was the first time, never tiring. They only stopped out of exhaustion, and then would lie quietly until they again found the strength to continue. They were insatiable in their passion for each other, as if they never wanted it to end.

They lay naked in each other's arms for many minutes before Maximilian spoke. "You're so beautiful, Zinnia, so desirable … and more than that. You're like a rare gift. I promise you'll always be provided for and protected like the treasure that you are."

These were the exact words that she had longed to hear. She squeezed him in her arms and rested her head on his chest. "And I promise that in my heart I'll love, no matter where my life leads me," she whispered. She paused, again wondering about something that she had not dared to mention before. She now felt compelled to finally ask. "Do you love anyone?" she whispered.

He did not answer.

"Are you decided on marrying Charlotte?"

"Yes, marriage is my destiny as a Hapsburg, my purpose in life. But you're the one I adore," he replied, kissing her neck.

"When are you getting married?" she asked in a shaky voice.

"The year of our Lord 1857," he said, adding the pomp to convey his own sense of intimidation at the prospect.

Later that night, Sophie lay in her royal bedchamber. Two fluffy white dogs were in the bed beside her as Zinnia pressed and massaged the Queen's feet. She was skillful in that art, and Sophie's eyes closed in relief. It was bedtime and she needed to relax. Her eyes opened lazily, glancing at a portrait on the wall of her middle son Maximilian.

"That's a true gift," she murmured as she looked upon the excellent painting of her favorite son. Zinnia looked over her shoulder at the portrait and carefully replied, "Beauty is in the eye of the beholder, my lady. The prince thinks you're far more beautiful than that portrait … and I think he's more beautiful than that portrait."

"Are you fond of him?" the queen inquired, raising her eyebrows slightly.

Zinnia looked cautiously into Queen Sophie's eyes. "I lost the right to be fond of anyone before I was even born."

"And why is that, my dear?"

Zinnia looked out the window, carefully considering her words before answering. "My mother was a maid and a dancing girl, an extremely attractive woman. She served an Indian queen …" She blinked at the memory, inhaling deeply and getting to the point. "Anyway, one of the queen's sons raped my mother, and that's how I came to be. My mother tried to give me poison after my birth, but the mosque imam—a mosque leader—rescued me. His wife had just had a stillborn child, and he presented that baby to the queen as me. She had that child thrown into the water to be eaten. The Imam then brought me up as his daughter. He's the old singer in my musical band," she said, glancing at Sophie's surprised face. "He also had a son who died fighting the British troops," she added.

"Oh … how did he die?"

Zinnia's heightening emotions made it difficult for her to speak, but she managed to continue with her head to the side, still staring out the window. "He was left all alone on a hill being defended by an Indian rebellion. The British charged that position. He was reciting the holy Quran when they took him prisoner. He was still reciting it when they hanged him."

Sophie's breath caught at the sad story, but her thoughts soon turned to her son. "I've heard that Maxi listens to holy Quran recitals from your old man," she commented. She paused, staring at the girl. "Maxi is Catholic, you know."

"Maxi has no religion," Zinnia insisted, forgetting herself and slipping into the use of a nickname for the prince. "He's above it, not below."

Sophie was silent, pondering this idea carefully. She wasn't sure if she should be angry with the girl for her insolence or grateful for the information. She finally decided to continue the conversation. Information was more useful to her right now. "How did you become a singing and dancing girl?" she asked, changing the subject.

"During the Bhopal uprising, we took shelter in a place called Begum Bagh, the Garden of Wife. The English troops entered and killed all of the natives with their bayonets. It was a horrendous time. I was spared, if you can call it that, picked up by a tommy. He wanted to earn money in England from my body or my crafts."

Zinnia's eyes filled with emotion and fire as she told Sophie her story. "You must understand that this was a huge turning point in my life, my lady. I had to choose which way I would earn the money that was required of me. He took me to London, where he used me to generate ten quid per day. He didn't particularly care how I got it, as long as he had it by the end of the day. It was my daily income from dancing, singing, and violin playing … I made sure I got my ten quid a day without selling my body, but I became a prisoner of that pimp. He had a wife and they constantly argued about me. When he wasn't threatening me about making my daily quota, she was accusing me of seducing her husband. There was no time to rest. I worked all day to get the money and spent most evenings listening to shouting and accusations. Maxi's fiancée finally saw me in a park and bought me from that man ... and then she sent me here."

Sophie extended her hand and rested it on Zinnia's head. "To me, you're Charlotte's gift," she said affectionately.

Zinnia bent and kissed her hand. The little puffy dogs sitting nearby were up in a flash, approaching Zinnia with threatening little growls. Sophie tried to back them off, but they stubbornly stood their ground to protect their mistress. The little dogs were so tiny and adorable that it was amusing to watch them try to be ferocious. Sophie finally called them off and the two women laughed.

The next morning, Maximilian stood by the window of his bedchamber, watching Zinnia work with the Schonbrunn gardener. She had spent a lot of time with the gardener lately, feeding her insatiable curiosity about how every flower was nurtured, the composition of the soil, every minor detail. She reminded him of himself at a younger age. Maximilian hurried down the stairs and out into the garden. Even covered in dirt, she was stunning, her hair slipping enchantingly from its pins.

"Good afternoon, Zinnia," he greeted as he helped her up.

Zinnia's dark exquisite eyes sparkled as she stood, murmuring a greeting in reply.

They walked down the garden path together, stopping by a row of huge hedges flanked by hundreds of flowers in white, gold, red, and yellow. Maximilian placed his fingers on her cheek, tracing the curve from her ear to her chin. His finger lingered there before continuing down her neck to the hollow of her throat. Her breath was taken away as he kissed her lips and whispered, "I must be with you soon."

"Tonight, my love, after dinner. Eight o'clock in your suite," she whispered, her eyelashes fluttering as he kissed her again.

"Yes, tonight ... I'll be waiting."

Zinnia looked around, kissed him quickly, and then hurried back to the gardener.

Maximilian sighed, satisfied with himself. As he stretched and looked over towards the maze, he saw his mother and father. Surprised, he managed a smile to them and continued on to the stables.

Royal Garden, Vienna, Austria

The old emperor and Sophie sat in the Schonbrunn gardens sipping tea. It was a lovely morning in Vienna, and the palace gardens were at their best. A beautiful water fountain cooled the breeze that played lightly over them.

"Maxi was enormously glad to come home," Franz Karl commented.

Sophie nodded. "His heart is always here when he has to go away."

"Not in matters of the crown," he quipped. "He'll always be your baby, forever longing to be in his mother's arms."

"He'd make an excellent emperor somewhere," she said smiling, always the doting mother.

"Wrong," he snapped. "He has ideas that are too … un-royal."

"For example?"

"For example, he hates the police, the army, secret services, strong government, the ESTABLISHMENT!" he answered, his voice swelling with every word. He had a sip of tea and collected himself. "He'd like to see no government, or very little of it anyway … an invisible, 'un-hurting' government, as he calls it."

"Those are futuristic ideas, not wrong ideas," Sophie cajoled.

"He wants to see ordinary people treated like emperors, as if they were somehow equal to royalty. He wants to build palaces and hotels for them, casinos and golf courses. He wants to see people in control of their own destinies. You know that'll finish us kings. His ideas attack the deepest roots of monarchy."

"Or he's simply making monarchy acceptable in the future. I've talked to him about what's been on his mind. He knows the Hapsburg situation. The empire is being challenged from three directions. Maximilian says we're no match for the Prussian army now. In Italy, the empire is being challenged by Sardinia. France is hell-bent on a military match with us. Max thinks we're about to lose our dominance in Italy. In the Balkans, the Hapsburg position is being threatened by Russia. Max thinks we should even consider befriending the Muslims."

Franz Karl frowned but said nothing, letting her continue to inform him about their son's logic.

Sophie added cream to her tea, stirring it as she continued. "He says that we've failed to create an ideological basis for the empire's existence. We've failed to curb domineering national groups, and now we're failing to satisfy the demands of the rising middle and industrial classes. So he says, 'What am I doing at sea?'"

"I didn't want to be the emperor either," he interrupted. "It's not my cup of tea. My elder brother abdicated and I was made an emperor, simple as that. It quieted the revolutionary forces of that time, served its purpose. But kingship is uncompromising. It doesn't take the wishes of the people into account … so here Maximilian may be absolutely right."

A maid brought them a fresh plate of sweetbreads, and the old man took one for himself as he spoke. "My grandfather had a great advisor, Matterneich. I didn't have any. I renounced my emperorship to quiet dissent. It looks as if we have to take Maximilian as our advisor now, but his ideas are too wild. He doesn't run with the king's hounds. He runs after them or away from them. Based on that, I abdicated in favor of Joseph. He's a fresh face. He's friendly with Prince Felix Schwarzenberg, Bach, Bruck, Stadion … all strong men. The revolt's been suppressed in Lombardy, but its spark has crossed the Alps. We're about to see even Vienna fall to the rebels."

The empress was shocked. "What about the royal family if Vienna falls?"

"We'll move to a safer estate," he replied, looking up and seeing her incredulous expression. "Sophie, we've crossed our fingers. Now let's see if the new emperor can stave off the dangers confronting the empire."

"The proof is in the pudding," she added, not liking the sound of that approach. Restless now, she got up and put her cup of tea on the trolley. Gesturing to the flowers surrounding them, she tried to explain her opinions. "Maxi or Joseph … both are as mature and complete as these flowers. They'll excel in whatever they put their minds to. But this is a vicious world, Karl. I'm fearful of what that could mean. Joseph is tough, he can stand slaughter and do slaughter. Maxi's too peaceful. He was hardly four years old when you put a uniform on him, put medals on his chest, paraded him around as a soldier king. And he's still being decorated even now. He's an archduke, but he's no Caesar … he's more like Alexander the Conqueror as a boy. If you asked him what he prefers, he'd say he likes to be around us, caring for us and sharing his happiness with us. But Maxi and Alexander have one thing in common—they both love their mother. I suppose that shows that even pampered darlings can be conquerors of the world."

"He's no pampered darling," Franz Karl fumed. "Look at him carefully, at the way he sets about the business of warfare and his forward policies." He paused. "He may even be right in his views, but are we prepared to put it to a toss? Certainly not! We've come this far, seven hundred and fifty years of rule, by a certain formula. We have a certain trademark on it. You know the saying: 'Put a Hapsburg as your king and live happily ever after.' We don't want to make exceptions, and certainly not in my time." Franz Karl rubbed his tired eyes and then closed them, concentrating. "Alexander the Great didn't leave any heir, you know. He asked his generals to fight it out, the fittest to rule. Before going to his greatest battle, against the Persian emperor, he sold all of his belongings and gifted away all of the cash and gold. Someone asked him what he'd kept for himself and he replied, 'Hope.'" Snorting at the very thought, he set his teacup down with a jarring clank.

"There, there, dear," Sophie placated him. "You're right, Maxi isn't pampered. He's a gentleman." She squeezed his hand affectionately. "He's coming here to say goodbye. He has to report for duty and I don't want any bitterness between father and son. Please don't be so angry."

"I'm angry because we Hapsburgs have stuck to the business of running an empire throughout our history. It's taken us seven hundred years to collect what we now have, what Maxi now has, and he dares to question its morality? I think perhaps he's bitter because I nominated his elder brother as the emperor. And what was I to do? Franz Joseph is better qualified, better prepared ... and he's the next in line!" He paused, looking in all directions as his thoughts raced. "I know we have to find Maximilian another land," he continued softly. "We have many to choose from. But he's funny. Wealth, estates, gold, kingship, emperorship ... he wants to give it away. We organized regiments to break up oppositions, and now he wants to break up the regiments. We declared that a Hapsburg king is all you need to live, and he wants to make kings subservient to the collective will of the masses. We make great palaces for ourselves, and he wants them made for the poor people. We select and train enforcers, but he hates them. We show power, majestic power, and he wants to be humble, walk like a common man. Sometimes I wonder if he's even my son. Isn't he too common to be a king?"

"Sire, how can you ask if he's your son?" she adamantly asked, offended. "Of course he is. But kings will soon be obsolete, as Maxi says. They had better be flexible enough to accommodate the kingship of the masses. Besides, a single person controlling the welfare of his subjects can make wrong judgments, bad decisions. I agree when Maxi asks if Parliament is being so bad. I think he's two or three hundred years ahead of his time."

"That's wishful thinking," he mumbled. "When's he coming here, anyway?"

"Within an hour or so."

"You're so close to Maxi. Perhaps you can fathom why he's so much against empires. What does he want?"

"He's not as against empires as you think, Karl. He's not a rebel. He doesn't want to topple any empire. He simply wishes that empires could be made more beautiful and stable. He plans cosmetics changes on the surface, but he also thinks about liberalism, human rights, more freedom, less control, constitutionalism ... people more in control of their ambitions."

"But how do you think that would affect Austria?"

"His ideas are very simple," Sophie said plainly. "He says Austria is landlocked and small. There're hills and valleys. The government should own the wood in the hills and make roads in the valley to carry that wood away to markets, be timber merchants. After that, it shouldn't meddle in other people's businesses, nor tax them. It shouldn't have embassies, and it should be a country without visas. No expenditures above timber. He suggests such tactics for Austria's other lands as well. Simple, 'rule of thumb' policies."

"But that strikes at the traditional roots of the empire and its emperor," Franz Karl seethed.

"That may be, Karl! But Maxi says that empires are bursting at the seams. New ideas, communism, democracy, they're all knocking at the door. He wants emperors to go one, two, three steps ahead of new ideas. Build palaces for the poor, make tourist resorts, think internationally, trade instead of fight," she responded firmly.

"Please tell him to see me before he leaves," the king commanded, getting up to leave. "Or rather tell him to see the new emperor before leaving," he corrected, referring to Franz Joseph.

"He'll leave after the dancing duel—he is presiding as judge." Sophie said.

Sophie was left alone in the garden. She sat back down at the table and sighed. The discussion had not gone the way she had hoped it would …

The Dancing Duel

Zinnia now had a full month to prepare for the royal dancing duel. She removed the furniture from her rooms and set it up for a dance rehearsal.

She was even given a maid, a young girl of thirteen years named Julia.

Zinnia practiced with guidance from her friend Mianji, the old musician. Julia lingered in a doorway and watched with fascination as Zinnia began to warm up.

"I want you to concentrate more on the inner you," Mianji corrected her. "Really listen to the music, then show the audience what the music is saying through your dancing."

"Then reveal the passion of your soul," Zinnia said along with Mianji, predicting his favorite line. The old man blinked in surprise at the echo as she laughed and turned to him. "Are you disappointed in my style, Mianji?"

"Of course not," he said with a smile. "I've seen many dancers whose techniques might be flawless, but they don't at all reflect the song they're dancing to. You must let the music speak to you and decide what it's saying to you. Then let that reflect on what you want to say to your audience. This is the music of your youth. It's the first music that you ever heard as a baby. You're an expert at it. Don't be reluctant to move on to the next level."

Julia watched Zinnia pause and listen to the music. Her eyelashes fluttered as she tried to give in to the rhythm, then moved fluidly into a sweeping dance. Her movements were more instinctive this time, at once aggressive and graceful. Julia exhaled in amazement when the Indian girl completed the dance. "Oh, that was beautiful, my lady."

"Thank you, Julia," Zinnia said, wiping perspiration from her brow. "You're young and easily impressed, but as always, my old friend is correct. The music and my heart must drive the dance. I must continue with more concentration."

Both dancers' hours were filled with choreography practice and stretching. In the evenings, when their muscles were exhausted and their feet ached, they turned their attentions to the costumes they would wear. Adele spent hours with Greta and her mother applying tiny seed pears to the girdle she would wear. When she finally nodded off, the other two women continued to work carefully on the costume, with only a dim lantern light to illuminate their fine stitches. Her costume was made of a delicate fabric, with a great deal of embroidery work that was white-on-white. The lightness of the costume's fabric enabled flaring of the circle skirt during the pirouettes Adele had practiced.

One day Adele was fretting about the competition, full of self-doubt. "Mother, may I catch a glimpse of this other dancer? I want to see her style and how beautiful she is. It will help me for the competition."

Adelaide looked at her daughter thoughtfully. "Yes, we can do that. This afternoon, Zinnia has requested the use of the Grand Gallery. I think we can watch her unnoticed."

After the noon meal, Zinnia gathered her singers, musicians, Mianji, and Julia to begin work on her routine in the Grand Gallery. Adele and Adelaide peeked from a doorway at the far end of the gallery.

The musicians included a man playing the *darbuka*, an hourglass-shaped Arabic drum made of ceramic, with the head made of goatskin. They played a short introduction and she began her dance. It consisted of varying pitches and paces. Her feet tapped the floor in a carefully choreographed rhythm, allowing her ankle bells to add to the song. The music was very powerful, with loud and resonating beats. Zinnia placed her right hand on her breasts and swayed very slowly. She tossed her long hair from side to side and swirled around in a circular motion, moving like the gentle waves of a calm ocean. She then used her graceful arms and hands to tell the story of a girl whose lover was a fisherman off the sea.

"Well, what do you think of her?" Adelaide whispered. "She seems quite beautiful and accomplished."

Adele frowned. "I'm willing to pit my charms and talent against hers." She suppressed a smile. "We'll just have to let Maximilian decide," she added, her eyes twinkling with a special secret knowledge.

Zinnia and Julia took a final shopping trip later that day. Zinnia selected a lovely *surya tika*, an ornament composed of a chain with a hook at one end and a pendant at the other. It was designed to be worn in the parting of the hair. She also chose several anklets of silver.

"In much of my dancing, the footwork is one of the most important elements," she explained to Julia. "Moving my foot in certain ways can produce a wide variety of charming harmonies from the anklets. My mother called it the 'music of the ankle bells.' Indian women love to adorn their beauty with jewels. We love the feel of jewelry as we dance. The flow of the veil and the brush of gold on the neck are inspiring in the dance." Zinnia chose red heart earrings with rhinestones and gold trim, as well as a gold collar necklace with red rhinestones and yellow gold bangles. At a fabric shop, she purchased maroon silk with slightly darker cotton to wear underneath. She also purchased burgundy silk to make a tight-fitting, short, bodice-like blouse.

"I'll cover myself with a red dye and make elaborate red *mehndi* patterns. It's an ancient Indian art. It's usually applied to the hands and feet. Men in India say the patterns evoke thrilling, erotic sensations."

Julia blushed.

"You must help me," Zinnia said.

Julia's eyes widened and she shook her head slightly.

Zinnia chuckled. "Don't worry, I'll train you. You'll help apply designs drawn on my forehead, hands, and feet. Henna is an important ritual, and it may take up to six hours. We'll buy fresh red powder henna, rose and orange water to wash my hands and feet before application … then we'll need one cup of brewed black tea that's been left to sit overnight … and the juice of a lemon that's been left to sit in the sun for at least twelve hours."

Julia nodded, trying to memorize the list. "My, it's so complicated! But I'd love to help." She smiled shyly at Zinnia. "I'd love to become a dancer like you one day."

Zinnia looked down at the girl and smiled. Her little servant had quickly grown to adore her. "After this duel is over, I'll teach you, Julia. I could teach you for years about the hands and arms alone, how they tell the story. My knowledge comes from five hundred years of Indian dance tradition. I can even teach you how to make costumes. Color, shape, and ornamentation are almost as critical as the dance itself."

As the day drew closer, more time was spent on the costumes. Adelaide and Greta searched the local shops to find the exact items needed. They planned an elaborate white hip belt with a thousand tiny seed pearls. The under-layer of her white costume was made up of diagonally cut pantaloons with ruffles on the edges. Vertical ruffled harem pants would accentuate her undulating hips and synchronized foot movements. The circle over-skirt was designed to feature Adele's shapely legs. The costume was carefully assembled to impart a sense of grandeur, femininity, and regality in its splendid fabrics and colors. Adelaide applied greenish-gold shades all over Adele's eyes, then lined them in kohl and rubbed perfumed oil over her body.

Zinnia applied a reddish bronze tone to her face, lining her eyes with a crimson lip pencil. She emphasized her eyes with kohl powder. It had been used in her culture from time immemorial, both to brighten and strengthen the eyes. It was smudged and blended with her eye shadow, giving her eyes more depth and definition. She then prepared her hair. She parted it in the center, pulling it up on the sides to create a braid. The *tika* was carefully placed high in the part. The rest of her long raven hair fell to the middle of her back.

Sophie and Adelaide entered the Grand Gallery of the Schonbrunn.

"I've always loved this room, my lady," Adelaide gushed.

"Me too," she said with a nod. "It reminds me of the wonderful times gone by." She gazed at the high frescoed ceilings, elaborate cornices, and rich stucco decoration, thinking of the grand imperial balls they held in that gallery over the years. The palace had 1,441 rooms, including the superb assortment of Baroque and Rococo staterooms, but to her, this was the grandest of them all. "I love to come here some days just to admire the frescoes. It's one of the largest and most glittering Rococo halls in Europe," she boasted as they looked up at the ceiling's frescoes.

"Who did this lovely work on the ceiling?" Adelaide asked, her soft voice echoing from the walls.

"It was done by Gregorio Guglielmi. He was a famous Italian artist," she added. Adelaide nodded, though she had already known of his work. "We'll light the hall with a thousand candles and the mirrors will reflect the light, illuminating the ceiling and reflecting on the dance floor," Sophie said, her eyes shining at the thought.

On May 13^{th,} one royal coach after another entered the gates of the Schonbrunn, unloading family after family of Europe's royalty. The guest rooms of the palace were ready. Bowls of rich chocolate candy, fruit, and pots of strong coffee in silver service sets awaited each visitor. Butlers and maids scurried around to cater to their every need.

That evening, the Grand Gallery was filled with people assembled from twenty-two royal families of Europe. The room was sumptuously furnished, the candlelight glittering off of the sterling silver and fine Venetian crystal. Gathered on the former emperor and empress's right was a large group of family members and Austrian dignitaries. The men were in dress uniform and the women were adorned with the most fashionable silks, satins, and royal jewels.

The "master" of ceremonies was Adelaide. She rose to speak and the crowd of nobility became quiet. "Ladies and gentlemen, I would like to present to you our most honored guest, Prince Nikola of Montenegro, also know as Grand Duke Peter Nikolajevic. He is a close cousin of Russia's Tsar Alexander III, who has referred to Nikola as the 'sole true and loyal friend of Russia.'" She paused as Nikola stood and nodded among welcomed applause.

"And next," Adelaide continued, The crowd applauded after each introduction, trained well in just how long to continue the applause so that the next introduction could be heard. Adelaide went on to introduce the former emperor Franz Karl, the former empress Sophie, and their three sons. Maximilian was dressed in the formal Austrian naval uniform.

Empress Elizabeth, or "Sissi" as the family liked to call her, sat beside her husband in a Rococo chair. She sat the toddler Prince Rudolf in her lap and played with him. He was adorable in his miniature sailor uniform.

"To the left of the royal couple are dignitaries from all over Europe," Adelaide continued. She introduced many more people, moving down the line of people seated by the emperor and empress. King Francesco II of the Two Sicilies; Prince Johann II of Liechtenstein; the Dowager-Empress of Russia, who was a frequent guest. The Count of Paris, Sophie's first cousin, gave the Austrian Archduchess Marie Clementine a possessive gaze as he was introduced. On his right stood Queen Amelia of Portugal. Next to her was Ludwig, King of Bavaria; Antoine, Duc de Montpensier; Infant of Spain and Infanta Luisa of Spain; Queen Maria II of Portugal; and finally her husband, King Ferdinand of Saxe-Coburg-Gotha of

Portugal. All of the dignitaries were seated with the two uniformed Hapsburg princes, Maximilian and Ludwig, who were seated in the middle to allow them a better view. They smiled and poked each other frequently, excited about the upcoming "duel of dancing beauties."

"After a musical interlude, we shall begin the dancing you have all come to see, the dancing duel," Adelaide announced. There was a polite round of applause from the guests, most of whom were focused on their next dancing partner.

There was a set of waltzes. As Sophie had planned, the scores of candles caught the glitter of the frescoes, sending their light into the mirrors and reflecting on the dance floor. It was lovely, like a dream. At one point, Adele peeked from around a corner and waited to catch Maximilian's eye, beckoning him over.

Maximilian excused himself for a moment, ducking from the hall without a little irritation. A cousin of Charlotte was at this event, and he did not want to ignite any jealousy or hurt her feelings.

Adele did not yet have on her costume. Its beadwork was so delicate that they planned to put it on her at the very last minute. For the time being, she was covered in a lovely silk robe of gold thread. Her golden hair fell here and there in careless ringlets, shimmering against the gold material. Maximilian's irritation faded as he eyed her up and down.

Adele smiled impishly and pulled him into a side chamber, closing the door. She was terribly jealous, watching him dance with the many lovely ladies, and she was determined to get some special attention herself.

"What is it, Adele?" Maximilian insisted, trying to hide his arousal.

"What is it?" she asked innocently. "I thought you'd want to wish me luck for the competition."

"Of course I wish you all the luck in the world, my dear."

"Have you seen my competition?" she asked, trying to read his eyes.

"No, I haven't. I hear she's a foreigner, Indian, I think," he replied.

She looked deeply into his eyes and decided he was being truthful. "Is it possible you'll find her more beautiful than I am?" she asked, pouting in her typical way.

"Oh Adele, don't be silly," he snapped.

"Are you sure?" she pressed, backing into a corner and pulling him towards her. "You won't admire her body more than mine?"

Maximilian said nothing as she untied her robe and let it part two inches across her breasts, resting on the creamy skin.

"Adele, you know better than that," he scolded, glancing nervously back at the door and shifting from foot to foot. "How can I help myself?" She opened the robe more, almost revealing the nipples. The bottom of the robe shifted opened further to reveal the rest of her. She knew him all too well. As intelligent and considerate as he was, there was only so much he could stand, and he stopped protesting. "You were my first and only. I want to give myself to you whenever I can."

Maximilian slipped his hands under the robe at her shoulders, sliding it back to fall to the floor. She leaned against the wall, her creamy skin glowing softly in the lamplight. "Your first and only ..." he repeated cryptically, alluding to her "secret" that she had not yet explained.

"Yes," she whispered, catching his hint. "It's not really that complicated," she explained before taking his hand, kissing it, and placing it on her breast. "The sultan used a trick you may know about. Horse owners keep two look-alike horses, a slow one and a fast one. They build up bets with the slow one, then use the fast one to win all the gold. My Egyptian master was that kind of horse owner. He found a girl at a circus in Germany who looked enough like me to pose as me. He put her in my bed to entice the prince."

"He switched you?" he asked, surprised.

Adele smiled. "He often kept two similar girls to blackmail powerful men. He has two harems in two separate cities. Besides, it's not hard to fool a foreign man. Blonde women are a rarity there. It's easy for them to assume it's the same girl if you match a rare feature like that."

"I see. What about the spoils of this kind of war?"

"My master took half, and the other half was divided between me and my look-alike."

Maximilian thought that over for a moment. "Hm ... you know, if I didn't know you were a virgin the day I was first with you, that story would be too fantastic to believe."

"Believe it," she said with a smirk as she slid up onto a table to her left, sitting on it to lift herself enough so they were almost eye-to-eye.

"Switched ... just like that," he mused.

Adele leaned back and rested back on her hands, arching her back so that her breasts pushed upwards in her most tempting pose. Maximilian could feel perspiration start to collect at his brow. "Adele," he stammered, again glancing back at the door as his hands slid down her ribcage and back up to her breasts.

"Oh Max, be a little naughty. It makes it more exciting," she whispered as she wrapped her thighs around his hips. He slid up against the table and kissed her throat. She closed her eyes and tilted back her head, arching her back more and then even further down …

When the guests had completed their dances, they again took their seats, eagerly awaiting the contest. Maximilian had hurriedly composed himself, washing up and smoothing his hair before sitting beside his brother again.

Adelaide reappeared. "Most renowned guests and friends, I would like to present Adele." There was polite applause as the beautiful young lady walked to the front of the gallery. Ludwig snickered under his breath and poked Maximilian in the ribs again. Maximilian grinned at his brother and gave him a friendly shove to silence him.

Adele's pale blue eyes shone through the dark eyeliner as she slowly smiled and began her dance of introduction. Her white-on-white costume was soothing, showing her soft pink skin to best advantage. She seemed to everyone like some strange, celestial being.

Adele's Egyptian-style movements were very precise, with the hips held under the rib cage. Her dance used little space, her pattern and rhythm contained within the sphere of her body. She walked forward with a rolling double-hip thrust, rotated her pelvis clockwise with a vertical shimmy, one arm over her head and the other at the leading hip. She then moved backwards with shallow, precise undulations as her hand movements told a story. It reminded the well-traveled audience of something one might see in Egyptian hieroglyphs. She concentrated on the movement of her hips, spine, and shoulders; muscle isolations were an integral part of the dance. Her technique was flawless. Her circular skirt provided an elegant line and shimmered beautifully with every move she made. She used a full-body undulation, a wavelike movement that requires a flexible spine. Starting with the knees slightly bent, it began at the thighs and slowly moved up her body to the torso, front to back. Then she displayed the movement in reverse, with the wave beginning in the chest and moving down to the thighs. It evoked the image of a camel's hump moving slowly across the desert.

The audience was pleased with her beauty and unusual style. Even the women who were prone to jealousy had to admit that she was a sparkling talent. Sissi carefully covered her tiny son's eyes during some of the more provocative moves, but she smiled with delight at the performance.

Next Adelaide introduced Zinnia. From her intricate sparkling *tika* to her splendid golden necklace, colorful bangles, and shining costume, Zinnia was beyond doubt a vision. She carried herself well as she walked to the center of the dance area. The V-shaped effect on the front of Zinnia's skirt was flattering to her figure. It went up to the waist in the back, draping in the front to just below the navel, providing an elegant line that shimmered beautifully with every move that she made. Her embroidered *jutti* shoes matched the skirt to form a continuous line to the floor, making her legs appear even longer. Also matching her costume was a burgundy Charmeuse silk veil. The curved edge was trimmed with a sequin band shiny enough to capture the light, and she intended to use this to its best advantage.

She had exquisite posture as she positioned herself and waited for the applause to subside. Her introduction dance was the one Adele had witnessed earlier, the story of a girl whose lover is a fisherman off the sea. She was undulating and luminous, full of grace and originality. The dance was based on the broad and natural movements of running, turning, twisting the torso, and natural posing.

After a second musical interlude, the guests watched attentively as Adele came forward for her final dance. She traveled in time with the music, using ballet triple steps to center stage. Greta played her violin in accompaniment as Adele began her rondo with "the jewel," a side-to-side crescent with a hip twist on each side. She layered her movements with a head slide followed by sustained figure eights, working her arms, chest, belly, and veil—then, returning to the jewel, she began all over again.

The music slowed down and her dance became more sinuous, representing the baths of the Egyptian priestesses. The hem of her gown and the longer ruffled harem pantalets she wore underneath belled out. She finally shimmied from her shoulders to her hips towards the princes, then fell to one knee. Her veil drifted down over her, enclosing her at the end.

There was tremendous applause. Adelaide tried very hard not to beam as she waited for the audience to quiet down and introduced Zinnia for the final performance.

Zinnia's hennaed feet seemed grounded to the earth as she walked to the center of the floor. She had asked Mianji to leave the Qawalis for once and sing for her dance. His was a heavy voice, sweet and sour, almost hoarse, but he had good lungs and sang loudly. A violinist joined the old man's voice, an interesting contrast that set the tempo. The girls began to sing, "Hoo ooo."

Zinnia approached a swing set that had been installed that morning by the palace gardeners. She lowered herself on the seat and swung back and forth. Her thick dark braid unloosed itself from the crown of her head as she also began to sing. She was a work of art from the top of her head to the soles of her feet.

When she had set the mood, she swept out of the swing and moved closer to the princes. The dance she began was a joyous celebration of womanhood and the female form, yet she retained the smooth movements and hypnotic body rolls of belly dancing. She twirled first one way, then the other. Next she bobbed and floated around in a circle, undulating, and carried it into a spin. Zinnia's final dance showed her ability to explore and develop artistic expression and personal style. Her eyes showed her emotions throughout the dance, like a window to the music. She danced a one-hipped circle with recoil that evolved into a slow pivot with a gentle shimmy, a shimmy that became hip thrusts. She incorporated both Indian and Turkish elements with Oriental dance moves.

The men in the audience were in awe. Her dance spoke to them on an inner level that on one hand was close to spiritual, yet on the other hand caused them to daydream about what it would be like to take her in their beds. She danced to win the heart of Prince Maximilian. Her eyes gave way to the secrets of her heart.

Zinnia's musicians began to mix the sounds of Chopin into their composition, adding to it the nuances of their Indian culture and the special sounds of their foreign instruments. It was a fascinating interpretation, and the audience enjoyed this unique experience of actually predicting the following notes and humming along.

During the final note of the song, she performed several sharp turns, finally extending one magnificent veiled arm upward before she froze, as quiet as a statue. The only signs of a living, breathing woman were small drops of perspiration gathering in the cleft of her glowing breasts.

It was captivating. The guests were thrilled and showed their approval.

A sudden hush fell over the room as the royal brothers, Maximilian and Ludwig, briefly discussed the performance. Maximilian finally stood to pronounce the winner. "Ladies and gentlemen, Your Highnesses, I have been given the most pleasant but difficult duty of naming the winner of this contest. I have listened to the advice of my brother, who prefers blondes."

There was a murmur in the room as people laughed softly. Ludwig cocked an eyebrow and smiled devilishly.

Maximilian patted Ludwig on the back and continued. "I declare Zinnia to be diva extraordinaire and the winner of this duel."

The audience stood and applauded his decision. Maximilian walked to Zinnia and Ludwig set off towards Adele. The dancers were escorted to the former empress Sophie, who awarded Adele a beautiful bouquet of flowers adorned with a diamond necklace. She gave Zinnia the same prize, as well as a carved and gilded wooden box full of gold coins. Maximilian, impetuous as always, took Zinnia in his arms and kissed her deeply. Many of the ladies blushed while the men raucously cheered him on.

It was late, and Maximilian had completed an evening of drinking, dancing, and flirting. He was tired as he walked the many hallways to his chambers. Ludwig had taken a couple of girls and gone off to his own chambers, inviting Maximilian to join him. He had accepted the offer, but he had no intention of staying all night and possibly having his mother notice his impropriety. He was surprised when he closed the door to his chamber and turned around to find Adele standing in the doorway to his bedroom, her hands planted on her hips.

"Adele, what are you doing here?" he asked, the archduke in him giving him an arrogant tone. "I thought it was understood that you were only to come to my chambers when it was prearranged."

"Max, how could you?" she demanded, genuinely hurt.

He stared at her and then brushed past her into his bedroom, pulling off his vest and dropping it on a chair.

"Answer me!" she pressed. "How could you choose her over me?"

"I did no such thing," he snapped, sitting and unfastening his boots. "It was a contest."

"You know how hard I worked on my dancing! I thought you cared about me!"

"Adele, this had nothing to do with that, and you know it. I was to judge a dancing competition, and that's what I did."

"And she was better than me?" she retorted angrily. He lifted a finger to his lips to have her lower her voice, but she ignored him. "Perhaps I should have painted my body like she did! Maybe that would have been the edge I needed!"

Maximilian pulled off his boots and clenched his jaw, the anger rising in his throat.

"Maybe she got to you before me, is that it? Did she visit you earlier this week to pay the judge?"

Maximilian stood up and stared at her. "Is that what you did earlier? Pay the judge before the competition?"

Adele glared at him. "How dare you!" she shouted, lunging forward and beating his chest. He grabbed her wrists so firmly that she gasped.

"You WILL keep your voice down," he commanded in a tone he had never used with her before. She gaped at him, surprised. "And you will not chastise me like an old wife, do you understand?"

She stammered and then closed her mouth. Her eyes filled with tears. His expression softened. "Adele, you're an excellent dancer, we both know that. But this woman was better than you. Not by much, but she was better. It's that simple. Now watch your tone with me. It was never a matter of personal favor."

Tears spilled from her eyes. "I'm sorry," she whispered.

He took her in his arms and hugged her. "It's all right, Adele," he comforted, holding her tight. He was still somewhat irritated by her earlier tone, but he knew she was genuinely hurt and did care about her.

"Just don't do it again," she scolded.

He held her by the shoulders and looked into her eyes. "Adele … I'll do as I please. Do you understand?" His tone was kind but firm.

She stared at him, her blue eyes sparkling with tears. "Yes, sir," she whispered.

It was understood. They cared about each other, but he was a man of means and she a dancing girl. She knew she would have to have him in whatever way that he chose. She decided then that it would have to be good enough. This was the man she had given herself to. She was hopelessly in love, and there was nothing she could do to change that.

That evening at dinner, Maximilian was restless and distracted. He made polite conversation and then excused himself, climbing the long staircase to his suite. It was almost eight o'clock. As soon as he crossed the threshold, he could smell incense burning. It was a spicy but slightly sweet aroma, overlaid by the scent of a musky perfume.

"Zinnia," he whispered.

On the bed before him were a royal blue satin dressing gown and a golden platter of fruit. He removed his clothing and put on the silky loungewear before relaxing on a chaise lounge.

Zinnia appeared as if out of nowhere from behind three sunburst screens, carrying a crystal wine glass etched in gold. She kneeled at his side and handed him the glass, then gracefully stood as she hummed her hypnotic music.

Her gold-shoed feet gracefully stepped back four paces, each step an enticement. Now he could truly see her. Her skin has been dusted with gold powder, sparkling with the slightest move. Her raven hair was done up in an elaborate coiffure adorned with a gold mesh cap with a jewel left to dangle over her forehead. On her delicate ears were fragile golden chandelier earrings. Her hands, both front and back, were covered in an intricate henna design, and the wrists and fingers told a story as her body moved like liquid gold to the rhythm. Her fingers fanned alluringly across her dark, kohl-painted eyes as she flirted and hinted at the pleasures that awaited him.

She was a gilded delight.

Her dancing costume bodice was reddish-orange with a scooped low neck, showing her satisfying breasts to their best advantage. Her gold-dusted midriff was bare, and around her waist was a thin braided gold belt which dipped just below her navel. Her hips rotated enticingly.

Maximilian's world was simple now. His desire was fixated on this gorgeous woman who was doing everything for his delight and pleasure. This banquet of sensations affected him in such a way that he could barely remain still; nevertheless, he stayed where he was, knowing that was what she wanted.

Zinnia glided and twirled, and her white transparent skirt opened at the split in the center to show her long legs. She felt his arousal, and it sent shivers of pleasure to her very core. She smiled seductively and put her hands behind her head, letting her abdomen suggestively undulate rhythmically as she took tiny steps towards Maximilian. As she got closer, she removed one golden hairpin after another, the dark rich tresses falling alluringly to her waist.

He reached for her and started to rise but Zinnia gently pushed on his chest until he was reclining. Then she moved to his feet, kissing them gently. As she knelt on top of him, her attention drove him wild, but he remained in place. He had everything he had ever dreamed of and Zinnia was in complete control. All he could do was repeat her name over and over.

"Zinnia, Zinnia …" His breath caught in his throat. "My love."

With two fingers, Zinnia opened his robe, first to the left and then to the right, as she kissed his stomach, his chest, and then his neck, tiny butterfly kisses …

Later, the two lay exhausted in each other's arms. Maximilian was content, but conflicting thoughts played in his mind as he tried to reconcile the two kinds of love he had in his life.

"My wonderful Zinnia, how can I explain how I care for you both? Charlotte would make the best wife on earth, and yet here I am devoted to you. Do you think she could really understand?"

"Don't you remember? It was all her idea. She understands that men who have heavy responsibilities have special needs that common men don't have. Princess Charlotte loves us both. I'll not pretend that I don't wish our destinies were different, but I'm resigned to love you in whatever way that I can."

Maximilian called on his elder brother in his palace office and audience chamber, the Walnut Room. The name came from the costly and exceptional paneling of its walls. The two brothers greeted each other with a handshake and a great deal of slapping on the back, as brothers sometimes do when trying not to show too much outward affection.

"Maxi, you're being sent to the admiralty."

"Yes, Sire."

"After this assignment, I'm sending you to Italy as governor."

"Mother told me that."

Franz Joseph smiled as he remembered old times. "As 'military men,' we were naughty boys. Now it's time to show our worth."

"Our worth as what?"

"Well, as directors, rulers, and enforcers, of course," the emperor replied.

"I'd like to see a Parliament meet after two years. We could remain home, go fishing, or meet the people. The government shouldn't be seen or heard. I like minimum government, no oppressive policies. I want to see a happier populace, freer and undaunted in spirit." Franz Joseph eyed his outspoken brother. "Our traditions don't approve of that laxity," he admonished him. He worried about his brother's future when he spoke like that.

"But, Sire, that's why we have revolts."

"Oh Max, you're talking about a utopia."

"Not a utopia, Joseph. We're going to be rubbed into dust if we don't hear the new sounds."

"And just what are the new sounds?" Franz Joseph asked, anger rising in his throat.

"Laws that over-regulate aren't necessary. Taxes are a burden. Liberty is too precious to let go of. Kingships and emperors are breaking apart at the seams. People are going to rule themselves. We can't sell our ideas to them anymore. Poets, culture, literatures, ideas are more important than gold and armies. Those are the new sounds."

"Then what are we going to do?"

Maximilian smiled. "Live in a chateau with a few animals and servants. Our servants would charge us for overworking them, so we'll have to work on Sundays and holidays."

Franz Joseph returned his smile. "Come on, Maxi, you're not going to see that in Austria. I'm here, and I belong to the old school."

"That means our lives will be tragic. But we can still adjust, calibrate to the times," he added hopefully.

"Whatever happens will happen," Franz Joseph said offhandedly.

"Here, I brought a manuscript for what I see as a better government. I wrote it for you, sire," Maximilian said as he presented a document to his brother.

"I'll study it very carefully, brother," he promised, taking it from him. "And as for you, you're going from here to Belgium to see if we can bring a princess here to be your wife."

"Yes, sire."

The two brothers hugged and kissed. Maximilian walked away, silently stinging from his brother's hardness against his ideas. And he knew in his heart that Joseph wouldn't change.

Prince Maximilian was supervising his navy in war. He had spent the entire day in the operation room, finally leaving at two o'clock in the morning. Back in his annex, Adele visited him. She presented a colored pencil drawing of the prince with his mother. It was amazing, almost as if someone had taken a moment in time and frozen it to be admired forever. He was impressed and took her in one arm as he held up the drawing and examined it.

"I want to kiss the hand that drew my mother. Yes, she's that beautiful, the most beautiful mother on earth," he said fondly, his eyes smiling as he gazed at the sketch.

"All mothers are beautiful," Adele replied, pleased at his reaction.

"Yes, yes, all mothers are beautiful," he repeated with a large smile as he embraced her from behind, bringing her hand to his lips.

"You want to kiss my hand. Is that a 'thank you?' You know my heart belongs to you. Besides, you can't give me away to anyone else. I'm the property of Maximilian."

"Only he can give you away," Maximilian said as he turned her hands over and kissed the palms.

"But I remain yours?" Adele insisted.

"Yes," he said softly, thinking of Zinnia.

Adele turned to face him. "The charge for this painting will be a kiss on the lips."

"You asked for it." As he kissed her, it became longer, deeper. She took his face in her hands, insisting that her kiss should become more passionate.

Maximilian stopped in mid-kiss. "I left you in Vienna to look after my mother in my absence."

"I took that as my command. But your mother sent me here."

"My younger brother will now be alone in the palace without you," he added. Since his infatuation with Zinnia, he had allowed Ludwig to make advances on Adele. She was deeply hurt by this, but never said anything. In typical royal fash-

ion, the thought that this might have hurt her never really occurred to Maximilian.

"There are many others to look after him," she pouted. "He's a bore."

"You mean his prowess in the bedchamber, or otherwise?" he teased.

"Your Royal Highness knows your brother. I'm a dancer. I told you how he
must have a woman every night." She stamped her foot and sulked prettily. Maximilian laughed. "But as you love your mother, where am I to spend my love? To
me, you're Prince Charming," she said, clinging to him.

"Go, go. I have no time for this. I'm tired …"

Maximilian took the two-by-three-feet pencil drawing of his mother to his
writing desk. Putting a pen to paper, he inscribed:

> "God wanted to show His best creation to angels.
> He called them all.
> He took innocence, coolness, color, song, silence,
> Music, tenderness, rhythm, chirp, restlessness,
> Steadfastness, warmth, thirst, ambiance, sweetness,
> Darkness, tallness from the rest of his creation.
> The angels asked, 'And what is this?'
> And God said, 'A mother.'
>
> The angels saw the mother freely giving everything to her child.
> The angels then declared: 'Surely, only a mother can do that.'

> To my mother,
> Bouquet of roses.…
>> Presented with the pen of my heart,
>> Should I drown?
>> Your sweet memories
>> Can turn the ocean sweet.

> *Yours, Maxi*

He put a blotting paper on the freshly written note. Adele put her arms
around him, reading the note from behind. "Give me that sweetness of yours,"
she enticed him.

Maximilian waved four fingers of his hand. "Go, go. I want to sleep."

She was greatly disappointed, but remained silent and reluctantly left. In the morning, she returned to the prince's room, finding him ready in his admiral uniform.

"Call the carriage," he ordered.

She left to do his bidding with a sad heart and heavy feet.

The horse-driven carriage stopped before Maximilian's annex. He looked magnificent in uniform as he gave orders to his annex staff and then climbed deftly into the open carriage. His bags and a trunk were loaded onto a different cart, and the coach was soon moving out of the annex. "I'm going to the emperor," he told his ADC.

Vienna, Austria

The gilded gates of the royal palace opened. The royal coach drove down the main boulevard, approaching the majestic palace. To Maximilian, it was home, but to the world, it was one of the finest palaces of the world. "Where is the Queen Mother?" he asked a sentry.

"In the garden, Sire," the sentry answered with a salute.

He looked at the wrapped portrait one last time, then walked down the stairs to meet his mother in the garden. Sophie stood waiting for him alone. The magnitude of this moment dawned on her, and she was overcome with tears.

"Mother," Maximilian said, bewildered. "What's wrong?" He hurried to her side, alarmed. She was not one to cry easily, and it worried him.

She looked up at him through her tears. "Oh, Maxi, you know very well why I'm crying. These are tears of joy for your happiness. This is a momentous occasion for the entire family, and it's such a big step forward in your future."

Maximilian smiled, relieved, and embraced her.

"Go ... go on to Belgium, Son. We'll be following shortly."

Maximilian nodded and kissed her cheek before leaving the garden. As he started down the path, his mother's servant Adelaide met him. He smiled, appreciating the good qualities that he knew firsthand had been passed to her daughter. "Good day, Adelaide."

"My lord," she said in a hushed tone. "If I may, I would speak with you briefly."

Maximilian frowned at her demeanor but nodded, allowing her to lead him inside.

"What's the matter?" he asked, sitting and beckoning for her to sit as well.

Adelaide wrung a handkerchief in her hands, perching nervously on the edge of her seat. "Sire, it's about my daughter—"

"You needn't worry, I'm very fond of your daughter," he interrupted, somewhat amused. "She'll be well taken care of after I'm married, I promise you that."

"I appreciate that pledge, Sire, but there's more to it than that." She paused, unsure of herself. "You see, Adele was born in Bavaria because her father was … well, he wasn't of the proper station for the child of a servant."

Maximilian chuckled. "You mean he was of royal blood. Don't worry, I know the entire story. I think the traditional way of dealing with royal bastards is barbaric, and I certainly don't hold it against her."

"Yes, well, I think it's very important that you know just who her father is."

He scoffed. "That's certainly none of my—"

"It's your father, my lord," she interrupted.

Maximilian froze. His eyes narrowed in disbelief. "You mean …"

"Yes, sire, Adele is your half-sister," she said quickly. "I would have told you sooner, but I had no idea that you'd taken … such an interest in her."

He shook his head, still not seeming to believe it. As she examined his face, she finally saw recognition. "I'm sorry, my lord. Please accept my apologies," she said desperately.

He stood, staring into space as he waved his hand to dismiss her. "It's quite all right," he mumbled, and left the chamber in deep confusion.

Later that day, he saw Adele in the garden, her usual place to meet him when they were planning a tryst. She spotted him and their eyes locked as she glanced about for onlookers and then smiled to him. He stared at her and turned, walking away. The smile on her face fell and she frowned in confusion.

After that, Maximilian avoided Adele. She was hurt and confused, but kept her place and said nothing. Young Ludwig kept making his advances and taking her to his chamber regularly. Maximilian asked his brother to leave her be from now on, but he did not dare explain why. Ludwig, however, continued to be Ludwig, and made his advances as often as he liked.

CHAPTER 9

▼

BEHIND THE VEILS OF THE COURT

The court doctor scurried nervously down a long hallway, entering the antechamber outside the king's private rooms. He knocked on the door and a smartly dressed young man answered it.

"Tell the king that Doctor Gustavus is here to see him."

"Come in, Doctor," the king exclaimed, and the young man stepped aside. The doctor stepped into Franz Karl's chamber as he rose from his chair. "What can I do for you today?" the king asked, obviously in a jovial mood.

The doctor hated to bring him bad news, but he had to do it. "Yes, my lord." He looked at the young gentleman and deliberately coughed. "Well, um ... this is a matter of some delicacy concerning Your Highness's court. May we have some privacy?"

"Yes, yes, of course. You're dismissed, Stephen," he said to his page. The young man stood, clearly resenting his sudden dismissal, and left the room with a muttered, "Yes, my lord."

"Well, what is it? Is my family not well? My wife and sons?" The doctor still hesitated. "Good heavens, man, don't keep me waiting," he urged, becoming concerned.

"No, sire, it's concerning the dancing girl that the Belgian princess sent as a gift to your wife," he finally said, the words rapidly spilling over onto each other.

The king let out a disgusted sigh of relief. "Oh, her. I thought this was important."

"Well, you did ask me to examine her, and I did so, just as you asked, immediately … that is to say, post-haste …" Again his words came out rapidly. He seemed totally confused.

"There, there, man. Take a drink of wine," the king said, pouring him a glass and handing it to him. The doctor gratefully accepted it, taking a couple of gulps. "Yes, that's better," Franz Karl said, frowning.

"Well," the doctor started, then coughed, practically sputtering wine everywhere.

"No, no," the king interrupted. "Take a deep breath and calm yourself. You're making no sense at all."

The doctor took a few deep breaths and forced himself to calm down. "The … that girl, the dancer … She's pregnant."

The doctor was startled by Franz Karl's sudden laughter, which went on and on until he finally had to sit down. "Is this what you came about, Doctor?" he barely managed through his laughter. "Just how many of our female servants get pregnant every year?"

"But Sire, the girl says that the bastard is of royal blood," he said loudly over the king's laughter.

Franz Karl paused in mid-laugh. His eyes grew hard, his lips thinned. The doctor winced, bracing himself. The room filled with the king's thunderous shout, "What do you mean, *royal blood*? Surely she's not saying it's one of my sons! Let me see her! *Let me see her!*" he raged.

The king stormed out of the apartment, his face distorted with rage. The doctor trailed along behind him, wringing his hands. They were almost to the queen's royal chambers when Franz Karl slowed his march and willed himself to calm down, knowing it would be more prudent to speak in a quieter tone. He turned to the doctor and whispered roughly, "No one is to hear of this, do you understand me? Absolutely no one!" When he reached Sophie's suite, he straightened his clothing and took a deep breath, collecting himself. He opened the door and called out, in a caricature of himself in a good mood, "Sophie? Are you here, dear?"

Zinnia was alone in the bedchamber, cleaning up after her lady's toilette. She stopped while picking up a towel and walked to the king. Curtseying low, she replied, "No, my lord, your lady is taking a walk in the gardens. I can run and fetch her if you wish."

Franz Karl cut her off, speaking in a voice that was deadly calm. "The doctor says you're pregnant."

Zinnia's expression revealed that she was as shocked at the news as the king. She was silent, not knowing what to say, and finally hid her face in the towel.

"Who's the father?" the former king demanded.

"My lord," she said, the words catching in her throat as she agonized about how to answer. Franz Karl jerked the towel from her, his hand rising as if to strike her.

"Who's the father?" he repeated, louder this time.

She opened her mouth, struggling to speak. "Prince … Prince …"

"I don't want to hear the name. You've violated the royal law," he said, still in that deadly calm tone.

He stormed out of the chamber. Zinnia, now alone again, sank to the floor and wept.

Zinnia was busy cleaning Maximilian's room. She scrubbed and wiped everything thoroughly, working with an intense energy that betrayed her anxiety. Cleaning helped to get her mind off the king's anger with her. Working in Maximilian's room when he was far away also made her feel closer to him, like she was somehow attending to his needs. She paused from her work and put her hand to her swelling abdomen, feeling the tiny flutter of life. Maxi's child … what a joy it would have been under different circumstances.

As she returned to her work, a houseboy entered, bringing her a sealed envelope. She thanked him and waited for him to leave, then frowned with anxious curiosity as she opened it.

"I'll come to you at midnight. No lights. No noises."

Zinnia's eyes widened and she ran to the window to look upon the courtyard. No carriage, no sign that Maximilian was visiting. But who else could have written it? She smiled, knowing full well that, of all men, he would be the one to make a long journey just to arrange a tryst. She tucked the note in her bodice, continuing with her cleaning and humming softly to herself.

At midnight, she got up, anxious, and looked out of her small window. The quarter moon offered little light. She put her forehead to the window, looking out into the inky black night. After a few minutes, she wandered to her cabinet and got out her violin, playing it softly in the darkness. Slowly she began to sing, barely above a whisper.

"A love song it is.
On waves of Life.
Life is meaningless without our story. Lalala la."

The violin joined in sweetly. "Meanings of life, find in stories of love."

A hand softly covered her mouth. She was lifted like a bride, taken to the bed, and covered gently with her fluffy quilt. Her heart pounded in anticipation, taken with the treasure of his love in her heart. She smiled and kept singing softly. "Lalala la." It was her love song.

She suddenly came out of her preoccupation with Maximilian, realizing that something was wrong, very wrong. She instinctively pulled the quilt around her naked body.

"Who are you?" she asked, trembling. There was no answer, and that frightened her even more. Waiting for another tense moment, she finally slipped her legs over the edge of the bed to go light a candle. She froze when a strong hand clamped around her upper arm.

"Hello, baby." She was held firmly next to someone.

This isn't Maxi! her mind screamed. *Who is it?* Her heart hammered in her chest.

"Baby …?" she choked. He never used that term with her.

"Honey … thick and sweet honey dripping from my fingers. It's all right, it's your darling Maxi."

Now she knew this wasn't Maxi. It wasn't his voice, his demeanor, his anything.

"NO!" she shouted, twisting away from that voice and breaking free of that hand. "No!" she gasped, running from the bed. The man snickered from the dark. She grabbed the door handle, but it had been locked. "What makes you think I'm not Maxi?" the voice asked persistently.

"Maxi," she said, forgetting herself in her fear and revulsion. "You're not Maxi! A woman knows her man, knows her husband, even in total darkness!"

"Husband! Ha!" the man exclaimed. She saw the shadow rise from the bed, growing larger as he came closer. She went to dodge to the left but felt those hands clamp her arms again, dragging her toward the bed.

"No, no, no, no, no!" she screamed. The wind was knocked out of her as she was thrown over the edge of the bed on her stomach. The hands pushed down on her back, holding her firmly on her stomach. One of the hands began to wander, stroking and squeezing her.

"Husband …" the voice repeated mockingly. "Just who do you think you are, whore?" the man asked, squeezing her bottom so hard that she gasped in pain. The hands lifted her small body again, flipping her over. She suddenly felt the oppressive weight on top of her. She screamed again, but the hand slapped her and then clamped over her mouth. She could barely breathe, and tears streamed down her face as she felt the man push inside of her. There was no use in trying to escape; the worst was already being done. She squeezed her eyes closed and thought of Maxi, where he must be, how happy he'd be when he discovered she was pregnant with his baby … any fantasy, however outlandish, to keep her from being there. She was NOT there! She was far away, safe, and Maxi would never let anything bad happen to her, ever …

The man shoved her aside and stood. "I'm finished," he announced crudely, his voice dripping with contempt. She curled up in the bed, wincing at the sound of the door being unlocked, opened, and closed again. Finally, the only sound in the dark room was her sobbing, muffled by a pillow in her shame.

The next day, a man and a woman came to her bedchamber. She had never seen them before. They stood over her as she clutched the collar of her robe modestly, trying to hide the trembling of her hand.

"So you're the slut, the dancing girl," the old doctor said, slightly wrinkling his nose as if he smelled something disgusting. "You're to be medically examined."

"I'm a guest here," she replied boldly. "The prince won't tolerate my abuse at your hands."

"The prince isn't here, and guests eventually leave. You're here permanently, yes? Now you must receive a medical exam."

"Who are you?"

"I'm the emperor's physician," he replied. Zinnia knew that was a lie. She had seen the emperor's physician several times, looking in on Sophie. But she knew there was nothing she could do. She looked at the woman, who only stared back. She wondered why the woman was there but dared not question the tight-lipped doctor further, assuming that she served as a witness to the ordeal.

Her robe was stripped away, without any pretense of consideration for her modesty, and a rough, hasty exam was performed. It was over in a matter of minutes, but for her it seemed an eternity.

"Who's the father?" he asked bluntly, closing his black leather bag.

"What do you mean?" she asked, desperately feigning ignorance. The unknown woman smirked.

The doctor could barely hide his disgust. "You're obviously pregnant. Do you know the punishment for servants who get pregnant in the palace?"

Her face turned ashen as the realization of what he was proposing sank in. "No, no. Just wait until Maximilian hears about this."

The man turned a knob on the wall and the gaslights brightened the room.

"Can you keep it a secret?" she begged. "Just keep it secret long enough for Maximilian to be told, please!"

"I have my orders," he flatly replied. "You'll be put in a tower room on top of the castle with a supervising matron. It'll be said that you've gone to meet your people back home. There you'll give birth to your bastard and crush the new-born," he explained with chilling pragmatism. "You'll put the pieces in a pitcher and it'll be dumped in the city sewers, or put into an acid jar."

"Do you think I'd do that?" she asked, shocked.

"You can't give birth to a royal bastard. You and I both know that."

Zinnia began to cry. "Then why did the royals use me? If it's so wrong, why did they do it?"

"Because they're royalty," he explained, irritated. "They're the law. We just obey their law."

"They're the law? What am I?" she sobbed, small tremors shaking her body.

The doctor's face twisted in disgusted hatred. "You're a useless bitch, that's what!"

Hysterical, she spat in his face.

The doctor flinched and closed his eyes. He had a handkerchief in his pocket, but he was so full of revulsion for the Indian whore that her spittle was the last thing he wanted on anything of his. Suppressing the urge to beat her within an inch of her life, he grabbed the lapel of her robe and tore at it, finally ripping a piece free and using it to wipe his face. She shrank back and sat on her bed, scooting into a corner with her back against the wall.

The doctor left the room without another word, the unknown woman silently following behind him.

Two days later, Zinnia sat in a chair, again weeping. They were cutting off her hair, and she sobbed as the dense, three-foot-long tresses fell to the floor in curly black bunches. They continued their sadistic humiliation of her by shaving her head, then her eyebrows. She was given a plain, deliberately ugly dress to wear. By then, her eyes were red and puffy from crying. She wordlessly accepted the dress and put it on.

The order finally came for Zinnia to be moved into the rooftop lodgings of the castle, where she was to stay for the remaining months of her pregnancy. As had been planned, the palace staff was told that she had returned home to India. She was to give birth to the baby and then crush it … no body, no grave. A royal matron, one of the doctor's servants, was appointed to supervise the entire thing, and she stayed near Zinnia constantly.

The time crawled by. Zinnia desperately waited for Maximilian to come rescue her. Sometimes she paced; other times she cried. It sickened her to think about what might happen if he didn't arrive in time. "No," she told herself, "I can't think that way. He'll come and free me. He has to come!"

Finally, the birth was imminent. Maximilian was still far away, with no word of a visit. Zinnia was moved to what seemed to be the darkest tower room of the castle. It was a large room with iron bars in the windows. She spent most of her time alone in bed, wrapping the blanket tight around her to keep warm.

Her austere and callous matron continued to linger nearby, looking for signs that the Indian was going into labor. When Zinnia felt the first pangs, she said nothing, and still remained quiet when her water broke. She finally cried out when a labor pain gripped her with a sharp stab, and the matron rushed into the room.

"You silly girl," the woman snapped, seeing that she had been hiding her labor. "Did you really think I wouldn't find out?" The matron acted as a midwife, and Zinnia's labor was long and hard. When it was over, she demanded the woman give her the baby. She whispered her thanks to Allah as she took the child tenderly in her arms and gazed down into its sleeping face.

The matron was carrying a heavy water pitcher to the bed.

"I can't do it," Zinnia said flatly, clutching the baby. Her eyes narrowed in disgust at the very thought.

The matron loomed over her in a threatening manner. "The baby has to be killed. If you don't do it, you can be killed, too."

"Then kill me. I can't do it."

Exasperated, the matron left the room and sent for the doctor. By the time he reached the tower room, he was furious.

"You will kill it!!" he screamed at the top of his lungs. Zinnia flinched but did not speak, only clutching the tiny bundle in her arms. He stopped himself and took a deep breath before continuing in a calm voice, as if speaking to a slow child. "You've committed a crime. You're to remain silent about the baby forever. You'll be wedded to an army officer who's being posted to Mexico." Zinnia's eyes widened in shock. She was speechless. "Those are the orders you have to obey. Your crime is promiscuity with royalty. You have to disappear."

Even her greatest persuasions couldn't melt the heart of the enforcing doctor. Zinnia was weak after the difficult labor, her body bruised and torn. Still she refused, sensing that, by law, they could not do the deed themselves. Their insistence that she must do it reinforced her suspicion that it had to be done by her, and she shook her head obstinately and held the bundle protectively against her bosom.

After a full twenty-four hours of influence, threats, coercion, even being struck on the head and shoulders, she fell asleep, exhausted. When she awoke, the baby was no longer in her arms. She was dizzy, feeling as if she were dreaming. In the spinning room, she saw the baby spread onto a table beside the bed. The matron was wrapping Zinnia's fingers around the handle of the water pitcher.

"Do it quickly and don't look at the child," the matron advised. "It'll be easier."

Zinnia blinked, trying to make sense of what was happening. In her delirium, they were starting to make sense. She knew that, even if the baby lived, she would never see it again. It probably wouldn't live for long either, simply disappearing so efficiently that no one would even believe her if she suggested that a baby had ever existed. In that moment of exhaustion, she did not pull back as the matron held her hand and guided it, wrapping it around the neck of a heavy candlestick and killing the child. The poor infant was crushed and the pieces put into the pitcher, which was carried away by the matron on a trolley.

Zinnia was an emotional ruin after that experience, destroyed by her actions and her deep regret. *If only I had been strong enough to resist*, she thought to herself over and over again.

She turned to the only activity that brought her any real solace. She sang quietly, wretchedly, alone in the chamber.

John Michael Best was a Belgian officer. He looked forward to the adventure of going to Mexico, but hesitated to leave on such a long mission without a bride. The army had assured him that if he took a wife, her passage would be free. John, thirty-two years of age, was an honorable, well-bred Catholic, and he wanted a wife with whom he could share his nights and days. He understood the loneliness of being a soldier posted so far from home. Up until now, he had been busy achieving all he could in his commitment to the service of his king. There had been little time to think of marriage.

On duty in Commander Picard's office on a bright Monday morning, John's mind wandered to the pressing issue of marriage. He wondered who might make a suitable wife, someone who would not mind being taken so far from home. His thoughts were interrupted by his commander, who strode into the headquarters. "Good morning to you, Colonel Best," the commander greeted him.

"Good morning," John said with a snappy salute.

"King Leopold was sharing a bit of correspondence from Emperor Karl, this morning in his office. I thought of you."

"Of me, sir?" John answered, stunned.

"Yes, he has a bit of a problem with a court dancing girl," he said with a chuckle. "Quite a lovely one, I understand." He watched the young man's face as he spoke, enjoying John's reaction.

"I assure you, sir, I've had no dealings with a court dancer," John answered firmly.

Picard turned towards his office door, suppressing a grin. "Come into my office, Colonel Best. I have something of consequence to discuss with you."

John was flabbergasted. Never before had his superior officer spoken to him in such a familiar way. He followed him into the large office and stood at attention.

Picard sat in an overstuffed chair, smiling. "At ease, Colonel."

John responded with a parade stance, his upper lip beginning to dot with perspiration.

Picard laughed. "No, son, sit down and relax. I'm not going to court martial you. Would you like a smoke?"

"No, sir," John answered, bewildered.

"I'll keep you in suspense no longer. The reason I thought of you when the dancing girl was discussed is because I know you're a bachelor."

"Yes, sir."

"Well, your brother officers have shared your concern at going abroad without a bride. Is it true you have no one in mind?"

"Yes, sir," John replied, baffled by the direction this conversation was taking.

"This girl happens to be in need of a husband, a husband stationed far away from here ... a bit of coincidence, don't you think?" Picard said, observing John closely. "What do you say if I arrange a meeting with the girl tonight in the officers' club?" His eyes softened fondly as John stared at him in wonder. "I've always liked you, John. If I had a son, I would hope he'd be like you. This seems like the least I can do for you before you leave."

Deeply flattered by Picard's remark, John found his voice. "Sir, yes, sir. Is there anything more you would like me to know, sir?"

"No, just be at the club at eight o'clock. Everything else'll be arranged. I'll bring the girl myself to introduce you. You're dismissed until that hour," he answered with a broad smile.

At a quarter until eight o'clock, John stood outside the door of the club. He was wearing his sharp dress uniform, the one he had made specially to take to Mexico. He absentmindedly kept brushing his shoes against the backs of his legs, but they already shone like mirrors. For the sixth time he looked anxiously at his watch. As he waited, thought after thought assaulted his mind. Just why did this girl need a husband? Could she be pregnant by a noble who was trying to get rid of her? Or had she found disfavor at the court? The commander said she was lovely. "I wonder ..." he thought.

It was five minutes before eight o'clock when he finally grasped the door handle and walked into the building. Sitting in the middle of the room was Picard, and beside him was the most astonishing beauty he had ever seen. She was a vision in a lavender and black dress, an Indian veil of the same colors over her head.

The commander certainly didn't mislead me about her beauty, he thought.

Picard stood and introduced the couple to each other. "Colonel Best, I'd like you to meet Zinnia. Zinnia, this is the esteemed Colonel John Michael Best, one of our best officers."

Zinnia was grateful for the mannerly way in which that was done. Someone had left her a sliver of dignity, finally. She smiled demurely from under her lashes. "Good evening, Colonel."

Picard interrupted, "I'll be going home for dinner with the family. I'm sure John will take good care of you." Picard then gave John a wink. "See to it she's at my door by eleven o'clock. You can tell me tomorrow of your decision."

"Yes, sir," John answered, saluting the commander as he left.

Zinnia and John sat quietly for an awkward moment, the tension so thick that they could not move.

After a long silence, John began. "Zinnia, I know this arrangement is as unusual for you as it is for me. First of all, I want you to be assured you'll have a choice in the matter—at least as far as I'm concerned. Marriage for me is a permanent commitment that isn't to be taken lightly. If we marry, I'll give you everything that's due your position, and I'll try with all my heart to love you and care for you. Is there anything about you that I should know?"

Zinnia was taken aback by his honesty and kindness. She blushed and adjusted the veil, making sure it covered her short hair. "John, I can't speak of love, but now that we've met, I know you're a sincere man. There's no hindrance to this marriage. I bring no baggage of any kind, other than some memories that will fade with time. I would be honored to marry you. I'll promise you this: I'll honor you, I'll care for your home, and I'll conduct all of my marital responsibilities. I'll never betray your trust."

John was silent for a moment. He then hesitantly reached for her hand and held it as if it were a rare jewel. Zinnia looked into his eyes and thought, *Allah is merciful. He has sent me a careful husband with a kind nature. I'll be safe with him.*

Several minutes went by while they began the long journey of getting to know each other. It started with more silence, and then John stood. "It's a warm evening. Shall we take a walk? There's a lovely lake close by."

Zinnia stood in answer, and they walked hand in hand out into the night.

At nine o'clock the next morning, the commander saw Zinnia at a late breakfast.

"Good morning, Zinnia. How did your meeting with Colonel Best go last evening?" he asked with a smile.

"Well enough. He seems to be an honorable man," Zinnia answered in a noncommittal manner.

"Honorable? I would think so. He's a fine officer." He stirred his coffee and then looked sidelong at her with a sly smile. "Is there any message you would like me to deliver?" he pressed.

"John knows my mind on those matters. Talk to him," Zinnia answered.

"Well, well, 'John,' is it? I take it you got along smartly?"

"Yes, sir. We have an understanding."

"Grand! Good to hear it."

In two days, John was to leave for Mexico, so there was little time for ceremony. John wore his uniform and Zinnia her traveling clothes, taking their vows in front of a judge in Commander Picard's drawing room. The whole process took less than ten minutes.

On board ship the next day, Zinnia and John strolled the deck, taking in the ocean air.

"How are you today, wife?"

"Well, thank you. And you?"

"Good. I do have a question, though. Just what did you do to cause your exile from court?"

"That's in the past, John. We must now look forward to the future."

"Zinnia, I need to know. It'll ease my mind. You know what they say, 'Confession is good for the soul,'" he said with a tentative smile. He was pressing gently, but he knew something terrible must have happened. On their wedding night, he had discovered that under those veils was surprisingly short hair. When he had asked her why it was so short, her eyes had filled with tears. Yes, something had happened, and he had to know.

Zinnia resisted. "If what I did is a sin, it's between me and God. I'll repair it. I'll decide ... I'll set things right."

"But I'm your husband!"

"I take responsibility for my destiny, John. Life is difficult, but I'm stoic. I'll not choose to give in. I remain unconquered."

John looked at his wife with a curious expression. "What a thoroughly brave statement. I see you differently now, Zinnia. You're not a refugee from failure, but a soldier with a plan."

"You see, John, others can't judge humans when they sin against God. The clergy has made gold out of other people's sins, but sins aren't for sale. If you sin, you set it right with God, not man."

"What wisdom from one so lovely," John stated softly, his eyes soft with tenderness. He placed his hands on her shoulders and looked deeply into her eyes, finally kissing her forehead. "Oh, Zinnia," he whispered.

"Oh Zinnia, Zinnia." Maximilian was whispering, too, but on the high seas, as he tossed and turned in the grip of a high fever.

CHAPTER 10

▼

A ROYAL WEDDING

In the year 1857, Prince Maximilian arrived in Belgium to see King Leopold I. He was given a full royal welcome and led to an elaborate suite that included several servants to care for his every need.

The next day, the engaged couple rode happily in a coach, King Leopold in another coach beside them. As they passed along a public road, the king began one of his lessons.

"Look at the subjects carefully," he taught. "They face six problems: food, clothing, shelter, sex, leisure, and a socio-political system not based on force. The first five problems are personal, with each person having his own requirements. The last problem gives birth to a collective problem, which in turn gives birth to a contract. Who, how, what, where, when … can mankind have a system without force in its surroundings?"

Maximilian smiled, thinking this lesson strangely familiar to him. Leopold was again carefully practiced, as if reading a speech.

The king continued with enthusiasm, enjoying the sound of his own voice immensely. "In history, man has put his neck into various yokes, but each yoke has exacted a price in blood and frustration. In which yoke does he pay the smallest price for obedience to an authority? That's the main political question of humanity. I think a good, kind, and noble king can do that."

Maximilian sparred, sneaking a wink at Charlotte. "Kings require an establishment, my lord, a structure in place to support their will. They work to make people obedient to them. Force demands obedience and punishes defiance. Mankind is leaving kingship behind, sire. Mankind has gotten away from those who have force, and now the kings want it back. This chills the blood of each peaceful person."

The king fell silent, disappointed that his rehearsed lesson did not seem to have the dramatic effect he'd hoped for. This prince's ideas fascinated him, but his bold, outspoken nature sometimes rankled the king, especially when he did it in front of others.

Leopold might have chosen differently for his daughter, but Charlotte was in love, so he was allowing the sixteen-year-old to make her own choice. Part of him was just happy to see her coming out of her shell and enjoying herself more, but another part of him missed the old Charlotte. Yes, she'd been a sad and serious girl, but they had seemed to have more in common back then, and their time together was something he missed and greatly treasured. Seeing her married was the proudest day of his life with her, but it was also the saddest.

On his second visit to Brussels, Maximilian talked with Charlotte about his liberal, idealistic, and Byronic ideas. He showed her the drawings for the villa Miramar, being built in medieval style near Trieste, and fascinated her with the stories of his travels to exotic places.

The royal wedding between Prince Maximilian and Princess Charlotte took place in the most glamorous style. The entire European royalty attended the lush affair, which promised to be the subject of gossip for months thereafter. They were married at last on July 27, 1857. Departure of the couple, their families, and guests to the cathedral for the blessing began at 10:45. The road was lined with excited people, happy and proud to see members of the royal families. The route wound from the Grote Market to the Kanselarijstraat, then finally to Cathedral Square. At 11:15, the royal coaches reached the cathedral.

They exited the coach amid much pomp and ceremony. Charlotte was lovely and petite, with dark eyes and hair. Twenty-four-year-old Maximilian was tall and as fair as Charlotte was dark. His full and luxurious blond beard was the talk of the gentry as they entered the cathedral.

The cathedral was filled with thousands of white azaleas, camellias, rhododendrons, and hydrangeas in honor of the royal couple. The cardinal led the nuptial mass in the cathedral of Saint Michael and Saint Gudula. The religious service had a classical character, with the music of Johann Sebastian Bach and Belgian composers. King Leopold entered the church holding his daughter on his arm, wearing the uniform of a lieutenant general of the Belgian army. He beamed with pride.

Maximilian was dressed in the full uniform of an Austrian admiral, with the collar of the Order of the Golden Fleece around his neck. He was as handsome a bridegroom as any young girl could have wished for. Charlotte was a glowing bride in her wedding dress of white and silver brocade with a stunning Belgian lace veil.

A lovely mass was followed with a traditional wedding sermon. It was a solemn occasion, but also indescribably beautiful. At 1:25 that afternoon, the couple and royal procession left Cathedral Square, traveling for an hour and a half before finally arriving at the royal palace in Brussels.

At 2:00, the couple and their parents appeared on the balcony of the royal palace. There was a reception for the guests, followed by the official photographs. At 3:00, there was a wedding luncheon. The combined nobility and royalty of Europe were fed on twenty-four-carat golden plates, spoons, and glasses.

After a marvelous dancing show, they all came out singing in the garden. Each of the royal houses was presented with a horse, complete with a royal crest on his apron, as a gift from the emperor. By 5:15 that evening, the family photographs were being taken, and then the royal couple finally rode back to Laeken Palace in a beautiful gilded coach, amid all the splendor due to such an occasion.

It was not quite over for the exhausted couple. At 6:30, there was a grand reception at the royal castle in Laeken. The finest Austrian crystal goblets brimming with champagne were prepared on magnificent heavy gold serving trays. The newlyweds were toasted again and again, as is still the tradition now.

The gift horses, tied to their coaches, left the palace in the morning. The church bells rang as Maximilian picked up his wife amidst cheers, taking her into the bridal chamber. The door closed firmly behind them.

"Where's the lop-off?" the princess asked.

Maximilian laughed. "No lop-offs anymore. I'll have the main course from now on."

Charlotte tried to sing the love song bursting from her heart, but she was overwhelmed at the effort and only managed to murmur a soft "Tut, tut" before Maximilian stopped her with an ardent kiss.

The days following the wedding were taken up with so many banquets, balls, and receptions that Maximilian and Charlotte did not have a moment to themselves. They left Brussels on July 30th and traveled across the Belgian frontier into

Germany. They embarked on a river steamer at Bonn and traveled up the Rhine to Nuremburg and up eastern Bavaria to where a flower-decked boat was waiting to take them down the Danube to Vienna, bound for the majestic Schonbrunn Castle.

They were finally in Austria and boarding a canal ship, properly decked and laden for the royal couple.

"Everything is so perfect. Is there anything missing in our honeymoon?" Charlotte sighed, watching the sun set on the Danube.

"The singing *choonga*. She's missing," Maximilian said wistfully.

Charlotte was thoroughly charmed both by the luxurious palace and by its elaborate grounds. "What a beautiful garden," she murmured. "It's so green and bright. The wind ripples over the grass like waves on the ocean." She was nervous as they stepped down from the coach and entered the palace, her anxiety mounting further as they walked towards the dining room where she was to meet Maxi's family for the very first time. Charlotte was talking rapidly, giving Max little time to respond. It was more of a stream of consciousness than an actual dialogue.

"Oh Maxi, do you think they'll like me?"

"But of course they'll—"

"Is this dress right for the occasion? It doesn't make me look like a child, does it?"

"Anything but a—"

"I'm so short! I have to be aware of those types of things, you know. You have to help me."

"Yes, dear," Maxi said as he opened the door to the dining room, smiling to himself.

The ambiance of the red dining room was at once luxurious yet intimate. The table was set with the Hapsburg rose pattern, with royal blue bands etched with large pink roses. Austrian crystal stemware covered the table alongside Hapsburg silver. Flowers were artfully arranged on all of the tables. Charlotte was impressed. She had always thought her father's palace was beautiful, but with all of the gold embellishments and treasures from throughout the world around her, she had to admit that Schonbrunn was even more beautiful.

Maximilian began the introductions. "First let me introduce you to my mother and father." He did so with all of the appropriate titles accorded each one. Sophie was the first to move towards Charlotte, her arms outstretched. She kissed her on both cheeks and embraced her. Franz Karl stood back until Sophie was finished, then he stepped forward.

"Let's have a look at you," he said in a friendly tone.

Charlotte tried to straighten her dress and smooth her carefully pinned hair as he appraised her, walking her to a bank of windows bathed in sunlight. "Yes, Maxi, you were correct in referring to her as a royal beauty. Welcome, my child."

She smiled and blushed a tiny bit. "Thank you, Your Majesty."

"No, no," the emperor insisted. "Call me Karl."

Sophie then took over the introductions. "Charlotte, this is my eldest son, Emperor Franz Joseph, and his wife, Empress Elizabeth of Bavaria. We simply call her Sissi," she added with a smile.

"Hello, Charlotte," Sissi said with a sincere smile. "I know we'll become good friends."

Sophie continued. "And this handsome young man is Ludwig, Maximilian's younger brother."

Charlotte curtsied sweetly. "I'm so glad to meet you all at last. I'm certain I'll be happy here."

A week later, Charlotte and Maximilian were walking in the Schonbrunn gardens. The path they walked had been carefully trimmed and maintained by hundreds of royal gardeners throughout the years, each trying to outdo the one before him with his skill and labor. Each small stone pebble in the walk had been smoothed by a team of two men pulling a large roller. The walks were lined with tulips, pale yellow ones lifting their heads towards the sun in contrast to neighboring brilliant red ones with fist-sized blooms. While walking through the spectacular park at the bottom of the garden, Charlotte spied the garden maze that had been built in Maria Theresa's time.

"This is an amazing place," she exclaimed.

"You know, as adults, this is a peaceful maze with a wandering path ... but I remember it as an adventure, from back in the days when Franz, Ludwig, and I were boys."

"I wish I could have been a little mouse, so I could have seen you play. But of course you wouldn't have seen me," Charlotte giggled.

"To us, it was a safari in Africa, a dangerous battlefield, or mountainous waves engulfing our ship. Not being able to see landmarks over the tall hedges was magical. It was our paradise. It's so thick we seemed a thousand miles away from the eyes of our parents and governesses." After finding their way through the maze, they climbed up some stairs to overlook the confusing maze and all of its dead ends. Max was as excited as a boy on Christmas morning. "I want to be the first to show you the ruins of the 'glorious place,' as you so aptly named it." They strode with purpose towards Neptune's fountain and the Gloriette.

Charlotte laughed at his little-boy eagerness. "Ruins! Surely you jest. These grounds are exquisite, just perfect."

Upon rounding the next turn, she saw the ruins. There was a large Roman arch with fallen columns, statues, and stones. The fountain in front of the ruins contained statues of a Roman man with some women, talking and gathering water.

As she gaped at the scene, a strong gust of wind came suddenly upon them, raising her skirts to scandalous levels. She squealed, one hand slapping down the skirts as her other hand jerked to her head, trying not to lose all of the hairpins from her elaborate coiffure. A fast and hard rain shower fell from out of nowhere.

"It looks like an umbrella," Maximilian observed, watching the billowing skirts. Charlotte giggled and ran ahead of him to a small building built in the neo-classical style.

He took his time in catching up, amused and enjoying his young wife's embarrassment. When he reached her, he could see that her wet garments were clinging to her body sensuously. Her beautiful dark hair hung in damp ringlets around her shoulders. She fretted as she tried to set things right.

"Stand still, don't you move an inch," he said in his most commanding voice. "You're enchanting. This is a sight a man doesn't see every day."

He leaned his tall body over her, resting his face on her forehead to breathe in her fragrance. He then kissed her, tiny kisses all over her brows and eyes. He was so tender and sincere; she was left weak from the power of his nearness and great affection. He spread his cape on the cobblestones for her to stand on, and they stood in the tiny building to wait out the rainstorm. It drummed on the roof in a rhythmical humming sound. They were truly alone—a rare occasion for people of their station—with no family or guards staring over their shoulders.

Charlotte returned each of his kisses passionately. Her body was hungry and she shivered slightly from both the damp air and her own anticipation. Maximilian slowly untied her bodice as they kissed, opening it to reveal her breasts. She shivered as the cool air touched her bare skin. He took one of her breasts tenderly in his hand, tasting the nipple gently. She moaned, her body aching with desire as he kissed and suckled her, lifting her and setting her gently on the ledge there. The brief storm blew outside with the gentle rumble of thunder as his hand slid up her skirts. Their passions grew with the wind, their young bodies and minds lost in their mingling as one. They lay in the little building, watching the sun return to dapple the cobblestone walk outside. Charlotte rested in the crook of his arm, as lazy as a cat. Her eyes drifted around the room until she spied a beautifully carved "M" in the stone wall of the neo-Roman building.

"Oh, I see now," she teased. "You've had so many young maidens here that they finally built this structure and engraved an "M" in remembrance of you."

They laughed as they straightened their clothing and prepared to continue their walk.

With Mother

"Well then, Mother, I got married … but what comes next?"

She eyed him warily. "Yes, now you're married off … but I hear you're fond of someone else."

"That someone else is my mother," he replied with a wink.

Sophie didn't respond to that. She watched her son as he sat down and cuddled one of her small, white Bichon dogs.

"Your brother wants to send you to Italy as a governor, to acquire knowledge of the governance. Your father agrees. He says, 'Enough battlefield medals. Let him be a king. Let's see how he does it. Italy's a fine training ground.'"

"In that case, it's clear to me that I'm not seen as fit to be the next in line to the Hapsburg throne," Maximilian stated flatly. "He wants me to go experiment elsewhere, being a king or turning out to be a joker."

"What makes you say a thing like that?"

"During the past seven hundred years, the old Hapsburg monarchs learned a few tricks of the trade. They knew how to present themselves as better kings and emperors. They said that a Hapsburg had no divinity, that he was closer to the people he rules. They learned how to wriggle out of bad situations, and they allowed dissent. No more Thirty Years' War between the Christians; let's focus on the Muslims, on Turkey. Then they united the crusaders against the Turkish empire. But they never marched against the infidel; it was just a ruse to knit all of the Europeans together."

Sophie frowned, not understanding what he was trying to say.

He saw the uncertainty in her face and sighed, trying to find better words. "The government is so dry that it would crack the faces of our ministers, should they ever smile. Mother, all of our territories are contested by internal rebellion and external encroachments. Are they beating a dead horse? Dissent is the roadmap by which we see how the world has progressed. I'm not a dissenter, Mother. I just want to be with the world." He looked hurt, and she sensed it was because he knew that his brother wanted him far away from the possibility of influence on those who could help him to the Hapsburg emperorship. It was a show of distrust, all but proving that Joseph's influential ministers were indeed whispering into his ear about Maximilian and possible intrigues.

"My dear boy, don't you see that you'd get a chance to put your policies in place in Italy?"

"Yes, but I'm being pushed out on purpose. If my policies are so sound that I can try them in Italy, why not implement them here?"

"Maxi, just go to Italy," she urged.

"Fine, I'll go," he said, ending the conversation. "Where's Zinnia?" he asked, looking around the suite.

"Oh my dear ..." Sophie hesitated. "I regret to tell you this ... but she went back to India. There's a war going on there now, and ... oh, it's so difficult to tell you this, dear, but I've heard she may be dead. It's possible that her kinsmen killed her for living with a tommy." She watched his eyes widen ever so slightly, and her heart broke at having to lie to him. "It's part of their culture, you know," she added helplessly.

"I don't believe that," he said firmly, staring out the glass doors and into the garden. "This news is too hard to bear," he mumbled, his eyes becoming glassy. He fell silent, scarcely noticing when his mother reached out for his hand and squeezed it. He stood and walked onto the balcony. It took several minutes to compose himself.

When he caught his breath, he stepped back in, staring mutely at his mother's worried face. He finally replied, "We'll have great gala nights of dancing and music. The future belongs to dancers and musicians." His strong voice wavered a bit. "We'll miss her."

"So I can tell your father that you're willing to go back to Italy?"

"On one condition," he said, turning to his mother. His eyes were blazing. "My brother must learn what happened to Zinnia."

Sophie blinked in surprise. "A throne is given to you, but you're left with a desire to search for a lost dancer? Does that signify anything?"

He stared for another moment, then sat in the chair across from her and took her hand. "Mother, I have a confession to make."

She was surprised at his reaction. "Your secret is safe with me, son," she replied, her brow furrowing.

"Mother ... I love Zinnia. It might be uncomfortable for you to hear that, but I love her."

"Love, a word of a thousand meanings. Does she love you?"

"A thousand times more."

"But Maxi, you're a prince. That kind of love … with that kind of woman, it's outside your domain."

"I know that," he sighed.

"And what about Charlotte?"

"Oh Mother, she's the best wife I could ever have. But if there's a chance that Zinnia is alive, she may someday return to you. Please, let me write letters to you, and you keep them for her in case she comes. I'll send presents, jewelry. Just keep them in case she comes. Tell her to sit before you, dressed up as my bride, and have her sing that old song, 'Oh, Where Has Love Brought Me.' Please, Mother, I beg of you, do this for me?"

Sophie was moved by his desperate pleas. Her hand lifted from her lap and tenderly touched his cheek. "Oh, my poor son, I wish you weren't a Hapsburg."

Maximilian finally wept, dropping to his knees before his mother's chair and lowering his head onto her bosom. Sophie felt a lump in her throat as she leaned forward and encircled him like a swan taking her chick under her wing.

"I'm such a self-centered fool, Mother," he moaned through his tears. "I should be grieving my poor Zinnia, but all I can think about is how lonely I'll be without her."

Sophie hushed him softly, murmuring comforting sounds as she gently rocked her body and held her dearest son.

That same day, Maximilian told Charlotte the news he had received about Zinnia. They were both deeply disturbed and found it difficult to show a happy face in public for some time after that. But the passage of time coupled with important futures to plan served to distract them from thoughts of the Indian dancer. She was more than a servant to them, especially to Maximilian, but she was still a servant, as well. He and Charlotte had both been raised on the assumption that they were more important than any servant in their grand estates, and this was a belief that subconsciously guided their actions, despite Maximilian's idealisms about the common man and his plight. They put the dancer's memory in the backs of their minds and returned to the business of day-to-day life. It was the only way they could continue with their public existence.

The prince's bedchamber walls were paneled in rich wood, draped with tapestries depicting several hunting and naval scenes. Charlotte was lying on the large bed, writhing with lazy pleasure on the furs that covered it. Maximilian leaned over the bed and embraced his new wife. "I've been evil, a sailor's kind of evil," he warned her.

"Can we place a wager on it?" she answered with a wink, making him laugh.

"I'm a sailor, lady, and sailors have a woman in every port!" he confessed.

"And I've been a lonely princess. I could get whatever I wanted and I didn't have a mother to watch over me. But you had an observant mother ... so how could you be so bad?"

"My mother sleeps, my dear, and she's a collector of beautiful maids. I have easy access to all of her sleeping beauties!"

Charlotte embraced him passionately. "Try this sleeping beauty, my prince."

He chuckled at her drama, tracing his finger along the curve of her breast. He abruptly stood then, turning to leave. "That's a good idea. Sleep now, and I'll come back at midnight."

Charlotte squealed and threw a pillow after him, laughing at his joke. "You'd better be here at midnight, or perhaps I'll give up on my charming prince!"

Maximilian grinned as he closed the door and walked down the hallway. He became more thoughtful as he gazed at the dozens of Hapsburg family portraits lining the hall. His pace slowed a bit as he passed them, looking at them as if they might tell him something to guide him. He was surprised when he snapped out of his musings and realized he had reached his intended destination, his mother's suite of royal apartments.

Sophie was sitting where she usually was when he paid her a visit in her suite, on her chaise lounge reading a book. She looked up in surprise. "You're in the wrong room, Maxi," she quipped, laughing at her own joke.

"I'm in the right room. You're my first love, Mama."

"All right, give your first love a hug then."

He did as he was asked. It was a very long hug.

She directed Maximilian towards a settee beside her. "Sit awhile and we'll talk. How's your new bride? She's such a lovely girl."

"She's quite well. I couldn't be happier with her."

"What did you like in her that made you decide on marriage?"

"First, her father's advice. I became a bit bored with his speeches, but I still usually liked them. He's a wise ruler."

Sophie chuckled at his youthful interpretation of the king of Belgium.

"Another reason was her personality and charm," he continued. "And then, finally, her lop-off."

"What's a lop-off?" she laughed.

"It's a complicated story, Mama. I won't speak of it now. But Charlotte is definitely the woman I've chosen."

"And what was it about her specifically that made you decide?"

"Her naked beauty," he replied, that familiar twinkle in his eye.

"Well, isn't it time you left to go enjoy it?" she said, again laughing.

"There's a lifetime ahead to do that."

"Well then, what was so important about her father's advice?" she inquired, stretching on the chaise.

"Many things, Mama. He's like a developer of beauty and majesty. He'll pull down the best palace in the world in order to build a better one in its place. That excites my imagination. I want to do that with the monarchy, pull it down and build something even better in its place. That will require collecting the best wisdom and expertise in the world. It's like collecting the best bricklayers, wall makers, designers, decorators … You need them, in order to build things better."

"So you're fixed on fashioning a better lifestyle for everyone?"

"Yes. Not just for kings and emperors, and not just for the rich and powerful. It would be for the poor, the people. I want to improve their lives."

"That means you'll be pitted against the establishment. But then, that's the way the Hapsburgs have always ruled."

"Yes," he agreed with conviction.

"The establishment has power. They'll turn against you."

"I'm aware of that."

How he worried her lately! "How would you fight their power?" she asked.

"Through the power of the people."

"You can't mean emancipation?"

"Yes, Mama."

"Will the people follow a king emancipator or a Garibaldi emancipator?" she asked, referring to the dictator general who had fought a bloody takeover in Volturno.

"That's my challenge—to find out, Mama."

"You're a risky king. Your brother can't risk making you his heir, if he can help it."

"Joseph is excellent here. You were right when we talked about it before; I have to look for another pasture."

"Napoleon's asking for you to be the Mexican emperor."

"A Mexican emperor with a French army occupying the country with me?"

"A king needs an army in order to keep himself on the throne, Son."

"Should I take the treasury and give it to the army and police? Take money from the people, whose power I'll need?" he asked, exasperated.

"Maxi, the army and police grant you the power you need," she retorted.

"They're the aristocrats I hate to associate with. They're so easy to purchase."

"Oh, my boy, what serious talk at such a time! You have a bride waiting! Go see her naked," she joked. "Enjoy your young bride. Go now, go ..."

Maximilian kissed his mother, plucked a flower from the vase beside her, and tossed it to his mother's beautiful maid with a twinkle in his eye.

He entered his room at midnight as promised and found Charlotte wide-awake, waiting for him in the huge bed. She wore a beautiful negligee of white lace and a devilish smile. He picked up her nightcap of matching white lace, slipped a flower into it, and placed it on her head.

She looked at the mirror and, seeing that the cap was crooked, offered him an affectionate laugh.

He picked her up and carried her to the next room, which contained a small swimming pool. Setting her next to the pool, he said boldly, "My first command, my beautiful bride, is to strip off your clothes!"

"At your command, sire." Gracefully, she removed her negligee and stood naked.

Maximilian came closer, holding her face with two fingers and smelling her hair.

"My second command," he said in a low voice, his face only inches away, "is to give me your pleasure ..."

He kissed her deeply, lifting her again and suddenly throwing her into the pool. She went with a splash and a shriek as he dove in after her. He led her to deeper water and they swam together, twisting together like two coins in a gambler's fingers.

They ate their breakfast the next morning in the Marie Antoinette room, which glowed with wall candelabras of Bohemian glass. The walls were white with gold paneling, adorned with a Gobelin tapestry based on the famous painting by Vigee-Le Brun, showing the French queen with her three children.

"See how my mother's had the room decked with flowers? You're sitting like a flower. It's difficult to find you amongst them!" Maximilian said, pleased.

Charlotte smiled. "This reminds me of a story my father told me. When I was a child, my father used to fill my room with dolls. It was difficult to distinguish me from those dolls ... until I winked at him." She smiled at the memory. "Oh, my dear father."

Maximilian closed his eyes, smiling as well. "Let me imagine it ... what are you? A doll or a rose?"

Charlotte chuckled and Maximilian peeked open one eye. "Perhaps you're both." He stood. "Now have the best breakfast of your life. Come."

They entered the adjacent room. The table had been laid out for only two people. He rang a bell and a long line of waiters came to offer breakfast dishes. The butler formally listed the names of the dishes offered.

"This is indeed the best breakfast of my life," Maximilian exclaimed, lifting his fork to his mouth. He was pleased that his new bride seemed enchanted by his carefully planned breakfast.

Charlotte sighed, relaxed. "Before I left Belgium, my father picked three cooks from the kingdom and they made a breakfast like this one. My father said, 'Your first breakfast must remind you of me saying good morning to you.'" She lifted her glass. "So good morning to you, Father."

Maximilian also lifted his glass. "To His Majesty! Your father is quite a connoisseur of talents. He organizes talent for higher achievements."

"Yes," Charlotte agreed.

The romantic young groom could not help but notice that her skin glowed a soft creamy white in the morning light, just the shade of a magnolia blossom. "You know, I wanted his advice on organizing an emperor's job, and on how to develop 'good feeling' among the people."

Charlotte pouted playfully. "When you visited my lands, you were picking me, not advice on your job."

"Your father helped me pick both," he said, laughing broadly.

"Is there any dish you've missed in this royal breakfast?" she asked pleasantly.

"Yes … " He picked her up and commanded all of the servants to leave. "This exquisite pudding." He placed her tenderly on the table. A small sharp pair of scissors was taken slyly from his cuff, and he began to gently snip away at her bodice. He started on the right, going down and across her stomach to go back up again. When he was done, he tossed the scissors aside and lifted the bodice from her, revealing her creamy breasts in the morning light. He caressed them gently, brushing his fingertips over her rosy nipples. She arched her back, eagerly, offering the swollen breasts to his lips while her fingers buried themselves in his hair. Accepting her invitation, he leaned over and took one of her erect nipples into his mouth.

"Tut, tut," she said in amusement, writhing in pleasure.

The newlyweds walked in the garden, one of the best kept in all of Austria. When they reached its farthest point, Maximilian gestured, directing Charlotte's gaze to the sight of a new palace gleaming in the distance. "That is a gift to us from my father. We're going to live there," he commented, pointing. "We're not even going to carry any clothes there. It has new clothes, new shoes, new cutlery … everything new."

"And this newly eaten pudding?" Charlotte joked, blushing.

"Doll," he countered.

Charlotte set her jaw stubbornly. "No more doll, no more baby-doll, no more virgin girl. Just a wife, God have mercy on you!"

"God have mercy on both of us!" he chimed in cheerfully.

Suddenly she turned and pulled him by the arm, almost dragging him to the bushes nearby. "Come, prove your manhood to me! Take me right here, right now, and let me see that manhood you want to satisfy!"

She used her hands skillfully, watching his face to see what pleased him, and climbed over him, kissing his face and neck. It was a wild scramble in the bushes, as if two wild animals were wrestling in the tall grass. The two began to writhe in sex, and she began to sing in imitation of their lop-off. "Tut, tut … tastes so sweet you … tut, tut … " She found herself singing almost exactly like her friend, the dancer.

Back in the palace at dinner, the princess was at her best, the epitome of elegance and refined manners.

"What's this?" Maximilian asked, marveling at her demeanor.

"Royal etiquette," she replied, her eyes flashing a lovely green. "I get daily lessons in it."

"And what was that?" Maximilian asked, gesturing towards the gardens and what had happened there earlier.

She had a very special smile on her face. "Tut, tut?" she said. "That … was an oven crackling with fire."

"Fire-cracker? Or sex-cracker?"

The princess lifted her head and clearly replied, "Etiquette is for here. What I do in the bushes is my sweet will. In this palace, I'm a princess. Outside … I long to be a country girl taken by her beloved in the flower beds." She called in a musician and asked him to play some romantic violin music.

"So what was that in the bushes?" he asked again, ever so softly.

"Tut, tut … you taste so sweet, my lover … yes, the oven is hot," she replied breathlessly.

"What should be our code word for a rampage inside a flower bed?" he whispered, grinning.

She blushed. "The oven is hot?" she suggested. The violin started playing.

"Not again!" he exclaimed with pleasure, causing her to laugh and shush him.

She placed her arms around his neck. "It suddenly came to me today, I can sing."

"I'll remember that, too," he said, kissing her neck.

"Fashion me a brooch showing an oven on fire, then be careful of when I wear it," she proposed cleverly.

Maximilian was overcome with laughter and finally replied, chuckling, "Yes, I'll do that. Smart girl."

CHAPTER 11

▼

ASHES TO ASHES

Mexico

Inspector Carillo's superintendent of police, Diego, was visiting the police station. Everything was looking in top shape, with the policemen dressed smartly in their proper uniforms and shining silver epaulettes. The now superior police chief Diego complimented Carillo for his top-notch inspection, advising him to relax.

"Let the city be run by private contractors," Diego said.

Carillo listened to his advice in amazement. "What about police rules and the law?" he asked.

"Relax," Diego said, amused.

"But that'll bring up a mafia," Carillo said worriedly.

"You can offset that with another."

"That'll start a gang war," Carillo objected.

"Then the gangs will finish each other."

"How? They can band together to become an overwhelming force."

"The police will be facilitated in its work by the members of both gangs. They can inform the police about all activities in the city."

Carillo listened carefully. He was sure now that the police chief and all of the judges and magistrates were extortionists. "Well, how do you get a bail for a murderer?" he asked, and then answered himself cynically. "By getting money from the murderer in advance ... half for the police and the other half for the judge, right?"

"Relax ..."

"How can I relax if the people are never going to see the murderers punished?" he asked in exasperation to the cool-headed chief. He stepped closer to Diego and lowered his voice. "The people will take the law into their own hands ... anarchy! The police are designed to make sure that nobody takes the law into his own hands! Sir, you should resign," he said abruptly, forgetting himself in his idealistic outrage.

"You could go to jail for punishing the murderers," Diego said, still in that calm, chilly tone.

"How?"

"You'll save the murderers from the wrath of a mob. The murderers will snatch weapons and wave them towards the mob, maybe kill one or two. The mob will run away. Those murderers will then attack you. If you win the attack, you'll be charged as their murderer."

"You know the police law," Carillo reminded him solemnly.

"I do, and I know far more than that. The judge can't punish without evidence. The barman always wins." Carillo's eyes narrowed in anger. "I was taught that honesty is the best policy, that truth must prevail ... that sincerity wins in the end, and that the police were made to ensure that no one takes the law into his own hands. Now you're telling me something else."

Diego thought about this for a moment before replying. "Not something else, Carillo. Something more. Honesty, rules, truth ... they come late, often when the entire foundation on which an honest man stands and lives is wasted. An honest officer will be put down and punished. He can't beat the dishonest world at its games."

He saw the anxiety in Carillo's eyes and patted his shoulder. "Relax. Seek advice from more experienced men. Beat the dishonest man at his own game. Crush the bad opponent with his own weight. Honesty, rules, straightforward- ness are only half the game. It takes more than that to win the game."

"So there's deeper wisdom in asking a police officer to relax, not to be tense?" Carillo muttered, partly to himself.

Diego gazed out the window and shrugged. "Yes. Look outside. It's spring- time. Life is short, so just relax. Why take on tension, worries, and headaches? Yours is a twenty-four-hour, seven-day job. If you take on all of that tension, your life will become miserable."

"But what about my *duty*?"

"Relax, Carillo," the older man answered.

"What about my duty?" Carillo insisted again in a lower tone. "What about my oath to see that no one takes the law into his own hands? My duty to ensure that citizens sleep peacefully, and to see that justice is done?"

"That's the job of the judges," Diego snapped.

Carillo knew that he was pushing the man's patience, but he could not help himself. "Their jobs depend upon my job. I have to take the criminal to them, along with the evidence. If I relax, the mafia will start charging money for delivering justice. That will make the judges redundant. Your philosophy is suited for someone who shouldn't be in police service. I have to be honest. I have to catch the criminals. I have to make sure that no one is too afraid to file a criminal report. I have to put the criminals away in jails so that others can sleep and work peacefully! Your recipe is to relax, just let it happen. That'll fill the jails with innocent and poor people. The rich and the clever will overtake the others. That would be a free-style fight."

"Duty. That's the bug," Diego snorted.

"Yes, sir, that's the bug. The soldier must fight. He can't relax or run away. The police officer must fight crime."

"Oh dutiful one," Diego retorted sarcastically. "You'll see what your duty does for you. Have it your way, but I'm not responsible for what happens!" he exclaimed, leaving Carillo's office in a huff.

Father Antonio Villar was a tall man with straight black hair and piercing dark eyes. He was the firstborn child of the ruling Spanish elite, dedicated from his birth to the Catholic Church. His family was vastly wealthy and gave him the best education available. He never had to earn money; to him, it was only a tool, whether it was his mother's gold or a peasant's pesos dropped into the alms plate. It was known from the beginning that he was to gain power and prestige in the Church, perhaps even have a place in the Vatican. He had already climbed to the prestigious rank of bishop.

Villar was a sort of uncrowned king, a priest living in splendor. He even had deputies loyal to him in the police department, and one of those men was now the superintendent of police, Officer Diego.

Deputies were excellent police officers. They could speedily solve several cases, then keep four or five special ones and make sure they were never solved. Villar also had paid informants to make sure the justice system stayed on his side, despite the actions of the occasional self-righteous officer like Carillo.

It was midday when the janitor entered the cathedral in search of Bishop Villar. He was a paid informant who worked at the local school, and he had news about one of the teachers there, Señora Pilar Covas Molina. She was a widowed woman in her early thirties, an energetic teacher, one of the children's favorites. Earlier that day, a very serious student named Manuel had come to her with a story of bribery and revenge against his family, instigated by Bishop Villar. Señora Molina had suggested that his family go to Inspector Carillo for help.

Bishop Villar frowned. "This woman will bring me trouble."

"Yes, Father," the janitor nodded.

He thanked the janitor and paid him his fee, excusing him. Later that day, he contacted one of his friends at the police station and informed him that it had been brought to his attention that Señora Molina was teaching heresy in the school. This was an absurd charge, but that hardly mattered. Three days later, the young woman was kidnapped from the school in order to be deported.

The woman's mother, Maria Covas, had been asked by Carillo to file a report, but she refused. She knew the risks involved and sought only to protect her grandson. Carillo and the older woman stood in her house, the missing woman's son now clinging to his grandmother.

"Señora Covas," Carillo urged her, "you have to file a report if you want us to find who took your daughter and return her safely."

"No one took my daughter," she objected, barely concealing the fear in her eyes.

"My grandma's lying!" the frightened boy cried out in frustration. "That man took my mother!"

Carillo leaned down and set his hand gently on the boy's head. "She wants to protect you, son. She's a mother, and her daughter's been kidnapped. But she's a grandma, too, and she loves you. She's afraid for you."

The boy's eyes welled with tears and Carillo comforted him. The woman looked down at the boy, then at the kind officer, so unlike many of the others at the station. She could see that he was a good and honest man. He truly wanted to return her daughter and see the wrongdoers brought to justice.

"All right," she said softly. "I'll register a complaint."

Carillo immediately gathered policemen and went to the cathedral, arresting the bishop. The bishop's men offered resistance but were quickly overpowered. The second deputy quietly informed headquarters, and the bishop quietly sent someone to inform Carillo's top police chief.

It was a fast process after that, so quick that Carillo barely had time to figure out what had happened. The police chief told a colonel what was happening, and the colonel then had Carillo arrested. The charge was murder; he was accused of killing the missing schoolteacher.

Carillo followed the guard through the cobblestone and mortar building. The smell of the dark and sweltering interior struck him with disgust and grief for his son Vail, who had been recaptured and was now locked with him inside the horrific Mexican prison known as Los Cerrillos, or "Little Hills." Inside of the large room were ten iron cages, each nine feet wide and six feet deep. Very little air got into the room, and only a small amount of light managed to shine through the tiny cracks in the iron-welded seams of the cages.

When he saw his son, he was overcome with grief. Vail reached his arms through the bars and they clasped hands, their foreheads only separated by the bars. Vail was so dark from his years away from home that the finer details of his face almost could not be seen in the dim light. For a few moments, Carillo could only hold desperately to his son's hands and squeeze his eyes shut. He finally took a deep breath and looked through the metal at the young man. His eyes were full of love, but also held a sort of angry edge, as if to say, "I tried so hard to dissuade you from being a revolutionary. Now look where you are!"

"Father ..." Vail said, managing a smile.

Carillo leaned forward and opened his mouth as if to speak, but then hesitated when a guard nearby nudged him and nodded, hurrying him along. He nodded back and watched the guard walk away before turning back to Vail. "I only have a few moments before the guards return and make me leave, so listen carefully. This is not the way to fight a foreign occupation, son," he urged him, squeezing his hands tighter.

Vail pulled his hands free from his father's grip, stubborn to the last. "How do you suggest we do it then? Ask them to leave?"

Carillo shook his head and sighed, wiping his sweaty brow. "There's more than one way to approach it. You can protest in ways that won't get you hanged at least. Strikes, wheel-jams, posters, letters, hunger strikes ..."

"Killing them all is quicker," Vail asserted boldly with his head thrown back.

Carillo hushed him and looked worriedly to his left and right, but no guards seemed to have heard him. "Yes, killing them is another way," he agreed in a whisper, "but silently, secret murders, pain for pain. Then you'd be labeled a terrorist and be hunted down by dogs. No, son, the best way to do it is to walk with them and help them draw correct conclusions in your favor, draw the conclusions that you want."

"There is no best way, Papa. Look at you! You live by the letter of the law and yet you're also rotting here in prison!"

At that moment, the jailer's keys rattled the walls of the cell, causing tiny iron particles to dust their clothes in red.

"I have to go now, son," Carillo said, his eyes red and rimmed with tears.

A look came over Vail's face that Carillo had not seen in such a long time that at first he was not sure what it was. He finally realized that Vail was afraid, his eyes wide and lost like a little boy's. He tried to speak, but a guard was rushing Carillo out too fast for him to understand what his son was saying. As he was pushed towards his own cell, he could hear his son shout obscenities at the guards. His voice was hard, angry, and more like the person that had gotten into that prison in the first place. Carillo stumbled into the darkness and heard the cage door close behind him. He exhaled hard and angrily wiped the tears from his eyes.

Meanwhile, Carillo's other son, Vickers, remained at the military academy. He was still the complete opposite of his older brother. Now a young man, he was mature beyond his years as well as conscientious and duty-bound. He adjusted to life at the academy quickly, though he missed his little female friend back home. She was called Pupi, a sweet girl who looked up to him like a brother, despite their different backgrounds. In his daily letters, he would ask Pupi to report all of the activities in his family. She always replied the same day that she received his letters.

She was a charming girl. Vickers was thinking of marrying her.

Vickers went on leave from the academy and took Pupi to a lovely garden in town, the most romantic place he could think of nearby, to ask for her hand in marriage. He was stunned when she refused him.

"But why, Pupi? You know me better than any girl, and I think I know you better than any boy."

"Because you're rich and I'm poor," she replied simply. "I don't want to be … promoted that way." She looked up at his disappointed face. "Besides, we're more like brother and sister."

"Sister?" Vickers scoffed. "That's hardly how I think of you." He took her face into his hands and smiled, his eyes softening in appreciation at her beautiful face and form. "Please, Pupi, meet me after dinner? Please."

His voice was so gentle yet so urgent. She could not help but nod weakly.

Pupi and Vickers rendezvoused just outside of town at a stream. The water was so clear that they could see the rocky bottom ten feet below. They held hands and walked slowly up the stream, soon reaching a sandy area and removing their shoes to walk in the water. Vickers surprised Pupi with a playful splash of cool water all over her shoulders and neck. She squealed and began a barrage of water by kicking her feet towards him. By the end of that, they were both soaking wet.

After tiring of their game, they sat on a large flat boulder and dangled their feet in the water, leaning back on their hands so that their faces were lifted up to the sun. They were quiet for a while as the sun slowly dried their clothes.

"It's so lovely here," Pupi sighed. "Do you remember how we used to catch crayfish and minnows when we were kids? We'd play with them for hours and then release them back into the stream."

"Yes, I remember," Vickers murmured as he leaned over and took a slow kiss from her lips. "I remember other times too, when we were older," he added with a sweet laugh.

Pupi looked up into his eyes, choosing her words carefully as she stood. "Yes, I remember those times, too. I always admired you. You were my knight in shining armor. I dreamed of being older and meeting you like this."

"Well, you're not dreaming now," he reminded her, standing and enfolding her in his arms. They stood embracing each other for a while until she gently broke away. "Please sit down and let me speak, Vickers. I can't think when you hold me that way."

"Think?" Vickers said with a laugh. "Who's asking you to think?" He leaned forward and tried to put his arms around her again.

"No ... no!" she said, finally breaking free and splashing more water as she roughly stepped to the other side of the boulder and sat cross-legged on it. "Would you please listen to me?"

"Yes, Pupi," he said with a grin that reminded her of the days when they were school children.

"Vickers, you know I've been fond of you all my life ... but we're no longer children. Esteban Lonzo has asked me to marry him and I said yes. I've been trying to tell you for some time, but now our marriage is only a month away. I can't delay it any longer."

"Marriage ..." Vickers said with an expression both hurt and surprised. "Surely you're joking. I thought I meant something to you."

"Yes, Vickers, of course you do," she urged, leaning towards him and pleading with her eyes for him to accept this, to somehow be all right with this. "But you see, I'm like one of those minnows you played with as a child. We had fun, but now you have to release me and let me go ahead with my life." She stared down at the water, tears stinging her eyes. "You've attained your commission. You're an officer now, high above me in station. It can never be between us. Please let me go. I'll always think fondly of you, but Esteban is a wonderful man who'll be a good provider. My family and I have agreed and the marriage is already arranged for."

Vickers was silent for a while, letting the facts sink in. He finally looked up at her, almost to her eyes but not quite there, too hurt to look right into her eyes. "I had no idea. I still think of you as my little Pupi of my school days. I thought …" Vickers's words trailed off with a shrug.

"School days are long gone, Vickers. We have to leave them behind now," she said softly, stroking his hand affectionately. Vickers slowly composed himself. He knew what she was saying made perfect sense. His plans to marry her came more from a lack of thought than a presence of it. It hurt, but it had to be. Pupi caught the change in his eyes, knowing him well enough to recognize the flash of acceptance in them. "Friends?" she asked with a smile, holding out her hand as if to shake his.

Vickers took her hand in his and raised it quickly to his lips for a brief kiss. "Friends," he agreed. "May I walk you home?"

"No, we have to go our separate ways now," she said, putting her shoes on. "Come to the wedding?"

"No," he said with a firm shake of his head. "That's asking too much."

She stared at his face with a slight nod, hiding the sadness in her eyes. "Goodbye then, friend," she said softly, turning and walking out of sight past the trees. He watched her leave, still sitting on the boulder.

"Goodbye," he said, though he knew she was gone and could no longer hear him. He stayed there for some time, thinking to himself.

Another six weeks passed and Vickers was about to get a one-month leave. As the day approached, he received a letter from Pupi informing him that the Anti-Terrorist Court (ATC) had sentenced his elder brother Vail to death. Stunned, all he could do was wonder why his father had turned his own son in to the authorities in the first place. He quickly sent off a letter asking his father why.

His father's letter in reply arrived the day before Vickers's leave began. His answer was simple:

"Son,

As a police officer, it was my job to put criminals away. Do not harden your heart against anyone because they stand by their convictions.

Please pray for your brother, as I will.

Love, Papa."

Vickers reached home and rushed with his mother Maria to visit his father and elder brother in jail. His father was still awaiting conviction from the court on the false murder charge. Vickers gave them both sandwiches to eat, intentionally leaving his army issue pouch behind for Vail with a subtle wink. It contained a compass and a map with a ring drawn around a village in red ink.

"Ramos was rewarded for killing the leader of that village," he whispered into Vail's ear, nodding at the map that could be spied through the slightly opened pouch. "Go help them to avenge their leader's death. I'll be there in one week."

Vail nodded and slipped the pouch under his shirt. It was easy in the crowded mob of prisoners and their friends and family, all huddled and talking at once with just a few guards to watch over them. Easy too was retrieving the thin steel cable coiled in one of the sandwiches. It could be wrapped around two fingers and used to cut through steel. Vail calmly noticed it and took a large bite of the sandwich, separating it from the food with his tongue before putting it in his shirt as well. Vickers backtracked from the death-row cell, not even sure his father had noticed any of their subtle exchanges.

After one week, Vickers kissed his mother goodbye, telling her he had to go back to the academy. Unknown to her, he stopped on the way at his friend Galeno's village, immediately renting a two-acre farm from his friend's uncle. He and Galeno then went to work digging a bunker and making it livable. The opening was only a square two feet wide, covered by a wooden plank. The plank was covered with grass to make it flush with the ground and well-camouflaged. Then they dug a tunnel that led to a nearby forest. Air was provided by perforations in the ground along the way, studded by wooden covers and some straw. The entire project took days of exhausting work, but they both looked satisfied when they were finally finished.

"Perfect," Vickers said breathlessly, falling back on his haunches and surveying their work. "Revenge." He then efficiently left Galeno with a number of instructions and a packet of notes, returning to the academy.

His first letter after his return to the academy was from Pupi, who wrote that Vail had broken out of jail and escaped. Vickers knew where Vail was heading, that he planned to be the leader of an underground guerilla group. It was a well-knit clan, closer to the American border and in touch with arms-dealing smugglers. Vail claimed to need such things to "rise against the devils." He sought to officially join the anti-dictator resistance led by the liberals under Juarez.

"You always wanted to have the world your way, Vail," Vickers said to himself as he stared at the letter. "Do what you like, but first go take care of Ramos and get revenge."

Vail immediately went to the village his brother had prepared for him and arranged to have Ramos executed by the village's guerilla unit.

Carillo's elder son, Vail, was trying to locate Benito Juarez, who was living in the wastes of Mexico. He had searched for him endlessly. The young man was deep red from the sun. The small fire he had made was set up with a spit to roast the rabbit he had caught. The smoke worked its way along the ceiling of the camouflaged cave he had lived in now for some time, beneath a hill.

His father had turned him in for working with the rebels against the government, but he had escaped. Other prisoners who had known of his plan told him that it was only a matter of time before the police picked him up again, but he had seen the twinkle of admiration in their eyes as they watched him stubbornly plan the right place, the right time to get away. One of them finally warned him that the guards were going to be supplemented with a few more staff members soon, so he had left before it became impossible. It was earlier than he had planned, but he managed to get away.

Now he was in total isolation and did not dare to contact anyone. His anger towards his father was mixed with feelings of love, and he missed him. He bit those feelings back. Anger was better. It made it easier for him to hide and bide his time when he focused on the anger rather than the pangs of homesickness.

This time of isolation was actually good for him, he suspected. He was learning to survive by his wits.

Isabel Lopez lived in a gracious hacienda just outside of the whitewashed village that was Vickers's small hometown. Her father was a wealthy landowner who had been widowed only the year before. He now spent many hours in front of a large painting of his beautiful late wife Deborah, which hung over the massive stone fireplace. Much of the time, he was in an eerie one-sided conversation with her, usually about their three lovely daughters. The girls had tried to stop their father from speaking to the painting at first because it had frightened them so much, but they had left him to his conversations more lately since there seemed no hope of stopping him.

During one of those "talks," he decided that he should offer Isabel's hand in marriage to Capt. Vickers, who was now the most sought-after bachelor in town. Years had passed since Vickers's graduation and commission as an officer. He had worked his way up and was eventually given the keys to the treasury as the representative of state, in charge of its gold.

"Deborah," he said earnestly up to the portrait, "I miss you so much. Our eldest daughter Isabel is now thirteen years of age, almost a full-grown woman. You'd be so proud of her. She's a woman of fire and magnetism! She loves bullfights and spectacles. And the men ... I've seen the way they look at her. It almost makes me mad," he added with a smile. "Yes, it's time that we decided her future."

Isabel hastily entered the room through the grand entrance, almost as if she knew she was being discussed and wanted to put a stop to it. She was dressed in a red and gray afternoon dress in flowing silk, and spoke rapidly like the excitable young girl that she was. "Oh, Father, you should have been to the bullfight today, it was so thrilling! While I was watching the grand entry, all caught up in that and not watching the bull, it escaped! Before anyone knew it, one of the picador's chestnut stallions was terribly gored, but the horse was brave and galloped anyway. The blood was everywhere and I'm afraid the horse will have to be shot. That's just a tragedy, don't you see? A real tragedy!"

"Slow down, little one. Take a deep breath and let me look at you," he comforted her, checking her arms, feet, neck, and auburn head for any signs of injury. "Good, you're not harmed in any way. You're fine," he said absentmindedly.

"No, Father, not me. Don't you see? It was a magnificent horse that was hurt," she said softly after she saw the fear in her father's eyes. "See, Papa? I'm fine."

"Fine ... yes, I see you're just fine. I'll hear all about your adventures at dinner. Go find your grandmother Lucia, I'm sure she's in the kitchen. Tell her your news," he said, smiling blankly as she slipped from the room. He then sank wearily into an overstuffed leather chair, looking once more at Deborah's painting. "See how lovely and spirited she is? We must make arrangements."

Isabel walked into the old kitchen where the aroma meant home, family, and grandmother to her. The round elderly woman was dressed from head to toe in black, making bread in the traditional Mexican way. She greeted Isabel with a warm smile. "What was all that noise I heard? Your voice and then your father's?" she asked as she continued to knead the dough.

Isabel's amber eyes became rimmed in tears as she related the story to Lucia, including her father's overreaction to her safety. "Oh, Grandmother, must I walk on eggshells forever? Papa's so emotional nowadays. Sometimes I think I should keep every worrisome detail of life from him. How long will it take for him to recover from Mother's death?" Lucia wiped her hands on her full-length apron as she sat on a stool and gestured for Isabel to join her. Isabel sat on a stool beside her and placed her head on the woman's bosom as she listened.

"You must remember, Bell," she advised, using her affectionate nickname for Isabel, "your father was deeply in love with her. They were friends who shared all of their thoughts, and now he feels lost without her."

Tears slipped slowly down Isabel's cheeks. "I miss her too, you know ... and now I miss them both. He talks to Mother's painting even more that he does to his own daughters. Doesn't he know we're *all* hurting?"

"Yes, Bell, he knows. He's handling it the only way he knows how. Time will bring him back to you, you just have to be patient." She smiled down at the girl, lifting a clean corner of her apron to dab the tears from Isabel's eyes. "But let's talk of the future. Someday soon, your father will find a handsome man for you, and we both hope it'll be a man you can love as deeply as your parents loved each other."

"But Grandmother, how will I ever love anyone with *las dueñas* that Father always has me surrounded with?" she asked petulantly.

Lucia chuckled. "Your mother had chaperones, too. It's our way, our tradition. Your father doesn't want you to be burdened by advances from men, advances that might be hard to deal with at your age. Don't all of your friends have chaperones, too?"

"Yes, but—"

"No buts," Lucia insisted. "You have a careful father who has your happiness at heart." She gave her a long hug and kissed the girl's beautiful reddish hair. "Now away with you. I must hurry if we're to have dinner at the usual hour. Tell Olivia to stop churning the butter and come help me. I'm sure we have plenty by now, and before you go, please stir the beans," she chattered, back at her breadboard and lifting the dough.

Isabel did as she was told and then wandered out to the courtyard. She was happy that she had stopped to chat with her grandmother, but now she was happy to escape the heat in there and walk in the slight breeze of the afternoon. As she walked around the gated area, she occasionally glanced through the intricately carved gates towards the village.

"I wonder if poor girls there have all the problems I have," she wondered to herself. A small stone fell at her feet. She stopped mid-step as three more tiny pebbles fell at the foot of the gate. "Who's there?" she called cautiously. A strong masculine voice answered. "It's Vickers, remember?" She paused, her eyes widening in surprise. Vickers finally went on to describe who he was, amused. "I gave your chaperone my handkerchief today when the horse blood got on your shoes."

"Vickers," she said, as if trying to place the name, but she was really trying to hold back her excitement. She remembered him well, and though she was naïve, she was also flirtatious. "Come closer so I can see your face."

"Yes, señorita," he said, approaching the gate and reaching a hand through. It held a red rose. "I brought you a rose as red as blood … in memory of our first meeting." With a quick glance over her shoulder to be sure that no one was watching, Isabel took the rose from the handsome young officer. When their fingers touched, she thought she felt a spark of electricity, and the eyes of the young man made her think that perhaps he had also felt it.

She knew she mustn't speak to men, but she was flattered and spoke in a whisper through the gate. "How delightful," she said with a curtsey and a mischievous smile. "It's nice to meet you. I'm Isabel. My father owns this village and the land around it."

Vickers lost some of his confidence and became almost speechless when he gazed into her amber eyes. "I, um," he stammered. "I'm Capt. Vickers. I've known about you and your family for months now. My family comes from this village. I was hoping we would get a chance to meet."

"Well then, if you're from around here, you know we can't meet like this. If you're interested, you must speak to my father," she answered with a daring twinkle in her eyes.

Vickers was elated. "Yes, I will next Sunday. Watch for me at mass." He then disappeared from sight, the small opening in the iron gate revealing only a road and some grass at its edge.

Isabel smiled at the rose and held it up to her nose, delighted at the effect she had on Vickers. The fragrance was sweet and familiar … a little too familiar. In the next moment, she realized it was the Don Juan rose that grew outside the gate. "He gave me my own rose," she whispered to herself in surprise. "That rascal!" she laughed, walking back to the kitchen with a dreamy smile on her face.

At dinner that evening, she retold her story of the bullfight, this time to her father and two sisters. She was careful in telling the story, leaving out any mention of the young officer. Her father was preoccupied as usual, but her sisters seemed excited by the story and asked many questions.

After the meal, their father rose from his seat. "Wonderful meal, Mother Lucia. I'd like to see you and Isabel in the drawing room as soon as you're able." Lucia and Isabel exchanged glances. "Of course, Son," Lucia agreed.

Later that evening, Don Lopez sat with his mother-in-law and daughter in the drawing room. He explained to both of them his plans to offer Isabel's hand in marriage to the handsome Vickers. Both women were surprised and excited about the turn of events.

Lopez at last turned to Lucia. "I understand it's out of the ordinary for me to make this decision without talking to you, but it's what Deborah and I both want." He then returned to his leather chair in front of the painting. Both women knew they were dismissed.

As Isabel got into bed that evening, she placed the red rose into her prayer book and gently set it under her lace pillow. She marveled to herself at how wise her grandmother was, and how nothing was a coincidence in life. Everything seemed to happen for a purpose.

From Vienna, Maximilian and Charlotte had traveled to Trieste and then on to Venice for a week. There they found a bustling city full of traffic. There was much to see and do. It was a swirl of activity, of newness and surprises at every turn. They watched as the locals went about their business. The city burst with ideas and adventure.

Charlotte was enchanted when she saw Venice, and she wrote enthusiastic letters to Brussels. It was a tonic to her, since she needed something to get her mind off the poor dead dancer. She bloomed in its atmosphere, though she soon found out that her fairytale prince had no intention of changing his habits now that he was married. Often he left for "diplomatic negotiations," his cover for what were actually wild parties.

In 1859, the Italian Freedom War broke out and Maximilian and Charlotte were forced to flee Venice. Charlotte was grief-stricken when the people of the city, who had before been so kind and welcoming, degenerated to the point that they outwardly hissed at her in the streets. She was sad when they had to leave and always missed the feeling she had when they had first arrived. The archducal couple mounted a carriage two miles outside the city of Milan, proceeding to Monza. Maximilian was wearing his admiral uniform while Charlotte sported a red velvet crinoline trimmed with heavy lace, along with a diamond crown decked with roses. They entered Lombardy in full pomp, living at Villa Medici, about eight miles outside of Milan.

Palace Wien-Schonbrunn, Vienna—November 1857

Franz Joseph I, emperor of Austria and king of Hungary, sat talking to the Queen Mother, Sophie Friederike Dorothea von Hapsburg. It had been six months since Maximilian had left to assume his duties in Italy, and Sophie was ambivalent about the whole affair. She had wanted him to go to Italy, to get away from the controversy and intrigues of the Vienna court, to have a place to stretch his own wings. But he had left under such sad circumstances as to sour the entire thing. There hadn't been a gala to see him off, no toasts and celebrations as she had anticipated. Everyone was still in mourning for the little princess when he left, and it would have been wildly inappropriate. She missed her Maxi, and another part of her resentfully wondered why her eldest son didn't simply wait awhile longer to send him to Italy, so that it could have been a happier exit. She kept these thoughts to herself as she listened to Franz Joseph discuss Maximilian in Italy.

"I sent Maximilian as viceroy in Italy because we needed him to suppress revolts there. I thought perhaps his unique ideas on governing could assist in that. The problem now is that his liberal policies are starting to shake my establishment, even the army. I have to discuss this with Father. Should we allow him to do as he pleases? Or should we simply command him to rule in the traditional ways?"

"It's an excellent training ground, but Maxi's been writing to me and saying that he misses us."

Franz Joseph scoffed, frustrated. "A king can't be his mother's pet."

"Maxi isn't like that," Sophie replied calmly. "He simply loves his parents so much that he would even abdicate a throne for just one hug from us." Her eyes softened lovingly, proudly as she said the words.

"I know that, Mother. At least he wouldn't stage a coup, but his methods of keeping control over Italy are being questioned."

The queen leaned forward and looked him in the eye to make him pay careful attention. "Son, the way to understand Maxi is to imagine someone who says, 'I'm more capable in building a palace on this site.' He'd have to select the best architects and feed them from his hands. He'd lay unique designs, better foundations, better looking, comfortable, and secure structures."

"He'd make a fine developer!" he retorted.

"Yes, Sire, fine indeed."

"But can he help save this empire? The empire his ancestors worked so hard to build?" He paused, shaking his head with a frown. "He's risking it all with his new ideas."

"If he's to risk it, let him lose Italy. We're already losing it. Garibaldi is the revolutionary down there. He's the one spreading nationalist ideas. Let's see if Maxi can win that debate."

The thought wasn't a comforting one. The emperor walked away, his face etched with concern.

Maximilian served there as an Italian viceroy. They were happier there, and Charlotte loved the Italian people so much that she even took the nickname "Carlotta." Later that year, Maximilian was seized with a restless desire for adventure and left for a botanical expedition in distant Brazil. No amount of Charlotte's protesting could stop him, and she spent months alone waiting for him. Only the affections of the Italian people helped her through the long time without him.

They spent two years in Milan, but in 1859, Maximilian's brother, angry over his liberal policies, dismissed him. Shortly after that, Austria lost control of its Italian possessions, and war broke out against France and Piedmont-Sardinia. Maximilian was relieved of his post as governor-general and watched his brother give full power to the military. Deeply resenting his dismissal, the ousted couple retired to a private life in Trieste. Maximilian found himself suddenly idle, so he threw himself into helping to build a ship-making port at Trieste; however, his main activities were in designing and building the château of Miramar for Charlotte and himself.

On his arrival in Trieste, Maximilian wrote a letter.

"Dearest Mama,

I hope this letter finds you well. You know I love you more than anything in life and it pains me not to see you. Pretend that I am giving you the fondest hug and the sweetest kiss you can imagine.

On our journey, we passed over a natural bridge on the way into Trieste. The countryside is beautiful. Our entrance into Trieste was magical. I remember the first time I came to Italy with Franz Joseph and Father. The beauty is still here, but the welcome was warmer. Charlotte looked as perfect as any royal imaginable. She wore a bright red silk gown from Paris, and of course I was dressed in imperial uniform. The crowd seemed genuinely glad to see us.

As you know, I've always said that all I want from life is a castle with a big garden on a beach, and now we are in the midst of building it. Our new palace is being built on a cliff off the sea. It is the finest view of Trieste imaginable. It will have the finest of everything. You'll want to come and visit after it's completed.

The climate is mild here. Charlotte is happy and is taking to her duties enthusiastically. I will have to watch her or the people will grow fonder of her than I. However, as we both are aware, there is no doubt as to who the real ruler is in our little family.

Upon arriving, the carriage took us to the medieval cathedral of San Guisto on the side of San Guisto Hill, in front of a castle of the same name. The castle terrace has fabulous views of the city of Trieste. Then we traveled to the site of our castle, which shall be called Miramar. The sun shone all day. The temperature was perfect as I walked through the woods and gardens surrounding the castle, the air astir with a sea breeze. Lazy clouds drifted overhead, and the pungent fragrance of boxwood hedges filled the air. The castle is going to be made of white Istrian stone, which will make it visible from a considerable distance. The cliff it's being built on, which had no vegetation whatsoever at the time we began, is being cultivated with numerous tropical species of trees and plants. The garden, when finished, will offer a chance for an interesting stroll among botanical species and an important collection of sculptures along its numerous paths. We also paid a visit to the future stables and the greenhouses, where we plan to create a butterfly garden.

Mama, do you remember the little sphinx I brought back from my cruise to Egypt? We will place that on the corner facing out to the Adriatic Sea as a kind of a watchdog. I believe that is a very clever piece of styling that you would appreciate. We stayed only a few hours, since it is still being outfitted, but I can assure you it will amaze you with its wonderful view of the Bay of Grignano and the Adriatic and beyond.

Love as always,

Your Max."

Maximilian stamped the letter with his emblem, sealing it with wax. He stared at the empty stack of pages on the desk and then thoughtfully lifted his pen, starting another letter.

"Dearest Zinnia,

Life without you is impossible. I hope by this time you've returned to the Schonbrunn and are in my mother's company. Although you belong at my side, at least I would have the comfort of knowing you are safe and well.

How could you have left without talking to me, the one person who loves you best in the world?

If only you were with me! I should like to take you in my arms simply to hold you and feel your presence. If you were here, I would kiss your hands and forehead. That would make me the happiest man in the world.

You would enjoy Italy, I think. The weather is warmer than Vienna. Charlotte misses you too. She understands our relationship well. Everything would be perfect if you were here. Please write me soon. It is my deepest desire to hear from you.

Your loving Max."

The royal couple found that the Austrian empire was far from popular in northern Italy, but despite resistance from the military authorities, they began to slowly win over many Italians. Maximilian's liberalism aroused less enthusiasm in Vienna, however, where he was increasingly seen as being in opposition to his imperial brother's government.

A great deal of time passed, with Maximilian and Charlotte whiling away their time at Miramar. The finishing touches to Miramar kept the archduke busy, as there were always new gardens to design, new birds to have sent for his aviary, but it was simply the filling of idle time. It kept his mind off his sorrows and gave him something to do besides drink and think too much. Charlotte became impatient, envisioning herself spending the rest of her life looking at the sea and waiting to die.

For a long time, Maximilian managed to push away the sorrow of Zinnia's possible death, but with every unanswered letter that he wrote, his heart felt a little harder, a little emptier. When Adele began to send letters begging him to allow her to join him in Italy, he ignored them at first, not even bothering to read them. That was an entire other affair that had weighed on his heart, but now in his depression over Zinnia, he felt a loneliness despite his love for Charlotte. He began to drink more, which deepened his depression.

One night, after drinking too much wine, he had finally written Adele a letter, granting her permission to join their household in Italy. Within the month, the eager girl had arrived, along with all of her belongings. She had fought bitterly with her mother and did not understand why she was so against her daughter's leaving, aside from missing her, but her mother had not told her the truth. She had finally left, hoping that time would calm her mother down and make her see that this was a good move for her.

Maximilian was gracious enough to her and saw to it that she was given an especially nice chamber for a servant, but he did not visit her and she was left only to wonder why. She saw that he was drinking a lot and finally decided that he was sad over the loss of Zinnia, the dancing girl. Adele's heart burned with jealousy and she searched her mind for schemes to work her way back into his heart, to be the woman whom he loved above all, even perhaps more than his wife.

In the end, it was Maximilian's drinking that provided the opportunity she sought. One night, in his usual place, his study, he actually thought he could hear the distant sound of Zinnia singing one of her enchanting songs. The hour was very late when he began to stagger about the hallways, trying to hone in on the place that the singing was coming from.

He finally approached a door that muffled the distinct sound of a young woman's voice and opened it. It was dark in the chamber, but he could see the silhouette of a naked woman in front of the window. His rational mind was gone, blissfully drowned in a bottle until morning, and he approached the woman with a slight stagger.

Adele smiled as he approached, then stood and took him into her arms. He hugged her fiercely and carried her to the bed. She was lowered very gently onto the mattress and was soon covered with kisses, responding with kisses of her own. Their lovemaking was hurried and desperate, as if at any time they may be separated.

Maximilian awoke the next morning with tears dried on his face. He was confused about where he was and horrified when he saw Adele sleeping beside him. He quickly left and never said anything about it, but the drinking continued. Now that the taboo had been broken, he found himself returning to her bed now and then, and over time more often, again and again ravishing her and pretending that she was his beloved Zinnia.

Charlotte was bewildered by his melancholy and often criticized him for drinking too much. One night he was so drunk that he actually told her how much he loved Zinnia and they fought bitterly about it. She was torn between jealousy and her own affection for the Indian dancer, and his frequent nighttime absences hurt her deeply. Lately when he was drunk, he had even begun to talk of suicide, and which was the best way to do it.

She felt that somehow the beauty of Trieste was going to ruin them, that it was a poisonous place where they had far too much time to think and linger on pain and regret. The life of the idle rich was not for them. She was determined to find a way for them to get out of there and serve a useful purpose somewhere.

Whispers from Mexico were becoming more tempting now. They offered the opportunity to have the titles and station that they both felt they deserved, at least more adventure than redesigning gardens and redecorating rooms. Nevertheless, the pull was not yet strong enough, and in 1859 when Mexican "monarchists" approached Maximilian, he did not accept their offer.

CHAPTER 12

▼

AN EMPEROR FOR MEXICO

France, 1861

In the Chateau de Versailles, Napoleon III and his wife Eugenie sat listening to a report from his foreign minister. Also present was the French ambassador from the United States.

"Sire, President Lincoln has been sworn in as the sixteenth American president. He's in distress with the Southern Confederacy."

"Did our ambassador report his inaugural address?" Napoleon asked.

"Yes, sire. I have a copy here of that address. The important points are underlined."

Napoleon took the manuscript from his minister and read it carefully.

"Now this is interesting," he said, beginning to read part of it aloud. "'In your hands, my dissatisfied fellow countrymen, and not in mine, is the momentous issue of civil war. The government will not assail you. You have no oath registered in heaven to destroy the government, while I shall have the most solemn one to preserve, protect, and defend it.'"

Napoleon stood and walked to the window, staring at the document. "What do you make of this, my friend?" he asked his minister.

"That there's going to be a war. Lincoln's War," the foreign minister replied.

"It also means that President Lincoln considers secession to be illegal," Napoleon said, expanding on the implications. "That he's willing to use force to defend the federal law and the Union. Five more states have joined the Confederacy, and only four are left in the Union. I suppose this all means that this Kentucky frontiersman from an undistinguished family is going to fight off secessionists," he said, not attempting to hide his amusement.

"Precisely," the ambassador interjected. "President Lincoln has called upon the states to raise 75,000 volunteers."

"Even after Union troops surrendered at Fort Sumter?"

"Yes, sire."

"Then it's civil war," Napoleon stated. "I'd like to see President Lincoln's personal and political biography, as well as the Louisiana Purchase Treaty."

Eugenie's eyes widened in surprise. "You mean to question the treaty? That's been in effect for … nearly sixty years now."

Napoleon nodded and waved his hand at that trivial detail. "Yes, well, maybe we can wrest Louisiana back. This would seem a good time to strengthen our positions in Mexico as well. We sold Louisiana for a song, so perhaps we can pay Mexico's debts to the Europeans by getting it back."

He paused, staring at the document. His mind raced with the possibilities. The minister and ambassador were granted leave to retire from the monarch's presence while he roughed out the details.

Benito Juarez's wife Margarita and his sister Josefa sat at a round table in the president's dining room of the Palacio Nacional, drinking coffee. They chatted while they helped themselves to sliced fruit and pastries from a tiered server with lead crystals. The table was decorated with a tablecloth of ecru lace.

The room was comfortable though not lavish, with a sitting area at the far end of the room. The coved ceiling was outlined with burgundy velvet swags trimmed in gold, softened with sheer ecru drapes. The Queen Anne style furniture was upholstered with burgundy brocade.

"I dreamed of this day as a servant girl," Josefa said. "When I told Señor Maza of my dreams back then, he said that 'if wishes were horses, beggars would ride.' But in my heart I knew Benito would go all the way to the top. Today he rode his carriage into Mexico City and soon it'll be official; he'll be president of Mexico for his second term. Now we *all* ride!" she added stubbornly, smiling at Margarita. "Do we know the official date of the ceremony?"

"March 21st … I should find a suitable outfit, as you should, my dear," Margarita replied.

"I care little for those things," Josefa said indignantly. "It's Benito's day, but I'll be sure to look presentable."

"I'll never forget the acclaim of the people on New Year's Day when he triumphantly entered Mexico City," Margarita said with pride. "The people must continue to be proud of our nation."

Juarez stood nearby between a large mirror and a portrait of himself. He chuckled at the women's conversation and approached the table. "It doesn't matter what you ladies or I wear. The only way to save Mexico is to improve the national spirit. And how? By changing the structure of society and the efforts now being made to obtain and consolidate the benefits of *la paz*. Under its patronage, the protection of the laws and the authorities that stand for the rights of all the people of the Republic will be effective. We'll be assured that the towns and the government respect the rights of all. Between individuals, like between nations, the respect to the other person's right is *la paz*."

After the inaugural address, the family met in the dining room. Josefa removed her bonnet and placed it on the president's piano as Margarita poured a small glass of wine for all. Juarez removed a bright red sash emblazoned with the Masonic emblem of the 33rd degree along with the medallion of the presidency.

"You should be very proud of yourself," Josefa said, her hand coming to rest on his arm. "I am, and I'm extremely contented."

"Yes," Benito agreed. "I'm very happy to begin my work. We have to rid ourselves of the colonial corporatist system and establish a modern, liberal one in its place." He sat with his drink, his expression serious. "We're faced with many serious troubles. The opposition's army may still be intact, and Congress has to be convinced that I'm worthy of their trust. Tax revenues have fallen to a disastrous low, and we're immediately faced with new difficulties. Trade is stagnant."

"But Mexico has many riches," Margarita objected. "We're a source of great wealth, especially gold and silver."

"True, but it takes money to mine and men trained to do it. Many men have been killed over the last several years in our struggle, not to mention tens of thousands of orphans. That's laying a heavy burden on Mexico's people and their economy."

"But surely Mexico has reserves," Margarita pressed.

"We had a war with America and our own civil war. Not to mention the fact that we've borrowed heavily from England, Spain, and France. The general coffers are virtually empty."

"Empty," Josefa repeated breathlessly. "How can that be?"

"Our government's been corrupt, and war is extremely costly both in money and men. Our revolution was led by simple men rising up and demanding their fundamental rights. Our state of mind during that time had to be about unity and a common goal. We couldn't stop to weigh the cost. We had to focus on victory. England, France, and Spain are our creditors now, and they're demanding full repayment. The French government claims $600,000 in damages suffered by French subjects during the civil war."

"$600,000!" Margarita exclaimed.

"As a solution to that problem, I'm considering putting a two-year suspension on the payments."

"What about the properties of the Church? Surely we can sell some of those," Josefa countered.

"Very few have the resources to buy. Besides, flooding the market made property values fall. That's not my plan for the Church property anyway. My dream is to use some of that land to set up institutes of free public learning. Only through learning can the people of Mexico hope to support a democracy."

On July 17th, Juarez declared a moratorium for two years on all foreign debt repayments by submitting his plan to Congress. Congress found itself obligated to suspend payment on all agreements previously entered into with foreign powers. America was in the middle of its own civil war and was in no position to collect its debts; however, the very next day, the representatives of France and Great Britain entered a formal protest on behalf of their governments. On July 25th, when their demands were not satisfied, England, France, and Spain suspended all diplomatic relations with the Mexican administration.

Juarez soon went to address his old academy, the Academy of Science and Arts, where he had spoken years before. There he was recognized as the first head of government, appreciated for his efforts in recasting an independent election commissioner, a judge of the Supreme Court who was selected from some of the best liberal thinkers in Mexico. He had also subjected his government to a poll so that the people could give their government feedback about its performance.

The academy commandant expressed his appreciation for those democratic gestures and then asked el presidente to speak. BJ, as his close associates knew him, stood before the assembly and addressed the academy.

"Let us consider why people fight, why there are so often civil wars. Why does terrorism flourish? These are very serious questions and deserve reasonable answers." He paused, slowly walking up and down the stage, as was so often his habit.

"During elections in a country, charges of rigging the votes fly across the political landscape. Elections become controversial as the losers blame the opponent for cheating and the referee for being partial. This prevents genuine democracy from putting down its roots. Yes, part of our problem is repeated army interventions that have blighted political development in Mexico. It hits democracy in the face if the rewards of electoral victory are very lucrative. Then nobody wants to lose. The consequences of defeat are that political rivals are mercilessly harried, shot, or hounded out of the country by the victors. A loser is vulnerable to trumped-up charges and pressurized to join the ruling party." No one could deny that, which had been seen all too often in their country in recent years. A murmur of assent hummed beneath his words.

"Then there's the role of bureaucracy. An officer who doesn't ensure the victory of the official candidate is swiftly transferred to a bleak and profitless post. That's punishment without being charged, without being given the chance to defend himself. Therefore the civil servants don't wait for orders to surrender their conscience. When told to jump, they only ask, 'How high?'"

"The previous election authorities hardly ever ruled against the candidates of the ruling party. This shows their lack of a spine, for the most part. It's the same for the higher judiciary, where they hardly ever used their power unless there was some personal profit involved. It's therefore virtually impossible to unseat the sitting government. Democracy is involved in *changing* the government, not solidifying it. What we've been facing is a sitting government that can't be changed without military intervention."

"Or divine intervention," a member of the assembly added. There was soft laughter around the room.

Juarez nodded. "Exactly, sir. What chance does the opposition have? And then when the rulers bypass the constitution, they fall prey to fighting. Call it civil war, terrorism, military intervention, it's all the same."

"But how do you fight against it?" a man asked, echoing everyone's thoughts.

Juarez paused. "How indeed. That's what I'm trying to discover, gentlemen."

By late 1860, the Mexican conservatives had been faltering, and in January 1861, Juarez was finally able to return to Mexico City. He immediately reassembled the election authority with great deliberation, selecting a group of liberal conformers that included Jesús Carranza and Juan N. Alvarez. Juarez submitted to another general election and was constitutionally elected as president.

The day in 1861 that they launched his second presidency arrived quickly. In a speech, Benito Juarez said to the triumph of the Republic, "Mexicans, let's direct all of our politics here. My reforms will be a turning point in liberal policy."

Margarita rose and gave her husband a small peck on the cheek. "Yes, dear, but of course you're right. As always, you've thought everything through."

A month later, a servant came to the door while the family was eating dinner. "El Presidente, there is a man with a message here to see you."

"Oh my, must we be interrupted now?" Margarita said.

"Hush, dear, I'll see to the matter," Juarez replied with a soft but firm voice.

The servant was worried that he had irritated the president. "I told him you were busy, but he insisted it's urgent."

"It's quite all right, bring him in."

The servant left and shortly returned with a man in uniform. He made a quick and sharp bow. "I'm sorry to bother you at this time, sir, but our spies have discovered important information about England, Spain, and France."

"Yes, officer, what's the information?" he asked, hiding his impatience.

"The information's been confirmed, sir. All three countries are gathering forces and sending their armies to collect their debts."

The Mexican Congress soon assembled for a high level meeting with Juarez and Josefa, along with one of Juarez's most trusted men, General Ignacio Zaragoza. The general reported that Spain and Great Britain had agreed to withdraw their troops in exchange for suspended payments at a higher interest rate, but France refused to leave.

Josefa stood to address them. They were familiar with the small woman now, and they knew that she spoke the mind of their president. "Men of Mexico, we've fought too long and hard to allow foreigners to take away our liberty now. We must once again gather together our forces and defeat them. Our men are brave and willing to fight. They only await your pleasure. Let's use our liberty to fight for freedom."

Congress rose to its feet and the loud debates began. Juarez thought the shouting men were objecting to her words, but he had misjudged their reaction. There was soon an overwhelming majority voting to go to war.

The next day, President Benito Juarez told his army to stop the invasion, so the military officers laid a clever trap.

The Battle of Puebla in May of 1862 was a remarkable one. The French army was the greatest in the world at that time, with 4,000 strong and well-trained men who were equipped with many of the best weapons of war. The French army began its advance towards Puebla, a small town of many farmers south of Mexico City. The village had to make their own army with very few guns and bullets, led on May fifth by General Ignacio Zaragoza. His army included 5,000 ill-equipped Mestizo and Zapotec Indians who only carried hoes and farm equipment.

As the unsuspecting French marched towards Puebla, the general employed about 1,000 farmers and other villagers. He spoke to his new recruits on horseback. "We must make haste to wet down this large plaza. The plaza is the main entrance to the town. It's our goal to make it impassable. Find as many buckets as you can and form a line from the two wells. Our bucket line will create a quagmire."

After two hours, the villagers had soaked the entire area. General Zaragoza was pleased. "Now gather together every goat, chicken, and cow from the area and turn them loose to trample in the mud." Herds of animals trampled the plaza until the mud was a foot deep. The bog acted like quicksand, taking all of a man's strength to pull a single foot from the sticky, sucking mud.

When the French entered the plaza, they became bogged down to the hubs of their wagon wheels and could not move. There was mass shock and confusion. The raged and poor Mexicans surrounded them, fighting until the French had no choice and finally left. They had defeated the great French forces with cunning, strength, and determination.

An ocean away, Napoleon III was informed of the Mexican victory. He was stunned and incensed. The next day, he dispatched another 30,000 troops.

One year later on the 17th of May, Puebla was finally captured after two months of fighting. The fall of Puebla meant easy access to Mexico City, and the French soon swept into the capital in June of 1863.

Congress met with the president, who again brought his well-spoken sister Josefa. Juarez gave them information about the location of the invading French and then handed over the podium to his sister.

"Gentlemen, there's only one way to preserve this government. The Mexican army must be disbanded, sent north to U.S. borders." There was a grumbling in the large room and she continued in a louder voice. "El Presidente Juarez must set up his headquarters at El Paso del Norte, just across the Rio Grande from El Paso, Texas. This will give us time to reorganize and strengthen our position. We'll leave, but always keep in mind the day of our return to retake our position. In addition, all of our army's men and officers should be paid one year's salary and carry their weapons and ammunition with them, so that there's no confusion about our intent."

There was a heated discussion at this unusual approach. Some thought it incredibly cunning, others foolish, while even more agreed that there was little else they could do. On May 31st of 1863, Congress gave President Juarez "extraordinary powers to last the extent of the foreign invasion." That night, Juarez left with a few advisers and ministers, heading towards San Luis Potosí. Four years of danger awaited him before returning to Mexico City.

By 1863, Napoleon III was pushing his French army deep into Mexico under his general, Elie-Fredrick Foray. He was aggressive and carried out the commands of Napoleon to the letter, soon capturing the capital, Mexico City. Napoleon was ecstatic at the news and rushed to get his plans set up as soon as possible.

A Mexican delegation met with Maximilian to convince him that, as he had desired, a written document would be forthcoming, reflecting the wish of the Mexicans to have him as their emperor. The ubiquitous lawyer Jose Marie Gutierrez, who had been Juarez's rival in the Reform War of 1857–60, headed the delegation.

Vienna

Maximilian entered the stateroom of the emperor. All of the servants and officials were cleared from the room as they greeted one another. Once the room was empty, they each assumed their true positions.

"I forbid you from accepting this emperorship in Mexico," Franz Joseph bluntly stated as they sat, getting right down to business.

Maximilian blinked in surprise. "My lord, this is a unique opportunity for me—"

"If you accept this throne, you'll lose all of your noble rights in Austria," Joseph interrupted.

"What's behind this threat? I can't usurp your throne, and I wouldn't, even if I could."

"Be careful of your decision. You know I have the power to remove you from the succession to the Hapsburg throne. It's not an idle threat."

"What good are these titles without the freedom to rule?" Maximilian reasoned. "And it seems now that you truly have no intention of sharing even the smallest part of your vast kingdom with me, although I don't know why. With the situation being what it is, I'd think you would welcome my help."

"Help, is that what you call it?" Joseph sternly protested. "You're much too liberal with freedom. You'd empty out our treasury just to feed and house the rabble."

"I'm now torn between the opportunity to try my mettle as an emperor or simply stay here and wait for you to change your mind."

Joseph was silent, knowing what he said was true but not budging. His silence confirmed his younger brother's statement, and Maximilian stood. "I see you're not going to discuss this with me, only issue commands. If you'll excuse me, sire, I'm tired from my travels."

Maximilian stayed for only a short while to rest before returning to Miramar. The icy silence during state dinners with his brother was more than he could bear. He had tried to request an audience with Joseph to discuss the matter further, but he had been shut out and did not speak to him again. He was both relieved and intensely frustrated by the time he left to return to Italy.

Upon his return, over a meal on the terrace, Maximilian shared his and Joseph's conversation with his young wife. Princess Charlotte was bored with their inactivity as of late and urged Maximilian on to the Mexican throne.

"Max, you know our talents are being wasted here. I love Miramar as much as you do, but you don't honestly want to spend the rest of our days just sitting here, do you?" She saw the confusion in her husband's eyes and pressed on. "You can go on all of the botanical expeditions that you want, but you can only do so much to make up for an idle life. We're young! We're royals in the prime of our lives! And now it looks like Mexico is going to give us the proof that you want, to show that it really wants you as their emperor! Let's go show your brother that you had it in you all along to be one of the best rulers this world has ever seen. Let's change Mexico and make it a part of the civilized world, where the people can have all of the freedoms you've been dreaming of ..."

She carried on for some time, knowing just how to use her words to ignite his passion and idealism. He moved from confusion to certainty, a pattern he would follow frequently in the years to come.

Maximilian's affair with Adele carried on as she continued to serve as a meager replacement for Zinnia. A small part of her knew that was all she was to him, that she would never find the place in his heart that she wanted, but her love for him drove her to accept whatever she could get. Most of her relationship with him was based on the love she held in her heart and the fantasies she held in her mind.

Suddenly word arrived from Austria that changed everything for her. Maximilian's mother Sophie had discovered that Adele was Franz Karl's daughter, and she indignantly insisted that Adele be married to an old servant back in Austria. Adele was shocked at the news but too in love with Maximilian to think rationally. Despite letters from her mother urging her otherwise, she refused to leave Italy and Maximilian behind. It was finally decided that she would marry an old horsekeeper on the grounds and live nearby, and she had no choice but to agree.

Their wedding was no more than a dry ceremony, with the bride actually biting back tears through most of it. The old man did not care, too excited at the prospect of having such a young and voluptuous wife. His excitement was cut short on their wedding night when she refused to share a bed with him.

It remained that way for some time, she refusing his advances and he becoming more and more infatuated with his forbidden fruit. After two months of agony, watching her walk about in all her beauty and being unable even to touch her, he surprised even himself by dropping to one knee in front of her as she tried to walk past. She looked down in surprise.

"My dear, it's breaking my heart that you don't want me!" he moaned. "I know I'm an old man, but you're my wife and you have a duty to please me."

Adele sniffed. "Get up, old man. I've told you a thousand times that it's never going to happen." She brushed by him in disgust. He staggered back to his feet and limped after her before regaining his balance.

"Please, Adele …" She left the room. "I'll do anything!" he shouted after her.

After a brief moment, her head peeked back into the room. "Anything?" she repeated.

"Oh, yes," he insisted, approaching her cautiously.

"Fine. I want you to deliver messages to Maximilian."

The old man scoffed. "Love letters? Do you take me for a fool?"

Adele appraised him closely and traced her hand lightly over one of her breasts.

His eyes followed her hand. "Adele, you know that if the Queen Mother found out about it, I could be in a world of trouble."

Adele raised her eyebrows doubtfully and began to slowly unlace her bodice.

"Uh … what if I get caught?"

"You won't," she replied softly, opening her bodice and untying the lace of her dress.

He walked over to her and lingered, like a bee around something sweet. "Are you sure …?" he asked weakly as she slid the dress down just to where her breasts began to swell.

"Positive," she whispered, letting go of the dress and letting it fall to her feet. She leaned against the door and let it close softly behind her.

His hands opened and hovered over her breasts. "Oh … oh, all right," he whispered, caressing her breasts and kissing her neck. She leaned her head back and arched her back as he began to kiss her breasts and suckle her nipples.

Adele closed her eyes and thought of Max. "Only for you, dear," she thought to herself.

Upon landing on the shores of Mexico, the French army pounded the outskirts of a city there with their cannons, which were lined up to fire simultaneously. They encircled the town and quickly obliterated it. Each home held a family with its own tragic story.

A farmer on the outskirts of the town ran into his house, desperate to evacuate his family. The sudden cannon fire smashed the wall of his small kitchen, and the roof collapsed into half of the building. There was sudden silence as a massive cloud of clay dust covered the area.

A ten-year-old boy named Mace lifted his head and squinted through the rubble and dust. He could hear squeals and cries muffled by debris, and began to frantically dig in search of his brothers. He found his two-year-old brother first, screaming in terror and buried in roof tiles and rags. Mace extracted him as gently as he could, but the boards and stone scraped harshly at his soft skin.

The next person he found was his father, but the head was lodged firmly under part of the wall. The boy shook him desperately, but his father was dead. The boy's eyes widened in horror as a scream rose in his throat. He froze when he heard more muffled cries, then turned and continued digging. His mind screamed that he had not seen his father, that it never happened, and he clung to that thought as he continued his search for survivors.

When he was done, he had found two of his brothers, two-year-old Pepe and five-year-old Tiago. Baby Pepe whimpered a tiny wheeze as if he had no breath. Mace took a curtain from the ground and used it to drape over his father's body, not wanting the younger ones to see. He then took off his shirt and put it around Tiago, finding a chunk of bread the child was eating before the attack. He turned to offer it, but Tiago shook his head frantically, heaving gulps of air as the panic and dust got the better of him. Mace rolled him over onto his chest and pounded his back. Coughing and sputtering, the boy gasped for breath, tears in his eyes. He grabbed Mace by the neck and sobbed in silence. With his brother clinging to him, Mace managed to reach for the blanket still wrapped around Pepe. He picked Pepe up under the arms and blew small gulps of air into the toddler's mouth. Moments pass without a response, so he took both brothers, half dragging them, to a nearby spring. He plunged Pepe into the cold water, causing the boy to reflexively gasp and take in some air. He came out of the water screaming and angry, flailing his arms in indignation. His two older brothers laughed with relief at his tiny rage.

Mace removed all of Pepe's wet clothes and took his shirt back from Tiago, swaddling Pepe and rocking him to sleep. The toddler's angry cries quickly faded as exhaustion took over. Mace then threw the wet clothes into the branches nearby to dry, hurrying in the failing light of dusk. All of the children were exhausted from their ordeal, and soon Tiago was also asleep.

Mace could see through the dim light the bodies of his mother and grandparents strewn around the yard, two missing limbs. He was badly shaken and suppressed a cry, but his determination not to let the little ones see the desecrated remains gave him temporary strength. He placed Pepe beside Tiago and tiptoed away when he was sure they were sleeping soundly. He collected the bodies and dragged them to a deep pit on the far side of the spring. His eyes remained blank as he pretended one moment that he was moving firewood, then the next moment goat carcasses. Anything else. After two hours of plodding labor, he wearily limped back to his brothers and fell into a deep sleep, cuddling Pepe in his arms.

At dawn, Mace was awakened by the sound of growling and barking. It was the villagers' dogs left without owners, fighting over one of the chickens from the coop. He saw the ruins of the farm in the morning light with its broken-down fences. Picking up a broken branch from a tree, he swung it high above his head and shouted ferociously at the animals. The lead dog took this chance to grab the bleeding bird into his mouth and race towards what was left of the town. He sank to his knees and lowered his head to the ground without even the strength to weep at the desolation around him.

Mace stayed in that position for some time, how long he could not say. He finally lifted his head when he heard Pepe crying and realized that he was famished. "My brothers must be hungry, too," he thought to himself. He went to the hen house and found three eggs, carrying them to his brothers. They watched him curiously as he broke them open on top and fit a twig into the little holes, stirring the yellow contents. He had seen his father do this once on a hunting trip. He put the first egg up to Pepe's lips, and the boy began to suck eagerly. He offered the second egg to Tiago, but the younger boy made a face and refused to eat. Mace sighed and then held up the third egg. "Drink it down in one gulp like this," he said, tipping back his head and swallowing it all at once. Tiago hesitated but was truly hungry, so he finally followed his lead and did the same.

Mace took a large leaf from a nearby bush and formed it into a cone, folded at the end to make a cup. He walked to the spring and used it to bring back cool water. Tiago drank first as Mace fashioned a second cup for Pepe and filled it for the child. Both boys drank ravenously. When his brothers were satisfied, Mace went to the spring for himself. He lay on his belly as he had seen the farm animals do, making a cup with his palms and drinking his fill.

Mace worked all day making a lean-to. He used the old stone fireplace as the foundation, with many pieces of wood that had been thrown to the wind by the explosion. The day was sunny but not too warm, and Tiago played with Pepe under the shade by the spring. Mace gathered scraps of rugs and blankets to make a doorway. He was proud of himself as he placed a small three-legged stool next to the hearth, building a small fire from the embers of the previous day and scraps of wood too small to use in his makeshift building. It was late in the day when he returned to the henhouse to gather more eggs, finally bringing his brothers into the little shack he had fashioned.

They ate their meager fare and fell asleep by the fading fire.

In the late night hours, a clap of thunder and drops of rain on their faces awakened them. Mace looked wearily up at the raindrops leaking through the primitive roof and began to weep hopelessly. He stopped quickly when he heard Pepe scream. A snake had crawled into their meager dwelling, and Mace once again reacted automatically. He clutched the three-legged stool and struck the reptile furiously over and over again, continuing long after the creature's head had been pounded from its body. He finally slowed down and then stopped, laughing in relief. His laughter soon took on an edge of hysteria as he whispered repeatedly, "I'm not strong enough, Father, not strong enough … not strong enough!" He then began to weep again.

Tiago saw the desperation in his brother's weary eyes and leaned against him, whispering over him, "But you're strong, Mace, you're strong. You're strong and brave. See? The rain stopped," he said encouragingly as the shower tapered to an occasional drop. "In the morning, we'll go into town to find someone." They huddled together, wedging themselves into the fireplace to keep warm.

As the sun rose, they held their two-year-old brother turn by turn and took to the road. They soon grew tired from trying to hold the wriggling child and set him on the road to follow them. Pepe was happy to be free to move about, stretching his arms out and laughing as he sang, "Danza! Danza!" He would spin in circles as he sang, occasionally staggering or falling, and then get up and start his spinning dance all over again.

They made it just past a copse of trees when they saw a pack of jaguarundi. The cats circled the boys. Pepe was still too dazed and dizzy from his game to see them yet. He gasped in surprise as two of the cats leapt forward and took him by an arm and a leg. Mace's heart felt as if it would pound right from his chest as the sound of his baby brother's screams filled his ears.

Tiago screamed as well as more of the cats attacked him and his older brother. The two cats that had Pepe dragged the terrified boy into a patch of bushes. Mace kicked viciously at the cats that were attacking Tiago and himself, desperate to get to the ones who had Pepe. The cats backed off of the road and trotted to the bushes for an easier meal. Mace ran to the bushes to try to rescue his brother, ignoring the blood that covered his own limbs. He lunged towards the bushes but jumped back when one of the cats snapped at his hand.

He froze when he saw what was left of poor Pepe. The boy had been torn apart by the jaguarundi. Mace's body began to shake violently as he watched the cats stomp the child's remains, overcome by their hunger and ignoring Mace. They picked at the body as Mace stayed, locked in horror. One of the cats clamped its teeth around the toddler's neck and began to gnaw on it. Mace turned and ran screaming, stumbling back to Tiago on the road. Two cats broke free from the bushes and stalked them. The bloody children ran until their lungs felt as though they would burst.

Two young men came running with machetes from the ruins of town. One took a sweeping cut towards the first cat and partially decapitated him, chasing the other cat as it ran away howling into the hills. The young men picked up the boys and finished the walk to town, carefully setting them down in the shade of a battered shop front. They tended Tiago's and Mace's wounds as best they could. When they were sure the boys weren't dying, one of the men reached into his sack and handed them a loaf of bread and a few ragged apples. The taller of the youths gave Mace a jug of watered-down wine and then turned as they made their escape into the hills.

The boys began to eat in silence, staring straight ahead. They finally grew tired and lay down on the step of the storefront. Their sleep deepened to unconsciousness, and they lay there for two days. Mace finally lifted his heavy head when he heard a small keening sound. He shook his brother awake and they looked about, confused, finally realizing that the keening sound was the cries of their great-aunt Alma.

"I've been searching for days for you, my poor little ones, and here you are!" she cried, lifting them into her arms and rocking them over and over on her ample breasts. The blood that covered the boys told her that there was no point in asking about little Pepe. They were clearly too stunned to reply. Her powerful arms held them up firmly as she walked down the ruined street. "Half alive, sleeping in a roadside shop front! Miles from home! My poor little ones," she sobbed.

The shouts of wailing mothers rose in a din above their cries.

The following day, the French army ordered the city to hand over the resistance soldiers of General Diaz. When the people failed to comply, they commanded that everyone evacuate the city. The boys left with their great-aunt, but her husband and all of the males over fifteen years of age were ordered back into the city.

The prominent political leaders were summarily jailed or executed, and the lesser political leaders were commanded to address the populace and advise them to cooperate. At one point, a Mexican dignitary tried to pacify the crowd as they evacuated, but they angrily shouted, "Traitor!!" and refused to listen.

The firing squads were in three layers: lying on their bellies, sitting on their haunches, and standing as they shot their guns. They were chillingly efficient, mowing down the crowd. It was chaos, some jumping over walls and others dying as they tried to follow behind. Some were blinded. Some had broken arms and legs. Women shrieked, cried, wailed. Men shouted. Children died. Once the town was evacuated, every male over the age of fifteen was killed by the troops, who went house to house to accomplish the task. Outside of the town, the evacuated women, children, and elderly were left to be preyed upon by looters, rapists, soldiers, and animals.

The music that the sage had heard was becoming even clearer.

The horror was unfathomable. How could Maximilian possibly come to places like these ruined towns and presume to rule them? The French army had so horribly ravaged the people that the populace was likely to view him as merely an extension of the terrible men who had destroyed their families and their lives. It was a bad political situation from the start, but the wool was already being pulled over Maximilian's eyes with the rigged vote and the document they were preparing, the lie that said Mexico wanted him as their emperor.

The French army then opened a general offensive to rout Juarez's forces. Their operation room was full of French officers and generals who were supervising assaults at several different targets. The bombardment destroyed many peaceful cities and their populations. Blood and misery were everywhere.

In one city, a woman came out of her adobe hut, lunging towards the firing squad nearby. A neighbor held her fast, restraining her for her own good as the woman lamented, "Juarez, Juarez! See what they're doing to us? You said we'd have peace with the invaders! Occupiers … goddamn you murderers!! Oh God, oh God, where are you??"

The men were put into lines along an adobe wall and then shot by the firing squad. As they fell to the ground, one civilian shouted, "Viva, Juarez!" He was grabbed by the neck and taken to a pole, where soldiers quickly put a rope around his neck and hanged him. Two other pro-Juarez politicians were beaten and put into jail, later shown to be armed revolutionaries.

All that remained of their cities and towns were mass graves.

Juarez entered what was left of a town. The carnage was indescribable, with the corpses of women and children piled up in carts. They were being taken to a mass grave, where the soldiers pulled the bodies out by the legs or the neck and threw them into a ditch.

Juarez sat with his militia in a broken town square not far from the mass grave. Someone in the militia was speaking nearby. "Revenge! We take revenge, we counterattack!"

"No, no," Juarez said in a commanding voice. "I'm the leader here, I'll make those decisions." The men of his militia looked at him and listened as he continued. "This is our struggle against a foreign power. We don't want Mexico to become a place for an international war. We're a responsible command. We're going north so we can be in sufficient control of some territory. From there, we'll engage in guerilla war. Right now, we're incapable of carrying out a sustained and concentrated military operation. We're disbanding now and we'll escape to the north. We'll hide our weapons. Then and only then will we fight a guerilla war. Nothing will happen unless we want it to."

An hour later, Juarez was reviewing dispatches and other documents in the dusty office they had made for him in the back of a bank. General Diaz approached Juarez, handing him a proclamation to sign.

After reading the document thoroughly, Juarez looked up at Diaz incredulously. "But surely you don't believe in this?"

"All my life I've fought these reactionaries, and now you're asking us to disband and escape to the north," General Diaz replied. "Sign it and I'll attack."

Juarez stared at him intently. "You'd disobey?"

"Your armies go by the rules you set," Diaz stated proudly. "I'll go by my convictions."

Juarez took his time and finally asked the general, "What then, when your convictions change?"

Diaz kept silent.

The Juarez forces began the long retreat north in darkness. General Diaz hid his troops inside a flowing canal, the men using reeds to breathe as they hid under the water. They waited for some time before ambushing the French column crossing the stream. They went on to blow up storages and attack headquarters, finally pushing in for a house-to-house, close-quarter battle. They managed to kidnap a French officer in the process, but Diaz was soon betrayed and captured.

He was tied, beaten, and thrown into jail, taken out from time to time for merciless interrogations.

Juarez was so despondent on his way north that at times he actually thought about suicide. During the long march, everyone blamed him for the death and destruction that Mexico was suffering, wondering aloud why he hadn't managed to negotiate as he'd planned. He swallowed his own personal feelings and continued with the plan, ordering the disbandment of the army so that it could transform into a guerilla army in the north. They completed their retreat and hid their weapons.

Meanwhile, the French army conducted their plebiscite, asking the people if they would vote for Prince Maximilian von Hapsburg to be their emperor. The entire system was a fraud. Pressure was put on the peasants at every turn. An old man walking with his young son was seen putting his vote in the box. He had voted "no" and a French officer had found out. The old man was violently questioned and his son beaten. The old man cried, "We want Juarez! WE WANT JUAREZ!!"

A nearby officer screamed, "Juarez is dead! And we're sending you to meet him!" He turned to the soldiers nearby. "Shoot him."

"My father isn't a politician! He's just an old man!" the man's son shouted.

The officer stared coldly at the young man and turned away, snapping over his shoulder to the soldier, "Shoot him, too."

French Marshal Bazine stood before his staff, Colonel Lopez, to give his opinion of newspaper coverage on the vote. "Prince Maximilian obtained 99% of the vote, so it's fair to say that it's an overwhelming consent."

Colonel Lopez raised an eyebrow. "But why was there such low attendance?"

Bazine laughed. "The plague, of course," he lied.

Italy

Maximilian and Charlotte sat by the opulent castle of Miramar, entertaining guests at a poolside musical concert. Light from the gaslights reflected in the pool as the soft strains of violins filled the evening air. People milled about in their gowns and suits, accepting delectable hors d'oeuvres from the many servants winding their ways through the crowd.

Maximilian was in his element, charming the crowd with his numerous stories and anecdotes. Charlotte beamed at his side, pleased that she was able to enjoy herself among others and forget about her daily boredom, if only for that night.

An ADC approached the archduke in the middle of one of his exciting stories, waiting patiently while the Hapsburg finished the story and caused an eruption of sycophantic laughter. Maximilian then excused himself and stepped away from the crowd, taking a telegram from the officer. "It's from Napoleon, sire."

Maximilian opened it with interest, Charlotte craning her neck from a conversation to peek curiously at her husband. The telegram read:

> "Overwhelming consent. Take emperorship. Good luck.
>
> —Napoleon III."

"Overwhelming consent?" Maximilian repeated. "What does that mean?" He looked at the ADC, confused. "Napoleon's forces attack Mexico, they fight back valiantly on May 5th ... and now they report overwhelming consent? Are these crafty generals trying to make a fool out of me?"

By then, Charlotte had slid next to her husband and read the telegram in his hands. "You can easily find out the authenticity of this," she said, scanning the paper.

"How?" Maximilian asked her with a look of surprise, as if she had appeared out of nowhere.

"By going to Mexico to see things for yourself, Maxi."

"And find out that we were tricked by a general putting his pistol into the mouths of the people to get that overwhelming consent?" he scoffed. "I think not. What if the general there and his policy directors in Paris are determined to cause a civil war in Mexico to weaken the people resisting them there? They will be doing things instead of avoiding things. How would you know?"

"Maxi, Austria has very extensive espionage. Put it to good use. Get to know the facts."

"Everyone seems to be in a hurry to push me to an emperor's throne. Am I going to be the fool?" Maximilian agonized over his decision. Charlotte took his arm and led him down the garden path, away from the ADC. "Look, the French army is already there. The people probably hate them. If you can liberate those people, you might strike your roots there."

"How can I strike my roots there when the situation hinges on the Confederates winning the civil war?" Maximilian reasoned. "The North is far too organized and industrial to stand up to. That Lincoln is preaching emancipation from slavery in the South—"

"More states are joining the South," Charlotte reasoned. "Lincoln only has a few states."

"And what if Lincoln wins? That'd make Napoleon withdraw his army and forget about the Louisiana Purchase. We'd be left utterly helpless and exposed."

"But my dearest Maxi, Lincoln is not winning, he's losing. His own life is in danger."

"It's certainly a very odd telegram," Maximilian concluded, walking back up the path and handing the paper back to his ADC. "Perhaps it's a fraud."

Maximilian and Charlotte both felt the need for counsel, and since Charlotte wanted to visit her father, they made the long journey to Belgium. Charlotte was excited as they traveled past the vast orchards to her parent's palace in Laeken. As they passed through the gilded gate, the familiar domed roof sitting above the grand columns loomed majestically ahead. Charlotte scarcely waited for the carriage to stop before leaping out and embracing the old man in livery. The duke of Brabant, who ordered that the king be notified of the royal couple's arrival, greeted them.

A house servant entered King Leopold's library. "Pardon my interruption, sire, but Archduke Maximilian von Hapsburg and Princess Charlotte have arrived."

The king eagerly went to the door, careful not to appear in a rush to his staff, and greeted his daughter with a kiss and an affectionate hug. He turned to Maximilian and pounded him sturdily on the back.

"Good, good! You're here at long last! Come in, come in! Sit down! Andrew, bring us a bottle of champagne, the best. We must celebrate." Andrew returned with a chilled bottle and three champagne glasses. After the drinks were poured, Andrew backed out of the room and gently closed the door behind him.

The princess sat on her father's knee as she had done years ago when she was a child. "Oh, I love you, Papa," she gushed, hugging him tightly. "I've missed you so much!" King Leopold returned her hug, ecstatic to see her after so long. It was a while before they were able to separate themselves from each other enough to take their own seats and pick up their champagne glasses.

Leopold finally looked at Maximilian. "So you're going to Mexico?"

"Yes. I've received a letter from Benito Juarez, the rebel leader there. He wants to negotiate."

Leopold rose and left Charlotte in the most comfortable chair, crossing to Maximilian. "By the time you reach Mexico, the French generals very well might have changed that situation," he warned.

"Anything is possible," Maximilian admitted with a shrug.

"One of the Belgian officers on General Bazine's staff told me a story about his trickery. Bazine blockaded certain Juarez areas and didn't allow food and supplies to reach the populace. The mayor concluded an arrangement with him to hand over one hundred of Juarez's men in return for lifting the embargo. The one hundred were handed over and Bazine tortured them, obtained information from them, then shot every last one of them. Then he attacked the real targets with artillery. In one night, some twelve hundred shells landed on those peaceful locations. The people went mad with rage."

"A perfect example of a general's rough-handed way of dealing with politics," Maximilian lamented, shaking his head.

"Those kinds of generals create revolts, my son."

"Juarez can't fight the French army. He probably expects that I'll give him a better agreement."

"Maybe, but Lincoln isn't losing the war. And now he's supplying arms to Juarez, which means a bitter guerilla war ahead instead of Juarez's surrender. My resources also tell me that Juarez's deputy has asked him to step down because he's an Indian. Imagine how you'll fare as a European."

"But sire," Maximilian debated, "I want to go in order to control General Bazine. He's a typical military man. He's the kind who'd brush all of the dirt under the carpet. Hell, he's one step ahead of that devilry; he'd even perfume the carpet. He'll have his way, attack Juarez or his deputy and try to scuttle the opposition with sheer force. Force is all he knows and submits to. He's a cunning fox."

"Then go," Leopold acquiesced. "You have a slight chance, if you're a wise ruler."

"I'll take that. I believe I can be successful as emperor. The odds aren't that bad as yet."

"As yet," Leopold repeated menacingly.

"You're known for good advice, sire. Any advice for me?"

"I have someone who can give better advice than I. Let's go to him," Leopold replied.

"We could call him here."

"We need him, Maximilian. He doesn't need us. Since his advice is worth a crown, I would think you'd be willing to travel as far as the other end of the world only to get such good advice."

The king sent Charlotte off with a kiss on the forehead to the suite of rooms he was having prepared for them. "Go, child. Rest and we'll meet for breakfast first thing in the morning." She complied hesitantly, unhappy to be left out of the talks but having no choice in her customary role as a woman. She left for her suite, determined to interrogate her husband later about what happened.

Leopold walked the archduke out to the stables and they sat in a royal coach, always kept ready for such surprise trips. They traveled to the house of the sage with bodyguards accompanying on horseback. On the way there, Leopold explained the sage to Maximilian.

"He wanted to marry a girl, a young girl at his old age," Leopold laughed. "He said she's willing to marry him, said he's good for her even as an old man."

Maximilian smiled.

"He said that her parents are the only impediment," Leopold added, laughing.

"Funny," Maximilian laughed.

"Human."

Maximilian stuck his head out of the coach and looked at the road ahead. The sage's house was near. As they approached, there were beautiful pigeons flying around the modest home. Maximilian frowned at the pigeons, always a stickler for protocol and courtly etiquette. "In France, only the princes can keep pigeons," he said with disapproval.

"Oh, he asked me permission to keep pigeons," Leopold replied, smiling. "It's a small concession to make."

The coach halted before the door. The king got out first as some of the men accompanying them knocked upon the door. The old sage greeted them at the door and brought them inside, nodding curiously to the young man.

"My dear friend, let me introduce my son-in-law, Prince Maximilian von Hapsburg, from Austria."

"I'm humbled, sire." The sage bowed low before the archduke.

"What's happening here?" the king asked, looking at the disheveled room and up at the rafters, where the cooing of pigeons could be heard.

"The cat pounced on my pigeons and tore open my best one," the sage replied sadly. "The other pigeons flew to the rafters, and there they've stayed ever since. They haven't been down since last night, not even to eat or drink."

"Why?" Leopold asked curiously.

"Fear changes their psychology completely, sire. They won't come down now."

"Hm," the king hummed, staring at the frightened birds.

The sage picked up a dead pigeon. It looked like it had been a strong enough bird, but its wing was now broken and it hung limp in his hand. "This pigeon was a jolly good fellow when he had no fear. He used to flit around, flirt with every female pigeon, eat, make a run for the sky, and then somersault to impress the ladies. Fear changed his entire lifestyle," he explained. His underlying meaning was obvious. He took a small knife from a drawer and started to skin it.

Leopold watched for a moment. Taking note of the sage's preoccupation, he finally said, "We could come again. I see you've enough troubles of your own right now." The sage once again noticed his company and stated emphatically, "Sire, your son in-law is going to be the emperor of Mexico, yes? I read the news. He's come to you for advice." He paused, looking directly into Maximilian's eyes. "He shouldn't go there."

Maximilian was stunned by his abruptness. "Why?" he asked, bewildered.

"You're a falcon, sire. Can you lead pigeons?"

"The Mexicans aren't pigeons," Maximilian pointed out emphatically. "They braved the invading armies. They're courageous."

"No, they're not pigeons," the sage agreed. "The elite minority is inviting you there. They're the pigeons. As soon as their French protectors are gone, they'll leave you and side with the Juarez forces, your opponent. They'll not look at your handsome face; they'll only kiss the ugly face of Juarez."

Max looked greatly disturbed by the sage's counsel. He excused himself and went out to wait in the coach while Leopold concluded his visit. All the way back to Laeken, he sat quietly, deeply concerned, troubled, and dejected.

Word was carried to Napoleon III that Maximilian was "actively listening" to the delegation. With no time to waste, he ordered that the rigged vote stating that Mexico wanted Maximilian as their emperor be arranged. When word of this reached the ears of Emperor Franz Joseph, he was furious, and immediately summoned his brother.

French troops entered the Mexican capital in 1863, and an empire under the Austrian archduke Ferdinand Maximilian Joseph von Hapsburg was declared. Republican forces retreated to the far north, and for four years Mexico would have two governments.

Schonbrunn Palace, Austria—1864

It was evening in the royal palace. The royal family sat in a lounge next to the great dining hall, in the empress's salon of gold and white. An unusual clock tick-tocked on the mantel. It had two faces so that the time could also be seen while looking into the mirror. Maximilian was reading a newspaper. He found an interesting article and called for the attention of his family, his mother Sophie, sister-in-law Sissi, and wife Charlotte.

"Interesting, listen to this, it's about democracy," he said, standing and bringing the paper to the sofas where the ladies were sitting. He sat beside his mother and read it aloud.

"If fifty men with one voice term the day as night,
The twenty have to agree, accept the wrong as right.
This is the democratic age.
Who can question or debate?"

Sissi laughed and waved her hand, continuing the verse playfully,

"If fifty-one declare a cow as a beauty queen,
The forty-nine must acquiesce, or in vain simply scream."

Now Charlotte laughed and added,

"If the majority elects an owl to be their president,
Need must the minority accept that good sense?"

Maximilian enjoyed their rhyming and concluded,

"This is the democratic age.
Who can question or debate?"

The family laughed, everyone in a good mood now.

Their laughter died off as Emperor Franz Joseph and his father entered the lounge. All rose to bow, Sophie smiling sweetly at her husband. The house butler, a member of the royal guards, entered wearing a uniform and a royal sash. He saluted the emperor. "May the dinner be served, sire?"

"Yes, please," Franz Joseph said nodding.

The NCO energetically saluted and walked away. The kitchen servants brought their trolleys full of delicious food and pastries to the dining table, a rich and shining oblong slab of mahogany decked with silver trophies of the household royal regiment. As always, it was heavily decked with lovely flowers.

As Sissi sat down beside her mother-in-law, Sophie, she said, "We're helpless emperors and kings. This is the democratic age."

Sophie touched her sleeve with a small gesture to as if to hush her.

Sissi looked questioningly at the former empress. "Have I said anything against the etiquette, ma'am?"

"As you well know, we never discuss politics at the dining table," Sophie replied softly.

"My husband is gloomy today," Sissi said, moving to excuse herself from the table. "I only wanted to cheer him up."

Franz Joseph took the clue from Sissi and acted cheered up. "Sissi, what was that joke you told the other day about women coming to Parliament?"

"Oh, yes," Sissi laughed, sinking back into her chair. "They would stand flaunting their jewelry, adjusting their hair, and filing their delicate nails. Their speeches would include talk of ribbons and lace. The economy of their daughters-in-law would also come up for debate."

Now everyone was laughing. This was the calm before the tempest. After dinner, Franz Karl asked Sissi and Sophie to leave. They nodded and were quickly gone, leaving Charlotte as the only woman still in the room. The doors were closed and guards stood outside to forbid entry to everyone.

Franz Joseph turned to his brother. "What's your decision, Maxi?"

Maximilian looked at his wife and extended his hand to hold hers. "We're going."

"Is that good judgment?" Franz Karl asked.

"Everyone, including my own father-in-law, has told me not to do this," Maximilian replied. "They say I'm not Mexican, that I'd just be the facade of an occupying French emperor."

Franz Joseph pressed him. "The French sided with our enemies in Italy, went to war with us, and cost us two-thirds of our empire. This entire Mexican affair is just the latest bait to overthrow the Hapsburg dynasty. Would you be a partner of the French against the Hapsburgs?"

Maximilian sighed. "There's more to it than that. Look, Joseph, we've lost such a vast empire in only two years. Here's a chance to dig our roots into a new land, a vast land! If we can't grow in Europe, perhaps we can grow in the Americas."

Their father interjected, "You're well-intentioned, son, we know that. But you're being beguiled by scheming manipulators into believing that you'd be ruling over a population that genuinely adores you."

"God makes out of nothing, but man makes out of something," Maximilian insisted passionately. "I have that 'something' to make it work."

"For example?" his father asked.

"For example, I can ask Juarez to be my prime minister. We have common ground in education, humanitarian ideals, representative governments …"

"You failed to mention your most common ground, son."

"Which is?"

"Both of you want to reduce the powers of the Roman Catholic Church."

"Yes, that's true. So?"

"So the powerful conservative classes would be against you, Max. If your French armies leave Mexico, they'll sell you to Juarez."

"Why would the French armies leave when Napoleon wishes to undo the Louisiana Purchase? That would give him back everything in the United States west of the Mississippi!"

Franz Karl continued, patiently trying to reason with his son. "Napoleon once lost his emperorship. He made mistakes for which he paid. Now he's making another mistake, investing his forces and money in a far land when he's in danger in Paris itself. Would Mexico be more important to Napoleon than France?"

"Of course not," Maximilian grudgingly replied.

"Therefore, he'd pull his troops out of Mexico," Franz Karl concluded.

"I can abdicate in the worst scenario."

"To do what?" Franz Joseph interjected. "By accepting this emperorship, you've already abdicated all of your Hapsburg positions and titles. Besides, why put yourself in a position where your only choice would be to abdicate?" Franz Joseph shook his head. "I need you to strengthen the available Austrian empire. I can post you anywhere you decide. That would keep you close to the family."

Maximilian sat quietly, but he was faintly shaking his head. Charlotte watched the entire discourse like a tennis match, her head turning right, then left, then right again. Franz Joseph leaned in his chair and spoke in a softer tone, but his point was still firm. "You don't belong to Mexico, Maxi, not even to any of its ethnic tribes or minorities. The people there are up against an occupying power, France, our enemy. That enemy is trying to force a civil war inside of Mexico now to divide them. America is fighting a civil war, too, but when it's over, they'll become powerful allies for the Mexican people."

"That's the situation, exactly—" Maximilian started, but his brother continued.

"After the plebiscite, you'll be the government, not the opposition. You should join the people instead of being the occupying army's figurehead. If you like, I'll abdicate in your favor here," he offered.

Maximilian embraced his elder brother. "I made a commitment and I must honor it. After the plebiscite, I have to honor my part of the deal."

"You don't want to be counted amongst the martyrs, do you?" Franz Joseph asked, frustrated.

"Of emperors or ideas?" Maximilian responded.

"Ideas," his brother clarified, sighing and rubbing his tired eyes. "All right, tomorrow we'll decide the date and time for your de-investitures. You have to resign your commission, your titles, all links to this empire."

Maximilian walked to Charlotte and smiled hopefully. "Tomorrow it is. Let's go, darling."

Franz Joseph nodded to his father, who had the doors reopened. They walked out to the lounge where Sophie and Sissi were having coffee. As the men entered, Franz Joseph assumed a more cheerful demeanor and said to his wife, "Who?"

Sissi laughed.

"The Fulfiller," he said ominously, and Sissi smiled uncertainly.

The next day, Maximilian formally resigned from all of his titles and commissions. The papers were drawn up and officiated, leaving the prince with no direction to go but forward. Franz Joseph met for one last talk with his brother at Schonbrunn. He had secretly waited to file the papers of renunciation, hoping against hope that this one final meeting would allow him to tear them up and throw them into the fire.

The luxurious drawing room known as the Blue Chinese Salon was lit and ready to receive the Hapsburg brothers. The lights from the great hearth and candelabra caught the dramatic blue from the numerous detailed prints inlayed into the walls, as well as the two large Chinese vases decking either side of the fireplace. The furniture was upholstered in a matching brocade of light blue and white. The emperor, looking at his brother, said:

"With a wild dreadful roar
He unsheathed his deadly sword,
Raised a loud deafening laugh,
And thrust the steel into his heart!"

Do you want to do that?

The brothers were bathed in the relaxing blues as they entered, both in full dress uniforms so formal that they included their swords. Maximilian's face was flushed with excitement. He wanted to go to Mexico, his hopes of obtaining an emperorship rekindled.

"You truly look like an emperor today, Joseph," Maximilian said with a smile.

"I *am* an emperor," Franz Joseph reminded him dryly.

"Yes, you are. I admire the royal uniform, especially when it's completed with the sword," he said, nodding at Franz Joseph's red and white attire. "You remember we were dressed in royal uniform from the time we could ride a horse. We were a sight, you and I in identical uniforms," he reminisced with a smile.

"Yes, well, Devin made sure we were always properly dressed," Franz Joseph said.

They both nodded with a chuckle as they thought back on their old schoolmaster. Devin had been very strict and took his duties very seriously. He made sure that a significant portion of their days was taken up with marching, drill, ceremonies, and a great deal of standing in formation. This was alongside the riding, fencing, dancing, and gymnastics that had been part of their physical training. He had instructed their parents, the emperor and his empress, that the princes were to be on the drill grounds and maneuver fields as early as four o'clock in the morning. They would return for lunch towards ten or eleven and then devote their afternoon to military studies of one kind or another, especially military strategy.

Maximilian frowned to himself in concentration. "I remember that one book you read religiously, The Officer's Manual in the Field. It was all worn and you had it memorized by the time you were ten years old ... what was the name of that other one, your second favorite book?"

"That was The Manual of Bayonet Exercise by McClellan," Joseph replied proudly. "I also liked System of Cavalry Maneuvers in Line."

Maximilian nodded. "And from four 'til seven o'clock, your time was taken up by barrack room inspections, reports ... and the other thousand-and-one duties incidental to regimental life. I much preferred to spend time with Mother and the gardener," he added with a wink. "But all the same, old Devin told us time and time again that as crown princes, our work would be exceptionally heavy, that we were expected to learn in six months what those of lower ranks and positions took years to learn."

"And that we did, or so we tried," Franz Joseph said with a nod as he remembered all of their work. "At the very least, we learned discipline."

"But is that what we should've learned?" Maximilian wondered aloud.

"What do you mean?"

"Well, discipline teaches conformity. The dress, the drills, and the parades ... they all require you to conform. That's not teaching leadership. Even the leaders become ordinary soldiers with that approach."

"Ordinary soldiers?" Franz Joseph repeated, not sure if Maximilian was also referring to him in that statement.

"Well, think about it, Joseph. Where would Napoleon have been if he'd been a conformist? When he was sitting on the coast of English Channel and getting ready to attack England, did he do as was expected? No, he secretly turned and marched into Austria, knowing full well that he'd be up against Russia and Austria together. But he dared, and look what he gained. He defeated Austria, entered Vienna and visited this very place we are standing in. Imagine that! He didn't conform, he won; and later, when the Russian army came upon him, he didn't run; he defeated them as well. Would Napoleon have been like that if he'd conformed? We're teaching our kings to be foot-soldiers, not thinking commanders. If we drill them like soldiers, what do we expect? Should we teach them to obey and then expect them to have the independence of mind, the resoluteness, and creativity to do extraordinary and far-seeing things?"

Franz frowned. "Well, not all great and creative things are accomplished by looking forward into the distant future, Maxi."

"But if not the leaders, who would do it?" Maximilian asked his brother passionately. "Who'll reach forward and grasp at what has the most meaning? Who'll bring the truth to the people?"

Franz Joseph shook his head. "It's not the truth that matters; it's the whitewash, Maxi. Nothing succeeds like failure, so long as you wave the flag hard enough and keep the whitewash coming. That's the way rulers reward themselves when they fail." He glanced and could not help but smile at his brother's astonished face. "Rulers must be artful, know how to earn a 'Thank you, sire' even from failures."

Maximilian fell silent a moment, frustrated at his brother's vastly different point of view but determined to stay in a light and happy mood. He patted his brother's arm as he swiftly changed the subject and enthusiastically went back to recalling their school lessons. "My favorite part of the lessons was marksmanship. We really learned confidence in both ourselves and our weapons with that part, I think. We perfected the fifteen one-second movements to load and fire a musket. I believe that was when I was about eight years old."

"Yes," Joseph smiled. "I couldn't help but laugh when you struggled with that musket, twice as tall as you." He sat by the fire and poured himself a brandy. "And remember when you got us three days off from our teacher Cavin? By throwing his eye glasses into a tree?" They both laughed at that as Maximilian sat in a chair beside his brother, enjoying the fire.

"I wasn't the only one flirting with trouble, Joseph. Thanks to you, we always seemed to know when the palace girls were going for a swim in the canal. Remember when they caught us watching them bathe naked?"

They laughed for a while at the memories of their past misdeeds. Maximilian fell silent and stared at the fire, then spoke softly, thoughtfully. "Mother always said you were obsessed with the concept of honor, and that you were too honest because of that. But she also said that you were unexceptional in some ways, that you possessed the qualities of an infantry captain instead of a leader. She thought you went against her golden rule of never surrendering until defeated in battle. She said it was always better to be destroyed in war than to surrender territory in peace."

"Yes, Mother would have made a great general," Franz Joseph said with a soft laugh. Maximilian's words were blunt and somewhat harsh, but Franz Joseph had long gotten used to it. Maximilian meant no harm, and only spoke whatever was on his mind. It was one of the reasons Franz Joseph felt that Maximilian's prospects in politics were limited, but it was a character trait that could not be changed. His mother's thoughts about him came as no surprise either, as she had many times said those very words to his face, though in softer tones. It was certain that she and her favorite son Maxi spent hours at a time trading opinions about even the smallest of his decisions as emperor. It was part of his duties as emperor to tolerate such things, something his father had already prepared him for when he passed down the title to him. "I still have a picture of you," Maximilian said, interrupting his brother's thoughts, "an image of Archduke Franz Joseph. You were getting your military training at a one-pounder field gun, surrounded by military instructors. You were a child soldier, wearing a white Austrian fourth infantry regiment's uniform, a Hoch-Deutmeister, complete with a sword ..." His expression softened from fondness to a touch of sadness. "You know, the sword stands for the authority of the office. I want an emperor's sword someday."

"But you have an exquisite sword, brother," Franz replied fondly.

"You know what I mean, Joseph. I want an emperor's sword. That's what we were born for, trained for. I'm incomplete without it, it's my destiny." His voice and eyes were transformed from soft and sad to bold and full of excitement.

"You're still determined to take the emperorship of Mexico?" Franz Joseph asked. "Even if it means losing everything?"

"Yes, Joseph. There's been a plebiscite there, and over 90% of the people voted to have me as their ruler."

"It surprises me to think that a country as divided as Mexico could agree on anything right now. Your plebiscite has no legitimacy."

"Well, that's exactly what they did," Maximilian insisted. "I have no cause to doubt it."

"America's fighting a civil war of their own, Maxi, and when that's over, they'll side with the Mexicans."

Maximilian nodded soberly. "Yes, that's the situation."

"You've renounced your ties, your titles, all of your noble rights in Austria … what's left?" Franz Joseph asked, his hands thrown up in exasperation.

"Joseph, the blood that flows through my veins is Hapsburg blood just like yours, emperor's blood, and it *must* have some fulfillment!" Maximilian insisted as his spirit took fire. "I know you could forbid me to go, but you also know I'd go anyway."

Franz Joseph paused and stared at his brother, struggling for patience. "You know that the bureaucrats in Mexico are going to lead you down an entirely different path than you have planned." He saw his brother bristle but continued. "They'll get you to rule through positivism, try to control the public thought. It's part of the new approach on the rise, attempting to change human nature—"

"Human nature can't be crushed, that's impossible."

"But a dictator does succeed in crushing and changing human nature when people stop questioning whether his pursuits are selfish."

"I've read Karl Marx, Joseph. He feels the same way I do about—"

"Oh, Max, enough idealism! Think logically, please! Just let me abdicate in your favor," Franz Joseph interrupted, his eyes pleading.

Maximilian stood and turned away. He would do almost anything for Franz Joseph. As brothers, they were as close as two people could be, but as men, they had separate lives to live. His jaw was set. He had decided. His destiny was in Mexico.

CHAPTER 13

▼

GOOD INTENTIONS

The young couple prepared to leave Austria for their journey to the New World. Maximilian had finally been appointed emperor of Mexico, and almost everyone in the court congratulated them with false enthusiasm. Both Maximilian and Charlotte believed that the Mexican people wanted him to be their new ruler. They were blissful and optimistic.

It was finally the morning of their departure for Mexico. Maximilian was dressed in the latest fashion of the day, quite the dashing gentleman as he entered his mother's suite of rooms.

Sophie was also impeccably dressed, wearing a morning dress of golden lace. She had been weeping, her beautiful eyes red and puffy. When her son entered, she attempted to compose herself, patting her hair carefully and examining her face in the mirror. She fought to be strong. It took a great deal of energy and strong determination, but she stood and pulled herself up to her full height. She looked every bit the royal lady as she greeted her son with a kiss.

"Maxi, my loving son," she said, forcing a smile. They exchanged kisses as they had always done. "Are you sure this is what you want?" Sophie stammered weakly. "There's still time to change your mind. You know I'll miss you terribly. When you left before, I always knew you were only a few days away if I needed you. But this ... this Mexico is halfway around the world. I fear I'll never see you again!" she finally said. It was all too much for her and she began to weep.

"Oh, dear lady," Maximilian cooed, taking her into his arms. "Yes, this is what I want … this is what I've been waiting for all of my life." He tucked a finger under her chin and lifted her head, lowering his head to look into her eyes with a tender smile. "I'm happy, Mother. Please be happy for me. Everything's been prepared and the ship awaits me even now."

"Yes, I suppose I've planned all your life for you to take over a throne somewhere. And I'm happy for that.. Forgive my mother's weakness," she sniffed, dabbing her eyes. "It's all just so final. I mean, are you sure the throne is waiting for you? You have assurances from the Pope? The French and the Mexicans?"

"Yes, I've been assured that there's been a vote of the people. They want me, Mother, and not just the aristocrats. The French army is standing and waiting for me, and the Pope has given his blessing."

"Oh Maxi!" the queen cried, heartbroken. She embraced him and wept uncontrollably. For a while they both wept, feeling the inevitable loss of the connection they had always felt so strongly.

"I have to go," he said at last, holding her by the shoulders and at an arm's length. "Can't you see this is what we've both wanted for so long? It's a chance for me to use my skills in a way that will make a difference in the lives of the Mexican people. I'll make a great emperor, Mother."

"Yes, I know you will," Sophie said. Exhausted, she sat on the chaise lounge.

"I'll write you often to tell you all about my supreme skill at government. You'll see! You know I'm well trained for emperorship. You've been my greatest teacher, Mama, my unyielding support," he said, sitting beside her.

"Yes, yes, of course, you'll be marvelous," she almost whispered, trying bravely to smile.

"Then give me one last kiss. I mustn't keep my future waiting any longer," he said, fighting to control his voice. "Promise me that you'll put off all this weeping."

"Yes, Maxi. Yes, of course." She gave him another kiss and followed him to join the family at the front of the palace. "Goodbye, Maxi. Go now, goodbye," she said, her enthusiasm more believable this time. As he climbed into the carriage and began to move down the road, she called after him, "Don't look back, Son! I won't weep!" She lied to make him feel better, to give her son a happier departure. She continued standing tensely with the family until his carriage turned the corner and was out of sight. Clapping a hand over her mouth, she hurried back into her suite and sank into her lounge, a broken soul. It was a long time before she stopped weeping.

The young couple was soon headed for their new home. After leaving England, they had boarded an Austrian vessel called *the Novara*, a sharp-looking ship painted black with the cannon slots painted white. The captain ordered the cabin boy to raise the Mexican imperial standard, and they finally set sail for their new home, bound for Vera Cruz. Maximilian and Charlotte were excited and optimistic, their enthusiasm bolstered by a royal send-off. Their cousin, Queen Victoria, had ordered her garrison at Gibraltar to fire a salute as their ship passed by, though she would not officially endorse his move to Mexico as emperor. They had received a blessing from the pope, as well.

Charlotte watched the coast of Europe slip away for the last time. "Do you ever think we'll see our homeland again?" she asked Maximilian.

"Our homeland is Mexico now. Its people are our people," he replied with ardent idealism.

The waves of the Atlantic had calmed quite a bit overnight and were tranquil compared to the days before, allowing Charlotte to finally overcome the seasickness she had succumbed to for the first two days of their trip. It was the third morning of their voyage. On board the frigate *Novara*, both Maximilian and Charlotte gazed towards the west.

Charlotte's personal maid Louise was doing quite the opposite of her mistress, standing at the stern of the ship and looking east, back towards her home. Her thoughts lingered on her mother and father, whom she had left behind. The sea breeze scattered the small tears that tried to well up in her eyes.

"Good morning," the sage greeted her happily from behind.

"Oh," she said as she turned around, a bit startled. "Yes, good morning."

"Perfect morning for a sail, don't you think?" the sage commented, his eyes quietly scanning her face.

"I suppose so," she said distractedly. "Do you think we'll ever return home?"

"If that's your real desire, I don't see why not," he replied, still watching her beautiful face, her small hands that wrung her skirts nervously. She stood about five feet tall, sweet and young with glowing skin flushed by the breeze. Her hair was the color of sand and hung in tiny curls around her face.

"Did you know that the direction you focus on when traveling tells a lot about your thoughts?" the sage asked with another gentle smile.

"Really?" she asked, turning and finally looking directly at him. His face was kind, if wrinkled. His eyes were bright and his smile sincere. She felt somewhat comforted by his presence and offered him her hand in greeting. He bowed from the waist and brought her hand towards his lips in a feigned kiss.

"I suppose it's time to formally introduce myself," he said. "I was sent to watch over those two by King Leopold," he said, gesturing to Maximilian and Charlotte. "They all call me Sage. You can too, if you wish."

"It's good to meet you, Sage," she said, blushing sweetly. "I'm Louise Kiss, originally from Hungary and the daughter of a soldier," she added, explaining her slight accent.

"And what is the Hungarian daughter of a soldier doing in the service of a Belgian princess?" Sage asked curiously.

"I was brought to Belgium when my family went there on order of Emperor Franz Karl. I met Princess Charlotte during a winter festival when we were both ice-skating. I was eighteen and she was fifteen at the time. We got along famously, and she asked if I would be interested in becoming her maid and living in the palace."

"Asking an eighteen-year-old if she would like to live in a palace is like asking a pigeon if it would like to fly," he commented with a wink, grinning in amusement at her candidness.

"Yes," Louise answered with a toss of her curls, "and my home was scarcely a palace. Besides, she was extremely kind to me and I knew the money would help my parents."

"The answer of a kind and dutiful daughter … and a beautiful daughter at that. I like that."

Louise blushed and finally smiled. In an instant, the sage was enamored with the young woman. *This is going to be a much more pleasant cruise than I imagined*, he thought to himself.

A week later, the ocean was strangely still and there was no breeze to help the ship along. They were at a dead standstill. The sea was like a polished mirror, reflecting the ship back up to itself. Both the crew and the passengers were getting bored and restless.

The captain ordered the deck swabbed for the third time, simply to give the crew something to do. The men broke out the wooden buckets bound with black metal, and the lye soap. They climbed down onto their knees and began their rhythmic scrubbing of the worn planks, but the captain could hear their light-hearted mumbling and noted their discontent.

"Cookie," he barked at the cook. "Get out some of our best provisions and prepare a feast tonight. It's hard for men to be testy when their stomachs are full."

"Aye aye, sir."

"Midshipman Jolla?"

"Yes, Captain?"

"Pull out that crate of hurricane lamps. I want this deck to glow like a spring evening. And tell Antle to pull out his fiddle, we'll have dancing tonight."

"Aye aye, Captain."

A few hours later, the men began to harass the cook. They were hungry and impatient.

"What are ya doin' in there, Cookie? When'll it be ready then?" one of the older sailors shouted.

"Back off, you blocks," the cook shouted over his shoulder. "It'll be ready when it's ready."

Just before the sun set on the horizon, the ship decks, now swabbed clean, had been filled with long tables holding a delicious feast. The captain personally sat the royal couple at their special table. "Come, come, Empress Carlotta, you start the festivities," the captain urged her. "See what a meal we've prepared."

Charlotte smiled when she heard the captain use her Italian nickname. "Oh look, Max! Oranges and lemons, and your favorite roast. And see how the lantern lights play on the water. It's quite radiant," she exclaimed, looking about her with glittering eyes.

"It certainly is," Maximilian agreed, enjoying his wife's delight.

Sage and Louise followed the royal couple, impressed by the abundance of choices spread before them on the tables. They were seated with the ship's officers.

The lesser ranks occupied their own tables and soon took them over with their good-natured antics, pushing at each other and laughing.

"Hey, Frank!" one crewman cried. "Leave some for the rest of us!"

"You manage your own lot, you!"

"Hey, Cookie ya been hidin' a real cook under decks. This grub ration almost tastes real." There was loud laughter at this, and even the officers smiled.

A little later, first mate Antle played his fiddle. He started with some merry sea-going tunes, later moving on to songs of home, of wives and sweethearts left behind.

"You look beautiful this evening," Maximilian said, beaming at Charlotte. He stood and offered her his hand, leaning in closer to whisper against her flesh, "Dance with me, wife." She looked up at his refreshing smile and stood. They walked closely, arm-in-arm, towards the middle of the deck. The sweet strains of the violin accompanied them as they began a slow and affectionate dance.

The sage watched them glide about the deck and leaned over to Louise. "Would you humor an old man with a dance?"

Louise gave him a lovely smile as she took his hand and rose. "You're not so old, sir. You move pretty fast, if you ask me."

"At my age, you have to take short-cuts. Minutes count," he joked.

Her bright eyes flashed humor, her smile letting him know there was still a chance. They walked towards the deck, between crates lashed down on deck.

"You wouldn't toy with an old man's affections?"

"What makes you think I'm toying?"

The sage laughed quietly. He escorted her down the stairs to the deck and admired the romantic scene. The lanterns glistened on the water, catching as a sparkle in the young lady's eyes. He took her in his arms and they danced as if time were not a fact of life, as if it would go on eternally. It was a lovely evening, and they danced for several tunes. They later wandered off to a private corner of the deck to refresh themselves in the breeze from the ocean, enjoying a vibrant conversation. At the end of the evening, Louise allowed him a goodnight kiss.

Throughout the trip to Mexico, Maximilian spent his time writing a manual of court etiquette, which he saw as of great importance to the monarchy. He wrote about all the plans he had to keep his people healthy, happy, and prosperous. He wrote of even greater dreams and plans to have a benevolent monarchy that could be an example for the world to follow. When he was not working on this, he studied Spanish, knowing it would be crucial to facilitate business and to appear more acceptable to the people.

One afternoon, Maximilian and Sage were sitting on comfortable chairs on the deck. First mate Antle stepped forward and addressed Maximilian elaborately. "Your Royal Highness, Prince Ferdinand Maximilian Joseph, would you desire me to play you a tune?"

Max paused at his formal language. "I'm changing the rules and court etiquette. Just call me 'Majesty.'" He smiled. "Please do play something for me," he added.

Antle blinked in surprise and bowed. He turned and returned to the upper deck, where he took up his violin and began to play away.

Sage looked thoughtfully at Max. "Why not 'comrade' as Marx suggests?"

"Oh, Marx. He calls us imperialists, moneylenders, usury top guns," Maximilian chuckled.

"What do you think about that, sire?"

"Well … it's true, quite frankly. The bankers are the usury top guns. We may or may not support them, but they're very rich because their principal amounts continue to grow and grow. They're the moneylenders. They must have leverages from us to get their money back with interest. Yes, we may be called imperialists. But imperialism brings health to a sick society."

"But sire, the Church claims that role for itself."

"Ethics exist in both the law and the Church, but the law covers ethics more extensively. Jesus gave no commands regarding environmental laws, security regulations, bankruptcy, court systems, or dispute resolution. That's what we handle."

"But the kingdom of the Church is more lawful, more powerful, and wealthier."

"Yes, but we kings do take from them."

"Kings go bankrupt, sire. The Church doesn't."

"And why's that?" Maximilian asked, curious about the sage's opinion.

"Because it costs money to maintain a king. It costs nothing to maintain a bishop."

"Yes, I suppose that's true. We collect taxes which people resent, but they maintain their bishops voluntarily and with pleasure."

"That makes kingship vulnerable."

"Yes, in the long run, a king has to pay for his armies, as well as his police and other agents."

"Then why start a kingship in Mexico? Isn't it rather like playing cricket on bad turf?"

"Well, what do you suggest we do?"

"Bring money to overwhelm money," Sage replied bluntly.

"How can we bring money into Mexico?"

Sage hesitated as he thought that over, and then replied, "Can we bring money through regulating? Stock exchanges? And perhaps maintaining an army of businesses."

"Yes, we can do that ... once we have some ground to stand upon in Mexico, of course."

They both gazed out at the sea for a while, each deep in thought. Sage finally turned his head back to Maximilian. "Why are Your Excellencies going to Mexico? What's the central idea? Is it a military conquest to put the Hapsburg dynasty there, or maybe France, with you at the helm? Gold? What's your aim?"

Maximilian thought his questions were rude, but kept his reaction to himself. He collected his thoughts and replied sincerely, "Placing a monarchy there is my aim. Politicians are greedy and therefore corrupt. A king or an emperor is above that. He doesn't need money, increased strength, or even the people to constantly support his every move. Monarchies must aim to make people stronger and more prosperous, to look after the people. It's the best form of government."

"But in a democracy, don't the people elect their leader?" Sage asked. "They call him the president or the prime minister, but he can't wage war or raise money. Only Congress has that power, and they can't violate the wishes of the people. With all due respect, sire, I believe that the era of kings is fading away. Kings are being reduced to 'war-you-can't-make' positions."

Maximilian frowned slightly, but continued to listen.

"Sire, if kingship is your aim, who will be your archduke?"

"I can have a Mexican as my heir, for political reasons," Maximilian replied.

"But why not leave the Mexicans to their own will? Why should you impose another king over them?"

"Kingship is better," Maximilian stated flatly.

"The Hapsburg style of kingship?"

Maximilian didn't answer.

"Sire, you are roughly half my age. You have your own ideas. You probably never had a mentor, yet you are imagining a future where you have neither a mentor nor money nor tools. I had as many ideas at your age, but my ideas, thanks to my mentor, began to die or fade or prove to be wrong.

"I'm now left only with one good idea, solid and based on common sense. It has stood the test of time. Your opponent Juarez has a better idea in *democracy*. He got it from the American Constitution. The idea is that there shouldn't be a king. People are the king, that's the new idea. It's the future, Sire, as kings must live in palaces and have the best food."

His eyes softened as he regarded Maximilian's bewilderment at his advice. "Sire, measure your ideas with his. It's not your royal blood, or even your heir that counts here. Either you beat Juarez at his ideas or you've lost. Forgive my frankness, but ruling isn't as simple anymore."

"My brother thinks that in case of failure, a ruler has to keep the flag waving harder. His ministers will not tell the truth, though they know the truth, or answer questions posed to them truthfully. Instead they will wrap the answers in make-believe half-truths. If they get stuck, others will supply them the acceptable arguments. There are lots and lots of suppliers, available to power brokers, ready to throw in bad spare parts for lies."

"Wave the flag harder, tell lies, hide the truth, answer deceitfully, wrap up lies, put forth accepted arguments … but how can you hide money and blood spilt in that process? More money, more blood, more money, more blood, till treasures are emptied. The lies run out ... then alone dawns the truth. If lies could hide, liars would be emperors."

Small Louise appeared on the deck, interrupting Sage's thoughts. Maximilian noticed the man's eyes catch hold of the woman and follow her as she walked along the deck. She glanced their way and saw him looking at her, greeting him silently with a shy little smile as she made her way to a group of royal servant girls.

Maximilian smiled, relieved at the change of subject. "Did you light a torch of love in her heart?" he teased.

Sage smiled appreciatively back at Louise as she stood at a distance, every now and then stealing a look his way. "Love can't be torched or extinguished, Sire. It has its own game plans."

"And what's the game plan that triggers love?"

"Sincerity comes first. It wins in the end. Attraction comes next, for it makes someone finally turn his or her head and take notice. The third essential is a sort of passionate look—"

Maximilian chuckled at that. Sage smiled at his reaction. "It's true," he insisted. "Everyone has a kind of passionate look. The fourth and the most important element is the thought of 'What will they say?' which of course really means, 'What will they say if I get into this game?'"

"And what exactly do you mean by that?" Maximilian asked with a cocked eyebrow.

"This lovely little woman, young, inexperienced," he said, gesturing with a nod to Louise, "you could get her first, but I couldn't. Why? She's judging each of us in her head. 'What will they say if I sleep with the emperor, or marry him, or get him to court me?' If she chooses me, they'll break her bones, never let her hear the end of it. If you give her the nod, she can become part of your life but not mine, no matter how much I might want it. Love can't be extinguished once it's begun to shine. That means it also can't be torched."

Maximilian turned and appraised the girl, giving her a very careful look. "No, women aren't built that way. We men come from one world, and women from another one entirely. They feel differently than us. She'll ask herself, 'What do I get from it?' rather than, 'What would they say?' They want to know if he's presentable, good-looking, smart, intelligent, caring ... all of the advantages of a relationship."

Sage shook his head. "That's what they consider for marriage, Sire, not love. Those are worlds apart. You can marry a woman without loving her."

The emperor mulled that over. "How true," he finally agreed. "You did say the little woman may fall for me, but since someone will break her bones, she wouldn't dare fall for you." "Common sense," Sage said with a knowing nod of his head.

"What if I went to her and ordered her to marry you, promising the girl her weight in gold every year?"

Sage considered that for a moment. "She'll choose, then either come to me or refuse me."

"Therefore, choosing is involved?"

"Yes, Sire."

"Therefore, humans can be driven to some corner if you show them advantage or survival there."

"Like sheep or cattle, yes."

"So what you're telling me is that humans are still living in a poultry market, eating their daily meal and thanking God for it ... but they don't know the butcher."

"Yes, Sire."

"She's just a hen in a poultry cage."

"Yes," the sage agreed, looking at Maximilian closely.

"All you need is my weight to get her?"

"I think so."

Maximilian nodded, enjoying his flight of ideas. "So every person builds his own weight, some quickly and others gradually. By avoiding sin, he builds it more rapidly. Every giant tree starts from a seed, every movement from an idea."

"Right."

"If I go to her and say to her, 'I want you in bed with Sage tonight. After that, I'll post you as my ambassador to your country,' what do you think I've done to damage her entire reasoning process? Advantage sown in her mind, though it could demolish her personality. She'd be an ambassador who bedded her way to it. Just by putting in her brain the devilish idea of self-interest?" he asked, observing Sage keenly.

"She has to balance between a sin that is beneficial and a refusal that shall not demolish her image of herself."

"So a decision is involved?"

"That explains human frailties. They normally will choose sinning that brings them advantage rather than refusing the advantage, in order to uphold the image they have of themselves."

"We call that life," Sage concluded. "That's why life is run by the sinful majority."

"Yes, good people are in the minority and rare."

"I didn't know you could think that straight, Sire," he joked. "Yes, a devilish idea can make someone think differently. A brother will oust his brothers from their father's business when his wife presents a devilish idea which he accepts."

"So logic can include presenting devilish ideas imperceptibly?"

"Or hiding truth imperceptibly. The people do resist, men know that. How to break that resistance? One way is to put them in a civil war. The lesser the better. If you will ask your general why you haven't pacified the people, the general will ask for more troops and money. Pacification doesn't require troops or money; it just requires accepting and guaranteeing the rights," Sage conceded.

"So a good-looking idea may take one to hell, and a bad idea to heaven," Maximilian concluded. "A good-looking idea can actually be a bad idea. Here comes human judgment of men and matters."

Sage chuckled to himself. He corrected his headdress consisting of a handkerchief.

"Sins start self-interest," Maximilian said as he stood, by now enjoying the sound of his own voice.

"Sins start selfish, self-serving self-interests, yes, but sin demolishes the image one earlier had of himself. One builds an image of himself. That shatters that image. That is the cost of sin," Sage corrected as he rose with the emperor. They began to stroll along the deck.

"The more that image is lost to sins, the more one gets corrupted, until he takes it as matter of course."

"That is why there is no dearth of hired villains."

"Answer me this," Maximilian demanded good-naturedly. "What should God do when one single idea can churn human life?"

"Sit and watch," Sage answered wisely.

"The tornadoes of human emotions require men to learn to be sensible."

Louise passed them as she returned to the front of the boat. She gave Sage a wink and a sincere smile, motioning for him to come to her.

Sage watched her pass with another smile, sighing as she rounded the corner. He turned to Maximilian. "Sire, I hope that if she comes to me today, it'll be of her own will, not from of any coercing on your part. It would be a much more satisfying adventure for me," he said earnestly.

"Done," Maximilian said with a chuckle. "If nothing else, I want your desire to be satisfied."

Sage was dismissed, and he wasted no time in hurrying to the front of the boat to meet up with Louise. They passed the afternoon in pleasant conversation, listening to each other's thoughts and showing concern for each other, touching each other with kindness.

It was nearing the dinner hour and Louise finally took her leave, going below to prepare for their meal. Sage was surprised to see Maximilian still on the deck, smiling at him slyly over a book he had been reading. Sage returned to the young emperor's side with a sheepish grin.

"You know, Sire, anything is possible," he concluded hopefully.

That night, Sage was eager to fall sleep, hoping for a marvelous dream of his dear Louise. When his eyes closed, he thought of her, allowing his lustier thoughts to flow in the privacy of the small ship cabin. He imagined her creamy bosoms pushing out of the bodice that plunged just enough to allow them to plump out invitingly. He fantasized lowering that bodice and freeing those lovely bosoms, spying the tender nipples hidden beneath and tasting them under the moon and the stars …

He began to shift left, then right, as a powerful dream overtook him.

He was standing at the prow of the ship and could only see the water coming at him. The sea, wide and endless, its stormy, churning water and waves, looked like broken ribbons of music coming towards him. He could not make out the tunes, but they grew swelled as they flowed towards him, growing louder and louder. He soon found himself swallowed up in those hundreds of tunes. They seemed to give him some message, some meaning, but he could not understand it. Then colors seemed to be added to the oncoming waves, first gray, then black, orange, and finally red. The red water overtook all of the other colors, coming from the direction the ship was traveling. He soon became aware of shrieking sounds, like a bird, a falcon shrilling over all of the music. A Qawali was added to it, an almost imperceptible voice singing an ode, lamenting, crying, wailing, and weeping. "Is that Maximilian's mother?" he thought to himself, but he could not see or hear her anyone, nothing but the red water, the wave of music, the strange and detached wailing.

The intensity of the dream awoke him suddenly. He was badly tangled in his bed sheets, his shaking body covered with sweat. Pulling free of the damp sheets, he stumbled to the porthole and looked out anxiously. The ocean looked normal, its calm and dark waves glittering under a clear sky full of stars.

Sage knew the dream was of great consequence, and he immediately sat at his little desk and took out his pen and paper to record as many details as he could remember. "I must decipher its meaning," he thought to himself as he finished writing down the details and stared at what he had written. The mood of the dream had been ominous, leaving him anxious and sad.

He began taking further notes as thoughts occurred to him. A bird ... a symbol of intellectual flight, ideals and intuition. Seeing a bird in a dream meant that someone wanted to cheat you. Seeing birds flying away meant that sadness and loneliness awaited you. Watching predatory birds flying meant that your enemies were waiting for a chance to attack you. The ocean was a sign of mixed fortune if it was choppy, but if very rough or stormy, it was a warning that real courage would be needed to overcome your obstacles. The color red had deep emotional and spiritual connotations. It could mean you had to stop and think about your actions, but it could also mean sin, rage, and the Devil. It was an indication of raw energy, force, vigor, intense passion, aggression, power, and courage. Dark red further stood for greed, energy, anger, hate, blood, and willpower ... black symbolized the unknown, unconscious, danger, mystery, darkness, death, mourning, hate, or malice ... gray indicated fear, fright, depression, ill health, ambivalence, and confusion. Annoying music meant that you would meet unpleasant people or be under extreme tension.

Sage set down his pen and carefully examined the symbols and their meanings, both to him and to Maximilian. He did not sleep again that night, working arduously until dawn.

The next morning was clear and bright. Maximilian was up early, walking on deck when Sage found him.

"Good morning, Sage," Maximilian greeted him familiarly.

"Good morning, Sire. I must talk with you as soon as possible. It's a matter of utmost importance—"

A bugle sounded on the deck, cutting off his words. A ship had been sighted. Sage studied the distant ship for a moment and then turned back to the emperor. "If it's one of your ships, I'd like to go back home, Sire."

Maximilian blinked in shock. "Wha—but I thought you and Louise were ... why do you want to go home?"

"You're going to put down a plant in Mexico, an Austrian emperorship. Austria's lost two-thirds of its empire in the last few years. Your family may have need of me, Sire."

Maximilian shook his head, confused. Sage noted the disappointment in the young man's eyes and went on to explain. "My Lord, you're wise, but have no practical experience in growing an empire. The man opposing you, this Juarez, he's come from adversity, while you come from affluence. His hundreds of prayers must have been wasted, left unanswered. Only now he's come to see the charisma of luck return to him ..."

He frowned, his words coming out jumbled and unclear. Maximilian walked alongside him and waited, listening attentively. "Juarez is going to win, Sire. If Lincoln wins, he wins. If he refuses to be taken under your wing, he wins. You have old ideas, ancient ideas, however gilded they may be. He has ideas whose time has come."

Maximilian opened his mouth to speak, but only a bewildered puff of air came out.

"There," Sage said, pointing towards Mexico. "That's your test of quality."

"But won't you at least accompany me?" Maximilian asked softly. "See the match?" he added with a weak smile.

"The match between kingship and democracy? Or between a hard-baked veteran and a novice?"

"Very recently, we were having a very good discussion about women, marriage, love," Maximilian wondered aloud. "Then Louise finally made a definite move towards you, and now you want to go home ...?"

"Sire, that entire discussion made me realize that you'll be busier with state banquets than with battlefields. I've been listening and observing you during this trip."

The young man was too astonished to be angered by the sage's tactless summary. He winced, obviously hurt.

"Besides," Sage added, trying to make him listen, "I had a dream last night." He went on to tell Maximilian about his dream, though he only told the portions that he hoped might persuade the young man to change his mind. "I've proven my methods in dream interpretation, Sire. The boat on a stormy ocean may foretell some setbacks in business affairs or troubles at home. The storm itself is a symbol of strong feelings and fears that have my emotions in an uproar. Being in a storm means that someone will face a hard fight and the best defense is a good preparation. Struggling through a storm is a sign that you need to be prepared for problems and losses. Listening to a storm roaring outside denotes bad news ahead," he explained.

"A dream?" Max interjected. "Your dread is based on a dream? What significance could that possibly have?"

"I admit, prophetic dreams are difficult to interpret, but this dream contained passionate wailings, horrid melodies, attacking witches, scapegoats in red clothes, all coming …" He shuddered visibly. "My deepest and most ardent intuition tells me that a willing victim will suffer for a cause. That made me realize that someone high and noble will be martyred in the direction our ship is sailing." He paused, both men knowing full well who the martyr he spoke of was.

Maximilian stared at the western water, towards Mexico. "What do you think I should do?" he finally asked, his voice barely a whisper.

Sage placed his hand on Maximilian's shoulder, his expression grave. "Come with me, Sire. Let's go back to Austria. Save what you have today."

"Desertion?" he asked in awe.

"No, Sire. Avoiding a battle where the odds are piling against you. Counting the cost."

Maximilian frowned. "I thought you'd help me win the coming war, and now you want to leave me?"

"You are not a general, Sire. Indeed, you do not have a good general. That is the sole requirement of your political situation. This could be a plan against the Hapsburgs."

"How's that?" asked Maximilian.

"Sire, this whole matter is possibly Napoleon's ruse," he said urgently, trying another approach. "A ruse to finally shatter the Austrian monarchy."

"But Napoleon is paying for all of this," Maximilian argued impatiently.

"He can shorten his payments by withdrawing his army from Mexico. Then where does that leave you? In an armed struggle you are likely to lose."

Maximilian frowned, beginning to shake his head. "My motives are exalted, not just for an odd piece of land far away from Austria or France," he explained. "I'm not fighting over possessions. I want to resolve Mexico's internal struggles. Its people have suffered enough already."

"Kings and conquerors always go out with exalted motives, Sire. Kingship has been decomposing for the last two hundred years. The time is coming soon when all of the royalty around the world will be left with nothing except their pretensions. They want to maintain themselves in power despite internal struggles. That's the truth. The dream I saw was the suffering sea of humans, humans whose lives are colored with the bloodbaths of their rulers. The shrieks I heard are the mothers whose sons have been butchered and shot. I can't take sides with kings and their generals. I'm a humble citizen," he said, his head lowering wearily. "Let me go back and take care of my ailing wife and pigeons."

"I'll take my chances. You can go back, old man," Maximilian replied bitterly. He turned abruptly and trod away, his shoulders slumped in disappointment at the lack of support from his own friend.

Sage stared dejectedly at the floor, wanting to follow the young man and lift his spirits, to tell him that this was only told out of concern for a dear friend. But he did not follow Maximilian, did not even look up from the deck. He knew there was nothing he could say to make things right with the emperor or to make him feel better, not without compromising his own thoughts on the matter. He sighed regrettably and returned to his own cabin to gather his belongings.

After three hours, Sage had made ready for his transfer to the new ship, which had indeed been a vessel of the British empire. He said a tender goodbye to Louise, trying to explain his quick departure to the confused girl, but she did not understand. She was bitterly disappointed, knowing that now she would always wonder how their newly budding romance would have turned out.

Maximilian stood nearby with Charlotte beside him in obvious confusion. She moved as if to speak and then hung back as Maximilian strode confidently to Sage, his back straight with formality. "Sage, you've been a good advisor and a good friend. Give my regards to the family. I'll miss you."

Sage offered the emperor a courtly bow, quoting a verse.

> "When brick is burnt
> Then things happen rightly;
> These soft, fragile hearts
> Are not suitable
> For laying any foundations,
> Or construction."

Maximilian gazed at him a moment as he ended his verse, noting that the sage was still trying to gently persuade him to change his mind even with poetry. They embraced quickly with a lot of shoulder pounding, the emperor trying to keep from getting too sentimental.

"Please take this as a token of my esteem," he said, handing Sage a gold watch and adding his most princely of bows. "Martyr? A willing victim will suffer for a cause," he said, reminding him of the dream.

"Is it you, Sire?"

Maximilian said nothing as the sailors from the other ship grabbed Sage's belongings. They grouped around him and helped him climb over the side and into the small dingy that was to carry him to the returning English ship.

Just above the rush of the waves, Sage could hear the music from his dream. A chill went up his spine, as he repeatedly looked first at the sea, then at Maximilian.

As if he just now realized that his advisor was really leaving, Maximilian leaned against the ship rail and asked, "But Sage, how can I prepare? Precisely what should I do?"

Confused, Sage just sat in the boat as it was lowered into the water. Maximilian watched Sage move away from the ship as one of the sailors took the oars and cut through the water. He stayed at the rail, watching sadly until Sage was aboard the English vessel and gone, only a speck on the far horizon.

In the doorway leading below, Louise fell against the doorframe. "What did I do to cause this?" she thought wildly to herself. "What could I have done to keep it from happening? Why did he leave?"

Charlotte approached her tenderly, still confused herself about what had just happened. "Oh, Louise," she said softly, placing a sympathetic hand on the girl's shoulder.

Tears welled up in Louise's eyes, blurring her vision. "Love wasted is the true crime," she whispered, and rushed away to her cabin.

Sage reached England in good weather and caught the first ship to Ostend, Belgium. Charlotte's father, King Leopold I, met him there. The old king ordered that the sage be placed in his personal carriage, and they were quickly off.

Leopold noted the weariness on the sage's face. "What brought you back, Sage?" he asked, concern deepening the lines of his face.

"I apologize, sire, but I'm famished and weary from my journey. These old bones, you know. May we first have a bite to eat, and then I'll report?"

"Of course," Leopold replied, always gracious. "But just tell me my daughter's well?"

"Oh, quite well and happy, Sire."

"Wonderful," he said with a sigh of relief. "Dinner will be served immediately upon our return."

They were soon having coffee and pastries after their dinner. Household servants surrounded them, catering to their every whim. The palace guard lingered as well, standing dutifully by the large, intricately carved wooden doors. Leopold nodded and the servants retreated back to give them more privacy.

"Now why have you come back?"

"I wasn't needed there, Sire."

"Who told you that, Maximilian or Charlotte?"

The sage gave him a solemn look. "God, Sire."

Leopold's eyebrows arched. "Does God speak to you?"

"He speaks to everyone."

"How? I never heard him," the king replied.

"Our minds receive his words."

"Well, what has He told you about my daughter and son-in-law?" he asked dryly.

Sage sighed and stared at the table with an almost imperceptible shake of his head. "I tried to explain to your son-in-law that I'm nearly twice his age, and that, when I was his age, I had many ideas. I had time to chase those ideas. Time went by, and now I no longer have ideas to take me for a ride." He looked soberly up at the king. "Maximilian still has such ideas, and they're definitely taking him for a ride."

"I sent you with him so that you could help him draw sound conclusions."

"Yes, Sire, and at first I had no real doubts about all of this ... then they started, like the tiniest of pebbles in your shoe. They first became only noticeable, then later they were obvious. When I expressed my doubts to Maximilian, he was too full of his own ideas to hear mine. Young people defend their own ideas, guard them jealously. They shoot down ideas other than theirs. That's why they must make mistakes, waste time, and repent in their old age. A young man's brain is like a battlefield's frontline post, defended and vigorously guarded. As soon as some old fool advances an idea, strange but solid, young people don't analyze it on its merits. Instead they guillotine it on their minds' chopping block."

Leopold nodded vaguely in agreement, listening.

"You see, Sire, I needed to travel a few days with your son-in-law to make my analysis of him. When I saw how he thinks, I advised him to return to his lands, to forget his feast and eat homely broth. He lives in dreams, not reality. His ideas will wreck him. I didn't want that to happen under my guard, so I came back."

"How could you know all this about him in a few short days?"

Sage stared off, as if looking again at Maximilian. "During the voyage, Max told himself repeatedly, 'I'm sure I can be the philosopher king that the Greeks once spoke of. I'll be just and improve the plight of my people.' He worked on his Spanish diligently and worked hard to learn the names of the elite ... but sadly, he chose to spend his time beginning work on writing new court etiquette. He hadn't so much as glanced at the books and documents on Mexico that were offered to him. They were brushed aside like a child dismisses tedious schoolwork for something more enjoyable. That alarmed me, sire. He should know that those documents are the most important of all his tasks. That showed me how he plans on approaching his rule, and that gave me cause to worry. Plato said, 'It is a king's obligation to know his people in order to serve them better.' I'm afraid that he has no knowledge of his people or what he's getting into."

Leopold stared soberly at the sage. "What do you think Maximilian should do when he reaches Vera Cruz?"

"First he should assess the damage done to his monarchy by the French generals ... they've done more to alienate him from the people than anyone else so far. Then he should assess the civil war going on in America, and the chances of the South in their rebellion against the North. Then there are the slave issues ... these are all political issues, sire. Generals or the new monarch have no expertise in that. If the North wins the war, the South will be crushed, and the North will then be free to help Juarez. If Napoleon withdraws his forces from Mexico, Juarez will get the money and weapons he needs to defeat Maximilian."

"What should Maximilian do to ward off Juarez?"

"I tried to explain this to Maximilian. He should try to persuade Juarez to share his government with him."

"But Juarez is being hunted like a fox. Everyone is searching for him."

"That's the first obstacle, Sire."

"And what's the second obstacle?"

"Would Juarez be willing to allow a monarchy to weld itself to a democracy?"

"What's the harm? Juarez has humble origins. He may be all too pleased to stand beside an emperor."

Sage shook his head. "Emperors and kings just don't understand democracy, Sire. Democracies start by accepting that the rulers must change. A monarchy can't accept that belief."

"But Maximilian isn't an old style king," Leopold objected. "He doesn't believe in the idea of absolute kingship. He has pro-people ideas, much like Juarez's ideas."

"That makes their struggle more deadly, Sire."

"More deadly? How?"

"Juarez hustled out a dictator, Santa Anna, and spared his life. He wouldn't spare Maximilian if he wins."

Leopold began to look more alarmed. "What should I do?" he asked anxiously.

"Call your daughter back the moment Napoleon calls his armies back from Mexico."

"And Maximilian?"

"He'll abdicate, but his colonels won't let him do that."

"Who would deny an emperor?" Leopold asked haughtily.

"They can sell Maximilian to save their own necks."

"What about the generals?" the king asked, shocked.

"The French generals will come back to France and the Mexicans will be shot."

"What are you?" Leopold asked, rising. "A sage or God himself?"

"I'm just a normal, humble, poor old man who tries to think correctly. I'm just a gardener who grows ideas."

The king gripped the top of his chair firmly. "What about the elite Mexicans, the rich aristocrats? And the European minority as well? They have a great deal of power, and they're well-entrenched there."

Sage nodded. "Yes, they have a vested interest. They'll salute the rising sun, and then they'll betray Maximilian. If Lincoln wins and Napoleon pulls his troops, they'll be singing the local tunes."

Leopold gave Sage a cross look. "I sent you to help him, to guide him."

"As much as I may try, he isn't a man to be guided, Sire."

The old king sunk back into his chair, deep in worried thought.

CHAPTER 14

▼

THE ARRIVAL

"Land! Land, ho!" the voice of the sailor echoed across the waves at dawn. Charlotte quickly rolled out of her berth and rushed to the porthole. The shoreline of Mexico rose faintly above the waves, a welcomed patch of green. With an excited smile, she clutched her rosary and whispered a prayer to herself, Psalms 46, which she had learned when studying the Old Testament as a child.

"Oh God,
Oh God, our hope and strength,
A very present help in trouble.
Therefore we will not fear, though the earth be moved,
And though the hills be carried into the midst of the sea,
Though the waters thereof rage and swell,
And though the mountains shake at the tempest of the same.
There is a river, the streams whereof make glad the city of God,
The holy place of the tabernacle of the Most High.
Amen."

With the demeanor of an excited schoolgirl, she almost hopped up and down, waiting for her maids to finish dressing her and attending to her toilette. Maximilian had already risen and she was eager to share this moment with him. How long they had waited for this day! Here they would finally win the acknowledgement that their blood bestowed upon them, a respect that was never quite achieved back in their native Europe. She had eagerly read everything she could find on Mexicans and their culture, and now she would test that knowledge against the reality.

One of her maids leaned forward to hurriedly complete tying Charlotte's last bow as she rushed from her cabin in search of her husband. It did not take her long to find him; she simply went to the first spot it seemed natural to go on such an occasion as this: to the prow of the ship, facing the land that slowly loomed closer and closer.

Maximilian smiled down at her as she bumped next to him affectionately, the sunrise blazing orange and red in the sky behind them. "Are you as excited as I am?" Charlotte whispered, her face flushed.

"Compose yourself," Maximilian teased. "You're an empress now."

"Yes," she agreed with a small laugh. "Forever your faithful Empress Charlotte."

"No, not in this land, or so I hear. The Mexicans have already taken you as their own, and from now on you'll be Carlota."

She beamed, pleased. "Then Empress Carlota I shall be!" she exclaimed. He took her hand and squeezed it, both of them savoring the moment.

The frigate *Novara* dropped anchor at Vera Cruz on May 28, 1864. The water was a dazzlingly clear azure blue, with brightly colored fish seemingly suspended in air. The sun was high in the sky by the time they stepped onto the land, yet there was no one there to meet them except for the royal guard. The couple frowned in disappointment as they scanned the docks and the shore.

"Max, where is everyone?" Carlota whispered.

Maximilian turned to the head of the royal guard. "Where is everyone? We expected a customary greeting."

"I apologize, Sire. The plague is still about, and the people have been forbidden to congregate in large groups." A group of French officers stood nearby, all smiles and congratulations in their attempt to somehow fill the void and provide them a proper welcome.

A Mexican horseman galloped up to the French officers. There was a flurry of words, and finally the horseman persuaded one of the officers to deliver a letter. The man took the letter and turned to do as requested, turning back in surprise as the Mexican rode away as swiftly as he had come.

Eager to be the first to meet the emperor, the officer walked briskly forward and handed the letter to Maximilian without checking the contents, offering a sharp bow from the waist. "Welcome to Mexico, Emperor Maximilian."

Maximilian nodded and accepted the letter. He opened it and scanned it quickly. "It's from Juarez," he said in surprise to Carlota. "Perhaps he's decided to join us." He cleared his throat and read aloud, "Archduke Maximilian von Hapsburg, I have come to know all the treachery you and the French have been up to …" He glanced awkwardly at those around him and finished in a lower voice. "Do not dare to set foot in the capital, Mexico City. That is my final word. Signed, Benito Juarez, president of Mexico."

Carlota laughed carelessly. "The poor deluded soul thinks he's still the president. After lunch, let's continue on to *our* capital."

Maximilian chuckled nervously, but it was astoundingly easy for him to fall in line with her and let the letter go as nothing more than the demands of a desperate man. He felt giddy knowing that he was on the final leg of his journey to emperorship. They ate their lunch with childish delight at everything new around them and then continued on their journey to Mexico City in spellbound awe. The air was clean, with a faint sea breeze murmuring among the fresh green leaves. The colors were crisp, bright, and clear. Every minute, it seemed something new appeared to fascinate them. Cockatoos, parrots, quetzals, and beautiful landscapes went by like works of art paraded past for their pleasure. The mountains loomed nearby in deep blues and purples, in contrast with the sky of perfect blue and streaks of pink near the tops of the mountains. They had made their choice. It was a new day, a far new world. Maximilian was daydreaming of his grand plans for Mexico, to turn it into a new state based on his ideas. Thoughts of other projects to promote tourism and give his people a happy life went through his mind, and he began to think out loud with Carlota.

"We should develop a democracy like the English monarchy. We'd support a free press. We could even use Juarez as a prime minister and have basic administrative units with an industrial base. I think if we set things up correctly, we can use exports to support our treasury. I wouldn't have to levy any taxes, except for a just sales tax." Carlota nodded approvingly as he carried on excitedly.

Mexico, 1864

A major of Colonel Alfonso rushed through the town square, past several spectacular murals depicting various social and political issues in dazzling colors that were now muted in the dim light of the streetlamps. He knocked on the colonel's door and was given permission to enter. Alfonso, a deputy of General Bazine, was drinking in his flagstaff house.

"Colonel, sir," the major said, "The 'double eagle' has landed. Emperor Maximilian is in Mexico."

"Who brought the news?" Colonel Alfonso asked.

"The liaison officer from the Vera Cruz garrison," the major replied.

"And where is he?"

"In the office." The major turned back to the door to open it.

Colonel Alfonso brushed by him in haste. "I'll come to the office right away," he said, rushing out the door and to his own quarters to get ready. His wife was in her bed in her nightdress, watching him whistle as he got out his uniform and boots. She squinted her eyes, suspecting something, and quietly slipped from her bed. She tiptoed across the room to peek around the corner, finding her husband taking out a small wad of notes from a powder box. She cocked her head curiously but silently returned to her bed, pretending she hadn't seen anything. When the colonel was finally clad in his uniform, he came to the bed and kissed her. "Will you come back soon?" she asked softly.

"No, darling," he answered in a brief mumble. "Important matters at the office … I may sleep there."

"All right, dear," she replied with a smile, and gave him a little kiss.

Alfonso reached the headquarters and found the lieutenant officer waiting for him. After a while, the colonel slipped out and knocked at a door. A beautiful woman opened it and smirked at him as she leaned against it, the glow of the fire in the hearth giving her head a golden halo.

"Who's inside?" Alfonso asked cautiously.

The woman giggled. "Just my friend, Maggie."

He shut the door and went straight to the bedroom. The two women kissed the colonel one after another and then took off their clothes. The older man sat in a chair between the two young women.

The first woman stood behind him and rubbed his neck and shoulders. "Tough tour of duty, Colonel?" she asked as she kneaded the muscles. Her dog approached him and began to bark at him. He came closer, barking louder. Alfonso became aggravated and finally picked the dog up, tossing him out the first story window and into a flowerbed.

Outside, Alfonso's wife stood with two sentries from the flagstaff house. She caught a glimpse of her husband tossing the dog out of the window. The light inside the room allowed her to watch him, though he could not see her in the blackness of the night.

She asked the house sentries to knock at the door, but they refused apologetically. Irritated, she briskly stepped up to the door and knocked on it herself. She continued knocking, but no one answered the door. She finally waited outside the door impatiently until her husband emerged. She ran inside the half-open door as the colonel could only grunt and look behind him, too confused and flabbergasted to stop her. She went straight to the bedroom and caught both the naked women in the bed. Enraged, she picked up one item after another and hurled it at them. The women scrambled from their bed, but the colonel's wife cornered them between the wall and the bedside table. "Who are you?" she seethed at them, lifting a pillow as if to swing it at them. Beneath the pillow was a wad of notes and a carved rubber strap-on penis. She dropped the pillow and clutched the notes and the phallus in her hands. "What's this?" she shrieked.

One woman ducked behind the table. "Your husband pays us monthly. That's the money," she explained, nodding at the wad of notes.

"And this?" the colonel's wife demanded, lifting the phallus towards them.

The second women glanced at her companion, who replied, "That's mine."

"I don't care what you are," Alfonso's wife snapped. "How long have you been living in this army guest house?"

"This is the fourth month," one of the women replied. "We've been here since after the plebiscite. We came to the polling booth and voted no. After the officer on watch saw that, he took us to the colonel, who ordered our interrogation. We were in his custody for four months …" She stared at the angry woman and added desperately, "We're poor women. This is how we now earn our livelihood."

Alfonso's wife thundered, "But he … this son of a bitch is absolutely impotent!" She turned and saw that her husband stood only a few feet behind her. "Don't I already know all too well about your impotence?" she shouted, grabbing the scruff of his neck.

One of the women, relieved that the woman's anger was shifting to her husband and away from them, added as she gestured to the phallus, "We use that between ourselves. I had it in my bag and he volunteered to do it for us."

"You bloody swine!" his wife screamed as she began hitting him and tearing his uniform. The guards rushed in to investigate the noise, but were sent away by the embarrassed colonel. He begged her to calm down and go back to their house. She responded first by slapping him so hard across the face that he stood stunned, his hand on his cheek. As he stared ahead blankly, she grabbed a vase and broke it over his head, knocking him onto the bed. "They do tremble before their wives," one of the women jeered.

"And bosses," the other added, laughing.

"Shut up, you two!" Alfonso bellowed from the bed.

"No, don't shut up! Blackmail him! Get him court-martialed! He wanted this third tour of duty. Now I know why. Easy to get women. Eat him alive!" his wife shouted to the women. "You impotent son of a bitch, what do you get from them that I can't give?" she screamed, looking back down at him. The colonel looked down feebly, examining his torn uniform. "What do you get?" she yelled insistently.

Finally one woman answered. "Sex."

"Sex?" she asked incredulously. "Get out, you bitches!" she screamed. "Out! Out! OUT!" she shrieked, hurling things after them.

The two women shrieked and ran for the door. As they burst through the doorway and into the courtyard, the sentries gave the passing naked women exaggerated salutes, grinning broadly.

Alfonso looked about wildly, knowing it was almost time to meet General Bazine. His uniform was ruined and his hair a mess. Bazine was very strict about proper conduct, and the colonel could be demoted or imprisoned, subject to who knew what other harsh punishments. In desperation, the colonel knelt on the floor in a back room, opening some locks and climbing down into a small underground bunker. The light from above spilled in to reveal two beds, upon which two of Juarez's men were laid in chains. He fumbled with his keys and opened their locks with one hand as his other hand held them at the gunpoint. Pointing the pistol at their heads, he ordered them to rise and go upstairs with him. They silently obeyed and were led out and through back doors to the far rear of the army house.

Colonel Alfonso stared at them for a moment, as if building his courage. The men stared back at him curiously and waited. He finally shot each of them in the head, and then fired three shots in the air. Wincing to himself, he pressed the nose of his pistol against his own shoulder and fired, falling to the floor with a cry. Despite his pain, he quickly placed the revolver close to one of the Mexicans and arranged himself on the floor as if he were badly wounded.

"Terrorists … killers … guard … guard!" he cried as the sentries burst into the room. Soon a group of soldiers was assembled, and they helped him to the hospital. There the doctors removed the bullet and stopped the oozing blood from his shoulder, bandaging it carefully. When they were finished, the colonel asked the doctors to help him reach headquarters. Three young doctors helped him to the adjoining square where the headquarters were.

Alfonso entered the building, limping between the doctors as he raised his head and saw General Bazine waiting for him. He saluted pathetically, exaggerating his wound. A group of officers in attendance stood up from their seats at the table, concerned.

"What's happened to you?" the general asked, surprised. "Terrorists, sir," Colonel Alfonso gasped. "They captured me in my flagstaff house ... tortured and shot me. It was a close-quarter fight. I was lucky to get out alive, sir."

"You deserve a medal for that," the general remarked. "Why were the terrorists in your flagstaff house?"

"They were trying to rescue General Diaz, probably," the colonel lied off the cuff. "Or perhaps they were there to kidnap some soldier who could give them a tip about Diaz's location. It could be a plan to make his escape possible, sir."

The general ordered a report prepared for submission to the coming monarch, Maximilian. He then turned to his officers gathered in attendance and commanded, "Let's show Emperor Maximilian that we're fighting valiantly and with great honor. Even our senior officers are facing the terrorists, and with first-rate courage." He turned back to the doctors. "Tie more bandages on him, make him look terribly wounded. We'll have him brought on a stretcher to receive a gallantry award from Maximilian himself. That should be a performance," he said with a contented smile. "A proper investiture ceremony."

General Bazine frowned at Colonel Alfonso. "Here today? But he was expected two days from now."

"Probably a good sailor, sir," Alfonso commented.

"I see," he responded, concentrating. "Order and allow only the selected elite to go to the reception. Put two regiments in civvies between 'the eagle' and the Mexicans, and tear up the blockade report. All papers concerning the embargo, the negotiated settlement, and executions are to be burned. Send the impounded assets by ship to France. You're personally responsible to me to see that it's done."

"Yes, General, sir," Colonel Alfonso replied, giving a sharp salute with his good arm. He turned on his heel and silently went over all that he had to do in his mind. He had to hurry if he was to get everything done and still have time to get on a stretcher and pretend to be seriously wounded.

General Bazine changed his mind and called the colonel back. "Execute Diaz immediately."

His ADC interjected, "That could be construed against you, General, sir. Diaz is an important person. I recommend we begin to try to win him over to our side."

Bazine stared at his ADC for a moment and then patted the nervous captain's cheek. "Good advice." Colonel Alfonso cringed, taking out a pocket mirror to look at his own face. His left eye was black and swollen shut, an injury from his wife that he hoped would impress the arriving monarch.

Their trip finally took Maximilian and Carlota into Mexico City, where they were received with much more splendor. Maximilian was enchanted, and Carlota gazed with wonder at the many sites. On their way to the national palace, they were forced to skirt near a section of town where the people were forced to live in profound poverty. Looking to their left, they could see that suddenly the brightly painted walls were faded and peeling, the cobblestones chipped in places. The driver maneuvered them away from the scene, but not before they took in the desperate plight. It had not occurred to them that many of their European countrymen lived in similar conditions, and they were shocked at the squalor in contrast to the magnificent haciendas of the upper class.

A young mother moved slowly down the street, her four tiny children wrapping their thin arms around her legs. Two of the children were weeping, perhaps out of hunger, as she tried to drag along a chunk of fly-infested bone she had just retrieved from the trash of a nearby hacienda. As she rode by sitting on the velvet seats of her carriage, Carlota stared at her. The two women's eyes met, and Carlota was astounded at the desperation she saw in the eyes of the woman, unlike anything she had ever witnessed before. The woman's eyes were deep with fathomless sorrow, devoid of hope.

Tears flowed down the cheeks of tenderhearted Carlota as she turned to her husband. "Oh, Max, we must come to the aid of these poor people! Did you see that woman with all of those hungry babies? I pity them, my heart goes out to them," she said, shaking her head and staring out again. Her eyes lit up with hope as she turned back to Maximilian. "I believe this is a sign from God, Max. Let it be my mission to help these mothers, and your mission will be to build new housing for the poor. Perhaps in doing this, God will grant my prayers of a son, a Hapsburg prince for you and Mexico."

Maximilian solemnly dried her tears with a lacy silk handkerchief. "My dear, I make a solemn vow to be the best ruler any people of the world could have. And I'll see to it with all the power I possess that the lives of these people are changed forever."

The driver slowed down and came to a stop in front of the ramshackle Palacio National. It resembled a meager barracks with broken windows. The entry door stood open, unattended. Nearby, a stack of straw was covered by a brood hen.

Maximilian called for a colonel in the royal guard. The man came hurriedly as other men rushed about to make the entrance a little less unsightly. "Is this where you expect us to stay?" Maximilian snapped at the colonel. "The very thought is preposterous!"

"I'm sorry, your Majesties, please forgive us. The Mexicans were supposed to ready the palace for you, but there must have been a miscommunication as to your date of arrival."

Maximilian stared hard at the man, searching his eyes for traces of a lie. The man simply stared back in wide-eyed astonishment, and the emperor realized he was wasting his time. The first task a military officer had to master was hiding his feelings and the truth. Searching his face would do him no good either way. He waved his hand in irritation and stepped out of the carriage, scanning the dilapidated grounds with a sigh. "Very well, let's at least see if our quarters have been readied."

The colonel nodded and stepped back while Carlota was assisted out of the carriage. They stepped inside and wandered into a large courtyard, surrounded on all sides by three levels of stone balconies and rooms beyond. The yard itself was parched and barren. A small and squat Mexican man busied himself sweeping garbage into small piles, using a bundle of sticks tied together.

Carlota was at once relieved to see a servant on the grounds and irritated that such basic cleaning had not been completed before their arrival. An archway on the far side of the yard revealed an enormous garden, though she could see that it was overgrown. With an exasperated sigh, she closed her eyes and raised her face to the sun. "At least that's in working order for us," she mumbled to herself, trying to keep her mood light.

They were led to a series of chambers that had been set aside for them. They were both silently thankful to note that at least this space had been swept and the windows opened to air out the rooms, though the walls were as yet bare of tapestry and the stale odor of past cigars and pipes lingered. Soon, men were lugging up furniture, basic pieces to get by with until proper shipments could arrive from Europe. Until now, the pieces they brought in would have seemed spartan in comparison to their personal bedrooms, but now these tables and chairs seemed to glow when set next to the dark and unpolished wood that covered the walls.

Still the young couple vowed to make the best of it. They knew this was going to involve a lot of work, and Maximilian mused that the state of the palace merely reflected the neglected state that Mexico had been in for too long, reaffirming the need for their presence. Carlota smiled as Maximilian made a gesture as if to roll up his sleeves, as if to say that he was ready and willing for the work ahead.

They took a simple meal that evening, since the kitchen was still being set up, sitting at the window of their bedchamber. Roast chicken and fresh bread were laid out on the small table, as well as wine and chocolates that Carlota had brought from Belgium.

"This is surely the strangest meal I've ever had," Carlota laughed, setting a chocolate next to her chicken.

Maximilian nodded. "Wine with your chocolate?" he joked. Carlota laughed.

"Oh, look!" Carlota exclaimed, looking out the window. "We have a marvelous view of the gardens."

Maximilian glanced out of the window and chuckled. "I'm not sure that's a good thing."

"Oh, Max," Carlota said, still smiling, "I'm not worried about the garden. You're a wonder at designing them. I know that soon enough, it'll be a beautiful view."

He returned her smile and took her hand, loving her for her undying optimism and faith in him. Perhaps this would not be so bad after all. Her enthusiasm was contagious, and he was so positive about the things to come that he even ignored the bold rats that lingered near the walls, smelling their food.

Very tired from their long trip, they soon went to bed. The sun had set and they knew that there was much to do the next day. Maximilian took Carlota into his arms and they soon dozed off.

"Max! MAX!!" Carlota shrieked. Maximilian sat up straight as an arrow, his heart pounding. Carlota jumped from the bed and shrieked again.

Several cockroaches covered her white nightgown. She jumped and trotted, knocking them off, and then danced on her feet, afraid that they would run back up her legs. Once he got over the shock and saw that she was all right, he struggled to stifle a laugh. "That's it," he announced. "There have to be better lodgings somewhere." He rose and disgustedly brushed a cockroach off of himself as well. It hit the floor and ran to the hearth, shining disgustingly in the firelight.

They were soon in the game room, eyeing the billiards table.

"Well, what do you think, dear?" he asked Carlota. "Shall we brave it?"

"If it's the best we have, then I suppose we have to," Carlota said, her eyes scanning it doubtfully.

Maximilian gave her a tender kiss on the forehead but kept his hand playfully near her breast. She ducked with a grin to the other side of the pool table and rolled one of the balls towards him. He laughed and rolled two balls back. They continued this, at first slowly and then more assertively, both of them flirting with their eyes.

There was a soft knock on the door. Maximilian looked up sharply from their game. "What?" he asked in a perturbed tone of voice.

A plump old woman peeked her head into the room. Her arms were piled with stacks of sheets and silk comforters. Her old voice shook with fright. "They told me to bring this bedding. It's our very best, Your Majesty, and freshly laundered. Would Your Highnesses like me to make your bed now?"

Maximilian and Carlota stifled uncontrollable giggles. He composed himself enough to finally reply. "Yes, come. Her Majesty and I will step out on the balcony. But do it quickly and then leave." They left for the balcony, still giggling behind their hands.

"I hope she's as experienced as she looks," he whispered, taking Carlota into his arms.

"And I hope she's as proficient as you are," she said softly, lowering her head and looking seductively up at him from under her lashes.

They were soon alone in the game room, now a makeshift bedroom. The pool table was a strange but charming bed, topped with pillows and a silk comforter.

"Now I'll take advantage of an old marriage custom," Maximilian said, picking up Carlota. "I'll carry my wife into our new home and consummate our love once more."

He lifted the beautifully petite dark-haired woman and placed her gently onto their makeshift bed, climbing in beside her. They lay back onto the fluffy pillows and Maximilian gave her a long and gentle hug. "In Mexico, they call that *abrazar*," he whispered. "And they call this ..." he whispered, leaning down and kissing her slowly and tenderly on the lips, "... *besar*."

They continued to kiss, their breathing calm and steady, their hands sliding softly over each other's bodies. Carlota began to slowly remove his clothing, showing great attention to the exposed flesh. Her kisses lighted on his body like little feathers brushing here and there.

"I love you," she whispered breathlessly as she confidently caressed his body. "I can't live without you ..."

"Oh?" Maximilian murmured with a smile.

"I'd die before I'd let anything happen to you," she whispered dramatically, responding to the intoxication she felt.

"No, you'll live," he whispered, holding her close. "You won't die, and neither will I. But memories of the departed will haunt whichever one of us survives. That's what happens in life, especially to people in love."

"I feel haunted already," she replied with a glint in her eye, squirming under his hand.

His hands slid down her belly, caressing her until she moaned softly and arched her back. Their foreplay seemed to be in slow motion as he untied the lace bodice and opened it to reveal her breasts. She offered them to him with another moan as he lowered his head and kissed her gently, then played his tongue over her nipples. A moan finally escaped his lips as well as he pulled the gown down from her shoulders and slipped it off completely.

The balmy air flowed lightly over their skin, and Carlota shivered in anticipation as he covered her body with kisses. Everything remained in slow motion, each kiss, each caress, each thrust. The room echoed with their gasps and moans as he took her again, then again. Their lovemaking finally ended in a frenzy of passion and erotic pleasure.

"In Mexico, they call that *hacer el amor*," he said, his voice husky and breathless from their lovemaking.

She was roused gently by the sound of his voice from the half-dozing dreaminess in which she had been so luxuriously indulging. Her lips were full and dark in the dim light as she chuckled in a lover's intimate way. "In Mexico, the grass sandwich has more meat," she whispered.

Maximilian laughed out loud at that. They cuddled closely and listened to the drapes ruffle in the breeze. "One can be happily married to one but hopelessly in love with another," he mused.

Carlota slapped him. "Oh, Max, why do you say things like that? Besides, if you marry out of love, you're still hopelessly in love with your wife, is it not so? Love doesn't die."

"Have you ever thought about why it doesn't die?"

Carlota paused and then smiled sheepishly. "No," she admitted, having only uttered a romantic absolute.

"Heaven and earth are permanent, but people come and go. Love arouses the souls of heaven and earth. Love adds to the growth of your own soul, even after your body has perished. It's God's sweet music," he stated dramatically, caught up in his own romanticism. "When you fall in love, God is actually asking you, 'What are you contributing to my pleasures and satisfaction for creating this world?'"

"God's pleasures?" Charlotte mused. "What touches God?"

"Anything that arouses the spirit and the soul. Music touches the soul, too. Repentance touches the soul, love touches the soul. That's what touches God. He's collected all things that arouse the soul, like a good merchant. It's like the saying goes: the life we live is a ferment in God's barrel. Portent dark wines lift His soul." Carlota paused, still bothered by his initial statement. "Would you ever leave me for a beloved?"

"No."

She waited for more, but he did not offer anything. "Why not?" she pressed.

"Because I'm a gentleman."

"Meaning what?"

"I'm trustworthy."

Carlota sighed. Sometimes she felt like the only thing that mattered to him, the center of his world. When things were like that, she was in heaven. But other times, like now, she felt that he so loved to philosophize that he unwittingly said things that were insensitive and hurtful.

She knew he loved Zinnia. It was hard to be angry with that, since she had offered the dancer to him on that first night they had been together. She loved Zinnia as well, and she knew the Indian would do anything for either one of them.

Were there others? Maximilian was idealistic and impetuous. It was possible.

Carlota began to play the mind game again. To combat the temptation to confront him with questions about whom else he loved, she would focus instead on the fear of losing him if she did confront him. Then, to avoid that fear, she would focus on how much he loved her, on how, out of all the women available to him, he had chosen her. "All great men have their mistresses," she thought to herself. "They're just amusements, servants that a powerful man can grow attached to. It's not love, or at least not the same kind of love as a man has with his wife. *I'm* the one he publicly committed to for life. *I'm* the one who will bear his children …"

Carlota lulled herself into a calm and lazy contentedness with her mind game. As usual, Maximilian was totally unaware that such a struggle had occurred right beside him. He pulled her closer to him and sighed happily.

Soon they were both sound asleep.

In another part of town while they slept, a printing press was at work on the morning newspaper. A French senior military officer entered the newspaper office and strode up to the press. He took a freshly printed newspaper from the hands of the editor and began censoring it. It took several hours and a great deal of clever work and help from the editor as they removed all details of death, mourning, gossip, and talk in the town and taverns. Instead, a picture of a huge crowd was shown welcoming the royal pair into Mexico. Touched-up photos were included to give the impression that the many religious people of Mexico were welcoming a great Catholic monarch and his lovely wife. Some counterfeit letters were printed to show the positive changes that people were told Maximilian would bring, such as foreign capital, better laws, and living conditions. The French officer then appointed hand-picked military editors to write other such stories and publish many more newspapers full of propaganda. When the officer was finished, he had his staff reprint a censored newspaper, ready to be delivered to the national palace.

Early in the morning, Maximilian woke, the rays of the sun falling on his face. Carlota was still sleeping, so he carefully rose and left for the adjoining chamber. He called out for Izel, then Nelli, but there was no answer from either servant. He finally threw on a silk robe and began searching out the kitchens, looking for something to eat and drink.

After a few minutes of exploring, he found the large stone kitchen and called for the servants with a cheerful voice. This time, a young man named Timas and a slightly rounded woman named Milinal greeted him with a low bow.

"The empress and I require a meal on the balcony. We'd like to begin our reign here with some of your best traditional dishes. Surprise us. Do what you will, but make it the best you've ever done."

The pair bowed down a second time and said together, "Yes, Your Majesty."

After Maximilian left the room, the wide-eyed servants gave each other a look, then a shrug of the shoulders as they began preparations for a traditional meal.

When Maximilian entered their dressing room, he found Carlota dressed in a lovely morning frock, white with the bodice covered in tiny embroidered red roses. He eyed her appreciatively. "You look especially lovely this morning," he said as he kissed her neck.

"Thank you, Max," she replied, returning his kiss. "But I'm famished."

"Food will be here shortly. I instructed the servants to serve on the balcony, but now I must hurry and dress." He stared confusedly at a half dozen wardrobe chests, all filled to overflowing with the newest fashions from Europe. "Help me select something especially regal to wear."

The royal couple spent the next half-hour choosing Maximilian's clothing. They both felt that his first impression would be important to his monarchy. They finally strolled onto the balcony to discover a feast of Mexican dishes. The table was dressed in a finely embroidered tablecloth with matching napkins, and a silver table setting. Brightly painted pottery contained *tamales de dulce*, or sweet tamales, made of *masa harina* and pineapple. There was also *chorizo con huevos*, eggs with Mexican chorizo sausage, served with lettuce leaves, slices of avocado, tomatoes, and *queso fresco*. Lime wedges were piled high along with pickled jalapeño chiles and warm corn tortillas. There was plenty of Mexican coffee, sweet cream, and fresh water.

"I feel a little guilty for eating such a grand meal when I think of the eyes of that poor young mother we saw in town," Carlota said, her face somewhat distressed. "I must start today to work on my vow to help those poor people."

"My charitable Carlota, we're not in this city twenty-four hours and you're pushing for my cooperation on your vow. There's so much for us to do, but don't worry, we have the time and energy for it."

Carlota took a seat and picked up a book she had taken with her, reading it as their coffee was poured. She had a sip of her coffee and then rose regally from her chair, quoting from the paper, "Let men tremble to win the hand of a woman, unless they win along with it the utmost passion of her heart."

"Who wrote that? He must have had a wife with a cause," Maximilian mused, sipping his water.

"Nathaniel Hawthorne," she replied. "I'd like to read his novel on romance, The Scarlet Letter."

"Yes, I've heard about him, an American writer of the Transcendentalist school. He believed in individual choice and consequences, and he wrote with an emphasis on symbolism."

Carlota nodded and took her chair again, trying her eggs. They were strange, like nothing she had ever tasted, but she found them delicious. The spice would take some getting used to, but it was not at all unpleasant. She turned and looked out over the balcony, watching the clouds drift past the distant mountains. "Here we are, Max, finally. In Mexico City," she said dreamily. "You and I should travel the country to show the people our dedication to them, to win them over completely."

"Yes, we'll bring an era of peace and prosperity for our new country," he agreed haughtily. "I'll also send Señor Arroyo to seek an interview with the United States president, with a view to the recognition of the empire."

Carlota nodded approvingly at that.

Maximilian smiled at her confidence, at her beautifully strong face. "Carlota, you know I love you dearly, don't you?"

She looked up at him with surprise. "Yes, my dearest Maxi, of course I know that."

"Then I must tell you this," he said, hesitating to find the right words. Carlota frowned slightly and paused in her breakfast, listening quietly as he continued. "I realize that you're praying for a son to carry on the legacy, someone to groom as heir to the throne. And my prayers are with you, believe me, but we must have an alternate course in case that doesn't happen as soon as we wish." Carlota opened her mouth to speak and then closed it quickly. She did not want to have this discussion, but knew they had to have it sooner or later. "We have to look for an heir for our new monarchy. I've put a lot of thought into this, and I think we should adopt Augustín de Iturbide y Green. He's a descendent of an earlier emperor of Mexico, and we can groom him as heir to the throne."

A shadow of sadness fell across her face as a sinking feeling began deep in the pit of her stomach. She thought of her long-desired son, a son that may never exist. A part of her feared that if they adopted someone and groomed him, it would lay down some sort of curse to make sure that she never conceived a child. Her very logical mind dismissed that as silly magical thinking, but her heart cried out against the idea of adopting another's child as her own. Despite all of these thoughts swirling and screaming in her head, she relied on her court breeding and managed a smile. "Yes, Maxi, I agree. A son to train, yes, and to me, it will be a pleasure."

They were interrupted by a French military officer who stepped out onto the veranda to deliver their paper. Unbeknownst to the royal couple, this was the same officer who visited the printing press the night before.

Seeing the paper lifted Maximilian's morale. "Ah, our first Mexican newspaper!" he exclaimed, dismissing the officer with a wave and reading it eagerly. Carlota blinked at the sudden change of subject. Again relying on her innate court etiquette, she sighed and rose from the table, coming around to read the paper as well.

The French officer retreated from the royal couple and stepped out of the palace. A slightly built officer of lesser rank approached him and took a small sack from the man. "Take this to the ship," he said, and the smaller man left with a fast salute. The officer smiled to himself as he watched the man leave, bound for a ship he had privately rented and loaded with loot from Mexico. The Frenchman, along with many of the other French army officers, had nearly emptied Maximilian's treasury.

Earlier when Juarez had won victory against his civil war opponents, they had left Mexico City with all the treasury, gold, silver, anything valuable. Maximilian had yet to discover that there was no money in the treasury, just as he had yet to find out that he had no supportive army to bring about the changes he had promised.

All he had were loans from France and his own personal treasury. With extensive alterations yet to be made to the imperial residence, as well as the costs of the pageants and ovations that would soon come from his journeys in the provinces, the relief brought by the loans he had secured would be brief.

"Carlota, look!" Maximilian exclaimed, pleased. "The paper reports that the Catholics are eager to meet with us!" Carlota laughed, charmed by his enthusiasm.

Understanding

Juarez waded through the ankle-deep water that had inundated his hideout. He had found a cave far in the north, dusty and dark but perfect for his needs. The dustiness was gone from an unusual rain that had flooded his hideout. He firmly grasped the upper arm of an old companion who had come to bring supplies, helping him through the slippery mud to the entrance of the cave.

Now and then, someone, usually a farmer or his son, would visit the cave to bring him news from the capital, or a gift of a pot of soup or a loaf of bread. They kept very quiet about his whereabouts, and most of Juarez's men did not even know where he was. The people loved him, and they protected him in that quiet and subtle, yet fiercely determined, way that many country folk of his nation had.

Here he would wait, moving when necessary and biding his time. That was something he had: time. He was not so sure that Mexico's French-appointed emperor had that luxury, and that was what he was betting on. He was patient, and so were his people. They moved with the slow and quiet confidence of people who knew deep in their hearts that someday, somehow, their time would come.

"The rain has stopped," the old man observed as he hobbled through the mud and squinted up at the gray sky.

"It never rains that much here," Juarez marveled, pulling his feet from the mud that sucked at his boots.

"Is God testing us by pushing us from a palace to a cave?" the old man asked helplessly. "By making us look at our dying friends and family members? Is He cruel?"

"No, He's not cruel," Juarez protested softly.

"Then why all of this? Why all of the devastation?"

"He tests people, tests how a society reacts to its tragedies."

"Why test mankind?" the man complained.

Juarez smiled at the man's grumbling. "Because He gave mankind two special gifts: the ability to choose between actions, good or evil, and the ability to intelligently weigh and make those choices."

"So?" the old man asked in irritation as he looked at the muddy ground. "What does that mean?"

"It means that He put tremendous responsibility on our shoulders. We have to be sure that we don't abuse our gifts by rejecting God or by hurting each other unnecessarily. He could have decided things otherwise."

"Otherwise?"

Juarez nodded. "He could just take away our sight or cripple us right now. And then how would we cross this water?"

"Hm," the old man mumbled, taking the reins of his horse and allowing Juarez to help him mount the horse. His eyes softened as he looked down at his old friend. "You be careful. I'll come again as soon as I can."

"Thank you for coming," Juarez said, clasping his hand, "but I don't think it wise for you to come back here."

The old man stared down at him, then finally replied: "We have bayonets everywhere, but we can't sit on them."

"I guess you are right."

"In the mountains, a woman was mourning. When asked why she wept, she replied, 'My husband's father was killed here by a tiger, my husband also, and now my son has met the same fate.' 'Then why do you dwell in so dreadful a place?' 'Because here,' she answered, 'there is no oppressive ruler.'"

"That is what Confucius said: 'Oppressive rule is more cruel than a tiger.'"

"An oppressive ruler is a more dangerous risk." He gave Juarez's hand an affectionate squeeze and turned the horse into the dripping grove of trees. He was soon out of sight.

Juarez sat on a trunk and read a week-old newspaper by the light of a lantern.

"Now the French have their pleasing Catholic princely face," he mused to himself as he squinted at the paper, his voice echoing off the walls. "He's the perfect choice to red-carpet their occupation … their atrocities. Of course he'll eventually have to be scapegoated," he added, not without some amusement, taking out his canteen and opening it slowly.

A flash of pity danced in his thoughts for this European, whose hopes were as high as his insight was lacking. He ignored the pity and let it pass, knowing that it would not help him in accomplishing what had to be done. It would also not save the emperor from the lion's den he was already trapped in, aside from Juarez's rebellion. That ship had sailed, and there was no use in dwelling on emotions like pity and compassion.

He finally stood up, restless in the cramped confines of his rocky home, and paced up and down the small path. "Is this prince a good judge?" he wondered aloud.

The old man sat down, and then finally nodded.

"Can he spot the devils in his flock?"

He knew by then that Maximilian had no treasury, and was strapped with an opportunistic class of men who held a vested interest. The Church would soon start collecting funds in the new emperor's name, and the army would make sure that they looked heroic. "Hmmm … the real issue is that the Americans are fighting amongst themselves, and in the meantime, others have come to benefit."

He dwelled on that thought. When America's civil war ended, many things were going to change, and quickly. He nodded pensively. "So this is understanding," he murmured, nodding to himself. "Reading what kind of future lies in the womb of the present."

CHAPTER 15

▼

THE BEGINNING OF THE END

Carlota stretched languidly as she looked out the window. The sun was high in the sky, warming the wood floor in a pool of golden light. Carlota lifted her head, vaguely confused at the unfamiliar feel of the air. Her senses spoke to her. She recognized the odor of tropical flowers, and then heard the soft strains of some distant music.

In a moment she remembered where she was: Mexico. She was in Mexico! Her heart skipped a beat at the sudden realization. She glanced hurriedly around the room, but Maximilian was nowhere to be seen. A small chuckle escaped her lips when she realized that she was lying on a makeshift bed on the pool table. She climbed down from it in a rush, grabbing the silk ivory robe that matched her nightgown.

Her feet padded across a rich carpet of red mixed with greens and blues. She whisked past a large arrangement of exotic flowers that had been placed in a costly Talavera vase, a lovely piece that would take her days in her excitement to even notice. It was expertly painted with graceful orange flowers and accents of blue, pink, and green.

The room showed signs of their recent arrival, with clothing left hanging on chairs and trunks stacked here and there. She practically tripped over a trunk that stood open on its side, cursing softly to herself and then giggling. "Why am I in such a hurry?" she thought to herself.

Carlota leaned over the trunk and sorted through it for something to wear. She selected a pretty white day frock sprigged with tiny blue flowers, then pulled out some fine linen undergarments to wear with it. An elaborately embossed basin and pitcher stood ready on a washstand, and she quickly washed her face and got dressed.

As she fastened her dark hair into a graceful coiffure, Maximilian strode into the room. He picked her up and swung her in a half circle. Carlota squealed and hugged him tight.

"Good morning, Empress Carlota," he said with a boyish grin, setting her back on her feet and bowing slightly at the waist.

Carlota responded with a lavish curtsey. "Good morning, Emperor Maximilian." They both laughed.

"When is breakfast?" Carlota asked. "I'm starving."

Maximilian took her by the elbow and led her out onto the sunny terrace. There a colorful table awaited them, spread with flowers and fruit. A dozen servants clad in white stood at attention, helping them to sit and then scurrying about to bring them their breakfast. Once again the food was strange but delicious.

"This is wonderful. I wonder what it is," Carlota mused as she carefully wiped her mouth with a brightly colored napkin. It seemed to be some sort of egg dish, though there was a garlicky sauce on it and some kind of vegetable that she could not yet place.

Maximilian nodded. "There are so many things we have to do today. What would you like to begin with?"

"Well, of course I should direct my maid in unpacking, and then I'll have to set up some sort of order in our sleeping quarters."

He smirked at her term for the makeshift bedroom. "Yes, this place has a great deal of potential. We'll make it into an imperial palace, just you wait and see. I've decided to name it Miravalle, in memory of our beloved Miramar."

"What a lovely idea," Carlota murmured, spearing a chunk of pineapple.

"Carlota, I'm alive with plans for this place and for this entire country. It's all I can think about. This is our new country. From this day on, we're not European, we're Mexican," he declared enthusiastically. His head swirled with ideas, and he pushed on before Carlota could reply. "For one thing, we should do something about the railroads. It seems they've been trying to build one here for quite some time, but the revolutions keep stalling its progress.

Maximilian ate some of a pastry, frowning and concentrating to himself before he continued, thinking out loud. "I also think we should link this castle to the city."

"Castle?" Carlota interrupted. "I wouldn't call it that yet, darling. It still looks very much like an old military academy."

"True, that's what it *used* to be," he replied confidently. "I have bigger plans for this place than that. We're going to renovate from top to bottom, spare no expense. That winding old road leading up here is going to be widened, with trees planted and gaslights lining it like a proper street. We'll extend it all the way to the city, like an official imperial residence." He paused, his eyes glinting. "And guess what we'll name this new avenue?"

Carlota smiled. "What?"

"Avenue of the Empress."

Carlota laughed. "That's very kind, but it's your notion. I think it should be called The Emperor's Avenue, so everyone will see what you can do. These kinds of projects are your forte."

Maximilian beamed, his pride getting the best of him. "We can work out the naming later, I suppose. For now, I must prepare for my first meeting with Marshal Bazaine," he said, standing.

Carlota nodded soberly. Bazaine was the head of the French military in Mexico. It was crucial that he establish a good working relationship with him, and Carlota silently wished him luck.

"I'll be setting up a makeshift office in the observational tower."

Carlota again looked surprised. "You mean that circular tower on the roof? It's a shambles up there." The tower jutted from the roof of Chapultepec on the topmost level. The locals called it the *Caballero Alto*, meaning "the tall knight."

"It won't be a shambles for long," he reminded her. "The view is spectacular from there. I can see for miles, and I couldn't think of a better spot to work out of. You busy yourself with putting things in order. I'll return when my meeting is finished." He gave her a quick peck on the cheek and hurried along the balcony towards the stairs to the upper level.

Maximilian spent the next hour in his tower, sorting through a virtual mountain of correspondences. He was finally interrupted from his work when one of his personal guards came to the door. "Sir, French Marshal Aquiles Bazaine to see you," the young soldier announced with a salute.

Maximilian dismissed the young man and appraised Bazaine as he entered the room. He was short and plain looking, his body thickset. Maximilian gestured to a straight-backed chair to the left of his desk.

Bazaine saluted him formally. "Good morning, Emperor Maximiliano," he said before taking a seat.

Maximilian laughed. "Maximiliano, is it? I thought Juarez called me 'The Austrico.'"

Bazaine shook his head. "No, sire. You were 'Austrico' before the Treaty of Miramar last March. Since then, according to the treaty terms, you resigned commitments and rights to the crown of Austria."

Maximilian cocked an eyebrow, slightly irritated at the man's quickness to correct him. "Well, I did come in an Austrian ship."

"True, but not with Austrian funds. Your brother required a written promise from Napoleon III for the support of the French army before he allowed the *Novaro* to take your entourage to Mexico. Your brother maintains control of that ship, so you cannot use it for Mexico."

Maximilian suppressed the urge to shake his head at the man's insolence, but he also knew that it was important that they start off on the right foot. "Tell me, Marshal Bazaine, exactly what is the French army here for?"

"To protect your emperorship, sire."

"At your earliest convenience, I would like to see your commanders."

Bazaine hesitated. "They've been instructed to stay away from politics, sire."

"I beg your pardon? If they're here to protect me and my government, surely I have to at least meet them."

"They're busy in field areas, sire."

Maximilian could feel his ire rising. "Do we need all of the commanders in the field right now? What are we trying to do here? Beat my nation into submission?"

"The commanders are not your nation, sire. You'll meet your true ward tomorrow night, the Regency."

"So I'm to meet my masters tomorrow night?" Maximilian replied sarcastically. "I have to object to your attitude, Marshal. I'm here to ensure the welfare of all my subjects, not just some."

Bazaine shifted awkwardly in his seat. "Sire, all of your subjects are fighting a civil war right now. Most of your subjects are Juarez's terrorists. The French army has had to stomach criticism of even its supporters here."

"A civil war? Right now?" Maximilian repeated incredulously. "No one told me that."

"One of Juarez's top men was hanged today. His last words were, 'We do not want an emperor, no matter how liberal.' He was quoting Benito Juarez, so you can see how resistant these people are."

Maximilian could see that the marshal was getting agitated just thinking about the Mexican sentiments. He stayed silent and let Bazaine continue, sensing that he would get more information that way.

Bazaine shook his head in disgust. "If you'll pardon my saying it, sire, this damned country was ruled by a European dynasty hundreds of years ago. We were supposed to come here to sow the second coming, but all we've gotten is resistance. The second coming will occur though, and they'd better learn to accept it. That's what the ceremony tomorrow night is for: to call in the beginning of the second coming of Europe."

"And what if I don't care to engage in such a ceremony?" Maximilian asked, straightening in his chair.

Bazaine shrugged. "I don't believe that's an option, sire."

"Take it or leave it?" Maximilian asked dryly, managing a smile.

The marshal was surprised at Maximilian's humor. "Um … yes, sire. Take it or leave it."

"I'm not here to insult the good name of a Hapsburg," Maximilian said, shaking his head and leaning back in his chair. "I have to leave it."

Marshal Bazaine blinked in surprise. "Which means your supporters will be even more disappointed," he said firmly. He opened the pocket of his uniform and slipped out a check. "I've been told to deliver this to you. It's a check for 500 million Mexican pesos. It was promised to you by a unanimous vote in a meeting of the Regency of Mexico. It's intended to pay for the start-up of your government, which officially begins on the twelfth of June." He placed the check on the desk and slid it towards the emperor.

Maximilian stared at the check, startled. "Who are these people? The Regency of Mexico?"

"The notable citizens, the old families made up of prominent people. They're the ones who brought you here. They're paying for you," he answered matter-of-factly.

It took Maximilian some time to soak that in. "I'm perplexed," he finally managed, standing and walking to a turret window. He stared at the mountains in the distance as he thought it over. "Have I renounced Austria to protect the interests of these men? Was the plebiscite a fraud? I thought I took this throne in good faith, on the vote of the people of Mexico. But I see now that my best intentions are of no use. I wanted to approach my leadership with honesty, uprightness … a desire to lead Mexico into an age of peace and prosperity."

A small, sad smile lit across his face. He felt like a fool, like he should have known better and had instead fallen for a classic ruse.

"Was it my fate to be deceived?" he asked, turning on his heel and walking towards Bazaine. "This group of rich men, this *Regency* as you call them, will they now prevent me from following my own character? Will they keep me shuttling and oscillating between my liberal ideas and their own conservative agenda?" His back stiffened stubbornly. "How can they prevent me from ruling Mexico as I see fit?" he challenged.

Bazaine shook his head, seeing he did not yet completely understand his predicament. "Sire, your government can only work where we have French garrisons, mostly major cities and supply arterials in Vera Cruz, Puebla, Queretaro, and a few other places. You have no choice but to stay inside safely."

Maximilian pushed the check back towards Bazaine. "I won't do it. I intend to work for all of my people, not just a few. I'll recruit a national army. I could even open negotiations with Juarez."

Bazaine stood. "Good luck to you, sire. Tomorrow evening, the Regency will be arriving to meet you. You must thank them for the support of this town, the check. They intend to see the Grand Hall once again witness the glory of a European ruling dynasty in Mexico. That's what they expect and what you should provide for them." He left the check on the table. "On the twelfth of June, your government begins with that money." With that, he saluted and left the room.

Maximilian was speechless.

When Maximilian returned to his rooms downstairs, he was a changed man. He had gone upstairs as the new emperor, ready to rejuvenate the country with countless ideas. He had returned a mere puppet, a showpiece. They had duped him into accepting the Mexican crown; that was all too clear to him now. These elite men had their own agenda, and so had the French. Maximilian was to be nothing more than a foolish facade for their nefarious aims. Here he was, a Hapsburg prince who had renounced the Austrian throne and all his titles, thrown by deceit into a civil war which neither the French army nor the elite were interested in. He was expected to live on the purse of the Mexican and foreign elite, to run a government for the interests of a few and against everyone else.

He was shaken out of his dream.

"I'm nothing more than a red carpet," he thought to himself, another wry smile on his face at the very irony. "But who can help me? Or who even would?" he wondered. It did not take him long before he thought of someone, the person who was always there for him no matter what. "Mother," he thought. "Surely you can do something to help me." He decided that contacting her would be his first move.

He rushed out to find Carlota, the only other person there who he would dare discuss this with right now. She was in the garden, and her face was immediately full of concern when she saw his expression as he approached. "Max, what's wrong?" she asked, standing.

"Oh Carlota, it's all such a mess," he moaned, sinking into a chair and rubbing his temples.

Carlota moved behind him and stroked his shoulders. Her expression was one of alarm from behind him, but she kept her voice deliberately calm. "What happened?"

"They've tricked us. They want nothing more than for us to behave ourselves and serve the upper class."

He explained the situation to Carlota, once again thankful to her. She was always so strong, not like many other women of the court who had to be left out of serious discussions. She always listened when he needed to talk, was strong when he needed support. In many ways, she reminded him of his own mother.

After an emotional discussion, they decided to get his mother's support. They sat down together and composed a letter to be delivered immediately to his mother in Vienna.

"Dear Mother,

I miss you. This is a lovely land full of potential. But all is not what it seemed. I find myself in a difficult place in my new empire. The government's coffers here are empty, and I now find my personal funds for the imperial household depleted. I refuse to be a marionette dancing on the stings of the rich minorities. I must at least seem to have my own funds to assert my rightful authority.

You always have the answers. Please, dearest one, contact me as soon as you can with any advice and help that you can muster.

Your loving son,

Emperor Maximilian I of Mexico."

The former empress Sophie was dressed for the day and walked towards her study, a delightful room with white paneling and blue velvet furniture. The sun flowed in mellow columns through the windows and onto the polished wood floors as she entered her study, but even its warm illumination could not distract her from thoughts of her middle son, now the emperor of Mexico. She felt a hollow spot in the pit of her stomach, a vacant place below her ribcage that she could never quite ignore when she thought of her beloved Maxi.

She sat at the pearl inlaid French writing desk that looked out across the manicured lawn of the palace, facing the Gloriette that glowed the imperial color of Schonbrunn yellow. Taking out paper and pen, she meant to write him yet another letter today. She stared at the blank page and wondered if he had even received the first letter yet. She sighed heavily as her personal servant Adelaide entered with a light step.

"Your Majesty, the weather's lovely today. Later on, would you like to take a stroll in the garden?"

"No, no, Adelaide," she mumbled, waving a hand. "It's kind of you to care for me, but I have a million things on my mind."

Adelaide stood above her quietly as Sophie stared out of the windows at nothing at all. Her face was hard and her eyes began to glitter with tears. When Adelaide placed a hand softly on her shoulder, she could no longer hold back, and tears spilled from her eyes. She covered her face with a handkerchief to hide her face, but Adelaide felt that she was a close enough friend not to be required to leave her alone as other servants were expected to do. Instead, she kept her hand on her shoulder, quietly soothing her.

They remained that way for a few moments. Sophie hated crying in front of anyone, but at least it was Adelaide. She lowered the handkerchief and wiped her eyes with a sniffle. "I will not spend another moment in this self-indulgence."

"I have something to cheer you up," Adelaide offered, pulling an envelope from her pocket. "The post has arrived, and I think you'll be interested in this envelope in particular."

Sophie laughed as she snatched the letter gleefully. "How can you leave me to suffer when you had this all along?" she teased.

"Sometimes you need to express how you feel," Adelaide offered, but Sophie was too excited to think about that.

"It's from Mexico," she confirmed, examining the address. "It's from Max," she added, stating the obvious as she savored the moment. She tore at the folds as fast as she could without accidentally tearing the words inside, eager to read something from Max.

She slowly read the short message, cradling the paper in her hands. A smile crept onto her face. "Ah, so my boy still needs me after all," she murmured to herself, pleased. "Those poor things have no idea what it takes to run an imperial palace."

She paused, thinking over what to do. She finally nodded to herself and began talking in her usual confident tone. "You must help me arrange outfitting the royal couple for their new reign in Mexico. They need the correct linens, furniture, and all kinds of household goods befitting their station. They've never had to arrange for such things."

"Yes, Your Majesty," Adelaide said as she took paper from the secretary's drawer and began taking hurried notes.

Sophie smiled again. "He may be halfway around the world, but I can still see to it that he lives a civilized life." She began dictating to Adele. "They'll need the proper crockery, table cutlery, serving pieces, table linen, china, furniture, blankets, bedding … they should be placed in leather cases and then packed in crates to protect them during the long voyage."

Adele nodded, writing as fast as she could.

"Louis Bonaparte commissioned his royal purveyor Christofle to make a dinner service for them already, nearly five thousand pieces in German silver. It's all monogrammed 'MIM' for 'Maximilian Imperator Mexici.' We should stay with that design, and we'll continue the MIM monogram throughout."

She stood and paced, energy revived in her limbs now that she was back in her element. This was the next-best thing to having her son there. "As for bed linens, we'll send two dozen sets. Across the entire front, there will be embroidery, and it should continue partly down the sides. Of course each will also have an elaborate MIM monogram in satin stitch."

Adele wrote furiously, only nodding from time to time.

"We need a dozen banquet cloths of Point de Vence work, broderie anglaise, and satin stitch with filet lace borders. With that, we'll have twenty dozen linen napkins with a filet lace border. In one corner of each should be the monogram, again in satin stitch embroidery. Then four dozen round linen tea cloths with punch work of roses, and a wide bobbin lace … ten dozen large, round lawn linen coasters with lace borders of roses … and a large selection of pillows, quilts, and coverlets. And monograms, don't forget to monogram everything!"

Adele's notes were as thorough as Sophie's instructions. Her hand ached from writing, but she was glad to see her lady so alive again.

The next several days were a frenzy of activity. Sophie sought advice from many experts, including those who could advise on the best way to run a government, as she assembled a team to send Maximilian what he needed. She even visited polo matches, where many in attendance were former players who had been good friends with her son. They were eager to support his emperorship of Mexico, and she garnered a great deal of support there.

Sophie had the royal purser arrange for the crockery, linen, washing, and furniture for her son. Before shipping everything, she personally oversaw the packing list with the royal purser.

"We've procured silk and Rococo furniture, including everything that's 'movable' in a house," the purser reported. "Here's the list, Your Majesty."

Sophie looked over every piece and checked them off the list as they were placed in the crates.

> *"Boudoir (Louis XVI)*
> *Salon (Louis XVI)*
> *Marqueterie Cabinet Writing Table (Riesener)*
> *Writing Table (Marie Antoinette)*
> *Cylinder Secretaire (Rothschild Collection)*
> *Pair of Armchairs (Louis XVI)*
> *Carved and Gilt Settee and matching Armchair*
> *Sofa En Suite*
> *Secretaire with Sevres Plaques*
> *Clock by Robin (Jones Collection)*
> *Set of Four Italian Sedan Chairs."*

Sophie was nowhere near finished. She continued going to polo matches in Vienna and from there called all the wise and capable administrators to ask them for advice. She requested them to fit out ships, arrange funds, recruit servants and volunteers to serve as royal bodyguards, collect household equipment like party crockery and kitchen utensils. She even had the royal bodyguard volunteers fitted out with horses, swords, and other weapons, arranging their dispatch by ship from Trieste.

Sophie had done everything in her considerable power and capability to help her son build a monarchy in a foreign land, to help fulfill Maximilian's dream. She advised him of her efforts in a letter.

"Dear Son,

I hope this message finds you well. I have arranged for shiploads of support, bodyguards, personal staff, crockery, cutlery, household stuffs, cooks, a doctor, and many others that will be helpful to you. You will also find contact language via newspapers. There will be other shipments later.

Your namesake, your sister-in-law Sissi's father, Duke Maximilian Joseph of Bavaria, sends you his best wishes and the following advice:

'The state is one language, one religion, one culture. Your state does not coincide with the nation of Mexico; therefore, you should build spontaneous pluralism in Mexico, hold your own culture out boldly. To do that, you must build your office opulently, get builders to create gilded halls and magnificent tables. Float elegance and start inviting the common people for dinners. Build Mexico City as a cosmopolitan city. Raise your own army and supportive institutions. First, pay attention to correcting the judiciary. Make sure that the high and mighty are reduced to ordinary citizens. This justice will resound in state dinners. Mexicans will like that. Then the monarchy can spread its roots.'

As for my own advice, how can I improve on perfection? You are and will always be a magnificent Hapsburg, born of and destined for success.

I shall write again soon.

Your loving mother."

Maximilian was soon sent the letter as Sophie continued to report her activities.

"Dear Son,

I have received a letter from King Leopold, as advised by his sage, asking you to meet Juarez as soon as possible. The sage advises that as emperor of Mexico, you should order a republican government instead of a monarchy, appointing Juarez as your prime minister. I am forwarding King Leopold's complete letter to you.

I have been thinking a great deal about Duke Maximilian's advice regarding an opulent display of your culture, and I have many ideas on how this can be achieved. First, have 'whole city parties' with waiters who bow to the people. Arrange for ornate cafes, gas lamps, beer taverns, chocolate cakes, apple strudel, Lipizzaner dancing horses, and the music of Mozart. Have the bodyguards I am sending appear to be guarding them as well as yourself. Simply immerse the city in the air of Venice and give the ordinary citizen a feeling of royalty. The more people start kissing your hand, the more rapidly your monarchy can spread its roots.

Below is more specific advice I have gathered from several sources:

1.   Organize the royal mint

2.   Next organize the postal system.

3.   Make volunteer clubs for helping the monarchy with money and labor. Be wise, reading and listening to their advice.

More soon.

Your loving mother."

That particular letter made it all the way to Mexico before it fell into the hands of French General Forey. He frowned at the words as he sat in his armchair beside the fireplace. "So they're sending a royal bodyguard," he thought to himself. "Well, we'll just have to make sure that they become absorbed into the French army." He turned and dropped the letter into the hearth, watching it burn thoughtfully. "Don't think for a moment that you'll be able to use us," he whispered. "We're here to use the emperor, not the other way around."

After writing the first letter to his mother asking for help, Maximilian had consulted Carlota about how to handle what he had started to call "The Second Coming Dinner." She had wisely advised him to attend the dinner and to learn more about the Regency, and to ignore his urge to boycott the entire affair out of protest. He trusted her opinion and promptly ordered clothes and robes befitting the show that was to be held.

The following evening, he entered the Grand Hall accompanied by the sounds of bugles and cheers. He walked slowly, surprised to see huge paintings on the walls that had not been there before. He inspected them closely as he passed, finding small number chits pasted to them by the museum staff. "Museum pieces, eh?" he thought in amusement. "It looks as if the Second Coming is nothing more than an artificial transplant."

The hall was packed with the Mexican elite. The head of the Mexican Regency was ironically a German hardware merchant, a senior member of the Boker family. Maximilian sat with him on a dais, inclining his head forward to speak with the much shorter man.

"Are you German, sir?"

"I was, Your Majesty. Now I am Mexican."

"A Mexican conquistador?" Maximilian asked dryly.

"Not exactly, sire, but we have business interests from Europe to Canada, the United States, Mexico, and Argentina. We're hard-working immigrants who only want peace and prosperity for Mexico."

"We have a common ground there," Maximilian replied with a nod.

Boker smiled broadly, appearing relieved. "Yes, we do. I am always at your service, sire."

Expert servants in carefully tailored white uniforms served tea and coffee.

Maximilian took a cup offered to him. "If I may ask, how much did you pay to hire me?"

Boker's face flushed red and there was a long pause.

"How much?" Maximilian pressed.

Boker finally straightened in his chair and found his voice. "Each of us here paid ten million Mexican pesos, sire, but that was simply to help you put down your royal roots."

Maximilian looked him directly in the eye. "Strange, I'd thought people had paid to hire me."

Boker shook his head and tried to appease the emperor. "Your Majesty, try to understand, we have a diaspora here in Mexico. People have settled here far from their homelands. They look to me for leadership. I helped them draw the conclusion that for the next several generations, we have to work hard and think hard to achieve prosperity."

Maximilian sipped his coffee thoughtfully. "*Your* prosperity?"

Boker again shook his head. "*Mexican* prosperity, sire. It will trickle down to the masses."

"So a tumultuous political climate doesn't help your business, is that the root of this? Stabilize the government so that you all can prosper?"

The German reluctantly nodded. "Yes, sire. That's why we wanted an emperor."

Marshal Bazaine entered the hall in his blue patrol ceremonial uniform. Everyone except Maximilian and Carlota stood up to cheer. By that time, Bazaine was the most popular man in the army. He had risen through the ranks in the military and had a reputation for being both intelligent and resourceful.

Bazaine walked straight to the emperor and offered his hand. Maximilian allowed a handshake, though with only three fingers to stubbornly show his position. "Sit down," the emperor said, gesturing to a chair a great distance away. Boker rose and saw to it that the marshal was comfortably seated before returning to the dais.

Maximilian continued their previous conversation, ignoring the marshal's insulted glare. "So you need a positivist regime, an iron hand, lots of ropes to hang people, plenty of firing squads?"

"Only to remove the shadows of danger around you, sire," Boker replied.

Before Maximilian could reply, the German was called to the platform to speak officially before the crowd. There was great applause as they greeted the esteemed chairman of the Regency, though the imperial couple managed only a distractedly weak clap as they watched him carefully.

The stout German cleared his throat. "We are here tonight to witness the second coming of European royalty, after centuries of unrest in Mexico." He paused as the crowd cheered heartily, their unleashed enthusiasm making it hard to believe that this was a ruse. Maximilian actually wondered if many had forgotten the ruse in the heat of the moment and bought the romantic idea for the evening.

Chairman Boker smiled and waited for the cheers to subside before continuing. "As the elite families of this nation, we must work with our emperor and lord to help bring peace and prosperity to both his government and our own livelihoods. This in turn will help the downtrodden people of this country to build better lives and futures." He emphasized this part, staring at the emperor as he spoke the rehearsed words. Maximilian's face was an unreadable mask.

"In order to begin this task, each family must begin by building separate and private cultural enclaves, according to your own homelands and specifications. Build your own shops, schools, and hospitals. With that as your base, you can then engage in cross-cultural trade. Identify local or hybrid supportive elements, then hire them whenever possible. In this way, we can keep our own identities while helping the local people around us to participate in and thrive from our endeavors."

Carlota frowned at the blatant self-interest of his speech.

"Finally, we should aim for assimilation. Our emperor seeks to establish a stable political climate, which his monarchy and our money can provide. We should do our part willingly and with great effort, having faith in our emperor's commitment to do the same. I, for one, hope that the era of Emperor Maximilian of Mexico will bloom and bring in a new age for this great country."

Again the hall rang with loud cheering and clapping. Maximilian and Carlota exchanged a subtle glance of disgust and detachment.

It was a long evening for both of them.

Not long after that ordeal, Maximilian received a letter delivered by an anonymous Mexican army captain. It was posted in Vera Cruz.

Pola.

Admiral Wilhelm Von Tegethoff.

My dear comrade-in-arms,

The bearer of this letter, Captain Vickers, is the son of a police officer named Carillo. He was known to one of my ship captains, and so I believe him to be a trusted messenger.

I went to Paris and met your mother there at a polo match. She told me about your difficulties, and I have decided to send you some advice that I hope will be most beneficial. I realize that I am merely jockeying here, with no direct concept of what you are enduring; nevertheless, I believe that a detached outside opinion may be far more useful to you than one entrenched in the dealings of your dilemma there.

First, I believe that you should establish yourself to the common people as a peaceful citizen, sharing your wealth with the native people. The sooner you earn their trust and respect, the safer you can become on all fronts.

Next, your weakest point is the French army. The civil war raging there is actually an armed struggle for self-determination against a foreign occupying army, a war of national liberation. The people are up against a racist regime supported by a minority. They are going to be helped by America and probably others. You should therefore either abdicate or move to the port of Vera Cruz. There you can generate enough revenue to help build a strong merchant and naval fleet. Your enemy Juarez won the civil war after occupying that revenue-yielding port. It is a valuable position in times of need. I can send support by ordinary ships via that port.

Remember Field Marshal Baron Ernst Laudon! There is a grand new portrait of him that now hangs in Feldherrenhalle. Try to keep his words in mind: "Battle victory changes fates."

More later.

WVT."

Maximilian promptly asked for a list of qualified officers from whom to select an ADC for himself. He scanned the list carefully and was sure to choose the name of Captain Vickers Carillo.

Juarez had fled the French intervention and the emperor Maximilian, going far north of Mexico City. He and his soldiers were reorganizing in the interior. Somewhere in the northern Mexican jungle, Juarez sat and read an old newspaper filled in abundance with the smashing impact of Emperor Maximiliano on the now-cosmopolitan society of Mexico City. He scoffed to himself as he read the shameless propaganda. The boldfaced lies would have sparked a riot among the common people if more of them had known how to read.

Vail entered the hideout carrying the last of his delivery. He was the son of police leader Carillo. The young man was an outlaw who served the resistance, faithfully delivering food and supplies on a donkey to Juarez each week. "Reading more of those lies? Why do you waste your time with that, sir?"

Juarez smirked at the young man. "Yes, they're lies, but it's important to know what image he wishes to portray."

Vail scoffed. "It seems a pretty predictable image. I may be able to get you better information, anyways."

Juarez lowered the newspaper into his lap, intrigued. "What do you mean?"

Vail grinned. "I mean that my younger brother has just been appointed ADC to the emperor."

Juarez frowned. "I'm confused. How could such an appointment come about? Vickers isn't one of his men. I would think the Austrian would appoint his own men for such positions so they can cheer him on, brag about him, sing songs about him."

Vail laughed. "My brother doesn't like royalty, I'm sure about that."

"Oh? And why is that?" Juarez asked.

"Because Vickers always says that there's a king's version of history set apart from the actual events."

Juarez nodded. "That's true. Kings have the language and the wiles to weave their own agendas under a cloak of unselfishness. They can spin their men around to their viewpoints, brainwash them. They use that to acquire funds. Wise men know that's a special craft that keeps kings on top. If the king has committed unlawful acts, his people may revolt or ask him to abdicate, or Congress can start an impeachment process. So kings buy their own Congress and write whatever version of history they desire. Once you hire the writers, you can change your image into that of a good man, a great leader and patriot, and finally a compassionate and determined man. No matter how deep the stains of his sins, these speech writers make him as clean as snow."

"But there always comes a day when his own party cries out for relief from the king's propaganda," Vail interjected. "They'll want to replace him."

"'But the Lord won't answer that day,' Samuel 8:18," Juarez quoted knowingly.

"Presidente, you know the Bible?" Vail asked. "Oh, I remember now, you were in religious study once."

Juarez shrugged. "Religion loves truth and so do I. We have to dig out the truth from falsehood. It takes courage and great understanding to do that. A dictator's men find out the truth because they can't stay fooled forever. But by then, the dictator may be too powerful to be uprooted. That's why we have to establish a democracy and free elections, so we can periodically remove those false prophets."

"And what about this king, sir, this emperor?"

"I pity him," Juarez replied thoughtfully. Vickers frowned as Juarez continued. "He's up against his own French army. They're here to collect money and domains, the Napoleonic glory of old. But they're not here to fight. A true Napoleon would have helped the American Confederates win against the Yankees, but they're not the mettle of Napoleon. They'll leave with gold and silver, we know that."

Vickers chuckled at the thought.

"That'll leave their emperor alone and without money. He can't have a 'King's Party' because he rules over his own entourage, not our people. In a few years, the people supporting him will be singing our song instead of his. He's condemned to become a pauper."

"But he's so well-connected, plus he's a Catholic prince. Our people are deeply religious."

"But don't you see? The Church will be flying *our* flag inside, not his," Juarez concluded.

CHAPTER 16

▼

FAERIE GLAMOUR

The next evening, Maximilian felt overwhelmed and restless. He wanted to go off by himself and pray. "It may be foolish to venture out alone when everyone says I'm in such danger," he thought, "but I have to take some time and think." His thoughts had been jumbled and confused since his meeting with Bazaine. He had to find a way to sort them out. He gave Carlota a vague excuse for leaving, which was easy enough since she was preoccupied with her servants and with setting up the household. He was soon walking along a quiet stone path, nearing the centuries-old forest that bordered the castle.

At any other time, he would have enjoyed the serenity of the woods, the sun low on the horizon as the birds took their last flight of the day. On that day, all he could do was think. The only thing he was becoming certain of was that the 500 million peso check that the Regency had given him had to be returned. It was hardly one year's salary for two thousand soldiers, and he had an empire to build. That would require far more money than he was provided with.

His thoughts drifted to Vice Admiral Wilhelm von Tegethoff, wondering if he should take a similar stance as his friend. Tegethoff was responsible for returning parts of Italy back to the Hapsburg family, and was quickly on his way up in the Austrian navy. He had been vocal in warning Maximilian that America would help Juarez in his struggles against any European emperorship. He had warned Maximilian not to merely settle in as a peaceful citizen, but instead to raise an army and sow his own roots there by force.

"Am I really just destined to be a red carpet here for a racist regime?" he thought. "Just a pawn to serve the interests of the rich, like Juarez said I was?" The bitterness crept back into his thoughts. He had been told that the Mexican people would think of him as their redeemer, someone who would bring equal opportunity and success to Mexico. It had all been a lie, and with his signature idealism, he had believed it.

He paused as the trees became scattered and he entered a clearing. Nightfall was casting a long shadow across the field as the mountains glowed with the last bit of the sun. It was breathtaking, having a sacred feel about it. Maximilian looked around to be sure he was alone, but the only ones who witnessed him were the birds and animals that had fallen silent but were everywhere. He kneeled down on the ground and lowered his head to pray, one hand reaching up to touch his cross.

"God, please help me to sort this out. My mind is at war with itself. I know you made me an emperor for a reason. Maybe you chose me to overcome all this and save this country. You placed me here for a reason; please help me to know what I have to do and how to do it. I need your wisdom and protection. I only want to be a wise and just ruler, but there are so many demands and uncertainties now. I'm in danger. I need you." His eyes stung with tears as he thought the words. "Show me the way, Lord. Please show me the way and tell me what to do."

His aide de camp, the young officer Captain Carillo, had been shadowing Maximilian silently. His brow furrowed slightly as he watched the emperor from a distance. The European looked as if he were praying, his head down and a hand on his lower neck. His head lifted, and for a moment Vickers worried that his presence was known. He slowly moved behind a tree so that he only had a sliver of sight through a bramble of branches, but the emperor merely stared at the mountain range as if deep in thought.

Maximilian suddenly spoke loudly, his words ringing across the field. "Lord, don't put me to shame. I place myself in your hands."

Vickers felt a twinge of empathy for what appeared to be a beautiful Christian character. He cautiously stepped out from the trees and skirted close to the emperor, kneeling. He waited a few moments, but the emperor was still unaware of his presence. "If I may be so bold, Excellency," he said softly.

The emperor was startled, quickly hiding his surprise but still staring at the young officer as if it were the first time that he had ever seen him. "Permission granted, Captain. I can use all the assistance I can find these days. Be frank."

"Choice decides outcome, Excellency. The Lord left the controls to us. He's given you the talents to solve your own problems."

Maximilian turned and looked into one of the most sincere faces he had ever seen. Such understanding in one so young was mesmerizing to him. His expression softened. "There's an old saying, Vickers. Every man at the top of his profession knows it. 'The wind blows cold on top of the mountain.' It means that it's lonely when you have no peers to converse with, no one who understands your situation. Do you understand?"

"Yes, Excellency. My father was chief of police. He told me more than once about his need to talk, and the absence of anyone to share with. I believe that's why he told me his problems. He knew better than to share with the men in his division about things that were happening in his work, things that were illegal or hurtful."

Maximilian felt a rush of relief so powerful that it was difficult to maintain his stoic expression. This was the first Mexican who had extended a hand to him, the first who had shown him any concern or kindness. "Perhaps you can be the person with whom I can share," Maximilian said cautiously. "As equals."

Vickers nodded in agreement, knowing the usual reply of "Yes, sir," was not appropriate from an equal, but not really sure how to address him.

Maximilian stared into the young man's eyes. A strange calm came over him. He was still overwhelmed with the problems of his emperorship, but he wasn't in distress anymore. For the first time in days, he felt truly relaxed. "Of course, we have to honor court etiquette in public, but when we're alone, I want you to continue to speak to me frankly and as an equal, all right?"

Vickers nodded again. Max smiled at his silence, suspecting the young man was not sure how to address him. "You can just say yes, Vickers."

"Yes," Vickers said awkwardly. Both men stared at each other until they were grinning.

Maximilian chuckled softly and sat back, leaning against a fallen log. He invited Vickers to sit beside him, which he quickly did.

"Vickers, I was afraid, I'll admit it. But I'm not afraid anymore. I know what to do now." He put his hand on Vickers' shoulder. "Proverbs teaches, 'With all thy getting, get understanding.' I believe you've helped me understand what I should do."

They sat quietly for a while as the last part of the sun crept up the mountains and was finally gone, leaving the mountains as a dark silhouette against a backdrop of dim stars. Maximilian finally stood and Vickers got up as well. The two began a leisurely walk back through the woods and towards the hill that led back to Chapultepec.

While walking, Vickers was careful to walk a step behind the emperor. Maximilian equalized their steps and put his arm around Vickers' shoulders as the two walked together.

"Where did you learn that wise advice you gave me?" the emperor asked.

"Our academy's director of studies was lecturing us once and completely shocked us by saying, 'I don't pray,' and then he told us why."

"And what did he say?" Maximilian asked, intrigued.

"He said that God gave us a brain and He also gave us time. He said we shouldn't abuse those gifts with jumbled thoughts and laziness. He said we can't compensate for our inadequacies by praying, using our incompetence and prayer haphazardly and yet expecting results."

"That's the truth," Maximilian agreed. "We have to use the gifts God gave us, and structure our prayer so that we do it in ways other than simply asking for something we should be doing ourselves."

"Exactly, Excellency. We have to work on that continuously, day and night."

Maximilian patted his ADC's back. "That's an interesting concept, and it rings true to me. I have to give it some more thought. Share some other wisdom you've learned."

Vickers thought it over for a moment. "For our prayers to be answered, we have to act correctly. We tend to make decisions during intense degrees of emotion, which is a mistake. Let the emotions pass, like a hurricane passes. Cool down and then decide. That helps to bring out God's blessings in our lives," Vickers explained.

"Yes," Maximilian mused. "I've done that before, reacted rather than acted. The reason I've done it lately is simply because I wish things were as they promised they would be when I came here."

"Wishes aren't horses you ride," Vickers interjected, getting more comfortable with the candid discussion. "They should come true because you acted calmly and deliberately, not because you reacted and then everything happened to work out the right way. That won't happen." He glanced at the emperor to make sure he was still allowed to speak openly; the European's face was relaxed and thoughtful. "And as for things in Mexico not being the way you'd expected, just remember that no one is going to put a crown on your head. You have to put it on yourself. Prayers don't bring luck to gamblers, and they don't crown fools as kings. But if you act carefully and use time correctly, you can rectify frayed affairs. My father taught that we often leave ourselves adrift, aimlessly wandering like cattle. We don't know how to occupy ourselves all the time. Will prayers do anything about that?"

Maximilian smiled and shook his head. "No, prayers won't help at all. I see what you're saying. You're a very wise young man, Captain."

They reached the door. "See you tomorrow, Vickers."

"Good night, Excellency." Vickers saluted and clicked his heels, then went to patrol the area before retiring to his quarters.

Maximilian turned in the doorway. "Just a minute, Vickers. There's one more thing I'd like your opinion on."

Vickers paused and stepped closer.

"What do you think I should do first?"

"I'm not a politician, Excellency. But from my understanding of what's needed, I'd say you should sow the seed of glamour."

"Glamour?" Maximilian asked in surprise.

"Yes, sire. Glamour includes charm, romance, and excitement. It's a magnet, attracting and enchanting. When my people see glamour from wealth, they see authority. The glittering trappings of royalty impress them. You want a tax base to fund a proper government, but you won't get any money from the masses unless they begin to accept your authority. Ordinary people bow to glamour. Start with this place, sire. It was the National Military Academy. Change it into a glamorous palace where ordinary citizens will be impressed. Then they'll listen to your ideas about changing Mexico, and then they'll agree to pay for your government."

Maximilian laughed out loud. "You know, I already had plans to make this place a palace, but I'd missed the advantage that could've had on the common people. You have very good judgment, my friend." He leaned against the stone wall beside the door and thought that over. "Glamour ... I'll need assistance to do it right, especially if it's for such an important reason now. I should invite my brother's mother-in-law."

Vickers' eyebrows arched. "She's good at such things?"

Maximilian nodded. "The Duchess Louisa Wilhelmina lives in Pest. She's actually known for such glamour."

"Where is Pest, Excellency?"

"It's actually Budapest. Back home we call it the 'Paris of the East.' It's two cities, Buda and Pest, joined by a bridge. It's one of the largest ports on the Danube."

"Oh," Vickers simply replied. He had never heard of such a place, and was starting to fully realize just how well-traveled this young European was.

"One of these days, I'll tell you more about it." Maximilian turned and put his hand on the door handle. "For now I should be off. I'll see you tomorrow, Captain."

Maximilian went inside and paused, enjoying the quietness of the house. He went up the stairs and used the long balcony to walk along the edge of the upper level until he came to the doors that designated his and Carlota's apartments. Each room had set French doors opening directly out onto the balcony, with etched glass in each door to let in the light. Now it only let in the mellow glow of the moon, which perched in a small crescent overhead. Again he paused, not wanting to break the spell of the quiet night, the gentle breeze, and the soothing darkness.

He finally unlocked the French doors leading to his bedchamber and went inside. There was a soft light in the corner of the bedroom, and he was surprised at what its mellow illumination revealed. There had been a dramatic change since he had left the castle. An exquisitely ornate, gilded bed had been centered against the back wall. It was flanked on either side with bedside tables, each of which supported a gold clock. Carlota had been busy in his absence, and she was now curled up on one side of the bed, sound asleep.

Maximilian turned slowly about and looked at the rest of the room. There were heavy velvet drapes of royal blue skirting either side of the doors. Also in matching blue were several pieces of furniture, giving the entire room a gold and blue theme.

Maximilian nodded appreciatively and walked over to his sleeping wife, kissing her gently on the forehead. Carlota's eyes fluttered open and she gave him a sweet, sleepy smile. "Hello," she whispered.

Maximilian smiled. "Hello," he whispered back. "It looks like someone I know received a shipment from my mother." He removed his overcoat and slipped on a smoking jacket, then sat on the bed by her side. "The room is lovely, my dear. You put a lot of time into it."

Carlota stretched lazily and straightened her leg until it lay over his. "I wanted it to look nice for you when you came home."

"What, you didn't like the bed I made?" he asked, pretending to be hurt.

She chuckled. "Oh, I adored the pool table, Maxi. It's my spine that protested."

They laughed and Maximilian pinched her thigh lightly to tickle her. She squirmed and finally came to rest on his chest.

"What kept you, tonight?" she asked casually, hiding her intense curiosity.

"I've been given a new understanding tonight, Carlota," he replied cryptically. "I know what I should do next now."

"Oh?"

He paused, his mind awhirl with ideas, much as it had been before his meeting with Marshal Bazaine the morning before he had met the Regency. "Do you remember Fagaras Fortress?" Carlota shook her head. "It's in Transylvania. It became a Hapsburg property during the days of Queen Marie Theresa. Years before that, a man by the name of Gabriel Bethlen made major changes to it. He redesigned it in the Italian Renaissance style. I think that's what this old place needs."

Carlota nodded. "Yes, you'd mentioned all the ideas you were having for this place."

"Well, my ideas are more exact now. I'm going to build it like a palace as well as a bastion. We'll create a great political center in Mexico. It's more than just aesthetics. We can do it in such a way as to transform the political climate around here." He turned and looked down at her. "And I need your help, darling."

"My help?" she asked, surprised. Maximilian usually coveted renovations for himself. He was a master at it, and was not one to give over control when he had a vision.

"Yes, you can use what you learned at Schonbrunn. Use the details of its rooms and gardens. We can use that check to make our house a glamorous political center. Power follows glamour." His eyes were shining in that familiar way. His hope was back.

Carlota smiled faintly at his childlike expression, at the sweet optimism in his voice. She nodded her head, catching his enthusiasm. "We can get paintings from Paris, glasswork from Venice …"

Maximilian's smile broadened as she continued.

"We can have musicians brought so they can play Mozart and other courtly music. And of course, we'll need soloists and dancers."

Maximilian was aglow with excitement. He gave her a squeeze. "I knew you'd be able to supply the details."

Carlota laughed and sat up beside him. "We can bring in musicians dressed in Mexican costumes, and we'll have colorful shows of folklore and fun!" she declared dramatically, stretching her arms over her head.

Maximilian laughed loudly. "What else?" he demanded.

"We'll have Tyrolean evenings," she continued, enjoying the game. "They'll be lively with singers and dancers, strictly traditional entertainment."

"Exactly, you read my mind!"

"Should we build a glorious white dome?" she teased.

"Such a wonderful idea!" he exclaimed. "I'll have the masons and architects look into that."

"You'll build over these rooms, another floor?"

"Yes, they'd be erected as an additional floor."

Charlotte laughed at his enthusiasm. She loved him when he was like this, forward-thinking, adventurous, striving. She looked deep into his smiling eyes and embraced him, then gave him a deep and meaningful kiss. "I love you, Maxi."

"And I love you," he answered, though he sounded distracted by his thoughts.

Carlota squinted. "You only love me for my ideas."

"What's wrong with that?" he countered. "How many men can you say love their wives for their minds? There are certainly worse fates for a wife."

"Oh, you're just using me," she groaned jokingly, sinking back onto her pillow and yawning loudly. "Can I sleep now?" she mumbled, her eyelids again getting heavy.

"No, not yet!" he exclaimed. "Are you mad? This is the best time for women, when their men are all worked up!"

His energy was at its height, and he flipped up onto his knees and leaned over her, hastily untying the ribbons of her nightgown's bodice. She laughed as he pulled her up into a sitting position and quickly pulled the nightgown back off her shoulders and ribs, arching her back and her breasts upward. She giggled, ticklish at first as he rudely kissed her throat and breasts, then her nipples. As he lingered there, her laughter faded and her breath became deeper. Finally her hand crept around his neck as she closed her eyes and moaned softly to herself. "I suppose I asked for it," she sighed, still amused as her arousal swelled thick inside her.

The next morning, Carlota and Maximilian sat at breakfast, and she found that his passionate attentions of the night before had done nothing to abate his manic pace. He appeared stimulated and reenergized. They were eating privately in their apartments, so she was lounging lazily in her peach silk morning gown.

"Carlota," he said, having called her by her Mexican nickname ever since they had arrived in their new country, "we need to prepare for our formal coronation. Our people need to see a solemn ceremony affirming our reign."

"Yes, Max. Don't worry, I'll take great pains to make the proceedings go smoothly and with much grace," she said with a false air of snobbery as she buttered a breakfast roll.

Seemingly unaware of her more casual demeanor, Maximilian nodded and continued. "Please have your ladies-in-waiting help make the arrangements. We need to show the people the traditions of a monarchy, plus the splendor and treasure of their own country. I've asked about investiture jewels and regalia, but it seems there aren't any. We have to correct this immediately. We'll commission a royal crown, and of course a consort crown for you. Those are crucial, darling. They symbolize royal authority. And for robes and regalia, we'll send for the finest tailors and jewelers in all the land."

Carlota smirked. "I already have grand ideas. We'll show them almost everything our monarchs have to offer."

Maximilian paused. "Almost everything?"

Carlota cocked an eyebrow naughtily and shifted in her seat, allowing her dressing gown to open slightly in the front.

His eyes wandered down from her throat, and he could see the points of her nipples pressing through the peach silk. It was obvious that she was wearing absolutely nothing beneath the morning gown, usually unheard of. "Oh, Carlota, be serious," he chided.

"Oh, I'm quite serious," she explained, hooking the forefinger of each hand into either side of the neckline and running them down the opening, making it wider and showing the swell of her pale skin. "One must have a contented monarch to ensure a successful rule." She finally opened the gown far enough so that her nipples were just peeking through the edges.

Maximilian smirked, his eyes darting up to her eyes, down to her breasts, up to her eyes again as he played along. "And what happens if the monarch remains unhappy?" he teased.

In her bawdiest manner, she stroked her own fingers gently across one breast, sliding easily over the rosy nipple. "Then I suppose the other monarch also becomes unhappy," she replied casually as she arched back into her chair and hooked her arms over the back of the seat, letting her breasts push fully out of the gown.

"Oh, you're terrible," he scolded as he rose from his chair and dropped to one knee beside her. "Just terrible," he repeated, closing his eyes and stroking his cheek against her smooth skin.

"I'm doing my duty, dear," she purred. "I just happen to love my job."

Soon, Maximilian had the finest craftsmen gathered. Tailors scurried about the room as their apprentices hurriedly brought in bolts of fine cloth and ermine.

The emperor and his empress spent hours on their selections for the coronation that was to take place the following week.

Later that day, Carlota met with her ladies-in-waiting. There was Doña Manuela Gutierrez-Estrada del Barrio, the first lady-in-waiting at the Mexican imperial court. Countess Paola Kollonitz was also there, the one who had accompanied Carlota to Mexico. Señora Dolores Osio de Sanchez-Navarro came from the family that owned the largest private estate in the history of Mexico, though the government under Juarez had confiscated it.

Others ladies present included Señoras Francisca Escandon de Landa, Rosa Blanco de Robles, Catalina Barron de Escandon, Guadalupe Cervantes de Moran, Luisa Quijano de Rincon-Gallardo, Soledad Vivanco de Cervantes, and Concepcion Lizardi de Valle.

Carlota was embarrassed to admit that she had not yet accomplished recalling all of their names, their foreign sounds hampering her efforts. She kept with her a sheet of paper scribbled with reminders about the coronation, and tucked in one corner was a list of the names of her ladies-in-waiting. She kept her thumb carefully over that part of the paper, not wanting them to be insulted that she did not yet remember all of their names. As they all sat down, she silently hoped that she would address the right ladies and pronounce their names correctly.

Refreshments were served before Carlota got to the business at hand. She addressed them as a group. "Ladies, I have so much to tell you, I really don't know where to begin. As you know, the coronation ceremony is only a few days away and there seem to be a million things left to do. You all should immediately find a suitable white gown. You're expected to wear small coronets covered in fresh flowers. This is an important occasion, so please wear your best jewelry."

"Countess Kollonitz, please help me train the other ladies in the procedure of the procession, and of caring for my train." Paola nodded and Carlota turned back to the group. She had managed so far to find a way to discuss things with them without having to use any of the Mexican ladies' names.

"The emperor and I have prepared a gift for all of my attendants for the occasion." From the Louis XIV table beside her she lifted a large, ornately carved box. She lifted its lid to reveal ten smaller boxes tied with scarlet ribbons. Her eyes sparkled as she solemnly kissed each woman on both cheeks and handed her a box. There were squeals of delight as the women opened their boxes and found dangling diamond earrings.

"Aren't they lovely?" Carlota agreed among their murmurs. "Just the thing to set off the flowers and your sparkling eyes," the empress said with a smile of excitement. The ladies began talking to each other about the many choices to be made.

The city was teeming with throngs of peasants dressed in vivid colors, chattering excitedly to one another. The vibrant crowd had assembled quickly, some coming from miles away to see this European prince who was to be their new emperor. Being everyday people with little sparkle in their lives, they were more interested in the spectacle than what it stood for. There was a feeling of excitement in the air, much like a carnival. Old men told stories of their memories of the last emperor, who had underwent a coronation in exactly the same place back on July 21, 1822.

The massive thirteen-acre Zocalo square, one of the largest city plazas in the world, was animated with countless people. On one side of the square, the National Palace was hung with streamers and draping cloths of many bright colors. On the other side of the square, the twin-towered National Cathedral of Mexico, one of the oldest and largest churches in the Western Hemisphere, was undergoing the last festive touches for the coronation. Tables and pulpits in the church had been temporarily moved into storage to allow for as much standing room as possible.

During the preceding month throughout the city, the way of the cortege had been decorated so that they would be in place during "coronation week." Building owners had decorated according to their means, allowing for a most extraordinary sight and hinting of the coming of a rare event.

The main doors of the cathedral were opened and the people started crowding in.

In Maximilian and Carlota's private apartments at Chapultepec, servants were rushing about to finish the last details of the idealistic young aristocrat and his wife's imperial toilette. When they had completed their tasks, they hurried out to the carriages.

The imperial couple proceeded with great pomp and ceremony from the castle and was escorted into a striking golden coach that would take them to the cathedral.

The court ladies exited their carriages first. Empress Carlota's ladies-in-waiting assembled and stood in attendance nearby, assembled in groups of five. Their court dresses were so elaborate as to compete with each other's, all white as had been instructed. Their skirts blossomed dramatically over concealed hoops, their décolletage necklines low and daring but made more subtle with ribbons and flowers. Again as instructed, they each wore small coronets, and woven through them were elaborate designs of bright flowers. Their diamond earrings, necklaces, and diadems glittered in the brilliant light. They stepped into the cathedral and waited inside for the empress.

People craned their necks to catch a glimpse of the glamorous people entering, all glowing snowy white and sparkling with their rare jewels. Several times people murmured that they thought they had seen the empress, so dazzled were they every time another striking lady arrived covered in glittering gems.

A grand march began playing, signaling the time for the ceremony. In Europe, a solemn hush would have fallen over the cathedral, but this was not Europe. The people were excited and began to cheer, threatening to drown out the music. The procession slowly began to enter, the crowd getting louder as each person stepped inside.

The first to come inside were dozens of children, the children of the Mexican elite. They were dressed in white robes and were there to light the candles at the golden "altar of the kings."

Next, the Bishop of Leon entered, carrying a gold-covered Bible.

Beside the bishop walked José Mariano de Salas, twice the president of Mexico (though his longest office was held for only four months), and more recently regent under another government. His gray mustache appeared white in the dimmer light of the church. He carried a gold crown made up of eight branches, each of which arched upward so that they came together under a globe of gold that was studded with precious stones. Other bishops, abbots, and many clergymen, all wearing gold crosses and some bearing the golden royal scepter, followed the bishop and the politician into the church.

Next came the bishop of Zacatecas, then various men of the court, more clergy dressed in their robes, and finally the empress. The friendly crowd cheered especially loud when they saw their empress walk slowly down the aisle with her train lifted gently behind her. The only Mexicans that stood by in quiet disapproval at all the noise were many of the rich people in attendance, who sat comfortably in balconies above the throng and clapped politely.

Behind the empress's entourage followed heads of state Juan Nepomuceno Almonte and Juan Bautista de Ormaechea y Ernaiz. Next were three men of high standing in the court, each carrying a velvet pillow upon which were the royal regalia arms and robes. After them came Louis Forey, the French general, who proceeded as far as the choir before pausing and turning to face the entrance.

At last, Emperor Maximilian entered with a cadenced step, and the crowd cheered louder than ever before. The walls seemed to hum from the din as he stepped down the aisle with all the grace of a man raised in the courts and experienced in military marches. Four mustachioed Mexican gentlemen, who bore the train of his long robe, followed him up the aisle.

Upon reaching the altar, the emperor kneeled. The four gentlemen carefully spread out his robe behind him and stepped back as Archbishop Labastida lifted the crown from the altar and blessed it with a special prayer. With slow and solemn ceremony, he placed it upon Maximilian's head and delivered the scepter to him.

By now, even the enthusiastic crowd had finally hushed at the holiness of the ceremony.

The archbishop began to administer the oath in sight of all the people. Maximilian placed his right hand on the Bible and held his left upright in the air.

"Señor, is Your Majesty prepared to take the oath?" the archbishop of Mexico City asked in a strong accent.

"I am prepared," Maximilian replied, his clear voice ringing through the large cathedral.

"Will you solemnly promise and swear to govern the people of Mexico according to respective laws and customs?"

"I would without reservation observe them all. I make a solemn promise so to do," Maximilian replied formally.

"Will you, to your power, cause law and justice, in mercy, to be executed in all your judgments?"

"I, Maximilian, now in the presence of almighty God, pledge that all of these things I shall perform, so help me God."

The emperor kissed the Bible and turned to a silver stand that was placed nearby. On it was the document containing his oath. He took up a pen from its stand and signed the document as written evidence of his vow.

After that, all of the bishops and archbishops swore their fealty, each saying, "I will be faithful and true, and faith and truth will bear unto you, our sovereign, Emperor Maximilian I of Mexico, so help me God."

Empress Consort Carlota was crowned next. Her ceremony was simple in comparison to Maximilian's, but the crowd remained silent in respect and affection for the woman who appeared so gentle and small as she knelt before the altar and received her little crown. Her demeanor was modest and shy, and they were enchanted. She seemed both hypnotizing and virginal.

Archbishop Labastida offered the Bible as he had for the emperor, and she placed her right hand on it as she raised her left hand.

"Señora, is Your Majesty ready to give your prepared oath?"

"I am." Everyone strained to hear her voice. It seemed small and delicate, yet it somehow reached every corner with ease. This was the skill of a lady of the courts.

"I, Marie Charlotte Amélie Augustine Victoire Clémentine Léopoldine, wife of Emperor Maximilian, swear to serve my nation and my husband in all soberness and fidelity. I do swear by the blessed Trinity and sacrament, which I am now to receive, to keep this, my oath."

The archbishop administered the sacrament and then addressed the people. "To the people of Mexico I present, by the grace of God, His Imperial Highness Ferdinand Maximilian Joseph, and Her Imperial Highness Carlota, empress of Mexico. God preserve a Christian emperor! Amen!"

"Amen!" the crowd shouted, erupting again in cheers and shouts. Some shouted, "Maximiliano! Carlota!" while others merely raised their voices in loud shouts and congratulations. Maximilian and Carlota exchanged a glance and smiled for a moment, no longer able to maintain their solemn faces amid this open expression of celebration.

The procession turned and left the cathedral in the opposite formation in which they had come, except that Maximilian and Carlota were the first to leave, their robes carried behind them. Music was playing and most of the people began to sing the national anthem of Mexico.

In the weeks following the coronation, Santiago Rebull and Franz Xaver Winterhalter created a coronation painting of the emperor and empress in their stunning coronation robes. Both commissioned artists were highly respected in their field, Winterhalter coming all the way from Germany.

The news traveled to nearly all parts of the globe.

Sophie sat at the breakfast table and read some of the articles about the coronation aloud of her son, Maximilian. She looked up from the newspaper and smiled, her eyes shining. "Well done, Max! Everything seems to be going perfectly."

CHAPTER 17

▼

THE ENTOURAGE

It was early morning. It had rained the evening before, and coolness still hung in the air. Maximilian had a light breakfast and eagerly went straight to his office, which was in the library. It had been newly decorated similar to his bedchamber, with bold royal blue satin and gold accents. It also had a pavilion where he could look out and catch a stunning view of the Mexican landscape, with the Sierra Nevada to the east and the Sierra Guadalupe to the north.

As he entered, he was pleased to see Captain Vickers waiting there, and the young ADC saluted promptly. "Good morning, Excellency. Your secretary had business in the city today, so I volunteered to help you." Maximilian nodded and Vickers went back to his work, filing papers and stacking correspondences on the walnut Biedermeier library table.

Maximilian sat down at his mahogany desk and picked up a pen to begin signing a stack of papers he had looked over the day before. As he worked, Vickers brought in a stack of files from the outer office and put them in a tray marked "Files: Press Cuttings."

When Maximilian was done signing his documents, he handed them to Vickers, then began leafing through the press cuttings that had just been placed there. One file caught his eye, labeled "Carillo—Prison for Doing His Duty." He examined the name carefully and finally looked up at his ADC.

"Vickers, isn't your last name Carillo?"

"Yes, señor."

The emperor frowned and scanned the clippings inside the file. "This police officer's been arrested, and the press claims he's innocent. Any relation to you?"

"He's my father," Vickers simply replied, standing straight with his hands clasped firmly behind his back. His eyes were neutral, but a small muscle in his right jaw quivered involuntarily, betraying him.

"Captain, adjust the oil in the candelabra, and open those drapes further. I'd like to read this more carefully." Vickers silently did as he was asked as Maximilian read the clipping for several minutes. "If this account's to be believed, this man wasn't treated justly," he concluded, leaning back in his chair.

"True, he wasn't, Excellency."

"Did you put this in the press?" he asked his ADC, eyeing him carefully. "Did you know this file would be sent to me?"

"No, sir. I didn't even know it was in the files," Vickers replied.

"You have my permission to sit, Vickers."

Vickers took a seat in a chair in front of the great desk, facing the emperor. He continued reading the cutting as Vickers waited.

"My," Maximilian murmured. "I see your father received a medal for arresting his own son. How odd … I've never heard of police officers arresting their own relatives. Your mother must've been fit to be tied. Did he come to regret it?"

Vickers inwardly sighed when forced to think about the conflict between his father and brother, but he kept his outward demeanor formal. "My father repents when he's out of uniform, sir. When he's in uniform, he's a different person."

"You think it's the uniform then?"

"Yes, Excellency," Vickers replied with a clear, unwavering stare. "It's the uniform."

Maximilian set the clippings down and cocked his head curiously. "Well, what power does his uniform have?"

Vickers repeated what his father had taught him as a boy. "A uniform means you belong to an organization, and when you wear it, you do what's best for the organization."

"Hmm … and would that include hiding dirt under the carpet?" the emperor asked, thinking about his own dilemma. "Protecting the good image of the institution by any means necessary?" His face was calm and deliberately casual, though one hand resting in his lap could not be still. His fingers rubbed together, then made a fist, and then rubbed together again. The other hand rested on the desk, and he willed it to stay still.

Captain Vickers leaned forward in his chair. "Señor, my father used to ask me, 'Would you kill a skunk and hide it under your bed?'"

Maximilian smiled and nodded. "I asked basically the same question to my inspector general. I know my generals and colonels do that. They don't believe in allowing their institution to have a bad name, and they certainly don't want me to see what they've shoved under the carpet." He settled deeper into his chair, satisfied with Vickers's answer. "I happen to think their attitudes stink like a skunk. In fact, I'm changing my entourage entirely. I want the truth, unconditional and undiluted. To have that, I'll need men who value the truth, regardless of what consequences that might hold for their institution."

Vickers nodded. "Those colonels and generals are taught that the institution is a sacred cow. But cows are meant to be slaughtered," he added with a smile in his eyes.

Maximilian laughed. "Truth has transparency, doesn't it?"

"It has, Excellency. It's a concept very important to me, and being in the military rubs against it sometimes." He also settled into his chair, relaxing. "Just yesterday I read part of a citation for a colonel I have to decorate in the investiture parade. I have to promote him, too. I'll be expected to speak about how gallantly my army is facing Juarez's army. My army calls them terrorists, but I smell a skunk there. That colonel could have violated his uniform for all we know, but he'll be celebrated regardless of how he may have acted."

Captain Vickers remained silent for a while, thinking that over. "A uniform means *duty*."

Maximilian smiled and leaned back. "Well, what *is* duty?"

Vickers smiled softly at his emperor's enthusiasm, but it was a sad smile that faded as he thought over his answer. "Not inflicting pain ... removing pain."

"Isn't that an outlandish definition?"

Vickers looked at the emperor. "Pain directly affects our quality of life. If you want to improve the quality of life, you should make sure there isn't any force or pain around you. If there is, remove it."

Maximilian's eyebrows rose. "Who taught you that?"

"My father and my grandfather, señor."

Maximilian stood and paced, staring at the carpet. "So rulers and all of their uniformed men have just two goals: to avoid inflicting pain and to remove pain for the people being ruled. Those are the only ways to improve the quality of their lives?"

"Yes, Excellency. Though they do have one other goal, the most important one: not allowing others to inflict pain."

Maximilian nodded, satisfied. He enjoyed talking with this young man. It seemed to clear his head and allow him to see things in a new light. "Young man,

I believe you may've taught me the golden rule of proper governance. I'm going to assemble my staff and entourage so that I can present the Mexican people with a government along those lines."

Vickers smiled. "Señor, I didn't teach you anything. My father—"

"Your father deserves a medal."

"If you would grant it, señor, my father first deserves his freedom, to have his name cleared."

Maximilian paused and sat on the edge of the desk. "Fill me in on the details. What was the charge?"

"The former regime had an old intellectual in the prison. One colonel hated his ideas and decided to have him killed. He arranged for it to look like the old man had attempted to escape prison, and they shot him in cold blood in the back. My father investigated the case and tried to arrest that colonel. Soon after that, he was charged with a murder, but of course he had nothing to do with it."

"And now you're the ADC of an emperor, and that emperor's been informed of a good police officer who's been thrown into prison for doing his duty?"

Captain Vickers kept quiet.

"Is your father against kings or emperors?" he asked pointedly.

"I don't know, to be honest. I've never talked to him about that," Vickers answered thoughtfully. "All I know is that he's against evil and supports ethics. He's a lawman of highest integrity; that much everyone knows. Even the press is saying that."

Maximilian paced a while, mulling it over. His face suddenly brightened. "I have an excellent idea!" he exclaimed. "I'll approach your father with advice about selecting my entourage. I'll ask him for names of people he recommends." He pointed at the young man. "First things first, have your mother file an appeal to me. That'll be a good start to reforming the judicial system."

"That's very gracious, Your Majesty. If you'd allow it, my grandfather is a judge and he lives nearby. He'd like to speak with you on the matter," Vickers said, his eyes shining.

Maximilian paused. Had this been planned all along? He decided against that conclusion. The entire family had probably pressured Vickers to approach the emperor about his imprisoned father, but had he? There had been ample opportunity before now, and yet he had not brought it up even once. He had only mentioned that his father was a police officer, and he had never elaborated beyond that until asked directly. When he looked into the young man's eyes, he knew that his instinct about him was true.

"Yes, I'd like that very much, Vickers. Bring your grandfather tomorrow and we'll have a talk."

Vickers nodded with a poorly suppressed smile. "Yes, sir."

"Now shall we continue with this correspondence?"

He and Vickers worked steadily until all of his correspondences had been properly answered, papers signed, and the filing complete. Maximilian stretched in his seat, stiff from hours of work at his desk.

"I'm going to have luncheon and speak to the empress. If you like, your grandfather can come tomorrow at ten o'clock."

Vickers saluted. "Thank you, Excellency."

The next day, Maximilian sat in a wingback chair beside the fireplace, warming his feet by the fire as he read a manifest of provisions for the army. Mornings in Mexico were at times surprisingly chilly, and the stone of the castle walls sometimes held the coolness from the previous night until long after it had warmed up outside. Carlota had adopted the habit of having a fire prepared each night in the bedchambers and early each morning in his office. As summer began, it seemed that would no longer be necessary, but every now and then it still was, and in any event, the fires were becoming a comforting habit in their new home.

The door opened and Vickers brought an old man into the side office. The ADC busied himself entering and leaving the emperor's office, carrying files and notes while the old man completed a petition. When the petition was complete, Vickers placed it in a new file and took it to the emperor.

"Excellency, I would like to present my grandfather, Judge Antonio Carillo. He's drafted this petition," Vickers announced softly.

Maximilian glanced at the clock and noted it was time to meet Vickers's grandfather. "Oh please, bring him in. I'd very much like to meet the grand old man," he said with a smile, rising from his chair. "Didn't you say he was a judge?"

"Yes, sir," Vickers replied, ducking into the hall adjoining the main study with the side office. Maximilian could hear shuffling noises in the hall and stepped forward for a better look. Vickers was walking with straight military stature beside an old man whose posture was a sharp contrast to his own. Vickers's grandfather suffered greatly from arthritis, and he used a cane to struggle up the hall. The emperor frowned and strode swiftly towards them to assist.

"Captain, you should have requested an audience in the council room so you wouldn't have to tire your grandfather so greatly," Maximilian scolded worriedly as he helped the old man to a chair.

"Yes, Excellency." Vickers took the reprimand with a slight smile as his emperor lent a hand.

Antonio Carillo was seated in a carved ebony armchair beside the fireplace, across from the emperor's own seat. As the old judge settled in, a spasm of coughing overtook him. The two younger men rushed about to get something to drink. Vickers handed Maximilian a goblet of water, who in turn offered it to the older man.

"Here, Judge Carillo. Drink this," Maximilian said with a voice that was both commanding and pleading. Genuine concern lined his face as he watched the old man take the goblet and meet his gaze with watery eyes.

The old man's face was full of wrinkles and looked very pale, but it did not look weak. The deep lines hinted at years of experience and skill. His eyes, though watery and fatigued, were sharp and focused. "Please don't make a fuss. It's cold and damp, and I'm just tired." His veined hands shook as he drank the last of the water and returned the goblet to Vickers. He straightened somewhat in his chair and waited for the emperor to have a seat, uncomfortable being served by one superior to him. "First let me thank you, mi emperador, for seeing me today."

Maximilian relaxed a bit, seeing that the man's breathing was more even and that the color was returning to his face. "How may I be of service to you, sir?" he asked politely.

Antonio glanced out the window at the incoming gray clouds. "It looks like more rain, and my old bones are feeling it today. I beg your pardon for not standing."

"Please make yourself comfortable, señor," the emperor said, waving his hand. "It's of no consequence. I've no intention of being that sort of emperor."

Antonio nodded but said nothing. Maximilian and Vickers exchanged a glance before Maximilian decided to make conversation to get things started. "Your grandson's become a trusted part of my government. I think he's wise beyond his years. I understand that wisdom was taught to him by you and his father."

"Yes," the old man agreed. "We've tried to teach him the proper path. In fact, his father is precisely why I needed to talk to you," he added, his shaking hands holding out his petition. "You know he's in prison, of course."

Maximilian nodded and took the petition, glad to have gotten the old man back onto the subject gracefully. "Yes, I read about it in my news clippings yesterday morning."

"I was totally shattered after my son was convicted inspite of his innocence," Antonio said as Maximilian opened the document and looked it over. "I fought my best for his case in court, against all of their false witnesses." Antonio glanced down and clasped his hands together. "But now I see the wisdom of the Lord. It says in the Bible that the Israelites wanted a king. They rejected the prophet Samuel inspite of what he'd done for them. God had provided well for them in the desert, helped them conquer their enemies, and led them to fertile lands. God deserved their praise, their undying devotion and thankfulness. Instead they asked for a ruler …"

Maximilian frowned slightly as he listened to the judge, not sure how to interpret what he was saying.

"I went door to door pleading for my son, Carillo. Today that rejection breaks my heart," he confessed, tears in his eyes. "Because I see the bigger picture now." He lifted his head and looked back into Maximilian's eyes. "Before now, I thought my son was doomed to die in prison because of Mexico's false judiciary. I've even made plans as to where he'll be buried, and who will take care of his family after he's gone. He's already died for me, I've already mourned him. But now I see you here, and I have hope."

Maximilian smiled and patted the man's hand, flattered.

"Mi emperador," the old man continued, "I think you've come to set this judiciary right."

Maximilian's smile faded as he was overcome with awe at this old man's faith in him. He had certainly grown up hearing people tell him every day that he was great, intelligent, capable, a true leader. What he had recently been lacking was any sort of faith from the people he was meant to rule in Mexico. It had shaken his confidence, made him yearn for someone to believe in him. Of course he knew that Carlota had nothing but faith in him, but he wanted that validation from someone more objective. And now here was this old man, a respected judge and lifelong Mexican, and he saw Maximilian as some sort of savior of a judicial system that had gone awry. This man did not question what country Maximilian came from, or even if he had a right to sit in this castle and make decisions about Mexico. He seemed to believe in him completely, and it both flattered and uplifted the young Austrian.

A sharp pain started in Antonio's hip and he slowly adjusted his position in his chair. His eyes were still spilling tears, and he was too tired to will them to stop. Maximilian got up from his chair and kneeled by Antonio, resting a hand gently on his shoulder. "Don't worry, sir," he said softly as the old man finished shifting and sat shaking slightly in his chair from the pain. "You and your grandson here have shown me what I need to do."

He stood and stared at the fire, resting an arm on the mantel. "I don't need an entourage at all. What I need to do is to find all of the Samuels rejected by the system. Here I am, someone without money, without my own army or police … and certainly without my own judiciary …" He turned from the mantel and faced Antonio and Vickers, who stood behind his grandfather's seat. "I need to trust in the Lord, just as you said. Trust in the Lord and collect his people."

Antonio nodded slightly, listening attentively.

"Yesterday I asked this young man a question," Maximilian continued, gesturing to Vickers. "I asked if his father was against kings or emperors. You ought to know the answer because he's your own son; you brought him up. I'd like to know your family's inner feelings about such rulers."

Antonio turned slightly towards the warmth of the fire with a small wince, using the time it took to hesitate in answering. He finally sighed and replied, "We've always been against kings and emperors, mi emperador. But my grandson seems to believe that angels have to sleep with Satan in order to learn how to use him."

Vickers flushed brightly when he heard his grandfather speaking so frankly to the emperor. His hand had been resting on Antonio's shoulder, and he gently squeezed the old judge as if to warn him.

Antonio reached up and placed his hand on Vickers's. He pulled it slightly, and Vickers stepped around the chair so that his grandfather could see him. The old man smiled as he surveyed his grandson, his eyes affectionate. "He has a different way of thinking. Yesterday I realized the wisdom of his point of view. And now today I've been asked by mi emperador to provide papers so that he can fight my son's case, even after conviction. Yes, Vickers is the wise one in my family."

"Tell me, judge, if Vickers is wise, does it also make him ethical? Is there a difference?"

The old man waved a hand. "Ethics can reject wisdom, señor. Of course, it's done at a cost."

Maximilian crossed his arms, interested. "Please explain to me why your family has been against monarchs."

"A very good reason," Antonio insisted. "It's well-supported by historical record, sire."

"And that is?"

The sun went behind a cloud and the room grew dim. Antonio leaned back in his chair and almost closed his eyes, staring into the fire as if reading from the blackened wood. "History records many kings, sire. Kings of Egypt, Persia, India, Germany, France … all over the world, there have been kings. All these kings had the power to declare war, and they did. They had their wars, thousands of them."

Antonio's eyes opened completely and he looked up at the emperor. "Those kings all had the power and wherewithal to sacrifice their own people as they desired, for gains or glory." His eyes squinted in contempt at the thought. "Mi emperador, just once, listen to a king from the past."

Maximilian obliged him, sitting in his own chair again and listening.

"Imagine that a king from long ago can actually speak with you. He's telling you that he's tired of peace, that peace is no policy. He wants the thrill of battle; see his enemies in the dust, armies running away from him, villages on fire, cities falling, all before his eyes! He wants to make his name terrible among the sons of men. He wants to be remembered like Alexander, Caesar, Attila the Hun, Napoleon, Ivan the Terrible … why should he remain the king of Babylon? Why not the whole world?"

He paused and stared at the emperor, as if daring him to imagine all that he had just said. "Now, señor, listen to an older, wiser man. 'Oh king, your country is prosperous, its people happy. Do not plunge them into ruins or despair.' The king of the past hears that, mulls over the wise man's counsel and good advice. After some time, he says, 'Throw that doddering sage to the wolves. Tonight we go to war.' And now imagine the sounds of rushing chariots, men on horses and on foot, the crying wounded, and war cries … try to imagine the sounds of the flames devouring the destroyed cities, the slaughter of women and children, and now the triumphant procession with the defeated monarchs chained to the chariots of the conquerors. Kings dragged in the dust. But the farms on both sides are neglected, the industry of the nation ignored. The towns are empty and everywhere there are graves, sick people, wounded people dying and screaming in pain."

Rain began to drum gently on the pavilion. Maximilian shivered slightly.

Antonio leaned forward in his seat a bit. "Sire, mankind has spent so many centuries on the sport of war. At last we've reached a state of wisdom by writing the words, 'Congress shall have the power to declare war'! The right to wage war was finally taken away from those greedy children and given to the people, the ones who actually pay the price of war. And those people want peace. That's a good enough reason to be done with war-hungry kings."

Maximilian scrutinized the old man with great interest. His words had a ring of truth to them, though he was not very comfortable with the idea that these greedy kings were actually his ancestors. "The right to declare war has always been a royal prerogative," Maximilian said. "It lies fairly and squarely within the legal powers and responsibilities, even the privilege of a sovereign." Antonio's eyes flashed and Maximilian felt the urge to qualify his statement and to explain himself.

"Yes, I agree there should be accountability to Parliament. Even in the modern era, a sovereign can address the Houses in Parliament to show the case for war, to legally justify it. Presidents in a democracy have that privilege as well."

Antonio shook his head. "Señor, a democracy is worse than a monarchy. A president given a few years of such powers can become extremely rich, receiving fat bribes under the table from foreign powers. That's why, when George Washington addressed the Parliament and relinquished his presidency, he declared that America couldn't afford to have special relationships among foreign powers. They shouldn't have any favorites, because then those favorites can use the American army for their advantage."

"I see," Maximilian replied, rubbing his forehead and not completely understanding.

"Sire, the prerogative you speak of will bring a king's country to many wars. Hundreds of years of political maturity demands that only Parliament decides if it wants war. After making its decision, Parliament has to hold a referendum asking the entire nation to clearly say yes or no to it. That alone would be a true democracy. People going to war without deciding on it themselves, without being convinced of its necessity, is pure kingship. It may be wrapped in a cover and called something else, but democracy isn't a set of clothes you can simply cast off; it's the naked body from which nothing can be cast off."

Maximilian shrugged. "That's reasonable enough," he relented. "But a king isn't a poor man like a president. He looks at power from a different angle than a man like that."

"Yes, but cunning advisors can blindfold that king and keep him in the dark," Antonio stressed, trying to make him see his point. "They learn his desires and then manipulate him. They fashion him as some sort of 'fulfiller,' reaping the benefits but putting the common people in endless trouble."

There was a pregnant pause in the room. It felt heavy, like the clouds outside that were full of rain.

Maximilian turned to Vickers. "What do you say about this?"

Vickers shifted. "Excellency, as I've said before, it's very difficult to judge matters or men. It requires wisdom."

The rain beat down on the stones and windowpanes. The fire cast a flickering golden glow on the paneled walls. Maximilian began to pace again. "What should be done with a police officer who's the son of such a distinguished thinker? Then again, who can arrest and convict their own son in the line of duty?"

"If I may be so bold, sire," Antonio said. "Such a man is more precious than all the gold in the world."

Maximilian pointed at the old man. "I agree." He carried the petition to his desk. "Your son Carillo is the one who'll make me a list of my principal officers." He picked up his pen and paused, looking up at the judge. "Sir, I must come to your house to sit beside you and have a meal sometime." He picked up his pen and took another quick look at the faces of Vickers and Antonio before signing the petition. Vickers took the signed petition to an adjacent office to file it and get an official receipt.

Antonio lowered his head and began to cry. Vickers returned and handed him the receipt. "Thank you, sire," the old judge said as he lifted his face from his hands. "It would be my greatest pleasure to have you at my table."

Vickers quickly brought his grandfather some more water and helped him to compose himself. As they left the office, Antonio paused and managed a slow and incomplete bow for the emperor. "Mi emperador, it's been an honor to meet you, a day I'll never forget."

Maximilian smiled and returned his bow, then offered his hand. "The honor is all mine, señor," he said sincerely. The man shook his hand and turned, taking time to leave the office and to disappear back down the hall.

Maximilian returned to the fireplace and stoked the fire. When that was done, he straightened and wandered aimlessly with a sigh, stopping at the window. The rain still drummed steadily against the panes. He pulled back the brocade silk drapery and stared out into the rain.

CHAPTER 18

▼

THE BUSINESS OF MEXICO

Mexico City—September 7, 1864.

In the days that followed the meeting between Judge Carillo and the emperor, Maximilian set out to clear Carillo's name. He was also working to exonerate Victorio Emmanuel, a member of Parliament who had been convicted and sent to jail. He called on the chief justice himself to find out the procedures needed to accomplish his goal.

The gentleman was polite and accommodating, explaining the American Judiciary Act of 1789 to Maximilian. It was the act that had constituted the Supreme Court and set it up as an appellate court, although it did have original jurisdiction in certain matters. Maximilian had enough of a political background to fill in some of the holes. He knew that an appellate court did not hear from witnesses and decide facts, but instead heard appeals on decisions made in trial courts that had already heard from witnesses. The decisions were somewhat limited as they now stood, since none of the evidence heard in the original trial was actually reviewed by the Supreme Court.

The chief justice suggested that the emperor sign an act that would allow for "writs of certiorari," which would empower the Supreme Court to demand records of evidence and testimony from inferior courts in order to reevaluate their decisions. Each writ was drawn up for a specific case, as necessary. Then the higher court could issue writs for petitions from convicts or their relatives, who normally had no right to appeal, so that the lower court's decisions could perhaps be overturned.

Maximilian took the advice and penned an act in the best language he could manage, ideally to make the judges more responsive to it. Upon discovering that the Supreme Court did not begin on a set day each year, Maximilian went so far as to sign a royal decree to set a date, hoping to speed up the process. Next came the tedious work of selecting writs of certiorari to be granted, then the procedures for granting them, studying the briefs, hearing arguments by the lawyers, and finally preparing written opinions. He also had to contend with the dissenting opinions of justices who did not agree with the decisions of the majority, something he would have to get used to, since it would only increase as time passed and the populace grew in number and outspokenness.

Exhausted by the process and worried that it would take too long to accomplish, the emperor finally drafted notes on how to simplify the process: "An immediate relative writes a petition to the Crown; the emperor asks only a duty judge to request the records from the lower court; the chief justice, with the aid of a large staff of judicial clerks, reviews the records and does all of the actual work on the case, circulating briefs and opinions to the other judges; the justices meet with the emperor at the jail one day a week, reviewing the cases and handing down their decisions in the presence of each prisoner."

Maximilian scanned his notes carefully, pleased with his idea. It seemed sound, like it would allow the Supreme Court to provide prompt justice. This would be a welcomed change in Mexico, and Maximilian strongly believed that it would go a long way in making the Supreme Court more honored by the people. He submitted his plan to the chief justice, requesting records for the cases of Carillo and Emmanuel. He also ordered that lawyers be recruited immediately to begin his new process.

The next day that any mail was delivered after sending the order, a letter arrived from the Supreme Court. It explained that a writ of certiorari had been issued for the records named, promising that justice would be administered in jail as requested. The emperor called his ministers, Civil Chief of Staff Felix Eloin, Marshal Bazaine, Judges Pena Ruiz, Delgado, and Vega, as well as others to his office.

The brocade silk drapery was pulled back to let in bright rays of sunshine as the elite group of men took their seats at the large library table. Maximilian, showing his affinity for all things Mexican, served Casa Madero wine from the Hacienda de San Lorenzo.

"A toast to truth and justice," he said dramatically, holding up his glass. The men stood and raised their goblets high. "To truth and justice," they repeated. The room fell silent for a moment as everyone took a drink of the wine, sunshine sparkling on the antique bohemian crystal goblets that bore the images of Agustin de Iturbide and Chapultepec Castle.

Maximilian set down his goblet and remained standing, getting down to business. "The chief justice has issued writs of certiorari to call up court records. In the case of former police chief Carillo, a thorough investigation of the statements and evidence of the case shows that his trial needs to be reevaluated." He scanned the room and noted cloaked surprise on more than one face. "I'm very grateful to the chief justice for his work in this matter," he added carefully, forcing politically correct nods of approval from everyone there before continuing his rehearsed speech. "In my opinion, according to the information provided, Carillo has been victimized by unjust procedures and wrongful imprisonment. One of Carillo's own officers undertook a campaign of defamation against his good character."

He paused to let his words sink in, finally leaning down and planting both hands on the table. "How do we proceed now, gentlemen?"

Judge Vega was the first to speak. His light hair and hazel eyes were reminiscent of an elegant European as he stood. "Excellency, just for the sake of argument, you know it's said that justice done should not be so summarily undone."

The emperor smirked. "Perhaps, but what if it isn't justice at all? What if a judge willfully and wrongly gives someone's property to another? Would you call that justice? As far as I'm concerned, that judge is a thief and should be dealt with accordingly. Any judge who wrongly passes a death sentence is a murderer, plain and simple. Justice demands truth, so why can't the truth enter a jail to be heard?"

Judge Vega nodded nervously and took his seat, apparently satisfied with the emperor's reasoning.

"Justice is served after due process, which means that the government must act fairly and in accordance with established rules." He clasped his hands behind his back and continued his speech in a confident tone. "It may not act unfairly, arbitrarily, on some unreasonable whim. But fair procedures are of little value if they're used to administer unfair laws. In Mexico, it seems that one is considered guilty until proven innocent. This section of the Napoleonic Code has been criticized for its de facto presumption of guilt. In fact, the Constitution of 1857 was liberal enough to declare, as I'm sure you're all aware, that 'the fundamental rights of man are the basis and purpose of social institutions.'"

Maximilian was actually secretly surprised at how quiet and subservient they had all been so far. Seeking to play on the aura of authority that seemed to linger around him, he walked over to his grand desk, the royal seat of the emperor's office, to silently remind them of who he was. He lifted some papers from the desk. "I've been sent two appeals, one for Carillo and one for another case, and they were examined thoroughly. A member of Parliament is in jail under a long sentence for reading an anonymous letter to his colleagues. According to the army's rules, an anonymous letter deserves to be thrown into a wastebasket, not given another thought. The chief justice has asked the army to observe its own rules on this matter."

Supreme Justice Pena Ruiz frowned thoughtfully. "What happens if an imperial commanding officer reads an anonymous letter? Would you put that officer in jail?"

Eyebrows rose all around the table, followed by a burst of laughter.

Maximilian smiled and paused until the laughter subsided. "The second case is regarding that outstanding police officer I just spoke of. He arrested and convicted his own son as a terrorist; such is his sense of justice and duty. What should be done with such an officer, a man who has shown such exemplary conduct both inside and outside of jail? He deserves justice." He straightened and lifted his chin haughtily. "My rule will begin with the resolve that, in Mexico, the richest and the poorest, the most powerful and the weakest, the most educated or intelligent and the most illiterate, will be equals, at least in the courts. That's the business I came to do in Mexico."

Judge Delgado stood, his chair creaking beneath his considerable size. "Post-conviction justice, Excellency?"

"Yes, Your Honor, post-conviction justice. That's the kind of justice that's even nobler." He slowly walked around the table as he continued. "Our judges send people to jail every day. If truth is slow in coming, either that judge or his superiors should always be ready to come back and answer for their decisions, and to remove malfunctions of justice. And it must cost the convict nothing."

"Excellency," Judge Delgado replied uncertainly, "there's no tradition in Mexico for that kind of justice. If the truth comes out later, why not simply let the convict appeal the court's decision and present his case before us?"

"I'm here to set a new tradition of justice," Maximilian explained, completing his circle around the table. "I think of the law as a flexible instrument, capable of accommodating social realities. It has to allow itself to be subject to reinterpretation. Why should the convict crawl to the judge after an unlawful conviction? The judge should be crawling to *him*. I hope to establish this new tradition quickly, without any cost to the convict. Perhaps it'll be duplicated elsewhere until the entire world has adopted it."

The men murmured amongst themselves.

Maximilian clutched the two files and walked around the table again. "Gentlemen, you represent the highest in appellate jurisdiction." He paused when he reached Supreme Justice Pena Ruiz, slapping the two files onto the table before him. "These are two simple cases. Kindly proceed, Your Honor."

Ruiz leafed through the documents for a few minutes, the emperor waiting quietly over his shoulder. The man finally looked up and nodded.

Maximilian nodded as well, announcing, "The accused may be brought into this court now, Victorio Emmanuel first." A guard at the door nodded and left the room quietly.

Within ten minutes, Victorio Emmanuel entered the royal office, also the court for now. He stood with his hat in his hands, eyeing Justice Ruiz, who stood and addressed him.

"The record shows that in your case, the evidence used against you was an anonymous letter against the army," Ruiz explained. "You were charged with treason, yet crimes of disloyalty cannot be treason unless the country is at war. Was it perhaps sedition? That would mean it incited rebellion against a lawful government, yet at that time the government was not lawful; brute military strength does not constitute a lawful government. No crime was committed."

Emmanuel blinked in surprise.

"Sir, I contend that you were actually doing your duty. It's the army's own law to ignore and trash anonymous letters, no matter what their content. Victorio Emmanuel is hereby set free," he said to the group of judiciaries. "Next."

Emmanuel did not seem to realize what had happened at first, since it had all happened so quickly. It seemed to dawn on him as the guard approached him, and he managed a small bow and a murmur of surprised gratitude as he was ushered to a seat at the other end of the room. He passed Carillo, who was just being led in.

Carillo was escorted to the same spot where Emmanuel had stood. He looked several years older, his eyes having lost some of their zeal of previous years. Justice Ruiz sized up the pale man standing before him. "How would you convince us that the judge overseeing your trial knew the evidence brought against you was completely fabricated?" he asked.

Carillo's dark eyes scanned the group of men at the table, lingering on the emperor. "Your Honor, I was convicted based on my confession, which was extracted by torturing both me and my family. Evidence obtained through torture should have been thrown out, but it wasn't. The judge was an interested party who found himself under pressure from military authority. My lawyer has evidence on file that he was approached by the same colonel I was going to arrest for murdering an intellectual in his custody. There was also no jury, and there was complicity in my department."

"Thank you, Señor Carillo," Ruiz said. "You may be seated."

Carillo sat on a chair that had been placed a bit closer to the table. He again glanced at the emperor, who gave him a small but encouraging nod.

Ruiz went through Carillo's file with exacting carefulness, taking half an hour. Beyond an occasional cough or shuffling of papers, not a word was said until Ruiz lifted his head from the case papers. "The previous decision is reversed and the court dismisses all of the charges. The accused Antonio Carillo is hereby set free. The police department is to reinstate him and to hold an internal inquiry on charges of complicity. Their report is to be sent to me within thirty days or I shall order compensation."

The emperor could not help but grin as Carillo's mouth opened in disbelief. Maximilian rose to congratulate his judges and both of the defendants. As Carillo shook the emperor's hand, he clutched it in both of his hands, kissing it in desperate gratitude.

Maximilian beamed. These were the kinds of moments he had dreamt of when imagining his days as emperor of Mexico.

The court was officially adjourned, though the only one who actually left was one of the guards. He was to send word to the Emmanuels and Carillos to immediately come to Chapultepec and retrieve their loved ones. The judges clustered into groups and began chatting over drinks, one of them kindly handing Emmanuel a drink and drawing him into his group's conversation. The man took the drink thankfully and straightened himself, still haggard from jail but otherwise as proud and respected a member of Parliament as he had ever been.

Maximilian likewise handed Carillo a drink and stood off in a corner with him. "I've met your father," he said over the drone of the surrounding conversations. "He's a grand old man to have a son like you and a grandson like Vickers."

"Yes, Excellency, my father's full of wisdom," he agreed with a nod. "Perhaps his entire vision for the police department will finally come to pass."

"Oh?" Maximilian said. "What vision is that?"

Carillo swallowed his first sip of the wine. He was surprised at the tang in his mouth after so long with nothing but warm and often rancid water. "For years, my father's wanted a law passed so that the police department has to be made responsible for everything it's been found to have stolen. Then the accountant general should be at the department's throat to collect it."

Maximilian took a step towards the window and stared at the garden below before turning on his heel. "What a superior idea," he marveled, a twinkle in his eye.

Carillo smiled. "My father said it's the best way to prevent thousands of thefts by the police."

Maximilian felt the same generous friendship with him that he had felt before with his son. "I've told your father that I'd like to visit your home. Eat food and gossip with your old man."

"I'm humbled, sire. By all means, my home is always open to Your Majesty."

Hours later, the rays of the sun fell on the office floor at a sharper angle. Now later in the evening, they were a deep gold color. Emmanuel and Carillo's families had arrived amidst embraces and tears. It was a moment Maximilian would replay many times in his mind, often to cheer himself up and to remind him why he was really here. The families had finally been reunited, and Vickers was granted the rest of the week off to escort his father home and get him settled in.

The judges had also gone home, but they were surprised to find that the guards normally posted outside their homes were gone. They were critical staff in those uncertain times, when judges of a new government were prime targets against the Mexican resistance.

Even Chief Justice Ruiz found that his guard was missing. He quickly went to the local guard post to ask where the guard was, and was told that they had been called back under orders from Marshal Bazaine. He immediately returned to Chapultepec, not daring the risk of waiting until the morning and leaving both he and his family vulnerable throughout the night.

When he arrived back in the emperor's office, he saw that Bazaine was still there, as if expecting his return and waiting for him. He stalked angrily up to Bazaine, his face flushed. "Why did you pull the guard from my house?" he demanded. Maximilian stood nearby, surprised and confused by the confrontation.

Bazaine's eyes were unreadable. "All of the judicial guards have been pulled," he explained, his voice unnervingly calm.

"But *why?*"

"If you can't protect us, we're under no obligation to protect you, sir."

Ruiz's eyes narrowed. "You think you can use this country's state of civil war to force the judiciary into doing your bidding?"

Bazaine waved a hand. "I'll instruct your guards to return tonight. But you need to remember that we're not here to turn our victory into a sudden defeat.

Mexico is ours by conquest," he said arrogantly, referring to France. "We put down the Mexican resistance a long time ago."

Ruiz looked appalled at the marshal's attitude. "Are you suggesting—"

"You should go now, sir," Bazaine interrupted.

The judge's face filled with rage. "Just who in the hell do you think you are? You're addressing—"

This time, Maximilian interrupted him by stepping between the two men. He made no effort to hide his disdain for the marshal as he turned to him. He paused and looked down at the several medals studding Bazaine's uniform, daring to reach out and lift one into his hand. "You're obviously a skilled soldier," he commented. "These medals prove your experience in European wars. Your predecessor brought you here as one of his divisional commanders." He let the medal drop back onto Bazaine's chest. "Marshal Forey did things that gave the Mexicans pride in themselves, and you didn't like that."

Maximilian stood at his full height so that he actually looked down at the marshal, trying to physically belittle him. "You realize that you're doing things that will get you into trouble after your monarch is gone … lots of trouble. Don't feel too invincible, Marshal. I've seen two Austrian marshals executed."

The men were interrupted by the swishing sound of Carlota's silk taffeta dress. "Gentleman," she interrupted, "things are getting a bit stifling in here. Please take some refreshment with us. The emperor's dinner is prepared."

Bazaine eyed the other two men suspiciously and received an equally hostile stare in return. They then turned to the empress, who waited by the door. She knew how lovely she looked in her dress. The pagoda sleeves flared dramatically to make her ivory hands looks even smaller and more delicate, and the fringe of blonde lace sewn throughout the costume struck a dramatic contrast to her glossy black hair. But the most influential thing she wore was a confident air of persuasion.

The men were angry, but also relieved that the moment had been interrupted. They knew that they had been trapped into an argument that none knew how to extract himself from, and each just wanted some breathing space. They assumed their political faces and accepted the empress's invitation, moving to the dining hall.

"Come now, while the food is hot. My cook is learning new ways of seasoning food with local spices. I hope you enjoy it," she said graciously, hoping it was edible. The cook's attempts had not been so successful in recent days.

Once they were seated in the opulent dining room, Carlota worked her magic and lightened the mood. She said all of the right things to these three powerful and arrogant men, things like, "What a lucky woman I am today, with three handsome and powerful men to escort me to dinner," and, "Judge Ruiz, how is your charming wife?" and, "Marshal Bazaine, I've yet to see a more striking figure in uniform!" An onlooker would have balked at her transparent flattery, but her beautiful face and airy voice soon had each man smiling and lowering his head, embarrassed by the flattery.

While dinner was being served, Carlota took a folded piece of paper from the pocket of her dress and passed it to her husband. Maximilian kept it in his lap and glanced at the other men now and then as he reviewed the note.

"Marshal, my wife was obviously raised to rule the same way I was," Maximilian said to Bazaine. "The empress has proposed a settlement agreement between you and me."

Carlota's eyes widened in surprise at his frank discussion of the note.

"How do you find it?" he asked, handing the note to Bazaine. The marshal looked mildly amused as he accepted the letter, his smile fading as he read what seemed to be a well-constructed and intelligent proposal. It was jotted down like a list.

"What is to be done now?

1. All French troops will move after direct agreement between His Majesty, Emperor Maximilian, and the French corps commander.

2. It is agreed that in any case of combined military operations (French with Mexican), the French will enjoy superior command.

3. The French commander will not interfere with any branch of the Mexican administration.

4. Every two months, the Mexican government will pay 400,000 francs to keep French army shipping open.

5. The French want an occasional naval show of force. Allow it.

6. The French have demanded repayment of the cost of their expedition (from 1862 to July 1, 1864). The cost is fixed at 270,000,000 francs. Agree to it.

7. France has asked that indemnity be paid to France for pay and support of its remaining army corps from July 1, 1864 onwards. Agree to 1,000 francs per person per year.

8. France has asked His Majesty, Emperor Maximilian, to remit 66,000,000 francs in loan securities at once. Agree to it.

9. Summary: Agree on fiscal demands, but keep the army corps commander away from the Mexican administration."

Below the list was a drawing of a heart with an arrow through it, evidence that Carlota had not expected anyone but her husband to see her list of ideas.

Bazaine lifted his head and smiled at Carlota. "My lady, you're both gracious and intelligent. We men could learn a thing or two about agreements from you. I believe your list appears reasonable. I'll be happy to sign this beside Your Majesty, the emperor, and let this be a gentleman's agreement."

"No," Maximilian interjected firmly. "An agreement must be formal, written with appropriate witnesses and seals."

Bazaine chuckled and rubbed his chin. "Very well, Your Majesty."

Justice Ruiz watched the empress's skill in maneuvering in the background, fascinated and intrigued at what the list contained. "Charming, yet brilliant," he thought as he watched her smile sweetly and lean back in her chair. He barely noticed the servants placing the first course on the table.

Carlota called for her personal servant, who soon appeared in the dining room. "Oh, Rosa, there you are. Please bring me the files lying on my bedside table." The dark woman nodded and hurried from the room. Very soon after, she returned with the files, curtseying after handing them over and quietly exiting.

The empress soon selected a paper to refer to, studying it and addressing Marshal Bazaine.

"Marshal, this civil war in America seems to be a witch that's caught America up into blood-letting. They've seen almost a thousand battles since '61. What do you think caused it?"

"My dear empress," Bazaine replied, "the issue of rights was the evil that afflicted that country."

"You mean the power to invade rights inspite of a Constitution?"

"Yes, and impair the value of their property."

"Passionate minds, wouldn't you say, Marshal? One group trying to trample rights, another group fighting for them?"

"Yes, Your Majesty," he replied, starting to feel a bit uncomfortable as he wondered where this was going.

"That has a familiar ring to it. What are we doing here in Mexico?"

The Marshal's lips formed a thin hard line. He kept silent.

"We're doing the same thing," she insisted, "and they're fighting back. You can say, 'Yes, but we're strong, unbeatable.' But they're still fighting back."

"They're weak," he insisted, looking at the food and waiting for the imperial couple to eat so that he could begin. "They've been beaten, rubbed into the dust."

"But still, *still* they're fighting back!" Carlota insisted.

He shrugged. "Yes, Empress."

"My husband is here to stop this needless blood-letting, to give rights to the people and add value to their lives. Do you understand that? Can you allow that?"

"No," he answered frankly but cautiously. "The Mexican people don't consider His Majesty to be their friend," he reminded her.

Carlota smiled. "The Hapsburgs have calmed many nations over the years. They've been tutored and reared for that job."

Bazaine suddenly stood and walked to the emperor's chair, holding out his hand. "Let's make that agreement Your Majesty's proposed. The French army won't stand in your way."

Carlota laid her hand in the crook of her husband's arms, preventing him from shaking. "So His Imperial Majesty will be given the freedom needed to repair the damage done to this country?"

Bazaine bowed formally. "Yes, Your Majesty."

"Anything required will be permitted without interference?" she clarified.

"Yes, Your Majesty," the marshal repeated.

Justice Ruiz shook his head in amazement.

Carlota lifted her hand from Maximilian's arms, allowing them to shake on their agreement. She settled in her chair again and smiled, snatching a roll from the basket like a mischievous child. Everyone followed her cue and began to eat.

Thankfully, the meal was a success. Her cook had experimented with cilantro, an herb that she found agreeable. It was certainly better than the marinade from the evening before, which had been so sour that she had been unable to eat much more than soup and bread. Their guests also seemed to enjoy the meal, though it was just as likely that they would praise it even if it were the worst thing they had ever tasted. That never occurred to Carlota, though. Raised in opulence and surrounded by false flattery, she had long ago done what many spoiled and rich royalty do, making a conscious choice to accept most flattery as sincerity so that she could enjoy the compliments.

Before their guests left, Justice Ruiz took Carlota's hand and gave it an elegant kiss. "It's been an enlightening evening, Your Majesty, simply fascinating."

Carlota smiled, again a charming girl. "Thank you, sir," she said with an air of adolescence, affecting a slight blush. Ruiz was enchanted, also blushing as he nodded and said his goodbyes.

After the two visitors took their leave, Maximilian and Carlota stood arm-in-arm beside the door. Maximilian looked at his wife appreciatively. "How many battles have been fought by Americans in their civil war? Nearly a thousand?"

"Oh, I don't know," she laughed with a wave of her hand.

Maximilian laughed, now wondering how many of her words had been show and how many were based on research. "How very skillful of you," he praised.

Carlota tilted her head back haughtily, jokingly arrogant as her dainty eyebrows arched. "Many ideas of men are rushed and obsessive, causing nothing but blood and frustration. Skillful ideas seek to prevent them."

Maximilian laughed until her arrogant façade finally cracked and she smiled, then burst into laughter herself.

CHAPTER 19

▼

A PRINCE IN THE DARK

The dark was so complete that it had to be hours after dusk. Crickets chirped loudly as four men met in secret to plan the fate of Maximilian's strange Mexican empire. They had staggered their arrival times to avoid suspicion, with Marshal Bazaine's aide de camp, Xavier Girard, meeting and escorting them in one at a time. He stayed nearby the proceedings at all times, always on guard. Bazaine's dimly lit office was decorated with fine French furniture and paintings of Napoleon III.

Marshal Bazaine was short and thickset. He was dressed for the meeting in an official French military uniform that threatened to overpower his own plain features with its dramatic black jacket and red trousers. His thinning gray hair was kept short, revealing a high forehead. It would have been easy to summarize him with a glance as an anonymous military dinosaur, just another older man whose best military years were behind him. It would be easy to do that until seeing his eyes, watching their cunning glitter and keen intelligence. He was a man who had been sharpened by years of service, not worn down. It gave him an air of unpredictability, as if he almost hoped you would underestimate him so that somehow, *somehow* he could show you how wrong you had been.

He began the meeting by welcoming his French division commanders. Field Marshal d'Herrillien, General Brincourt, and the youngest one were there, General Sebastian Moreau. All of the officers were highly decorated with rows of medals and elaborate epalettes and gold silk sashes. The lantern glowed sharply on their highly shined black leather boots.

As the clock struck ten o'clock, ADC Xavier Girard took up his post outside the door to ensure there would be no interruptions. "Have a seat, gentlemen," Bazaine said, gesturing to a massive table in the middle of the room. They settled into rattan chairs darkened with a deep mahogany finish and covered in rich padded leather.

Bazaine remained standing and paused to light his cigar. The men waited patiently. "As you know," he began, a puff of smoke pushing from his mouth, "I signed an agreement with His Imperial Majesty. Nevertheless, in a recent letter from His Majesty Napoleon, I've been ordered to set up a scientific commission in Mexico."

"A scientific commission?" General Moreau echoed. "What does that involve?"

Bazaine shrugged. "Study Mexico, devise ways and means to promote France's mission to civilize it. We already have all the tools we need, I think. We just need to execute it."

"Execute it?" Moreau again echoed. Bazaine's jaw clenched the tiniest bit. This younger one often got on his nerves with that echoing business. Moreau seemed not to notice his irritation as he leaned forward and rested his elbows on the table, a wisp of dark curly hair resting just below the eyebrow. "But that's completely the opposite of your agreement with His Imperial Majesty," he reminded Bazaine.

"He looks like a boy," Bazaine thought pettily to himself as he eyed the young man's errant hair in his eyes and nursed his irritation.

"We have to keep him in the dark," the elder Field Marshal d'Herrillien replied matter-of-factly, though in a furtive tone to stress their need for discretion to the younger officer.

General Moreau was still young enough to miss moments of discretion. "That'd be a breach of an agreement from the army's side," he said, shocked. "Do we really want to set that kind of precedent?"

Field Marshal d'Herrillien stood with a sigh and walked to Bazaine's side. "We're here to colonize, not to free these people. I have personal instructions from Napoleon to make sure that the Mexicans forget their nationalism, and we've been ordered to acquire their money by any means necessary. We're not Britain and Spain. They just came to collect a debt. We have more strategic aims that involve a very long stay here."

The field marshal continued as he walked to the wall and gestured to the large map of Mexico framed there. "Here's where we intend to dig a canal across Mexico," he said, poking at the map. "It'll be similar to the Suez Canal, and it'll give France dominance over all the trade in this region."

Moreau frowned and nodded slightly, listening. "Gentlemen, our mission is clear," d'Herrillien said plainly. "We live on their money. We use all their resources to build a greater France. Maximilian is just as bad to us as Benito Juarez is. But this is a unique opportunity for us, because we can keep Maximilian under close observation while we beat Juarez to smithereens. Then we can do what we please with the Austrico," he explained, his language for the emperor familiar and flippant to show his contempt.

Marshal Bazaine nodded. "The U.S. Congress is supplying the republicans. Juarez has one of his men close to American borders, and he continues to receive military and financial help from there. We're going to weaken Juarez by buying that man."

"That's something I can handle," General Brincourt offered eagerly, all but rubbing his hands together.

Field Marshal d'Herrillien continued. "On April fourth, the U.S. Congress officially opposed a monarchy in Mexico, but it's paralyzed to do anything about it right now because of its own civil war. So now we have to persuade Maximilian to sign our proclamation."

The officers grunted in agreement. The field marshal was referring to the Black Warrant, which would allow them to immediately execute any guerrilla caught in their war against the Mexicans. It would be a much faster way to deplete their numbers and cut out the tedious process of prisoner negotiations.

"We have to move up to Oaxaca and find a way to defeat General Porfirio Diaz," the field marshal said.

"That would be a major victory," Moreau agreed, stating the obvious. "He's a staunch supporter of Juarez."

"I can handle that, too," General Brincourt chimed in, a lazy smile on his face as he watched his hands calmly.

Field Marshal d'Herrillien nodded with a smile. "Request that in writing. I can get Maximilian to sign off on the operation."

"Sir," Brincourt nodded. It was as good as done.

"We have also to capture the mines in the north," he added, nodding at Brincourt. "If you manage to capture Oaxaca, I'll send you another division to capture Tacambaro and Guayama. Then you'll be ready for phase two." He pointed at the third divisional commander, General Moreau, who nodded and turned to nod to Brincourt. The man was still staring at his hands with the faintest smile and did not notice him. Moreau nodded to no one and stared at his own hands as well.

Bazaine leaned on the table and sighed. "Now on to another thing. We need to stop calling ourselves the French army. All military personal will now be called 'the Imperial Forces.' Instruct your press coordinators to censor the name 'French army' from now on. We'll have the stamp of 'Imperial Forces' on all of our uniforms, evening and working dress ... everything. That includes insignia, formation symbols, and signs. We'll have to write up a request very carefully, asking Maximilian to sign a proclamation. But the proclamation can't see the light of day until after we've reversed our battles against the guerrillas." He frowned and thought for a moment, then added, "In fact, let's stop calling Juarez's army the 'republican forces.' From now on, we should simply call them guerrillas, insurgents, terrorists. We'll plan and execute some acts of terrorism, then blame the guerrillas. That'll make it exceedingly easy for the press, which we need to have complete control over."

"So more dummy papers?" Brincourt asked, finally looking up from his hands.

"Absolutely," Bazaine replied. "We have to keep the emperor in the dark as much as the common folks. The Belgian and Austrian troops need to be absorbed immediately into 'the Imperial Forces' too, and stay under our command. We have to make sure that the emperor can't use them to his advantage."

Brincourt smirked. "Do you really think he's that capable?" he asked, his dark eyes gleaming. Young General Moreau stared at his face, at once feeling fear, fascination, and admiration for the cynical and brooding man.

Bazaine paused and turned to Brincourt. "Be careful not to underestimate him. Maximilian may be a spoiled royal, but he spent years in the Austrian navy and was well-decorated for it."

Brincourt's eyes narrowed slightly. "Maybe, but I'm willing to bet some of those awards were won by birth, not girth." His eyes flicked over to Moreau, who was still staring at him. The young man glanced away and lamely examined his fingernails. Brincourt smirked, amusing himself.

"We have to deny Maximilian any opportunity to further his own position or unite Mexico," Bazaine replied. "See, we have two fronts to fight: Benito Juarez and the Austrico. Hopefully the Black Warrant will finally tear them both apart."

General Moreau shrugged and thought out loud. "What happens if Lincoln wins a second presidency and the North wins the civil war?"

Field Marshal d'Herrillien answered, "Then we leave Mexico. We can ask Maximilian to abdicate." He paused, his eyebrows arching. "You know, I think it would be a good idea to endear Colonel Lopez to the emperor. He's a master at trickery. We could get him into the palace, start him arranging the royal dinners and so forth."

Brincourt laughed. "Lopez will lick their shoes and keep us informed."

The sun was rising. A Cassin's kingbird, grayish-olive with a yellow belly, perched on a twig and sang, "Come 'ere, come 'ere." The emperor was mounted on a beautiful white horse, wading through crops of cacao beans, corn, and sugar cane. He was heading towards Carillo's residence, eager to see how the man was settling in at home. The idea of seeing Carillo again fed his ego. It was not completely selfish, but he did enjoy playing the role of savior and seeing the grateful look in his eyes. It was something he had spent hours imagining on that long sea voyage to Mexico, and even before that in Europe; for now, this was only one of two men he had saved, and he clung to the feelings this evoked. When he saw the gratefulness on Carillo's face, he felt like a knight, but also humbled and part of a larger good. So it was not all ego. It was simply that everything in Maximilian's life, no matter how good or progressive, always fed his ego in some way.

Maximilian traveled long and narrow stretches of road before he reached the crest of a small hill and saw his destination. It was a small frame house with blank stucco facades, surrounded on three sides by Mexican live oaks. As he rode into the small courtyard, the chickens cackled loudly. He dismounted his horse, ignoring the guards who trailed behind and lingered at the road so that he could pretend he was traveling alone. He strode energetically to the door and knocked.

A young house servant opened the door, still wiping the sleep from her eyes. "May I have breakfast in this house?" asked the handsome rider with a smile.

Soraya, who had been present at the cathedral on the day of the emperor and empress's coronation, recognized the man immediately. Her eyes widened in shock and she ran into the house, leaving the door ajar as she bounded into Carillo's bedroom and tapped him quickly. "It's him!" she whispered breathlessly. "The emperor is at the door asking for breakfast!"

"The emperor?" Carillo mumbled confusedly, sitting up.

"Get up, señor! Come, quickly!" she urged, pulling the coverlet off Carillo in her excitement. "It's really him, señor. I couldn't believe my eyes!"

Carillo rose quickly, simultaneously rushing to the door and shrugging on his robe. He paused behind the somewhat opened door and tried to quietly catch his breath, smoothing his hair with both hands. A smile lit his face as he rounded the door. "Your Excellency, we're humbled," he said declared, bowing twice when once would have sufficed. "Welcome to my home."

Maximilian nodded and was escorted into the parlor. "Please sit here, señor," he urged, settling the emperor into the best chair in the room. "Shall I call my father?"

"Yes, if you please, sir," the emperor replied.

Carillo nodded and rushed out. The house servant, Soraya, lingered in the doorway and stared with wonder at the Austrian, then hesitantly withdrew to the kitchen.

As Maximilian's eyes grew accustomed to the dim light, he saw a simple, cozy parlor. There was a small dining table, big enough for four. The chairs were made of iron and upholstered with leather. The tabletop was made of glass, something new in Mexico. Resting on it were flower-shaped mats made of straw, with a rack in the middle that held small bottles of mustard, chilles, salt, sugar, vinegar, and honey.

Judge Antonio Carillo was more appropriately dressed when he entered the room. Maximilian stood and started to speak, but the old man was full of energy and began first. "Could we ever dream of such a morning when an emperor asks for breakfast in our house?" He was overcome with the very idea. "Soraya, you and the señora fix a big breakfast for our honored guest."

Maximilian cleared his throat, feeling the need to speak carefully to this man who had won his respect. "I came alone as a friend," he said, not really fibbing. The guard did not officially count as someone he "came with," but was simply a shadow that all royals learned to ignore. "I'm not an emperor today. I simply came to have breakfast with a friend, to ask about things and enjoy a good conversation."

"Ooooh, I see," Antonio replied, easing himself into one of the dining room chairs. "What would you like to talk about, mi emperador?"

Maximilian smiled at the man's title for him. It was quickly evolving into an affectionate nickname. He sat in a chair across from the man. "Just everyday sorts of things ... prices, sanitation ... the general mood of the people."

"The mood of the people is dreadful," he replied without hesitation as Soraya set a plate of hastily sliced fruit on the table. Maximilian's eyes darted appreciatively over the young woman's bosom and full lips as he listened to the man's reply. "They're saying that the French have an agenda, and that they're not here for your empire, but for their own. Prices keep soaring. The civil war is actually between the republican guerrillas and your French troops."

"Really," Maximilian replied neutrally, trying to sound interested but nonchalant. It got his attention all the same, and his eyes turned from the exiting servant and back to the old judge.

Antonio nodded. "The French don't want your image growing in Mexico." He paused and lowered his voice. "I'm afraid for your safety."

"Yes, I've heard that before," Maximilian confessed, rubbing his forehead. "My staff officers report the same thing."

"You're in a difficult fix," Antonio summarized bluntly.

Maximilian smiled weakly. "It seems I'm blessed with two Goliaths: the French army and their rivals, the republicans."

Soraya and Carillo's wife soon brought more trays full of food. It was to be a traditional breakfast, of course, with boiled eggs, sweet tamales, strong coffee, and bread with lots of butter. Maximilian cheered himself by watching the servant woman again. A wisp of black hair had missed her hastily assembled bun and rested on her dark neck. He enjoyed the duskiness of her skin, the liquid dark of her eyes. She reminded him of his dancing girl. The thought that he had never enjoyed a Mexican woman also occurred to him.

"Make sure your heart is braver than David's if you want to knock out two Goliaths," Antonio said around a mouth full of food.

Maximilian looked away from the girl and was confused for just a moment, having forgotten what they were discussing.

"You've made a commitment here," he added, forking an egg and waving it for emphasis. "If need be, you go down fighting. Remember what Goliath said to the shepherd boy? 'I will eat you and throw your carcass to the sheep.' That's the worst they can do. So trust in God and don't look back."

Maximilian blinked.

"You're up to your neck in it now, mi emperador," Antonio said with a smile, his eyes shining.

Carillo took a seat at the table, shooting a look at his father for his familiarity with the emperor. "Eat, señor," he urged the emperor, trying to lighten the mood.

There were a few minutes of silence as the group of men ate their breakfast. Maximilian finally spoke as he opened a roll and spread it with butter. "The first thing I did yesterday was to read the dossier the government had on you, Señor Carillo. I'm very fond of your son Vickers. He's an excellent ADC. But I was reminded in reading that you have an older son. Where is he?"

"He's a revolutionary, Excellency. He started reading controversial literature and discussing revolution in college."

"Eventually got involved in a train robbery," Antonio added.

Carillo nodded at his father's comment. "My deputy witnessed the robbery and told me about it. I arrested him and had him convicted. He escaped from jail and we don't know where he is anymore."

Maximilian looked up from his food. "He's a staff member of Benito Juarez."

Carillo was shocked. "Juarez? Are you sure?"

Maximilian nodded. "He's Juarez's personal attendant."

Carillo stared off at nothing. "I haven't heard from him in almost a year," he said faintly, as if to himself.

"I'm afraid there's more," Maximilian continued, trying to be tactful. The Carillos paused. "Your son has apparently vowed to kill your deputy. I don't know why though."

Carillo's face was grim and he glanced towards the kitchen, lowering his voice. "When my son and I were both in jail, my deputy came into my house and raped my wife. She told my sons about it later." He sighed and sank back in his chair. "I wouldn't expect anyone to find out such a thing without wanting revenge, but Vail was always one eager to find a reason for vengeance."

Antonio grunted his agreement. "He was always an angry boy."

Maximilian slid his plate to the side and leaned forward, lacing his fingers on the table before him. "Well, Vail is apparently staying with Juarez somewhere close to the American border."

Carillo clenched his fork and shook his head. "I swear, if I ever see that boy again …"

Maximilian cocked his head a bit. "What would you do to him if you ever caught him again?"

"I'd have to put him back in jail, señor."

"Really? You don't believe that the deputy should have to pay for what he did to your wife? Doesn't Vail deserve the right to have his vengeance?"

"Anyone who believes in vengeance shouldn't wear a uniform," he quickly replied. "I believe in duty."

Antonio grunted again, perhaps in agreement but maybe not. He only ate and listened.

After some consideration, Maximilian finally spoke. "What if I were to change your duty from police chief to master of the royal mint?"

Carillo shrugged. "I'd go where I'm ordered to go, señor. But I'm clueless about such matters."

"You'll learn fast; you're obviously very intelligent," Maximilian replied, his mind made up. "It'd be safer, and the wages should make your life more comfortable."

"Son," Antonio interrupted, "can't you see that he didn't come here for break-fast? He's here to reward your honesty." The old judge stood up and approached Maximilian, making a bow as deep as his arthritic bones would allow him. He reached for the emperor's hand and kissed his ring. "Mi emperador, I'm over-whelmed."

Maximilian smiled magnanimously. "Your son's honesty makes him more precious than all the gold in the world. I'd also like to invite you to take the hon-orable position of advisor to your son in the planning of my mint. I want you both to arrange for the minting of my new coins, and may they last hundreds of years."

Carillo and his father were at a loss for words. Soon they were both standing, staring in disbelief.

Maximilian smiled again. "It's settled then. Come tomorrow and I'll write the appropriate orders and take you to begin working on the royal mint." He raised his glass. "To the new mint master," he offered.

Each man, as if snapped from a spell, clutched his own glass and held it up as well. They had a drink and smiled at each other familiarly.

"My good friend Admiral Tegethoff said good things about you, Carillo. How did he know you and Vickers?"

"I have a relative in the shipping business. He often hires captains and stays friendly with many others. They receive their commissions through his friend-ship, señor."

"Where does he live?"

"In Vera Cruz, Excellency."

Maximilian nodded, deep in thought. He stroked his beard unconsciously. "May I have a pen and paper?"

Carillo got up hurriedly. "Of course, Your Excellency."

Maximilian wanted to write a letter to his mother, but he did not dare send it through his own registry, where it would be examined by the French and proba-bly discarded. They gave him space and privacy at a small desk in the adjoining room, finishing their meal as he wrote.

"November 25th, 1865

Mother,

I hope this letter finds you well. I miss you very much and love you always. I have gathered some information concerning Austria's war with Italy. Admiral Tegethoff and I spent five years building an ironclad navy together, and I have information that assures me he is a trusted man. From what I already know about him, he's capable of winning the Adriatic conflict that seems inevitable. Ask my brother to post him in the Adriatic Fleet.

Love as always.

Your son,

Maximilian."

Maximilian paused and added below his name, "MAXIMILIEN EMPERODU MEXIQUE." He closed the envelope and handed it to Carillo.

"I'll see to it that it's delivered, Excellency."

Maximilian then handed Carillo the pen and some paper. "Please take notes regarding your orders for the mint."

Carillo nodded and sat at the table, pen in hand.

"You're to mint twenty-two carat gold marriage coins, eight carat medals of honor, eighteen carat gold wedding tokens … create a design of my face and the empress's, the Mexican eagle, and the Aztec calendar. I want Mexico's gold to establish my image."

Carillo wrote quickly, nodding for him to continue.

"I want you to fashion some Cuauhtémoc coins. Use the updated eagle and go up to an assortment of thirty. Also replace the current Augustine gold coins with some memorial coins, and put our coat of arms on them." He paced, enjoying these kinds of tasks. "Also mint fantasy coins. I'll reach my people through their children; children are attracted to objects of fantasy."

"Yes, señor."

"Put the words 'MAXIMILIEN EMPERODU MEXIQUE' on the table of world jewelers."

"Yes, señor."

"See to it that you don't make me look an old bearded man!" Maximilian warned, patting Carillo's shoulder with a laugh.

Carillo and his father exchanged glances and smiled.

A half hour later, the emperor sat on a chestnut horse and Carillo on the white charger. He had protested greatly, but the emperor insisted that Carillo ride back on the imperial horse, with the emperor on Carillo's horse. They waved goodbye to the grand old man, Antonio.

"Excellency, I want to change our route," Carillo said as they edged towards the road. "We should travel in this direction."

"Why is that?"

"It's safer, with a covered approach running parallel to the track. Besides, if we go this way, you can see some beautiful estates."

Maximilian shrugged, hating to give in but grudgingly doing so. "I do have a guard with me, Carillo. There's no need for such precautions."

Carillo looked unimpressed. "Excellency, an assassin can find you by following your guard just as easily as by following you."

Maximilian paused. "You make a good point there, Carillo. Lead the way."

Soon they were in a sea of flowers, geraniums, petunias, and snapdragons resembling the gardens Maximilian used to see in Europe. The emperor evaluated the rows of plants and shook his head in disbelief. "Carnations …"

"Pardon me, señor?"

Maximilian did not respond. After a short distance, he saw a bed of geraniums. He dismounted the horse and picked one, examining the soil.

Carillo sat quietly on the white charger, not knowing how to respond to his emperor's odd behavior.

Maximilian examined the flower. "Pest-free, disease-resistant, enriched soil … only a European gardener grows plants this way." He got back on his horse and continued, Carillo shrugging and following. As they rode further through rows of chrysanthemums and poinsettias, Maximilian recalled the good feelings he used to have upon seeing neat rows of flowers like this. He saw cartloads of seed, bound in burlap, stacked along the edges of the track.

Next his gaze fell on a well-outfitted sausage factory, big enough that it must be exporting food. Soon after, he was shaken when he saw rows upon rows of hot peppers. "Hot Tepin pepper, 500,000 units," he said to himself. He remembered Zinnia laughing and saying, "Put one in your mouth and you can't argue anymore."

The next field was full of workers in white shirts, weeding Congo black peppers, also known as chocolate habanera. In the next few rows, he spied a different species and again surprised Carillo. "My God, a white cherry tomato! Zinnia ... this is Zinnia!"

Carillo was baffled, concerned that perhaps the emperor had too much sun.

Maximilian continued on and found tomatoes on bamboo, staked ten feet high: toothache plant eyeballs. He picked one and tasted it. It quickly numbed his mouth, confirming that he had been right in guessing what kind they were. "This must be you, Zinnia. This is you." He raced his horse towards the palatial hacienda that was obviously the home of the landowners. Carillo followed, confused but obedient.

"Where has love brought us?" Maximilian hummed, remembering Zinnia's song.

He stopped suddenly and wrenched the horse to face left, craning his neck and shading his eyes as he squinted towards the field closest to the house. A dark-haired lady wearing a veil was working there in a bed of nursery plants. Maximilian straightened his back and cupped his hands around his mouth. "Zinnia!!"

The woman turned. Zinnia was stunned to see Maximilian and dropped her little rake. Maximilian slid off the horse and charged towards her, finally catching up and embracing her closely. He held onto her for who knew how long, smelling the familiar scent of honey in her hair. When he finally pulled away, her face was dazed, her eyes glittering with tears.

"Max ..."

"Oh Zinnia, I thought you were ..." He could not finish, only wrapping her back up into his arms.

Carillo was flabbergasted as he sat on the charger nearby, far away enough to give them some space.

Zinnia hugged him back fiercely, then seemed to sag in his arms. Her shoulders heaved with unheard sobs, her face and voice buried in his chest. She finally pulled away and caught him by surprise by wrenching away from him and walking swiftly back towards the house. Her head was down and she sniffled, wiping her face with the back of her hand.

"Zinnia, where are you going?" Maximilian asked, confused.

"I'm not ..." She caught her breath and wiped more tears from her cheeks. "I'm Mrs. John Michael Best—"

Maximilian caught her by the shoulders. "Zinnia—"

"Mrs. Best!" she sputtered, struggling against him. He held her firmly. "It is too late," she sobbed. "Mrs. Best ... Mrs ... Best ..." she repeated, shaking her head and staring at her feet.

Once again, the prince, Maximilian, looked at her in awe. "Oh Zinnia, you're still so beautiful."

"No!" she shrieked, wrenching free again and rushing to the entrance of the hacienda. "No more Zinnia!" she shouted over her shoulder. "I'm married now. I'm Mrs. Best!" she screamed as if insane, banging the huge oak doors shut behind her.

Maximilian stared at the doors, too shocked at her reaction to notice the tears on his own face.

Paris, 1864

Napoleon III stood in his elegant office in the Grand Cabinet at the Tuileries. He wore a royal blue military uniform, standing before a large, Regency-style mirror with a letter in his right hand. He was addressing his cabinet ministers.

"Well, well," he said, flapping the letter. "Mexican Corps Commander Bazaine reports a transfer of fifty-five million francs to us. He also reports on details of other fiscal supports for our army there. Maximilian's government has apparently signed an agreement with him, too. They've changed the name of the army to 'the Imperial Forces,'" he said with a conspiratorial wink of his small grayish-blue eyes. "We're to receive one thousand francs per soldier per year for this change of name."

He held the letter up and scanned it. "It says here that Maximilian has to sign operational orders. Ridiculous! Are we going to sit on the fence to wait for his operational orders? I think not!" he said briskly, his long waxed mustache and pointed beard glistening. "We acquired fifteen million francs? from Mexico, plus what we received from selling the land west of the Mississippi. I hardly think his thousand francs per soldier will compare to that in the long run."

Napoleon paced in a manner reminiscent of Napoleon I. His Cabinet listened to his discourse patiently.

"I tell you, Americans will not stop their war cry of 'manifest destiny.' In our opinion, it's nothing but annexations, acquisitions, ceding ... precisely the same thing we're doing in Mexico! They're called enabling while we're called disabling. It makes me sick. And now this upstart Hapsburg *prince* wants us out," he said, spitting the word "prince" like an obscenity.

He walked over to the table and leaned on a chair there. "The English rebels have started fighting each other over rights and property issues," he said, referring to the United States. "And now they're paralyzed. We thought a civil war would put America away; we scrambled towards Mexico with that hope. We beckoned the southern states to come and join us, but they refused. And now this character, Lincoln! One of my own courtiers slapped his face over some illegitimate Hapsburg girl he was in love with, and now he's been elected for a second term! He's bad for France. With blood oozing from his head and face, he continues to supply arms and aid to the republicans under Juarez. It's a bad omen … both are bad for France."

"What's to be done?" a corps commander asked.

The room fell silent. One could have heard a pin drop.

Napoleon continued to think out loud, as if no one had spoken. "Lincoln says that opposition to government policy is protected and encouraged. Encouraged! We're hanging them, attacking them. We sent a red carpet, a Catholic prince, to cover up our mayhem. Our generals hate opposition, and now this Hapsburg is the opposition leader. Who should we deal with first?"

Edmond Drouyn de Lhuys, minister of foreign affairs, hazarded a reply. "Your Majesty, we have limited resources and the Atlantic Ocean separating us from our troops. In the final analysis, we talk about giving rights, but the Americans are teaching the Mexicans not to accept sovereigns who bestow rights. They think the people are sovereign and that they don't need rights because they already have them. Liberty is the new war cry."

"Yes, yes, we have a bad neighbor to the north. We face a bad philosophy from there." His jaw tightened. "Let's just face the truth here. We've managed to occupy Mexico, and we have our strategic goals there. So now we have a choice: forget Mexico altogether, or else make the Mexicans forget that they were a nation." He picked up a military baton and waved it angrily. "Or we can gain total surrender by force!" he shouted, striking the table. "We can just instruct the corps commander to bring back the gold if nothing else!"

The members of the Cabinet were tense but did not make a sound.

Napoleon struck the table again. "Let's do it! Let's make the Mexicans forget they were ever a nation!" He clutched the baton in both hands and seemed to visibly will himself to be calm. "Let's see which way the wind blows."

After the Cabinet members had left, Napoleon's secretary handed him a document. Napoleon signed it and affixed his official seal. It was a secret letter for his corps commander, Marshal Bazaine. He stood and followed the document with gleaming eyes as his secretary carried it out of his office.

"Bazaine, it's your job now to fool that Austrian carpet."

CHAPTER 20

▼

THE REUNION

A letter was delivered to the Indian lady who owned the vast agricultural estate. Zinnia looked at the envelope embellished with "MIM": Maximilian Imperator Mexici. She hesitated and even thought of throwing it into the fireplace. "John Best has been a kind, loving husband all these years," she thought to herself. "If I open this, my life will never be the same."

The light streaming through the window was golden, but her heart was as black as onyx. An agonizing quarter-hour later, she tore at the envelope with trembling fingers, her eyes darting to and fro and her mind a jumble of sights and memories. "Clear your mind and read the letter," she commanded herself as she held the letter up to the light.

"My beloved Zinnia,

Do you know I did not sleep that night? I was told that you had gone back to India. Then I was told that your kinsmen killed you. I was devastated, but still not sure what had happened to you.

I was only sure of my very deep love for you. I did not forget you and never failed to hold your memory in my heart.

I saw certain plants as we passed through your farmland, and I saw signs of your skilled hands among them. I said to myself that it had to be Zinnia.

The way you ran away after my embrace told me amply that it was you, though now married. But love is above marriage. It has no frontiers.

I have continued to write to you through my mother. For quite some time, she's been receiving the letters I wrote to you, in hopes that you would come back to me someday. She is my only confidante in this matter. She would tell you how I pined for you, how much I missed you from the last time I saw you in 1861.

Please visit us in the palace. Bring your husband, too. I would like to hear what happened to you, how you ended up married to an officer and living in Mexico.

Waiting, waiting, waiting!

Your prince."

She clutched the letter to her heart, rushing to her bedroom and dropping onto the bed. She wept uncontrollably, burying her face in the pillows to stifle her sobs. No! No! No! Her heart screamed over and over again.

Miles away in Chapultepec Castle, Señor Carillo was installed as Mexico's master of the mint. After taking an oath of office, the emperor gave him an envelope. "Please take this message personally to the Indian lady's house to ask her to come to the palace with her husband. This second letter is for her husband. It's an appointment letter to make them the official daily supplier of flowers for the palace. Then I'd like you to return and inform me of her reply."

Carillo nodded, silent about the emperor's choice of words in saying *her* reply rather than *his* or *their* reply. He returned later that evening with an exquisite bouquet of flowers and a letter from Zinnia's husband, thanking His Imperial Majesty for appointing them floral suppliers to the Crown. Maximilian impatiently paced back and forth as he read the message.

"Is she coming?" he asked Carillo, thinking only of his main concern.

"Her husband will be coming tomorrow, señor. I'm not sure about her. I didn't see her there."

"Kindly go back there tomorrow and ask her to come personally. Tell her that her best friend, Charlotte, is expecting her," he ordered, desperate to see her.

"Yes, Your Majesty," Carillo replied with a small bow. "I'll send my wife to her and let you know of her reply immediately."

"Good," the emperor mumbled, his restless hand moving across his brow absent-mindedly.

In another room of the palace, Marshal Bazaine and Colonel Lopez were arranging a fiesta in honor of the imperial couple. Bazaine suggested that Lopez organize a music, dance, and food fiesta for the townspeople as well. Lopez contacted Angela Peralta, Mexico's most famous female opera singer. She would later be known as the "Mexican Nightingale," an artist revered throughout the country. Nineteen-year-old Peralta accepted their offer to sing for the imperial couple, her last performance before her departure for a European tour.

On receiving a letter of acceptance from the young singer, Colonel Lopez went to inform the emperor of the fiesta and the planned entertainment. The Austrian seemed tense, then visibly relieved when he realized that the colonel had only come to discuss the details of a gala.

"It will be a marvelous occasion, my lord. You'll adore the artist. All of Mexico is raving about her talent."

"A national celebrity?" Maximilian clarified. He wanted to be sure that the event included the best that the country had to offer.

The colonel nodded emphatically. "Excellency, Angela Peralta is particularly famous for her inclusion of a high E-flat at the end of the triumphal scene in *Aïda*. She'll be accompanied by her troupe and plans to perform that scene."

The emperor was pleased to accept the offer and promised to pay for it from his own pocket. He was actually pleased because he would then have an excuse to see Zinnia. "Colonel Lopez, be sure that the Bests are invited."

"The Bests, my lord?"

"The royal florist and his Indian wife," he clarified, trying to sound casual.

Lopez thought it an odd request but said nothing about it. "Your Excellency, the royal florist has been working under me as a translator. He's a good man, but I'm afraid he's not well."

"Oh?" Maximilian said, his eyebrows arching.

Lopez nodded. "Six months ago, Señor Best became ill, and the doctors have recently told him he's dying of tuberculosis. The doctors have declared him close to death."

"In that case, send my imperial coach for the couple."

"Yes, Your Majesty," Lopez said, saluting. He hesitated, then used the opportunity to deliver a letter. "My lord, I have an urgent letter for you from the Imperial Forces' chief of staff."

Maximilian took the letter and read it carefully. It was a request for permission to take Oaxaca, the cultural hub of Mexico that was still under the control of republican troops. He finished reading the letter and wrote a note on the bottom of it, reading aloud as he wrote to inform Lopez of his reply. "*Yes, provided I am assured that Oaxaca will be taken without civilian casualties. I also add the condition that I can release the republican general Porfirio Diaz, who will take my message to Benito Juarez."*

Lopez was astounded. "But Excellency, Diaz is the bravest general Juarez has. If we release him, we'll have to face him when we attack Oaxaca."

"You ask one favor," Maximilian said, his voice full of conviction, "and you must return one to me."

The colonel took the note without another word. He clicked his heels, bowed, and left.

Diaz had distinguished himself as a strong right arm of the liberal cause; however, Maximilian had a plan.

After signing operation orders for the Imperial Forces to extend Maximilian's rule into the province of Oaxaca, the emperor visited the liberal General Porfirio Diaz in jail. He stepped into a dark cell and took a moment to let his eyes adjust to the dimmer light. After a few moments, he could make out wide shoulders and a deep chest, the figure of a man with impressive military carriage. General Diaz stood at attention with dignity as Maximilian looked at his face. He had a square chin and a wide, firm mouth fringed by a mustache. His high, wide forehead was hidden beneath black hair that hung down over deep-set, dark brown eyes.

"General Diaz, I'm releasing you. Go to Juarez and give him this," he said simply, handing the man a letter. "It's my offer for him to be my prime minister. I'd like us to unite Mexico and rule together."

Diaz blinked in surprise. "Juarez is dead-set against foreign conquerors. Why should he join you?" he responded, his shock removing all diplomacy from his words. "He plans to punish you as a warning to other foreign conquerors."

Maximilian ignored the question, staring in fascination at this man who knew the legendary Juarez so well. "You've been very close to Juarez, haven't you? How would you describe him?"

They spoke for a few moments in hushed tones, the emperor prodding him with little questions here and there to find out things about Juarez he would never have heard otherwise. Diaz described how intelligent Juarez was, calling him the best lawyer in Oaxaca. He described how Juarez had studied law, Church theology, Latin, grammar, philosophy, the arts and sciences, as well as public service. He even described how, as a student, Juarez had carried a whip with him; it was not so that he could whip others, but instead for others to whip him every time he gave an incorrect answer.

"He's capable of unsparing devotion, and he did wonders as Oaxaca's town councilor, a federal judge, the governor of Oaxaca, a law minister, and more recently as president of Mexico."

Maximilian sighed deeply. "Such a man would make a very powerful prime minister." His eyes looked as though they were looking at something very far away, and Diaz said nothing to disturb the emperor's thoughts. Maximilian's eyes finally met Diaz's. "I also want to do miraculous things in Mexico, General. I only wish for Juarez to know that, to know my sincere intentions. You could serve as an invaluable go-between for us."

Diaz stared at the emperor knowingly. "If you let me go, the first thing Juarez will do is post me as general against your troops."

Maximilian shrugged. "Probably. But you're the best messenger I could ever ask for, so I'll have to take that chance. It's very important for me to have Juarez as my prime minister."

"If I tell him that he can stand by your side as your 'number two man,' he'll ask me if he can fire an emperor," Diaz replied stubbornly, his jaw tense.

The emperor looked as if he were suppressing a smile. "General, the people hired me as their emperor. They must allow me time to show results," he explained patiently, as if to a child.

Diaz's dark brown eyes narrowed. "Who told you the people hired you? Do you mean that plebiscite? That was wool pulled over your eyes. They shot and hanged anyone who was against you before they even started that plebiscite. Napoleon's generals were in complicity with the elite Mexicans all along. Those elite were the ones who were really ruling Mexico, and they were the ones who wanted to bring you here."

"So the plebiscite was a fraud?" Maximilian repeated, still with that condescendingly patient expression.

Diaz leaned forward slightly, his dark eyes fearless. "One hundred percent fraud, and no substance." Maximilian's patient expression faded as the general continued. "They told people to stay home because of a plague, then troops came in civilian clothes to cast votes. Fraud is a small word for what they did."

Maximilian paused and stroked an eyebrow with one of his characteristically nervous hands. "Your leader has quite a record. He was deported to Havana, then New Orleans. He planned the overthrow of a Mexican dictator from there. Now he's fighting the Imperial Forces. Doesn't he care about his social position? His family? The comforts he could enjoy from a high station in life?"

"If I saw him today, he'd probably be eating an onion and a chunk of bread with a cup of water," Diaz replied. "He has very, very small needs."

Maximilian shook his head and waved his hand. "I'm setting you free, General, if you promise to deliver my message."

"I will."

"Fine then. You may have a meal with me before leaving."

Diaz bowed slightly, crow's feet appearing around his eyes. "And I'm to leave in what way after our meal? I don't trust French generals. They've branded me a 'terrorist,' so I'm sure they'd kill me as soon as I walked out of here."

"My ADC will accompany you with my Austrian Guard. They'll leave you near Oaxaca."

ADC Vickers and the Austrian Guard did just that, turning back once they reached the borders of Oaxaca State. As soon as they were out of sight, Diaz took a detour towards the north. He traveled a great distance and through hostile terrain, edging closer to the United States. Juarez's resistance fighters, partially made up of loyal Mexican patriots, had been pushed into the bare and sparsely populated northern regions. Diaz searched until he came into an area that widened and leveled out. His skilled eyes knew this to be the result of military organization, so he knew he was getting closer to where Juarez was hiding.

After some time, he managed to come into contact with resistance leaders and was led to Juarez within days. He finally stood before his leader.

Juarez smiled, relieved and pleased to see Diaz. "You escaped then?" he asked, clapping the general on the back.

"No, Señor Presidente, I was released by the emperor."

"Released?" Juarez echoed, confused. He offered the large man a seat and waved a servant away from the table. "Why?"

"He came to my cell personally," Diaz explained. "He asked me to send you an interesting message." Diaz smirked. "He wants you to be his prime minister."

"What?" Juarez's mouth hung slightly open in his shock.

"The emperor wants you to be his 'number two man,' señor."

Juarez's face was incredulous. He hesitated, then asked, "Can you fire an emperor?"

Diaz burst into a smile, unlike him in most other situations. He quickly regained control of his expression and resumed a more professional air. "That's exactly what I told that Austrico you'd say."

"What route did you take to get here?"

"They took me to Oaxaca and then turned back. I turned north after they'd left. I wasn't followed."

Juarez's eyes narrowed. "Are you sure?"

"Yes, sir. They tried to have someone trail me, but I lost them long before it was clear that I was going north."

"They're interested in Oaxaca. They sent spies with you, I'm sure," Juarez insisted, nodding to himself. "This is our military stronghold now in addition to our cultural one. And they're going to attack it as soon as we refuse their offer."

Diaz nodded. He felt sure he had lost anyone following him, but it could very well be true that someone still followed unnoticed.

"I exiled the archbishop of Mexico and the Spanish ambassador for helping the conservatives with money, troops, and moral persuasion. It seems they're back now. I want you to take over the defense of Oaxaca. Leave tomorrow. We'll plan a counteraction in the event that they attack."

"Yes, sir," Diaz replied, that smirk again on his face.

Juarez smirked as well when he noticed the usually stoic man's expression. "What's on your mind, General?"

"I warned him not to release me. I said that if he did, he'd end up facing me in Oaxaca."

"Did you?" Juarez exclaimed, laughing freely.

There was a pause, and Juarez soon got a thoughtful and faraway look on his face, not unlike the one the emperor had when he had spoken with Diaz in the jail cell. "How would you describe this Austrico?" Juarez then asked, giving Diaz a strong sense of déjà vu.

"He supposedly ruled the Lombardo-Venetian kingdom wisely. I know that Gutierrez-Estrada was the first to propose him as the best choice for Mexican emperor." He thought carefully about what else he had heard about the Austrian. "He's a botanist, knows the Spanish language. He asked for a popular vote before coming here—"

"Oh, I know all of that, General," Juarez interrupted, impatient. "What kind of *man* is he?"

Diaz hesitated, thinking that over. He shrugged. "Sincere and without guile, señor."

Juarez nodded quietly. He had heard as much, but hoped it was merely the propaganda of a new ruler. "He's appointed Iturbide's grandson as his presumptive successor," he said.

Diaz nodded. "He also issued amnesty for all political prisoners last week. He saved them from execution by the French court martial. An Austrian officer told me on the way to Oaxaca that he also plans to raise a Belgian-Austrian Corps to offset the French military power here."

"He has empty vaults," Juarez scoffed. "You can't do such things when you're poor."

"I said the same thing to the man who told me. He said that a European loan is being arranged."

Juarez leaned back in his chair. "That means he's at loggerheads with the French."

"Yes, the very ones who are supposed to help him get settled in here," Diaz added, at ease now. He lit a large cigar and offered one to Juarez, who accepted it. "He instituted a committee for the regulation of public affairs, too. He seems to have good intentions for the faithful administration of his government."

Juarez looked uncomfortable. "Is it true he meets with the common people?"

"Every Sunday. He listens personally to their claims and complaints. He's also been touring his provinces. He seems brave and fearless."

"I'm told he's affable enough. That'll win him moderates and jurists," Juarez said, always thinking of the political implications. "What else can you tell me about him?"

Diaz puffed his cigar for a moment. "He's progressive, a social reformer. He's abolished debt-peonage, moved to restrict child labor, and he restored quite a lot of communal land to Indian villages."

"Worthy improvements on his part. Tell me more."

"He appointed the empress as regent during his absences, and in the event of his death. Last month, he decreed compulsory education. He declared Catholicism the state religion, but with freedom for all other creeds, giving full toleration. He's following in your footsteps when it comes to church property and income. It seems to be alienating him from his most zealous supporters."

"He wants to rule well," Juarez said thoughtfully. "He seems wise in some ways. He's the best they have."

"Which means?" Diaz questioned, eyeing him curiously.

"It means we have to put up a more determined resistance. We have a worthy opponent, although a displaced one."

They sat in silence for some time after that, each smoking his cigar thoughtfully. They ate together, little more being said, before General Diaz was dispatched to Oaxaca.

Zinnia and her husband traveled to the palace in the imperial coach, accompanied by Colonel Lopez. When they arrived, John Best waited politely on the terrace while his wife visited Empress Carlota.

Colonel Lopez brought Zinnia into Carlota's living room. "Majesty, she is here."

Carlota stood. The two women stood facing each other for the first time in many years. Neither said a word. Maximilian finally entered the living room and broke the silence. "How are you, Zinnia?" he asked simply, too overcome by her nearness to be any more eloquent.

Zinnia bowed. "Your Majesty." She lifted a bag hanging from her belt and took out a silk satchel. In it was one hundred thousand British pounds. "Today Your Majesty has need of this," she said, handing it to Maximilian.

"I see, even a prostitute has ethics?" Carlota said in a mood uncommon to her. Maximilian was shocked but held his peace.

"I was never a prostitute," Zinnia objected. "I was your slave. I obeyed you, and now I'm returning your money so I can be your friend. Slave no more."

Carlota shook her head. "I sent you to Vienna and you immediately betrayed me by getting pregnant. Why?"

"I was pregnant when I left Belgium."

Carlota was shocked but clearly remembered the night years ago when she took Maximilian to her bed, pulled back the quilt, and said, "This is the 'lop-off,' my betrothal gift to you." It all made sense now. Maximilian had been the father.

Maximilian looked down at the money, a thick wad of sterling notes. "How did you get this money?"

"From honest labor, my lord. Soil, water, sunshine, careful agriculture, and God's blessing," she replied with characteristic simplicity.

"I'm bewildered by your progression from a dancer to a millionaire by mere labor," he replied, tossing the money on a table.

"Anyone can reach dizzying heights by labor and knowledge, Majesty."

"What should I do with you, Zinnia? Appoint you as my agricultural minister?" he asked jokingly.

"Keep the money and call me a friend," she replied.

"I should send you to raise a loan for me in Europe."

Lopez cleared his throat. "She's one of the best businesswoman in Mexico, Your Majesty," he interjected.

Zinnia curtseyed. "I'm just a woman, sire."

Carlota finally found her voice, walking over to Zinnia and embracing her. "A woman of substance now!" she declared, her tone now friendly. "Come, Zinnia, let's go to the garden and sit together. I'm sorry for being spiteful. I was hurt and missing you." The two old friends walked arm in arm to the terrace.

"Request permission to leave, Your Excellency?" Lopez asked.

Maximilian refrained from following them out to the terrace. He was jubilant with the outcome of the meeting and cheerfully clapped Lopez on the back. "Colonel, you're organizing the town fiesta and several more important duties of the Crown," he said, leading the man to the door to excuse him. "You seem trustworthy enough. Can you take on the role of commandant of my bodyguards?"

"It would be a great honor, Your Majesty," Lopez replied, amazed at the Austrian's naïveté. "I hope my life is lost protecting you."

CHAPTER 21

▼

THE SANCTIMONIOUS EMPEROR

Paris, 1864—Office of Napoleon III

William Lewis Dayton, the United States' minister to France, waited in the room adjacent to the emperor's office. Lewis had been appointed by Abraham Lincoln to travel to Paris and protest what Americans had seen as an infringement of the Monroe Doctrine. He passed the time flipping a French coin in his hand. It was one of the new mints, a gold ten franc piece struck with the image of Napoleon III. He wondered to himself if the real monarch would look anything like the glorious Caesar-like character on the coin, wearing a laurel leaf crown.

The chief of protocol, General Castelnau, entered the room and informed Lewis that the emperor was ready to see him. Lewis rose, a stately figure in his black suit, and straightened his satin lapels as they entered the emperor's office.

Castelnau gestured to Lewis. "Your Majesty, this is William Lewis Dayton, the United States' foreign minister to France."

Napoleon eyed the man closely with a slight nod.

Castelnau now gestured to the emperor and looked at Lewis. "Minister, this is Emperor Napoleon III."

"I am honored to meet you," Lewis said with a slight bow. His dark hair was carefully swept to the side, his appearance impeccable.

"Have a seat, Minister Lewis," Napoleon replied. "What can I do for you today?"

Lewis took a seat on a hand-carved French Empire sofa. He attempted a polite smile, to which Napoleon grimaced his mouth very slightly in an awkward reply. It was clear that there would be no pleasantries. "Sir, I must come right to the point," Lewis started, sensing that to be the best approach. "I'm instructed by my office to protest your actions. The Latin empire in Mexico is a flagrant violation of United States policy."

"A flagrant violation?" Napoleon repeated, his face unreadable. He could have been amused or offended; it was impossible to say.

"Yes, sir. The empire is represented by a puppet prince," he said, referring to Maximilian Hapsburg. "It violates the Monroe Doctrine, which forbids European intervention in the Western Hemisphere."

Napoleon leaned forward in his seat. "What has your doctrine to do with my activities?"

"With all due respect, our Monroe Doctrine is not the nonsense your actions seem to say it is," Lewis pushed. "You're clearly in control of the empire over there, and that violates United States policy."

Napoleon twisted his waxed mustache lazily. "Why do you involve yourself in the affairs of other nations? What do you have to do with territories beyond America?"

"Sir—"

"President Washington and Thomas Jefferson both warned your Congress against 'entangling alliances,' so why are you so interested in Mexico?" Napoleon interrupted. "You're spread from the Atlantic to the Pacific. You have enough territory to govern already."

"Sir, it's in direct violation—"

"Is the Monroe Doctrine a *law*? Certainly not!" Napoleon barked over Lewis' redundant reply, silencing him. "Name me anyone in Latin America or Europe who gives a fig about your Monroe Doctrine. Besides, how can Europe or anyone else threaten your country's safety? Has anyone attacked you?"

Lewis shook his head. "Sir, the Monroe Doctrine is a self-defense policy. Any attempt by Europe to extend its system into any part of our hemisphere will be construed as dangerous to our safety."

"Yes, yes, I've read the document," the emperor scoffed. "You're no longer a new and weak nation, so now you feel as if you can write anything you like and the world must abide by it. For 150 years, you've stuck to a traditional policy of isolation from the rest of the world, and now it's evolving into expansionism. Isn't that what you now call your Manifest Destiny?"

Lewis visibly bristled at the emperor's flippant reference to America's most reverent concept of expansion west to the Pacific Ocean. He shifted in his seat but allowed Napoleon to continue.

"You have a huge continent of your own, so focus on exploring and settling it. You also have a great many problems, so why not work on solving them before involving yourselves in world affairs?"

"Sir, never deign to dictate policy for the United Sates of America," Lewis said, his chin tilting upward defiantly.

"Nobody's trying to dominate you," Napoleon said in exasperation, an irritated frown wrinkling his face. "It was the French who gave you the means to obtain your independence in the first place, remember? And what do we get in return? You've come to see me and threaten France."

"No one threatened any—"

A guard near the door suppressed a smile. He was always amused when he saw men who had never tangled personally with the emperor.

Napoleon pointed at Lewis. "You expanded your entire continent from a mere thirteen states, and it is now triple that size. We gave you all of your states west of the Mississippi for a song. Then you snatched Florida from Spain. You took the Louisiana Purchase in 1803 for fifteen million dollars, doubling your size in a single stroke."

He continued to harangue Lewis about the United States' dealings in expanding its territory over the past several years, his contempt for their tactics obvious. He reminded Lewis of how the U.S. took Texas from Mexico in 1845, obtained Oregon the following year, defeated Mexico to secure California in 1848, extended the Southwest via the Gadsden Purchase in 1853, and then quickly acquired Arizona and New Mexico to obtain the best rail link to the Pacific.

"You see, Minister Lewis, we know all about your Manifest Destiny," he spat, saying the words as though they were an obscenity. "It disallows destiny to other nations, and I see no reason to discuss it with you now. It's nothing but bunk! Go settle your civil war first, Minister. Go, sir." He waved his hand in an insulting dismissal.

Lewis stood, his back as straight as a pole. His lips were set in a thin hard line as he looked down at Napoleon. "Excellency, be very sure that I'll be coming back here after the civil war to prove that our Monroe Doctrine is not 'bunk,'" he replied coolly. He stood and turned his back on the emperor, striding across the room. General Castelnau rose and escorted Minister Lewis from the room.

General Castelnau walked behind the American minister to the coach that was to ride him to the gates of the estate. They climbed in and faced each other, Lewis still in a foul mood and saying nothing. In an attempt to lighten the mood, Castelnau lit a cigar and offered one to the minister as the coach began to roll away from the palace.

Lewis looked at the cigar, then up at the general. "General, does your emperor think that Americans are at each other's throats?" he asked, absentmindedly accepting a cigar.

Castelnau frowned slightly and shook his head, not understanding the minister's line of thought. He offered a match and allowed the minister to light his cigar.

"Does he really think that Americans have blood flowing from their heads from internal strife, and that they're too weak to enforce the Monroe Doctrine?" Lewis continued through a thick cloud of smoke. "More than one nation has risen from a civil war to conquer the world."

"Which nation did that?" Castelnau asked politely, puffing on his cigar.

"You should read more history, General," Lewis snapped. "The Arab nation, for starters."

Castelnau maintained a patient air. "My dear minister, are you truly in a position to stop European powers from recovering their lost territories? I understand that you believe the United States is capable, but do you think that other nations are incapable?"

Lewis fumed but kept quiet. The coach stopped outside the gate. Both men stepped out.

"General," Lewis said, facing Castelnau, "We hope you remain the chief of protocol of France. Then you can watch your tiger become emaciated."

"This is uncalled for. I resent it," General Castelnau said, pulling himself up to his full height.

Minister Lewis stared hard at the general for a moment. Instead of replying, he threw his cigar into the dirt and stomped it. With a look of satisfaction, he straightened his lapels again and walked over to his own coach, getting into it without a word.

Castelnau shook his head in amazement as he watched the coach ride away.

Castelnau promptly returned to the emperor's office and told him all about what Lewis had said.

Napoleon again stroked his mustache. "We shouldn't take that Kentuckian lightly, General. He means every word that he says." He fell silent and gave it some careful thought. United States politics had been an important factor to him for some time now, and he had already weighed it very carefully.

He was particularly concerned with U.S. Vice President Andrew Johnson, a Democrat who was supposedly fond of saying, "As vice president, I'm nothing, but I may be everything." Republicans always extended presidential powers, being extroverts by nature, but Democrats were different. They lived within specified implied powers rather than trying to extend those powers. They were introverts, more worried about internal matters. Lincoln was the first Republican president to be elected in the United States, and Napoleon was convinced that was part of the problem.

"If Lincoln loses the election in the next term,"—or loses his life, he thought—"we could see a Democratic president in the United States. Then perhaps that president would be too busy with the civil war and other internal matters to meddle in our affairs right now. That could give us time."

"What should we do, sire?"

Napoleon's eyes squinted shrewdly as he thought it over. "Go to Emperor Maximilian," he finally said. "Tell him that I don't want him to behave like a sacred character, like some sort of monk. We have very little time left to consolidate our hold in Mexico. I'll pay for his Belgian and Austrian Corps. We'll arrange a loan in Paris. Get him to allow Bazaine the right of way. Bazaine is the right man there." He nodded, satisfied with his plan. "Go by the first available ship and get Bazaine to secure Mexico."

"A ship leaves in three days," General Castelnau replied.

"Go then. The sooner, the better."

Mexico City

It was midnight when Zinnia rose, startled awake by her husband's spasm of coughing. She quickly lit the lamps and gave him the medicine she kept close by on the bedside table. She was fast and efficient, this being a ritual she had done many times in the last few months. She felt his pulse and stroked her hand over his forehead, trying to calm him while they waited for the medicine to take effect.

The coughing was not subsiding, and by then his handkerchief was covered in blood. Zinnia helped him to change his position on the bed and repositioned his pillows. She pulled a chair over to the bed and sat next to him, holding his hand.

John was a shadow of his former self. He was gaunt and pale, having a hard time eating because of his fatigue and the coughing fits. They had been married for the better part of a decade now, but he easily looked twenty years older.

He caught his breath and lay calmly for a while, the new position and the medicine helping the coughing to pass for now. "Zinnia," he whispered, not daring to speak louder lest he bring on more coughing, "thank you for everything you've been doing for me." His pale fingers traced softly down her hand.

"Tomorrow, the emperor's personal doctor is coming to see you," Zinnia said, trying to soothe him.

John stared at her, his eyes becoming wet with tears. "Zinnia, if I die, I want to be embalmed, and then I want my body sent back home."

Zinnia blinked back her tears and gently wiped his eyes. "Don't talk like that, John," she whispered. "You'll break my heart."

"Let's be realistic," John pressed, his words soft and slow. "We have to face the facts. There's no cure for tuberculosis." His face became red, and she knew he was trying to hold back from coughing again. "All the doctors can do is prolong my torture," he said through another fit of coughing.

"Why you?" Zinnia said, crying openly now as she clutched his hand and watched him try to catch his breath. "You're such a good man. What sin did you commit to deserve this?"

He reached up and ran his hand through her long hair, his eyes smiling. "You want mercy," he remarked as if it were an outrageous desire. "The angel of death doesn't have any mercy," he said, attempting a joke.

Zinnia hunched over him and covered her face, crying. She was so distraught that she did not even lift her head when he began to cough again. She finally felt his hands on her face and looked up.

John's eyes were sunken and showed how much pain he was in. "Please," he whispered. "Get me some cold water."

Zinnia nodded and rushed to the door.

"Zinnia."

She turned from the doorway. "Yes, John?"

"I love you," he whispered, managing a slow wink that was meant to resemble the fast and playful wink he used to give her in happier times.

Zinnia managed a smile. "I love you too, darling."

She walked out of the room and went to the kitchen, then to the well outside. It always offered cool water no matter what the temperature was, and she knew that the coolness felt good on his ravaged throat. She focused on her task, not wanting to think any more about her husband's fate. Her face felt swollen from all the crying she had done in recent weeks as her eyes drifted to the darkness beyond the kitchen courtyard. In that darkness lay the hacienda fields that she and John had built together.

"Don't think about it!" she scolded herself, but the hot tears welled up in her eyes despite her best efforts to keep them at bay. *Why?* Her mind continued to wail. *Why?*

There was the loud pop of a pistol shot from upstairs. Zinnia froze. She finally let go of the well bucket and ran wildly back to the bedroom.

John still loosely held a pistol in his right hand, the smell of gunpowder lingering in the room. A crimson stain flowered across his chest. His eyes were closed but his lips moved slightly. Zinnia frantically leaned close to his lips as a trickle of blood made its way out of his mouth and down his cheek. "Goodbye, Zinnia. I love you," he managed to whisper. "Loveyouloveyouloveyou," he mumbled, trying to get the words out as he died.

Zinnia's eyes widened in horror, then she screamed. She beat the bloody mattress as she shrieked and wailed, then finally kissed his face over and over again, her tears spilling onto him. "Goodbye," she cried as she kissed him. "Goodbye, goodbye, goodbye …"

At eight o'clock the following morning, the emperor's personal physician arrived at the hacienda. The servants were waiting anxiously and told him about their master's demise. He asked to be escorted to the couple.

Zinnia was sitting on the stone floor beside his bed, rocking and weeping uncontrollably. The physician quickly assessed the situation and could see that it had been a suicide. Zinnia seemed barely to notice his presence.

The physician left for the castle and reported the matter to the royal couple immediately.

Minutes later, Maximilian came charging on his white horse towards Zinnia's home, followed by his bodyguard troop. Carlota followed shortly after in the royal carriage, another troop of bodyguards in tow.

When Maximilian stepped into the room, he paused, shocked at Zinnia's rocking and crying. A maid was cleaning blood from John's face as another maid brought porridge to Zinnia, asking her to eat something; she lifted her head, her face red and her eyes swollen, and pushed the food away.

Maximilian kneeled next to her and attempted to console her repeatedly. All she managed to say was that John's last wish was to be sent back to his hometown in Europe.

The emperor turned to an officer of his guard, relieved to have something useful to do for Zinnia. "Take him to the church and have the body embalmed." He knew that Admiral Tegethoff was coming from Austria in his ship, *Elizabeth*. He was due in six days, and Maximilian wanted to make sure that John was secured in his coffin in the church at Vera Cruz by then, so that the admiral could take him back.

"Yes, Your Majesty," the officer replied with a salute.

Maximilian then turned to Zinnia and placed an arm around her shoulder. "Be brave," he softly urged. "You must be brave now, Zinnia."

He instructed his bodyguard troop leader to arrange for matters in the household and for the preparation of the body, also instructing the servants to care for Zinnia. Then the emperor left for his residence as quickly as he had come. Carlota arrived soon after to console her friend.

"My husband," Zinnia moaned, "my dear husband."

Carlota burst into tears and hugged Zinnia. "I'm so sorry!" she whispered fiercely. "I know it seems impossible, but time will make this easier to bear." Her words sounded hollow to her. She honestly did not know what she would do if she lost Maximilian. The very thought made her feel as if she would go mad.

The two wept together. Unlike anyone else in the house, or anywhere else in the world for that matter, Zinnia's old friend was someone she could share her broken heart with.

Back at Chapultepec, Maximilian jotted notes in his memoirs. "Aus Meinem Leben ..."

There was a knock on the door. Maximilian slipped the memoirs into a drawer. "Enter."

ADC Vickers slipped inside. "General Brincourt is here to see you, Your Majesty."

Maximilian sighed. Brincourt was Bazaine's divisional commander, the man who had a pivotal role in ousting Juarez and his government. He was now entrusted with the task of securing the Oaxaca province and adding it to Maximilian's ruled territory.

"I'll see him in the library," he said, rubbing his forehead wearily. He was distracted, his mind focused on Zinnia.

General Brincourt wore the new imperial uniform. When the emperor entered the library, Brincourt addressed him with a crisp salute. "Majesty, I have good news for you. Marshal Bazaine has agreed to your demands and the Imperial Forces have been ordered out of seven regions. He's issued instructions not to persecute them, Your Majesty. They've been given full political clemency. The army is dismantling all of the roadblocks and closing military bases, and your revised peace accord plan has been accepted by the generals."

Maximilian smiled. "That certainly is one piece of good news."

Brincourt nodded as Maximilian walked over to a desk to retrieve some notes. The general's pleasant expression faded when the emperor's back was turned, only returning when they faced one another.

What he had reported to the emperor was only partially true. The clemencies that had been granted were merely being used to compile a list of men to kill later. Dismantling roadblocks would be helpful for them to sneak troops wearing Mexican garb into the area. The ultimate goal was to concentrate their forces in the Oaxaca region, all under the emperor's nose and under his orders for the opposite.

"Colonel Lopez was supposed to organize the first public fiesta with the Imperial Forces. How is he progressing? I want it memorable, with international entertainers and that opera singer," he explained vaguely, forgetting her name.

"ADC Vickers and bodyguard commander Lopez are coordinating with the imperial staff, sire."

Maximilian nodded. "More importantly, I want the minimum force necessary to be used to secure Oaxaca for the empire."

Brincourt hid his disdain for the emperor very well. He had been appalled when Maximilian's first reaction to his military news was to ask questions about the fiesta. At least he had finally gotten back to the matter at hand. "Detail orders are being prepared by the corps commander, Your Excellency."

The emperor nodded, then paused as the general lingered. "What else?"

"The divisional commander's house has been vacated in Orizaba, sire. The corps commander has asked that you … shift there temporarily, Your Excellency."

"Shift there?" Maximilian asked, shocked. "Why?"

"For your health and protection, sire."

"Well, what's so special in Orizaba?"

"The divisional commander's house is a secure fort. The climate's mild, and there are several healing mineral springs nearby. It's a good place for recuperation, very peaceful. It's not far from Citlaltépetl," he explained, referring to the majestic snowcapped volcano near there. "The tuberculosis sanitarium is there as well."

"Oh, I see," Maximilian replied distractedly, handing Brincourt the file containing the royal proclamation. "Let me repeat to you again, the imperial army is not to commit any atrocities. I want the people spared. My amnesty must be honored in letter *and* spirit."

"Yes, sire. No killing without due trial."

"No killing *at all*, General. It's crucial that the annexations be bloodless."

Brincourt opened the file and looked at the royal proclamation. "Sire, we need this signed before we can act."

"Never," Maximilian replied stubbornly. "I'll not have my hands soiled with Mexican blood." He massaged his brow, his expression impatient. "They're my countrymen now."

The general closed the file disdainfully, though the emperor was too distracted to notice his insolent slip. Brincourt left after a half-hearted salute.

Maximilian sat down in the dim office and tried to massage away his headache. "Zinnia should go to Orizaba," he thought to himself.

In another part of Chapultepec, Brincourt met with Marshal Bazaine.

"He wouldn't sign the proclamation," he explained with contempt. "He wants a bloodless annexation of the Oaxaca province."

Bazaine smiled and shook his head in wonder as they both sat down. Brincourt poured himself some brandy and sipped it, waiting for Bazaine to think it over and respond.

"Will he go to Orizaba?"

Brincourt shrugged. "He didn't object, but I'm not sure."

"Tell Lopez to persuade His Imperial Majesty to go to Orizaba. That dancing girl would be a fine distraction for him," he said, referring to the Indian woman Zinnia.

"I can do that," he said, holding up his tumbler of brandy.

Bazaine poured himself a brandy as well, and then stared at Brincourt. "Juarez escaped to Paso del Norte last time we cornered him in Oaxaca. He may not be there now, but all of his friends and relatives still are. They shouldn't escape this time."

Brincourt cocked an eyebrow, liking the sound of this.

"The emperor's Austrian and Belgian troops are under my command now, so we should take full advantage by having them inflict atrocities and cruelty of the worst kind."

"How do you know they'd do it? Maybe they're loyal to their emperor."

Bazaine chuckled. "Oh Brincourt, wake up. Mexicans can't differentiate between Europeans. Just get some Austrian and Belgian uniforms for your French troops. Kill all captured prisoners after an obviously token court martial. Let the crowd see that it's His Imperial Majesty's troops doing all of this to them."

Brincourt nodded, his demeanor as casual as if he had received everyday orders. "I can do that," was his typical response, said in a light tone.

Bazaine sipped his brandy and continued his orders. "I want you to have Mexicans collected from the royal fiesta. You can use them as decoys to infiltrate Oaxaca town. Round up Juarez patriots, and of course the Juarez family. Execute them immediately."

"Yes, sir," Brincourt replied, again in that routine tone. Nothing seemed to faze Brincourt. Bazaine liked that about him. It made things more efficient.

"Juarez's wife is at the top of the list for executions, so if you find her in Oaxaca, take care of that first. The next one on the list is his grandfather Pedro, then his uncle Bernardino, then his father-in-law Maza."

Brincourt took a pad of paper from his coat and began scribbling notes.

"All of the people from the village Ixtlan," Bazaine continued, "then one of Juarez's old mentors, Antonio Salanueva, and another one of his former teachers, Jose Domingo Gonzales. I want them all summarily shot by a firing squad."

General Brincourt wrote the names in his notebook. "I can do that."

"Oaxaca's Institute of Arts and Sciences is to be pulled down and made into a stable."

Brincourt smirked down at his writing pad. "I can do that." He looked up in surprise, since Bazaine had said the words right along with him. The men exchanged an amused glance before the marshal continued.

"All anti-establishment and liberal politicians, doctors, and lawyers are to be shot. I don't want any stone left unturned. Don't forget about the Belgian and Austrian uniforms, no slip-ups."

Bazaine topped off his tumbler with more brandy. "I want the bishop of Mexico and his churchmen to be spared. They're on our side, so make sure the bloodbath doesn't get carried away." The Church had helped the conservative troops with men, money, and moral support. "Have your spies contact them. They can help us locate the elected alderman of the town council."

"Yes, sir."

"No mercy, no prisoners."

"No mercy, no prisoners," General Brincourt repeated, sipping his brandy.

"We'll hit Juarez in Oaxaca, his province, his town, his village … even his family."

"Yes, sir."

Bazaine smirked. "The thing I like about you is your 'yes-sir-ing,' then your killing without mercy."

Brincourt looked up from his pad and grinned, lifting his tumbler. "Viva La France, sir."

"That's the spirit!" Bazaine declared with a rare grin of his own, lifting his own tumbler and clinking it against the general's.

The royal chief of protocol, French General Castelnau, met with Marshal Bazaine later that afternoon. Bazaine was agitated, pacing in the same room where he had earlier met with Brincourt. Word had reached him that the emperor was refusing to go to Orizaba, which threatened to interfere with his plans.

"We can't have him at the town fiesta if we plan to catch Mexican decoys there. If he even *thinks* he sees something like that, our plans will be jeopardized."

Castelnau watched his agitated pacing with characteristic calmness. "Colonel Lopez says there's an Indian girl he's interested in."

Bazaine nodded. "Yes, I know about her. Can we use that to somehow get him to live in the army house in Orizaba?"

Castelnau paused for a moment, already having given this some thought. "Well, we can start by having Colonel Lopez persuade the Indian woman to go to Orizaba. She just lost her husband, so he could come at it from the angle of a welcome change from her troubles. Then we inform the emperor that a dissatisfied liberal Juarista group member and one of his liberal generals are planning on meeting him in Orizaba. We'll put out a bulletin showing Orizaba as the location where the emperor can be found, which is why the Juaristas plan to meet him there. Make sure that the royal couple is told about this. When the emperor finds out, he'll leave the fiesta himself and go to Orizaba."

Bazaine laughed. Printing bulletins to pull the wool over the emperor's eyes was wickedly amusing to him, though it was nothing that had not been done before.

Castelnau nodded. "Get your best press team to draft them now. Send the press whatever best fits the situation. Stain the emperor's name to the point that he feels grateful to sign the proclamation."

"Stain it how?"

"Marshal, public opinion can be changed by design. First we create an accident, then we blame the liberals for it. That gives us a reason to exterminate them. We'll fashion a sanctimonious emperor for the public, a hypocrite entirely consumed with his throne. We'll have it appear that his sacred character has been corrupted, that he's become aloof. That should be easy enough if we simply let him enjoy dancing, music, women, until he forgets his holiness and piety. We'll paint him as the devil incarnate."

"Artfully," Bazaine interjected with a glint in his eye.

"Yes, artfully. We have a large reputation to destroy, so we have to be careful about how to do it."

"That's just it," Bazaine added thoughtfully. "The Hapsburgs have a solid reputation. How do we combat that with simple debauchery?"

"Melt his reputation in the furnace of that damned thing called *love*," Castelnau declared. "The Indian woman has the emperor's heart, so we have a valuable tool."

Marshal Bazaine smiled as he realized just how powerful a tool that Indian woman was. "This may not be so difficult after all."

THE END (Part I)

About the Authors

Saeed Tiwana is a free-lance journalist, famous for his insights into military strategy and philosophy. His first book was *Fundamental Rules For The Organization Of Military Victories*. His next, about the first Gulf War, was *Saddam Shall Live. The Prince & The Dancing Girl* is his first historical novel.

Sharron McGregor is a graduate of Owasso High School and Tulsa University. Later she received her Masters degree from Northeastern University. Her eclectic background of theater director and teacher of English, Speech, Creative writing and Humanities has been brought to culmination in the "Prince".

978-0-595-67985-0
0-595-67985-4

Printed in the United States
71850LV00004B/244-246